VOLUME I

Book One

"Regret is a form of punishment itself."

- *Tennessee Williams*

www.ALetterGuideforRebecca.com

A LETTER GUIDE FOR REBECCA

DISCLAIMER

This is a work of fiction. All of the characters, organizations, and events portrayed in this novel are either products of the author's imagination or are used fictitiously. Although its form is that of a purported Guidebook, it is not one. Space and time have been rearranged to suit the convenience of the book's fictional story, and with the exception of public figures, any resemblance to persons living or dead is coincidental. The opinions expressed are those of the characters and should not be confused with the author. Certain long-standing institutions, agencies, public figures and public offices are mentioned, but all non-public characters involved are wholly imaginary. Historical events cited may or may not be accurate and any deviation from the original historical account was for fictional literary purposes only. Any act, deed or suggested act by any fictitious character is intended to reflect the intent of the fictional story and fictitious characters only. Just to be absolutely clear, should anyone ever say to you, "Hey, are you the Real Rebecca?" The correct response should be as follows; "No, I am not Rebecca. Rebecca is a fictional character in a fiction book and I do not know a Derek Devon, and that is all I am going to say about that." 😐

Any references to Aliens, off world locations, or technology covered under the Galactic Copyright Law of 2024 or Galactic Patent Office located on SR-14537 in the Andromeda Minor sector have been adhered to. 😊

ISBN
978-1-7386519-0-0

First Published April 14th, 2022 by
Devon Publishing through Amazon KDP services.
www.ALetterGuideforRebecca.com
www.devonpublishing.com

A First book by Derek Devon

Preface

As a first-time author, I want to thank you personally for taking a chance with me and reading my book. For years I always felt I had a *'book in me'*, but never seemed to find the time to commit to sitting down and writing my book. Finally, in May after listening to a couple of TC's pod cast's *(TC After Dark)*, I found that motivation and began the task. Much of the book's genesis came from my own life experiences. It was both an exhilarating and rewarding process, especially allowing me to relive many precious moments from my past, if only now through the written word. Also, most of the locations and places are real, and I have been there and did most of what I wrote about if you strip away the sci-fi stuff. I hope that I would be able to foster in you the opportunity to relive your precious memories and moments, from your past, through the characters and their story in this book.

As a true pragmatist, I can think of no better measure to determine if this is something I want to continue to pursue or was a one-time self-indulgence and homage to the *'real Rebecca'*. So, I would like ***you*** to be the determinant factor. If you enjoyed this read and I was able to stir in you some of those old memories and feelings like I hope, then I would ask you to consider doing the following: First, leave a review wherever you purchased the book (Amazon etc.). Second, if you know two people who would also like this type of read, encourage them to buy the books or maybe give one or two as a gift. You will soon learn I am a fan of 'Networking' and the 'exponential growth' factor. Third, consider maybe writing something yourself *(Nudge-Nudge TC)*. The 'Letter Guide' series will be a 3-volume set with Volume one containing book 1 and 2. I wanted you to get 2 books for the price of one as my way of saying *"Thank You."*

One of my editors once asked me, 'If I could actually have what happened in the book really happen to me, would I truly do what I wrote I would do?' I can honestly answer, ABSOLUTELY! That is why it was such a pleasure for me to write. It's who I am, good or bad! Finally, I am preparing my sailboat ***'It-girl'*** for a circumnavigation in a couple of years, so if you see me out on the ocean, please, come and say hello and maybe enjoy a stout with me; or a glass of Port and cheese *(wink…wink)*.

Dedication

To my Mom and Dad, who I miss every day!

I Need Your Expertise!

I don't know if you will agree with me or not, but I think this book would make one hell of a movie or even a mini-series. I am an avid movie watcher and still frequent the cinema and whenever possible love to watch a new movie in Imax 3D. Often when a new movie gets released, I like to critique the actor selection for each particular role. More times than not, I find myself wishing an alternate specific actor would have been better suited for the role. And when a movie gets the perfect actor for a role, it's almost always a great movie or an outstanding performance (ie. Harrison Ford as Indiana Jones, Bruce Willis as Harry S. Stamper, Hugh Grant as William Thacker, Brian Denneny as Sherrif Will Teasle, Helena Bonham Carter as Bellatrix Lestrange, Tom Hanks as Robert Langdon, Sigourney Weaver as Ellen Ripley, George Clooney as Old Derek Devon (😉), and I could go on and on).

So, if you go visit the book's website:

www.ALetterGuideForRebecca.com

There is a section that will allow you to enter your recommendation for a particular actor you believe would be a great fit to play the selected role. I hope you will allow me to tap into the enormous brain trust that is out there and who knows; Maybe one day the book will become a movie and the casting director will use your suggestions. I thank you for the consideration and to those that share their opinions, a very special thank you!

As a first time novelist, making the New York Times best seller list is a major milestone and with your help, maybe this book can do what Harry Potter did for the fantasy genre for the Science Fiction genre. I invite you to enjoy this ride with me.

If I am ever fortunate enough to have a famous actor or actress *(or influencer)* read this book, and you liked it, please let your adoring fans know. I would be extremely grateful...... 😊

Table of Contents

WARNING: This Book may be addictive to certain readers!

The Beginning.......

Hey Dimples,

Before I get into the specifics, of why you are now in the possession of this two-volume 'guide', as I now like to refer to it, I think it would be wise if I first do, a little Mea culpa with you. I know you must have wondered over the years, how I could always be so sure of myself, and more times than not, you often would comment to me, sometimes in a nice way, and sometimes in a not-so-nice way. But the comment was the same. "How did you know what would happen?" Or, a slightly different version, but essentially the same point: "You are the luckiest SOB'! I recall the look on your face when I was in the exact spot needed to catch 'Joe Carter's' winning world series homerun ball in '93. Well, my pretty dimpled 'it-girl', love of my lives and girl of my dreams (which you will soon find out just how much); It means "buckle your seatbelt, Dorothy, 'cause Kansas is going bye-bye'!"

Not sure if you will get that reference, but I assure you, it fits perfectly. So, I want to say from the bottom of my heart, with no BS attached, or conditions, that I am so sorry that I did not meet your expectations and needs recently. You could say I was not my usual self for a while (wink, wink). It was never you; it was me. There is nothing I would not do for you, and I know deep down that you always have known that to be true. I hope after reading this guide, you will understand me in a way I never allowed before. I often justified it to myself, with the rationale, that I was somehow protecting you, but I know deep down, in the place I hate to look, I was doing it because I was afraid. Afraid of losing you again.

The first time I 'lost you' did not go well for me. It brought out a person I eventually realized I never wanted to see again. It also led to a lifetime of regret and self-isolation at times. Unfortunately, because of my brokenness, I seemed to lack the ability to simply move on. It took me two lifetimes to figure that out, but I hope that the corrective path I eventually took was the right path. I know this guide is going to answer that question for me, and I think that it's probably enough Mea culpa.

Here comes another one of my TV quotes, (just to warn you), "With great power, comes great responsibility" (Or more accurately, "They must consider that great responsibility follows inseparably from great power"). First, old Ben Parker, the latter, 1793 French National Convention. There are, or maybe were, some things I needed to do, but I have been, for some time, encountering a much different set of circumstances than I had previously expected and had planned for. In some cases, for a long time. I want to also apologize to you, Becca, for passing on this enormous responsibility to the only one I have truly loved through two lifetimes. I know it was never equally reciprocated, but the one constant in my lives was my unwavering love for my 'It-girl'.

12757982! That was once our special number. I always loved that number, but, at some point, decided it was too schlocky to use with Derek 2.0. I was wrong! It was a great number and you're going to have to learn to love it as well (I just made a very satisfying-looking face with a grin). I never thought, or expected, that I would not be able to complete my plans myself. If you are reading this, then we can assume I have most likely died or suffered a major medical misfortune before I completed everything that I worked this lifetime expecting to achieve. After that, I was hoping to transition to sailing around the globe, with you of course, into our gray-haired years. My lawyers must have acted on my instructions and would have provided you with the details. I don't feel it is helpful for me to speculate or prognosticate on how you would have received that information or the nature of my fate. I will simply say that maybe in the future, I will learn the answer another way (Wink, Wink, you'll get it later).

I have struggled with how best to explain to you what I have tried to do, what I have already done, and what's left to do. If, after reading this, you should decide to end my desired quest, then I would support your decision. Any thought to continue my work is yours, and yours alone. No strings attached, no guilt, just your own private choice. The responsibility I have left you is not for the faint of heart, or without future risk to both you, the kids, and our families. I am sure you will have had a visit from a few men in suits asking questions and giving their condolences. I try to edit this guide every 6 months to ensure it is as reasonably current and relevant as possible, knowing that this day may eventually happen. When I first began writing it (at age 12), it was only a few pages, written with my H2 pencil, in my special Black duo-tang booklet. Fortunately, I knew from prior experience the best hiding spots in the old family home. No one would ever see this guide until now.

While I have always maintained this secret, even from you, if you feel you need to seek another person's counsel, to assist you with my request, I will ask that you do it on a very selective and confidential basis. Please, Becca, finish reading this guide before you make that determination. One of my most difficult challenges was not bringing you into my confidence about my secret. My rationale was based on trying to make sure I could protect both you and our families from any potential danger associated with my secret. You have no idea the number of times that I wanted you to know what I did, and why I did it, but just could not risk it, or more importantly, risk you or the kids. There is no one in my 'lives', that I believe knew me as well as you did (Except maybe my new buddy Tank). You know I have always had a bit of a 'unique' side to me, and you first mentioned it to me at our first school dance when I recall you said, "You're very different from the other boys."

To maintain my secret, fulfill the required tasks, and try to live a 'normal life' without any consequences, was, as it turns out, not possible. I managed to complete many of my objectives and for the work I was able to complete, I can pass on this guide knowing I made a difference in a good way. You are about to discover how far-reaching those choices I made have changed the world as 'we' could have known it and how I used to know it. You're the sole keeper of this knowledge now.

Changes have consequences Rebecca and consequences make change!

Yours forever and now eternally,

Derek 2.0 😊

12757982

1

June 24th, 2024: It was on this particular day that my world changed. If you're trying to search your memory to see if you can recall that day, it is a day that has great meaning for me and none for you. I don't mean change in a small way; I mean changed; Changed that I could no longer return to the life *(world)* as I had known it and lived in it for 118 years. It's not a typo, I said 118 years *(And you better not start calling me Mr. Jangles now; I'm grinning)*. I promise you, it will make sense shortly, but for now, I need you to just keep reading. I promise you that I am not nuts and it will certainly make more sense to you soon. First, back to June 23rd *(the day before the big day)*.

I was driving up north to my buddy's fishing camp to help him install an off-grid solar system to power his camp. I once introduced you to Al and Laurie at a Pink Floyd concert, sometime around 1985, if you recall. I knew Al was a huge Pink Floyd fan, and I wanted the opportunity to see my old friend. I arranged to have our seats beside theirs's. It was funny seeing Al and Laurie for the first time again. They, of course, had no idea who we were. I wanted to maintain a friendship with Al, but there just wouldn't be enough time to connect with all my prior friends. I will be introducing you, Rebecca, in this guide, to a few 'acquaintances' that I once had very long and special friendships with. Some you will know extremely well, and some you will have never heard of. Now, back to the start.

Al and his wife Laurie bought the fly-in fish camp a few years ago and have been working on improving the camp during the summer seasons. I met Al and Laurie through Luke Mattson's dad when Joe Mattson was a CA. I was pretty good with computers and had helped Joe with his office computer automation. Al, who was a client of Joe's, needed help with his business computer issues. So, Joe suggested I may be able to help Al. Well, I helped Al and Laurie, and we soon became good friends.

Al retired a few years ago and bought a custom-built condo in Cabo San Lucas, where he and Laurie now spend their winters. They also have a very nice home located an hour and a half south of their Fish camp. From May till November, Al and Laurie bounce back and forth between their house and the camp. Laurie is active in a 'Save the Swan group' and Al keeps busy with the fish camp renovations, growing his select cannabis and drinking a few beers. I got a call from Al a few weeks ago, asking if I had time to give him a hand installing a solar system at the camp. Al knew I had some familiarity with the technology, as I was in the process of doing something similar on my 41-foot sailboat named 'It-girl'. If you're asking yourself if it's the same 'It-girl' the answer would be yes (*kind of*). Lithium batteries certainly have made it easier to change the old propane systems to an eco-friendlier electric power system.

It-girl enjoys 1600 watts of solar panels to power its 30,000-watt-hour lithium battery bank, which runs my fridge, stove, cooktop, ac, dishwasher, washer-dryer, water-maker, freezer, and all the other electronic needs on the boat. I bought the old Morgan Out Island, with the plan to renovate the entire boat and turn it into my soon-to-be future floating home. I was planning on retiring in a couple of years, and then heading out for a full circumnavigation when I hit 65 and taking my full pension. Little did I know that this plan was about to change. Or I should say take a ***divergence***.

The phone alarm went off at about 5 am. I got out of my bed in my 1-bedroom rural apartment which oddly enough is about 12 minutes from your childhood home and began my usual morning routine. These days, getting out of bed comes with plenty of moans, huffs, and puffs and walking, like the late Tim Conway character from the Carol Burnett show. *(If you smiled Rebecca, then, I know, you know, the character I am referring to)*. Age has not been kind to this body. Arthritis, joints wearing out, decades of physically abusing this body, and playing far too many sports, have taken its toll. I am still proud I can strap the old blades on and hold my own on the ice at my age. The younger guys can certainly skate circles around me, but most are good sports and try not to make me look too pathetic or complain about my tendency to clutch and grab to compensate. Every once in a while, I still find some of the old magic and can demonstrate I wasn't a pylon in my younger hockey days and do a little of the 'old dipsey doodle' and stuff the puck into the net. Unfortunately, those moments seem to be decreasing on the ice, and increasing as old war stories in the post-game bar reminiscing, we love to do after hockey.

I packed up what I planned to haul into Al's camp the night before, and I knew I would be passing Micky D's on my way out of town, so no need to brew up a cup of coffee for the road. I seemed to have overcome most of the aches and pains by now and made my way down the stairs to my truck. I bought a 2014 Ram quad cab a few years prior when I still had the Muskoka cottage. It was a shame I sold the cottage, but I told the kids that if they were not going to use it, then I was going to sell it. You always enjoyed the cottage, and I know my grandfather was crazy about you. I think he liked you back then, more than I did *(I just smiled)*. My memories of us at the cottage provided me with many years of great memory surfing, as I like to call it. It got me through some tough times. I am pretty sure, although it's been years since I wrote this section, recalling doing a little re-exploring of the cottage days, in more detail, in the early chapters of this guide. Please appreciate that I have tried to continuously edit this section, to keep it current, except around the time of the 'Great Re-set', but the rest of the guide was written chronologically from when I was 12 till now *(when ever that is).*

So, it's the early morning of June 23rd, and with my Micky D's large coffee with just milk in hand, my phone tuned to my CNN–Smerconish recording from yesterday, which I missed, I was on the road. I always thought if Smerk and I met in another life, we would be friends. He likes a good cigar, loves to fly fish, and our political views are almost always spot on. Although I would have forced him earlier in his life to add a 'leg day' routine *(I am sure he would be pissed about that comment if he ever knew I said it and tell me to F-U, then ask if I would now buy my roses from, I hate Steven Singer* 😊*).* I was heading up the 400 to meet Al at his home. From there, we would take his truck to the parking area he uses to access his camp. The camp was a fly-in access-only camp, but if you didn't mind a few portages, you could hoof it in, in a few hours. To fly in from the Beaver location *(Beaver plane that is, complete with a childish snicker)* was 15 minutes, but cost $750. Al justified the hoof in as a great way to get some exercise. I think it was more to offset the many Blue Light beers he would be consuming at the camp. For me, it was both the enjoyment of the exercise and the adventure of the trip. Since I did not get in that often, I had a tendency to haul in a few culinary delicacies. Like a nice big ribeye steak, some jumbo shrimp, and a few quality bottles of Chilean Carménère red wine, from my personal collection. It usually added up to about a 50-pound backpack, and I won't speculate on the calorie count. Oh yeah, I almost forgot, a few choice cigars. One of 'my' bad habits I justify as an homage to my grandfather. Gramps loved his cigars and since he lived to be 94, I figured it was safe to enjoy a few a year.

God knows how many kilometers I trolled, and how many cigars I smoked at the old cottage. They were great memories, but nothing close to my memories of you and me at the cottage. I guess I should apologize now for my unfortunate tendency to get caught up in some of the old *(prior)* memories, but as you may be able to tell, I still regard them as priceless, and would never want to forget them. If it's any consolation, it is all about you, anyway! Sort of! I arrived at Al's around 8 am, and we loaded my stuff from my truck into Al's truck.

I said, "Hi Laurie, how are you?", who was sitting on the front stoop drinking her morning coffee.

"I am good Derek, now that I have got some coffee in me. Looks like you and Al have some decent weather for your trip," she replied.

"Ya, I brought my battery-powered sleeping bag, just in case it gets a bit cool during the night. Unfortunately, my sleeping bag isn't large enough for Al to fit in to keep me warm," I jokingly replied.

Al was, of course, listening to our banter, and thought it was the appropriate time to chime in with, "You listen here fella, if it's that cold, we can zip two bags together."

We all laughed, and after a few more jokes and quips, we waved goodbye, headed out onto the gravel roadway, and started the second leg of the trip. Al and I always enjoyed each other's company and were never short of topics to discuss. I think we spent most of the trip, discussing the steps we needed to do with the installation, and I am sure, we had a few distractions with a few USA-political observations, some prognostication on the upcoming Leaf's hockey season, and still no cup. Al needed to make a stop at a Tim Horton's drive-thru, about 30 minutes north of his house, and get his breakfast feeding. I elected to get another large coffee and warned Al that there would be a better than good chance that we would need to make a pee stop before we arrived at the camp. Al certainly took advantage of the opening and said,

"You should have planned better in advance and put on an extra-large Depends," along with his usual grin.

"Well, maybe I did, but have already filled it with my first morning Micky D's coffee. What you should be suggesting is that I go into Timmie's and change my Depends to a new one," I replied.

We exchanged our usual laugh and continued back on our journey and discussed the installation. The drive is about 90 minutes from Al's house door to Al's parking spot to access the camp from. Al carries a Jon Boat *(flat bottom green tin boat)* in the back of his truck, which I think is about 10 feet. He also has a 4-stroke gas, 3.5 hp, little outboard to push it. Al parks at a resort, just off the highway, which is also a seaplane port servicing the area. Al contracts the Beaver *(seaplane and another childish giggle)* at the start of the season, to haul in supplies, including a bunch of cases of Blue Light.

During the winter, he hired a local to pull in a bunch of lumber by Skidoo, along with some other stuff. It was still a somewhat rustic setup, considering we needed to use a traditional outhouse to do our business.

Part of the reason for the Solar upgrade was the future addition of a proper composting toilet that could be put inside the cottage. Al had hooked up a propane water heater earlier that year so we could enjoy a hot shower when needed.

I know Laurie was looking forward to the convenience, although she is a trooper, and could rough it with the best of us. For Al and me, it would mean that we would not have to pee off the front deck, for our mid-way through the night tinkle. For now, it was the old-fashioned way, and I doubt I will see the indoor toilet in use until next season. Chances are, if it's in earshot of where Laurie sleeps, if I am there when she is there, I will most likely continue the off-the-deck ritual, and hopefully some version of an outhouse for those nasty times guys can have, after consuming large quantities of red meat. Al backed the truck up to the dock area, where we could slide the Jon boat down onto some sand. We slid it out, gently lowered it down into the water, and began to unload all the supplies.

The resort was a typical Canadian Northern resort, with the main lodge and several separate cabin complexes spread about. It looked like it was built in the 60s with periodic upgrades over the years. It is certainly handy for Al to access the lake from here, and the route requires us to boat roughly 3 km across the lake, where we beach the boat and lock it to a tree. From there, we carry our supplies, including the 3.5 hp outboard, which Al had fashioned a cute little two-wheeled cart to pull it on. From the first landing, we need to hike a trail for about 45 minutes to the next lake. There, Al has another Jon boat that we will use to cross the next lake and perform the same process. We cross a total of three lakes before we reach the final trail that takes us to Al's private lake. Al enjoys the entire lake to himself. No neighbors. The entire trip takes about 3 hours. Carrying the 50 lbs backpack makes the trip a bit of a grind heading in. Fortunately, my old body can still perform the required task, although I am sure there will be a few Tylenol extra strength on the diet for tonight.

I recall on the last lake crossing asking Al, "when are you planning on buying your float plane to fly in on? We've discussed a Cessna185 a few times. The bright red hue from your face suggests sooner rather than later, or you better add a defib unit to your near future purchases."

Al replied, "Once I drop a few pounds, the trip won't be as grueling as it seems to be at the start of the season."

"But the season started 2 months ago, buddy! At this rate, you will be closing up by the time you reach your imaginary weight goal. Maybe it would be easier if you just bought some larger jeans to transition into, to give you the illusion of weight loss", I teased with the customary stunned look.

"Well, I guess I could always bring me back a couple Mexicans for the summer to carry me in.... certainly would be cheaper than the plane, and give Laurie some variety," he replied chuckling.

We both laughed out loud and knew our brand of humor could be seen as a bit off-color or politically incorrect. Fortunately for us, it was just us. Besides, Al and I were equal opportunity bigots. We didn't care about race, the color of skin, or sexual orientation; If you're a dick, then you're a dick! The last trail section into Al's cottage always seemed to go fastest. I guess it was the anticipation of finally getting there and dumping the backpack that helped with the adrenalin boost. As the cottage finally came into view, I felt a bit of relief and my f'd up shoulder would certainly appreciate unloading the backpack. As we approached the cottage, we passed by the good old outhouse. Unfortunately, it will be well used by us, I was sure. I just hope Al and I don't share the same bowel movement schedule this trip, or even better, my schedule was 15 minutes before his *(Another childish grin Rebecca).*

Al's place is located at one end of the lake, which is somewhat elongated more than round. I would guess the length-to-width ratio would be roughly 4 to 1, with the length being about two kilometers. The lake is host to bass and pike and a couple large snapping turtles. On the last trip to the camp, I enjoyed some fried Pike bites and expect the same tomorrow. Al has become fairly proficient at cleaning pike, which is generally considered very hard to clean *(no bones).* I am sure, Rebecca, that you remember our trip into the West Arm of Nipissing years ago. It was the first time we tried, you-know-what *(and that's all I am going to say about that; Ha-ha, made you blush!).*

Sorry, back to the information. Al and I arrived at the camp around 1:30 pm and decided to immediately get to work for a few hours before we would quit for dinner and drinks. At our age, once we stop for dinner, good luck getting us to go back to work. Tonight was going to be simple: hamburgers and hotdogs with a side 'salad in a bag'. Beer for dessert. I packed in a few Kilkenny and a couple of Guinness. Al was a loyal Blue Light guy, while I loved the thicker stuff, as you know. Tomorrow I was planning on cooking our ribeye's sous vide, with a side of blackening on the Barbie. Ever since I discovered 'sous vide', I have never gone back. Another bonus I brought with me across time, I guess. I know you always appreciated and enjoyed my cooking. I have always loved cooking, and I think asking for, and getting, an Easy Bake Oven as a kid was a strong sign. That 100-watt light bulb certainly turned out a lot of chocolate mini cakes for the neighborhood guys.

Dinner was consumed, and drinks were flowing. Al decided to roll himself a little hash cigarette *(a favorite of his).* I *(as you know)* never got into any kind of smoke other than a good mild cigar. I always blamed the gas mask experience at U of Miami for my dislike of getting stoned. Although, it was responsible for me discovering Blimpy's Double meat deal. I knew that it would only be a matter of time before the guitar came out. Al is a very good guitar player and the two of us make a pretty good duo. I told him I would have to buy him a bass guitar or drum kit as a cottage warming gift.

Whenever I get a chance to jam, I can't help but remember the times I played with my dad's group. I know he was so proud of the effort I put into learning to sing and play drums and guitar. Funny how we tend to latch onto certain things in life. I loved my parents, but back the first time, I was more into what I wanted and less into what I am sure they were hoping for. I never made the effort to be the best I could be. I guess that is the one thing that most of us would be guilty of. But the second go-around was incredible.

I had brought in my 88-keys roll up piano keyboard that I hooked up to the Mini USB speaker. When I got everything connected, I broke into my latest arrangement of an old Eric Carmen song, 'All by Myself'. We jammed for a few hours and eventually Al had polished off his 12th or 15th beer and looked ready to crash and burn. He stumbled off to bed, and I decided to stay up and enjoy a cigar on the dock with a glass of Port that I also hoofed in. I was a bit of a lightweight that night with the beers, which afforded me the ability to have a snifter of Taylor Fladgate 20-year-old, and a fine Romeo and Juliette cigar. The only thing missing for me was a fine selection of sharp cheeses.

[If you are getting tired Rebecca and want to take a break from reading this guide, then this would be a good place to do it. I think you will want to be fresh for the next few pages…]

2 June 24th (Shortly after midnight): I had taken a chair, from the deck, down to the dock, and proceeded to set up my little private port and cigar area, when I first felt an odd sensation in the air. It had to be around midnight, maybe close to 12:30 when I detected a strange odor. I had never smelled anything like that before and proceeded to light my cigar. I brought my favorite lighter that my cottage buddy Hart gave me, and performed the customary 'end clip', with the clipper my cottage buddy Hart gave me also. Thanks, Hart *(I smiled)*! As I applied the required saliva coating to the cigar, I thought I heard a faint crying sound. I stopped for a moment and listened, as best as I could, considering my hearing was less than perfect, or some have accused me of being outright deaf. After a minute passed, and I was unable to hear what I thought I heard, I continued my cigar lighting ritual, complete with the lighting, cigar spinning, finishing with the flame to the end. Another perfect light job!

I took my first proper puff and took a look up at the sky. Looked like a clear sky, and the temperature was not that bad. I would guess it was about 10 degrees Celsius, with no breeze. Having enjoyed the first puff or two, it was now time for the first sip of my port. Every time I drink Port, I can't help but remember my great port hunt of 1993. Harley motorcycle, good friends, and plenty of Port hunting. I know I shipped back over 30 bottles, and I also know that half turned into excellent cooking vinegar. But to find a few 1882 Grahams private reserve winemakers only selection made it all worthwhile. I know my buddy Bernie was pissed-off at my find, but that is what differentiated me from the B-man. Fortunately for me, the label had fallen off and was hidden under a half-inch of dust at the bottom, or the shop owner would have never allowed me to buy the box. I paid him $100 US for the whole box, as is.

I was prepared to go anywhere while Bernie was more selective, and I think, interested in finding women than a lost rare bottle of port. We must have stopped into a couple of dozen, out-of-the-way wine and Liquor shops. I was head to toe, covered in 50 years of dust when I emerged with the old wooden box. The owner of the shop claims, he never knew the box was where I found it and had no idea how old it was. I think he was more concerned it was all just going to be glorified vinegar. Well, that is what makes Port hunting so exciting. One man's box of dust-covered vinegar is another man's pot of gold! I think Bernie, always felt I should have given him at least 1 bottle, as consideration for him being such a great guy. I decided it was better he learned the cost of taking the shortcut and womanizing over Port hunting.

I will never forget when I put the 2 other bottles up for auction, without fully appreciating what I had found. Part of me, still feels some guilt, that I had the nerve, to drink a $7,000 bottle of Port, with average cheese *(Yes, another giggle).* Looking back Rebecca, I wished I had taken you to Portugal and toured these iconic wineries. I know you would have loved the adventure far more than Bernie. I still have the letter you sent me when you did your European 'find myself' tour in the summer of 1981. I think we both know you never needed any finding!

After a few more gentle puffs, and a couple sips of my favorite late-night indulgence, I thought I heard a faint crying sound again, coming from the bay, beside the dock. There was enough moon to light up the bay that night, but I could not see anything but the lake. I tried to focus my gaze, in the direction where I thought the sound was coming from, but again, just lake. I sat in the chair, with my gaze fixed on the spot I thought the sound came from while continuing to take slow and small puffs of my cigar. I would estimate that it took about 3 minutes before I noticed a ripple in the water coming toward the dock.

My immediate thought, was the old Snapper Turtle that was living under the dock last year, was out cruising the water. Well, no big deal, mystery solved, and I was glad I had determined the source of the sound. Back to my sipping and puffing. As I relaxed again back into the chair, I started to stare up into the sky, and as I often did, started to think about you, Rebecca. I wonder what Rebecca is doing now. Did I do the right thing and not find out where she was living and force some contrived chance encounter at the grocery store. I think that was one of my favorite, 'What if's', to pass some personal quiet time, and I always enjoyed daydreaming about what I would say. When I sent you the text a few years before this, I was not prepared for your reply. I was somewhat devastated, but also part of me, fully understood why it had to be. Back then, I had always tried to convince myself that you deserved better than me *(I am sure Rebecca 1.0 would be agreeing with me)*, and if I truly loved you, and wanted what was best for you, then it couldn't be me. I have always wondered what a psychologist or psychoanalyst would think of my reasoning. Lucky for me, I was always too cheap to find out.

There was that sound again, this time a bit louder. I was sure it was coming from the middle of the Bay, but I could only see the lake. There was nothing there, so, what could be making the sound? I know a bullfrog can make a crying sound, but this was different, not a bullfrog, I could not see anything but the lake. As my curiosity got the better of me, I thought I might hop in the canoe tied to the dock, and paddle over to see if I could figure out the mystery. I was certainly not drunk by any measure and paddling out into the bay in the middle of the night could not happen, without a couple of additions to the trip.... my bottle of Port, and the fish cleaning knife Al left on the dock from earlier. Just in case it's the Snapping Turtle, trying to lure me out, pretending to be in distress, and then flipping the boat and eating me *(that was a joke, Rebecca)*. And so, my adventure began. I put the Port bottle on the edge of the dock, stuck the cigar into my mouth, and started the most difficult part of this whole process, bending down and getting into the canoe. For a guy that canoed almost every inch of Algonquin park, in his youth, during the numerous canoe outings with you at the cottage, one would think it would be a no-brainer getting in.

After some unplanned moans, and they were not pleasurable moans, I managed to slide my butt into the middle of the canoe, so I could rest it on the center yolk. A simple J stroke and I will be out to the middle of the bay in 3 minutes. After getting in, the next emergency was figuring out where I could put my Port Snifter. After scanning the canoe, my only option was to leave the glass and bring the bottle. At least it had a cork stuck in the end so all would be good.

There it was again. Yes, it was getting louder each time. And now with my 'on the lake' positioning, I would bet it was coming from the middle of the bay, some 200 yards away. But there was nothing but lake. I looked across the bay and could see the rock cliffs lining the shore all along the opposite side from where I was. Maybe the sound was occurring someplace else and was bouncing off the cliffs towards my position. I began to scan around the lake to see if I could pick up anything out of the ordinary that would give me a clue as to what was I hearing. Nothing. Just lake. As a true adventurer and fearless *(yuk yuk)*, I did what anyone in my situation would do when put into this perplexing position. I popped the cork and took a mouthful of the old Taylor Fladgate. A few puffs, and now I was ready to head to the middle of the bay. Might even be cool to lay on the bottom of the canoe for a while and stare at the sky. Who knows, maybe Peter Quill will appear overhead, or I guess, truer to the story, Yondo. If you smiled Rebecca, then you know you're a sci-fi lover.

I put the paddle in the water and made my first J-stroke. Still had it after all these years, Rebecca. Again, with another J-stroke. There was that smell again. I don't think I ever smelled anything like that before. Maybe there is some methane trapped under the lake and is slowly leaking out. Great, a few more strokes, and I could lose the water's buoyancy and sink to the bottom. Thank God, it's at best, 12 feet here according to Al. Al could have his own Bermuda Triangle on his lake. When I start to get a bit nervous, you probably noticed I tend to get a bit silly with my thoughts. Rest assured, behind those silly thoughts, I am soiling myself. Figuratively speaking that is. Truth is, as you well know Rebecca, both now and before, I always could turn off the scared valve, and when needed, the morality valve. I must have been subconsciously doing just that. My whole body went into its defensive mode. My Spidey sense was telling me, that I was not alone out here, but my eyes were telling me the opposite.

Another, bigger dose of that smell. As I began to bite down harder on the cigar in my mouth, my instincts had me reaching for the Rapala knife. I am a smart guy and have had many experiences in my life, certainly more than most, surely, I can figure this out. Weird smell, strange sound, almost full moon, no wind to speak of, Al in bed, Derek floating in a canoe in the bay. What could go wrong with this picture? Rhetorical question!

I can honestly say that what I felt next, was almost identical to the time my dad took me out in a canoe when I was about 6 or 7 on Lake Mazinaw. I was in the front, and dad was in the back. I don't think dad had a lot of experience in a canoe. We were fishing along the shoreline. Dad wanted to paddle to another spot, just up ahead, when all of a sudden, the canoe began to slowly rise at the front end, eventually rising right out of the water. It rose, which felt like feet, but based on my post-dad canoeing experience, probably a foot at best. The rise was not the issue, but the canoe slowly started to tip to the port side, *(left side Rebecca)* as the angle continued to increase, I must have realized I was destined to go into the lake.

Splash, I was in, luckily, I had a life jacket on, mother's orders, even though I was a good swimmer, but the scary part was the canoe landing on top of me upside down. While I wish I could tell you, I was strong and fearless then, truth be told, I started wailing like a baby. I felt my dad grab onto me and tell me, "Everything was ok. We just ran up on a stump and it caused the canoe to tip." With one arm, dad flipped the canoe back upright and with his other hand, grabbed me and stuck me on top of the partially submerged stump. The initial shock seemed over, and I believe I had come to realize that I was safe on top of the partially submerged log, dad was safe, and I didn't need to cry anymore. One good part of falling in water, then bawling like a baby, hard to tell tears from the lake water. As I sat on the stump watching my dad, he got to a shallow spot near the bank, then tipped the canoe in such a way as to empty most of the water. He then climbed up on the bank and got himself back into the canoe, where he was before our tipping. He grabbed the paddle, and most of the fishing equipment was still in the bottom of the canoe. Dad turned the front of the canoe towards me and told me to step in. I followed his direction, and with the tears now behind me, I noticed dad staring down into the water.

He said, "There it is."

I asked, "What?"

"Our fishing tackle box. It was not fully closed and must have sunk," as he continued to comment while maintaining his fixation on the location.

Fortunate for us, the fishing rods had cork handles and either floated or hung up on the yolk and seats. Our new challenge was not to catch a fish but to snag the tackle box. I don't remember how deep it was, but it was no deeper than the length of my dad's fishing rod. He was able to bring his lure, with the hook, right up to the tip of the rod, then use the rod to position the lure's hook, to snag the tackle box. It took a few tries, but dad managed to get the box up to the surface, grab it, and put it on the bottom of the canoe. I think we lost a few lures, but it was so long ago, that I can't recall that detail accurately. After that event, dad and I paddled back to the resort to change clothes and tell everyone about the near-death ordeal. Well, that's how I remember it. Dad's version to mom was less "Oh my god' and more laughing at us falling in. Knowing me, I am sure it has been told over the years with a variety of endings and recollections.

So, as the canoe began to rise at the front, I did what any experienced canoer would do, I plopped my fat 'hockey player' ass down to the bottom, from previously resting against the yolk, with the paddle now straddling the sides, and being used to offer me the ability to try and maintain the upright posture of the canoe, and balance myself in the middle. Unlike dad, and our canoe adventure, I was trying to prevent the bottle from falling in, or my cigar from getting wet. All kidding aside, what was even more baffling, was the front of the canoe was gone, or should I say about 3 feet of it. By this point, I can say that I had gone into full defensive mode. I turned off my fear valve. I thought I was ready for anything but was prepared for, not a thing. I found myself starting to test the stability of the canoe. I applied a little weight, shifting from port to starboard. Could I get it to wiggle? Nope, nothing. A little harder, and still no. I now made the decision, to reposition myself back up onto my knees. As I said, fear valve turned off, and one of the benefits of this, it also shut off my pain receptors.

I pulled myself up onto my usually 'painful' arthritic knees, with no movement from the canoe. But as I stared at the missing front of the canoe, my senses were telling me that the canoe was still in one piece. I simply could no longer see the front part. It looked like someone cut the front three feet of the canoe off, and I was looking at lake water that didn't seem to want to rush into the rest of the canoe. Well, my physics knowledge was telling me, that is not possible, but my years of watching sci-fi television, and movies, were telling me differently.

Rebecca, you must be at this point, already rolling your eyes and thinking that this is some elaborate gag or prank, or worse, that I am truly nuts. I promise you it is not, and, I am not nuts, and if you will simply force yourself to read 5 more pages, JUST 5, I am sure it will all make sense. You know how I hate the expression, "I promise you on the life of my kids" statement, so, I would never invoke that. But I will remind you, of that Friday, back during the first week of June 1977, when I saved your brother's life. Most will challenge me on that claim, but you were there. It was the first time we hung out *(as friends)*.

I will remind you of my unexpected arrival at old Gibson's Pond. By myself, for a swim, which just happened, to be the same day and time you, your brother, John, Matt, and Frank decided to play hooky that Friday afternoon. 'Let's go for a swim, on our way home from High School'. One of the many benefits, of using Martin Side Road to bike to school, I guess. I am sure that is where you developed your love of cycling. It was pre-planned since you had your bathing suit on at school. I could see it under your shirt that morning. Yes, I was checking you out at school. I needed to confirm if that was Gibson's Pond Day. Strange, you never did ask me why I would go to Gibson's Pond, swimming by myself, after that day. Was it just a coincidence?

Man, I remember that day like it was yesterday. One of my fondest memories since it was the first time I was able to gaze at you in a swimsuit *(since my return)*. No one looked better in a one-piece swimsuit than you *(I know you just smiled)*. I would credit the biking mostly, but I must confess after meeting your mom, it was also genetics. And we can't forget to mention your fabulous gait. A cross between athletic and sexy. If you ever wondered what you look like from behind, the closest example that comes pretty darn close would be Shakira 😉.

I detected that day, a bit of shyness when I swam across the pond to where you were sunning yourself. I certainly hope I wasn't gawking at you like some love-smitten horny young kid. With all the trees around the pond, it was the only spot you could get direct sun. What you don't know, is that I had been keeping an eye on you since grade 8. My grade 8, your grade 7.

I made sure not to let you catch me with my gazes. I am pretty sure; I was also invisible to you. I even made a point to keep my interactions with your brother 'Tonka' *(Todd, we just call him Tonka after what he did to his jeep)* to a minimum.

But I do remember meeting your parents for the first time at the grade 8 graduation although they did attend the big gala in 1974, I attended *(more about that later)*. I purposely went over to offer my congratulations to Todd on graduating, hoping he would introduce me to your parents. Your mom, who you got your looks from, and Dad, were extremely kind, and also congratulated me on winning Athlete of the year and highest-grade point average. I was planting the seed of acceptance, for the future. My digression into old memories is certainly lengthening this section of the guide. I will try to limit them, but they are putting a huge smile on my face as I write this. Not to mention my tendency to re-read the entire section every time I need to edit it.

Can you remember how I suddenly jumped up and began to run around Gibson's Pond, in the middle of our chat, to the other side? The guys were using the swinging rope to do flips into the pond that was slung over the huge willow tree branch. Can you remember, how I immediately grabbed the other end of the rope, which had been tied off to another tree branch, with about 4 feet of excess rope dangling down, almost touching the ground? Do you remember, I grabbed the four-foot section, and tried my best to wrap it around my waist, just as your brother started his swing. Then, we all heard the sound, of the lower branch holding the rope, breaking, and your brother landing in about 3 feet of water on his back instead of 10 feet of water with his feet, producing a rather large bruise on his backside.

It took Tonka a few minutes to get the wind back into himself while he was struggling to keep his head out of the water. Then, the rather loud painful scream when the pain from landing on his back made its way to the necessary receptors. By this point, you had gotten up yourself and were running around the pond to join everyone, who were now watching Tonka's face contort in obvious pain. What you didn't notice, or at least I don't think you did, was my eyes stuck to you, thinking, how you had grown into such a beautiful girl. But I knew deep down, I had done what I needed to do, and that our time together was soon to end for a while. We all kind of just stood there for a few minutes, just staring at Tonka, and all realizing what had happened.

Remember John and Matt saying, "If Derek had not been holding the rope, your brother probably would have ended up landing on a pile of rocks along the shore." That certainly ended the rope swinging session, and we all slowly entered the pond, to assess what happened, while Tonka did his best to try and laugh off the incident.

I said to Todd with a grin, "How do you plan to explain the huge bruise on your back to your folks?"

"Rugby," Frank chimed in. "You got it playing Rugby." We all laughed since Rugby would have been the last sport Todd would ever participate in. Great guy with a big heart but a small frame.

Do you remember the huge rope burn tattooed on my lower back, which took the weight of Tonka's swing? I am pretty sure you do recall since you were the one, that came over and pointed it out to me. I can still feel your hand touching my back. While you thought I was probably in pain, I can assure you I was closer to the ecstasy side of the scale than pain. Rebecca Hamlin just touched my naked back! It was somewhat short-lived, as the new, pervy old man thought, replaced that precious golden moment. You will understand this mental issue better shortly. Remember you asking me, how I knew the rope would break, and I told you I could see the rope fraying from where we were laying and chatting? I lied. I did not see any rope fraying. Think about it. The loose four-foot section hanging was completely hidden from us because it was behind the trunk of the huge tree. Try to find those lost memories to confirm what I am telling you. So, the question would remain, how did I know to run and grab the rope?

Please, I beg you. Read the next 5 pages and you will understand, that, had I not grabbed the rope when I did, your brother that day would have hit the rocks, broken his neck, and would die in your arms on that day. It would be a devastating event for you, your family, and I am sure reshaped your life, into the life I came to know and love. This was now a new lifeline, that I could not predict anymore, since I was the one who decided to alter it. I think you would agree from Todd's perspective, it was for the good, assuming you can buy into my explanation.

When we all decided the hooky fun was over and it was time to make our way back to reality, and our respective homes, I don't know if you recall me touching your hand when it was gripping your handlebar and saying, "I will be watching you." You never did comment on that either. I hope your creepo meter did not start going off. As we emerged onto Martin's side road, you guys all turned left, and I turned right. You guys were lucky. All downhill, while I had one of the steepest biking hills in the area. But unlike the old days *(Derek 1.0)* Derek 2.0 was all about being the best he could be and peddled up the hill as fast as my legs would allow me. While my heart wanted me to continue our chatting after that day, my brain, unfortunately, knew better, and it was not to be.

I began to move toward the front of the canoe so I could get a closer look at what I could only assume was some optical illusion. I moved forward on the other side of the yolk and realized that I still had my cigar firmly held by my teeth. I decided to let myself take a puff. I was now only a foot from the mystery of the missing section of the canoe. Suddenly, I had another major whiff of that odor I could not identify, and for a brief moment, I found myself unable to breathe normally. Then, I heard without any doubt, the odd crying sound, and I was sure it came from about 10 feet in front of where I was now positioned. I slowly moved my arm forward, to where I figured the canoe side should be, and it was at that moment, I can honestly tell you, I knew exactly what was happening and that my brain was right.

As my hand grabbed what I thought would be the side of the canoe, my forearm, and hand were gone. Just below my elbow was water, but my hand was grabbing the canoe, and I did not feel any water. I felt the canoe side. No doubt, I had my hand, which was no longer visible, on the canoe side. I stopped, and to prove to my brain that I was right, I slowly retrieved my arm and hand from the fake water and my world made sense again. High-tech camouflage. Bingo! Probably military, and I was sure that it would only be a few minutes, before a bunch of military guys appeared, and would take me into custody. I decided to relax, sit my ass on the yolk, grab my bottle of port, and try to enjoy a few sips, maybe a self-pat on the back before all hell would let loose. Why would the military be here at Al's lake? Maybe because they thought it was deserted, and did not know, Al and I would be coming in. But, if the military was doing some top-secret testing, then surely, they would have had monitoring going on. Maybe they thought they were safe behind this high-tech camouflage. Well, at least I am sure, they would have enjoyed our concert earlier. The crying noise was most likely a failing bearing.

Something was not right. No military yet. Odor dissipated but I again heard the odd crying-like sound, it was coming from behind the camouflage barrier. I started to examine the barrier, with a much more discerning eye, now that I was aware of what it was. I have always considered myself more scientist, than liberal arts guy, and can even point to a few inventions that I have designed and built over my life. I am referring to the ones that I invented not the ones I may have lifted. Boy Rebecca are you going to have a whole new perspective of me shortly. Now, my scientist curiosity was starting to kick in, and I thought it was probably about time for me to venture behind the curtain to look at the wizard. I figured why not do it with some chutzpah, so I grabbed the bottle of port and moved forward toward the missing section of the canoe. I assumed the canoe was still *(no pun intended)* in the water and did not see any need to go and get wet. After all, I am sure I was about to see some stunned faces when I broke through the high-tech barrier.

When I was 14, my best friend Luke Mattson and I, discovered an ad in the back of a magazine called Outdoor Life, for a blow gun. Yes, a blow gun. Luke and I knew each other through our early hockey careers *(Novice through Bantam)*. He played for a team in the city relative to where his family lived, and I played for a team that was based on where my dad worked. I played for the Westinghouse Bengal's. We both played in the same league. We were the same age, and in fact, he was 6 days older than me. He was captain of his team, and I was captain of my team. I think we had a mutual respect during this competitive time.

In the summer of 1972, his family moved out of the city up to good old Sherman Falls. We called it up the mountain. I only discovered this on the first day of grade 7, when we spotted each other in the hall of Senior Public. I get into far more detail about Luke and me further in the guide so I won't repeat it here. Suffice it to say, we became best friends as you know. Getting back to the blow guns. We had been working, shoveling snow at my grandmother's seniors' home, and had our own money saved, and our parents didn't care how we spent it. So, Luke and I ordered the blow guns. I think they cost around 20 dollars each. Turned out it was an aluminum tube, some drapery beads, piano wire, and instructions on how to make the darts.

One night, I awoke to a strange sound, coming from outside the house. I had never heard the sound before. It seemed to get loud, then slowly got weaker. When it was loudest, it almost shook the house. I came out of my bedroom, and it appeared that my sister was awakened by the noise, just like I was, and we met in the hall. Our bedrooms were beside each other at the end of the hall. I am sure we looked at each other and asked what was going on. Again, every minute or so, the sound got louder and louder, then got quieter and quieter, but always very noticeable. Mom and dad's bedroom was in the basement, so I guess they never awoke from the sound. I said to my sister, “Let’s go outside and see what was going on.” I could tell my sister, who was a couple of years older, was not a fan of the idea and was noticeably scared. Not knowing what it was, I decided it was best, if I was armed, and I retired to my bedroom, where I retrieved my only weapon, the blow gun and a handful of darts.

I proceeded to the front door with my sister, and I believe I was in front. We went out onto the front porch, and as soon as we emerged from the house, the sound level was almost deafening at times. Still the same pattern. Loud, then soft, in 1–2-minute intervals. What made it even more interesting, was the fog. Yes, believe it or not, we had fog that summer night. Clutching my blow gun, I said to my sister, "it sounds like it's coming from up the street, let's go and see if we can see anything." This for me was a defining moment in my life. When faced with a completely unknown event, that certainly had my sister scared to the point she decided to retreat into the house's front doorway, my curiosity seemed to trump my sense of fear. With my blow gun drawn, I proceeded down the porch steps, and moved west across the side lawn, reaching the paved road. The sound was coming from the northwest. As I made my way along our street, moving towards the ever-increasing drone of the sound, I realized that I loved the adrenalin rush I was experiencing. I was not in fear, I was in a state, I only can describe as, wonderment, and extreme curiosity.

I think if I was hearing a sound I could identify, such as a gun or missile fire, then I would hope fear would be guiding my decision-making. But at this time, in this situation, I started to let my imagination get the better of me and had my first thought it might be aliens. While in my defense, I loved sci-fi and had watched every Star Trek episode multiple times, and my thoughts of aliens turned out to be short-lived. By the time I had made it about 300 yards up the street, my brain had figured out what was happening. I think at that moment, I had a combined sensation of laughter and relief. Not sure what was more dominant, but laughter would be dominant when I retold this story over the years. See, it turned out, that not far from our house was an old air-raid siren tower. It had been built years ago but don't know the exact date. I don't think it was the 1940s but more the late 1950s. It was a long-standing fixture in our community and remained erect since the cold war, and for several years, after this event. Turns out there was some electrical malfunction, and for the first time since they stopped doing the test before I was born, it decided to do, one more swan song, for the neighborhood as the giant cone speaker began to rotate.

Having realized what it was, my attention now turned to getting back to the house before any of the neighborhood spotted me out in my pyjamas carrying a blow gun. I read in the local paper, that after that event occurred, they disconnected the power. So, I hope you can now appreciate that my decision to engage the barrier rather than jump into the lake and swim back to the cottage, was an innate act. I think it was simply in my DNA. You're probably shaking your head in agreement based on everything that we have been through, or should I say, I have been through that you know about.

I was about to put my head through the barrier when a reflex caused me to stop. My phone: It was in my jacket pocket, and I think I would like to do a little recon first before I stick my head through an unknown barrier. I already knew my hand and arm went in and came out safe, but I didn't want to risk my head yet. I unzipped my jacket pocket and removed my phone. I switched it from sleep mode, to active, and touched the camera icon. I had the phone on me, just in case, I felt like listening to a few songs on the dock. I had on my phone, the 'World's Greatest playlist'. Well, that was my claim, and I always challenged people to prove me wrong. The camera function booted up, and I pointed the camera at the barrier. The Lake appeared on the screen as I would expect. I hit the video record icon, and I slowly moved my hand and then arm through the barrier, until my elbow reached the edge of the barrier, but remained visible to me. For a split second my brain fired "War amps." My brain probably figured if I lost my forearm but still had my elbow, I could still get some prosthetic that would allow me to hold onto a hockey stick and continue my quest to make it to the show. *(I just giggled).*

As my hand penetrated the barrier, this time I took notice of the sensation and tried to figure out what was being used to generate the barrier. I was leaning toward some special fog-like gas, that had a unique crystalline structure, that allowed some projection of the lake to be displayed from behind, creating the illusion of looking at the lake. But what I felt was absolutely nothing. No temperature change, no wet or gooey feeling, no electrical static-like effect, just nothing. I would be dishonest with you Rebecca if I did not confess, that I did have the thought that I could lose my lower arm doing what I did. When I stuck my hand through earlier and grabbed the edge of the front of the canoe, I had not yet completed my usual detailed 'What if' scenario in my head. Funny, that is something I do very well, but it took a back seat at that moment, which was rare. It was another blow gun moment.

I let the phone video record for a few minutes, and I did my best to use a slow panning movement, in hopes of getting as much visual information as I could. I was also prepared for someone to grab my arm, or hand, at any moment, and take the phone, before potentially pulling my entire body through the barrier to the other side. I had instinctively anchored myself in the canoe, to make that situation, as difficult as I could if it was to happen. After a few minutes of panning and filming, I slowly pulled my arm back to my side of the barrier. As I did, I thought I felt something touch my hand. Might simply have been the barrier itself, and the effect of passing through it, but I couldn't disregard what my mind was telling me. I turned the phone towards me and touched the play icon. As I drew my attention to the screen, to see what was on the other side, I again heard a faint odd crying sound.

As the video began to play, I could not believe what I was watching. I swear to God Becca, which isn't saying much since I am a devout atheist, but what was on the video screen was impossible. It was a video of Rebecca and Derek, at the Hermitage, that day after we had our first fight as girlfriend and boyfriend. It was our first, what I would call, high school adolescent lovers spat, since, by this time, we had accepted that our sexual activity was restricted to everything but, you know what, at your request, I will remind you *(I giggled again).*

I was sitting on the top of the east wall of the ruins about 10 feet up, more specifically, the original servant quarters section, when you emerged, from the trees, bare ass naked, with nothing but a smile. To be honest Rebecca, I don't even remember what that spat was about, but it must have been somewhat contrived since you were able to quickly find me at the Hermitage. You always knew it was my fortress of solitude. Deer tracking, fort building, fishing, hiking, and just loving being outdoors with my best friend Luke. I could honestly say, I knew the Hermitage area like the back of my hand! I always try to go there every April 14th and place a red rose on the window ledge of the ruins east wall, which lets me, honor the day we became officially Girlfriend and Boyfriend. I still call it the greatest day of my life *(Although I think I have a few 'Greatest Days' when it come's to you).* I will ask you, do you remember the heart-shaped locket? But I know you would be shaking your head, no. I know you have been throughout this reading so far, often wondering, who is Derek talking about, because it certainly wasn't you most of the time. I promise the answer is coming.

How was this possible. I was looking at a video, of something that took place 46 years ago. There were no cell phones yet, and I know, there were no cameras at the Hermitage. I don't know how long I stared at the video, but, for a brief moment, I could not take my eyes off of you. You were 16, going on 17 in September, and WOW, you were so beautiful *(Not to suggest you're not still as beautiful)*. But how was this possible? I had done my best to retain my memories of you over the years and cherished a few photos of you I had in my memory box. The box you gave me. It had the Boutonnière you gave me from your graduation party, pictures from a mall photo booth, some pictures I took with a disposable camera, a couple you gave me, and my favorite, a few pics from our time at the cottage. I wish you could remember the one at the cottage taken with my gramps, and you wearing my high school football jersey and your/my favorite white cotton bikini style undies. *(Another giggle)*.

But the video of Rebecca was taken from multiple camera vantage points. There was the view of me looking down at you emerging from the trees, there was a view from where you were standing looking up at me smiling. There was even a view of me, coming down off the wall, and running over to you, telling you to quickly get your clothes on because people were coming up the drive. Fortunately, I could see up the drive from the top of the wall or it could have been a completely different outcome. *(I just smiled again)*.

I don't know for sure, but I have to guess, that it was about this moment that I first thought maybe I was going nuts or was already nuts in some hospital strapped to a bed enjoying this crazy dream! My military camouflage rationale was now giving way to me most likely having a mental breakdown. Even in this momentary state of confusion, I touched the phone again so I could replay it. There you were, birthday suit, smile and for a moment, I felt a lifetime of regret rushing through me. I thought, what a loser I was, as you stood smiling up at me. I had perfection, and somehow, I managed to screw it up. This is certainly not the time to start the whole regret montage. I would run out of computer memory if that was the case. I guess, buried in my brain, was the one question I never could answer with any sort of comfort or definitiveness that haunted me since the day you dumped me. ***Why did you dump me?*** You were the love of my life. I even gave up going back to U of Miami, because I did not want to be so far away from you, then you dumped me. No warning!

I often like to, 'go to my memory of you' driving over to my place the night before I was to leave to go to U of Miami for my first semester. You were on my lap, sitting in the living room when you said the words that would shape my life, times 2! "I think I am falling in love with you." Every day I was at University, I could only think of one person, you. I counted the days till the end of the semester, so I could get home and be with you.

You were my 'It-girl' Rebecca. Maybe, I was becoming too clingy, and I was suffocating you at a time you needed to figure out what you wanted to do with your life. I am sorry Rebecca, and I know none of this makes sense to you. Hermitage, being naked, my university saga. So, rather than confuse you more than you must already be, let me return to the events taking place on Al's cottage lake. There will be plenty of time to decide if I am just a nut job!

Ok, let's recap; some barrier capable of acting like perfect camouflage, or maybe, I should switch up my word choice, to calling it a 'cloaking system'. For the sake of simplification, I will define camouflage, as a stationary or static state, and cloaking is a dynamic state. I needed more data. I needed more time to let my brain process this unbelievable situation, so I decided to do another exploratory video, and see what comes next. I reset the video *(making sure I preserved the first one)* on the phone, hit record, and repeated the process, exactly as before. I pulled my arm back, turned the phone screen toward my face, and pressed stop then replay. This I was not prepared for. I was in my mental zone of no fear. Valve shut tight. It's what kept me from either fainting or jumping in the lake and swimming back to Al's and assuming the fetal position in my sleeping bag. It has always served me well, and I knew it was about to be tested like never before.

As the video started, I immediately knew when, and where this was. It was in the garden solarium at my mother's nursing home in 2003. We had just returned from the hospital, and I took my mother into the solarium, so I could process what just happened. You see Rebecca, earlier in the day, I went to see my mother at the nursing home, after she called me, and said she was having difficulty breathing. When I arrived, I found my mother lying in bed, struggling to get her breath. I immediately told the home supervisor to call for an ambulance. I went with my mother to the hospital. She was taken into the emergency ICU area, and a doctor started to take a look at her. I went to the waiting room, to do what everyone does in a waiting room, wait.

The doctor came out to see me after about 30 minutes and told me that they had given my mother some meds to help her breathe easier and they needed to send her up to get an x-ray. They said they were a bit backed up; it was going to take about an hour. I went into the emergency area to see my mom and see how she was feeling. She told me she was feeling much better and could breathe almost normally again. What a relief. I told her I was going to pop out for a quick bite to eat, and I would be back in an hour.

I was starving. I asked if she was hungry, and wanted me to bring her back anything, and she politely declined. I think she was exhausted from trying to breathe the last day or two.

What you also don't know Rebecca, is that my dad was in another hospital, and just had the lower section of his leg amputated as the result of his diabetes and was also fighting an infection that developed. I had been bouncing back and forth between visiting my dad in the hospital, and my mother in the nursing home, while attempting to start a new internet company. I moved home a few years earlier, to act as a caregiver for my parents, who were struggling with their health. Dad was on home dialysis, and mom was in her wheelchair. The only reason dad was able to do home dialysis, was the commitment I would be his home dialysis assistant. I became quite proficient in needling him for the IV line. Eventually, we all decided, it would be better for mom to go into a nursing home. Dad's health was on a slow and steady decline, and he no longer could assist my mother with her needs, to keep her in the family home. Home healthcare support only went so far. I had been there *(my parents' house)* now for 3 years. Originally, it was only going to be for 1 year, until my dad got his kidney transplant. Well, the transplant came, and unfortunately did not take, and this is where things were heading.

Dad did not have any chance at another kidney, and unfortunately, I was not a match for him being adopted *(And I checked)*. So, mom went into a local nursing home which made it easy to take dad to visit *(a 5-minute drive)*. This was their life now. Separate from each other, their health declining, and me trying to make up for all the youthful indiscretions that I put them through. Payback time! A great fringe benefit Rebecca, I got to spend a ton of time with them, while all my peers were building their own lives and families, not unlike you, not you but the other you.

So, back to the solarium. When I returned to the hospital after grabbing a bite nearby, I found my mom still in the same spot in the emerge department. My mom said she had the x-ray and was waiting to see the doctor. I spotted the doctor who I spoke to earlier and went over to the desk area to get an update. He noticed my approach and moved into a more private area to speak with me. He told me that they did a full chest x-ray and that they found my mothers, pre-existing, but presumed in remission, breast cancer that was diagnosed years ago, had somehow now fully metastasized. I had watched enough medical TV shows, to know this diagnosis, to ask the uncomfortable question, "How long does she have?"

As soon as the words "fully metastasized," emerged from his mouth, my body and brain went into the old emotional shutdown mode. Turns out that not only could I shut off the fear valve at will, but I could also shut off a few other valves. What the doctor said next, however, would prove to be one of the better tests on the strength of my valve shut-off capability.

"I would give her a few days, a week at best, but there is no way to know for sure. The chest x-ray was full of cancer. I was surprised how well she responded to the meds we gave her to alleviate her breathing difficulty," he informed me in a doctor-like, non-emotional, but caring tone.

As I tightened the valve all the way, I asked "Can I bring her back to the home for a few days, or are you keeping her here? Are there any treatments to help her be comfortable?" as I stared directly into his eyes.

He told me, "It would probably be ok for a couple of days, but as things progress, she will start to experience a lot of pain. She will need to start taking some pretty strong pain meds that will most likely make her sleep all the time."

The valve was holding, and my 'What if' planning brain kicked into high gear. First, however, another test of the valve's strength. I needed to tell my mom. I went back into the bed area she was in and pulled a chair up beside the bed. I grabbed her hand, and with every ounce of strength keeping that valve closed, I told my mom exactly what the doctor told me, except the part about coming home. I needed more time to plan for this. She wasn't upset, and even smiled, and seemed to be, on some level, at peace with what fate awaited her. I think she was probably more concerned about my mental state. After all, she's a mom. I arranged for Darts to come and pick us up, since mom was feeling much better, and could travel by Darts in her wheelchair, back to the nursing home. The doctor gave me a pill bottle, and an inhaler, gently shook my mom's hand, fully knowing her fate, and gave me the customary pat on the back before he turned and continued his duties.

We sat out front and waited for Darts to arrive. As we sat there, my mom turned to me and said, "Do you think I could come home to the house for a few days?"

I gave mom a reassuring smile and said, "absolutely."

Before I had finished the absolutely, I pulled out my blackberry and started making all the arrangements. Thankfully it provided me with the distraction I needed. The Darts van arrived, and I loaded mom on, and we began the silent trip back to the nursing home. Deep down, I was destroyed.

An emotional wreck! I just could never show her that. Losing your mom is always going to be the hardest life event, except maybe your child, which, thankfully, I had no experience with. If losing a mom hurt this much, then I can not imagine the pain of losing a child. It's a major shaping event.

We arrived at the nursing home, and I took my mom into the sitting area, in her section of the home. I left her for a few minutes so I could speak to the people in charge and let them know I was going to be taking my mother home for a few days. I informed them of the doctor's diagnosis, and I could tell, they were upset by the news. Everyone jumped into gear to help pack up an overnight bag, with all my mom's personal care items, as well as some clothes. Another worker handed me another large bag full of more nursing care-type stuff, anticipating, that I would not have anything at home. I had called her old CCAC contact who was still listed on my phone and let her know the situation. I asked if she could arrange for some, in-home health care services.

The plan by this point was to bring mom home until I could no longer safely care for her, and then transfer her to St. Peter's hospice section. With Dad in the hospital, I planned to repurpose his *(medical)* bed and move it into my mom's old room on the main floor. I requested a Darts van again, to take my mom from the nursing home to the house, a ride of about 5 minutes, but they could not get a driver there for an hour. So, with time to kill, we went out to the solarium.

I sat in the solarium, with my mom's wheelchair pulled alongside my chair, and I held her hand. We did not say much but I could feel the valve starting to fail. I knew what would happen if it did, and suddenly it dawned on me, that the last time I cried, was the rainy afternoon, you came to my house, in the old Gremlin *(and yes, I now hate Gremlins)*, and told me you wanted to break up. Yes, you once drove a Gremlin *(Minor giggle)*. The love of my life wanted to go away to her university in the fall, single. The pain I felt was devastating. Nothing I had ever felt before. I remember sitting there, crying like a little child saying, "Why?" "Why?" What a sight, two grown, not far from 20, young adults, sitting in a Gremlin crying. I think the pain was so great for me, that I needed to find a way to control it or suppress it. I am sure this was when I developed my valve system for the first time. Find the valve and turn it off. Simple. Well Becca, it was that simple. It took some time to develop the discipline, but I must say, it has served me well, in what I have had to do, and what I have done.

Unfortunately, the solarium sitting turned out to be my kryptonite. As I sat there, holding my mother's hand, I knew this was going to solidify my view on religion for good. What God would ever do something like this to my mother? If I ever came face to face with God, I would beat the crap out of him, for allowing this to happen to my mother. And anyone that would try the old, 'its god's design', you get the crap beaten out of you even more.

The old solarium moment certainly had several tentacles. First, exposing the weakness in my valve system, second, solidifying my anti-God view, and now third, my first contact with those responsible, for the mysterious barrier. When I played the second video, Rebecca, it was me, sitting in the Solarium holding my mother's hand bawling my eyes out just like in the Gremlin repeating, "it's not fair, it's just not fair."

I remember in the original, non-video version, my mother putting her hand on my head and saying, "It's ok. Don't worry about it. Just make sure you look after your dad." No tears, no anger, just a mom, being a mom and worrying about everyone else. Just having to write about it after all these years, is testing the old valve system. After the solarium, I never cried again, until your mom's funeral and it was only my eyes filling up this time, but with my sunglasses on, no one could tell. And you never spotted me in the very back. Then when old Emma had to be put down. I guess my valve system kryptonite is three-fold, Mom, Emma, and Rebecca. Although, you also get the credit for creating the beast! *(I smiled)*. I needed to add this to counter the potential failing valve.

In the video version on my phone from the barrier, it was my mother now saying to me, "It will be ok. They need your help. Go save them." Unlike the Hermitage video which was more of an exact replay of the event, this one had a new dialogue between my mother and me. While you would think my first instinct would be to ask, "who are they?" But it was my mom telling me. I don't have any reason for what I did next, and I can certainly tell you I have relived this moment over in my head for years, with the same outcome. I simply don't know, and most likely will never know. But what I do know, is what I did next was the right decision, and what I am doing now, telling you Rebecca, is the right decision.

[I know I said only 5 more pages, but as I write this, no shortcut can do justice to what I am going to ask of you. Going back and editing the 5 to 10 just seems wrong.]

I took the phone and returned it to my pocket. I took the cigar out of my mouth and put it on the seat of the canoe. I took off the summer jacket I was wearing and returned the cigar to my mouth. With all the necessary valves shut, I slid out of the canoe into the lake. A bit chilly, minor shrinkage most likely *(not that it mattered at my age - another giggle)* but, not too bad for June. I held onto the side of the canoe and began to slide myself through the water, along the canoe, toward the front. If this was going to be my final act in life, just like my mom, I was already at peace with it. I lived a full life, even though it was a life full of regrets. Better they find me bloated, floating in the lake, than in a nursing home drooling, wondering who I was. My helium exit plan was always going to be the best way, but if this is the day, I am ok with that. My only final regret would be never having the opportunity to tell 'that Rebecca', that the time we spent together, and those memories, sustained me, and made me thankful for the time she did give me.

My body started to pass through the barrier, and as my mouth came up to the barrier, I tried to take an extra deep breath, but the cigar was making that impossible as I began the transition. If I had to guess, the barrier would be only a few millimeters thick. After all, I had put my entire forearm through earlier. But to my surprise, the barrier was very thick. I was not as good as I use to be, holding my breath underwater, but was still able to get into the two-minute range with a little Zen help. Thankfully, my freediving over the years helped me maintain my lung capacity. I reached the bow of the canoe but could not see it. I closed my eyes when I entered the barrier not knowing what effect it may have on them. Blindness was never high on my, ‘I could live with that’ list. I could even live with being 'John Bobbitted', but to lose my sight, would be one of the worse losses to bare. Unfortunately, at this point, I was going to have to transition into treading water. It was very unfortunate, that the barely half-smoked Romeo and Juliette, would have to be sacrificed. I took a quick last puff before I let it go.

As I released myself from the canoe, I tried to maintain a straight line through the water. Thankfully, I felt comfortable I could tread water out here for some time but may have to lose the jeans shortly to lighten my load. I moved what I would estimate was another 4 feet, and with my eyes now open, the inside of the barrier certainly looked like a dense fog without any wet feeling. It had been a while, but I heard again, the odd crying sound, and it was certainly sounding like it was getting closer. Just as the sound faded, the barrier was gone, or should I more accurately say, I emerged from it. I am pretty sure, I know what you are expecting me to describe what I see, which will then, certainly cause you to roll your eyes and say, "I can't believe I let him draw me into some crazy fantasy prank.”

Well, Rebecca, any sane person would think exactly like you're thinking. So, to make it even more interesting, I won't say the word.

I will describe what I was seeing or believed I was seeing. About three feet, maybe four feet in front of me, is a large, I will assume, oval-like structure. Being so close to it, and because of its size, I have no idea its full length, width, and height. It appeared like it was partially submerged, but again, I could not tell from my vantage point. The exterior was relatively smooth, almost translucent, except for a couple of what appeared to be openings that protruded into the object.

I was back rethinking maybe military again, but visually, it looked more 'space-like' based on my TV watching and reading and not first-hand experience. I continued treading water and moved closer to the openings, hoping they were not some exhaust ports, and I was about to be incinerated. As I reached the opening, which measured about 2 feet by 3 feet, almost round, I decided to go to the next level of, "oh my god," and touch the structure. The material was like nothing I had ever felt before. My hand glided over it like it had absolutely no surface tension. It did not feel wet or slimy. I was beginning to rethink my thought of trying to climb into the hole and venture down. With the surface having no surface tension, I would simply slide without any ability to stop, down the shaft/hole. My luck, I would end up inside some new military jet engine. Well, even if I wanted to go into the shaft, there was nothing to grab onto, to pull myself up. I found myself, constantly rubbing the surface, trying to figure out what the hell it was. Suddenly, I heard the crying again, and this time, I could identify where it was coming from; the second shaft. I needed the canoe to assist.

The problem now was, where the hell is the canoe. I decided to try and retrace my route, which I estimated could be no more than 18 feet. I began my treading, and after a few strokes, I was back into the barrier. After another few strokes, I began to emerge from the barrier, and true to my natural directional instinct, the canoe was two feet to my right.

I grabbed the canoe, and tried to pull it towards me, but like before it would not move. Another mystery. Well, once again, using my hands, I slid along the gunnel toward the front to see if I could feel what was holding it. As I entered the barrier again, I slid one hand down the side, towards the bottom, to see what it was resting on. To my surprise, I felt nothing. I moved over to the opposite side and tried the same exploratory move there. Nothing. Well, I knew it may eventually come to this, but it was time to go under. Wished I had my mini scuba tank now! I sure hope that old snapper is not staying up late tonight. I took a deep breath and slowly submerged using the bottom of the canoe to hold me down, and in place.

As I held myself under the canoe, I began to stretch out my arm, and search for the thing holding the canoe in place. I felt everywhere. At one point, I used my head up against the bottom of the canoe, to hold my position, as I tried to cover 360 degrees with my two arms. I continued to work myself to the back of the canoe, from the underside and found nothing holding the canoe. When I reached the back, I came up and grabbed a fresh breath of air. Wow, another cool mystery. First, the barrier, then the structure, and now the invisible force field, holding the canoe. I moved back toward the front. I wondered if the aluminum was reacting with whatever the barrier was, like a magnet on steel. This mystery was above my pay grade. I was not yet ready to surrender my educational learnings, since I was sure, I was entering a new area of science. Well, a new plan developed, and so I grabbed the paddle, my Rapala knife, and since it was staring me in the face, my bottle of port. I know my adrenalin was at an all-time high, but in the forefront of my mind, I was starting to think about the potential monetization of this whole situation. I may be learning highly secret military stuff, but somewhere in that sci-fi over-exposed brain of mine, I was enjoying a little fantasy exploring with the old, 'Could it be… wait for it…. Alien?' A Close Encounter of the 'Al' kind. *(Another giggle, maybe an eye roll)*.

I headed back to the structure, and thought, that this may be a secret stealth plane, and the material was some new, non-reflecting, non-surface tension substance, that could not be seen by radar. The barrier was most likely some form of chemical reaction, between the material and the water. Maybe, it had to make some emergency ditch here, and since it was 100 percent stealth, the military couldn't find it. But where are the pilots and crew? Is it a drone? Maybe there's a reward somewhere. So, with canoe stuff in hand, neck of the bottle in my mouth, back to the structure I went. I was getting better at my travel angle, as I emerged almost exactly, as I emerged last time. When I got to the farthest opening, I proceeded to place the paddle up on the surface, but, as soon as I let go, it started to slide down the hole. I grabbed it before it went too far. My last effort was to try to wedge the paddle on an angle, so it would create a hold, to allow me to pull myself up, out of the water, and into the shaft opening. I put the port bottle down for a second, to adjust my hand hold on the paddle, and before I could move fast enough, it slid down the shaft opening.

Not to waste the opportunity for more intel, I stopped everything and listened to see if I could hear the bottle crash or hit something at the bottom. One Mississippi, two Mississippi, three Mississippi, and nothing. My luck, some air force officer would be enjoying a nice port later. I tried to wedge the paddle, but it would not hold its position. It just wanted to slide. Plan "B." Let's see what happens when I hit the surface with the paddle. Maybe, the noise will force someone to come, and inspect this part of the aircraft. I tried to put my arm over the edge, to balance me a bit, while I cocked my other arm to swing the paddle against the side. Well, it worked just perfectly. I was able to get a pretty good, and forceful 'Vladdy Jr.' swing with the paddle, but another mystery just emerged. No sound was emitted. I did it again, and again. This stuff also can absorb energy. Well, the mysteries kept growing and my resolve to get into this structure was equally growing.

Ok, now the big guns. Time to go and wake Al and introduce him to my new crazy sudoku. I didn't know if I would encounter the Lion from the 'Wizard of Oz Al', after encountering the wizard for the first time, or hopefully, it would be 'Leonidas Al', but with a 24-pack instead of a 6-pack. I swam back to the canoe and put the paddle in the canoe when I felt something touch my leg. Oh no, the Snapper was here. I attempted to kick the area I was guessing it would be in, but my foot didn't hit anything, and I did not feel any pain from an angry snapper turtle bite. Suddenly, whatever touched my leg before, now had a really good grip. It felt more like a Hydro linemen's horse cock. All crude joking aside, the horse cock *(Actually called Kellmen's Connector I believe)* refers to a special metal-weaved device that when you insert a large wire cable into it, like one of those overhead power transmission lines, as you pull on the other end, it grabs the line and the harder you pull the tighter it grabs. It's used to pull large wires through conduit. Probably need to show you one for you to fully understand how it works.

I grabbed the side of the canoe, to prevent whatever had hold of my leg, from pulling me under. I still had the Rapala filet knife in the waist of my pants, and to be honest, I was surprised I hadn't accidentally cut myself with it yet. Well, the leg-pulling increased, and I figured it was some military guy in scuba gear about to drag me under, to incapacitate me, before slapping cuffs on. I might have been able in my earlier days, to hold on a bit longer, but the pull was so strong, that it was either pulling my leg out of the socket or tearing every ligament in my fingers. In anticipation of the submerging, I forced myself to take a really good deep breath. As my head broke the water surface, I went into my free diving Zen mode. I had no idea how long I would be underwater and wanted to preserve my air, for a potential hand-to-hand, fisty cuff, with the frogman. I am sure they, or he, would have no idea how long I could hold my breath. Boy, will he be surprised! I don't know what prompted a flash memory Ingram to pop, but I thought at that moment, "Surprise, Surprise, Surprise" with the customary Gomer Pile drawl.

I hate being pulled backward, as it inevitably leads to me getting a nose full of water. Who needed Navage now? Without a mask in the evening water, I was as good as blind as to where I was being pulled. I tried to reach down, and feel the rope around my leg, but the speed was a bit too much, and I had to stay focused on keeping my body streamlined to avoid any drag. Drag equated to the loss of air. I kept my legs together, and arms crossed my chest, with hands grabbing my shoulders. It was probably around a minute so far when the water started to brighten, or should I say, I was entering an area that had light.

Based on a minute, and the speed I was being pulled at, I estimated we could have traveled, over one hundred feet, probably close to one hundred and fifty. That would rule out the two shaft holes, and I know the lake is at best fifteen feet deep in the middle. So, if my math is close, I could be anywhere. I started to slow, and I was comfortable with maybe, another minute tops before I would enter drownsville. Without any forewarning, I think I left the medium of water, and now found myself in a medium of warm air. Lights had dimmed again. I know it could have gone really, really bad, but fortunately, I was now breathing air, I think it was. Well, whatever it was, it did not kill me obviously, and my lungs could function just fine. It finally dawned on me; I was being pulled along by the same material as the hull. The Zero surface tension stuff.

Without the water, I was now free to try and contort my body, into a shape that would allow me to grab the thing wrapped around my leg. Well, mystery number four, or are we at Five. I kind of lost count. When I grabbed my leg where the attachment point was, I didn't feel rope, I felt *(by touch)* the same type of material covering the external hull of the vessel. Well as quick as it had started, the ride appeared over.

I was now in some sort of test tube-like structure. It was still fairly dark, but I could make out something, about twenty feet to my left. Not enough light, but something was out there. Now I needed to turn ON the valve governing the 'alien probing' experience. *(I could not resist Becca)*. I remained in the same position, in the giant test tube, when I noticed another light starting to blink. Then another light, and another. Soon, the entire room, or whatever you wanted to call I was in, began to reveal itself.

The room itself was cylindrical, like my test tube, but maybe ten times the size. The walls did not look solid, but more organic. The lights seemed to be embedded in the organic wall covering. I took a quick look at myself to assess my situation.

Feet covered with what I think is the same material the hull is made from, just like the horse cock device, I had previously described. It appears to be attached to the bottom of the clear cylinder structure I was in. I touched, what I assumed was the wall of the tube I was in, and again, a surface I never felt before, and can only describe as void of any surface tension. I can only assume, as a defense mechanism, my thoughts now turned to the idea that some big probe would enter my tube, and would go up, you know where *(that's all I am going to say about that – big grin)*. I was now glad I had not removed my jeans. Humour can sometimes be a welcome distraction. I can't explain what happened next, because I don't remember, and I was never able to find the time to ask. Whatever happened next, must have put me to sleep.

My next vivid memory Rebecca was being on a bed-like device with the hull material stuff fully engulfing my body. It was like a giant condom. Form-fitting, but the only part of me exposed was my head. I tried to move but was being kept motionless by the substance. While I had no mirror to guide me with what was happening on my head, I did feel something on my head. The other thing going on was a faint humming sound. As I lay there, I heard a voice. It was the audio of my mom in the solarium again.

"It will be ok. They need your help. Go save them," mom said just like in the video.

Funny how our minds work; I had this instant flashback to an old Jodie Foster movie called 'Contact'. Not sure if you ever watched it. Just in case you want to watch it, it was released back on July 11th, 1997. I am sure it's available online somewhere and may help you in the near future with a bit of context. I had pretty much ruled out military and was more leaning toward a nervous breakdown, or maybe this was some transition process you go through when you die. Maybe I was sitting on the dock and suffered a massive heart attack, and this was my brain letting go.

"It will be ok. They need your help. They won't hurt you," mom said. I was having my very own 'Field of Dreams moment'.

Wow, the message changed. Well since I am here, and probably dead or dying, why not enjoy the last ride I thought. So, I took a second to think about what I wanted to say, and decided the best reply was, "I am not afraid. I am just trying to figure out if this is real or am I crazy, or worse, dead."

"It will be ok. We need your help. You're not crazy or dead," I heard mom reply.

"Then please explain how we are communicating mom," was my next response.

I am sure you would agree that my little written dissertation so far would certainly make for a great National Enquirer piece, or maybe the makings for a good sci-fi book. But I think at this juncture, and I have given this a great deal of thought Rebecca, it's best to leave this storyline temporarily and provide you with something different to maybe help condition your mindset moving forward.

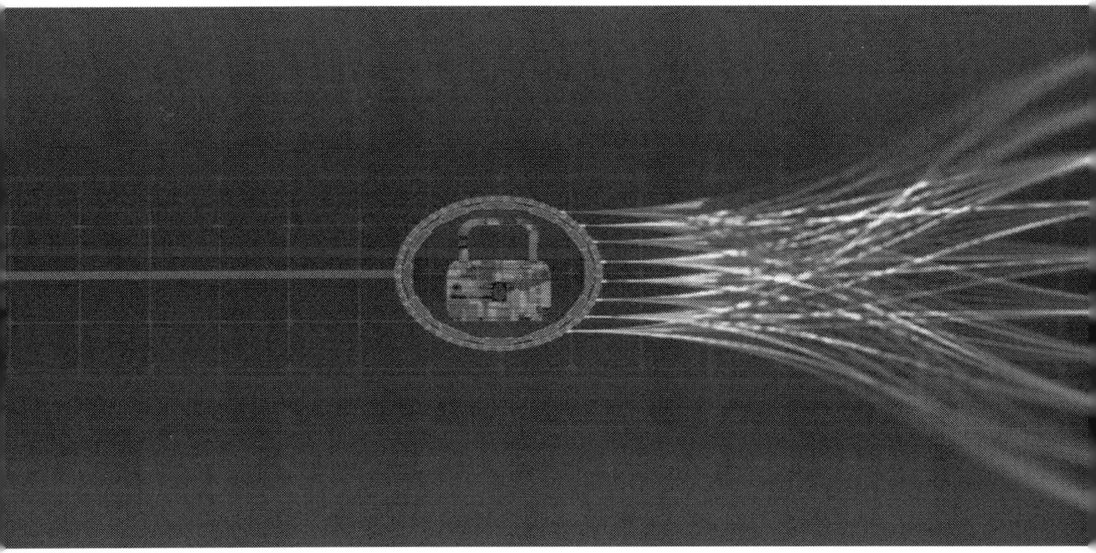

The Proofing Test

(Or stick your hand in the boiling water test)

3 It's straight forward Rebecca. All I did, was to put myself in your shoes, so to speak, to determine what I would need to experience, if there was any hope in hell that you may buy into this incredible fantasy, I have introduced you to. Please remember, that I am controlling when you get to read this *(more like I controlled the instructions to my lawyers)*, and I am the sole author *(Well, almost the sole author)*. I know what you know about me/us, and I am confident, that I have an above-average insight into how you think.

Converting you into a believer from your current Ms. Skeptic, I am sure, requires a very particular type of proof. Some proofs are achieved through a purely mental exercise, like for example the Riemann hypothesis, P versus NP problem, oh yeah, I forgot, they have not been solved yet. But if you think back to our calculus school days, we used equations to prove an answer. We can accept proof through physical means; Hold any object out in front of you and let go. We know from science, that gravity will cause it to drop at a rate of *(acceleration)* of 9.8 m/s/s, downward *(on Earth)*. But that is not always true. What if the object was a balloon? Then we would need additional information, like what was used to fill the balloon? Air or helium? Or was it water? So, as I am trying to illustrate, there are always potentially multiple requirements to achieve obtaining 'absolute' proof. This proof needed to be more of what I would refer to as the 'boiling water test'.

How can you determine if water is boiling hot? Well, if you saw vapors rising off the water you could conclude it was boiling. But what if instead of vapor from heat, there was a small piece of dry ice in there? We would still see vapors, but it was not from a boiling process. One workaround could be, if we put a pot of water on the stove, we watched it go from tap water temperature to a full-on boil, then we would reasonably conclude the water was very close to 212 degrees F or 100 degrees C. But that may also not be accurate. What if the water contained a large amount of salt? Then the boiling point would be higher than 212 degrees F. The difference in this example is you had the benefit of observing the entire process from start to finish, and therefore, could have a higher degree of confidence, that the water was truly just below or at 212 degrees, or if salt was present, even higher. The absolute test, however, would require one more step. Put your hand into the pot of water. If it hurt like hell, and then after you brought it out it turned red as a beet, and the skin started to bubble then peel, then you would have the ultimate proof. Do you Agree? So, Rebecca, you are about to watch the water come to a boil and then put your hand in it because it was the only way you would ever accept the information, I have been telling you was true.

So, without further ado, let's go have you stick your hand in the water! *(You know I am grinning through this whole section).*

1. The first thing I need you to do, go to the Volume marked Appendixes. This book of the 3 books you received is where all the relative appendixes are maintained. Go to the tab marked 'R' *(For Rebecca, he he)*. Splitting the guide this way, also makes it easier to follow instructions, without constantly having to flip back and forth, had it been included in a single guide. The other reason is so I could keep the parts separated for added security.
2. Now I want you to go to the date, that corresponds to the next date after reading this guide for the first time. Since my last edit, I am guessing the rows will be in the early 7,000 range. Maybe start on Tab 'R', page 16. When you find the correct date row, I need you to continue moving down to the date row *(below)* that corresponds to 'our favorite color'. As you see, each row has a different color of text. *(Warning, old thought dump)*. I remember when I bought you your very first dozen red long stem roses. It put a major dent in my wallet, but with the smile it put on your face that day, I probably should have bought you 10 dozen. Your mom and dad's expressions however were more in the "Oh my God, what is she getting into" look. Sorry, I just had to say that.
3. Write down the number sequence immediately to the right of the date box on a separate piece of paper with each number as a separate column.
4. Do not break a number into individual digits. If the number is 10 *(like your birthday)*, then put 10 on the sheet as a column, not 1, and zero as two columns.
5. Now for the magic. Under each number you have written at the top of the page, using "Our number," subtract the minuend from the subtrahend to obtain the difference. Or, in case you forgot our

math terms *(snicker, snicker)*, Subtract "Our Numbers" from each of the numbers you recorded above.

It Should look like this example:

10 12 24 36 40 53 <<<< Sample number from Tab 'R'
1 2 7 5 7 9 <<<< 'Our Number :)'
9 10 17 31 33 44 <<<< 'Your results for Tab 'S' instructions

6. In the future, if the number from Tab 'R', is less than the length of 'Our Number', then only use the same number of numbers starting from the first position going left to right *(Like above)*.
7. If the number exceeds the total number of 'Our Numbers', then simply repeat the sequence.
8. Now, record the new number sequence after applying the subtraction process and record them on a small piece of paper.
9. Now I need you to go to Tab "S."
10. Follow the instructions in Tab "S" exactly, and it will give you the last piece of information needed to utilize the number sequence in the way it was intended.
11. Now *(And I have a huge smile and am so proud of myself right now)* go and stick your hand in the water, to prove without a doubt, if I am a deranged madman loser or have been telling you the truth.

[I so wish I could be there to see the look on your face at that magic moment. Just in case you are wondering why the elaborate scheme using "Our Number." Firstly, it would require you to continue to use "our number," and hopefully put a smile on your face, and I suspect, force you to remember me forever (I'm grinning). Second, I needed a way in the early days, to protect the numbers, just in case someone ever got access to the guide by mistake or worse.]

I am sure your ability to complete the 'Proofing' experiment will take a day or two to complete, so I think it would also be beneficial, to provide you with, what I will simply call, a bit of a 'teaser'. Using the same page from Tab 'R', find the date you just used. Now, I want you to move up the rows to the next row that uses 'Our Colour'. Now follow the previous steps 3 through 10. I am pretty sure you know where this is going. You were always deceptively brilliant Becca, and I probably never told you that enough. Now jump onto the internet and do the appropriate search and see what you find. If you have found, what I hope you would find, then the 'tease' is completed. If it did not produce the required outcome, then there is obviously something much more complicated going on and I would fear, this guide could end up as some manuscript for a "B" level sci-fi book, not to mention the pending Proofing experiment is sure to fail.

However, I will proceed on the basis that the 'tease' was successful, and you're now starting to enter the next mental phase this guide intended too illicit. The process you are going through, and will continue to go through, until the Proofing test is complete, will be one of the most frightening and at the same time exhilarating experience you will ever have. Rather than try to describe it to you, I will simply say, enjoy it, and respect it. You will understand that statement a bit more when I can describe my experience with the same kind of mental processing I had to go through.

I would say, enjoy the next days, or hours, going through what you will be going through, but I will add a brief caveat to that experience. You are going to unfortunately be exposed to some very dark times in your life. Memories that you had previously buried in your brain's synaptic recesses hoping never to have to re-process them because they were so painful. It's what happens when we start to re-process old memories through a completely new filter system. Please do not let the process overtake your sense of what is real, and what is not. Or, what is right and what is wrong. As you move deeper into this guide, the process you are starting to go through will only increase and expand beyond your wildest expectations. I like to think of this moment as the moment of our re-birth. From this moment forward, you will be looking at everything through the eyes of a newborn. I should also say, what you will go through, can't be undone. But that may not be entirely accurate; that realization will come much later, I am sure.

End of Proofing!

Welcome Back Babe!

4 I am going to assume if you are reading this guide again, that I have either been successful in winning you over mentally, or it failed, and you wanted to see, just how far my madness could go. I will proceed on the basis, that you are a much wealthier person today *(Although as the sole benefactor of my estate, it's kind of a moot point)* than when you started reading this guide for the first time and have fully satisfied your prior *(understandable)* skepticism. But before you 'act' on the proof test, Read Tab 'W', for specific instructions on what you need to do with your ticket or stub. You must follow those instructions to a 'T'. I will get into the thought process that I used to develop this guide further in the guide, and there is an excellent section dedicated to *'Our Number'*. But for now, I need to return to describing what was taking place at Al's, or more specifically, inside that mysterious structure.

The obvious benefit for me now Rebecca, is I don't have to worry about saying something, that I thought previously, would have sent you running before I could give you the proof you deserved, and frankly needed. So, if you recall, *(I will recap a bit to save you from having to refresh yourself on the previous section).*

My next vivid memory Rebecca was being on a bed-like device, with that strange hull material fully engulfing my body. It was like a giant condom. Form-fitting, but the only part of me exposed was my head. I tried to move but was being kept motionless by the substance. As I lay there, I heard a voice, but could not see anyone. The room, if that is what it was, looked like a glass fish tank, and I was inside it. Maybe 4 feet wide, 6 feet tall, and 8 feet in length. On the other side of the glass, was fog, I think. The sound was the audio of my mom's voice in the solarium.

"It will be ok. They need your help. Go save them," mom said, just like in the video.

"It will be ok. They need your help. They will not hurt you," mom reiterated.

Wow: the message changed. I took a second to think about how I wanted to respond and decided the best reply was, "I am not afraid! I am just trying to figure out if this is real or I am crazy, or worse, dead."

"It will be ok. We need your help. You're not crazy, or dead," mom replied.

"Then please explain how we are communicating like this mom" was my next response.

"Telepathy," mom said somewhat authoritatively.

"And you are not really my mother?" I asked.

"No, just a representation we obtained from your memory to try and make this conversation easier for you," said the psychic interloper.

"And the video of me, and Rebecca, at the Hermitage, was also taken from my memory?" I asked.

"Yes, it was," came the reply.

"And why did you choose that memory?" I followed up with.

"We will be happy to answer all of your questions, but we have an emergency that we need your help with now, and time is of the essence," came a rather anxious response.

"Well, I think it will be a bit difficult for me to do much good, laying here in this, and I am going to now use the words, Alien condom," was my response.

"In order for us to fast-track what we need you to do, we are going to send into your mind, in a completely safe method, the information you will need to perform a specific task for us," my fake mother said.

As I was laying there, all of a sudden, I knew exactly what I needed to do. Not just some general instructions, but minute detail. It was like I always had this information, but I knew darn well it was all new. And it wasn't like a few pages of instructions, it was more like one of the volumes of Encyclopedia Britannica, and not the letter J, but more like the letter M. It was simply a series of instructions, but every possible question that the task would have elicited out of me was completely answered with unbelievable exactness.

The chair structure I was attached to began to move. The body suit I was in seemed to transform into a very stylish jumpsuit, complete with built-in booties and hoodie. I could not feel the material, but I could tell that there was an increase in the internal pressure of the suit. The chair turned sharply downward, and I was now on, some sort of drop chair amusement ride. I fell for maybe 15 seconds, and then the chair leveled out and continued to move in a forward motion. At least that is what my senses were telling me. And I even think my mind was controlling everything that was happening. My hoodie began to alter its shape and it now started to feel like some sort of dive mask covering my entire head. No need for goggles since I could already see everything in front of me, even though my eyes were closed. 15 seconds to impact, and I felt ready for it. Ten, nine, eight, seven, six, five, four, three, two, now. My body entered, into what I knew was water, but the suit I was in refused to let me feel it. It was game time friends.

I was now under the observatory, in about 25 feet of water. Al, you lied buddy! I began to kick my feet and my booty's had transformed into a pair of high-tech flippers. My hand coverings, also transformed into web-like appendages, that helped and improved my forward movement. It only took, about 20 seconds for me to reach my target. In front of me, I could see, but not with my eyes, three, of the type of cylinder I was inside earlier. The three cylinders looked out of place there, and I was now seeing the bottom of all three cylinders had damage to their seals. It looked like the bottoms had hit something, which damaged the side of the cylinder, as well as the seal at the bottom.

I could see a gas-like substance emerging from the damaged seal area. I was not able to see what was inside the cylinders, but knew from my latest studies, there would be one of my new friends in each cylinder. They to were wrapped up in some strange material, which was different from mine, but I knew they were still alive. My next job was to locate a spot on the observatory marked 'X', beside where the cylinders were. I think the 'X' implant was for my benefit. Once I found it, I was going to remove the cover, by pushing on it with my now bare hand, and immediately placed my hand into the opening. Inside the opening, I would then feel around for a very cold blob of material. Once I could get a good grip on the freezing cold blob material, I was going to use all my strength, and pull it out of the opening. As soon as that happens, there would be a rather large burst of a gas-like substance that would dissolve my body suit and return me to my jeans and t-shirt. So just before I made the big move, I took a few, really, deep breaths. Ok, one, two three, and yank.

Swoosh.... And I suddenly remembered, how cold the water was. I think down here, I was actually below a thermocline. Instead of 65–70-degree water, it was more in the low 50's or even high 40's. As the gas-like substance was released, the three cylinders seals at the bottom, immediately disintegrated, which caused the bottom of the cylinders to fall away. Suddenly, I saw three elongated sacks, about 4 feet in length, emerge from the bottom of the cylinders, and right on cue, I grab all three and began to swim away from under the observatory. I knew I needed to try and conserve my air as best as I could. Without the benefit of the previous body covering with the high-tech flippers and webbed gloves, it was just good old DD. Between the extra cold water, and the unfortunate drag of the pouches that used a material that had surface tension drag now, I fully expected I would be testing my lung capacity tonight, or maybe it was now this morning.

Suddenly, another gas eruption occurred which sent me into a bit of a corkscrew, but I did not lose hold of my guests, however, their sack material did not seem to be doing all that well now. I saw the landmark on the side of the observatory that I had been looking for.

From there, I needed to head down again, further under the observatory. My air was getting low, and I knew the gulping was not far off. I continued the swim as best as I could, with just my sock feet and waterlogged jeans, which I should have removed earlier, maybe even go full commando. I did my first re-breathing gulp and kept kicking. By this time, it must be coming close to two minutes since I had my last air intake.

If only mom could see me now. Here, being in my early sixty's, slightly overweight *(You know I am a big bone frame type of guy, not fat)*, and not in university fighting weight condition, favorite son, swimming with 3 new alien buddies, in a northern Ontario Lake, in the middle of the night. I hope the guys inside can read my mind and are having a gut-busting laugh over that last thought. Gulp 2, I kept swimming. Gulp 3, and I am starting to feel the carbon dioxide buildup, as my brain started questioning my ability to complete the task at hand.

Probably my last gulp, so keep your fingers crossed boys, if you have any, because I got, maybe 15 seconds left in me, then, we will all be floating down here. Just when I finished that thought, I felt that same stuff, that grabbed my leg when I was holding onto the canoe. Thank God! If I pass out, at least they will be able to pull me in.

Hopefully, they know how to resuscitate me as well. To make sure I wouldn't drop any of my passengers, I erected a bear hug around two sacks and put the other between my legs. As I began to pass out, I could feel the cold of the water dissipating. As I came to, I noticed I was once again back in the chair, complete with a new body condom covering me. And yes, that thing on my head that I still have not seen what it looks like. As I began to regain my mental composure, I heard my mom again, "Thank you for what you have done for us."

And as I usually do when in an awkward situation, I replied, "Well, I just happened to be in the area and had nothing better to do."

I was hoping of course, to maybe elicit a laugh, or maybe a chuckle or two, but only silence. Maybe it was not as funny as I thought to them.

So, I tried another, "How about those Blue Jays."

Then fake mom replied, "We have not seen any Blue Jays around here for a couple of days."

"That's because they are playing in New York this weekend," I responded with a bit of a giggle.

"Not to be pushy with you folks, but any chance we can meet face-to-face, assuming you have a face, and can you select another spokesperson. Hearing mom's voice was a bit unsettling," I asked.

I think they must have a sense of humor, because the next voice was my dad's, "Derek, we don't share a similar breathable surrounding. The thing you refer to as 'air' would kill you the same way your air would kill us."

"Why don't you transfer, into my brain, the same way you did before, with information about yourselves, a visual representation of what you look like and maybe where you come from and why you are here," I requested.

Dad went silent for a while. I just laid there since I could not move anyway. Dad returned with a reply, "Please give us a few minutes to discuss your request, Derek." Now I wish I had my phone, so I could play a few songs from my 'Greatest Song List of all time" while waiting. I hope it's not morning, and Al finds me gone and the Canoe stuck in the lake. I had not stopped, and attempted, a full-on assessment of what I was going through. It all happened so fast. While part of me was still wondering if I would wake up in some hospital, staring at rubber walls, part of me still wondered, was this my mind's final hurrah, before I left my body. I guess only time will tell, assuming they have time.

I heard Dad again, "Derek, your request is possible but the amount of information that we would need to transfer, may cause you some discomfort. Are you prepared to accept that?"

"For foreigners, you guys sure seem to have an excellent earth vocabulary. Not to mention your flawless English, however, a sense of humor does appear lacking," I replied hoping to get a bit more info.

"Our people Derek have been observing 'your world' for well over 75,000 of your earth years if you don't mind us using those metrics. We actually can communicate in every language with similar clarity and understanding, including a few of your water fairing mammals. You're currently in one of our observatory units which we use to study you from," dad explained.

"Well, I guess I will accept the pain and risk of the information transfer, but if I die, you will have to deal with my lawyer," I paused hoping for a laugh.

"We want you to know that we have in 'our own way,' been appreciating your wit and humor, but we don't tend to laugh as you do, we just sort of smile inside," was the explanation.

"Well maybe, while I am hanging out with you guys, in my lovely human-size condom, instead of just smiling inside, why not clap your hands so I know you got my joke," I asked.

"Sorry, assuming you have hands that is," I quickly added.

It was kind of like music to my ears, suddenly, I heard what sounded like, a bunch of people clapping. Wow, I have officially made true first contact. "In your face Cockrane!," I accidentally shouted, followed by another round of clapping,

I could not help but feel that I was bonding with these visitors. And I think, they were growing fond of me. I was not fearful, I helped them with a major problem, and maybe saved a few lives, I told a few great jokes and was no threat.

"Well, no time like the present to pump my brain with the good stuff," I said.

"Ok, it will take a while to complete the transfer. Much longer than the last one, but we will monitor everything, and if we see anything wrong, we will stop it immediately," dad comforted me with.

I did not get any immediate pain, but I did notice my head seemed to be getting warm. Like a 1500-watt heater was blowing at it. I hope I have enough free brain space, and they don't go and overwrite any of my old memories. Especially, those Rebecca memories I cherish. *(I know you smiled).* I kept waiting to see if I could access those new memory implants, but nothing. Just a hot head. I don't know how long it took but after about 15 minutes, which was a pure guess, I started to feel an uncomfortable pain in the front of my forehead. I wanted to touch it, but my hands were secured in that non-surface tension stuff. I felt the pain increasing but I did not want, whatever they were doing, to end prematurely. Time to turn that valve. I closed my eyes mentally because they were already closed physically, and after about a minute of doing my thing, the pain was gone.

I don't know exactly how long I was out of it, or if I was ever out of it, but the very first recollection I had, now being in possession of the new synaptic Ingram plants, was you Rebecca *(I meant the other Rebecca)*. She was sitting at the front of the old tin fishing boat at the cottage. We were out, somewhere on the lake I think fishing. She was wearing the old red plaid shirt of mine over the top of your favorite Mickey Mouse mini turtleneck. She's looking down at a book. I guess she was reading, and I was probably trolling. I have my disposable camera with me, and I stop what I am doing, and take a picture of her at that moment. You hear the click from the camera and look up. You lean back and I take another picture. You tell me not to take any pictures of your calf's because they are too big. Dimples in full form and that beautiful smile I loved so much came out. Our eyes lock and for a split second my brain tells me, 'You're going to marry her one day, Mrs. Rebecca Devon'. At that moment, I could sense the need for me to implement the valve system. I knew if I did not alter my thoughts, it was only a matter of seconds before I would begin to cry. And not some little whimper, but a release of 40 plus years of repressed emotional baggage. You don't maintain a 40-year love affair with a memory, without crossing over to the emotionally disturbed side *(You better have smiled!)*.

Where the hell is that valve lever? It must be here somewhere. It's always here for me. Why the hell did they stick this memory at the front of the line? I just made first contact, and I wasn't going to let them see me wail like I did that day in the Gremlin when you broke up with me. No way, I am far too proud to expose that to my new alien friends, but what happened next was truly, a gift of a lifetime. I started to cry. Yes, gradually at first. I think there must have been some internal struggle around the valve, but it did increase. I was now in a full-fledged, uncontrol bawling session, and all I could hear was me crying the words, "Why, why me?" I know none of this is making any sense to you Rebecca, but I think you needed to know some of this baggage, to understand the decision, I would be making shortly.

Suddenly, I was not alone crying. I could hear and feel others crying with me. It was my new friends, I think. Why would they want to experience such a strong emotion? I continued to bawl, but now knowing, I was polluting my new friends' minds with my emotional baggage seemed unfair, bad form one might say. After all, this was my baggage and mine alone. No one should ever have to go through what I put myself through. YES, we all know it was self-inflicted, and YES, we all know I chose to do it to myself, but I never intended to ever share it, not even with you Rebecca. Wow, I was exhausted. Emotionally spent. Where the hell are those new memories I was supposed to receive. Instead, I get an old memory they surely knew would send me down this embarrassing emotional path. Why?

All of a sudden, I start to hear clapping. My tears gave way to me starting to laugh out loud. I suddenly realized, that not only could they transfer information into my head, but they could also access my thoughts. And their clapping was the result of my previous thought, to myself. I was thinking, "I can't believe that some Aliens, traveled God only knows how far, to find me and make me cry like a little baby over a long-ago failed relationship. Someone must have lost a huge bet if that was the case." While I loved hearing my dad's voice in our earlier dialogue, I was now aware that I didn't need to use that vehicle anymore and that we could communicate non-verbally. Once I grasped this new realization, I also immediately knew, from the new upload, how to control my communications. There was even a private mode, not dissimilar to my valve system to restrict their ability to read my thoughts. I also understood that I would only be able to engage on a one-to-one basis with my friends, but they had the physiology and ability through many years of evolution, that allowed them, to carry on multiple connections simultaneously with each other.

"Harcourt, Harcourt Fenton," my imagination seemed to want to go to. I laughed and after a very slight delay, my friends started laughing *(clapping)* as well. I guess we have achieved full connectivity.

With our newfound communication protocol in place, strangely, I found myself being continuously bombarded with questions about you Rebecca, or I should start referring to Rebecca 1.0. Seems you had galactic admirers as well *(I giggled again which is a good sign).* Well, less about Galactic admirers, and more curiosity about why I would dedicate so much of my mind to memories of you. I think I was probably too late, to start using the privacy protocol, and I will assume they had already gone through the entire archive of my Rebecca memories. Some real, and some probably based on self-fabricated fantasy wishes over the years. I hope they can differentiate between the two. One of the most beneficial aspects of this type of communication is speed. When we verbalize our thoughts, it requires, not only thought but also a lot of motor control, to move our lips and generate speech.

My physiological restrictions, regarding that process, were now removed. All I can tell you Rebecca, is what a rush. A conversation or discussion that would have taken hours, probably days the old way, was completed in seconds, maybe even nanoseconds. I would love to provide you with a full transcript of our discussions, but it would be thousands of thick volumes. I could easily fill an entire law library. So, for the sake of maintaining my goal with your guide, I will only share the needed pertinent stuff.

I guess the first item you need to know, is where they are from, and is it true, that we are not alone in the universe? Wow, I have seen plenty of television shows, and movies depicting first contact with an alien visitor, some turned out good, and some, were not so good *(I just smiled)*. No, this was not going to be 'War of the Worlds,' or 'Close Encounter of the Third Kind.' More like a hybrid of 'Starman', 'The Last Starfighter', and a little 'Back to the Future' with a dab of 'Quantum Leap.' You can see a map, of where they are located, under Tab 'M'. They clapped at my choice of using 'M' for the tab, although I had not written or formulated the whole guide idea yet, or so I thought. Not sure you ever watched the TV show 'My Favorite Martian?' Obviously, we are not alone, but more interesting, is how many other planets my new friends found, that host intelligent life. I have a great section under Tab 'L' that will truly surprise you. I was shocked when I found out.

A question I posed, early in my conversation with them, was, 'why with all their obvious advanced technology could they not save the three people I was sent to help.' Well, turns out, that while they are advanced way beyond our comprehension, even 'super advanced' races can encounter unforeseen accidents. Before I get into the details of the accident, you will need to first understand, what they are doing here and how the whole spying on the human race works, from their perspective. Hopefully, this format makes it easier. Some answers are my interpretation, and some are their exact responses (some with clapping):

Q: Why spy on us?

A: Gather information on your species both from a physiological record as well as a developmental perspective.

Q: Why?

A: Maintain a galactic database we can use to assist in the development of emerging planetary expansion.

Q: Do they take DNA samples?

A: Yes.

Q: What else do they take?

A: A sample of everything. Plants, animals. Everything.

Q: Why?

A: So that if one day we *(us humans)* somehow destroy your planet or a natural disaster causes a global extinction of all life, they will have stored most of the original building blocks needed, to restore our planet to a healthy state.

Q: Why is that important?

A: The universe has a finite number of planets that are capable of supporting various species. Not all species are interchangeable with each other's home planet. We could not survive on your planet, and you could not survive on ours. There comes a time, when a species outgrows its home planet, and thus, the need to locate and inventory potential sustainable planets.

Q: Why not intervene/correct any problems before they become problems, like our current climate issues?

A: Wait for it....... You know it is coming...... Their 'Prime Directive' although they don't refer to it exactly like that .... *(Made you laugh)*

Q: Can they cure cancer?

A: Yes?

Q: Why don't they?

A: See Answer, 'Prime Directive'. Seems the old concept of non-interference is not just some sci-fi-movie concept.

Q: What does their Prime Directive limit them to, and why?

A: They cannot interfere in the evolutionary process of any planet. They can only observe and collect. It is, from a galactic perspective, that each planet must go through its own natural development *(Completely on its own)*, so they can learn from what they see, and record. To interfere would change the natural evolutionary process, which could then create, an even greater threat in the future, that was not natural for that planet.

Q: Why have they never revealed themselves before?

A: They have, but on a very limited basis *(See National Enquirer, giggle).*

Q: By having me help you, have you not violated your 'Prime Directive?'.

A: Yes, but we will fix *(repair)* that.

Q: How?

A: We will restore your memory to the moment you were sitting on the dock staring at the stars just before you thought you heard a noise.

Q: And?

A: You will not hear a noise, smell a strange odor and we will return to our work, and you will have no recollection, of ever knowing we are there.

Q: How long before that Happens?

A: Very soon.

Q: Why did you use the 'Derek & Rebecca' Hermitage memory for the first video I shot?

A: We needed to start the contact process and selecting that memory would generate from you, a base that we could build on.

Q: What base?

A: We knew from our memory probe of you that you had a *(very meaningful to you)* repressed memory. By showing you that moment, we knew that it would not only elevate your curiosity but would also act, to use an analogy that best describes our intent, like giving crack to a crack addict. *(Huge round of clapping)*

Q: So, you are not only explorers, and observers, you are now my crack dealer?

A: Clapping. A lot of clapping.

[Before I continue the Q&A Becca, I wanted to pause, to tell you the next section, will not only be the most fascinating but is going to form the foundation of how this guide started 'its own evolutionary' journey.]

Q: How were you able to travel such a great distance, from your home world to ours?

A: We can put it into terms you can understand, warp space. What you have yet to discover is the area of space occupied by what your top scientist calls dark matter. It is the dark matter that allows us to warp space.

Q: So, you can time travel?

A: That is a different question.

Q: What do you mean?

A: Time is as you would refer to it, a linear measurement while warping space is a physical process. They are very distinct and not related in any way.

Q: So, how does space warping work?

A: Rebecca, See Tab 'W'.

Q: Can you time travel?

A: What do you mean specifically?

Q: If you wanted to move yourself to another point on the 'linear' time scale, let us, say for the sake of discussion purposes, tomorrow at noon, and tell me what I would be doing?

A: No, not on what we would call the leading edge.

Q: Can you elaborate for me?

A: Yes, time, as you think of it, is linear. It has a starting point and an ending point. As a method of measurement, what you are asking, is, can we at any time, place ourselves, at a specific place along that timeline, and the answer is, yes. By warping space, we can warp it in such a way, as to emerge at a predetermined point in space, but also from your understanding, a specific point in time. What we can't do, is travel into a future that has not yet happened. That point in time is what we call the leading edge. The original-first timeline.

Q: So, are we at the leading edge now?

A: Yes.

Q: Then why not simply warp space, and go back to the point in time before you had the accident that caused the incident you needed my help with, therefore, eliminating any need to expose yourselves in a 'mental' sort of way to me?

A: We don't see how that would be beneficial. Going back as you asked, will only create what we would describe, in terms that you hopefully can grasp, a time divergence, a splintering of a timeline. Think of it this way, you have time which we will represent, as a straight line on a piece of paper. Let's make it, 10 inches long, and we will of course use your favorite H2 pencil. *(A short burst of clapping just happened)*. Now, place the pencil at the leading edge of time, which in our example would be the end of the pencil line at the right of the page. The left starting point of the pencil is the start of that timeline example.

Let's, now, establish a method of measuring time. We will use, 1 inch represents 1 year. So, our ten-inch line covers from right now *(the leading edge)* going back 10 years. Now, to illustrate what you want to know. You want us to warp space, and emerge let's say 2 inches left, on the line from the leading edge. As we said, yes, we can. But as soon as we emerge at that point in time, and cause any meaningful changes to the existing timeline, it will create a 'new second timeline' from that point. To again illustrate, we would start a new pencil line 1 inch above, exactly parallel with the emergence location of the first timeline. Now, fast forward two years, and our new pencil line, would be at the same parallel location, as the first pencil line. But while the second pencil line was moving through time, the first pencil line was also moving, at the same speed. So, when you go back 2 years, by the time you return to the previous leading edge, the leading edge is two years further ahead, or a 12-inch line now.

Q: Just to make sure, I completely understand this physics lesson, or maybe even Quantum-physics lesson, if we warp space again, and want to go back 1 year, a new timeline will occur, so we would have now, 3 separate timelines all moving at the same rate.

A: Exactly. Changes in timeline 2, will never change what happened in timeline 1. It is its own timeline or as some of your recent science fiction concepts like to refer to it as an alternate dimension. So, since there is no way to go back in time to fix a timeline, only create a new one, it would simply be a complete waste of time and resources. That is why we only care about the leading edge.

Q: Could I, after reaching the original starting point on the divergent timeline, the 10-inch mark, now warp space so I would emerge back on the 12-inch line just shy of the leading edge. Basically, return to my original starting position which is now two years further along?

A: Well, that is a very fascinating concept and in short, I will say yes, but that warp would produce now, what I will call for your benefit, a 'time distortion' effect. As soon as you emerge, you would cause another divergence, but this divergence would occupy the same space-timeline at the first jump. The problem occurs when the second divergent timeline meets the start of your new divergent leading-edge timeline. When the prior timeline meets up with the new timeline, if they are not perfectly synced, there will be an energy wave created between two competing events.

Q: Can you give me an illustration of what you mean?

A: Let's say you were in your bedroom when you warped forward and back to the original timeline. If you emerged let's say at your Friend Al's, cottage, then, when the timelines meet, what happens if you are at the Hermitage in the divergent timeline? You can't exist in two places at the same moment on the same timeline. The result would be a displaced energy wave created by the two-competing events. The two timelines are going to want to find equilibrium and any and all timeline differences are going to want to merge which would now create even a bigger energy wave. That is why it is outlawed by our people and only in a very rare case is it done.

Q: I get it, I think. No Jumping forward. Now to a new area of inquiry, and I want you to know how much I am enjoying this exchange, even though I know it will be wiped clean shortly, and I am sure it is like me having a chat with an amoeba for you. You also have the ability, to record our species' thoughts, and I will for discussion purposes, again use the term 'record' all our thoughts, memories, and experiences, exactly as they are stored in our brains?

A: Yes. Our technology can, what we would prefer to describe, map your actual synaptic pathways and Ingrams. So, what we ended up with, is an exact duplicate, of the entire structure of your brain in an organic-based computer like simulated 3-D print. Think of a 3-D printer, which could use organic material, to recreate an exact copy of your brain, what would you have? 2 Brains! One original and one exact copy. *(Another clapping fest just occurred).*

Q: So, when you reprint my brain back into my current brain shortly, you don't copy my entire old brain pattern, you simply remove all the new stuff that was added after the initial recording.

A: That would be a very insightful, yes. We certainly can see how you managed to graduate High School in 3 years.

[Q&A Paused]

Rebecca, what you also need to understand, is the above transcript I have written down for you, is only a sliver, of the entire conversation I was having. For every question, I would ask, I was getting maybe, a thousand questions from my new friends, that I was answering. And the remarkable thing about nonverbal communication, it all was happening in seconds or maybe minutes. But while they could map my mind, they also could intercept my short-term memory. If you recall grade 12 Biology, our brain takes input from our eyes, ears and sensory organs like our skin and first records them in what we know as our short-term memory.

At some point, our brain will decide, and please don't ask me how, since I don't know, and did not, unfortunately, ask, move selected information into our long-term memory area of the brain. I think purely from an intuitive perspective, our short-term memory only records new information and does not continuously add already stored information. Kinda like, if I was staring at a sunset, and thought "Wow, that is beautiful," it only records unique and new aspects and not everything I was seeing (again), since I already had stored the first sunset view, and our brain can stitch all those pieces together, anytime we want to recall it.

While they could access my memories, what they could not do, is access my immediate thoughts. I am pretty sure there is a delay between what I was thinking and when they could access it. My bigger concern was the forthcoming lobotomy I was going to have. Ok, maybe a bit extreme, but I can honestly tell you I did not want this experience to end.

[Q&A Resume]

Q: If I asked you to take me with you, maybe as a mechanic type tool, in your tool house, just in case you need me to help you again in the future, and I am aware, I would have to live inside some special room like some 'Bubble Boy' for the rest of my life, at least when we left this planet, would such a request be possible?

A: No, Prime.....

Q: .... Directive again. Damn the Federation of Planets rules. Where is Kirk when I need him to bend the bloody rules for me *(Another round of clapping)*. You informed me, that I could put my brain into a 'Private Mode', what does that do from your perspective?

A: It does not block anything, it's more like you post a sign at the doorway to your short-term memory, saying 'access only by permission, please wait.

Q: And what about access to my long-term?

A: Same.

Q: But you already have a full copy of my brain stored in your database somewhere?

A: Yes, but we would respect your request and not go back in, to explore.

Q: How do I know that you would not simply ignore my signage, and still access my short-term or long-term memory?

A: Prime Directive, but to provide a more comforting reason, understand, that we also have the same ability to probe the mind of each other, just like we do with you. Long ago, we decided that mind-probing while highly efficient, also removed our ability to retain private thoughts. Over the years, and I mean many years, our people/society found itself, pulling away from using the privacy protocol, but we still fully understand the importance of it, not just with your species, but with many others. As such, it is a protocol, that we hold dear, and to breach it would be unimaginable to us.

Q: Well, you could say our relationship is fairly new, and trust is built over time, but, due to your upcoming plan to re-integrate me back into my older self, I am willing to accept your word on the topic. How do I turn it on?

A: Just think about it. We will see your request and respect it.

[Well Rebecca, I took it for a test ride, and suddenly all the questions that I had previously been fielding, from my many new friends, stopped. I was in, as you can appreciate, new territory, but my mind, was still mine, and it wanted some privacy, to spend some time figuring out a plan that I thought was pretty cool and might provide me with the 'big fix' that I have needed for a very long time. But as you are going to see, that fix will have a direct impact on you. The current you that is, and you would know nothing about it, or have the option to tell me to f-off and leave you alone. By providing you with the information I have so far, I am hoping, that you would be ok with my idea, and maybe one day embrace it.

The Big Ask

5 I used the next few seconds to formulate my idea in my head and do the customary 'what if' scenario run throughs. I needed to flush out my idea, as best I could under the circumstance. At least I knew, it would certainly provide the ultimate test of the Privacy protocol. I think you already have figured out my plan, but just in case, here are the Coles notes. I figured, that since they would soon restore me to my pre-contact state, there was nothing I could do, with regards to the leading-edge timeline we were on. What I was hoping to get them to do, was allow me to go back in time, to a specific point in my life's timeline, and create a new divergent timeline. They seem to regard such a thing as a big waste of time, but to me, it would offer me the chance to go back, and right my wrongs so-to-speak, and hopefully live the life I had daydreamed I should have lived, if I ever got a do-over. Since my original self, would still carry on, completely oblivious to all this, and I knew going back, the way I wanted, would not undue what my original self had already been through, or interfere with my remaining years, why wouldn't I? For that matter, who would not love this opportunity.

Here was my one chance, to actually turn that lifelong desire, into something real. I knew it was going to be selfishly, only for my benefit, but the thought of being able to go back, and re-live meeting you again, was so powerfully strong, my brain quickly became fixated on that single desire. Rebecca 1.0, just like Derek 1.0, would continue on, exactly as it would, until our eventual deaths. But Derek 2.0, could now live a life, that I have been building in my dreams for years, to right my perceived wrongs, and maybe even fix a bunch of other events, that I would have the benefit of knowing would happen. Just because I would be inserted into the timeline, creating a new timeline, unless my actions some how impacted events within the new divergent timeline, the events should occur exactly as they have so far.

You have no idea Rebecca, the adrenaline rush I was experiencing at that moment, but as crazy as my scheme may have sounded, I knew I would need time to gather information, that would be useful to me, or should I say Derek 2.0's re-do. So, I would not only have to get my new friends to agree to my convoluted request to go back in time, but I would also need them to provide me with time now, to do my prep.

Step One; build up sympathy for where my current life is at. Step Two; Create the 'You owe me" guilt factor, and finally: Step Three; Convince them it would not violate any of their rules. Maybe even become a new cottage industry for them. *(There would most certainly be a lot of clapping if my privacy sign was not posted).* But there could be a small issue with them sending me back, with all my new memories and information. What happens if they send me back, with my pre-contact memory, rather than the new modified one? I decided, that would have to be a dance that I do, if, and when they may try to insist on it. From my perspective, as long as I could go back, that was goal number one.

Q: I have had to field a lot of questions about Rebecca. Why so many questions about Rebecca?

A: You had dedicated so many of your memories about her, some actual experiences and many self-contrived and they existed only as a fabricated daydream experience. Often memories lack context, or sufficient information, to fully appreciate or understand them to their fullest. Therefore, asking specific questions, help us better understand, what we could not deduce, just from the memory file so to speak. Context is the purview of the memory supplier.

[I had a brief moment of panic, as I just now realized that if they could access my 'made up' daydream memories of Rebecca 1.0, then they would have been exposed (no pun intended) to some pretty, I prefer to characterize as, 'out there' fantasies (Completely innocent I assure you!). I always knew in the back of my pea-brain, the day I stumbled on the Rebecca doppelganger internet 'Adult' star Jodi, would come back to haunt me (Major blushing happening). I am surprised, I have not been asked about some of the more colourful fantasies stored in my brain. I will have to assume, that they know the difference between real life experiences, and fantasy-based memory implants I may have created. I guess the best test for that, was the fact, no one had yet referred to me as Perve 1.0 (and that is all I am going to say about that)]

Q: What is your assessment of me as a human?

A: You, we would consider to be highly complex, extremely intelligent, and psychologically damaged stemming from back to your breakup with Rebecca and lasting your entire life.

Q: That obvious?

A: Yes! (Followed by some hesitant claps).

Q: Are you able through reading my memory experiences, also able to experience the emotions that are created from that experience like the bawling session we all participated in earlier?

A: Yes and No. One of the aspects of the evolution of our species, is the ability to focus our thoughts on wanting to always improve ourselves, and over time, emotions and emotional responses have been greatly modified towards a more, can I say, less impactful response.

Q: Do you guys feel love?

A: Again, as a result of our evolution, what you would call love, has been replaced with a sense of 'mutual well being'. And if I may anticipate your next question, yes, we procreate but not how you do it. Our process of bringing new life into our world occurs from a process of mutual assimilation of many specific traits that are contributed by many of our people. We then assemble that new life form resulting in what is probably best describe as a community generated new member. Our children have hundreds or thousands of parents from your perspective, and that has allowed our people to develop a much more harmonious and mutually respectful civilization.

Immediately after that answer, I found my friends once again peppering me with all sorts of questions about you and me. Rebecca 1.0 that is. But as I said earlier, one of the benefits of authoring this guide, is my ability to sensor my exchanges and not include many of the absolutely, full-on, red-faced blushing questions that had occurred. Including a very intimate sexual exploratory afternoon on Joey "B" at the cottage and our joke about 'poo babies'. If Rebecca 1.0 ever knew I allowed strangers to see what we did *(More accurately attempted)* that day, I would be in for a major 'Amber Heard' experience. So, unfortunately, you will have to use your own imagination to try and figure out what they asked me *(and that is all I am going to say about that)*.

Q: How long will you remain here after you return me to my prior self?

A: Based on your metric, we will be here another 23 days, 8 hours, 13 minutes, and 23 seconds.

Q: How close do you need to be to a subject, such as myself, to be able to perform your memory harvesting technology? And is the same technology used, to do either the recording, or the re-imprinting?

A: Yes, the same technology is used. Our 'reading' technology, that is the part where we take a 3-D image of your brain, is done by way of a unique radio wave, but not a radio wave like you're familiar with. Our 'radio waves', probably more resemble your x ray machines, but can act like radio waves. Just to provide a little more context, we have 3 observation posts currently collecting data on this visit, spread around your planet. The questions you were receiving, actually came, from all of the observation locations, because we are linked together using the same technology. Think of it as a giant permanent zoom call.

Q: How big is it, the tech that is?

A: Well, that is a bit of a difficult question, because part of the process is done, by linking our collective minds together, so we can equally share the work. The actual hardware part is about the size of a 24 case of Blue Light. The 355 ml size. *(And there goes some claps)*.

Q: If I did not come to Al's lake when I did, and if I did not head down to the dock when I did, would my friends in the tubes have died, as I know death?

A: Yes, but your decision to come down to the lake when you did was the result of us sending you a bit of a memory nudge, using one of your Rebecca memories, and then modifying it a bit to also include 'Your Song'. *(Ya Ya , Clap, clap, clap)*

That is right. I was motivated to go down to the lake, to have sometime to think about you, with the justification of a nice snifter of Port, cigar and yes, I made sure to bring my phone, with the 'Greatest Playlist of All Time', because it just happens to include 'Our Song'. *(And yes, it was the same for both Rebecca 1.0 and for you)*. Call me an old sentimental. "Hello, I don't even know your name, but I'm hopin' all the same, This is more than just a simple hello" *(Made you blush!).*

Q: I was quite a long way from you, so, how far can you reach with your mind sucking technology? *(One or two claps).*

A: I think we have been successful using it over 5,000 kilometers using your metric.

Q: Why the limit?

A: Has to do with gravity and solar radiation.

Q: So, we all agree, that through some manipulation by you, if I did not perform the implanted task, and rescue your boys, they would be dead. And I mean dead forever, and not reanimated using some tech you have.

A: Our real issue was not our ability to re-animate them, even if they lost all their air; the issue we faced was the gas like substance that you encountered that dissolved your suit, we initially provided you with. While that gas, was for the most part, harmless to you, and the rash you will develop in a few days, you will blame on not realizing you must have touched poison ivy walking out from Al's camp, is an instant killer to us. No reanimation and would have dissolved our people into a nasty liquid like material. Think of a human, coming into contact with your strongest sulphuric acid. The protective suits we have for just such an event, were unfortunately, stored in the compartment right where the damage had occurred, rupturing the gas containment feed line, going to what you would think was our engine. We had calculated an estimated timing, with a degree of certainty down to the millisecond, when the line would completely blow, and the gas would reach the pods, or what you have referred to as cylinders. The 'Crying' sound you heard was the periodic escaping gas bursts.

Q: What were they doing in the cylinders in the first place?

A: They are actual observation pods that we deploy out into the field. They are completely self contained, and our people can stay in them while observing or collecting samples, for up to a month, based on your perceived time. They were getting them ready when the observation post you like to call it, suffered, the beginning stage, of that gas line leak, causing our vessel to clip the rock cliff, not far from us, which started the chain reaction of events. Normally, the observation structure deploys what you would call landing legs, but the failed gas line, triggered our systems, to go into a brief holding pattern, which you do not want, when in the middle of a landing procedure.

Q: Do you, or your fellow observorites *(my new name)*, understand the earth concept of appreciation?

A: Here it comes, the shakedown *(followed with a huge clapping sound)*. Yes, we do and while our view of appreciation greatly differs from yours, since we all exist, to try and make the future better for everyone. We just do the individual pat-on-back thing.

Q: Your communication vernacular has obviously been improving and I would clap, but my hands appear bound at this moment, but I assure you, there is no shakedown. If this is it, and I am returned to pre-contact Derek, then I want you all to know, that our time together has been, do I say it, "Out of this world'. *(Biggest clap yet I think)*. But knowing what you know about me, especially my unresolved feelings regarding Rebecca, I would like to ask, what I am sure is a huge favour, but I hope, from your view, is no big deal based on what you have told me. I want to ask you, to take my current memory mapping, and go back in time and put it into an earlier Derek, yes, creating a new divergent timeline, *(who I will use as my guilt card)*, who saved 3 of your people, and yes, I am smiling and thinking hand clapping.

Wow, silence. Not sure if that is good or bad, but it was a strange feeling to feel so alone again, after being connected to so many minds. I am not sure how long it took for the reply, but it was quite a while in terms of their timeline. But as they came back online, I felt the person I was interacting with now, was different to the person I had, most of the more official discussion with. This person, actually came with what can only be described as oozing empathy, mental empathy. It is times like this, that you can not replace the face-to-face value of reading another person's face, to truly appreciate their sincerity. In my case that was not possible, as far as I knew, and while they knew what I looked like, I still did not know what they looked like. Slowly the table/chair I was attached to tilted up a bit and moved closer to the glass like partition. The fog on the other side began to dissipate and what I had not expected, happened.

You Becca, or should I say Becca 1.0, standing there, exactly as I remembered, that evening I dropped you off at your house, after our first date. I accompanied you to the front door, where we had our first real kiss. No cheek this time. I know it was not Rebecca, and I was fully aware that my memories were being manipulated, but not only did I not care, I wanted it to continue, all the way to the point when your mother yelled out the window for you to get in the house. If memory serves me still, it was about 30 minutes or more. The image was so powerful, that I was scared that I would start to cry like a baby again. I had so much emotional baggage in me, that seeing you was about to uncork a powder keg. But before that happened, you spoke to me. And yes, I know it was not really you, but one of the strangest things that happens over time was, I forgot the sound of your voice.

I had pictures of us, and you, but I never made any recording of us together *(Trust me, Rebecca 1.0 would be saying right now, Thank GOD)*, and had I known my future fate, God only knows, I would have had a video recorder strapped to my body. I once tried to reach out to you *(sorry Rebecca 1.0)* after my divorce in 2013, hoping to have a simple phone call, just to say hi. Just to be able to recapture the sound of your voice. Something as simple as a hi, would have rocked my world. But, as the relationship gods, still had it in for my happiness, my text message to you after 30 years, was returned, and not how I wanted, but how it needed to be. I still have your text on my phone. Yes, how pathetic I know. But for some reason I still periodically re-read it, and I still feel better after reading it than before. I think it will put a brief smile on your face, even though it's not you, so, here is the reply I got from Rebecca 1.0, on December 4th, 2017 at 9:17pm.

> ***"Hi Derek, what a surprise it is to hear from you. I hope all is well. I am sorry, I do not feel comfortable connecting, as the man in my life for the past 4 years would be understandably concerned, as would I if he was to connect with one of his old girlfriends. I hope you understand. I wish you well and a wonderful Christmas,"***
>
> ***Signed Rebecca.***

I guess one good thing, was you, or she, indirectly referred to me as 'her old boyfriend'. I chose not to add either the initial text I sent or my follow up reply, *(except to tell you, that I told her, 'That the man in her life was lucky and better treat her like a Queen')*. A bit too painful, but as I have said, I always knew, deep down, that the text she sent, was the right text. I think, I always knew, that I blew any chance, at maybe having a shot at getting together again and to see if there was any spark left, or the chance to create a fresh one, all because of that day in October of '81. One question I never did ask Rebecca 1.0 was 'When did she decide I was not the guy and decided to dump me without warning?' But, as will be revealed later in the guide, back then, it could never be anyway. My only hope now, was through a do-over.

What's truly amazing, is their ability, not only to re-create an exact likeness of you, but they were able to generate your exact voice, just like they did with my mom. Before the first word out of your mouth was finished, all my old Rebecca pathways lit up, and I could now remember your voice again, for the first-time in probably 35 years. If they do not grant my current ask, then I would certainly see if they would allow me to remember the sound of your voice again, and maybe to leave a copy of the Hermitage video on my phone *(I'm grinning)*. But as you have guessed, knowing what you already know, I heard the words I so longed to hear, "You can come Derek." I know it generated a tear or two, but they were tears of happiness not sadness. They made you smile exactly as I remember, with those cute dimples and beautiful eyes. I would never acknowledge that I was a broken man, because I did, actually have a very fulfilling life. I married, I divorced like you, I have great step kids and even great step-grand kids. I know I have had a positive impact on their lives, and have been extremely blessed, with a great group of great friends. I know, this entire situation is not even a couple hours old, but if it ever came down to having to choose to stay in the present or go to the past and Derek 1.0 would cease to exist, without hesitation, I would choose the past.

All of the emotions that must have flowed from me, at that moment, appeared to be received by my friends with open arms, even though, I still had no idea if they had any. It was odd that there was not a single push back by anyone. It was time to start the process of planning how this was going to take place. As it stood, my present Derek 1.0 would have my pre-contact memory re-integrated back into my mind and my life would continue in this timeline complete with my current family and friends and no Rebecca, except for my annual birthday text message which I am pretty sure she has on call blocking at the request of her lucky guy. Yes, I could always use another number, but to me, that would be disrespectful and as I like to say, 'Bad Form'. My current memory scan would then be transferred into my younger self, but I needed to better understand how this process would work.

Q: You obviously know how grateful I am, that you are prepared to give me this incredible gift. What are the steps involved with the process Rebecca? *(Fake Rebecca that is).*

A: We will need to know a time, and location, that your earlier self will be. Once we know, we can, for your conceptual benefit, program into our technology the necessary data to cause the space to warp, and to have the warp occur at the proper time and location.

Q: Does your whole ship have to go back through the newly created space warp?

A: No, with the geo-location established, we only need to open a warp fissure to allow us to beam or transmit the memory information to your earlier self. We use one of our drones for the whole process.

Q: So, your drone will fly to where my old self would be, generate the required warp in space, and at the intended time, have a crack large enough, then using your technology, transfer my current memory mapping into my prior self?

A: Yes, that is an excellent summary, Derek.

Q: Won't my retention of everything you have placed into my memory violate your Prime Directive?

A: Not at all. Think of it this way. You are actually going to a copy of yourself, which has absolutely no connection to your original self and the Leading Edge. The Prime Directive only applies to the Leading-Edge timeline.

Q: And by doing this, we will not disturb some galactic forces that could damage the Leading Edge in any way or hurt Rebecca 1.0 or Derek 1.0's family and friends?'

A: No, a single divergence is nothing and the two timelines will be just fine'.

Q: After you transfer me back to my earlier self, when I hopefully reach my current age, in about fifty years, and I would know in advance, that you would be here; could I perform the task, and save your people again, and then ask your copy-selves, to again take a new copy of my memory and do it all over again?

A: *(A lot of clapping again)* It was so nice to be able to have the conversation with the fake Rebecca, even knowing it was all taking place in my brain. I knew I had asked the right question, which provided them with some new stimulation, not to mention the big smile on your face *(Fake Rebecca that is, and I could not take my eyes off of you)*

A: *(Continued)* You have once again, proven to be somewhat of a human oddity. You seem to have developed a few fans here based on the comments that have been exchanged. Just to put you at ease, when we do the memory implant into your younger self, we always add a special, additional file, that would only be recognized by us, which would contain information, that would provide a divergent us, with all of the pertinent what, why and where data. But please understand, that once you are implanted into your younger self, you will always be outside of the leading edge, and can never return. Prime Directive, sorry. Your original copy will continue with exclusive ownership of that timeline until your death.

Q: One last request, and I hope it won't be a big deal. You previously said, you will remain here, in this location, for the next few weeks. I think you said exactly, 23 days, 8 hours, 13 minutes give or take a few seconds. Will you allow me to wait 22 days, before you do the procedure? I promise you that I will keep everything confidential.

A/Q: That is an odd request, but before we answer, why do you need time? Your, what you like to call, pre-contact self, will be returning to resume your leading-edge life anyway?

A: I realized, I wanted to complete some last-minute house keeping chores, which will assist me after my jump. I promise you that there is nothing I plan to do that will interfere with your Prime Directive in anyway. And since you already have the pre-contact memory dump anyway, you will always have the option at anytime, to do the procedure and restore all to what it was.

A: We have seen that you place a great deal of value on being a 'man of his word'. I think you continue to hold the rule that, 'A person's word is his life. Break your word, Lose your life.' So, we will agree to your request, but please understand, we will need to monitor your interactions, so we can fix any issues that unexpectedly may occur that may interfere with the Leading Edge.

I responded, “I would accept nothing short of that.”

“We will now return you to the water. When you feel the coldness of the water, take a deep breath. We will make sure you are away from the observation structure so you will be able to swim to the surface,” Rebecca instructed.

I asked my final question, “Is there any way we could do some sort of group hug first?”

I think they never expected I would ever make that request, but they gave me their version of a group hug, they had you sing, your line of our song, back to me, “Hello, do I smile and look away? No, I think I'll smile and stay, to see where this might go.”

Before the old tear glands could fill, I was being deposited into the water. The sudden shock of the water was no longer concerning. My excitement with what had just happened, overloaded everything. My brain was going a mile a minute, and part of me was still processing what was transpiring. Now added to this, was the realization, that I had no idea how much time had lapsed. I needed to start to prepare, for a variety of situations I was about to be thrust into. What do I do, if Al is standing on the dock when I surface, or worse, has already called the police to report my unexpected drowning? Great, just what I need, a police helicopter buzzing around my friends. Well, thank God *(who still has a beat down coming from me)* for the concept of buoyancy. Because I had taken a fairly good breath, in anticipation of the water dunk, once I hit the water, in order to determine what direction was up, all I needed to do, was to not move, and see what direction my body was headed. Then, simply assist with the last few feet with a couple of strokes and kicks.

As my head broke the surface, I immediately knew it was still nighttime, since the sun was no where to be found. Second, it appeared I was about 10 feet from the canoe, which was now fully visible. Damn, I never did ask how they were holding the canoe in place. I reoriented myself so I could see the dock. Please, no Al! No Al! First concern handled cleanly. I think it was instinct, but I let out a somewhat muted and short, “Thanks Guys.” I swam over to the canoe, and with one hand gripping the front, I started the process of bringing the canoe back to the dock. Once I reached the dock, I was able to climb out with the help of the dock ladder and proceeded to tie up the canoe. After I finished the last knot, I noticed my jacket was in the bottom of the boat; the paddle, and to my pleasant surprise someone put my bottle of Port back in. Or, had it never left? Why would anyone do that? Hold on a second; How would I know if it was real or had been some elaborate fantasy I concocted when I was drowning after falling out of the canoe.

Damn again. Old smarty pants forgot to ask for something to prove it was all really happening, and not some mental breakdown. I went from pre-panic, to my usual self-pat on the back for being so smart. My phone will have the proof! The videos should still be on it. Did they actually generate the video on the phone? or did they do it only in my mind? No video, then I am nuts; video, then a quiet celebration. If it was in my mind, they would be monitoring my thoughts right now, since I did not re-invoke the privacy option, and I am sure, they would immediately do what was required, to place an actual video on my phone.

I grabbed my jacket, unzipped the pocket, and removed the phone. I turned it on, and waited with some level of trepidation, for it to fully boot. Home screen appeared. My grandson's wallpaper picture was there, and I pressed the gallery icon. Up came the gallery page, and I hit the video icon. As I stared at the phone, a rather large smile grew on my face. My friends left me, one of the two videos. With the grin going ear to ear, I think Rebecca, you know exactly which one it was.

I retired back into the chair, dripping wet still, grabbed the Port bottle, popped the cork, took a swig, and proceeded to watch the video. I paused the video, at a particular point, and enlarged the picture view, which on my phone, was HD or 1080p. I sat, and stared at it for quite a while. While I know Rebecca, you think, I would have enlarged the picture of my 'special place', but you would be wrong. I was looking at just your face; smile and dimples in full force, eyes looking at me with such innocence. It would take a little time, but the reality of what was about to happen, slowly swept over me, and I sat in that chair for a while longer and quietly wept. Not tears of sorrow, but tears of joy. Seems someone forgot to turn a valve off.

END of the first part!

The Countdown!

Note to Becca; I wrote this countdown section roughly 2 years after my arrival as Derek 2.0. I apologize if at times I bounce back and forth between you and Rebecca 1.0 memories. You may also wonder how I knew a future event when I had not yet made the transference. Well, now you know. If in the future I get the time and inclination to clean it up, I will make a note of that.

6 ***T-minus 22 days:*** I got myself pulled together, as best as I could under the circumstances, while my brain wanted to begin figuring out the order of the next steps, my other part of the brain was telling me to take a deep breath, relax and go up to the cottage and get out of the wet clothes. Sounded like good advice, and to be honest, I was starting to get a chill, and the last thing I needed was to catch a cold. So, I grabbed all my stuff and made my way to the cottage. When I reached the grass section, just after you step off the dock gangway, I paused, turned around, and felt it was important that I begin mentally documenting everything. I stared towards the part of the Lake I knew my friends were and figure they must be busy making repairs to their Observation outpost/ship. I had turned on the privacy mode a little while ago, so I turned it off for a second and initiated a thought hoping they might be monitoring me. 'I am here and

available to help at any time if you think you need me again. Maybe take a quick recording of Al's memory, just in case you need to do a re-implant later."

I hesitated, hoping to get some type of acknowledgment, but to my disappointment, nothing. I turned the phone towards me and hit the video icon. Thankfully, Rebecca, your video was still active and alive! I am sure I will be doing a few 'reassurance looks' over the next while. I reached the deck, and I figured it was best for me to take off my wet clothes here and hang them over the railing. In the morning, I will transfer them to Laurie's makeshift clothesline, strung between a couple of trees. I was working on the 'story' I would tell Al in the morning when he spots the evidence on the railing. I was leaning towards, 'I accidentally tried to fart, ended up soiling myself, and went to the lake and washed everything'. That was more of a guy-type fake story, but I was not sure I wanted to expose myself to a good old ribbing from Al all day, if not, for years to come. Maybe I will shift the blame to Al and the poor job he did to tie up the canoe, and it was floating away from the dock when I went down there, and to save it I had to jump in. Well, as my brain worked a little longer, I knew to get some dry clothes on, get into my sleeping bag, warm up, and hopefully try and sleep a bit before morning.

Funny; I just realized at that moment that throughout my numerous encounters with my phone, I never bothered to check the time at the top. No time like the present! I grabbed the phone from the railing where I had put it and hit the necessary button on the side to kick it into gear. When I first looked at the time, I wasn't caught off guard at all, but my brain wanted to do some quick math to establish a reasonable approximation of how long my entire ordeal took. So, I went to the dock around 12:30 am; sat in a chair; not that long, lit the cigar; Had a sip or two of Port; noticed sound and smell; Let's say a maximum of 20 minutes; Get in the canoe; paddle; get stuck; not crap myself; go in the water; not crap myself; oh darn, forgot one of the most important steps, take video and see my girl. *(I am so giddy right now)*. Ok, back to the calculations; in the water; swim to structure; try stuff; back to canoe; Maybe another 20 minutes tops; Pulled under; dragged to structure; stuck in a condom; mother's voice; Hmmm. Now the guessing starts. Let's say 10 minutes. So, we are at about 50 minutes from first reaching the dock.

Chat; first memory dump; saving my new buddies; return to Observation post/ship; back in a condom; Man, I can't believe it was more than 5 minutes tops. After all, I only had two, maybe max, two and a half minutes of breath available. Second, chat; meet fake Rebecca; the big bawl weiner stuff; more chat and then dumped in the lake; Swim and get canoe; return canoe; tie up canoe; question my sanity; Look at the picture of the most beautiful girl in the world, ever *(Trying to make you roll your eyes)*. Having another verklempt moment; and walk to deck and strip. Full commando! No, 'Dirk Diggler', water was chilly *(Smile time)*. I will give that a big 30 – 60 minutes max. So, if my brain can still do simple math, the total best guess time would be, 110 minutes max. That would mean, the time should be around 2:20 am? But it's not. It's 5:30 am. Why the discrepancy? I grabbed my ass, more as a defensive joke gesture, but somewhere in that joke was a little nervousness. My new buddies would not go and violate me in that 'you know what way', especially after I saved their bloody lives. It would simply be bad galactic form *(I laughed)*. Perhaps the big memory dump took a lot longer than I thought?

Funny, how some old national enquirer story about alien abduction, would create an urban legend, that all Aliens seem to like to use the annus to access the interior of our bodies. Sorry, Rebecca, it's a guy thing I am sure unless I made you blush *(and that's all I am going to say about that)*. I would not characterize the time difference as overly concerning, but I will, hopefully, before the final transference, ask my friends about the time gap. For right now, looks like I will get an hour or two at best of sleep, assuming I can fall asleep.

Well, I can answer that question right now. I went out as soon as my head hit the pillow and was woken to listen to Al go through the now customary morning 'old man' rituals, with all of the moans, grunts, huffs and puffs, and finally the sound of putting the kettle on the stove to boil the coffee water. I heard the door open, and then close, and I assumed, Al was off to the outhouse to do his morning business. It will be interesting to see if he's awake enough yet, to notice the clothes on the railing. It was always funny how Al and I both shared the curse of the early morning rise. I have always blamed my dad for the curse since he would never let me sleep in as a kid. But it was even worse when I was of the age that I started exploring the pleasures of drinking and getting drunk and having a serious hangover in the morning. I would never be afforded the option of the old 'sleep it off'. It always pissed me off, pardon my language, that all my friend's parents would let them sleep in till whenever, but my dad was at my door by 9 am telling me to get out of bed, "because it was a beautiful day, and the grass was not going to cut itself" he always said.

Don't get me wrong, I did embrace the getting up early curse because it turned into a benefit when I was older. I usually got up at the crack of first sun peeking out over the night sky. I was not a fan of daylight-saving time and would refuse to turn my clocks back, and make morning, night till 7:30 am. It would not have bothered me if it was dark by 4 pm, just let me keep rising with the sun. Al was the same. It is not uncommon for us to chat on the phone before 7 am. Well, it was time for me to decide on the story I would use with Al regarding my wet clothes. Just as I was trying to pick one, Al re-entered the cottage and was now in the process of making our morning brew. I crawled out of the sleeping bag and took a look at the little thermometer on the wall near the window that faced the lake. 12 degrees Celsius, I can live with that, although as I have aged, I have become more of a fair-weather type of guy. I put on my work stuff and made my way out of my room about the time the Coffee was ready to drink.

"Morning. How did you sleep?" I asked.

"Well, I think I may have had a few too many beers by the look of all the cans that need to be crushed," said Al with a bit of a raspier voice than normal. What I will say about Al, he can certainly rebound from a booze fest better than I. Nowadays, it's a 2-day waister for me. On the first day, I feel like crap, on the second day I am at about 60%. Don't get me wrong, I still love to have a few drinks, I just can't do the excessive pounding that Al can do.

"Well after you retired for the evening, I went down to the dock for a snifter of Port and a fine cigar. I guess I nodded off with the glass of port in my hand and ended up spilling it all over me," I offered up as I watched for a reaction.

"Oh, was wondering why your clothes are strewn all over the railings. Thought maybe you crapped yourself last night after you went for the high note on 'Take on Me'", chuckled my portly little buddy.

See Rebecca, a guy thing! "Well fortunately for me I had to dunk the clothes in the lake to get the port stains out. Might have scared all the wildlife away being in my birthday suit and all. I guess we will see later if the stains came out, and if there was any evidence of the latter theory, it's gone now. Besides, I figured by the time we attempted that song, all our vocals were spot on like the original."

"I figured two more beers, and we would have been doing some Rush," laughed Al.

I thought I better do what I do best and get cooking breakfast. I was starving after last night's activity and was looking forward to bacon and eggs, Applewood smoked bacon! Al had bought a couple of large boxes of dehydrated hash browns, which I was looking forward to trying. He had mentioned to me before that he bought them, and claimed they were great. I figured if they were great, I would add them to my future sailing provisioning checklist. Breakfast up north always seems to be extra good, and this breakfast seemed to be a few notches above the usual. But while my tummy was saying thank you, my brain was still working through what happened last night. Part of me was still struggling with the whole, 'was it real or not' question?

So, I decided to show Al your picture Rebecca on my phone, to see if he actually can see you. And before you go and get bent out of shape that I am going to show you in your birthday suit, when I last had it open, I had paused the video and enlarged just your face. I promise I would never willingly show that video or any video involving you, especially bare ass naked *(I just smiled)* ever, even though we both know it was not you per say. Just to be clear on the issue, I will give you my word, that I would never do anything to hurt or embarrass you *(again)*. Once was enough! So, I thought *(Damn grin again)*

I grabbed the phone from the table where I had placed it and got your face shot ready as before. I said to Al, "I was going through some old photos last week, found one of my high school sweetheart Rebecca *(Yes, Al knows all about you, the other you, and just to prepare you, everyone does)*, and I found one that I had not looked at for probably 40 years."

I turned the phone around to show Al the new find, and as I did, I watched intently to see his reaction. With a fork full of eggs, he paused mid-shovel and said, "hang on." I held the position and watched as he reached for his cheaters and put them on. No real reaction on his face, and then he continued to shove the fork in his mouth with one hand and remove the readers with the other.

"Hate to tell you buddy, but I think you may be right, she was *wayyyy* too good for you," as he looked up with his usual fake innocent grin.

I simply smiled and was so relieved with the fact that he could see you, Rebecca, that I didn't even try to send back his way a witty retort. For me, that truly was rare. That was now, sufficient validation, that it was really, all real. T-minus 22 days and counting down. I continued to eat my breakfast when Al said the strangest thing, "You alright? You look way too happy for 8 am after partying last night."

While you would think, I would appreciate such a comment, it was actually, the opposite. Al was able to pick up a change in me, which I know was on full display. There is no way, a person could go through what I went through, without experiencing a life-altering change in themselves. It was imperative that I add a new valve to the system, a valve to turn off whatever I was emanating. I have 22 days to get through and needed to do those 22 days without any change in my demeanor, routine, or expression, or there may be an emotional volcano that would erupt.

So, for the next few hours, I worked very hard on trying to be normal, humble old Derek. Fortunately, I only needed to get through about 8 hours, then Al will be into his beer and smoke. After that, I will be able to use the old excuse, you were drunk, you were hammered, you must be f'd up to deflect any emotional or other leakages out of me. If the guitars come out again, none of my Rebecca songs tonight.

The day went fast, and I enjoyed the distraction. At first, I figured I would be spending most of the time dedicating my brain to figuring out what I needed to do over the next week. Instead, I found myself focusing on the job at hand, and seem to return to a more normal self. The day went smooth up till the moment Al dropped a wrench on top of the solar batteries. It was a bit comical to see him jump when the sparks flew. Fortunately, he had a plan of what was needed, since I gave him a lecture about an hour ago about how dangerous it was to have the battery terminals exposed, and that we need to put a non-conductive cover over them. He grabbed the broom that was right beside the batteries and used it to knock the wrench off before it fused to the terminals.

"Before you go and say I told you so, just remember who is going to clean some pike tomorrow for you," said Al with the startled look still engrained on his face.

"What me. I am not the kind of fella who likes to point out another person's errors and make them feel like they are some worthless turd, especially when pike bites would be on the line, besides, I am more than satisfied with the knowledge that you just soiled yourself and would need to clean your pants in the lake now," as we both laughed.

As you probably picked up on Becca, Al and I love to kibbutz a lot. I have found that I have developed over the years, different ways to interact with my different friends. I think it's a way of having some unique bond with that person which partially defines us. Humour has been very important to me over the years, sometimes to mask and sometime to help develop that unique bond I mentioned. Just before 4 pm, we had pretty much completed everything we had wanted to do and could start knocking off a few items from our Sunday list. We had planned to finish work

Sunday at noon and then put the cottage to bed before our hike out. I was hoping to reach Al's house by 6 at the latest to grab the truck and get my ass home. At 5, I put the 2 choice rib eyes in the sous vide bath, and yes Rebecca, I packed in my sous vide unit *(I am sure you are laughing at me now).*

I set the sous vide to my usual 128.5 degrees and set the timer to 1 hour 20 minutes. Ok, I will confess that I had also marinated, and vacuum sealed the steaks a week ago and flash froze them the night before the hike-in. I take great pride in my culinary skills and have always thought I could have had a career in hospitality as a chef until I managed that Night club back in the late 80s in my Derek 1.0 days. It was our New Years' eve bash at the club. I oversaw the club on behalf of the company, so it was 100% my baby. We had sold out completely, 500 tickets with a menu that included a beautiful prime rib dinner. The day fell on a Friday, and on Wednesday just prior, my head cook decided to hit me up for a sizable raise. I think he knew he had me somewhat over the barrel with New Year's in 2 nights. Well, head-strong young exec Derek decided to call his bluff. I told him that I would consider a raise in the New Year but would be basing the raise on some form of cost management savings metric. He was brutal with food waste that was killing my bottom line. While I appreciated it was a country and western nightclub, we still had a full food menu, and controlling waste was part of the job.

I detected he was not a fan of my position, but I stood my ground. I guess he thought he would have the last laugh and was a no-show for Thursday's shift. One of the bus boys told me that he took all his cookbooks and other personal stuff he had kept there Wednesday after closing, and I quickly concluded he quit on me. I called my boss *(Now good friend)* Mark, the president of the company that owned the place through a bankruptcy-type action. My job was to get it up and running, and once we had a year's worth of financials, we would then sell it hoping to get the initial investment back or as much as possible. After all, we were financial guys, not nightclub operators. So, with no hope of finding a chef to oversee the New Year's bash, and there was no way I would cancel it, I decided, being an overly cocky guy, that I had enough knowledge to handle it myself. I'm sure that 450 people that attended would agree I did a great job, food was cooked perfectly, but the 50 that I was unable to feed that gorgeous prime rib steak dinner to, would tell you otherwise, and a few did. It was not as bad as I took it. Most appreciated the full refund and understood the situation we were faced with, and I certainly was able to fill them up with every other bar food imaginable that night.

Seems I misjudged the number of roasts I needed to cook, and I also did not count on my serving staff handing out some stupidly thick helpings to many of their friends and acquaintances. One guy I swore had a 2-inch slice on his plate. In the end, my boss, and friend Mark, appreciated my effort, and we made a lot of money that New Year's. For me, however, I have always continued to punish myself for not being better prepared for all possible contingencies. After all, I considered that my superpower.

I calculated exactly, the amount of meat in pounds that was needed to feed everyone. The ticket buying process already separated the 'Primers' from the 'Chickeners'. Back then there was no such consideration for vegetarians. If you were a guy dating a vegetarian, then it was a bonus. You would get a double helping of meat in exchange for a few veggies. I knew the cooking calculations including shrinkage etc, and I had all the sides worked out as well. It should have been perfect; except I did not take into consideration the staff factor. Why? Never done anything like that before. Zero, hands-on experience. Not only did I not factor in the overzealous portions' sizes, but I did not figure on my staff sneaking food for themselves on the side. With 30 staff working that night, it added up quickly. I eventually found a bunch of plates under the bar which I knew was the bartender's handy work along with a bunch of plates in the staff change room. I was a good boss and already told the staff that I was going to take them all out for our own New Year's bash next Wednesday. It was like a slap in the face to me. They did not respect me the way I thought they should. I am telling you this because after that, I worked very hard on teaching myself the art of "What if scenario" processing. No more getting caught with my pants down again *(I wanted to make a joke Becca, but it would not work here!)*

I won't go and brag about how perfect the dinner was. These past few years, other than cooking a great meal for one every now and then, my cooking enjoyment was relegated to watching Katie Lee (*The second cutest girl in the world*) on the food network. Seems even she finally found her 'It-boy' Ryan and not me *(Sorry, I had to grin)*. But it was an awesome meal! What should have made me satisfied and happy, felt more like a wake. I would most likely never see my friend Al again after this. I mean the post-meet and greet Derek. I know that my pre-contact Derek would continue as if nothing changed, but it was weird to be thinking about the 2 separate Dereks that now existed. I was the new Derek now, and everything

I would do over the next 22 days would be unique to me, while still in the Leading-Edge timeline. I know my friends will do a suburb job stripping my memory down to the old Derek 1.0, but no matter how much I tried to intellectualize it, it came out the same, I am going to miss my buddy Al, the way I use to know him, because Rebecca, we both know that he is not part of my/our future except for a 'planned encounter' at a Pink Floyd concert.

7 ***T-minus 21 days:*** As you can tell Rebecca, it was not necessary to describe the rest of my time at Al's or the hike out and yes I had the rash they warned me about. I was still feeling down over my future loss. So, to change topics, I made it home by 9 pm and was able to make it to my favorite local sushi restaurant to grab dinner. I love sushi as you know. When I arrived home with sushi in hand, I immediately went to my computer and turned it on. I opened the bag and removed my food. I grabbed my 'real chop sticks', not a fan of the free wooden ones they give you, a proper wasabi dish, and a glass of water. I wanted to get down on paper *(actually computer)* some thoughts that I had during the truck ride back from Al's. I drove the entire way home without the usual Sirius radio on listening to CNN or Howard Stern. I sat and worked at the computer until midnight when I decided to call it a night. I wanted to start conditioning myself now, rather than in 21 days, so I went into the bathroom and did what I know you still do religiously, even today, as well as my first Rebecca, brush my teeth. I have never been a great tooth man and was always jealous of how perfect your teeth are.

Not that long ago, a buddy who I will not name to protect the innocent told me about spotting a picture of Rebecca 1.0 on the internet. While there was a brief 'gut feeling' that I would somehow be acting like a creepy old stalker, that feeling quickly gave way to my strong desire, to see what you looked like after so many years. Yes, at various points over the past number of years, mostly since my divorce, I would periodically do a little Rebecca searching on the computer. *"Ames, if this man shoots me... I want you to kill him... And I want you to go clear my browser history,"* flashed through my mind with a definite laugh to follow. Other than a blank Facebook page, with luckily a few 'Friends' posted so I knew it was your page, I was only able to source a few cycling (Georgian Bay Centurian area bike race) results that you participated in. It was this obvious expression, or lack thereof, that made me conclude that you were wanting to remain private and not participate in the social media world. I guess I will never know. It was great to see you and your fellow 'Girl's Night Out' gals smiling for the lucky world to see such a rare photo of you. I had not seen most of the girls since our 25th high school reunion. You looked almost like you did the last time we saw each other 38 years ago! I don't think I have held up as good as you, but I still have hair.

I changed into my usual pyjamas and climbed into bed. My last act that night was to play the video. It would turn out, to be something I would do each night for the next 21 days. And *NO REBECCA*! not with a box of Kleenex in hand *(Can't believe you would ever think that; grin, grin)*. Besides the dirty old man, disgusting pervert thought, I felt it was important to wait, till I could be with you again for the first time. It was my time to play the virgin card. I was well aware of how long this sudden desire for abstinence would be, but it just felt right and needed. I knew after the transference; I would no longer have access to the video and there was a very high probability that event would never be repeated. I was sure/hoping there were plenty of other ones, but this had a very special place in my mind, and I will one day, miss it.

You would think I would struggle to fall asleep each night, with what was going through my brain continuously, but that turned out, never to be an issue. I slept great actually and would discover in a few hours, that I found a new jump *(you could say)* in my step that morning. Today, Rebecca, I need to share some of the thoughts and ideas I developed when I was strapped to the table/chair and first used the privacy mode. At first, I was concerned if they listened in on those thoughts, especially based on the first couple, they may pull the plug on ever letting me come back to you. But before I get into specifics about my ideas, I want to discuss and pose a couple of 'What if's' directly to you.

Let's start with this hypothetical. Knowing what we know about the life and times of Adolf Hitler, and I already know, you know, what I am about to say, but here it goes; If you had the ability to go back in time when Adolf Hitler was a young boy, would you kill him? Thereby eliminating his future self from, committing the atrocities, we all learned about. Alternatively, would you take time, to try and influence his development, hoping you could alter his future, and never have what he eventually did, from ever happening? I know I like to use the term 'do-over', but I also think, "With great power, comes great responsibility" *(I think we both just rolled our eyes)*. All light-hearted observations aside, I don't know what you would choose to do. Really, me, Mr. Insight, the great 'Observationalist'. I have been battling in my brain with this very question.

Hypothetical number two; What if I told you, that a person in my current Leading-Edge timeline, was responsible for the horrific rapes and killings of multiple young girls over the span of 8 years, and was eventually caught, and convicted, because he and his sick wife videotaped the rape and killings of two of the victims. I want you to know, that my primary motivator to go back, for the 'do-over', was to be with you again. However, that being said, I also felt a great responsibility, for maybe interceding in certain events important to me, as well as some other major ones, to prevent them from ever happening. As I already told you, and you witnessed first-hand, I decided to do exactly that. Your brother Todd is an example. It's true, in my time, Todd dies, in your arms, at Gibson's Pond. It severely impacted you and your family. Your dad launched a bunch of lawsuits against the owner of Gibson's Pond land, the High School, each of the guys there, and their families. It was a very dark time. Thankfully, you and your family were able to recover, never fully, but to what I would call, a much more normal life. One I would become a part of for a while.

As a result, Gibson's Pond was fenced off and sold to a private developer, who, eventually buys up other lands down Martin Side Road, and the area goes from a great nature retreat for the town to housing. You and I, I am sure, will return to Gibson's Pond to kind-a re-create our first get-together. Can you picture no pond, and a fully paved Martin's Side Road? The school board settled the lawsuit, and your family eventually received some $3 million in settlements, but it took roughly 7 years to get through the legal system. You had dumped me just before that. Probably figured I would only be after you for your future wealth! *(Kidding, needed a joke)*. My point is, that was not your life, all because I will take certain information that I was privy to, and decided to act, with the goal, of correcting what I determined was an awful wrong.

This will be possible because I knew exactly what was going to happen, where it was going to happen, who was involved, and how it happened. I will use that information, and alter the future, at least the future I was coming from. I need you to do some sole searching, and decide if what I did was right, or wrong. The future as I knew it now may depend on it.

[Rebecca, please stop here and take a few days to digest everything before continuing. Trust me, it's needed and important to both our futures]

I am sure you have figured out; I decided to do exactly that. Come back to be with you and make as many fixes in the world as I could/can. Back to Adolf for a second. The transference only works from me to my earlier self. They cannot take my brain mapping and implant it into anyone, or I may have elected to bypass a 'do-over' with you, and go back to when Hitler was younger, and kill him! My choice in that hypothetical would be to kill him. No attempt at rehabbing. That is the only ABSOLUTE. Fortunately, I never had to make that choice. But over the next 21 days, I did exactly that. I selected a number, of what I like to call 'intercedings' *(my new favorite made-up word)*, and I will become an 'intercedealist'. Sounds much cooler than Time-cheater. Working on a crest for the front of my tights *(yuk yuk)*.

Back to the big question, what would you have done? So, over the next 21 days, I will be taking you through my selection process, my information gathering methods, the development of a supporting training regime, and most important, committing everything to memory. Remember I told you about my black duo-tang booklet that I started when I was 12. It was, my complete memorization transfer, from my memory to paper, immediately after my arrival. Your guide is a bit different. It was one thing to have the information, but it was another matter to be able to execute it *(pun intended)*. Your guide will focus on a 'Coles notes' like approach for each task I was planning/hoping to achieve. The following section of your guide will give you the basic information I gathered over the next 21 days. Today's task Rebecca was your brother's day. Off to the library to pull up all the old newspaper articles from that day forward, especially the stuff from the trial.

8 ***T-minus 20 days:*** Step one, compile the list. When my mind first generated the concept back when I was strapped to the table/chair, in the giant condom, after I had posted the privacy notice, I started the process. But not with saving Todd first but trying to figure out how I could 'cure cancer'. Yes, seems 'my mommy', placed a bit higher than your brother on my wish list. I think Rebecca, you will forgive me for that ranking. The challenge here, and now, was, that we have not yet found the cure for cancer, and my friends said they could not give it to me, but we have been making great strides in the area of early detection and excellent treatments. You know at some point, I would have gone through the mental exercise of believing I could save the entire world, but that was fortunately tempered, when my inner more rational voice said, "remember the prime rib new year's dinner." Seems we do learn from our mistakes *(I smiled).*

Yes, as I said, I consider myself more scientist than a liberal arts person, although one of my favorite post-secondary courses was surprisingly, a theology class at Mac. I could probably fill another dozen pages outlining what I found so enjoyable in the class, especially considering I still have the view, of a much-needed beat-down for God, but I think we need to be a bit more focused on the job at hand.

Another issue, and eventual limitation, will be the amount of information I can memorize before the transference. I was still working on, "should I memorize as I go, or wait and do it the last few days, so it would be fresh in my mind?" Now, for a little bearing of my soul Rebecca, believe it or not, Derek 1.0 was not a good student. When I was younger, before the age of 12, I seemed to have the ability, to absorb information that we learned in class very easily. Unless the teacher gave us an assignment that required us to return with either written content or assemble something for a presentation, I didn't need to do the traditional study step, that most students would perform each night, when they were at home. Rebecca, I will admit to you, for the first time, that this ability would also be a major deficiency for me throughout my prior life.

In retrospect, what it meant for me, which is a huge disappointment, was, that I rarely pushed myself to my limits. This fact, I will acknowledge, allowed for mediocrity instead of potential exceptionalism. I don't mean it in an "I am greater than you" sort of way, I mean, I never discovered what my personal best limits were, or could be. Getting a passing grade in school, in the 70-80 range was good enough. At least back then when entry to a university only required 70 percent. I am not sure even now, if this unfortunate ability, could also be construed as a form of laziness, or in the alternative, a mental deficiency. I was so afraid of the answer, that I never even attempted to look it up in the DSM-IV bible. This single issue has haunted me my entire life, and is responsible impart, for my strong desire for the 'do-over'. You're still the number one reason Rebecca, but this time, I would make sure, that I would correct this perceived flaw, and I would always push to be the best person I could be, both physically as well as mentally. Never in a braggadocious way, but in a doing way, by example.

I am starting to think, that writing this Guide for you, is also unknowingly *(now knowingly)*, providing me with a little cathartic therapy. At least from the Derek 1.0's perspective. And I promise, the last example to illustrate this point, was my getting accepted into U of Miami, not hopefully Harvard, that will be part of your life. So, I shot through High School in 3 years since we were on a semester system, and to graduate, all I needed to get my post-secondary honors graduation diploma, was 6 year 5 courses and 2 Canadian study classes. Well, easier said than done, unfortunately, and when it came time to submit my transcript to the U of Miami for acceptance after 3 years of high school, turned out my year 5 physics grade of 60 percent, and my year 5 calculus grade, did not meet their requirements to enter my program choice being Marine Geology/Geophysics *(Don't worry, I get into that topic later in the guide).* They would have let me into an arts program, but not science. And we know I am a scientist type *(Ha Ha).*

Most people, when faced with that situation, would simply postpone graduation for one year, and go back and take the classes again to upgrade. Well, that is not how I was wired. My solution was far easier. I would simply break into the guidance office and alter my grades accordingly. So, that is what I exactly did. I went from an overall grade point average of 74 to a new grade point average of 83. More than enough to get accepted, but not too crazy to draw attention. If you recall, back then, we did not have computers, it was all handwritten report cards by our teachers. Not only would I have to break in to steal my file, but I would also have to learn to be a master forger *(I just laughed at myself)* and then break in again to put the file back. Thankfully, you never had to deal with that Derek, you got the new and improved Derek, who was in the planning stages of becoming a time-crossing hitman! *(I giggled to deflect the tension at this moment).*

[The following section was updated after writing the preceding section]

You know about Tonka, and you know about my desire to 'cure cancer', but as we both know, my friends will not provide me with a cure. I am hoping to get a huge jump start on detecting the disease, and also, on getting a few experimental therapies made available to my loved ones that have been developed during this timeline. Yes, Rebecca, I will intervene not only with my mother but also with yours. I know our mothers are both gone now (In Derek 1.0 timeline) and it was hard on both of us to lose them, but in this timeline I am writing about, my mother died when she was 71 of breast cancer and your mother died when she was much younger from cancer as well. I was not part of your life when that happened, but I did attend the funeral from afar, so to speak, which was easy, since so many people attended that day, and I could easily blend in and go incognito. So, the next item on my list was helping our mothers live longer.

[End of new edit]

This single task would prove to be the most challenging, simply due to the vast amount of research and memorization time it would take. When I was doing it, I never thought about the influence I would have on the search for curing cancer, or the patents I would be stealing and calling my own. I love science, but having to read so many white papers, and published works on the subject of breast cancer, as well as ovarian cancer, took a few years off poor Derek 1.0's vision I would guess. I was already up to 2.5 cheaters. I read, googled, read more, watched YouTube, read more, eventually settling on a few key items. While I certainly pride myself on being a quick study, because it had to do with our moms, I was always feeling nervous throughout this one task. But as we know, I think I will do a respectful job. This task also was the basis for task 36, but we will get to that in due course.

9 ***T-minus 19 days:*** Task 3 was also a bit of a challenge, as it would be the first task, where I would be addressing the issue, along the lines of the prior Adolf challenge. I still could not provide you with any reasonable guestimate, on your choice Rebecca. The decision for this task was a no-brainer, and I know you would agree in principle. What was challenging for me, was the issue of deciding on how I would do the deed? Peter Bernard is currently rotting in federal prison, and I highly doubt he will ever see the outside for the remainder of his life. What I was having to explore within myself, forced me to take a really deep look into myself, which was turning out to be a very dark place. I know, I must have a valve for this that has been shut since its inception. Opening it was proving a bit unsettling. I am sharing with you Rebecca, some very dark thoughts, and I hope that they will not affect your memories of me, or us, in any negative way. But rest assured, I knew it would certainly affect me, for the rest of my life. Not in a bad way, but as a tool, and to keep that valve in check.

So, here it goes! And please don't think bad of me, although my gut knows differently. My preferred choice was going to be death by slow torture. And when I mean slow torture, I am not talking about letting him drown or a nasty poison, but rather, death by my hand, holding a butane plumbers torch, slowly burning every inch of skin off his body. And after the skin was off, I would use a spray bottle, filled with muriatic acid, to spray him down. Not too quick to make him pass out, but just enough, to watch him cry and beg for death. Well, Rebecca, that was what I was thinking. Probably also makes you question how you ever got involved with such an obvious sick, sick, emotionally damaged, obvious full-on psychopath, soon-to-be serial killer. I would be making Dexter look like an everyday petty shoplifter *(I needed to throw in a lightener).*

Don't go and judge me yet. It was only what I was thinking. We'll address what I decided to do, later in the guide. I thought it was important to demonstrate to you, that this will be a by-product of the process. Thinking about taking a life is extremely hard, but it will open up, the very recesses, of an inner darkness, that most aren't aware they have. You and I know that even you Rebecca, have a dark place. Not as dark as mine, but nonetheless, 'your dark place'. With Bernard, I had already made the decision to kill him shortly before he committed his first rape. I know you're thinking about, 'why not intercede and help him become a good person'? Because as the saying goes, "a leopard never changes his spots." A little theology lesson for you, it was used in Jeremiah 13:23, where the Hebrew prophet Jeremiah had originally said: "Can the Ethiopian change his skin, or the leopard its spots?" Besides, I was already ok with the notion of going to hell, since I knew heaven was out of the question, especially after I gave God his much-deserved beat-down.

So, once again, I need to go to the library and pull all of the Bernard news footage, and books, including interviews of his wife, who managed to get a plea deal of the century, for flipping on old lover boy. I was primarily focused on learning about his past, where he lived etc. It turned into an all-day thing.

10 ***T-minus 18 days:*** It has already been 3 days of information collecting, and I've concluded that I needed to find a better method for streamlining this process. At this rate, I would at best, only have the opportunity to fix, maybe 12 things, needing the rest of the time for memorization. I changed my approach today, and I decided to take the day and compile a full list, arranged chronologically by date, event, and by my new categorization system. So, Rebecca, this was the full original list;

1. **Task 1 – Make money and get in shape 1973-1976**
2. **Task 2 – Hockey Training**
3. **Task 3 – Get the list of Spec Carriers – 'Kids 4 a Cancer Cure' 1973**
4. **Task 4 – Reduce Workload 1973**
5. **Task 5 – First Charity Event 1974**
6. **Task 6 – Hockey and Grade 1975**
7. **Task 7 – Flamboro Downs 1976**
8. **Task 8 – Save Todd June 3rd, 1977**
9. **Task 9 – Save Elvis August 16th, 1977**
10. **Task 10 – Start Cancer interventions 1977 -1980**
11. **Task 11 – Iran Hostage Nov 4, 1979**
12. **Task 12 – John Lennon December 8, 1980**
13. **Task 13 – Ronald Reagan Shooting March 30, 1981**
14. **Task 14 – Air India Bombing, Brinks-Mat, Harrods June 23, 1985**
15. **Task 15 – Peter Bernard January 1986**
16. **Task 16 – Jane Hamlin & Dorothy Devon Cancer**
17. **Task 17,18,19 - Blackberry Investment 1991, Spyglass Investment, Bet on Blue Jays to win world series (1992)**
20. **Task 20 - World Trade Center Bombing, February 26, 1993**
21. **Task 21 – Nicole Brown hidden camera – June 12th, 1994.**
22. **Task 22 - Timothy McVeigh and Terry Nichols, April 19, 1995**
23. **Task 23 - Dunblane massacre - 13 March 1996**
24. **Task 24 - Princess Diana on 31 August 1997**
25. **Task 25 – Invest in Google.1999**
26. **Task 26 – Prevent Columbine High School massacre 1999**
27. **Task 27 – Stop September 11 attacks against United States by Al-Qaeda**
28. **Task 28 - Start Web Company Facebook. 2002**
29. **Task 29 - Space Shuttle Columbia Disaster 2003**
30. **Task 30 - Saddam Hussein - town of ad-Dawr, Iraq on 13 December 2003**
31. **Task 31 – Prevent Future President 42 – The 'Narcissist and Chief' 2004**
32. **Task 32 – Kill Kim Jung Ill 2005**
33. **Task 33 – Kill Putin 2006**

It was a very rewarding day developing my list, and realizing, just how much I was about to change my new future. What I had not planned for, was other potential collateral changes that could occur because of these changes. The most 'non-listed' impact, would not come from my memory, or knowledge, it would come from my wealth. Remember when I took you out for our first dinner as friends? In 1978, I took Rebecca 1.0 out for our first dinner at the same restaurant *(Sorry, a re-do memory thing)*. As I was waiting for her, in their living room, to finish getting ready for the big date, which I would like to point out was a regular occurrence. I recall your dad commenting to me how expensive the Sirloin Celler was. I think he was afraid I may not bring enough money with me to cover the bill seeing I had just turned 17.

The first time I went with Rebecca to the Sirloin Cellar, I was not that wealthy, and it put a major dent in my savings, especially with the added roses. But what pissed me off even more about that dinner, was her confessional a year or so later that she had left the table after the dinner portion and went to the bathroom and forced herself to throw up because she thought she would be too full if we made out later. I know it was not a bulimic issue, but it always bothered me. All that hard work flushed down the toilet! And worse, she would always order something different than me and then proceed to sample my entire meal. Sound familiar? I was just happy I ordered the cheesecake which she ended up eating half, and we did make out ☺.

11 ***T-minus 17 days:*** Hey, my hockey number day! Today, with my list completed, I was able to be more strategic with my time. Now, when I went to the library to do research, I could do it all at one time. Same for going to the bookstore to get required reading material and computer time to do research. My efficiency had greatly improved. Today was library day; the next three days are library days and not just 8 hours, I was putting in the entire day from open to close.

Still brush my teeth daily – 3 times most often *(Smile)*

12 ***T-minus 14 days:*** Ok, today was bookstore day, and not to be a bad grandpa, I visited with my daughter and my grandkids. Three so far and I would not be shocked if they try again for a girl. Three boys are great, but my daughter always wanted a little daughter too. Tonight, pizza and wings, and beer for the adults. While I was focused on the task at hand, I also knew that in 14 days I would be embarking on a new 'do-over'. I honestly did not know what I would do, as my new 'do-over' timeline reached that moment where they became part of my life. I figured since it would not occur until I would be 42, I would have plenty of time to figure that out *(Thirty Years)*.

I am also sure, at some point when reading your guide Rebecca, you will be a bit curious about what your other life was like for your other Rebecca, and we dare not refer to her as number one Rebecca *(Big grin here)*, let's go with pre-Rebecca *(Sorry, I lifted that from the Minority Report)*. To be perfectly honest, I always respected Pre-Rebecca's right to privacy from me. After all, I was factually speaking, only her high school sweetheart and somewhat limited post-breakup friend. I was so grateful she allowed me to drive her to the house she was going to move into, for the start of her soon-to-be University experience.

After the traumatic dump event, we did chat on the phone a few times, and she was still working at her dad's hardware store, which was only a good driver *(golf club)* from my house, as long as I could clear the Church. There wasn't any guidebook like this to teach us what we should do. It was learning by doing. I was out washing my car, she must have seen me from the road, and stopped by on her way home to say hi, and probably to see how I was doing. This was new territory for us. It was during that chat, that she mentioned having to go to her, soon to be, new University home in London, and do some stuff before her final move for the start of her university life. I took full advantage of the opening and asked if she would like me to drive her there, as friends of course. When she said OK, I knew I had to play it cool, even though inside, I was full of those wonderful butterflies she always gave me.

I picked Rebecca up later that week in my red TR6, and we drove to her 2 storey university house at 1192 Richmond Street in London, Ontario. I even think the last 4 digits of her new phone number was '0443'. When we got there, she was the only student in the two story house, even though she was sharing it with a few other people. Rebecca's spot was in the basement, with one other bedroom down there. I already knew we were staying the night, but I had no idea what I was going to do. I was still trying to be the cool ex-boyfriend and made myself at home on the only couch in the room. I kept myself looking busy as best I could, but most of the time, I would simply watch her do her thing. I knew that she was about to start a new chapter in her life, and while my heart refused to concede what my brain already knew, the heart always seemed to win the battle. It was that damn infection. That evening, we were both sitting on the couch chatting about Rebecca's class schedule, and the amount of walking she would have to do from her place, with the campus so spread out. What she didn't know, and I would never let her see, I was still so lovesick and devastated from the breakup inside. She gave me a look, smiled, and said she was tired. Being the gentleman that I wanted her to think I was, I was first to broach the unspoken issue and asked if she had a spare pillow and blanket for me. I would sleep on the couch. After all, we were officially, no longer girlfriend and boyfriend.

Rebecca returned the smile, went into her bedroom, and returned with a pillow and blanket. She put them on the couch and came over to the end where I was standing. Completely unexpected, she proceeded to give me a hug. At first, it was a simple goodnight-type hug, but it slowly turned into something more. Our arms went from a casual embrace to a stronger and stronger hug. Neither of us wanted to let go. We kept hugging with my nose taking in her scent. She always smelled beautiful, then we pulled away enough, so we could look at each other. This was not some post-breakup hook-up; this was more like some final last rights ritual.

When we went through that rainy afternoon in my driveway and began the testing phase on her theory of love, there was no goodbye hug, kiss on the cheek, or even a simple clutch of hands. I simply needed to get out of her Gremlin. I had stopped crying by that point and went into what I can only describe as some catatonic state. I closed the car door and never felt the rain hitting me. I stood motionless beside the car and looked at her through the rain-soaked side window. She was still crying as she put the car in reverse. She backed out of the driveway and as she drove away, she glanced through her side window in my direction. I stood there and just watched my entire world come crashing down on me. I did not make the first move, Rebecca did. She started to give me a passionate kiss which slowly turned into a very passionate kiss. We slowly changed our position from standing to sitting on my soon-to-be bed. After an inordinate exchange of saliva, I pulled back and said, "Are you sure about this?"

I could see the smile said yes, but the eyes said differently. Up until this moment, I had spent every waking moment, only thinking about myself, and my feelings and how I could win her back. I never gave any thought, to how Rebecca may be feeling. After all, we were inseparable for almost 3 years. I never asked, and we never talked about that moment. I can only speculate, that she was not yet 100% over me, but she knew she needed to do, what she so often said about 'true love';

"If you love someone, set them free. If they come back, it was meant to be; if they don't, then it was not."

I don't know whoever came up with that saying, but I would put them right up there with God and give them a much-deserved beating on behalf of all those people who would fall victim to 'then it was not'. It was never said, but I knew, this would be the last time we would ever be intimate. I slowly slid myself off the couch and knelt in front of her, positioning myself between her legs. Eyes glued on each other, we did not have to say anything, we knew what was going to happen. I reached over and began to unbutton her pants. She began to raise herself just enough to allow me to slowly slide her pants off. She grabbed the sides of my head with her hands, and gently pulled me back up for another passionate kiss. It was probably the greatest kiss, and the worst kiss, of my life. We both knew this was a final act, and we both seemed to accept it for what it would be. Our own special form of closure.

I reached down again, repeated the process, and slowly removed her always sexy white bikini underwear. I knelt there and stared, at what had become my favorite female anatomical part. Her legs worked themselves up my arms to rest on my shoulders which caused her to slide toward me. She gripped my head again with her hands and allowed us one last 'intimate dance'. I wish I could use the term lovemaking, but ours, never involved the girl of my dreams, having to surrender her virginity. Our lovemaking was more about the exchange, of making our partner achieve that incredible feeling, without the need for intercourse. From my perspective, it was and still is, much more intimate than the other way.

After I knew, I had provided my ex-lover, with what I was very skilled at doing, especially after almost 3 years of practice; I was always gentle, took my time, and eased her slowly to that final release. The realization, that I would never share this most intimate exchange ever again, almost brought me to tears, if it wasn't for the valve. Rebecca's valve. We held ourselves in that position for a few minutes, then I stood up and offered my hand to help her stand. I then picked her up in my arms, and in my mind, I carried her over an 'imaginary threshold' into her bedroom. I lowered her down, stood her on the floor, beside the bed, and asked where her pyjamas were.

She already knew what I was about to do, she told me to look in the top drawer, and pointed across the room. I returned with the pyjamas, and like some ritual dance, I proceeded to put them on her. Then I gently removed her top. I stopped for a moment and took a long look at her. Normally, she would put her hands over her chest in a playful innocent way only she could do. This time, she just stood there and allowed me a final last look. I put her pyjama top on and proceeded to do up the buttons. I then reached over to pull the bed covers back. I picked her up one last time and put her on her bed. I gently pulled the covers up and stood there looking at her, trying my best to etch this entire dance into my memory, not knowing how valuable it would be to me in the future. As I stood there, she reached over, and I am pretty sure, was prepared to touch me, you know where, but before she could complete the grab, I quickly intercepted her hand.

I smiled and got down on my extended knees at the side of her bed. I gently ran my hand through her hair and told her, "God you are so beautiful," I then looked into her eyes and we both knew we were going to finish our dance and I said, "you had a long day and I know you're tired."

"I'm not that tired," she said with a very Rebecca-like grin. I looked into her eyes and gave her a big smile. She knew exactly what I was doing and the fact she let me have that always provided me with a glimmer of hope. I got up and walked to the doorway and turned off the light. I wouldn't look back, because I did not want her to see the tears in my eyes. The next day she came out to the couch and woke me with a polite kiss on the cheek. I smiled, got up and folded the blanket, and carried it along with the pillow into her bedroom. When I came out, we discussed the rest of the morning schedule and by late afternoon, we were back on the road heading home. It was a quiet and somewhat lonely drive, but at one point we held hands for what would be the last time as well. We always loved holding hands in the car. I dropped Rebecca off at her house, and with her parents watching out the kitchen window, I got out, opened her car door, and she got out. We exchanged a very innocent quick thank-you hug, and I got in my car and left.

It was a few years since that final parting. I moved to Toronto, after my two-year vacation, where I mastered the art of leather crafting. I was hired by a gentleman, whom I met through a fellow vacationer. I think he liked the idea of having a "Bad Boy" around, and it certainly didn't hurt that I was excellent with computers. My first main job was to switch the company over from a mini-mainframe 'Dec System' to a desktop IBM standalone computer network. The company was a financial lending company, and one of the perks I had, was the use of the company limo now and then. We had continued to keep in touch periodically since the big breakup, including, during those dark days of my vacation. I remember the letters you sent me, sorry Pre-Rebecca, and when they arrived, I was on cloud nine. I would read it over, and over, and over. I still have every one of them in my special picture box.

So, I thought I would see if pre-Rebecca would be interested in meeting for lunch sometime, since she was now living and working in downtown Toronto for a stock brokerage house, after graduating with a business degree. Rebecca's dad was a very successful businessman, and I am sure it was a big influence on her scholastic post-secondary choice. I called her at work with the lunch proposition, with the excuse that I would be downtown myself for a meeting anyway, and it would be nice to say hello and catch up. I arranged to pick her up out front of her office and we would head over to 'The Market Place' restaurant not far from her work. At best, a 5-minute drive. I am sure she was less than impressed when I rolled up in a stretch limo. I still chuckle at her surprise, when my driver Steve, who had to listen to me all the way down from the office, a Coles notes version of my Love for pre-Rebecca, hopped out and said, "Hello Miss Rebecca, Mr. Devon is inside, and my name is Steve."

I swear I could read your mind, sorry her mind, and it was saying. "Why can't he ever do anything normal?" You really don't need any details other than lunch happened, and I felt it was more a sympathy lunch than a "Derek, I missed you so much, let's get married right now," lunch. Ok, maybe somewhere in between. I may have been a hopeless romantic, but I was never stupid. I arranged one more after-work drink at a bar named Sammy's, but as it turned out, she was there with a bunch of co-workers, and we did not get a chance to talk. Not like we used to. Strike two, and she happened to mention she was dating a guy, who, she just had to tell me, she liked. Great, I had officially made it to, 'Friend Derek' status. Seems they were both into cycling. But the pièce de resistance was a phone call Rebecca made to me about a month after the last time we were together, as friends. At first, I was full of the usual butterfly's, my mind was racing immediately to, "She wants me back!." Then reality came crashing down, "Hi Derek it's Rebecca. Do you have a second to chat?

"Absolutely, for you, anytime, anywhere," I enthusiastically replied.

"Our company is representing a client with a new offering, and I wanted to see if you would be interested in buying some stock," came out of the phone earpiece.

Well, she continued to tell me all about the great opportunity. I had stopped listening after the word 'offering'. I had my securities license already and knew instantly, that I was relegated to maybe one notch before a cold call. New agents are taught to call friends and family first with any new stock offer, followed by the old cold call white pages. I despised cold calling. So, the girl of my dreams now saw me as just another potential stock customer. I know I had developed a great valve system over the years but the realization that I was now simply a potential stock chump was devastating. Strike three, you're out!

I was much better equipped now, and there was no major flood or anything, just something I had not experienced before when it came to Rebecca, disappointment. After the disappointment, came the anger, and after the anger, was the hardest thing I have ever had to do. Admit to myself, that I was not the one. I was not her *'It-boy'*, even if she was still my *'It-girl'*. She has chosen a different path and it would never include me. That was the last time I spoke with Rebecca. Part of me wants to think, that she too, picked up from my voice, what had happened because I never had another great stock opportunity pitched to me. It took me a long time to sort through this personal revelation. I spent a lot of time at the gym beating myself up with heavy weights. My body appreciated it, but my heart was finally truly broken. All I could do now is remind myself, that I let her go, she never came back, therefore it was never meant to be.

I know you're wondering why all the filler to the original statement. Truth is, I don't have much intel on pre-Rebecca. I knew she eventually married her cycling boyfriend. Then I heard about her mother's passing. Then about her having children. First was a daughter, and then another four more, although the fourth turned out to be twins for a total of 5 daughters. I suspect with such a large family; Rebecca was a full-time stay-at-home mom. Her husband had a good job and made good money, so they did not need her income. I had always assumed that she would have been a career focused individual striving to be the best she could be. I never would have guessed in a thousand years she would ever chose to be a stay-at-home mom. I always figured her sister Brenda would have taken that route but turns out I got it backwards. Brenda went on to have a very successful career as an educator in the field of Nursing. I know it begs the question, "Why did I not just move on and forget her?"

I wish the answer was that simple, but it was not. I will address that mystery question later, but to finish off this section, Rebecca split with her first husband around 2013 or 2014 if you recall the text message, I showed you earlier. I was shocked to hear the news, especially having had 5 daughters. He was Italian, and unfortunately, I went for the old stereotype and figured he must have strayed from the nest but really have no clue what really happened. That issue, I knew, would always be a point of no return with Rebecca. From there, I will assume she is doing great, and I hope only the best for her as I leave and come to you. Who knows, maybe if Rebecca 1.0 one day becomes a widower, Derek 1.0 and her can hook up in the later years and change each other's diapers until they no longer know who each other are! *(Sorry, I needed to lighten up this section as it still hurts!)*

13 ***T-minus 13 days:*** Charting Day. With just over 2 weeks to go, I needed to do some pre-memorization prep work. I've assembled a ton of data and needed to start the distillation process. First, I need to chart all the important lotto numbers. Then the sports bets, followed by a few critical electrical schematics. Once I get the numbers charts done, I plan to start spending a few hours, beginning the memorization process. I don't want to overload the brain by trying to do everything in the last week. Well, the charting day turned into charting 2-days. On the evening of day 12, I began the first number memorization process. I knew from experience the best method for learning numbers for me. I liked to repeatedly write them down in groups of 3. I seem to be able to regurgitate in sequences of 3 better than 4. Each night, I would set aside time to test my memorization. Unfortunately, I needed to hit 100%. 98% just would not cut it.

14 ***T-minus 12 days:*** With the pace I was working at, combined with the fact I was a 63-year-old retired over-the-hill senior, today I finally broke. Well maybe burnt out was more accurate. It was fortunate we had a sunny and warm day. I have always loved the sun as you know, and I still claim I am half Italian, or maybe I better change it to middle eastern after disclosing Rebecca 1.0's Italian experience *(I know she would beat the crap out of me if she ever knew I said that)*. I still, have not, even to this day, asked for my adoption records. I am aware that they may help me with planning for some future medical catastrophe, but I always convinced myself that, on some level, it was disrespectful to my mom and dad. Maybe Derek 2.0 will have a different perspective *(wink wink)*.

I can never sleep in, but I can move to the couch and veg watching an old movie. My choice that morning was Notting Hill. I have always loved the movie and especially the soundtrack. Now you know why we always seem to have a copy on the PVR. By 11 am, I moved from indoors to the hot tub on the deck. I love my hot tub! After a couple of cycles, a couple snifters of port and a cigar, I retired to my sun chair and began drying off with the good old sun's rays. For some unknown reason, my body always was re-energized after a good sun-soaking. I had a bunch of friends calling wanting to do stuff, but I just wanted a me day. Day 12 was going to be Derek day. Finally, for a treat, I would order some takeout sushi and binge watch an old recording of the series, 'The Time Travellers Wife'. I figured Theo/Henry and I had very similar butts when I was his age *(You had to laugh at that Becca)*. I was in bed by 10:30. Watched my favorite video and was asleep well before 11 pm. Derek Day was now over.

15 ***T-minus 11 days:*** I think this was the first day, I began to question, my mental ability to memorize so much data. I did not want to alter my plan, but I knew, I needed to have a "Plan B" if I hit the wall with the memorizations. Problem was that I could not figure out a "Plan B." So, after wasting about 2 hours, I abandoned the idea and went back to school and studied my brains out. By the end of the day, I was spent. I collapsed into bed at 10 pm and out by 10:02 pm *(I needed the 2 minutes to watch my video, yuk yuk)*.

16 ***T-minus 10 days:*** It was frustrating, that during the night, I realized I needed to brush up on my chemistry. At some point, I would need to make some plastic explosive or more commonly called C4. I wanted to make sure I had the most state-of-the-art formula available on the dark web to memorize. The explosive material in C-4 is cyclotrimethylene-trinitramine (C3H6N6O6), commonly called RDX *(which stands for "royal demolition explosive" or "research development explosive")*. The additive material is made up of polyisobutylene, the binder, and di(2-ethylhexyl) sebacate, the plasticizer *(the element that makes the material malleable Becca)*. It also contains a small amount of motor oil and some 2, 3-dimethyl-2, 3-dinitrobutane (DMDNB), which functions as a chemical marker for security forces. To make C-4 blocks, explosives manufacturers take RDX in powder form and mix it with water to form a slurry. They then add the binder material, dissolve it in a solvent, and mix the materials with an agitator. They remove the solvent through distillation and remove the water through drying and filtering. The result is a relatively stable, solid explosive with a consistency similar to modeling clay.

My problem is that in 2022, I can easily find information on almost anything. But I will need some C-4 before the advent of the world wide web. In the early 1980s, the concept of the internet, tablets, and streaming was still a theory or at best, work taking place in a lab. So now I must figure out, what special tools I will need to achieve my objectives, that won't yet be available to Derek 2.0. Added to that, I will also need a list of key individuals that I will want to track down to either solicit some help or steal their research. Great, another setback!

17 ***T-minus 8 days:*** The official cut-off day to add any more data. Now it was strictly memorization. I never left my apartment for the next 3 days. Lived off boiled hotdogs and a tub of slaw which I think was long expired. I boiled the dogs because we also had a lot of rain, and I just was not in the mood to take the cover off the BBQ. I did manage to get a hot tub session in every day thankfully. Each night I tested my memorization. Some things I was doing great with, and some I was struggling with. All I could do was keep forging ahead. The pressure was building, and I was sure was taking its toll on my boyish good looks *(please smile*). I was feeling a bit guilty chewing through a few of Derek 1.0's remaining years at this pace and intensity.

18 ***T-minus 5 days:*** Today I got a call from a good hockey buddy, who informed me, that one of the guys we played hockey with, died last night in a car accident. He asked me if I would go with him to the house to sit with the family. One of the downsides of always being the captain of your hockey team is that even without the 'C', you still tended to act like you had one. I was always organizing stuff, picking the bar we went to, and now having to go and sit Shiva, although they were not Jewish. I felt obligated, and Derek 1.0 would be pissed if I left him with the fallout from not doing it. The good part was, that it forced me to finally shave and have a nice long shower, wash the hair, clean my nether regions and look civilized again. I went over for a few hours, and there was a steady stream of people including, everyone that played on the team. We may not have been the best hockey team, but our camaraderie was the best. Finally got home at 10 pm and hit the books for 3 hours.

19 ***T-minus 3 days:*** Well, today was the first day that I started to feel like I was going to have a panic attack. It was hitting me full-on that in 3 days I would be gone from this world and re-born in 1973. Not only that, but I still needed to finish all the memorization. I did something I did not want to do but was left with no options. I started to drink energy drinks. I hated energy drinks because they upset my stomach after a couple. Then by the second day, it would be 'all squirting out' you know where from my backside. Let's just say it was learned from doing! With using the energy drinks, I did notice my memorization process was improving and I was able to reproduce without a single error, the entire lotto number table, sports bets, key people list, and all the required chemistry stuff. What I was still struggling with, was the cancer information. I may have tried to bite off far more than I could handle on this topic.

Messenger RNA or more accurately written, mRNA, was all the rage these days and it has proven to be an excellent delivery system. Problem was that some of the science utilized equipment that would not be invented for at least 10 years after I needed it. Figuring out how I might overcome this hurdle had me reading hundreds of technical manuals that were way above my educational level. I was great with machinery and always prided myself on being able to tear an engine down to the block and rebuild it. There was little I could do, but keep reading, and try my best to retain the information. I didn't need to memorize specific data, but scientific approaches and methodologies. While it was a major challenge, I can give myself a bit of a self-pat on the back for a job well done.

20 ***T-minus 1 day:*** Well, I made it through the countdown, and I know I was able to memorize a ton of material. Numbers, dates, people, formulas, equations, locations, and even a few complex theories. I think it was the first time, I 100% believed, I could pull this whole thing off. Now the hardest part was waiting to see, if I was truly a gifted nut job-ready for a padded room for the rest of my life, or if everything that has happened is real.

21 ***T-minus 0 day:*** Even after all the memorization, the one thing I was most proud of, I had the smarts to write down the exact time they told me they would be leaving, 23 days, 8 hours, 13 minutes and 23 seconds. I asked for 22 days so by my calculation, I had roughly between 6 and 10 hours to go. I never did get a chance to figure out the time differential between my calculations and theirs. I spent the next 5 hours testing my memorizations a bit more but wanted an hour to make a few quick calls to hear the voices of family and friends that I may not see again for a very long time, and some I will never re-connect with. Yes, I know Derek 1.0 will continue, but the new Derek 2.0 was leaving.

The other final thing I needed to do, was determine exactly when and where I would do the transference to. I had thought about it and chose to go back to the end of August, just before I would attend Senior Public School as a new grade 7 student. Monday, August 27th, 1973. I knew I would be home since we would start school on Tuesday, September 4th, 1973. This would give me the best of both worlds. I was starting or in puberty and going into a grade that would allow me to prepare for the start of my transformation, from Derek 1.0 to Derek 2.0. I also grew, like 6 inches that summer. I figured I would ease into it, or it may cause some unnecessary questions. I knew I would be in my bed, in my bedroom as requested by my friends. The anticipation was something I never felt before. Imagine, tomorrow morning I would be waking up in my old bed, in my old bedroom, and most importantly, seeing my mom and dad again. Oh ya, also my sister.

I made my calls, and it was not as tough as I thought after convincing myself that for them, they still got to hang with Derek 1.0, and who wouldn't want that *(Trying to distract myself with humor)*. I figured my friends at some point would pop into my head and initiate the information exchange. I was hoping that I would have the chance for a few Q and A's, to fill in some missing information, as well as clear up some of the mysteries that remained. It was a nice wish but if they just wanted to zap me back then that was ok too.

As I waited, the funniest thing happened. With all I was about to go through, my mind turned itself to the question I had been purposely ignoring. When would I try to see Rebecca for the first time? Not face to face, but from a distance. I never did the old, "Let us look at old photos of ourselves with her." I think the oldest picture I recall, was her grade 9 school photo for the yearbook. I would be 12 and she would be 11. I knew where you lived and maybe someday, I could simply ride my bike, past your house, hoping to spot you outside doing something. Well, it appeared my fantasy daydreaming, of when I might first get a look at you was taking over. This eventually gave way to my brain wondering when it would be best to go on a date. I knew I would see you at Gibson's Pond in a few years, but I still had not figured out when would be the best time to make the move from friend to more than a friend. The last timetable was great, but I did not want to go through exactly what I went through the first time. That would defeat the purpose of my re-do.

Thankfully, I didn't have to go any further down that particular train of thought that day, because my friends had arrived.

[End of Pre-Transference Section]

The Transference

22 As I was in the middle of my thoughts about when I should first go on a date with you, I momentarily started recalling my 'original' first formal meet and greet at the old Collins Hotel with Rebecca 1.0. A mutual friend *(Kathy)* came over to the table that Luke and I were sitting at. Every Friday and Saturday, the Collins hosted a DJ dance party in their basement section which if my memory is not too foggy, could handle around 150 people. It was the place to go for older High Schoolers. Back then, you could buy a beer at 16 if you played on the football team and had some facial hair. No one would ask to see your ID. Well, most of us could. The official age was 18 and a lot of the patrons only ordered pop. I vaguely remember when the age was dropped from 19 to 18 in 1971 and all the comments from concerned parents about the impact that would have. Don't forget, I had a big paper route and got to see firsthand daily, the headlines in the Spectator. In 1977, I remember my buddy Ted was pulled over driving home from the Collins one night and officer Keith who was one of two posted police officers in our town, gave Ted a stern lecture and told him to follow his car to Ted's house, where Ted would re-tell the story that he barely could walk into the house he was so drunk.

Well, as Kathy came to the table and pulled up a chair in front of me, we exchanged greetings and entered into some unimportant chit-chat. Kathy lived not that far from my house, and we went to school together from kindergarten through high school. Kathy was a cute brunette who back then looked a lot like a young Valerie Bertinelli, and I had in the past thought about asking her out. I had known her for so many years, you tend to develop a friendship which can distract you from realizing, that she would probably be a great girlfriend. At some point during our informal chat, she decided to tell me about a girl that said she really liked me.

I wish my friends, could unpack that long-ago memory, and replay it for me. I now struggle, with a complete memory of that night. The girl Kathy was talking about was a young Rebecca. Rebecca 1.0. She asked if I would accompany her and go sit at her table and meet my admirer. I said sure. Luke and I exchanged a look that was silently saying, "way to go, man, someone actually likes you." I smiled and got up, grabbed my drink, which I think was a beer, and followed Kathy back to her table. We reached her table, which was roughly 5 tables from where Luke and I had been camped out, trying to look cool. The place was now full and buzzing and if you did not already secure a seat, you would be standing for the night.

There were 3 girls already sitting at Kathy's table. I gather there was some pre-planning on seating, as I found the only chair left after Kathy sat down, was directly across from this really cute girl, with an adorable, dimpled smile. Big, beautiful eyes and a friendly, warm and inviting look, with perfect white teeth. I sat down, put the beer on the table, and pulled the chair in a bit. Kathy then introduced me to the other girls. I knew her friends already, but the cute one in front of me, I don't recall meeting before.

I said, "Hi Rebecca, I'm Derek Devon."

"Hi Derek, I am Rebecca Hamlin, I think you know my brother Todd," she said with a sweet, kind voice.

"So, you're Todd's younger sister," I replied.

"Well one of them. He's a year older than me and I have a younger sister Brenda," she said as she smiled.

After a quick math moment, I deduced that Rebecca was a year younger than me. I do wish that I could remember our chat, but I just don't. I know we went up and had a few fast dances during the night and were doing what all first timers do. Sit at the table with each other for the rest of the night and wait for that first slow song, which would allow us, to hold each other for the first time. The song we chose, was Meatloaf's 'Two out of Three Ain't Bad." I know it was a special moment for me, and we did the traditional dance setup, my arms around her waist and her arms on my shoulder allowing us to dance and look at each other without any other body contact. I had a pretty cool slow dance move, but with this being our first ever slow dance, that move would not be appropriate.

There was certainly a very natural comfort level between Rebecca and me that night. Exercising, the globally recognized male wingman rule, I am pretty sure I completely abandoned Luke for a while, but eventually went and brought him over to join us at Kathy's table. Luke was very popular with everyone, especially the girls and we always joked over the years, that he was our version of the 'All American, Ritchie the C' type. I think Luke liked Kathy and I think there was a bit of attraction for her too. Finally, we were reaching the end of the night. The last call had already been made at 12:45, which meant, we were about to hear the last two songs of the night *(it was a Collins thing I guess)*; 'Ballroom Blitz' by The Sweet, followed by the song I was waiting for, the 7 minute and 54 seconds, 'Stairway to Heaven' by Led Zeppelin. The entire table got up to dance to the Blitz, knowing that when it finished, the single people went back to the tables leaving the dance floor to the lucky couples for the last dance of the night.

As Page's guitar sound started, Rebecca went to put her hands on my shoulder, assuming I would hold her waist as we did for 'Two out of Three Ain't Bad', but I had planned to use 'my move' now. I took Rebecca's right hand and brought it up to my chest and we interlocked our hands, with the back of our hands facing each other's chest. My other arm proceeded to work itself around to her back, allowing me to pull her in towards me and feel the back of her bra through her shirt *('I think there was movement Jerry', not sure if you will get that reference, but I was smiling).*

Her other arm found its way over my right shoulder. I was about 6-8 inches taller than Rebecca, so her arm was fully extended. With being so close to each other now, in order to allow ourselves to sway back and forth to the music, it would require that one of our legs each found its way into the other's private area. As we moved back and forth, we were able to allow ourselves to perform the dance, sometimes called grinding. With the newness of our relationship, the amount of pressure we would allow during the dance was just enough to feel each other's thigh rub that very special area, but not too hard to meet the level of a true grind.

We both allowed ourselves, to give in to that moment in a way that we both knew was the start of something that would turn into a long and special relationship. But the final tell, was when she allowed the back of my hand to come into contact with her slightly protruding chest. I had never had a long-term girlfriend, sure there was always those adolescent necking and feeling up a girl stuff before, but when the back of my hand touched her chest, without any push back, I think she had just infected me. And to think, it all started that night, at the Collins for Derek and Rebecca 1.0.

Infection: Ground Zero Location

The Arrival

23 "Last time we chatted, you couldn't stop thinking about your Rebecca, and as soon as we re-connect after 22 days, you're still thinking about your Rebecca," said the voice of my old, new friend.

"I know, think of it as a disease. That girl infected me that night and I have been a lovesick puppy ever since. I would ask you for a cure, but we all know, that would violate the Prime Directive," I responded with a touch of sarcasm. But what I didn't know at the time, nor did my friends, my infection was not limited to me!

"I am one of the 'life-forces' or 'pod people' you saved 22 days ago. I would like to personally thank you for your sacrifice on behalf of myself, and my two fellow shipmates," said the voice in my head.

"It was my sincere pleasure to be in a position to be able to assist with that emergency, and while I am sure you think the assistance, I provided is appreciated by you and your people, I want you to know, that allowing me a second chance to go back and have a re-do, is of far greater value to me," I replied.

"So, you're saying that our lives are not as valuable as you getting to see your Becca again?" I was challenged *(followed by a large clapping sound).*

"I am very sorry for my choice of words, and of course, there could be no equivalency between saving a life and my desire to have my do-over," I said somewhat apologetically with a big smile added.

"We know what you meant, we just wanted to have some fun with you," my friend rebutted *(More clapping).*

"The exact time I would suggest, will be at 2:00 am the evening of Monday, August 27th, 1973. I will be at my home, in the first bedroom right of my house's front door. I will be asleep in my bed. The bed will be oriented along the wall separating the front hallway and the bedroom. My head will be at the end of the bed closest to the front wall of the house. Is that specific enough for you," I asked?

"You had us at, August 27th," said a different friend this time *(Another round of clapping).*

"Gee, I leave you guys alone for 22 days and you all become a bunch of comedians," I shot back with *(clap, clap, clap again)*. Little did we know that it was evidence of the infection.

"Before you do the final procedure on me, I would like to ask for a short Q&A with you guys again. Is that possible?" I proposed.

"That would be permitted, no time like the present," came a voice.

"Is everyone going to be online with us," I asked?

"No, we have divided ourselves up today to allow us to better complete some last-minute, as you like to say, housekeeping things," was the reply.

"So, who do I have the pleasure of kibitzing with now?" I responded.

It was kind of like some military roll call that happened. One by one a different type of voice introduced themselves, and it was funny, I could uniquely differentiate each voice. They have never interacted with me by giving themselves a name, but I found myself being able to differentiate each voice, just like assigning a name. Knowing we had a small intimate group of 6, rather than their entire accompaniment seemed to put me at ease. I was also getting comfortable with my ability to communicate with them and could even direct a specific voice with a specific question.

I wish I could have recorded our initial exchanges but again, it would take reams and reams of paper and I think I need to stick to what I believe are the relevant topics.

Q: "When the canoe I was in, first encountered your barrier, what was holding the canoe in place?" I asked, now having completed my prior stored unanswered question selection.

A: "The substance you like to call a barrier, is actually, a purely organic substance, with a unique feature which allows us to manipulate its cells at a very microscopic level. This ability, you can think in terms of nanotechnology, now imagine that those little nano guys can disassemble any part of a cell and re-assemble it however it wants, or we program it to," replied Morpheus. In my mind, I assigned a descriptor to each voice to allow me to select the voice more easily with whom I wanted to interact with.

Q: "Can I extrapolate on that explanation and apply it to all of your surroundings, barrier, observation structure, internal cylinder, etc.?", I quickly shot back.

A: "For the most part yes. But we do have certain application requirements for what you would call an inert nonbiological substance. In those unique applications, we use the same nano-tech approach to manipulate atomic configurations. Imagine being able to arrange atoms from a carbon formation to a lead formation. Or even better from your perspective, lead into gold," replied Tank. And yes, I thought it may be a bit funny to use the characters from the Matrix. I always loved that movie, just in case they would pick up on my naming convention.

Q: "How do you control the messaging to the nanotech?" I now asked Trinity. I was trying to include everyone in the discussion, secretly building up my knowledge of my new friends. And the voice with what I perceived had the highest pitch got Trinity.

A/Q: "Why do you want to know," came Cypher's voice. I am not one to judge a book by its cover, but out of all my voices in my mental interactions, Cypher was the only voice that caused my Spidey senses to perk up.

Q/A: Feeling the conversation was getting maybe into a touchy area, I thought it was the right time to shift the tone back to a less tense exchange. I replied to Cypher, "Well it got me thinking that instead of going back and having to go through all the emotional crap I was sure to put myself through, maybe I can simply build my own personal Rebeccabot! Imagine, fully programable, will look identical, and I could switch her from her beautiful 34 A's to a pair of 36 DDs at any time, or even better, I could download the doppelganger Rebecca into Rebeccabot" *(greatly suppressed grin. I know that you are shaking your head, but remember Rebecca, I was doing my best to switch the tone and you know I would never actually do anything like that, snicker, snicker. Besides. If original Rebecca ever heard me say that she would be giving me a beat-down).*

This time, The Oracle spoke to me, "Now Derek, we all know from your past experiences with us that you would never change a thing about Rebecca. She was perfect in your mind, even after the breakup, you never had a single thought or fantasy at any time, involving changing Rebecca, especially in any physical way. So let me see just how well I know you, even with your privacy sign posted."

Oh, oh, time to double-check all the valves and make sure they are closed good and tight. I would never openly admit anytime that I had a very unhealthy obsession when it came to Rebecca. First, I was sure Rebecca had emptied all of her memories of us, either when she fell in love with her first husband or even before that. Rebecca was built with more of a single focus, while I was much more of a multi-focused guy. A true multitasker. I had hoped at one point that the old saying, 'opposites attract' would work for us, but we all know that never happened.

My mind immediately started to work on trying to figure out their end game with this exchange. Our Q&A's were always of a light and friendly manner but this one had taken on a more serious and potentially probative vibe. I already conceded that I was no match for their obvious superiority and what was even more of a concern, I was most likely only exposed to a fraction of a percent, of their total abilities. Why are they wasting their valuable time quizzing an amoeba? They must be getting something out of our exchange, or they would have simply 'beam me up Scotty' to 1973 as promised.

"OK, let's hear your insight into me Oracle," I said.

"The nano-tech would never be used to build you, as you called her, a 'Rebeccabot', but it would be a game-changer in the area of medical science, specifically, curing cancer. You would build a little army of Nanos and program them to find and dispose of every cancer cell in your mother. You would also use the same Nanos to fix your father's issues and finally, you would personally adapt the tech to try and keep yourself as young and as healthy as possible, potentially living three lifetimes," Oracle responded.

"Oracle, you are truly insightful, and you would be correct on your assessment of my use of the nanotech, except for one thing," as I gave an extended pause to the moment. "I would do both!"

"So, you are saying you would make a 'Rebeccabot'?" he asked with a puzzled vibe.

"No, I would give Rebecca her own nano-tech, so she also would be as young and healthy as I would be, so we could enjoy a very long and healthy life together, maybe even 4 lifetimes and cure her mother," I replied with an added smirk.

I quickly asked Oracle before he could reply, "Did you just lose a bet with Cypher?"

The exchange went completely off-line it appeared, for much longer than I hoped, and it immediately got me thinking, 'Did I just screw up my chance at the Transference now?' But fortunately, my starting paranoia ended when I felt all of my friends clapping at my response.

"As your buddy, Luke seemed to often tell you jokingly, "You are something else" *(And another round of clapping).*

I decided that I could open up the possibility through the Q&A of potentially saying something that could destroy my plan, without me ever knowing why. So, with that realization, I elected to return to the task at hand, getting on with my transference.

"I am ready for the Transference anytime you guys are," I said.

"Agreed, we still have a lot of work we need to attend to after your processing as well," said Trinity.

"So, how will this work," I asked?

"To be honest, I have never been involved with a transference like this before. To us it is an utter waste of time and resources," the Oracle chimed in.

"I am starting to feel like I am about to be some experiment," I replied with some trepidation entering my thought tone.

"Don't worry my friend, you are in safe hands today. The procedure for us would be analogous for you to putting a thread through a hula hoop," Tank said.

"Well in anticipation, I made sure to put on an extra absorbent depends," I said jokingly with a bit of nervousness thrown in.

"From your perspective, we would suggest that you get into your favorite chair and watch some TV or YouTube. We will do the rest and you will not feel a thing or be aware of what is happening. Once the transfer is completed, you will most likely remain asleep as your 12-year-old self till morning," Morpheus explained.

"When I wake in 1973, will I also have my 12-year-old self's memories, meaning, will I know what I had done the day before?" I asked.

"As we said, this is new territory for us. I would think based on our scientific studies, once your new memories are integrated, you will be able to access those old memories fairly easily. Remember, we are not adding to your 12-year-old self, we are completely replacing everything. But also remember, you already have those memories stored in your brain, you just have not been able to easily access them through the passage of time. Hopefully, those pathways will begin to open almost immediately," Tank replied.

I must take just a brief pause Rebecca, to let what was about to happen to me, truly sink in. I was about to go back in time, with all my 63 years of memories and experiences retained, and be placed in a 12-year-old adolescent, not yet a teen body. When I first see my parents, I will be mentally old enough to be their parent. Every moment moving forward I will have previously already experienced. At least initially. I know that I will be battling the urge to want to experience everything through the eyes and body of my 12-year-old self.

Think about it! I could tomorrow, remove the engine from my dad's car, tear it down and re-install it. I will be able to play the piano immediately, and not that bad either, guitar, drums, even bagpipes if we owned any. I can cook amazing meals that my parents would only experience at a restaurant. I know how to skydive, fly a plane, shoot a gun, really, well; I know how to write computer programs, and there aren't even computers yet. Imagine having to sit in a grade 7 math class when I could probably teach the class far better than the teacher. I can speak Spanish, almost fluently, French just so-so. Think about it. There will be absolutely nothing that I will encounter, that I have not already encountered before. Don't get me going on my physical abilities. I am a 3rd-degree black belt in Shotokan. I can drop grown men in seconds. I can shoot wings off a fly! *(Well not really, just needed a momentary comic relief thought).*

The list never ends. TV? I have seen all the shows. Movies, seen a ton. Music, I know the songs before they will even be released. I could pick up a guitar and sing future hits, long before they become future hits. I know my single greatest challenge will be to repress those desires and simply be a 12-year-old boy again. Spoiler alert, easier said than done. What I did manage to figure out were ways for me to re-direct much of those desires into other private areas. It wasn't always perfect, but it would give us the fort! *(I am really smiling).*

"Ok gents, time for us to do the deed!" I announced.

"Before we part for good our friend, we wanted to give you a little farewell parting gift. Our way of saying thank you and best of luck with your new future," said all 6 of my friends in unison.

I went over to the lazy boy and assumed my position. Once I pulled the lever and the footrest came out, it almost felt like I was in a space capsule about to be launched. I wanted to start singing 'Major Tom' but just as my mind was searching for the lyrics, my gift arrived. They must have picked up on my memory deficiency with my first meet and greet with the original Rebecca. Suddenly, it was full 4K. My full memory of that night at the Collins, from arrival to departure. I just hope that they send it through as well.

Derek Devon 2.0 – Day 1, Morning to noon.

24 I can still remember that morning like it was yesterday *(I seem to use 'Like it was yesterday' a lot, made you smile).* I don't recall dreaming, and it seems, that 12-year old's don't need to get up in the middle of the night to pee, due to an enlarged prostate *(I smiled).* My first memory was the smell of my room. It immediately triggered a bunch of old pathways to light up. Then my eyes opened, and I was staring at the rock wallpaper on the wall beside the bed. I always loved that rock wallpaper, and it was probably an early indicator of my love for geology. The clarity of the paper and the detail were incredible. No squinting, no slightly out-of-focus issues, just pure 12-year-old perfect vision. I was a side sleeper most of the time. Then the entire realization of the last 23 days set in. I was frozen in bed. What the hell am I going to do. As soon as I open that door, I will probably see my mother, my father, and my sister for the first time in years. I lost my parents in 2003 and 2004 and I have not seen my sister for close to 10 years. I could feel nervous sweat forming on my forehead, and then the worst thing that could happen happened. My mother opened my door and said, "Rise and shine."

I was petrified. And trying my best to use my little person voice I replied, "Ok, I will be up in a second."

"Your dad will be out of the bathroom in 5 minutes if you need to use it," she mentioned.

Great, she even left the door wide open. I could hear the bathroom sink running and my mother's voice at my sister's door, along with a gentle knock. Why did she get a knock, and I got the open door without a knock treatment? Well, I have little choice now, but to get up and go for my first walk-through of the old home. As my feet touched the floor, I sat on the edge of the bed and did a complete scan of my room. My friends said I would recall 12-year-old Derek's current memories but there was nothing. I stood up and went to the window and opened the drapes. As they slowly pulled apart, my old neighborhood opened up before my eyes. Good, neighborhood intact as I remember it. My next move was to quickly make my bed, before I would venture down the hall to the kitchen, for my first 'close encounter of my parent's kind' *(Thought it may get a smile out of you).*

I pulled the bed away from the wall slightly and re-positioned the covers nicely and neatly. Military-grade bed-making as always, with a full sheet tuck. I remember several years ago watching CNN and one of their Military analysts wrote a book, and in it, he talked about the process of

'Making your bed." When fresh recruits enter the service, one of the first lessons they try to instill, is developing a routine. The best way to teach, and start, is by making your bed as soon as you get out of it. Breaking down your day into individual tasks will help you better prepare and complete them. It was kind of the same idea used in the movie 'What about Bob'. Baby steps! I pushed my bed back against the wall and turned to see my dad at the bedroom door standing there looking somewhat bewildered and confused. Oh no I thought, he can tell I am not his Derek but an imposter. As I stared at him, with what must have been a look of fear, or certainly nervousness, he said, "What did you do?"

"Nothing, why would you ask that?" I replied.

"You made your bed; you never make your bed. I have seen you go weeks without making your bed," he said with a suspicious look.

"Well Dad, I have decided to try and act a bit more mature now that I am going into grade 7," was my reason.

"Well good for you. Let's see how long it lasts," dad replied as he pulled away from the doorway and headed down the hall. Mom and dad's bedroom is in the basement, and I am guessing we have not finished the downstairs bathroom yet, thus Dad using the upstairs *(main floor)* bathroom. Having passed, my first direct contact with one of my parents, I was feeling a bit more at ease. Besides, if I ever tried to tell them the truth, I am sure it would result in some form of electroshock treatment.

Ok, what next, I thought? I didn't need to use the bathroom yet, so I thought I would wander down the hall to the kitchen and try my first face-to-face with mom. As I entered the kitchen, mom was at the stove making what appeared to be soft-boiled eggs. Dad liked his soft-boiled egg and a cup of instant coffee before heading to work. That would make the time about 7:10 am. I looked up at the kitchen clock and bingo 7:12 am. Dad would be up in 5 minutes to quickly eat his egg and then head off to work.

"Good morning mom how are you this morning," I asked?

"Oh, what did you do? First, your dad laughed and then said you made your bed this morning, and now you are asking me how I am?" mom challenged me.

"Well as I told dad, I am going to try and act a bit more mature now that I am going to be in Senior public," I replied.

"Well, let's see how long that will last. Can I get you a bowl of Alphabets for breakfast or would you prefer a slice of toast with peanut butter?" came mom's query.

Mom was in her usual house coat and slippers. No hair net, so she has not been to the hairdressers lately. Whenever mom goes to the hairdressers, she wears a hair net for a week. Mom's routine was to get up at 6:50 am with dad. Mom would come up to the kitchen and start making dad's breakfast and at some point, make a trip down the hall to wake me and my sister. I guess I will see my sister Ann shortly. After surveying the kitchen, I said to mom, "Don't worry about my breakfast today, I will get it myself," I said.

"Well please try to keep the mess to a minimum," mom replied with her back to me.

"I knew dad would be up in 3 minutes, so I decided to get myself a glass of OJ and walked to the fridge to look. No OJ, just a jug of milk. Maybe I will get a cup of coffee instead. I asked mom if there was any hot water left in the kettle.

"Yes, why do you need it? Are you making Quaker Oats?" she asked.

"No, I thought I would have a cup of coffee with dad," I replied.

She turned and gave me her displease glare and said, "Little boys don't drink coffee, it will stunt your growth," with a bit of a snicker.

"But I am going into grade 7," I smiled and replied to her. "Well, a glass of milk it is I guess."

I went to the cupboard and grabbed a glass. I was right beside my mom and wanted so badly to just give her the biggest hug ever, but I knew that such an act would force another questioning of who I was. I went to the fridge and got the milk out and poured myself a glass. I put the milk back in the fridge and went to sit at the table beside where dad sat. Right on cue, I heard dad coming up the steps and he took his seat. He was wearing the usual dress shirt, tie, and slacks with his grey blazer most likely hanging in the front hall closet. Dad grabbed his coffee, took a sip to see how hot it was, and then went back for a big gulp, which meant it was not that hot. I sat and watched intently.

The last time I saw my dad, was at the hospital, laying on the operating table absent of all life. Just a pale white expressionless face. My Sister and I were both at the hospital after receiving a call that dad had suffered a heart attack, and they were going to have to operate. We drove immediately to the hospital, and when we got there, he was already under the knife. Dad had been going through the 3 stages of diabetes. First, you lose your kidneys, then various extremities, and finally your life. It had been so long since I watched his routine, that I sat and just watched. I am sure he picked up on that and asked, “What’s up with you this morning. First you make your bed, then you sit there and stare at me, and zero complaints.”

I had already processed his passing in my mind and justified it as ending what was a very unpleasant life. Losing mom was devastating for him and I think he was just being dad, and in his way, being a stubborn Englishman to the last breath.

The surgeon came out of the operating room and came over to where my sister and I were sitting. I stood up, and my sister remained seated. The surgeon told us, “Your father suffered a very severe heart attack, and is currently on life support. At this stage, the only option we have would be to open up his chest and have direct access to his heart. Or, if you prefer, we can leave him as he is, disconnect the life support, and see if his heart will support him.”

In simple terms, the doctor was saying; ‘Pull the plug or Hail Mary?’ I knew dad’s quality of life sucked, and I was so happy, that I was able to take him out of the hospital just last week for a trip to Port Dover. He was wheelchair-bound and just had a section of his leg amputated about 3 weeks ago. Dad had been in the hospital for about a month. It was part of his final life’s schedule. 3-4 months in, 2 at home. I picked him up in the morning and put him in his green Coupe Deville Caddy. He was so proud of his Caddy. I drove him out to Port Dover, and we planned to enjoy a nice perch lunch on the beach; Well, looking out the restaurant window at the lake would be more accurate. When the waitress came over and asked if we wanted to order any drinks, I said I would like a coffee, and then dad gave me a bit of a shock, in a funny way, and proceeded to order a glass of sherry. I gave a bit of a chuckle and said to him, “You better not go and get drunk, or they will ban me from taking you out again.”

In all my years, I never witnessed my dad drunk. I saw him enjoy a few drinks, but never drunk. Even when I was playing drums in his band, he always had a glass of some liquor drink between sets, but never drank like the other guys in the band. I was underage and was relegated to the managers' office between sets with a pop. Dad always had an affinity for the water. I think it was where I got it from. I had bought him a 26-foot sailboat as a retirement gift, and he had a few great years sailing his boat at the cottage. We sat there and chatted about stuff. Our food came, and we both loved every bite. After the fish came the dessert. I passed, but dad got a rice pudding. I hated rice pudding. Must have been an English thing. Dad grew up through his forming years, in England, just before World War II, and eventually moved to Canada just after the war ended when he was 15.

He was a gifted sax player and over the next few years was the major breadwinner for his family, while they lived in Simcoe Ontario, playing sax in a 16-piece band. He was the first chair, or I prefer to call him, lead sax guy.

After the rice pudding was consumed, I said to my dad, "Was everything to your liking or would you like another glass of sherry?" Dad looked at me and I knew by the look on his face that he was fighting back tears. I never meant to cause him any emotional stress, and being a proud Englishman, making them cry would be sacrosanct. I wish I could have given him my Rebecca valve, but he chose to turn and look out the window for a while to collect himself. I turned to look out as well to give him his dignity of overcoming the urge to cry. I cheated a bit and could see from my periphery that he had taken a Kleenex out of his pocket and dabbed his eyes. When dad felt most of the evidence was gone, he said to me while still looking out the window, "I miss your mother. I wish she could have been here with us. Thank you for taking the day to bring me out here Derek," he added.

Damn, now it was my turn to deal with the urge to cry. Thankfully, I had my infallible Rebecca valve, and I made sure it was good and shut. I am not saying the eyes didn't well up a bit, but my composure was a bit stoic and measured. "You're welcome dad. I know firsthand what they feed you at the hospital. Nothing like Lake Erie perch to wash away hospital food taste," was the best I could get out under the circumstances.

We drove back, and you would think that it would be a bit of a bummer, knowing you're going back to the hospital, but dad had a positive outlook and was reminiscing about fishing at the cottage. This summer, the cottage was severely neglected because of dad's health issues, and my need to be his mule at the hospital. I dropped him off, and when we parted, he was already telling the nurses all about his day at the lake with his son. I would add his favorite son, but as you know I was his only son *(Needed to lighten the mood).*

So, my sister and I needed to make a joint decision and I could tell she was very upset and would not be helpful with debating what was best, so I took lead and crafted a self-serving leading question. "My dad has fought the good fight this far doc, I think he would want you to do everything you can. Would you agree with that assessment Ann," I asked?

I knew my sister would go along with anything I said under the circumstance, and with a short nod, the surgeon who was also my dad's cardiologist turned and returned to the operating room. It was at best another 30 minutes, and he re-appeared with the look that told you everything you needed. As doctors do so well, he proceeded to give us the bad news.

"Well, we opened him up and tried everything, but the damage was just too severe to his heart muscle. Would you like to take a minute and go and see him," he asked?

"My valve was holding but my sister did not have one and she was very upset. Giving comfort to my sister was not something I ever had to do before. I looked at Ann and then I gave a nod to the doctor. Ann got up still crying and we walked together into the operating room. There was my father, my hero, dead. Lying there with a sheet pulled up covering his chest area but his head was on full display. We walked over to the table and just stood there for a moment. We had already gone through a rehearsal with my mother about 9 months ago, so it was not completely foreign to us. I grabbed my dad's lifeless hand and squeezed it and said, "You're with mom now dad." It was not my intention of making the matter even harder for my sister, but my remarks caused her to go from a gentle whimper to full-on convulsions. I placed my hand on her shoulder and held it there for a moment. The convulsive whimpers had ended, and we walked out of the room. I stopped where his doctor was waiting for us and told him thank you. That was the last time I would see my dad's face until today.

"Just trying to figure out my schedule for the day I guess," was my response.

"Well, if you're feeling energetic, you can pick up the backyard," as he smiled at mom.

That's right. We have a dog. Where would Tiny be? There's food on the table. I am betting, dad already put her out in the backyard when he got up. Great, poop duty. Starting to feel like home again. They know I hate picking up the dog poop. Our family always fed our dog back then, canned dog food. Canned dog food equates to wet poops. Must add to my new list of things to change and get Tiny on good dry dog food. I am looking forward to seeing my old pal. We lose Tiny in another couple of years, I think.

"Time to go" he said. Dad gave me a little pat on the shoulder, leaned over and gave my mom a kiss on the lips, and went to the front hall closet where he grabbed his grey blazer.

"Is dad driving with Uncle Bill to work today," I asked my mom?

Mom was sitting at the table spreading marmalade on a piece of toast with her cup of instant coffee beside her plate. My mom was not too tall. I was now taller than her after my 5-6 inch spurt this summer. I remember just 3 weeks ago having to get a new pair of shoes. Dad refused to get me any shorts since we could cut the jeans to convert them from the flood look to the jean short look. The real challenge was to make sure they were not too short, or your friends would call you 'a fruit', and not too long or your friends would call you 'Poindexter'.

"When do you want to go to the store for your school supplies? and yes, your dad is driving Uncle Bill today," my mom asked.

"Whatever works best for you mom," I replied. And then the stare. I am sure the way I was talking, not the voice, but my vocabulary and diction were different. It was less a 12-year-old, and more like an adult, I was sure. I can't wait to see my sisters' reactions. Uncle Bill was not my uncle, just a friend, and co-worker of my dad. They both worked at Westinghouse and carpooled. Mr. Charles across the street use to carpool with them but he has been off work recovering from some operation of some kind. I used to run over to Mr. Charles's driveway when Dad dropped him off after work, and dad would let me sit on his lap and drive the car from Mr. Charles's drive to ours. It was only 2 doors down, but it was a regular routine.

"Mom, I can't find my other pants that you were going to fix the loose stitch," my sister yelled down the hall.

"Look in the spare room on the bed," mom replied.

"Any luck?" mom yelled.

"Yes, but the stitch still looks like it's going to come undone," came the voice that I was starting to remember.

My sister and I have not had a close relationship for a few years. I think we were regular brother and sister types until she reached 13. She was 2 years older than me and now nothing I do is right. She has become the master complainer. I would characterize it as plain miserable. And I was about to get reacquainted with it. Hopefully, she will just ignore me as usual, and all will be good. "Is Ann coming shopping with us mom?" I asked.

"I Don't know, I will ask her when she gets to the kitchen," mom replied while sipping her coffee.

"Is Ann, excited about starting high school," I asked?

"I think she is. All the kids that used to go to the catholic school will now be going to the high school, so Ann can walk to school with Trish and Penny," mom explained. Trish and Penny were Ann's closest friends and lived a couple of houses away.

"Are there any other big family plans this week that I have forgotten about?" I asked.

"No, just your Grampa and Ian are driving down on Saturday to show your dad his new car," mom said.

"Red Cadillac, 1965 I think," I commented to mom.

"How do you know what type of car he has? He hasn't even told your dad yet?" mom questioned me.

Well, my first mistake, and I knew better. I have to ask more questions and say far less. "I think Gramps had mentioned last time I saw him he was thinking about a car like that. I was just guessing," I countered.

"Well make sure you are around the house when they get here. Ian always likes seeing you," mom reminded me.

"Absolutely!" I said.

"Absolutely, what kind of words are you using now?" mom asked with a puzzled look.

"I heard it a few nights ago on a TV show and thought it was funny," I replied. I never heard squat, but a great deflection took the focus off me. I will have to use that more often. The excuse, not the reply!

Well, you know who finally made her way into the kitchen, and as soon as she looked my way, she gave me the old scrunched-up facial expression that said, 'what are you looking at loser'. I decided there was no time like the present to begin my resolution to build a new and hopefully loving relationship with my sister. I would have flashed her some counter facial scrunch for sure, but today I started the new me and said, "mom said you might come to the store later to get some school supplies. Would you be able to help me pick out stuff for my grade 7 needs, I would appreciate your expertise?"

Both my sister and my mom stopped immediately and stared at me. My mom probably from my word choice and Ann from the 'who is this person' type look. I picked up my glass of milk and took a drink hoping to force a change from the bewildered stare. My mom was first to act and said, "I am sure Derek that your sister would love to help you, wouldn't you Ann."

It was, quite comical, looking at her facial expression because she had no idea how to respond. As most people put in the same position would do, she turned to open the cupboard and mumble, "Maybe." I know her brain was processing what just happened, and I am sure I must have had a big smile on my face.

So, I have somewhat successfully made it through the family encounters, one left to do. I got up and went to the back door and took a look for Tiny. There was Tiny lying on the patio stones doing what Tiny did best. Very little. I can't blame her. We were never the dog-walking type of pet owner. Walking a dog back then was not very common. I don't even think we had invented the poop bags. Note to self, invent the poop bag. The responsibility of the poop pick-up rested on the poor property owner the dog decided on leaving his mark. Most people walked their dogs along the sidewalk that paralleled the road hoping the deposit would be made on the city ditch side and not the property owners' lawn.

As I approached Tiny, a very strange thing occurred, with her head still lying on the patio stone, her eye caught my eye and she immediately jumped up, or more accurately, lumbered up and proceeded to give me a growl. I stood still and smiled and instinctively held out my hand in a non-confrontational manner. Tiny slowly approached me and gave my hand a sniff. She paused for a moment and then I could see her tail start to come to life. It didn't take long but the hugs and patting followed. I am convinced that Tiny somehow knew that I was not her buddy from yesterday but was somehow different. I raise this issue because it happened with a number of dogs and cats in the neighborhood. It made my first, 'new' paper delivery, and collection day, very interesting.

With my meet-and-greets all completed, I needed to do two things. First, try and figure out what I was supposed to do, as my memories were still Derek 1.0's, and my 12-year-old self memories, from yesterday, have not surfaced. Second, I need to block time to write down my memorizations before I start forgetting stuff. I went back in the house, and it appeared mom was now down the hall re-inspecting my sister's claim of a faulty sewing job. I decided to throw myself together a quick breakfast, as I was starting to feel a bit famished. After all, I did just travel 51 years *(I just giggled again, Rebecca).*

So, let's see what was in the fridge for my first breakfast in Oz. I went through the fridge and found enough stuff to throw together a quick western-cheese hybrid omelet, although the ham would have to be baloney. I diced up some onion and baloney and sliced up some cheese. I went to the stove and grabbed the frying pan from the drawer under the sink. I would need a lid as well and found one that would work. I grabbed some butter and was ready to make my breakfast. It was mostly mechanical, but I was doing my usual clean-up as I went. It took the usual 10 minutes, but my meal was ready, and I only had one pan to wash. I sat at the table, then got up and went back to grab a top-up to my glass of milk. It was about that moment that my mother reappeared in the kitchen and looked at my plate. As I returned to my seat with my glass of milk, my mother sat down at her seat, and I could tell was in a bit of a shock-like state. She was staring at my plate while trying to figure out how to put her cup of coffee up to her lips.

I could tell I once again was way out of her comfort zone with how she remembered me yesterday, so I did what I would be doing often, I told mom, "I watched 'The Galloping Gourmet' make this on last weeks show and wanted to try it. Don't worry, I have cleaned up the mess and will do the frying pan when I am done." Mom sat there, and kind of had that look on her face that said, 'Who is this stranger'?

I finished my breakfast and put my plate and glass in the dishwasher, washed the pan, and put it away. I know mom was trying very hard to pretend not to watch me so intently, but I was well aware and thought I would have a bit of fun with the moment and turned and walked to the table and asked if she was done with her plate. It was probably more instinct than anything, but I could hear her voice say, "ah, ok,," followed by a respectful amount of delay until she also added, "Thank you." I took her plate and put it into the dishwasher and left her with the remaining *(cold by now)* instant coffee. I would have loved the opportunity to be a fly on the wall and watch her process everything. All I knew was, that I had a grin ear to ear.

I went back to my room and needed some time to re-orient myself with where everything was. I also wanted to see if I could find something to write in to transfer my memorization onto. My folks had bought me a complete bedroom suite about 5 years ago that includes a bunk bed, desk, and dresser with mirror. I was getting a bit old for bunks and dad and me, more dad, converted the bunk bed into a single with the help of a hand saw. I also knew I had a bunch of boxes stuffed under the bed as well as in my closet. I left my door slightly ajar and began conducting my inventory. The top desk drawer had all my important stuff like my paper route customer billing cards, coin change holder, cash box, bank book, and most importantly, a brochure I grabbed last winter when our family took a vacation to Myrtle Beach. What only my closest friends knew, if you opened the brochure, there was a really good-looking girl in a bikini standing and smiling at me. She was a brunette and what I realized for the very first time, looked a lot like you Becca.

Each week when I picked up their payment for the week's paper delivery, I would use a handheld hole punch to mark the card. Most of my customers usually gave me a dollar tip except for old Mr. Findley. He only would tip me with 25 cents, or in the summer, a box of something from his garden. Great guy but wicked body odor. I knew that my 42 papers would not be enough and would have to try and get someone else's route to add to mine. I needed to greatly increase my cash flow until I started work at the Racetrack if I was going to be able to start executing my plan.

I opened the cash box and counted about thirty-six dollars mostly in ones and twos. I checked my bank account balance, and I had a personal net worth of 466 dollars. I think I was saving up for a new bike. I did the same with each drawer and by the time I was done, I am pretty sure the old pathways had started to come back to life. The next step is bathroom time. I walked across the hall to the bathroom, and just before I went in, I gave my sister's door that was closed a knock and said, "Do you need to use the bathroom before I go in?"

We all knew what I was saying. She replied with a less than usual angry bark, "No." So, in I went. Closed and locked the door and proceeded to see if my butt would remember the old toilet seat. Our toilet was the same for my entire life through to the Mid '90s when I would remove it, when I renovated the bathroom into a giant shower, with a new lower profile toilet. My mom suffered a stroke when I was 4 and the resulting post-stroke impact was severe osteoarthritis, resulting in her becoming wheelchair-bound in 1985. Well, let us hope my efforts will make that either never happen or delayed for many years.

The seat appeared the same, although truth be told, they all feel the same. I did my business, and everything worked as I remembered. I did, however, take extra care, to do an excellent job with the wiping, hoping to end the former skid mark era *(I chuckled)*. Finally, it was time to begin my new habit, in honor of my girl, and brush my teeth. Now you know why I had such great teeth. After my final spit, I decided to do a quick personal check on where I was, with the whole puberty thing. I pulled my pyjamas down along with my 'Tighty-Whities', junior addition, and inspected the old package. Boy is it small *(I laughed again)*. In hindsight, I should have asked my friends if they could have added an inch or two after the jump. I know you always said it was perfect, but based on my 63 years of personal experimentation, for purely scientific purposes, another couple inches would not be a bad thing. After-all. I was going for above-average this go around. Yes, some pubic hair was starting, and I don't think I have had the official wet dream experience yet. But I will know for sure when I get those damn new-old memories available. I finished up in the bathroom and returned to my room.

In my search, I was fortunate to locate a duo-tang folder and some blank-lined paper. I put around ten pages into the duo-tang and found my favorite H2 pencil pack complete with manual sharpener. I grabbed my bike backpack and put the duo-tang and pen in the large compartment. I decided I wanted to do the memory dump in private, and around here is never private. I put on a pair of shorts and t-shirt, and socks and found my runners under the bed. I went looking for mom, to tell her I was going to go for a bike ride and asked when she wanted me home.

She said, "lunch of course. Where are you going too," she added?

"Spring Valley. I think some of the guys are meeting there for a game of ball (Baseball) ," I replied, knowing it was a lie.

"Ok, don't go and ruin your clothes again, your dad is done with the pre-school shopping spree. Can you let the dog in please before you go, and don't forget you promised your dad you would clean up the backyard," she added.

"I will, I will, and I will," I shot back. Let her figure out that combo.

I went out the front door and stood on the old porch and just took a minute to survey the view. Church in front, Water-tower behind, the street in front and Livestock Auction still there and stinking. I knew already the wind was from the east. I also knew that one day the Livestock Auction would be townhouses and the water tower would be replaced with housing. Maybe I would even be the one to do it. But first, time to get my bike and get my butt to Spring Valley. I opened the garage and there was my old bike. The Wedge! A cool three-speed with a shifter on the crossbar and the old banana seat. I won the bike a year ago selling new Spectator subscriptions. I was fortunate that my hockey coach had mentioned that he was finishing off the building of a multi-story apartment complex on the mountain. As I said, I was a quick thinker and was just smart enough to negotiate a deal that would allow me to exclusively canvas the building for new Spectator customers. The top personal subscription person would win a new bike. Typically, the winners in the past hit the 30-40 range. I was able to set a 'new record' of seventy-six new subscriptions out of the 98-unit building.

As much as I loved the bike, I knew I needed to move up to a 10-speed asap. At least until I reach fifteen when like before, I will get my motorcycle license. I grabbed the bike and walked it out, then closed the garage door. I suddenly realized I had promised mom to let Tiny in, so I ran around the back and let my buddy in the house to continue what she always did, nothing. I went back around to the drive and grabbed my bike.

I sat my ass on the seat and off I went. The bike was ok but to be honest, it was not much for speed. Poor leg to peddle angle, and the gearing was Micky-mouse. It would have to do for a while, and off I rode. My route was streamlined through the requisite bike shortcut paths and I knew the route from Spring Valley rink at the top down to the ballpark below. I gave myself a bit of a test to see how fast I could get there. I estimate it took me 12 minutes door to diamond.

The baseball diamond was not my actual goal. I had another location in the Spring Valley Park, that was kind of an out-of-the-way spot that few people knew was there. I discovered it a year ago while hiking through the park with a friend and his family. I was following this cool ground formation thinking it would make a great toboggan shoot in the winter. As I reached the top of the hill, I discovered down the back side an old gravel pit. I mean a small gravel pit. But cut into the one side was a cave. Not huge, maybe 10 feet wide by 6 feet high and max 10 feet deep. It was probably bigger years ago, but erosion was slowly shrinking it. This would be the one place I doubt anyone would visit today, allowing me full concentration for the memory dump.

I had a watch with a broken wristband that I had also thrown in my pack. I pulled everything out and started writing down everything I had memorized. Once it started to flow, it just kept coming and coming. Other than a brief distraction of a hawk checking me out, I wrote non-stop for 2 hours. I took a 5-minute break to give my hand a rest and check the time. From my location, I estimated it would take me 30-40 minutes to get home knowing I had the Spring Valley hill to ride up. I know they called them 3-speeds, but the first gear was more like eighth gear on a real 10-speed. I gave myself another 30 minutes and then home I would ride for lunch. Didn't want to piss my mom off the first day.

I realized on my ride home, that I wanted to start immediately with a physical training program. Both to help with hockey but also with my new 2.0 self. Derek 1.0 was no slouch, but Derek 2.0 would test his limits. I arrived home on schedule, put my bike in the garage, and went inside. I saw Mr. Kearns across the street cutting the church grass. I sent him a wave and he sent one back. I walked in and announced my arrival. "Hi, I'm home for lunch."

Derek Devon 2.0 – Day 1 Noon on.

25 "It will be a few minutes; I am making you some macaroni and cheese. What do you want to drink?" came a voice from the kitchen.

"Is Ann eating with us?" I asked.

"No, she is over at Trish's having lunch," was the answer.

"Ok, just going to hit the bathroom and clean up for lunch," I said passing the entrance to the kitchen. I could smell the cheese already, and I knew making Mac and cheese was as much for my mom's benefit as for me. I knew it would take some work, to start to convert our family diet, from high carb to outright healthy. If anyone could whip this family into shape it would be Derek 2.0 *(That last part was some self-deprecating humor)*. I popped in the bathroom and turned on the shower, stripped out of my soaking wet clothes, and jumped in for a quick and dirty washdown. I figured 3 minutes tops. Out I jumped and oh, oh. No towel. Great, now I would have to streak to the closet. Was not all that bad, the closet was right beside the bathroom.

"Did I hear the shower going?" mom yelled.

"Yes mom, I was sweaty from the ride home," I responded.

"I don't think there are any clean towels in the bathroom. Get one from the closet.

"Thanks, mom, great suggestion," I yelled.

With the towel wrapped, I picked up my wet clothing and took it into my bedroom. Hmm, no hamper I have never had a hamper. My hamper had been the floor, till mom picked everything up. Note to self, buy a hamper. They can't cost that much. I found some fresh clothes and dressed for lunch. I went back to the bathroom to give my hair a quick brushing when I stopped to look at my wonderful full and thick head of hair. The last time I brushed it, the brush would have passed through probably 1/3 of the volume and it was all silver-grey now, but still a full head of hair, unlike Rebecca's bald first husband. I gave myself a couple quick 'Joey's', 'How you doing' nods and with a single chuckle-like grunt as I headed to the kitchen.

I went over to the stove where mom was performing her magic by adding extra cheese. She always shredded it from dad's old fort cheese stash. "Smells great mom," as I elected to give her a small kiss on the cheek.

"I don't know Derek what has gotten into you today but you're starting to scare me," she said as she pulled the pot off the burner.

"Oh mom, don't you deserve a little 'Eddie Haskelling' every now and then," I said with a joking tone.

"How was the ball game," she asked changing the topic.

"Well, a bit of a disappointment, only two other guys showed up, so we ended up going for a short hike in the park," I told her.

"I hope you didn't put any wet clothes on your floor. You know how quick it marks your dad's floor," she said as a warning.

"No, I have them on my desk chair and was wondering maybe I should buy a hamper for my clothes now that I will be in senior public?" I asked.

"If I had known going into Senior Public would change you like this, we would have had you skip some grades long ago," mom said with her grin.

My mom was high school educated and went from High School to working at Westinghouse as a secretary. She used to be able to type like eighty words a minute or something considered fast. After her stroke, it took her a few years to re-learn to type and I would guess her word output now was in the high twenties. Mom never let her stroke make her bitter or use it as an excuse. Her view was, 'it was what it is, live with it' attitude.

But what most people didn't realize, was my mom was very witty in her own way. I am sure I will notice that side of her a lot more.

Mom put a bowl in front of me and again asked what I wanted to drink. Not to miss out on our earlier banter, I said, "Coffee with just milk please," with a grin added.

"Ok, milk it is. Do you want the quick as well," she followed up with?

"I think I will drink my milk in pure form for lunch," I said.

"You are acting so weird today," she said giving me a bit of a look.

I wanted to continue the banter and maybe even segway into me telling her how much I loved her, but that type of talk in our house would certainly get me a one-way ticket to the sanatorium. We were English for God's sake! Shake hands, pat on the back, and the odd, 'way to go' were our preferred responses. I grabbed the spoon and went in for the kill. I was certainly hungry, and it did not take me long to reach the bottom of the bowl. Mom on the other hand was always a slow eater. Last to the table and last to leave the table.

"That was delicious. Great idea to spike it with dads' cheese," I said. Mom had her mouth full and the best I would get was a part smile. Normally, I would get up and leave after I finished, but this was going to be the start of having real family dinners. Dinners where we all sit around and talk about what happened that day and any other topics we want to add to the mix. I remember my very first dinner invite at the Hamlin's. It was a Sunday dinner, and I think we had a roast. I was of course on full display and only knew Becca and her late brother Todd. I had met Mr. and Mrs. Hamlin at my grade 8 graduation, but other than a couple of meets and greets at the front door when I picked Rebecca up to go out on a date, that was about it.

I was sure that there would be some probing questions tonight, after all, I was their eldest daughter's first-ever, 'going steady' classified boyfriend. Although, that big event would happen on April 14th, and this was March. But, what was a first for me was sitting at a table having dinner for close to 2 hours. I loved that. We talked about all sorts of things and I did my best at maintaining a reasonable Eddie Haskell level for the entire dinner. They sat me beside Mike, Rebecca's oldest brother, and Rebecca directly across from me and her younger sister Brenda beside her. I am sure that her folks caught us a dozen times ogling each other. I think I was a pretty safe bet for them since they watched me get 2 awards at my grade 8 graduation. I also appreciated that they brought that meeting up and were not uncomfortable mentioning Todd. Well as dinners go it was right at the top for me.

I quietly sat watching my mom eat her lunch and did my best to look busy sipping my milk and every now and then attempting to scrape one last itsy-bitsy tiny spot of cheese from the bottom of the bowl. After about 5 minutes, I could sense that mom was a little uncomfortable with me sitting and watching her for so long. This was a first for her, I am sure. But to try and break up that uncomfortable vibe, I decided to start to tell mom about how excited I was about getting back to school. I started to reminisce about some of the people I had not seen since the end of June, and my plans to play a bunch of school sports. I got talking about adding a pre-hockey session workout regime into my schedule and I think it was about that point that mom turned me off and finished her mac with a few head bobs thrown in for my benefit.

"What time are we going to the store?". I asked.

"No later than 2:30, your dad gets home at 4:30 and I need to have the dinner ready by then. It's a school night. We are having lamb chops tonight," mom said.

"Can't wait. I will be in my room for a bit, but will be ready to go at 2:25," I told her definitively.

"Ok, maybe do yourself up a list of what you think you may need," mom suggested.

Off to my room, I went. The real reason I needed to go to my room was to continue my entry into my Duo-tang. I thought I was about a quarter done and wanted to get it finished asap. I was confident that, if required, I would pull an all-nighter after I went to bed. The time went quickly and I had already gotten all the number sequences out and was now working on the formulas. The cancer stuff was going to be the most difficult since it was all theories and processes. I kept an eye on the time, and at 2:15, I put my Duo-tang away in one of my secret spots, the cold air exchange duct on the floor.

When I got to the kitchen, no one was there so I took the opportunity to wander into the living room. Funny, the first time I have been in there since my return. I saw dad's piano against the wall and couldn't resist sitting down and twinkling the old ivories for a second. I forgot that I had taken a few lessons a couple of years ago and just never got into playing the piano. Dad never pushed it on me, and I believe next year I ask for a set of drums. I sat down and played a few cords to make sure the piano was in tune. I knew it would be perfect. Dad has perfect pitch. As I played a few more cords, I don't know what inspired me, but I felt like playing a song from the musical Phantom of the Paradise called Faust. I always loved the song and as schlocky as the movie was, or will be, I liked it. And what was even funnier, it doesn't get released till next year.

As I started to play the song and was coming to the start of the vocals, it suddenly dawned on me, my voice was more soprano now that I was in my pre-puberty voice-changing phase. Well as all good musicians do, I quickly adjusted the key to better fit my vocal range. I figure I would be sounding more like Michael Jackson and less like Winslow Leech. I started to sing;

I was not myself last night couldn't set things
right with apologies or flowers
Out of place as a cryin' clown who could only
frown and the play went on for hours……..

As I ended the first chorus of the song, I realized my mom and sister were standing at the living room entrance looking at me with a stunned expression. I think I looked as surprised as they did but for different reasons. I figured I better try some damage control and said, "What do you think of the song I am writing," I asked?

"You never wrote that song, you probably don't even know what half the words mean," the old party pooper replied.

I gather mom was more stunned at my piano playing and never listened to the lyrics. I didn't have a plan to diffuse the moment, so I got up, smiled, and said, "The store awaits."

As I squeezed past them, I knew they were still somewhat dumbfounded by what they just witnessed and more importantly heard. I am sure for my sister; it was going to manifest itself into another thing she will be jealous of. My hockey has been for some time, a major source, of shaping her attitude. Mom and dad loved coming to all my hockey games. I know they were proud of their son, especially at the level I was playing. Come the fall I will be back playing on two different house league teams as well as 2 select traveling teams in two different leagues. So far, we have been lucky that our game schedules never conflicted, and each of my coaches was ok if I had to miss a practice to play for my other team, in a game that is. And Dad and mom would always get me to my practices, even the 6 am ones.

I proceeded to the driveway and waited for mom to get to the car, and I asked my sister what seat she wanted.

“What do you think loser,” was her choice.

I knew that relegated me to the back seat. So, I climbed in, and mom and Ann got in the front. We had two cars, both station wagons. Dad needed the station wagon to haul his Hammond organ around to his gigs. Add the old Leslie to the mix and the back was completely full. As I got older, it used to be one of my workouts each Friday. Load the organ from the living room into the Wagon. We called the old blue Pontiac ‘Old Betsey’. And Old Betsey in a few years would become my prized make-out location during my dates. At least it was for Rebecca 1.0 and me. My ‘do-over’ however was going to have a few improvements.

The ride from our house to the store was only 5 minutes. But with mom’s health, walking there and back would be difficult. So, a 5-minute drive it was. Mom must have been still processing what she witnessed in the living room and asked, “When did you learn to play like that. I thought the last song you knew was chopsticks?”

“I had asked dad a while ago to show me some chords and I have been secretly practicing whenever you guys go out and I am home alone,” was my reply.

“Well, I am sure your dad will be excited to hear how well you’re coming along with it,” she said.

And right on cue was my sister, “Oh, you're just so great, you can’t do anything wrong,” came a sarcastic voice from the front.

“Ann, don’t treat your brother like that, or you can sit in the car,” mom said with her chastising voice.

I elected to just shut up and not add any gas to the flame. Eventually, I hope I can change the direction of my relationship with my sister, but right now, I had bigger issues coming my way.

We arrived at the store, and went in, looking like two students getting ready for school. I already had a good idea of what I needed for next week, and if I needed anything else, then I would simply ride my bike here and buy it with my own money. This trip was more for mom. She always loved getting us our school stuff. Both paper goods, as well as clothing. Mom grabbed a buggy, and my sister took off to start her search. She would find something she thought she needed, and then would return to the buggy and drop it in. Mom and I stuck together and made the rounds. I got a pack of student workbooks with lined pages inside as well as a few pads of graph paper. The entire trip lasted maybe 30 minutes and we were on our way home with our school supplies.

As we reached the turn onto our street, I was looking out the side window when all of a sudden, I suddenly realized, damn, 'I have a paper route'. As the wagon made the turn, I was staring at my stack of Specs bundled and wrapped sitting at the corner waiting for me. For the next 150 yards to our driveway, I was blaming this sudden realization on my friends and their less-than-perfect tech. I decided I would grab the collecting punch cards and use them to help me refresh the route. Problem was that not all of the houses in the neighborhood subscribed to the spec. Added to that, I also had 2 customers who only got the paper on Wednesday *(Flyer-day)* and Saturday, the other flyer day along with a bunch of other stuff. As soon as the car came to rest, I jumped out and yelled at mom, "Gota do my papers."

"Ok, don't forget about your promise to your dad," she said with a bit of a grin.

I sprinted down the street and grabbed the bundle of papers, put them on my right shoulder, and jogged home. I think I was still using the original shoulder carry bag you got from the Spec to carry the papers. The normal process was to fill the bag with as many papers as would fit, and I could carry, then ride my bike to the end of the street and deliver the first bag. Retrieve the bike and repeat. I could not recall how long it took me back then, but figured since I was still blanking on the whole - 'What the hell did I do yesterday?', amnesiatic state, no time like the present to get my first official workout in.

I opened the garage and surveyed the walls and spotted the carry bag. I grabbed the bag and my bike up against the wall and moved them out to the driveway area where I had dropped the paper bundle. My route covered three streets all fairly close to the house. I opened up the bundle of papers and did a quick count. Forty was the count. So, no paper for my two Wednesday & Saturday customers. I loaded twelve papers in the bag along with the customer punch cards. I rode the bike up the street and stopped in what I thought was the most strategic location allowing me to do a circle covering both sides of the street ending back at my bike. With the bag on my shoulder, I ran. It was awkward trying to run with the carry bag, but I got my arm around the bag as well and it helped reduce the bag's movement. As soon as I reached the first door, I started to recall some of the old habits of what location my customer preferred getting their paper delivered to and what hedges could I jump, and what lawns I was forbidden to step on.

It didn't take that long to perform the delivery and even though Mondays were always the lightest paper of the week, I thought I could speed up the entire delivery process by strategically dropping a pre-determined number of papers first, then simply run the route on foot. Note to self; need a 2-wheel cart to pull behind the bike! I did not time the delivery but would guess it was a max, of 20 minutes. I think before, I would take 45 minutes and an hour plus on Wednesdays and Saturdays not counting collecting. I was thankful one disaster was avoided. I could just picture sitting at the dinner table when Mr. Taylor would phone the house and do the old, "Hello, this is Mr. Taylor up the street and I was just calling to see how Derek is feeling?" knowing darn well that would immediately result in my dad, giving me the 'stare of death' as only dads can do with the reply, "Hi Ben, I can guarantee you that Derek will be dropping off your paper in a couple of minutes." Not today! I put the bike away and was now ready to keep my promise to my dad.

I figured I had maybe 30 minutes before dad got home and decided to pick up all the dog crap in the back. Tiny was back outside and was asleep as usual on the patio. I went to the rear garage door and grabbed a shovel and stiff rake. We had a side garden, and I had allocated a small section where I would dig a hole and then dump the dog poop into it. I hated the smell of disturbed dog poop. Dog poop that had sat long enough usually forms a poop skin, which keeps the stench in. As soon as you break the skin, odor city. Having had several dogs over the years, I have reached the stage where I have to bend down and pick it up with my hand with an inverted poop bag. My shovel and rake system didn't seem too bad. I finished the de-pooping in about 15 minutes and put everything away and headed back into the house.

Mom was busy making dinner, my sister was doing who knows what in her room, and as much as I wanted to get 15 minutes in on the writing, I thought, why not take Tiny for a short walk up the street before dad gets home. I went into the kitchen closet and found the leash. I told mom my plan, and she gave me a face look like 'what are you trying to prove.' When I hit the patio, Tiny knew the sound her leash and collar made, and she immediately got up and came to me with her tail wagging. I put the collar and leash on, opened the gate, and headed out on my first official walk with Tiny. I wasn't sure of her breed, but she was a big 90 lbs gentle chubber, with a heart of gold, unless you hit my mom. If Tiny is in the room and you go over to mom and raise your arm like you were going to hit her, Tiny would run over and give you her best growl and bare her teeth. It was always a cute show to do for the company now and then.

I was coming down our street when I spotted my dad's car coming the other way. He would beat me to the driveway, but I would arrive by the time he closed his car door. As I came down the driveway, he had stopped to wait for me. I kind of knew what he was going to ask. "What's with walking Tiny?" he asked.

"I was in the back picking up his deposits as promised and as I passed by him, he turned to me and said, Derek, would you please walk me today, I need the exercise," I responded. Dad's eyes rolled and he gave a bit of a grunt-like noise close to a micro laugh, he put his hand on my shoulder and transitioned into a smile and we walked together into the house. As was customary, I made the official announcement, "Daddy's Home," in a funny, do I dare say light in the loafers' voice *(Not that there's anything wrong with that)*.

Dad hung his blazer in the closet, and I took Tiny's leash off, and she went to her favorite spot this time of the year, the back door stoop. Mom was where she always is at this time of the day, in the kitchen preparing dinner. Our dinner ritual was the complete opposite of the Hamlin's. Normally dad gets home at 4:30, we sit down to eat at 4:45, and then I take off outside by 5 to finish playing with my neighborhood buddies, who eat at the normal time of 6 pm. Dad would usually retire to the living room to grab a short nap before he had to leave for night school at 5:45. He seemed to be always taking night school courses. While we did not enjoy the hours-long family gathering over a meal, my dad did instill in me another great gift, the ability to learn by reading.

Dad always taught me that you can do anything you want in life simply by reading a book about the topic. Well, maybe studying the topic intently is a more accurate description, and it may also entail multiple books. I always revered my father as a very bright man. Book smart is an appropriate term. But he was not some small in stature nerd that one might attach to a book-smart person; dad was six-foot 1 inch in his prime and a thick big boned man. He played rugby in his youth and had hands of steel. Mostly from playing the piano. While we did not share the same genetics, I always use to claim I was built like my father, broad-shouldered, which would be an asset in my formidable football years. As part of the new family health program, dad did play tennis a bit, and I was hoping that would be my first connection to a new healthy dad.

While dad gave me the book smart gene *(Just kidding)*, my gramps gave me my practical genes *(Just kidding again)*. My ability to tear down any engine and rebuild it was my Gramps gift to me. I was only 11 last year when our lawn mower engine quit running. Gramps just happened to be staying with us for the weekend, and as he always loved to do, decided to tear it apart to see what was wrong with it. Gramps was a heavy equipment mechanic who learned his trade during World War II. That particular Saturday morning, I found Gramps in the garage with his toolbox open, working on the lawn mower. We exchanged pleasantries, and before long, I was his right-hand man in this tear-down. I think he was excited to see my interest in what he was doing, and with his Lapalina Lilly protruding from his mouth and his English racing cap perched on his head like Jackie Stewart, he proceeded to strip the old Briggs and Straton 3.5 hp engine down to the block. I am pretty sure, a few years later, I determined that the problem with the engine was a plugged carb needle. But Gramps figured, why not teach his grandson about engines, and it also allowed us to give it a thorough cleaning and restore it like new.

Dad came out at one point and saw I was helping Gramps and I could tell was glad I was getting exposed to that part of life. He was working at weeding the front garden and I was glad he decided to let me work with Gramps rather than recruit me for his job. It took us about 4 hours to strip and rebuild the motor and carb. Gramps was a pretty good teacher and let me do a lot of the actual hands-on work. The other lesson I picked up on was, to make sure you have the right tool for the job. Gramps had everything in his toolbox right down to the ring compressor and cylinder compression tester.

In my later years, I gave myself the mechanic nickname, 'old one pull' *(And not that kind of pulling Rebecca!; I smiled)*. I prided myself on fixing an engine and having it start on the very first pull. Anything else, I considered myself a failure. Gramps and I had completed everything and were ready to see if all our hard work paid off. Being the proud educator that day, Gramps gave me the honor of the first pull. Back in those days, they had not yet added a priming bulb to those motors. Gramps being the great mechanic, knew the issue with the vacuum pressure on those motors and had added a mini-inline priming bulb to our old Toro. I gave it a couple of squeezes, smelled gas, and then positioned myself to make the pull. Foot on the footrest and away I tugged. I think, I had not made it to the halfway point, of the full length of the pull start cord, when the engine began to fire. I looked at the engine and listened to it for a minute. Wow, it was running smoother than I ever remember. I turned and smiled at Gramps with my head nodding. I then had to turn to see the look on my dad's face, who was pulling weeds about 30 feet from where we were, just outside the garage door. Dad looked at me and gave me a big smile, and that Englishman nod of approval. I turned back to Gramps and said, "Sounds really good."

Gramps with the stogie still in his mouth replied, "the rings are worn, and you will need to change them out next year along with the spark plug. Other than that, it should last you another 10 years, just make sure you change the oil every year." I was so proud of Gramps and me for getting the lawnmower running, and from that moment on, our two strokes and eventually 4-strokes would never see the light of a lawnmower repair shop. Next year I start finding older broken riding lawnmowers and do a complete rebuild and then sell them for cash! Well, that was then, and now is completely different with a new plan.

Dad proceeded to walk into the kitchen and as was the tradition in our house, dad would give my mom a kiss on the lips and ask, "How was your day?"

I took the opportunity to head to the bathroom to wash up before dinner. I don't think I ever washed up before any meal before. All cleaned up, I headed back to the kitchen to see what everyone was doing. As I entered the kitchen my dad turned to me and said, "Your mom told me you taught yourself a song on the piano?"

Oh, Crap. And if you ever wanted to see an example of how good I was at figuring out a solution to a problem, here it is.

"Ya, I have been secretly practicing a bit the last few months," I admitted.

"Why the secrecy," dad asked?

"Well, I was disappointed in myself for bailing on the piano lessons before and was too embarrassed to tell you I wanted to try it again," was my answer.

I knew by my dad's look, that he was still skeptical about the whole story, and did what any skeptical first-class musician would do, make me prove it. "I think we have at least 5 minutes before supper is ready, is that right honey?" my dad asked my mom.

"Yes, 5 minutes is about right," mom said as she was preoccupied with the meal prep.

So, I tried to show no fear and began trying to figure out the best way to handle this situation. I knew darn well I created it, and now I need to fix it. The distance from the hall to the piano was about 20 feet. As I reached the piano, I pulled out the bench and sat down. With the confidence of a concert pianist, I hit the D/F#, C/E, Am7/D, Am7, D#dim7, Em, F, D cords in that order. I selected a song that I would be able to do justice to with my pre-puberty high vocal register and I chose this song because it required less piano skill than Faust. Although now, I struggle to do it in the original key. I then started to sing;

The road is long.....
With a many a winding turn
That leads us to who, knows where,
Who knows where....

I ended after the first verse and chorus and turned to see my dad's expression. My dad seldomly had the expression of 'What the 'F' was that?', and my dad also had his valve on for maintaining his appearance of, 'No big deal'. So, he quickly tried to throw me his best curve ball with, "You learned that all by yourself?" I am sure that part of him figured he had me now and was about to expose my secret, that I was an imposter, but he had no idea that this was his son 2.0, and not the previous deficient son 1.0. I opened the piano bench and pulled out a music book my dad bought about a month ago titled, 'Greatest Hits of the 70's'. I started to flip pages and finally got to the great comeback page of all time, " He ain't heavy, he's my brother " by The Hollies, complete with cords and Lyrics. Seems my memories are starting to arrive.

My dad was still in his secret 'shocked zone' especially because my performance was close to perfect, but as usual, you never saw it. I could tell he was in that zone by this remark, "I thought that was a good buy." I got up and figured I would wait to hear his next comment.

We both walked silently to the table, and sat down, when mom said to my dad, "He sounds really good don't you think?"

Now most people, would have been satisfied, and expecting a simple, 'Yes, he played very well and sang in key too', type response. But not my dad, he's book smart. He knew exactly what my ego needed.

"Well, I thought it was fairly good, but his intonations were a bit off, and you need to learn to use the peddles properly; way too much sostenuto and missing some una corda, but overall, a very good start." In piano speak, it was like music to my ears, dad had just made the first move, and I knew the second move.

"Well, I was hoping, now that the cat is out of the bag so to speak, that you might have some time when you're not too busy, to help me improve my playing. I do love the piano," I replied.

Well, some people will say, 'I love you so very much', others would give big hugs and kisses on the cheek, but in our house, my reply to my dad was equal, or better, than both of those combined. The proof? Dad's reply had a little verklempting going on, "I would be glad to anytime." Our dance was complete. And not only did I plan on spending some great times together on the piano, but I would also plan to go and play occasionally with his band. I think that was a huge moment for both of us.

Dinner was great, and funny how my love of food came with me. I guess it must be stored in our brain. Mom always cooked our meats in the traditional English style, 'well done', meaning over-cooked. I am sure, I will help her see the light over time, to the medium-rare experience. Our table chat was mostly about school, and it was good to hear my sister taking the lead and chatting about some of the clubs in high school she was going to join. When we were done, I said I was going to go to my room and organize some of the new school supply purchases. Dad had night school and most likely would head to the basement couch for a short nap, mom would putter in the kitchen, maybe fold laundry, then sit and watch TV while knitting. My sister, back to her room, and as usual, chatted on the phone with her friends for a couple of hours. She was on the phone so much, dad put one in her room.

Once I got to my room, rather than pull my duo-tang out of the secret spot, I just continued, on separate sheets and would insert them tomorrow or later tonight. I finished the last page around 2:30 am, had my door shut, and was under my covers, with my camping flashlight. I got out of bed and put the papers in the bottom drawer of my desk quietly and went back to bed. I lay in bed staring at the ceiling thinking over my day. It was my first day and it was everything I had hoped for and more. And before I end this over-bloated section Rebecca, the other Derek's memories all returned by the next morning, and not soon enough, as I had promised to go over to Nookie's place and help him work on his tree fort in his backyard.

I needed you to understand what happened that first day. It's the hardest day because it's the first. The rest get easier and easier and more interesting and more exciting. Remember, 'change has consequences, and consequences make change'.

End of First Day 

Note to Rebecca:

From here forward I will be using a different format. As much as I would love to write about every little thing that I would experience differently for the first-time, I do not want to turn this into a multi-volume 'Life and Times', book. It's a guide! A guide YOU need! The format may change at some point but for now, I will try to present the information too you as follows;

Major Task Heading; Date or Date Range; Sub title; a paragraph or two (inside joke I guess), followed by updates. Some tasks will occur over time and may need to be worked on in parallel with other tasks. Any update will be placed inside square brackets and if a particular update was of a major concern, I will write it down in caps. I am aware that you will be reading this guide long after these sections were first written, however, what I want you to watch for, is any odd trends or patterns that I may not notice at the time. Especially if you see me make references to changes from my prior timeline.

It sounds a bit trivial to look for these potential anomalies, but I fully expect the actions that I will be taking will eventually alter my prior future events. As the frequency of this phenomenon increases, Tasks that I have previously planned for may not occur as I studied from my past. I am highlighting this point because mitigating risk is all about my reliance on knowing the past and developing my plan based on that information. You will need to do the same analysis.

Lastly, try to enjoy the information I present by comparing what I wrote with what you actually experienced. If I were in your shoes, reading this guide, I think the accuracy of my predictions would provide a different insight into me. Just a suggestion Dimples! So, as my You Tube sous vide steak master would say, 'Let's do it."

Task 1 – Make money and get in shape!

(Tuesday, August 28th – September 2nd, 1973)

26 ***Orientation and Planning:*** I had exactly one week till my first day of school. Over the rest of my arrival week, I was able to fulfil my earlier-self commitments, as well as ride my bike everywhere to re-acquaint myself with my territory, but through my new aged lenses. The most significant change Rebecca was my first meeting with all of my neighborhood friends and their families. Having lived my prior life growing up with these people and knowing who I would, and would not, have a lasting relationship with *(before)*, as well as being exposed to some of their older self BS, had completely corrupted my perspective. Unfortunately, not in a good way. My next-door neighbor who was a couple of years older than me was a prime example, and you know exactly who I am talking about. We grew up playing sports together and hanging out as most kids do growing up as next-door neighbors. Our parents were friends and they even on occasion took their summer holidays where and when we did. He was the person back when I was 6, told me my parents weren't even my parents, which sent me running home crying, telling them what he said. Finding out you're adopted at 6 is a very confusing experience.

It was two days after I got back that I had my first encounter with my 'not future' friend. Kevin was heading into grade 9 like my sister and I'm sure was busy getting ready like everyone else. I was at the side of the house climbing our maple tree, trying to get another workout in, when I spotted him cutting his grass. I was trying to move around the tree using only my arms like a monkey. He gave a quick wave as he passed not that far from where I was. I hung by one hand and proceeded to wave with the other. I then re-gripped and continued with my workout. I was able to travel a lot further up the tree than I originally thought I would be able and eventually was a good 15 feet off the ground. Once I got to the highest point I could manage, based on the branch configuration, I stopped and held one branch while I stood on the other. I took maybe a 3-minute breather and watched old Kevin cut the grass.

What was new for me and would be a regular theme Rebecca, was when I was watching him, my brain was thinking, 'What a loser he will be. A full-blown alcoholic in 6 years." In fact, old Kev would be put on my 'Sheldon Cooper's', Mortal Enemies list. I don't want you to think for a moment that it did not enter my thought process what you would have tried to tell me, 'Maybe instead of condemning him to that destructive life, try and nudge him towards a better and more rewarding life, especially with your newfound superpower, of advanced knowledge'. While part of me knew you're probably right, the other part was less forgiving and generous. It exposed another side of me that may require some modifications to my valve system.

By the end of the week, I was already establishing a pretty good workout program just with what I already had at my disposal. The maple was a great multi-directional monkey bar set. Paper route had good legs and a bit of cardio and finally, I started to sprint each evening around the block. The first few times was a single sprint, actually was a ½ sprint followed by a gradual speed decline for the second half. By Sunday night, I found the happy medium that allowed me to traverse the route at a full run speed. I was still 12, and building the upper body muscles, would have to wait a year before adding heavy weight training. After all, I was still growing and developing. As exciting and rewarding as the first week was for me, I am sure it was equally exciting and rewarding for my parents. I was doing dishes, making my bed, cleaning, folding laundry, and walking my buddy regularly. The only downside was the negative influence it was having on my sister. She was not a fan of Derek 1.0, now she most likely despised Derek 2.0 even more and it was not lost on me, and I was still trying to figure out a course correction for us.

Well, you know what they say, 'A strong body makes the mind strong'. I am sure old Thomas Jefferson did not have my financial issues or he may have added, 'Strong body makes a strong mind which makes a thick wallet' *(he he)*. I was sitting on a personal net worth of just shy of $500 but knew I needed far more to be able to pull off a few of my selected do-overs and new-do's. While I expected I would be in good shape for money in 1976 using Tab 'R', I needed to figure out some alternative money-making opportunities between now and then. Don't laugh, but I researched the date for the patent for the intermittent windshield wiper. Turned out that Robert Kearns invented it in 1967 and then sued Ford Motor Co. in 1978 and Chrysler in 1982, claiming patent infringement. I would expand my paper route by an additional 54 papers in a couple of months bringing me to a total of 96. I won't complain but it was slave labor for a man of my age *(I smiled)*. So, this week, I decided with the 3-year window, and financial drought facing me, I would try something more grandiose. 'Amway' or should I say, 'Devonway'! *(And yes, I smiled)*.

Yes, I once sold Amway and got to meet Jay Van Andel and Richard DeVos and their spouses at a convention. While I eventually quit the

Amway cult, it had taught me quite a lot about multilevel marketing as well as how to sucker people into spending their hard-earned money buying bogus motivational tapes, books, and other 'upline' self-revenue generating tactics. Amway was all about growing the business through recruitment, not selling products. The product was just a tool used to grow the distributor base. I am sure I could write a good book about the Amway cult, but most likely others have already done so. I recall a few about 'Cultism In Amway'. What I planned to do was a bit different. I knew the value of building a large network of friends and acquaintances, especially if you would one day be in a service field like real estate. I planned to build a network, not through multilevel marketing but through single-level marketing.

It was a very simple plan, but it would leverage a couple of key things. One, I would build the network using already existing networks. Two, I would provide a means to supplement the existing sales network by adding a new, non-competing, replenishable product like 'Amway'. And third, and most importantly, I would wrap the whole concept up in a 'Student Mentorship Initiative'. After all, every parent would love to support a young person in learning the importance of earning their own money while delivering a needed service. Finally, for all my hard work, creative thinking, and execution, I would take a small percentage, leaving the lion's share of course in my fellow young mentors' hands. Dare I say a 'Win, Win, Win'. A win for the youths, a win for the parents, and a win for yours truly.

Fortunately, as any 12-year-old knows, the first step to such an endeavor is to write a rock-solid business plan *(Hope you smiled at that one)*. I did what every freshman grade sevener would do with a fairly extensive chemistry background, that was capable of formulating good old laundry soap. And since I was at it, why not invent the cling-free dryer sheet. Actually, a gentleman Conrad J. Gaiser and his wife, Audrey, first developed the dryer sheet back in the mid to late 60s, but it was not a big success due to several technical issues with the process of 'coating' the fabric sheet. The why, and how I knew this, don't ask, but P&G would perfect the manufacturing process and start selling the first successful fabric dryer sheets in 1975. Most dryer sheets are made from a nonwoven polyester material coated with a softening agent that has a long hydrophobic chain. Fatty acids, fatty alcohols, and alcohol ethoxylates are all possible softening agents. P&G uses quaternary ammonium salts of fatty acids as its primary softening agents, whereas Unilever, which *(Will eventually)* produces Snuggle dryer sheets, uses a stearic acid. So, with my fortunate cling-free knowledge, I would manufacture my own sheets to go along with my own version of 'Oxi-clean' based laundry soaps.

Oxi-clean is oxygen bleach, or sodium percarbonate, which is made from sodium carbonate *(also known as soda ash)* and hydrogen peroxide. It works by releasing oxygen once it is exposed to water. This release of oxygen lifts stains and dirt off whatever you're cleaning. So, all I needed to do was locate a white label type manufacturing facility and convince them to manufacture my formulation and get paid after the products are delivered to our customers. In addition to that, order some business cards and a few brochures promoting the benefits of supporting 'The Student Mentoring Initiative' and the plan was ready. Just kick back and wait for the money to roll in *(Yes Rebecca, I was being a bit facetious)*. But I did manage to write out a draft business plan this week which had me earning a 10% markup on all products. Look at me, I had my very own 'Sigma Iotia II experience'. Kirk would be proud of this time-cheating "Krako' grabbing 'A piece of the action' *(Sorry, another Star Trek flashback)* idea. The markup was the difference between what the manufacturer charged me and what I sold it for to 'The Student Mentoring Initiative' under an exclusive 5-year supply agreement of course. Not bad for my first business venture!

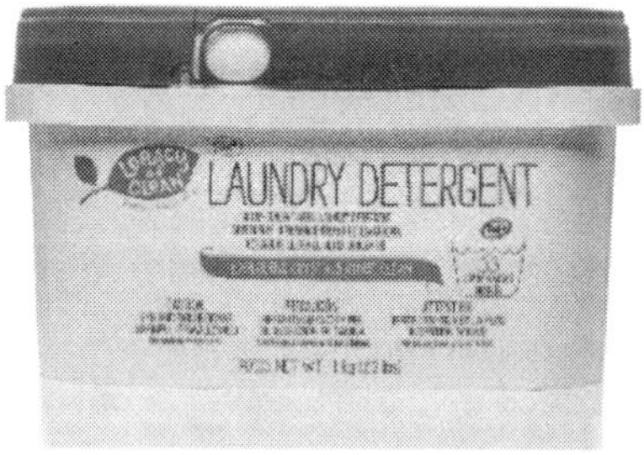

'Devonway' Is Born!

Task 2 – Meet Luke

(Tuesday, September 4th – September 7th, 1973)

27 ***The first week of School:*** Today was sure to be a very exciting and exhilarating next 10 hours. I would be meeting all my old friends from public school, new friends I had known from hockey, a few catholic kids whose parents decided to send them to Senior Public instead of the Catholic middle school, and finally, grade 8 kids that think they have the world all figured out. An unexpected enjoyment was the thought of seeing my old teachers for the first time again. On the last tour, I developed a great relationship with a few and planned on expanding on that experience. But what I was most looking forward to, was meeting my future best man and best friend, Luke Mattson. Today, we are going to run into each other after 2nd class in the hallway.

Mom had made me my lunch just for today as I usually rode home for lunch; my sister was looking nervous enough to forget to give me the usual morning insults. Dad was gone, and I was chomping at the bit to get going. I would ride my bike and if the timing was right, I would exit my driveway at the exact time a couple of next-door neighbor kids would be passing my place. I had taken the time to select my attire for the day. I wanted to make sure I was looking as sharp as any 63-year-old 12-year-old could look. I wish I could say it included my 'Dirk Diggler' bathroom mirror self-admiration nod, but that inside joke would have to wait a few years, after all, I was still growing *(You had to have laughed at that along with an accompanying eye roll).*

Well, got a kiss on the cheek from mommy, a tail wag from Tiny, and finally the missing insult from my sister, "Who are you trying to impress in those clothes?"

"I just want to set the same high standards that you did when you went to Senior public, the teachers would expect nothing less," I replied with a look of 'Don't mess with the Zohan'. I wish I could have taken a picture of her expression because it was priceless. She had no idea how to respond so she just turned and headed across the lawn to meet up I assume with her fellow neighborhood minor Niners.

I hopped on my bike, knapsack on, and was slowly peddling down the drive waiting to see who may be coming up the street for me to join the ride. The bike ride at a slow pace took about 15 minutes to reach the school. At a full-out pace, I could do it in 5 min. Almost on cue, rounding the corner was Sarah Miller and June Kapskey. Sarah lived 4 doors away and June lived across the street in the next survey east of me on Douglas. I would be adding their house to my paper route soon. June was nice but seemed to always dress like some carpet bagger. Baggie clothes that would never show off her form. It was a shame because June's family had an inground pool and I was treated to a few gawks delivering the paper to her in a bathing suit.

Sarah on the other hand was a year older and we had already done a little exploratory adolescent touching. The first time was this summer when we went to the golf course to do some ball hunting. It was something we used to do for fun. If you found a dozen golf balls, you could sell them to local golfers in the neighborhood for $5. On this particular outing, we were hiding behind a bunch of bushes waiting for the golfers to leave the hole so we could scour the fringe of the fairway for lost balls. As we were sitting there, Sarah asked if I had ever seen a girl's boobs before. We were good friends and grew up together and hung out a lot over the years. I looked at her and answered honestly, "No."

Well, she then took it up a notch and asked me, "Do you want to see mine?" I am sure the expression said all that needed to be said, and she proceeded to pull her shirt up showing me her bra. Well, some may be disappointed at looking at a bra, but being that this was my first actual face-to-face volunteer flash, it was great! What I was not ready for was her next request, "I need you to undo the back of my bra for me," as she turned her back to me.

"Ok," I robotically responded. Wow, another first. I looked at the back of the bra and said, "How does it work?"

"You just have to lift the one side and the other side down where they overlap," she instructed.

Well, I reached out my hands and made my first attempt to unsnap her bra. And to my surprise, it opened. Now most boys would have been satisfied with achieving this milestone, but as we know, I am not normal. Instead, I started to examine the clasp mechanism to see how it worked. Told you, all science! Once the clasp was open, Sarah turned to me and lifted her bra up exposing her breasts. Not sure if it was a guy thing or just me, but I wanted to touch them.

"Can I touch them?" I asked innocently.

"Ok, but don't squeeze them, they are a bit tender today," she informed me. So, today I felt up a girl for the very first time. I was glad it was Sarah because our relationship allowed it to be more exploratory and less sexual. Our adolescent curiosity would culminate in a couple of weeks in our pool when she would grab my you-know-what, followed by a full-on hand inside the bathing suit for my first flesh-to-flesh touch. I of course had to reciprocate and had my first hand-to-you-know-where experience. It was far more a playful act and not sexual yet. That was supposed to happen in a few weeks from now when Sarah would come with me to my grandfather's place. We would end up riding in the back of the wagon as the back seat would hold my grandfather's old stereo which completely blocked my dad's rear view mirror view of the back of the wagon.

And as all, or most adolescents do, we undid our pant zippers, and both reached inside to re-examine our pool anatomy class experience. The difference now was that we both would have new and strange feelings happen. Our finger exploration lasted for about 30 minutes. First, it was just touching lightly, and then something different happened. It grew and Sarah got wet! While I had no idea what I should do, Sarah did assist with trying to guide a finger to a particular spot. It was more her moving my hand and less me doing it on my own. At some point about 20 minutes from the house, Sarah must have hit a magic button because I had this unbelievable feeling, and then she pulled her hand out and gave me a disgusting look. It slowly dawned on me what happened and when I looked down at the crotch of my pants, I had this large wet spot clearly showing through. Not a little dime-size spot, but a spot the size of my hand. Sarah and I both knew what happened, and we had heard about this biological process in the school yard chats the last couple of years.

Realizing that my parents would immediately know what happened when they saw the crotch of my pants, I needed to figure out what to do. Sarah's look went from disgust to more of a grin as she knew what the panic on my face meant. It took her a while to move the grin from funny to concern since my parents would know that Sarah who was a year older was an active participant in the whole affair. She reached over and took the cuff of her shirt and tried to wipe the area, but it didn't do a thing. After several tries, I figured out the move and whispered it into her ear. Looking directly into Sarah's eyes I said, "Dad, how much longer till we get home because I have to go to the bathroom."

"Not far, maybe 15 minutes, and I am sure you can hold it," he replied.

I was smiling and Sarah was also giggling when I said, "Ok, but no promises." Well, the plan was set and as soon as the car stopped in the driveway, I jumped out the back of the wagon before mom or dad had opened their doors and sprinted into the house. Luckily, Ann was home, and the door was unlocked. I ran to my bedroom and grabbed another pair of jeans and Tighty-Whities and ran into the bathroom. I was hoping that my parents would not notice I changed jeans and fortunately, all my jeans were the same. Levis. I put the evidence under my bed and would wash them later. I ran back outside and said, "Made it," with a big smile. Dad looked at me and said, "Great, now you can give me a hand getting the stereo out."

Sarah was standing by the back of the car watching everything and when I got close to her, I noticed that the crotch of her pants was also damp looking. Her pants were lighter in color, so I did not notice it in the car. Using my eyes, I tried to get her to look down at her crotch. After a couple of eye gestures, she figured out my code and looked down. She immediately looked up with a slight fear and quickly said, "Thanks Mr. and Mrs. Devon for taking me but I better get home." She quickly turned and walked down the driveway so mom and dad would never get a chance to see her evidence. We did talk about the event later and laughed at the whole thing, but there was never any relationship-like feeling between us. While I suspected Sarah had been doing a little 'home research' regarding her special spot, I had officially become a man! Ok, maybe a boy with all parts now working as they should.

So, as Sarah rode up, I knew it would now be a different ending in a couple of weeks and certainly not a 'Happy Ending' *(You must have laughed Rebecca)*. I had made a mental challenge with myself to see if I could remain a 'virgin' and save myself for the first time to be with you, Rebecca.

We rode to school, and I am sure we discussed all sorts of first-day back topics. As we got closer to school and the neighborhood street networks began to converge, our little pack of 3 bikes was now close to 10. Most of us knew each other and exchanged head nods or simple 'Hi's'. When we got to the bike area at the senior public, there were already a ton of bikes. I found a spot on the fence and locked up the wedge. When I started to look around at the other bikes, I quickly determined it was time for an upgrade to a 10-speed! I walked over to the front of the school to meet everyone and exchange some bonding banter.

What was funny, was the first person I came up to, I put out my fist expecting a fist bump. Problem was that the fist bump I was sure had not yet been invented. So, as Kyle gave me an odd look I said, "Fist bump man," with a smile. Kyle, I guess didn't know whether it was a joke or some new senior public thing and reciprocated with a clenched fist. What I had not noticed, was a bunch of other classmates had observed the new greeting ritual and as I came over to say hello, I got a few fists pointing my way. After a few fist bumps, I arrived at Mike Lang, a hockey buddy, and put out my fist which he slowly copied but this time I blew my fist up with the sound effect, "Boom," followed by a good laugh. I am sure he thought I was nuts.

I am not here to suggest that I invented the fist bump, but I will be observing over the next while, strictly for scientific purposes to see how contagious it becomes. The doors opened and we all went in. The grade 8's went to their pre-assigned home rooms while 'us Newby's' all went into the auditorium to pick up our class assignments and schedules. Tables were spread about with different alpha signs posted. I went to the table with the 'D' and a teacher was standing there and asked my name. I responded, "Derek Devon ma'am."

She gave me an odd look but found my paperwork and handed it to me and then told me to go over to the table by the stage and get my locker assignment. My first instinct was to ask, 'why did they not include the locker assignment with the class schedule paperwork'. So, I walked over to the stage and stood in a line to wait for a locker assignment. While I was standing there, Luke Mattson walked over and was now standing behind me. I immediately recognized him and wanted to give my old buddy a big hug, but I knew better of course. My mind immediately began to process this. I am not supposed to meet Luke until after the first class and it was upstairs. Maybe he was behind me last time and I just didn't notice him. So, not to disturb the time-gods, I refused to let myself turn and do our introduction. I eventually went up and grabbed my locker assignment and was off to unload my stuff in my locker and go to my homeroom class. I was lucky that my locker was in the east wing and not the west wing. I arrived at my locker and immediately surveyed who was near me that I knew. Turned out not that many.

I gave a bunch of head nods and grabbed my binder and pencil bag and headed into my homeroom. My homeroom was Mr. Hodgeson who I previously had a great relationship with. So far, everything seems to be as it was, except maybe for the almost Luke encounter. The first day was generally a non-school workday for most classes, but there are always a couple of teachers who want to try and set a tone day one. Last time I sat at the back of the class with all the cool guys! Well, Derek 2.0 was going to take the front row closest to the window. I took my seat, positioned my binder, and placed my pen case on top. I already knew Mr. Hodgeson was going to sit at the front of the class with his butt on the desk and give a brief chat about what to expect in grade 7 English class. Then he would go around the class and ask each person to introduce themselves and have everyone tell one interesting thing they did over the summer. He started at the desk closest to the door which meant I would go last. When he finally got to me, I rose and took a couple of steps towards him and held out my fist. He stared at me and was wondering what I was doing. Then a classmate yelled out, "Fist bump." Mr. Hodgeson was a very sharp man, and it didn't take him long to figure out the move and proceeded to extend his fist somewhat tentatively. I touched my fist to his and said, "Very nice to meet you Mr. Hodgeson, I have heard you're a pretty good English teacher as well as a good hockey player."

I knew it was a bit of an Eddie Haskel move but I wanted to set a new tone. I was not the cool kid sitting at the back pretending I was being inconvenienced with his teachings. I was going to try and change the class dynamics. I figured it would not be overnight but why not start it now. Besides, when I now looked at Mr. Hodgeson, I was looking at a peer not a teacher.

Mr. Hodgeson stared at me and said, "I had Ann in my homeroom. I gather she is now in Highschool. As far as hockey goes, maybe we will get a chance to meet on the ice this year," he said with a grin.

"Yes, she is officially a minor niner," I replied. "As far as my summer went, the most notable event, was I grew 6 inches, in height that is," as I showed a bit of a grin with a 180-degree slow head turn to see the look on my classmates. Mr. Hodgeson's expression was stuck between letting out a good laugh and shock that a grade seven student could deliver such an adult-like one-liner with a strange vocabulary for a 12-year-old.

His last act of the class before dismissing us was to ask us a question. He proceeded to take a 'BB-Bat' taffy candy stick, or closer to lollipop off his desk, and held it up. I never liked them, but in the past, won a few and would suck on it in class, more to rub it in the eyes of my fellow classers and not because I liked it.

"The first correct answer will get the reward," he smiled.

"Give me an example of an Intensive or Reflexive Pronoun," he challenged.

I sat there and bit my tongue. He repeated the challenge, and no one put their hand up to give it a try. He smiled at the class and said, "Good news, before you complete my class, you will know the answer."

After a quick bang on the desk he said, "Class over. See you tomorrow."

I let most of the students exit the class and as I walked by Mr. Hodgeson, I reached beside him and picked up the 'BB-bat' and said, "He calls himself a teacher," with a grin.

I can honestly say that Mr. Hodgeson was flabbergasted by my act. He just looked at me with a confused expression. As I reached the door, Mr. Hodgeson said with a grin, "He thought himself a hockey player."

As I exited the class, I knew in about 5 minutes, Luke and I would meet for the first time. As I made my way up the stairs to the second floor for my math class, I was now constantly bumping into people I knew and it was a non-stop, "great to see you," fest.

As I reached the top of the stairs, I entered the second-floor hallway, and exactly as I remembered, Luke was walking toward me. I proceeded to walk directly at him, and our meeting went exactly as it had previously. I told him as I had before that we should ride home together so he could see where I lived, and it was not a major routing change for him. After school, we stood down by the bus area to meet a few more buddies and I made sure to introduce Luke to everyone I knew. We rode home and by the time we got to my place, all was good in the universe again. The best buddy's bond was complete.

Task 1 - Continued

(September 7th, 1973)

28 **Work on business plan for 'The Student Mentoring Initiative':** I had another idea regarding my business plan and all the working parts it required. One of my major steps to executing the plan was going to come from my-soon-to-be new friend, Father Sean O'Sullivan. Ok, Sean O'Sullivan. He would not enter the seminary for a few more years. Sean was a local boy who attended a Hamilton Catholic school and was constantly in the papers these days when he decided to run for the conservative Party for our riding of Hamilton-Wentworth. What I remember about Sean was a story about a chance meeting with John Diefenbaker when he was about my age. Diefenbaker became a mentor to him, and the two exchanged correspondence for many years. In 1970, Sean was elected President of the Ontario Young Progressive Conservatives, and in 1971 became Youth Adviser to Premier William Davis. Finally, in 1972 he decided to run for office. What made Sean remarkable, he was only 20 years old. Sean always reminded me of a young Guy Lafleur. He just needed to grow his hair longer. The reason I referred to him as Father Sean, was in about 5 years he resigns from politics to pursue religious studies and become a Catholic priest.

I knew when I decided to go back that I would be making many changes to my last life's selection of friends and acquaintances. Unfortunately, I would have to forego many in order to achieve my planned objectives. I also was aware that I would be adding many new friends and acquaintances and even some lifelong friends. Sean would be one of the hardest choices for me.

I could use a person like Sean to mentor me at my age which would not only give me instant cred but could in the near future open some valuable political doors and lay the foundation for some of my needed future endeavors. The only negative about this Rebecca, Sean will pass away in his late 30s from leukemia. I don't know if my cancer intervention will be of any help. It will always be active in my brain but for now, I needed to be Youth Director for O'Sullivan's election campaign. Time to put my soon-to-be Youth Mentoring alumni to work.

Task 3 – The Eddie Haskel Initiative!

(October – November 20th, 1973)

29 **'How to kiss ass and not get any brown stuff on your lips!':** School was great, and I was enjoying my new attitude about school, and it was rubbing off on a lot of my friends. I started the new 'Student-Teacher' hockey rivalry. I recruited most of my hockey buddies that were in grade 8 and grade 7, forming a fairly good team. We scheduled a once-monthly battle of kids verse teachers at the Double Rinks. We had the speed, but the teachers had the size and much craftier skills. We lost 8-7 in the first match. Teachers loved it and I think we kids enjoyed the out-of-school bonding with people we use to view as the enemy. The teachers all knew who initiated the event and I was developing a bit of a rep among the teachers as 'The Student with potential'. To be honest, all I wanted was access to them whenever I needed any help with my plans. After all, I was only a 12-year-old, soon to be 13!

Had my first what I would like to describe as a working meeting with Blane Simmons at the Spec. 'Blaner' was the circulation manager in charge of all paper delivery boys. He was about 6 feet weighed about 300 pounds and was sporting a wanna-be beard that we kids would call peach fuzz. Blane liked me ever since I made him look good with the new signup campaign last year. In order to get Blane to support my idea, it was going to be his idea, well eventually, our idea. I needed access to Blane's list of paper delivery people so I could recruit them for my near future 'The Student Mentoring Initiative' plan. I couldn't just tell Blane my master plan because he would have explained to me that the Spec's circulation network was private, for them only to abuse! I needed a backdoor approach, and 'Kids 4 a Cancer Cure' concept would be my vehicle. I proposed that in January, the Spec through their network of paper delivery people, conduct a fundraiser for McMaster University's Cancer research department, primarily Leukemia *(I recently decided after meeting with Sean that this area, for now, was the right move).*

I would recruit a printer to provide all our printing needs and the Spec would notify all their paper delivery minions of the added labor requirement in January. The fund-raising campaign was simple. We would ask each of our newspaper customers when doing our weekly money collection if they would donate to the 'Kids 4 a Cancer Cure' charity. With a $5 donation, we would give them a 'I supported Kids 4 a Cancer Cure with a $5 Donation' button to wear making sure that they knew the month of January was 'Kids 4 a Cancer Cure' month. After they gave the $5, we would hand them their button along with another button that read 'I supported Kids 4 a Cancer Cure with a $10 Donation', along with a mail-in envelope and ask if they could find one more supporter. But it was my Doctor Evil side that knew the human adult psyche; once a large majority of doners looked at the $10 button, they would request to up their donation to $10 from the $5, and some even asked for a few additional buttons and envelopes to solicit family and friends. My theory will be put to the test in a couple of months.

My end of the deal with Blane was to recruit a printer and, for that matter, could print buttons as well. Hopefully a one-stop-shop. The less Blane had to do, the greater the chance of success. So, back to my new networking idea, and I happened to grab a short chat with Sean when I was in the campaign headquarters at the beginning of October picking up more handout cards. I had recruited through school and hockey over 150 students who would go and paper their neighborhoods for me. I also was able to get a large number of teachers to help out and I was pretty sure half of our church. My efforts did not go unnoticed either. As soon as Sean spotted me, he was the one that came right over. When I asked if he had 5 minutes to chat, he said, "For you, the Network kid, make it 10," with a smile.

I already knew he would win, so at every chance, I would jokingly say, "Prime Minister Sean O'Sullivan, has a good ring don't you think?"

He would smile and immediately say, "Let's get this first step completed" with a quick pat on the shoulder.

I told Sean about my involvement with the Spectator paper boys fundraiser called, 'Kids 4 a Cancer Cure'. I then asked him if he knew any printers in the area that may want to donate a little printing time and paper to help us with our fundraiser *(Networking Becca, it is all about networking!)* Sean paused for a second, got up, and went to his desk. He opened the top drawer and pulled out what I will guess was his Rolodex. Mine was a plastic container with a growing number of my mom's blank recipe cards. He flipped through a few cards and finally found the one he was after. He pulled it out and walked back over to me and handed me the card. "Mr. Simpkins owns a fairly large printing business downtown, and just so happens, lost a child a couple of years ago to Cancer," he said.

"Do you know what type of cancer it was?", I asked.

"Yes, Leukemia," he added.

I took the card and told Sean, "Thank you for your help."

"No Derek, thank you for all you are doing. It is amazing what you have accomplished for our campaign and now you're helping with a cancer charity as well. Maybe I should be saying, "Prime Minister Derek Devon has a good ring don't you think," with a big grin.

"Touché Sean, Touché," I quickly countered. I knew as I got up and walked out that my buddy Sean was thinking, 'Who is this kid?" Well, Sean, I am The Intercedinelist! Keeper of Advance Knowledge, able to write a business plan in one day, and most importantly, The great Gretzky eliminator! *(Yes, I actually was thinking this, and yes, back home for a workout).*

I called Mr. Simpkins and introduced myself. I was pleasantly surprised that Sean had already taken the time to call him and let him know some kid would be phoning him to request a meeting. Sean was insightful enough to know not to tell Mr. Simpkins any details but simply as a courtesy to Sean, would he give me a 5-minute meet and greet. I arranged to take the bus downtown on Saturday, and he was willing to arrange to be at his office that morning. We met and before I finished with the end of my pitch, he leaned back and reached for a picture from his bookshelf. He looked at it for a minute and then handed it to me for a look.

"That's my boy Trevor," he said with a bit of a crackle in his voice.

"Looks like he was a lucky kid, Sir. You certainly have a beautiful family there" as I looked over at the rest of his pictures and smiled.

"It has been just over a couple of years since the Leukemia took him from us," as he then looked at the other pictures.

"Sean said you're only 12 years old. Is that correct," asked Mr. Simpkins?

"I turn thirteen January 9th sir, so closer to 13 than 12," I explained.

"Where in Sherman Falls do you live," he asked?

I gave him the coordinates and he stopped for a moment and then started throwing a bunch of names my way to see if I knew any. Sherman Falls is a small town and between School, baseball, hockey, and church, I think I knew three-quarters of them. He then told me, "Usually I would have my secretary Betty work with you on this, but I think I would like to get my hands into the mix and help out personally on this endeavor of yours if that is all right with you?"

I looked as old as I could and said to him, "If you need me to come down here and help you set up the printing presses or cut stock, just say the word and I will be here."

He let out a good laugh and said, "Wouldn't surprise me one bit. But I will go one better, if you're looking for a summer job, I think I could find a job for you here." Well, I think Mr. Simpkins and I are going to do a lot of business together!

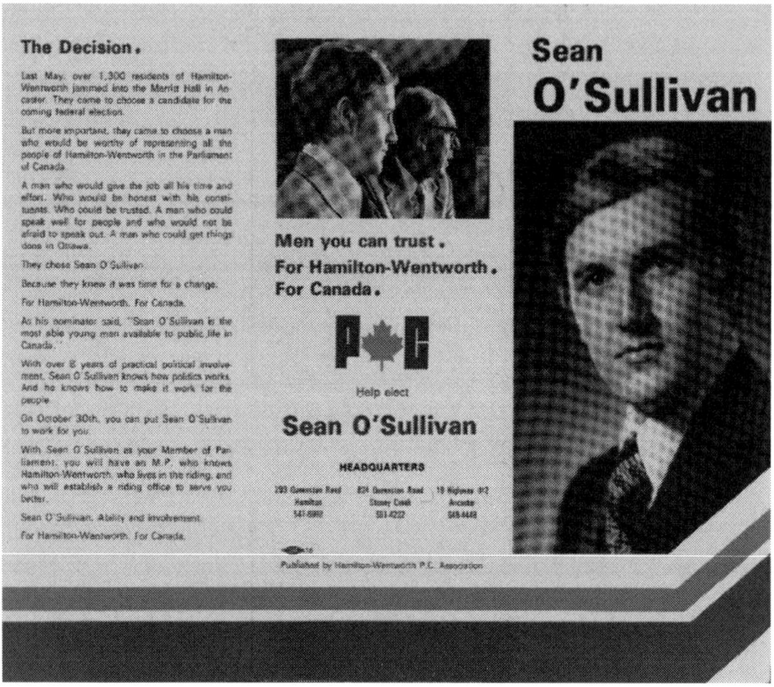

Sean Patrick Paul O'Sullivan
(January 1, 1952 – March 9, 1989)
Father (Pun Intended) and all around great guy!
☹

Task 4 – Reduce the Workload!

(November 21st – December 15th, 1973)

30 ***Focus man. Just focus!:*** I will admit today that I have in the past been accused of taking on too many things, and you Rebecca have often accused me of this as well. Taking on more than I could manage effectively is more accurate. I pride myself on my ability to multi-task and with the many new freedoms, I can have as a 12-year-old, going on 13, was proving a bit problematic. A normal kid my age was going to school, coming home, and playing with the neighborhood kids. Maybe do some homework, catch a TV show, rinse and repeat! But that is not what a 63 soon-to-be 64-year-old Thirteen-year-old does. With my time issue, I have already replaced my cardio with a run from school to home alternative and with the additional papers, my delivery requirement has added another hour to my chores. My hockey workouts are now reduced to 3 days a week and with my on-ice hockey season now underway, we are gone by six o'clock with either a practice or game most nights. The only good news is all the work I have been doing so far, my game is noticeably better not to mention my overall puck sense on the ice.

Sean won the election, and that time investment was over, but the 'Kids 4 a Cancer Cure' took over that time slot and then some. This weekend Sean was holding a riding volunteer thank you dinner and he insisted I be there. I had an afternoon game and would need to head straight home to shower and get ready, Dad and mom were invited. I had a science project that I needed to put a few hours into, and it was not something I could throw together at the last minute and get a 90. Added to all this, I was also trying my best to maintain some form of social life. Seems the new Derek 2.0 was in demand for a number of my fellow student's home parties. I was even getting a few grade 8 invites.

I knew how important the 'Kids 4 a Cancer Cure' fundraiser was, not only to everyone I convinced to help out with it, but also to my 'Bigger Plan', 'The Student Mentoring Initiative'. I have been back now, for less than 5 months and have already done what I wanted to avoid, overextend myself. It was not a physical issue, I had plenty of stamina, it was a social issue. Yes, I was becoming popular and part of me was enjoying it. Maybe not physically, but it was nice to walk through the halls and see so many people interacting with each other in a good way. I think me and 'My Boy's' *(Smiled)*, had all but eliminated hallway bullying. Even the teachers seemed to have a better attitude this time around. Mom and dad had certainly adjusted to the improved me in a great way and even my sister was starting to show signs of change. Who says a positive attitude can't be contagious? Ann had started to jog around the block, and I think she has used some of my homemade workout equipment now and then.

Anyway, Rebecca, I decided to hold off on adding any more tasks for a while, until I get myself a more even-keeled life schedule. I was comfortable completing all my promised contributions for 'Kids 4 a Cancer Cure'. Christmas was not that far away and that always meant a bunch of hockey tournaments. And yes, the Silver Stick revenge match. My first 'Listed' major task was to get a job at Flamboro, followed by Gibson's Pond in June 1977, and then trying to save the King's life on August 16th, 1977. I loved Elvis and wanted to see if I could do something. That gave me another year and a bit to Flamboro, four till Tonka, and four and a half years to Elvis. And most importantly, when would I first look at you?

Unfortunately, there may be bigger time gaps in this section, but I will try to put anything I think would be of interest to you in here even though they are not tasks. I will use the heading Update until I have an actual task to report on.

[Met with Blane and the Spec team helping with the 'Kids 4 a Cancer Cure'. Turned out Mr. Simpkins knows the Editor and chief of the Spec and my little strategic plan to access the carrier list was turning into a major media event. I was thankful I could shift the attention from Blane who did squat, over to Mr. Simpkins who was now Co-chair along with Peter Gordon the president of Stelco; who also knew Simpkins from the golf club and apparently after a few Scotches one night asked to be a part of the effort. The Spec was going to run a full-page article next week announcing the charity and you can't have a huge city-wide event for such a noble cause without a grand ball! Complete with a silent auction, band, and the token kid that came up with the whole idea, yours truly. This was a problem. The last thing I needed was to have that kind of attention on me. I am sure Mom and Dad would be super proud, but I needed to get out of this situation. So, I did what any almost 13-year-old would do, I called Sean to see if he was going to be around the area anytime soon. I had his direct line in Ottawa!

Sean said he would be home in two weeks, but that was too long to wait, so I told Sean I would come to Ottawa to see him. When I told my parents, Sean asked if I could come to Ottawa for a special dinner gathering, and they bought it considering my contribution to his campaign.

The only issue was that Dad could not take me due to his band commitments and Mom would never drive beyond our hometown. I tried to convince them that I could do the trip on my own, but unfortunately for them, I was still 12, and not 63. I phoned Sean's office in Ottawa and left a message that I was not going to make it but would most likely see him over Christmas. Plan 'B'! 'The Trevor Simpkins Annual Dinner, honoring 'Kids 4 a Cancer Cure' Charity. I called Mr. Simpkins and arranged to meet at his office after school on Thursday. I got home from School, did my paper route, and grabbed the bus downtown.

Mr. Simpkins and I were more like a father-son now and he always greeted me with a hand on the shoulder and his new favorite line, "How's my budding entrepreneur doing?", with the requisite smile. I was certainly flattered but deep inside I knew if I told him I was a 63-year man in the body of a soon to be 13 year old, he would have thrown me out his window. We sat at his small boardroom-style table, and he asked if I wanted a pop. I told him no thanks and then got right to my request. I could tell that the whole idea of wrapping my brainchild around his late son was stirring some emotions in him. I did my best to make the pitch sound as compelling as possible, but he was not yet on board with the plan I could tell.

He turned to give me a serious eye-to-eye contact and surprised me when he said. "It's a very nice gesture Derek, and may I go even further and say how much it would mean to our entire family, but Derek, this is your baby. You came up with the idea, you put all the pieces together, manipulated a few people along in an impressive way and now you want to simply hand it to our family?"

I paused and gave him a big smile. I continued to smile and then replied with, "Mr. Simpkins, I am almost Thirteen. Do you remember when you were Thirteen? Yes, you're correct on almost everything, but you are not taking anything from me, you would be giving me a great gift. You would be helping me keep my thirteen-year-old life. If they make me the poster kid for this, I can kiss that all goodbye. What we have built is not a one-off, it's going to be annual, will grow even bigger and every year I will get put on display. Do you have any idea what that would do to my social life? All I want to do, is be a kid, play hockey, experience school, hopefully, meet girls, and live an 'out of the spotlight' type of life. So, I am not asking you to take anything, I am asking you for your help. And I can't imagine a better symbol for this wonderful cause we built than your son."

I knew I hit a nerve and I was pretty sure he did not have a Rebecca valve. He got up and walked slowly over to the window. He stared out a while, I think he was collecting himself. I just sat there and gave him the dignity he deserved. After about 3 minutes, he turned and said something that made me feel good, “You and Trevor would have been such great friends. I will want to discuss it with Mrs. Simpkins before I commit, but I am pretty sure we would be honored with your request.”

The mood in the room was a bit heavy and as usual, when I get myself in that position, I had to come up with an ice breaker of some sort, so I replied, “Trevor and I may have become great friends, but he would never get around me on the ice.” I got up and walked over hoping to give Mr. Simpkins a handshake, but this time and the only time, he hugged me, complete with the old guy pat on the back. Not a long hug, just the right amount of time to signify our soon-to-be lifelong friendship was official.

I hopped on the bus and headed home. Mission accomplished; I hope!]

Hamilton Place -Site of the Gala!

Update – Showdown in Simcoe!

(December 15th – December 30th, 1973)

31 ***The 'Greatest' meets 2.0!:*** Yes, it's my birthday on the 9th, and my folks will want to have a party of some sort, but to be honest, I would prefer just to have some Chinese food from Lee's and hang with the family. Christmas was great, and Gramps and Ian had made the trip for our usual Christmas family turkey dinner. New Year's was always Dad's band playing at the Boat Club, and mom and I ordered Lee's Chinese food. It was a tradition, and I wanted to keep it that way. I knew in a few years; I would swap that tradition for the new habit of chasing girls. I was busy with the Charity stuff, and hockey took up a lot of time. But I am sure you're curious how the 'Battle in Simcoe' went? Regarding personal satisfaction, some may think the 'Kids 4 a Cancer Cure' Charity event and the anticipated over a million dollars raised will be the big item; wrong! It was my revenge match.

You see, Rebecca, I knew already that I would most likely never reach the skill level to make the NHL. I would have needed to get my friends to graft a pair of Crosby clone legs onto me. Maybe a farm team, but you need a natural ability, and I do not believe I have it. Luke has it but I don't. I was born with what Kinesiologist calls slow-twitch muscle. Old Ben Johnson, however, was the epitome of fast-twitch. I was big for my age and had a wicked slapshot. But the closest I would come to the show was going to be Simcoe. The great one would never know it, but it didn't matter. I would. I had spoken to coach Rick at practice before the Tournament weekend and asked if he would match me up with 'The Great One,' junior addition that is. He surprisingly agreed, and it would be Mono a mano. I was both super excited while also a bit nervous. I had been building up this rematch for years in my brain, and now it was going to happen. Funny how one event when I was 12 could etch itself into my psyche and fester for 50-plus years. I was always super proud of Wayne's accomplishments, but this was different.

The drive down to Simcoe was exciting for my dad, and he wanted us to go early so he could show us the old farm and some other local landmarks that had some significance to him. We did the exact same thing about three years ago when I was playing novice. We got to Simcoe about 2 hours before game time, and that was enough time to do the site seeing and get me there at least 45 minutes before we would take the ice. Dad and mom did not realize any of what I had done or was about to do today. As far as they were concerned, it was just another game. They enjoyed the whole hockey parent experience and had their usual fellow parents they would sit with. I went to the assigned dressing room and entered the room. Coach Rick was already in the room along with his son Jeff who was already putting his socks on.

Coach Rick knew it was me without even looking and said, "Your guy scored eight goals yesterday against the best team in the tournament."

While some may have taken the info and started to sweat, I had worked far too hard and had traveled across time to get scared now. I simply said, "Game on," and took the bench by the shower.

I was aware that I did not officially get into the 'real men' club since not inviting Sarah to Gramp's. But this afternoon, win or lose, I was going to take a shower after the game. I brought a towel and a bottle of shampoo. After today's game, I would enter the 'real men' category the only other way. The dressing room was unusually quiet, and it was not how I wanted my fellow warriors to prepare for battle. So, as all team captains would do when faced with the biggest game of all time, I pulled out my dad's cassette player, which had really great sound (and fresh batteries). I pulled a garbage pail to the center of the room, flipped it upside down, placed the cassette player on top, and told the Coaches I needed a few minutes with the guys in private. Normally you would think the coach would tell me to go, and you know what myself *(In a non-swearing way, of course)*, but today, they surveyed what I was setting up, smiled at each other, and said, "10 minutes!"

By this time, everybody had stopped getting dressed and sat to see what I would do next. This was genuinely uncharted territory even for me. I put a previously pre-planned tape in and hit the play button, making sure I rotated the volume wheel to full power, baby! And the magic started. I had selected the motivational song to prepare for battle, Marvin Gays' 'Let's get it on'. I ignored everyone, and they just sat there trying to figure out what the hell was happening. As the music started, I entered into my groove phase and did my coolest dance back to my bench area. With the music blaring, I began to get dressed and mouthing the words to the song. Everyone sat speechless for the first 30 seconds, and then slowly, one by one, everyone started to get dressed to the song's beat. Head bobbing, guys pretending to mouth the words, never knowing the actual lyrics, I was sure. It was a truly spiritual moment.

When the song ended after 4:56 seconds, we continued to get dressed in silence, absorbing what we had just done as a team. After about a minute, I stood up and said to the guys, "Win or lose today, guys; I want you all to know that I will be leaving everything on the ice today. When I come back to this room, I will hold my head high and know today was the day I gave it my all."

We, as a team, never chatted about that moment. And it's been a few practices and a few games since the Tournament, and we all have decided it was such a 'one of a kind' special day that it deserved to be placed into our memories and never spoken about again for a while. The Ricks came back into the room and knew what was played due to the volume level. They quickly scanned the room and figured out we were now in the zone. They quietly walked around the room, giving each guy a gentle slap on the side of their shoulder pads, and said, "Get it on."

It was customary for Coach Rick to give us a pep talk the last 5 minutes before the Zamboni left the ice. Today was exceptional, we all knew it, and the two Ricks grabbed their clipboards and said, "2 minutes," and exited the room. I had lived a full life, Rebecca, but after the door closed, the entire team sat there, fully dressed, helmets on, and just went around the room making eye contact and giving the nod. When the nods had finished, I got up and went to each guy and hit their shin pad with my stick. First me, then my assistant captain, Daryl Eastwood. Then my other assistant Captain, Mike Hempworth. Then from my left, going counterclockwise, each guy got up and continued the ritual ending with Glen, the goalie getting up and following the entire team to the ice. We all lined up for the first time without pre-planning, making a gauntlet for Glen to skate through. Each of us gave Glen a tap on the pads as he passed with a nod. The parents in the stands just stood there in shock, trying to figure out what was happening. Brantford was already doing their warmup, and all stopped to check what we were doing. As soon as Glenn reached the end, we all broke apart and did our pre-game warmup.

I know Rebecca that all this is probably meaningless to you, but to me, it was a moment in my life, ok, second life, that truly moved me. And I had no one to share it with at the time other than with you here and now. I know the guys will undoubtedly retell this day over their lives because it was that extraordinary; how could you not. After the warmup, the game began. Wayne was out first and had his customary position on the left-wing. As promised, Coach Rick had me out as well. When the puck dropped, we managed to get control and took it into Brantford's end. I was on the right defence and awaited my first contact. We managed a weak shot on goal, and after the rebound, their defenceman, as practiced, passed the puck up to Wayne. Wayne took the pass just past the board side hash mark and turned to begin his skate up the left side (My right skating backwards). Last time he was able to blow by me just after the red line and then curl in and take a shot on Glenn.

Today, however, was much different. I was skating backwards and was already at my full speed, which eliminated Wayne from blowing past me. Wayne quickly surmised that approach would not work and quickly changed his game plan and made a sudden turn left (his right), to try to get me to keep skating back towards the goal, which would give him a laneway to launch a screenshot at Glenn. Sorry, buddy, too many tree climbs, chair jumps, and wrist strengthening. As Wayne moved laterally, I immediately adjusted my direction left and maintained the perfect distance to prevent him from loading up for a shot. I saw my new agility and movement momentarily caught Wayne off guard, and for a split second, he did not notice my stick was swinging across the ice and would shortly knock the puck off his stick into the left boards where we were about to pick it up. That was the theme for the first period. No matter what he tried, I had a counter, and the result was no goal for Wayne in the first period. The good news for us, Hemper got our only goal on a misdirected snapshot.

When I returned to the bench after the first shift, Coach Rick came over to me and did something he had never done before. He bent down and said in my ear, "You own him." Those were our only words for the rest of the game. By the second period, the Brantford coach, Mr. St. Armand, knew our strategy and decided to try and throw at us a counter-strategy. It turned out that the counter strategy was to get me out of the game. Their first effort was their largest player, a right-winger who tried to take a number of runs at me. The last effort did not go that well for them. I had followed Wayne into the corner and had pinned him against the boards with the puck in his skate. Suddenly out of my peripheral, I caught old number 12 lining me up for a good hit into the boards. At the last second, I shifted my position just enough to allow my unsuccessful combatant to miss me and hit Wayne. Wayne and my assassin both fell to the ice. Wayne appeared fine, but their bruiser was hurt badly. I think when he realized what was about to happen at the very last moment, he shifted his weight away from Wayne and ended up hitting the boards with his back.

The assistant coach came out and tended to Wayne's first Semenko or McSorley type. I skated back to the bench and waited to see if Wayne would stay out or head to the bench. He went to the bench, which allowed me to do the same. While Wayne and I continued our chess match, Brantford managed to get a goal, and the game was tied 1-1. With One minute left in the second, we got our second goal of the night. Compared to the last time, 2-1 was looking pretty impressive. We got a flood between the 2nd and 3rd periods, so we all returned to the dressing room. The Ricks came into the room and gave us a short assessment report, and then Rick looked at me and said, “They're all yours.” As they exited the room, everyone waited to see what I would do. I grabbed the cassette deck and flipped the tape over. I again put the player on top of the garbage can that had not yet moved and hit play. The song started, and after the intro, I started singing along;

I never knew how complete love could be
'Till she kissed me and said, baby
Please, go all the way……..

I was enjoying that moment so much I didn’t care what anyone thought of my singing or song choice. But when I got to the main chorus and started selecting individual guys to sing to from my seat, complete with finger-pointing; I could tell they knew this was a once-in-a-lifetime moment. With everyone bobbing their heads to the music and a few playing imaginary drums using the bench, and the odd air guitar, I was sure the Ricks were right outside the door with their ear pressed up to see what I would do.

When the song ended, I walked over to the cassette player and grabbed it to put back in my hockey bag. As I sat back down, the room was silent. After about a minute, Hemper said, ‘Hey Cap, I am going to give it my all.” Then, Easty did the same, “Hey Cap, I am going to give it my all.” One by one and not in any order, everyone gave me a shout-out. And just like it would be written in a movie, after the last guy finished their shout-out, Coach opened the door and said, “Game on”!

I wanted this game to have a happy ending, Rebecca, but it would not happen today. At the 12-minute mark, Wayne’s centreman took a run at me, and when I shifted to avoid the collision, I bumped into Wayne; he hit the ice and rolled around. The ref’s arm went up, and I just got a 2 min interference call. It only took Wayne about 45 seconds to get the tying goal. After that, not only would I need to continue to shut Wayne down, but I would also have to avoid at all costs any penalty.

Around the 5-minute remaining mark, another player charged at me in front of our net and proceeded to drop his gloves and put his hands up for a fight. Back when I played, we didn’t have Swedish masks covering our whole faces that always irked Don Cherry, and the metal cages were still a few years away. No, in 1973, it was pure face! Ok, we did have a mouth guard. Hemper was on the ice and quickly knew the move and threw himself between the other guy and me and took on the role of my Semenko. Both guys got thrown out of the game, and each team had a 5-minute major for fighting and a 10-minute misconduct. We would be finishing the game 4 on4. Our hockey had not yet started using off-set penalties.

Wayne stayed out, so I did too. The puck was dropped in our end, and fortunately, we got control. Our best four players were on the ice, and I assumed their best four were on the ice. We battled for the first 3 minutes, and then Wayne went off. I jumped off for a break, and about 15 seconds later, they scored a goal from the slot. We pulled Glenn for the rest of the period and fortunately did not allow an empty netter. Wayne stayed off the last minute, so I sat as well. It was bittersweet, Rebecca. I was so proud of everyone, and I think the parents just watched one hell of a game. Maybe even the game of the Tournament. With the loss, we would not play them again and would be playing in the consolation round. We lined up for the handshake, and as was the protocol, I was first, and our goalie was last. I skated up to their team, and Wayne was not first. It was the winger who tried to run me earlier. When we reached each other, I looked at him and said, "Good luck with the Championship game." He returned a nod and was on to the next guy. Wayne was third to last, and when we met, I looked at him, and he said, "Good game," with a grin. I replied, "See you in '88." He gave me an odd look, then turned and continued the handshake ritual. Brantford went on to win the Tournament again and Wayne was MVP again!

I was first in the room and sat down. I was spent, as was everyone. Glenn was taking it badly and looked like he was going to cry. The Ricks came in along with our manager Brad. Everyone took off their helmet and gloves and sat in place to see what Rick would say. But I could not resist taking the lead and said, "I was never prouder of you guys. Glenn was a rock, and every one of their goals was pure luck. Hemper, thanks for watching my back. Everyone did what they said and left it all on the ice. Winning would have been nice, but before you get yourself down from the loss, just think, they are the best team in the Tournament. Every team they have played has lost by at least six goals. They barely beat us 3-2. I want you guys to know that I will remember this game, on this day, with this team, for the rest of my life." I took my seat, and the room was utterly silent. Coach Rick stared at me and didn't say a word for a while. Then he walked into the center of the room and said, "Coaches don't say this much, but today you did something no team has done to Brantford for a long time. Limit them to 3 goals. We play the consolation game in 2 hours so get a bite to eat and be back here 30 minutes before the game."

We won the consolation game 9-2, Hemper had a hat trick, and I bagged 1 goal and three assists. As I came out of the dressing room, I had my bag on my shoulder and went to the area the parents were. I put the bag down against the entranceway wall and went to find mom and dad. As I was looking around, I felt a hand grip my shoulder. I turned to see who it was. It only took me a second to realize who it was. As I smiled at him, he smiled back and said, "good game, son, you did something not too many players could do." At that moment, Rebecca, I suddenly felt this inner peace come over me. Vindication of sorts. I replied, "Thank you for those kind words, Mr. Gretzky, but your son is truly a one-of-a-kind and will one day be called the Greatest One!"

Derek 1.0 had met Walter often over the years at various hockey events in the area, and I remember the last time I saw him at the Gretzky Center in Brantford at a kid's hockey tournament; was the fall of 2020, I think. A buddy of mine's kid was playing. I always wondered if Mr. and Mrs. Gretzky would have preferred to see Wayne be a Leaf, at least for a while. Toronto was more our hometown than Los Angeles. I knew Wayne was a huge Gordie Howe fan, and they had become good friends. I was sure Detroit would feel like Wayne was stepping on his hero's toes, but it just always seemed to be a bummer he went South. Back then, that was! This time, he would make history here and with my bud Luke at center.

We got a chance to chat a bit at that Tournament, and it was a very sad day a year or so later; the day that we lost the 'Greatest (One's) Father'.

Some of the Greatest Ones Records

MOST GOALS: 894 (1,485 games)

MOST GOALS, INCLUDING PLAYOFFS: 1,016 -- 894 regular season and 122 playoff

MOST GOALS, ONE SEASON: 92 – 1981-82, 80-game schedule

MOST GOALS, ONE SEASON, INCLUDING PLAYOFFS: 100 – 1983-84, 87 goals in 74 regular season games and 13 goals in 19 playoff games.

MOST GOALS, 50 GAMES FROM START OF SEASON: 61 – 1981-82 (Oct. 7, 1981 to Jan. 22, 1982, 80-game schedule); 1983-84 (Oct. 5, 1983 to Jan. 25,1984, 80-game schedule

MOST GOALS, ONE PERIOD: 4 – (Tied with 10 other players) Feb. 18, 1981, at Edmonton, third period (Edmonton 9, St. Louis 2)

MOST ASSISTS: 1,962 (1,485 games)

MOST ASSISTS, INCLUDING PLAYOFFS: 2,222 – 1,962 regular season and 260 playoff

MOST ASSISTS, ONE SEASON: 163 – 1985-86, 80-game schedule

MOST ASSISTS, ONE SEASON, INCLUDING PLAYOFFS: 174 – 1985-86, 163 assists in 80 regular season games and 11 assists in 10 playoff games

MOST ASSISTS, ONE GAME: 7 – (tied with Billy Taylor) done three times – Feb. 15, 1980 at Edmonton (Edmonton 8, Washington 2); Dec. 11, 1985 at Chicago (Edmonton 12, Chicago 9); Feb. 14, 1986 at Edmonton (Edmonton 8, Quebec 2)

MOST ASSISTS, ONE ROAD GAME: 7 (tied with Billy Taylor) – Dec. 11, 1985 at Chicago (Edmonton 12, Chicago 9)

MOST POINTS: 2,856 –1,485 games (894 goals, 1,962 assists)

MOST POINTS, INCLUDING PLAYOFFS: 3,238 – 2,856 regular season and 382 playoff

MOST POINTS, ONE SEASON: 215 – 1985-86, 80-game schedule

MOST POINTS, ONE SEASON, INCLUDING PLAYOFFS: 255 – 1984-85; 208 points in 80 regular season games and 47 points in 18 playoff games

Walter, Wayne and Phyllis

Task 5 – The Grand Ball Part I

(January 1st – February 15th, 1974)

32 ***Finishing What you Start!:*** As far as my usual technique of the self-pat-on-the-back goes, 'Kids 4 a Cancer Cure' Charity was formulated to provide two essential tools for my tool belt. First, Networking. Second, a copy of the Spec's carrier list. When I first formulated the plan, I did not plan for it to be this successful. With all of Hamilton's elite business people planning to attend the Gala, there was no shortage of press and publicity. The who's who of Hamilton would be there, and I just got a call from Betty, Mr. Simpkins's secretary informing me that Premier Bill Davis was planning on attending. I am assuming that may be more related to Sean than anyone else.

The big day was set for Saturday, January 26th, and the location was moved from the Stelco banquet facility to the newly built flagship of Hamilton's cultural elite, Hamilton Place. I was now 13 but looked closer to 15 people were telling my parents. Dad was struggling with the decision to miss his own gig on that Saturday by coming to this event. Mom certainly wanted to go and gawk, I am sure. Parents have a keen eye for what their kids are up to, and mine were no different. They watched how much time I put into it, and I guess more than once over dinner had been my sounding board. Eventually, Dad decided to attend, especially when he found out that his boss's-boss would be attending.

Believe it or not, Rebecca, I was still basking in the glow from the Simcoe showdown. I got the usual family gifts for my birthday, but I did not expect the dozen or so additional gifts I received from my new key network contacts. The Simpkins, Sean, Coach Rick, even Blane. All tasteful with some business-type theme. The best was an electronic pocket organizer from Mr. Simpkins. The last thing I needed was a suit and tie for the big night. I fully expected this would turn into a match with mom and dad. They had their vision of how I should look, but I had mine. In anticipation of this eventuality, I, being of some 63 years in mental age, took it upon myself to hire a tailor to make me a suit. I knew exactly what I wanted; it would not be a 1974 look. Mr. Mattson had a tailor who also was a client, and I asked Mr. Mattson if he would introduce me to him. Luke and I tried to spend as much time as possible hanging out, but all my plans had cut into that. We did get our first hike down to the conservation area after a big snow storm the second week of December, but I was sure I was a dozen trips behind Derek 1.0.

Mr. Mattson arranged to drive Luke and me to see Angelo, his tailor, on Saturday after our hike. It was close to Christmas, so I was expecting Angelo the Tailor would not get to my suit until the new year. I was expecting to use my own cash to pay for the suit. It was the cost of taking mom and dad out of the process. When Mr. Mattson introduced me to Angelo, he told him I needed the suit for the 'Kids 4 a Cancer Cure' Charity gala. Mr. Angelo, as I now like to call him, asked me, "What are you doing going to the Gala?, you're just a boy".

Let's just say that Mr. Angelo was old-school Italian and did not hold back any of his thoughts. He had this seamstress tape measure around his neck, a white shirt and tie, 1940s fat pinstripe pants, and a vest. I was already at least 3 inches taller than him. But before I could answer, Mr. Mattson responded for me.

"Ang, you will be making a suit for the kid who came up with the whole 'Kids 4 a Cancer Cure' idea. He's a paperboy himself and thought, why not unite all the paperboys and raise money to fight cancer."

It seems my little secret was not as stealthy as I thought. I appreciated the support from Mr. Mattson, but I did not go there expecting a freebie from Mr. Angelo. Mr. Angelo grabbed my arm, led me to a wooden box, and told me to take off my coat and shoes and stand on the box. I followed his instructions, and Luke and Mr. Mattson walked behind us. I had, only as young Derek 1.0, ever had off-the-rack suits from Eaton's or Woolworths. Derek 2.0, however, was very familiar with a tailored suit and proceeded to speak tailor speak with Mr. Angelo. He was very impressed with my knowledge of suit design and the specific terms associated, such as a 'panel.'

I had three mirrors in front and could see Luke and Joe, who were now seated in a couple of chairs watching our banter. My idea for a suit would be a 1950's Bobby Riddel style. I also planned to wear the same suit at my grade 8 graduation. I told Mr. Angelo this and asked that he leave some extra material in the right spots in case I needed to have a bit of letting out with my potential growth factor. I knew everyone else at the Gala would wear the most current suit look, and I wanted to ensure I stood out. When we got to chatting about the suit jacket, Mr. Angelo felt it was necessary to give some push back. I wanted a very short jacket, almost like a matador would wear, and he didn't like that approach. We eventually agreed on a compromise, and I negotiated a 1-inch round collar at the top instead of the lapel look.

When it looked like I was done with the measurement and design chat, I asked Mr. Angelo how much it would cost. By this time, my net worth with the added paper route was close to $750. I was hoping it wouldn't be more than $350. Mr. Angelo put his hand on my arm and gave me a squeeze. He said, "My niece's little girl has cancer. This suit is on the house as my contribution to what you are doing."

"Mr. Angelo, I have a 96 paper, paper route and can afford to pay for this suit," I replied.

"Nonsense, young man, your money is no good here," he said with a big smile.

I knew the Italian way intimately and would not insult him by arguing. I would just happen to be in the neighborhood a few times in the future and drop him off an excellent block of cheese or a bottle of rare extra virgin olive oil. We finished up, and Mr. Angelo handed me a card with a date and time for my follow-up fitting on the first weekend of January following New Year's. I shook Mr. Angelos' hand firmly and thanked him for his generosity. When we got to the car, I asked Mr. Mattson if I could treat him and Luke to a Harvey's hamburger on the way home. I loved their salt-saturated burgers. We drove to Harvey's, went in, and the man behind the counter said, "Hi, Joe'.

It seems he was a client of Mr. Mattson too. This time I insisted on paying. We returned to the Mattson's,' and the snow was starting to come down. They had forecasted 12 inches overnight, and I knew I would be needed to shovel the snow at Gram's senior complex. I asked Luke if he was interested in helping and could make a few bucks. He was all over the offer, and that was the first of many snow-shoveling jobs we would do together. I made a point to thank Mr. Mattson and wished I had extra tickets for him and Mrs. Mattson to attend, but I had already given them to my strategic targets for the night. It was sold out, and good luck finding a ticket. I had asked my sister if she wanted to attend but knew what her answer would be before asking.

I rode my bike home through about an inch of snow and parked it in my spot at the back of the garage. I went in and could smell mom's cooking. I dare not mention to her that I just ate a Harvey's burger with fries. Tonight, was liver! Mom knew my sister and I hated liver and usually made us some fish sticks in the oven. I went into the kitchen and said, "What smells so good?", with an added smile.

"You know darn well what we are having," mom said with a little attitude in her voice.

"I know I have not been a fan of liver in the past, but if you have enough, I would like to try some tonight," I said.

"I think I may have just enough, but I don't want to go and waste it on you wanting to try it. If I cook it, you have to eat it," she challenged.

"Deal I said," with confidence. "Maybe you will even let me cook it for myself?", I asked with a definite leading question.

"I don't care who cooks it, but you must eat it, or your father will have a word or two for you," mom warned.

I have been slow to bring my family into the health zone with all my distractions. I wanted to add liver to my diet, just not cooked until it was converted to shoe leather. I grabbed the liver package, took out a piece, and put it on a plate on the counter. I went to our spice shelf and grabbed a few spices I knew would help add some more flavor to the meat or organ. I could tell that mom had one of her secret mother's eyes checking me out. She was almost done with the stovetop and placed the cooked liver on a plate in the oven to keep warm. The other element on the back of the stove housed a pot with green beans. I grabbed the frying pan and took it to the sink for a quick wash. I brought it back, and mom was now setting the table, but her secret eye was still watching me. I did my number on the liver and poured some oil in the pan and a generous butter dollop. When the pan was hot enough to show signs of smoke and the butter was now brown, I placed my liver in the pan. It sizzled immediately, and I knew my mom was dying to tell me I would burn it. Instead, she walked over to the kitchen window and cracked it open an inch.

After no more than 2-3 minutes a side, I turned off the element and slid the pan to the cool part of the stove. I grabbed a pot lid, covered my liver to keep it warm and let it rest. Dad must have smelled the liver and suddenly appeared at the top of the basement steps. As he entered the kitchen level, he said, "sure smells good, honey."

I replied before mom, not to miss a chance at a bit of kibitzing, "Thanks, Daddy."

Dad passed me standing at the stove and gave me a fake shot to the gut. Mom had a kitchen spoon in her hand and decided to join the fun and gave me a reasonably hard whack on the upper arm and said, "Your father was talking to me."

Well, since mom wanted to join the exchange, I figured she was fair game and replied, "I think he was smelling my liver, mom," with a bit of a smug attitude. Mom countered with her only move left, another whack on the upper arm and the devious grin she showed every now and then.

We all sat at the table after taking the food out of the oven. Mom warned us the dishes might be hot. My sister wandered in and surveyed the table and knew it was fish sticks tonight. As I took the frying pan and transferred the liver to my plate, she gave me her 'What the 'F' are you doing' look, although I am pretty sure we were a few years before her foul language period started. We loaded up our plates and began to eat. Mom and dad had one eye on me to see my reaction. I cut a corner of my liver and put it in my mouth. Not a bad job, I do say so myself, I thought. Dad took a look at my liver and then down at his. He then asked mom, "Why is Derek's liver different?"

Mom, feeling slightly offended, said, "Your chef son wanted to cook his own liver tonight."

Dad put another piece of liver in his mouth and began the ordeal of the chew. Well done, the liver needed a fair amount of teeth work. Mine, on the other hand, was moist and tender. After a couple more bites, dad asked if he could try a piece of my liver. Looking at him, I said. "I don't know, dad; I have my own secret blend of 11 herbs and spices."

"Very funny," he said as he reached over and cut off a fairly large portion for just a bite. We all kind of stopped our eating to catch my dad's look. Mom especially. Dad cut a bite from the piece he stole and put it in his mouth while his expression said, 'Wow, best liver I ever tasted,' his voice said, "Not bad, but I prefer your mom's," with an added personal smile directed at mom. You know that I will be watching our next liver day closely to see what mom will do.

I decided to tell mom and dad that the committee had agreed, as a way of saying thank you, to pay for a new suit for the Gala. Mom was first to speak up and said, "That was very nice of them. Do you need me to go with you to Eaton's?", she asked.

I replied, "No, they want me to use a shop downtown. Probably have some deal with them worked out."

"Let us know if we can help," mom finished with.

The meal was completed, and Ann and I started the clean-up as agreed to after a few major insult sessions. We worked out a deal to do the clean-up every other day. Mom and dad liked the arrangement; to be honest; I was still trying to figure out a move to get a better relationship with my sister. Ann always bolted as soon as the dishwasher was loaded, and I remained to do the detail work.

The following day, Luke and I did the snow removal stuff, walked over to Mrs. Finley's place, and shoveled her drive. She was a paper customer and, in her early 80s, lived in the house she had bought new with her late husband. I always tried to help her out whenever the opportunity was presented. As we shoveled, she came to the front window and waved. Once we were done, she would open the front door and yell for us to come and get a couple cookies. She had a little bag with about half a dozen cookies. I always told her it was not necessary, but I was sure our accepting them meant more to her. With shovel on the shoulder, we headed back to my place to hang for a bit.

I bused to Mr. Angelo's for my fitting, stopped by this cheese shop on Barton not far from his shop, and bought a nice piece of Parmigiano-Reggiano for $5. I went in the front, and Mr. Angelo was tending to another older gentleman on the wooden box. He spotted me and said, "Grab a seat, young-fella, I won't be long." As soon as my butt hit the chair, I heard Mr. Angelo tell his customer, "Vinny, this is the kid who started the whole 'Kids 4 a Cancer Cure' event. And he's only thirteen."

I smiled in the direction of the mirror facing me. I slightly chuckled when I thought I was probably not far off Angelo's age. They started to discuss the Gala, and Angelo was talking about his niece, and I just sat there quietly with the cheese on my lap. The gentleman customer got off the box and sat beside me to put his shoes on. When he had the shoehorn in his last shoe, he turned and said, "You like fish?"

"Yes, I love fish, especially jumbo shrimp," I answered.

He reached into his pocket, pulled out a business card, and handed it to me. I read the card, and it said, 'Agro's Fish Market.' Mr. Agro was getting a suit.

He said, "When you're done here, come down a couple of blocks to our warehouse. I want to give you a little something."

"That is not necessary, Mr. Agro. I appreciate the offer, but I don't think it will keep on the bus ride home," I informed him.

"Nonsense, I will look after that issue for you. I expect to see you in 30 minutes," he said with a bit of a demand to his delivery.

"He'll be there, Vin; he's a good kid and would never insult such a generous offer," Mr. Angelo added.

I extended my hand and exchanged a firm handshake as Mr. Agro stood up. Mr. Angelo led him to the door, opened it, and his friend Vin patted him on the shoulder. Mr. Angelo returned and told me to take off my shoes. He ducked into his back shop and came out with a suit bag. He hung it on the stand and opened the bag. He took the pants out, told me to put them on, and pointed to a change room. I went to the change room and switched to the suit pants. I came out and walked over to the box and got up. I knew the legs needed to be hemmed and a slight take-in in the middle of my upper butt. The black material he selected was perfect. Mr. Angelo did the required tailoring white pen markings and a few pins and told me to put a shirt on that was on the chair beside us. I took the shirt, went back to the change room, and switched shirts. The shirt was the same color as the pants but had a different sheen. I tucked it in, came out, and walked back to the box.

I was busy admiring myself in my new digs when Mr. Angelo held the jacket up for me to put my arms through. I slipped it on, and I am sure he could see the excitement in my eyes. Mr. Angelo hit it out of the park. It was exactly what I had described. He told me to turn sideways, then the other way. He sauntered around the box and looked me up and down. Once he was back behind me, He said, "How does it fit?"

"Mr. Angelo, you are a magician. It fits perfectly, and the material is unbelievably soft and silky, but not silky. The shirt has the perfect contrast, and the collar is amazing," I told him with a constant nod.

He reached back in the suit bag and came out with two ties. He told me to hold the tie-up like I was wearing it and to turn and face him. He looked at the first one and gave a head nod from side to side. He handed me the second one, and I held it up to my neck. He looked, and a smile said it all.

I turned to look using the mirrors and immediately understood his reaction. Wow, I could not believe how cool and much older I looked. Mr. Angelo said, "What do you think now?"

I turned and smiled and said what I hope was the most flattering thing you could say to a tailor, "I think I have found my tailor for life." He gave a decisive nod and said, "Well, young fella, you are going to turn heads at the gala, and I am sure a few ladies will be checking you out."

I stepped off the box and went to the change room to switch from 007 back to a 13-year-old bus rider. And when I say 007, I mean Daniel Craig 007! When I came out, I handed Mr. Angelo the clothes, and he took them to his back shop. I walked over to the chair and grabbed the cheese. When Mr. Angelo came out, I presented my gift to him. He took a look and said, "That is not necessary."

I was starting to learn the Italian dance, and I replied. "I insist; you don't want to hurt my feelings now, do you?" I knew he liked the exchange and gave a nod and took the cheese into his back shop. I put on my coat just as he emerged from the drapes. He walked me to the door, and as he opened the door, he said, "Go two blocks that way, and on the opposite side of the street, you will see the sign 'Agro Wholesale'. Go around to the back and knock on the green metal door." With a quick pat on the shoulder, my new tailor for life and I parted.

I walked down the street and made my way to the back door. I knocked, and in 30 seconds, the door opened, and a young guy in his 20's said, "You must be here to see Mr. Agro?"

I gave the obligatory nod, and he said, "Follow me."

He led me through a warehouse area to the front of the store. Mr. Agro was sitting at a desk doing some work. He spotted me and came over to shake my hand. He then went behind the counter and pulled out a small Styrofoam box measuring about 8 inches by 8 inches and 6 inches high. He had fashioned a small plastic handle on the top and handed it over to me. When I took it from him, I realized it was pretty heavy.

"It has enough ice to get you home. If you want, one of my boys is heading up to your area in about half an hour. He can drop you near your house if you want to hang out here and wait." Some may think that was a very generous offer, but I first thought, 'how did he know where I lived?' The second thought I had was, 'why the whole friendly old Italian guy act?' Besides those questions, if my parents ever found out I took a ride in a van with some stranger, I am sure my freedom to venture anytime by bus would end. Rather than insult Mr. Agro, I would play on his sense of family.

"I appreciate the offer Mr. Agro, but it is my mom and dad's wedding anniversary next week, and I need to stop and get them something at Jackson Square," I said.

He smiled, nodded his head in acceptance of my excuse, walked from behind the counter, and extended his hand. As we shook hands, he said, "My wife is dying of cancer."

Now I knew. Gee, seems like everyone had some relationship with cancer. As we stopped shaking, I replied, "I am very sorry to hear that. My mother had breast cancer, and I know how difficult it must be." I turned and left through the front door and began my journey home. As I started to walk, I suddenly realized that I had just reverted to my old Derek 1.0 when I replied to Mr. Agro. Note to self; Think before you speak!

I arrived home, and mom and dad asked how the shopping went. I told them I met Mr. Angelo, and he needed to make a few alterations to my suit, but it would be ready next Wednesday. I handed the box of fish to dad and said, "A little treat for us tonight."

Dad looked at it and said, "Where did this come from?"

"The store where I got the suit was near a fish market, and I knew how much you loved fresh fish, so I went in, and the owner Mr. Agro, helped me pick out some stuff, and it only cost me $5," I fabricated.

Dad opened the box and looked inside. He took it over to the sink and drained the melted ice water off. He returned to the table with a plate and started taking the contents out. First, I saw a colossal jumbo shrimp. It had to be a 3-4 count. Then another, and another. When he was done, we had 12 2-4 count huge jumbo shrimp on the table. He stopped and said, "Five dollars?"

"Yes, but he was apparently a friend of the guy who owned the suit shop and maybe gave me a special discount," I countered. I was never proud of the deceit I needed to employ, but I did have some satisfaction at the speed I could think of a plausible story on the fly. Dad then pulled out a fillet. It was a thick white fillet of cod. My dad's favorite. He pulled out three more, and the box was empty. I knew dad and I would be feasting on this tonight while Mom and Ann would have to fend for themselves. They hated fish, although Ann would eat fish sticks.

Dad looked at me and said, "You selected the cod?"

"Of course, dad!" I smiled, knowing I had no idea what Mr. Agro had given me.

"That has to be $20 to $30 worth here," he added.

It was close to 3:30 pm, and I knew Saturday dinner was closer to 5:30 than the weekday 4:30 pm time slot. I told Dad, "Let me give it a shot tonight."

He knew I was referring to cooking the fish and immediately deferred to mom, "As long as it's ok with your mother."

I looked at mom, and I am sure she thought, 'I am done fighting with my son about cooking' and said, "Ok, but you clean up any mess."

I decided to cook the cod two ways: one deep-fried and one baked. I looked in the cupboard to assess the oil situation; unfortunately, we didn't even have a quarter cup left. So, I got my winter clothes on and headed to the store for a jug of oil. I was out the door before dad could hand me money. By the time he got to the front door, I was already gone. From our house, there was a shortcut, but it required me to traverse a large fence. The grocery store was at the end of a tree line that boarded a field on the other side of the fence. Using the shortcut, I was in the grocery store in 5 minutes. I went to the isle where the oils were and spotted a large can of beef lard. Wow! Bingo! Any Englishman knew the only way to make real fish'n chips was with beef lard.

I grabbed the tin along with a smaller vegetable oil. I walked to the second aisle and located a hot Horseradish jar. Finally, I went to the produce area and grabbed the smallest bag of russet potatoes. I went to the cashier and paid for everything, and being the great planner I was, I took the knapsack off my back and bagged my stuff. I left and was home in about 8 minutes. All total, I was gone for around 30 minutes. When I got home, the kitchen was empty, and I figured I would prep the taters and get them blanched. I threw together a cocktail sauce with the Horseradish and made a fish coating just like old Grampa Lewis used to (but that is another story). With all my prep done and pot and pan setup, I was ready to go. I figured it would take me 20 minutes from start to table. I had about a half-hour to kill, so I decided to head into the living room for a bit of piano playing to relax.

As I pulled the bench up to the piano, I stopped to figure out what I wanted to play. As I started to peruse my Greatest Playlist of all time mentally, I came to the song I needed to play. It was our song, Rebecca! Not our first dance song, but our song. I knew that the song would not be released until 1979, but I didn't care if it caused some uncomfortable questions from my dad. He was in the basement doing something, and 'chances are' *(Big eye roll),* he would not know that this Johnny Mathis and Denise Olivor song would not happen for another five-plus years.

As I began to play, I knew that with all the stuff going on in my life, I found myself thinking less and less about us. And that bothered me. I also was not big on having to sing both parts. My falsetto was not great as my voice was starting to show signs of changing. I played it, and it was nice to get a moment to just think about you. After our song, I figured I would take a risk and played Styx, 'Come Sail Away.' I was in the middle of the second verse when my dad came in and sat down and listened. I disregarded my plagiaristic thievery and belted it out, complete with a couple of voice-changing misses, but overall, it was good. Maybe not Derek and Al good, but good, nonetheless.

"I don't think I have heard that song before," dad said.

"Oh, just another up-and-coming band called Styx," I replied.

"I like it. Do you have the music for it?", dad asked.

Oh-oh! Dance time! "I am sure I have it somewhere. Let me look after dinner and see if I can find the book it was in," I replied, trying not to look nervous. As I got up, Dad took the bench and started playing the song. He has such a great ear; he can listen to a song and sit and play it almost exactly. I sat there and listened to him play the song. Eventually, since dad was not a singer, except for church choir, he started to add a few of his favorite runs into the song, and before you knew it, it did not sound the same. Kind of the same but enough that if he played it in public, I think he would be safe from any litigation *(I smiled)*.

Dad kept playing, and I retired to the kitchen and began the procedure. Mom came in after 10 minutes and pulled some stuff from the fridge for her and my sister. Everything was amazing, and I knew my mother and sister would want some of my fries. The first course had to be Shrimp Cocktail, and I cleverly arranged the shrimp around an old martini glass with the cocktail sauce in the middle. The shrimp were great as we stuffed them in our mouths. After dad had sampled the two different fish offerings, he said, "Your fish'n chips taste just like a real fish'n chip shop's."

"And the French fries are just like we get at Grampa Lewis's," mom added.

"And the baked Cod, dad?", I asked.

"Different, but in a good way. I don't think I have had baked cod before," he said.

"I hope you guys appreciate all the hours I have put in watching the Galloping Gourmet and let's not forget my Easy Bake oven training," I said with a chuckle.

Well, dinner was excellent, and generally, things in the Devon household were progressing in a rewarding direction. The big night was next week, and once that was behind me, hopefully, I could return to focusing on my other tasks.

Next week shot by, and it was now Saturday, and even this '63-year-old, Mr. Experience', was having some nervous butterflies. Mr. Mattson happened to be at Mr. Angelo's during the week and grabbed my suit, which I picked up yesterday. I knew the suit would be a hit, but what would really be the Pièce de resistance; would be a great pair of Black Italian leather wingtip shoes. And yes, I did make a stop on my way home from Agros's at an Italian shoe store and bought myself a pair for $149. I know the owner was shocked when I pulled the money out of my pocket. But I deserved it and, more importantly, wanted it. Yes, I knew my feet would grow out of them long before my grade eight graduation, but damn it, I am a 63-year-old man and can treat myself to such luxury once in a blue moon *(I am laughing, girl)*.

The event was to start at 6 pm, and I was asked to be there half an hour before the doors opened, which meant mom and dad would have to wait outside for half an hour. I was confident I could get them in and to their seats early. Mom and dad were downstairs getting ready. Dad had finished the basement bathroom, and he and mom were using it now. It still needed a lot of work, but it was functional. I retired to my room and began the process of transforming myself from a 13-year-old DD to a new stylish 13-year-old DD. I never liked that nickname and always preferred 'Cap' *(Yes, Mr. Evens. I was the first Cap now!)*. I guess in the near future, I will try to figure out a cool nickname and try to get it to stick. I had my shower, and even gave me a blow dry using mom's hair dryer. You know, the hair dryer with the corrugated hose going to a large hair cover thing-a-ma-jig.

I was ready first and strolled out to the living room. I took a seat and was so nervous. I got up, went to my Gramps old stereo that he had given us, and looked through the stored albums. I flipped through the 15 or so jackets trying to decide what to put on when my fingers reached an old Billie Holiday Album called Lover Man. I pulled it out of the jacket and loaded it on the turn table. Hit the play button, go to the corner chair, and sit down. If you get the chance, Rebecca, go and listen to it. Or maybe one day, in the not-so-distant future, we will both listen to it together. See if you can envision this picture. I am sitting in the corner, in my new James Bond-level suit, new Italian wing tips, and listening to my first Billie Holiday song. Dad was the first to enter the living room, and I sat there with a grin on my face.

He looked at me and said, "when did you buy a Billie Holiday record" with a very puzzled look?

"I didn't. It was inside Gramps stereo," I replied.

Then mom came in and said, "let's get going. We don't want to be late," looking around the living room.

I stood up, walked over to the record player, and turned it off. As I turned toward mom, she gasped and said, "Hud, our boy is all grown up." She gave me a big hug when I reached her location and said, "I want my little boy back." Hud was what everyone called my dad now. His full name was William Hudson Devon, but I guess a long time ago, there were far too many Billy's or Bill's that Gramps started to call him Hud.

Dad laughed, knew we needed a tension breaker, and said, "You want to go back to having to wash his underwear?"

Mom released me from her hold and gave my dad an open hand on his arm, and said, "Oh Hud, don't encourage the boy."

We all left the house and got in the car. It was just around freezing, and of course, the great planner forgot he did not own any nice overcoat that would go with a suit. Dad had gone to the closet, grabbed one of his dark trench coats, and said, "Try this on."

I put it on, and I looked foolish in it. My hands didn't even make it out of the sleeves. I took it off and said, "Give me my Bengal jacket. I will take it off once we get there." So, old Mr. Style left the house in his James Bond suit and hockey jacket. The ride went fast, and my parents were chatting about a bunch of what-ifs and who-ifs as I stared out the window and lost myself in my thoughts. It's been almost six months since the Transference, and I wonder what Derek 1.0 was doing. Probably down on 'It-girl' getting her ready for the big circumnavigation. What was Rebecca doing? Probably still with her new Mr. Wonderful and still 100% mind free of any 'Us 1.0' memories.

Task 5 – The Grand Ball Part II!

(January 1st – February 15th, 1974)

33 I was fortunate that Dad had already been to Hamilton place as the lounge piano player between show breaks. He knew where to park, and since we were earlier than most of the guests, we had a close parking spot near the doors. We got out of the car, and I took the Bengal jacket off and tossed it in the car. It was chilly, but my adrenalin was keeping me plenty warm. We walked to the doors and entered the first lobby when Betty from Mr. Simpkin's office spotted me. She immediately came over and said, "who is this dapper young man" and gave me a big smile.

She then extended a hand to my mom and introduced herself, "Hi, I am Betty. I believe we spoke a couple of times on the phone."

Mom grabbed her hand and said, "This is my husband Hud, and I am Dorthey Devon," with a smile added.

"You must be so proud of this young man and what he has accomplished," she said proudly.

Dad was first to respond and caught me off guard with, "My son can do anything he sets his mind to," along with a pat on my shoulder.

"I can't believe how old he looks now. Just last week, Betty, he was my little boy," mom said on the verge of crying.

"Betty, is there a place my parents can sit and wait while I go and attend the pre-opening meetings?", I asked. Betty was ok with me calling her Betty and had previously lectured me about calling her Miss Betty, being that she was only 33 and still single.

"Absolutely! Mr. Simpkins is in the main hall with the other dais guests, and I am sure he will want you there. I will show your parents to their seats," Betty said reassuringly.

I gave my mom a quick hug and dad a pat on the side of his arm. I walked into the big hall and stopped to take it all in. This had just opened last year and was my first time here. Well, Derek 2.0. Derek 1.0 brought Rebecca 1.0 to a Doctor Hook concert here in 1980. As I looked around, I spotted Mr. Simpkins and a group of people up at the front. I waved and walked over to them. Mrs. Simpkins looked at me and said, what would become the night's theme, "Who is this fine-looking young man?"

"What style of suit is that you're wearing, Derek? I might have to get myself one of those", he asked.

I reached into the inside pocket and pulled out a business card I had grabbed from Mr. Angelo's expecting exactly what was happening and handed it to him and said, “Mr. Angelo has a small shop down on Barton Street and, as you can see, is a master craftsman. I would highly recommend him if you’re ever looking for a one-of-a-kind suit.”

The next voice I heard was Sean’s, and he said, “Look at you, Mr. Style. Out to break a few lady's hearts tonight, and I will take a card if you have another one,” he said as we did our fist bump greeting.

“Hi Sean, great to see you, and thanks again for all your help making this happen,” I said.

“Me, I did nothing but meet this kid,” he replied with a laugh.

“Well, he got me here, Derek, and it’s a pleasure to meet the brains of this group,” as the other person extended his hand to me.

“Mr. Davis, or I should say, Mr. Premier, it is an honor to meet you, Sir, and we can’t thank you enough for taking your valuable time and making this event that much more special,” I replied.

“I told you, Bill, was I spot on or what”, Sean jumped in with.

Everyone but me laughed, and I was obviously out of the loop. Mr. Simpkins knew I was wondering what was happening and said we should quickly review the night's seating plan and program. The dais was going to sit, myself on the far right facing the audience, Sean beside me, The Premier beside Sean, and Mr. Simpkins, who would be the MC for most of the night except for a brief bit by Billy Van. On the other side of the speaker’s podium was our Mayor, Mr. Cops; beside him was Mr. Gordon, the President of Stelco, John Warner from the Spec, and the last man at the far left was Doctor Eugene Crossgrove from McMaster University’s Cancer research department. The next item was to review the order of speakers, and it was the plan to divide the evening into two parts. Pre-dinner introduction and a short speech by Mr. Simpkins followed by a presentation by Dr. Crossgrove highlighting the facility and his work and ending with Mayor Cops welcoming everyone and announcing the dinner. Not on the list, but there was Father Gibson, who would lead us in a pre-dinner prayer of thanks.

After dinner, the first speaker was going to be Billy Van for a few funny stories about Hamilton, followed by Mr. Gordon, who would chat about the importance of supporting the cancer fight. The next speaker was the Premier, who would talk about some of the wonderful government programs his government was initiating in dealing with cancer research. Then Sean would take over and do a special tribute to Trevor Simpkins and the Newly Minted Trevor Simpkins Memorial Foundation, which would focus on having an annual charitable event like this every year. And inserted into the program, which completely blindsided me, was a special plaque presented to me, along with the unveiling of the total amount that the 'Kids 4 a Cancer Cure' has raised to date. I was not happy reading this and gave Mr. Simpkins a tug on his sleeve and quietly asked him if I could have a quick word.

"Derek, I know what you are going to say, and believe me, I tried my best to avoid this, but the Premier told Sean he wanted this award presented, and he is going to do it himself. It seems the Premier had a lengthy chat with Sean about you, including the work you did for his campaign, that I was not aware of," he said somewhat defensively.

"Sorry, Mr. Simpkins, I should have known you would try your best, but I wanted to let you know that I would be calling you and your entire family to come up and accept this honor together with me," I told him in a friendly way.

"You do whatever makes you feel comfortable son," he quickly responded.

What Mr. Simpkins did not understand; I was about to do my best Sammy Maudlin impression, a full two years early. Yes, I was prepared for a certain amount of praise, and there was nothing I could do about it. But I also knew that this night would quickly be forgotten in a couple of weeks. It was showtime in 5, and I wanted to go and say hi to mom and dad because they would not see me until after the event, when the schmooze and silent auction hosted by Billy Van would take place. I went over to Betty and asked where she sat my mom and dad, and she pointed to a table right in front of the dais where I would be seated. I did not notice them being seated. I walked over and asked if everything was good and told them about the latest twist. Mom started to cry, and dad said, "If anyone tonight deserves an award, it is you," complete with a firm grab on my shoulder. The lights started to dim, and music began to play as the main doors opened for the guests to enter. I smiled, gave my folks a double thumbs up with a silly 'Mike Myeresk' grin from Wayne's World, and retreated to my seat.

After about 15 minutes, Mr. Simpkins got up, went to the Podium, and said into the mic, "Good evening, and thank you to all of the generous donors and supporters of such a wonderful cause….."

I don't need to detail everything Mr. Simpkins said in his speech Rebecca, just the good stuff I know you will get a laugh from. Dinner was excellent; I selected the prime rib, and my piece was cooked perfectly. Everyone else had drinks, and Mr. Simpkins enjoyed a nice glass of Cab

Sauv while I had to sip pop. Now that was unfair. I would have loved a nice red at dinner. I was regularly getting a wave from mom, and dad would smile at me. After the dinner was done and hats off to the caterer, they served everyone and cleaned the tables off in an hour. We had been there about 2 hours now, an hour and a half for the guests, and I figured we were down to the last 20 minutes. Everyone scheduled to get up did a great job, and it was about the time for the plaque presentation. I was watching the Premier, and he had been reviewing his speech notes. I was a bit worried when I saw how many cards he had.

Mr. Simpkins took the Podium, re-introduced the Premier, and got the crowd to give him a standing ovation. He got to the Podium and pulled out his card and began. He did not yet identify me by name and kept referring to me as 'this remarkable young boy.' He talked about Sean and the campaign and had a remarkable amount of detail about what I did for Sean. I knew Sean was his source, but then he started into the 'Kids 4 a Cancer Cure' story, and after reaching, what I think was the end of the speech, he stopped and said what I was not expecting, "I would like to introduce everyone to the people that are truly responsible for this amazing young man, his mother and father, Mr. Hud Devon and his beautiful wife, Dorothy." As the spotlight found their table and my parents were coming to grips with what was happening, the Premier said, "Please stand up and let everyone see you amazing parents."

Thank God my dad was a professional musician and did not have any stage fright. I figured dad would be able to stand and smile at everyone, but what threw me was my mom. She stood up and had a smile from ear to ear. She put her arms up and started to wave to everyone, even doing a complete 360. I was busting a gut right then and just a few seconds ago had even thought they might soil themselves when the spotlight hit them. As the Premier clapped at the Podium, the entire room stood and gave my mom and dad a standing ovation. I stood up and must have had the most fabulous look of satisfaction you could ever have imagined. As I was standing, Sean's hand grabbed my shoulder and gave it a good squeeze. The ovation lasted close to a minute, and then the Premier started the end of his speech.

"Finally, I think it's time to meet this remarkable young man, and I would like to ask Derek Devon to come to the podium and accept this plaque as thanks for being such a fine young man with a heart of gold, and I am sure, a great future in the Conservative Party," the Premier said with a chuckle. As the crowd laughed at his joke, that bloody spotlight hit me, and as I got up from my seat, the whole place rose and began to clap. It was the loudest clap of the night, and as much as I may have enjoyed the admiration demonstrated, I really wanted to shift this unwanted attention to the Simpkins Family. I started walking to the Podium; Sean stood up and gave me a big hug, then Mr. Simpkins; thankfully, the Premier was already at the Podium. As I reached the Podium, everyone from the left side came over and hugged me. Even the Mayor, who I only met tonight. After all the hugs, I reached the Premier, and I think he picked up on the fact I was all hugged out and put out a fist for a fist bump. I knew Sean set him up. As our fists touched, the Premier pulled his hand back and gave me an exploding hand, complete with the required boom sound effect. I think I laughed and turned to see Sean laughing.

I took the plaque and told him it was my greatest honor to receive this from him. He didn't realize that he was about to be the first victim of my Sammy Maudlin show. Without warning to the Premier, I went to the mic, thanked everyone, and asked if they would all please take their seats. The Premier didn't know what to do, so he went back to his seat. Once the clapping stopped, I removed the mic from the holder and quickly assessed how much mic cord was under the Podium. It looked like maybe 20 feet which would be enough to reach Mr. Simpkins' seat. As I slowly walked towards Mr. Simpkins, you could hear a pin drop. Everyone was wondering what I was going to do. As I reached his seat, I waited for a second for the spotlight to catch up. Once the light hit us, I was on!

"I want to thank the Premier for taking time out of his busy schedule so he could be here for such a special event. Maybe next year he will return as Prime Minister," as I gave him a big smile.

"Yes, I had an idea. But the only way that idea could ever become, what we are all enjoying tonight, is with the dedication and selflessness of the leaders in our business community. Mr. Simpkins took a simple idea and transformed it into what we all hope will be an annual event. I am fortunate to have a great mom and dad to guide me, but I could never imagine the pain and anguish a parent would go through with the loss of a child." I took a pause and then said into the Mic, "Phil, do you still have the picture of Trevor available?"

With unbelievable timing, Phil turned on the projector, and there was Trevor, larger than life, on the theatre's screen. It was a pic of him that I had explicitly told Phil to use, sitting up in his hospital bed with a huge smile. The family was celebrating his birthday that day in the hospital. Mrs. Simpkins had me look at her entire album of Trevor.

I continued my speech, "I never knew Trevor. But I learned all about Trevor's influence on his family, both in loss and in life. We're here today not to give a few dollars to a valiant cause; we are here to make ourselves feel good. And the way we do that is by celebrating Trevor's life, his battle to the end, and his memory. This plaque is not for me; this plaque is for the people who will continue to make this happen yearly. This plaque will be our connection to this family, to their loss, and their future work in the fight against cancer. I would like to ask the entire Simpkins family to come up here and join with all the other people who made this event possible and help unveil the total amount of money raised so far."

Right on cue, the entire Simpkins family got up from the two tables they occupied, and the crowd rose to their feet and began to give a tremendous applause. At this moment, my main man Phil hit the play button on the tape I told him to make, And the music started to play through the entire hall's sound system. Then to the right of Trevor's pic, Phil had the Lyrics appear. And I said, "everyone, please join in," and I started to sing the song into the mic just loud enough to get everyone else singing in the room.

I see trees so green, red roses too
I see them bloom for me and you.
And I think to myself what a wonderful world.
I see skies ………

As the song finished, the family was now on stage, and it was a big hug-fest. Everyone on the dais was hugging everyone, and the entire auditorium was in the Kumbaya zone. I walked over to the Premier, handed him the mic, and said, "Would you please do the honor of announcing how much money we raised, to date?" The Premier took the mic and addressed the crowd in a very emotional and personal way. I thought I was doing a great Sammy Maudlin, but the Premier had a few Sammy moves himself. I want to believe my speech inspired his word choice, but I will leave that up to you, Rebecca, to figure out.

"Everybody, do you want to know how great you all are? Do you want to know how much greater you will have to be next year? Well, take a look at the screen and see how great your generosity is."

If I needed another job, I think I could have been a great stage director. Phil hit the play button again and the room filled with the sound of a drum roll, followed by a huge number appearing on the screen. The Premier read it out with pride, "Three million, seven hundred and forty-eight thousand, two hundred and sixty-nine dollars." There is a bit of an inside joke Rebecca. It was Sixty-five dollars, and I changed it to Sixty-nine *(he he. Hey, I am just Thirteen years old and that one was for Ronnie)*. Everyone was clapping for each other, and it was remarkable that my need to get the paperboy list would wind up making so much money.

The schmooze was equally insane, and I could not get my mom out of there. Who would have known that my shy mom loved the limelight? I think every female in the place came over to shake my mom's hand. Dad had his boss's boss come over, and the two of them were chatting in the corner, sipping on a rum and coke, I think. Once the lights came on and we knew the show was done, everyone could not wait to grab a drink. I didn't know what I wanted to do but decided I needed to thank a few people personally. Tonight, my cred was worth a lot, so better leverage it. The first stop was to find Phil and thank him for a great job. Then I tracked down Blane and gave him all sorts of praise. He actually had a date, and I think the fact that I came over in person and heaped a ton of credit on him won me his loyalty for life, and maybe even 'get him some' tonight *(Smiling)*. The Premier had left, but I was able to say thanks in person. He smiled and told me he might have to hire me as his speech writer. The Simpkins were now the night's stars, and it was so rewarding seeing everyone wanting to come over and learn a bit more about Trevor.

I had one last person to thank before I would plant the seed for Task 10. I spotted Sean chatting with Father Gibson and a couple of other politicians from around here. As I approached the group, Father Gibson pulled out this little camera and ordered us to get together for a group picture before I could get a word out. Sean and I were side-by-side in the middle, and Sean's other friends all tucked in close to us." Father Gibson said, "Everyone say Rugelach." I think I was the only one who got the joke and laughed. He snapped the picture, and before anyone would interfere with my need to have a quick chat with Sean, I said, "You got a couple of minutes."

Sean gave me a yes gesture, turned to his group, and said, "Father, tell them the one about the Priest, the Rabbi, and the leprechaun." As Sean turned back, I said to him, "There is no joke, is there?" We both laughed and walked to the wall for some privacy. "I just wanted to thank you for everything you did for me and this amazing opportunity. I think over the next while; we will be busy with our own lives and work. You in Ottawa and me in school being a 13-year-old again. I wish you were thirteen or I was twenty because I think we would have been great friends," I confessed.

I never saw Sean get too emotional, but he was definitely welling up a bit. He hugged me and said, "you, my 13-year-old going on 30, friend; I can't wait to see what you are going to do with your life. I know you are not a fan of praise, so I won't give you any. But I want to give you one small piece of advice. Maybe not advice, but something to think about. With great power, comes great responsibility."

All I could do at that point was smile and say, "Interesting words to ponder." I walked with Sean back to the group and said to Father Gibson as I was leaving, "Did everyone laugh when you said pot of gold?

Sean chuckled, and that was our last chat, and I was sad it may be for a long time. I went over to mom, who was now chatting with Mrs. Simpkins, put my arm around her, and waited for an opening. Mrs. Simpkins smiled at me and said, "I was telling your mom what a gifted speech writer you are."

I smiled and said, "It's all in the genes." I then asked mom, "I am beat. Any chance you and dad will be leaving soon?" Well, I knew that would get her motherly instinct motor running, and she hugged Mrs. Simpkins, and they said they would get together in a couple of weeks. Mom and I went over to dad, and I was sure dad picked up on what we were about to ask, and he quickly said to his boss's boss, "Well, I think I am being summoned to get my son home to bed."

They shook hands, and dad put his hand on my shoulder and asked if I was tired. I confirmed the assessment, and we walked out of the hall, each holding mom's arms. Yes, Rebecca, I had to sit through a 30-minute plus ride home with my folks heaping praise on me to the point I just wanted to tell them to shut up; it was not that big a deal for a 63-year-old Teenager and fake kid to do what I did. To defuse the issue, I decided to counter with a request I knew would shut them up. I asked, "How can I get a better relationship with Ann?"

[Got a name and lead at the Gala for a white label manufacturer in Toronto that may be interested in making my soap and dryer sheets.]

[The total raised for the Charity, including the silent auction and a few last-minute guilt donations was $4,035,664 *(I did not change the 64 to show you I was maturing)*]

[Almost forgot, I arranged for a meet and greet at the Gala with Doctor Crossgrove at McMaster first week of March. Task 10 seed was planted]

UPDATE – ☹

(February 15th, - March 30th, 1974)

34 ***Mrs. Agro!:*** Just wanted to add a short update. I got a call from Luke, whose dad asked him to tell me Angelo had called and Mrs. Agro had passed away. I had been seeing Mr. Agro every couple of weeks to get my seafood fix. He always was generous to me, and when he read how much the charity had raised, I could tell it gave him some joy during this difficult time. I did not know him that long or spend much time with him, but we seemed to have some old 'Wop' bond between us. I arranged to attend the funeral with Mr. Mattson, and Luke decided to tag along. We arrived at the catholic church, and it was packed. I was sure it would be standing room only, and as we were walking in; Mr. Angelo spotted us and came over to lead us down the side of the pews to a bench he had saved about 20 rows back.

I shook Mr. Angelo's hand, and we exchanged a head nod. Not many words were spoken today. We were sitting there, and I was reading the service card and trying to figure out what songs I should find in the hymn book. As my head was down, I felt a tap on my shoulder. It was Mr. Angelo who pointed to the row's end. Standing there was Mr. Agro's oldest boy, gesturing for me to come over to him. I got up and slid past everyone seated. When I got to the aisle, Chris, Mr. Agro's son, asked me if I would follow him to the front. I had no idea what was happening but just followed along like a lost sheep.

I thought the family would be in the first row, and maybe Mr. Agro wanted to say hello. The first two rows were empty, and he continued to walk to the left into a side room. In there was the entire Agro clan, and Mr. Agro was sitting in the corner alone. Chris asked me to go over and say hello to his dad. I was honestly feeling weird about this, and for a split second, I was panicking that Mr.Agro would hand me a box of seafood. When I got about 6 feet away, he looked up, and even with all the sorrow in his eyes, he managed a smile. As I reached him, he did not extend a hand and simply said, "please take a seat." There was a chair beside his but not touching.

I took the seat and let Mr. Agro take the lead. He reached into his pocket and pulled out a rosary. He kissed it, handed it to me, and said, "This is for you." I could tell he had his own Rebecca-type valve and would not let me see any tears.

"I don't understand, Mr. Agro," I said.

"It was my wife's, and when I had told her about meeting you, she followed everything that was being written about you in the papers the past months, including the piece about the Simpkins boy. She told me she wanted you to have this. She thought it would help you growing up in some way. I told her I didn't think you were catholic, but she said it didn't matter, that you would know what to do with it."

What Mr. Agro did not see was just how angry I was. Thinking about what he and his family had to endure with this bloody cancer shit was boiling my blood. I already had my big plan to beat the crap out of God if I got to see him face-to-face for what he put my mother through. Now all I could think about was I was about to add a second beating. I took the rosary simply out of respect for Mr. Agro. I knew how much this meant to him, and there was no way I was wired to say no. I extended my hand, and he placed the rosary in it. I clasped my hand closed and got up. We looked at each other, and I gave the nod. He returned a tortured smile. I transferred the rosary into my pocket of my suit jacket, yes, the same suit jacket, except I had bought a nice overcoat since the gala. As I walked away, I went and shook the family members' hands and said, "I am very sorry for your loss."

I went back to my seat and sat. Luke nudged me and asked what had happened. I pulled out the rosary and showed it to him. Mr. Angelo and Joe were eavesdropping as I told Luke, "Mrs. Agro wanted me to have this." I put it back in my pocket, and I think Luke knew I did not want to say anything more on the topic. The service took place, and we left. Mr. Angelo, for the first time, hugged me with a pat on the head. We would not attend the internment and drove home. As we headed up the Sherman Falls hill, Mr. Mattson said, "I didn't know you were so close to the Agro's."

I replied, "Neither did I," and that was all that was said.

[Had my meeting in Toronto with my White Label soap maker. We have come to an arrangement, and I was going into his office next week to play around with some formulations]

[Never guess who I bumped into at school last week. Tonka Boy! It felt weird talking with him and, to be honest, uncomfortable. I could tell he was testing the waters with me to see if we could be friends, and all I could think about was not disturbing the timeline. We have not had any classes together yet, but Frank and I were in the same class. I asked him if he had been invited to Sherry Krugger's big house party coming up. He said no. Danger averted. I was going to go. I told him it was nice to meet him and maybe we could do lunch with Frank next week. I told him I mostly went home for lunch but tried to do one lunch here each week.]

UPDATE – Confessional Part I

(April 1st – April 30th, 1974)

35 ***Sherry Krugger Experience:*** One of my promises with this do-over was to implement an open and honest communication protocol with you. I know you're thinking; what a hypocrite, you're telling me about a lifelong secret that you kept from me? But I would respectfully disagree with that proposition. Yes, I did keep an unbelievable secret from you, but I told you why, and I am sure as this guide expands, it may even be more justified, and potentially very troubling developments may emerge. I have decided to share things with you that I never did when we were together. We both had experiences that we never shared over the years. I never volunteered who got my virginity the same way you never told me. Truth be told, we both preferred not knowing, but what I will be asking of you now, you deserve to have the full story; Good and bad!

NO, Becca! What I am trying to explain, are the changes based on what I experienced or did my first go around, hoping I will make this one better for me but also better for you. The challenge I am currently facing was a battle between the brain and adolescent hormones. My brain was that of a person who lived 63 years already, complete with all the memories and experiences. But the body I was occupying was still only thirteen years new. A few months ago, I decided to alter my development with the notion I would be waiting for you. There was no Sarah experience this time. Turns out my body was telling me it had different plans. And therein lay the rub *(Pun Intended).*

I was invited to a house party at Sherry Krugger's and knew I would be subjected to all the trappings of adolescent emerging sexuality. Spin the bottle, slow dancing, truth or dare, sneaking behind the furnace to an awaiting air mattress, and on and on. Drinking would be a grade or two further ahead, but I was a very popular student now and the fact I was going to a grade 8's party was proof of that. Being as tall or taller than most grades 8's and being in great physical shape did not hurt, but I was going through this mental debate that was frustrating the hell out of me. You know I am the King of 'what if' scenarios. And everyone had the same outcome; a feeling like I would be cheating on you. We will not meet *(if my plan remains the same)* Until June 1977. It's April 1974! I also expect that you will have gone on a few dates before we eventually do date if your past have any similarities. I am ok with that, although, there was one date from that past you told me about that I did not enjoy finding out about. As I write this, all I can do is think about the Seinfeld episode with Elaine and the line, 'He took, IT, out' *(and that is all I am going to say about that, although it still pisses me off that you touched it)*.

Sorry, don't know where that came from. Anyway, back to the issue. If I go, I will almost surely have my adolescent brain, defeat my other brain. And I am not talking about that brain! If I don't go, I am afraid that at some future time I may simply spontaneously explode *(Made you laugh)*. You know what I mean, and I will justify it based on my first Rebecca 1.0's attempt at humping my leg behind her house in the woods so she could depressurize that day! Being a bit more mature this time, I decided to employ your own philosophy sort of. Remember, 'If you love someone set them free; If they come back then it's meant to be; if they don't, it never was', or something like that. And NO, it's not some deep-seated payback *(I giggled)*. I decided that you would tell me to go. To be yourself and enjoy the adolescent experiences when they are meant to be experienced. That I was not cheating on you, or my memory of you. Thank you, Rebecca, for being so wise and selfless! *(I really hope you are smiling right this moment)*.

Fast forward to Sherry's party. What made Sherry's party special was her parents were out of town and her older brother was looking after her and the house. He was going to have a few friends over upstairs, while she would have a couple over in the basement. Well, turned into around 30 in the basement and 20 upstairs. Ted was I think 5 years older and was about to graduate high school. As long as we didn't burn the house down, the two zones would remain separate. It was a wet night and my dad agreed to drop me off on his way to a gig that night. The rain was supposed to end a couple of hours later. When I arrived at the door, I knocked, and Ted answered. He knew who I was, and I only knew him from a few times he either dropped Sherry off at school or picked her up. Sherry was what one would call a Yenta! Well, a good-looking Yenta but was not my type. I was sure she invited me because of my recent articles in the Spec and a couple of episodes of CHCH news.

I had been trying very hard to fly under the 'Popular' radar, but the residual effect was lasting a bit longer than I wanted, but one could argue it had a few benefits like getting invited to a grade 8 party. Ted smiled and said, "Hey man, I didn't know my sister invited you."

I smiled and joked, "She told me you had invited me."

"You break me up. Come in and I want to introduce you to some of my friends before you descend into the dungeon," he replied as he led me into the living room.

There were only 4 other people in the room, and I recognized 2 from hockey. Tim Bellows played on the Bengals at the Midget level when the Bengals played in a tournament in California last year. He gave me a wave. The other hockey guy played summer hockey last year, and my practice was right before his. It was a hockey mutual respect type thing. I gave a nod and listened to Ted do the introductions. After the requisite 'Nice to meet you." I asked Ted for directions to the dungeon. He pointed to a hallway and said, "The door on the left." As I left and was headed down the hallway, Tim yelled, "Remember the Bengal way." I chuckled. The Bengal way was, 'Never apologize, admit to nothing but always say you're sorry and it will never happen again. There were a few legendary stories about some of the older kids' parties when the team did these March break special hockey trips.

I descended the stairs into a fairly dark basement. It was a fully finished basement and Mr. Krugger owned a car dealership and had a few bucks. While Ted's party would not kick into full gear till, after 10 pm, there were already about 25 people downstairs. When Sherry asked me to come, I did what every grade seven kid being asked to go to a grade 8's party did, I asked if I could bring my wingman! Yup, Luke was supposed to be there and since the Krugger's lived in the neighborhood behind the Mattson's, he would have walked over. Being that this was my first official real party, not the parent-arranged birthday parties, it was exciting even at my age *(wink wink).*

I spotted Luke about the time he spotted me. He was talking to one of the guys that played with us against the Teachers each month who was a grade eighter. I think Luke and I were the only grade 7 kids. Sherry spotted me walking to Luke and ran over to say hi. As I was about to thank her again for the invite, she threw her arm around my shoulder and said, "I want to introduce you to some friends. We went to a private girl's school together from kindergarten to grade 6."

I gave Luke the requisite eye roll signifying in our own language that said, 'Later'. She led me over to the couch which was facing away from us and forced me to stand in the front. There were 3 girls sitting on the couch and Sherry did the hostess thing and introduced me but failed to tell me their names.

"This is Derek Devon, the student that started the 'Kids 4 a Cancer Cure' event," Sherry said. I was getting used to that introduction and as I like to do, was trying a unique response each time just to keep me from saying, 'Just shut the F up already with the bloody 'started the 'Kids 4 a Cancer Cure' crap'!

Looking as sincere as I could, I responded with, "Shouldn't these ladies be upstairs at Ted's party?" Two giggled and one rolled her eyes as to say, 'What a phony'. Sherry gave me a little push and proceeded to give me a quick overview of where everything was.

"Snacks, pop, bathroom, and the only bedroom in the basement," with a devious smile.

I turned and said, "Excuse me ladies, but I think I need a pop. Can I get anything for any of you?" They all kind of giggled and said they already had a pop. I turned and went to the pop location and after getting a grape crush, headed over to see Luke. When I got to Luke, the first thing out of my mouth was, "Who's the girl on the couch at the far left?"

"No idea," Luke replied.

"Did you notice she is the spitting image of Lindsey Wagner from the Bionic Woman show?", emerged from my lips.

"The Bionic what?" he replied.

That's right, it will be a couple of years, so I modified it to, "I meant the Paper Chase" which just happened to be released last October. Before Rebecca 1.0, I had a crush on 3 TV stars. Lindsey Wagner *(The Bionic Woman)* and Baily Quarters *(Jan Smithers)* from WQRP and your potential doppelganger, Pam Dawber who will star in a series called Mork and Mindy. I liked to say I was into the librarian look *(Are you rolling your eyes?)*. I know I am the author of this guide and I control what goes in and what stays out. But I also realize that when you read this, I am most likely dead and free of having to face any potential rath from you *(Big smile happening)*. So, I will venture where I know I shouldn't but really, really want to go. I will not be telling you anything you are not aware of or will become aware of since this issue could be described as 'defines who I am'.

I said, "Luke, I gotta get a look at her ass." There, I said it! If I am true to my innate self, I am sure in a few years you will be introduced to the 'Butt Hicky Monster' *(I can't believe I am writing this. I feel like a little immature kid)*. A nickname you will give me! And who knows, I may finally get around to penning a textbook called 'Buttology – The Science of Kiesterology' *(Work with me, Beautiful Butt girl)*. The slang word keister is best known today as meaning the buttocks or ass *(or arse, smiling yet)*, but in the past, it has also meant a satchel or traveling suitcase, especially a satchel that can be secured with straps and a lock. And it could also refer to a safe or strongbox, particularly one within a larger vault. The word comes from the German Kiste, meaning box, and with a slang sense of the buttocks. The German word comes from the Latin cista and is cognate with the English word chest. In my Derek 1.0 final days, the larger Latin butts were in fashion like J Lo or Kim K. I never liked the large butt and would take a Shakira over them everytime *(I would say you could read more under Tab 'K' but that would just be too easy).*

So, you know where I am going but I think you will get a kick out of knowing what I was thinking now.

I told Luke, "Let's move over to the other wall just in case she gets up. She will most likely go where the pop and snacks are."

We repositioned ourselves and began the waiting game. The angle was just enough so I could get a much better look at her, but not too obvious yet. I felt like a little kid again. It was a good feeling and I have been doing way too much old man stuff, so it was refreshing to allow my adolescent self to take lead. I was trying very hard to maintain the nonchalant look, but old Sherry had been watching me very closely from the other side of the room. About 15 minutes into my stocking 'Lindsey', Sherry walked over with a grin and said, "I am guessing you like someone on the couch Derek?"

I quickly gave her a look that implied, "What, me?" What I did pick up on was Sherry didn't know which one I was 'Party Stocking'. She just concluded it was one of the girls on the couch. As any Yenta knows, all you had to do was say; "Tell me which one you like, or I will go over and tell all of them you have a secret crush on them," she threatened with a devious smile attached.

"How do you know it's not Luke," I countered?

'Because Luke came in and went immediately over to talk to Rob," she replied.

"Well Sherry, I am not saying you're right and I am not saying you're wrong. Let's just say, that I may be a bit curious about the girl closest to us, whom I may point out, you failed to introduce to me by name. I don't think I recognized her from school."

"Oh, Tina. She goes to Mount Mary Catholic school at the top of the hill." I knew where Mount Mary was and the first other male adolescent thought was, 'she must wear a school uniform' and Frank Zappa's song, 'Catholic Girls'. You know Rebecca, I am simply trying to throw in a bit of humor to deflect the always-present feeling that I am cheating on you!

Before I could get another word out of my mouth, Sherry yells over to Tina and says, "Tina, I forgot to introduce you earlier, get your butt over here for a second' *(And yes, I am smiling inside due to Sherry's choice of words)*. I am sure my adolescent side had a blush going but instinct had me stand upright, try to look like it was no big deal, and not crap my pants. Tina turned to the other girls and said something and then all three decided to get up and walk over. Unfortunately, the middle couch girl got up first which blocked any chance of a rear view! *(If that did not get a smile, then I don't know what will)*.

Luke and I stood there grinning at each other both thinking, 'look at us on display for 3 grade 8 chicks. The first girl arrived, being the middle couch girl and Sherry said, "Derek and Luke, this is Cindy. We went to school together, but she now goes to Father Loftus."

Tina was next, "Derek and Luke, this is my best friend, Tina. We have known each other all our lives and she goes to Mount Mary". I smiled at Tina and had my real first eye-to-eye contact.

"This is Dawn, and she goes to Senior Public. Her dad is good friends with my dad", she finished up with.

Both Luke and I said hello and we found ourselves all standing there wondering what to say. We don't do handshakes yet so no flesh-to-flesh encounter. After the appropriate amount of uncomfortable silence, I decided to initiate a conversation. "Why Mount Mary Tina and not Sherman Falls High?"

"My dad works at McMaster and my mom preferred I go there," she answered.

"Her dad is a doctor at McMaster," Sherry added.

"What is his area of practice," I followed up with, with odd looks being given to me by everyone.

"He is a surgeon," Tina said.

To keep the conversation going I followed up with, "Where are you girls going to High School?"

Dawn, I think felt left out and replied first, "Sherman Falls High for me."

"Same here" Cindy seconded.

"Mount Mary is a beautiful property. I love to hike around that area," I said, now thinking, they were thinking, I was some Peeping Tom. And since we are on the topic, your dad Rebecca is going to find the wallet of another high school admirer under your window in a few years. I will give you his initials, KR. Assuming I don't decide to add him to the list! But you already know that.

As with all pre-high school parties, the girls returned to the couch, and Luke and I went back over to where Rob was sitting now. The one good thing about the parting, I got a look at Tina as she walked away. I can safely report that there were no knocker knees, no TEA, and no major thigh rub. I was not a fan of her choice and fit of her pants. They were some sort of light color fake jeans and were about a half size too big. It was very hard to really see if she possessed one of the all-time most cherished by the males of the world, a 'Gap' *(Well if you're not going to bust a gut about now, I will)*. While I would need a bit more distance to capture her full gait, and put her in tighter pants, I would have to award a preliminary Rebecca rating of 8.0! In case you forgot what TEA stands for, it is the acronym for 'The Edible Ass'. A situation where a person's pants go up the crack of the ass. A condition that women with a perfectly shaped rounded spade derriere never experienced *(All I can do at this moment is shake my head in disbelief I am writing this down. It must be those thirteen-year-old hormones controlling my thoughts)*.

After about a half-hour standing in our little packs, Sherry turned off the music and told us to listen to her. She announced that a bunch of people want to dance so if the guys could help move furniture around to open up the middle of the basement for a make-shift dance floor, it would be appreciated. We of course all pitched in, and in 5 minutes had our version of The Dance Party. I could not resist moving over to the stereo with the thought of being the DJ. I think I had a much better knowledge of music than anyone else there. I grabbed another Grape Crush and went to the stereo and started flipping through the records as well as some 8 tracks. About 6 records in I spotted the Rascal's album 'Groovin'. I am hoping Rebecca you know what my plans are for that record.

I pulled it out and put it aside for later. I then took out 'Don't Shoot Me I'm Only the Piano Player. That would be the album to start with. I loaded it on the turntable and set the needle to my DJ-inspired spot. I turned up the volume and looked to see what type of reaction it would get. When the kazoo sound started, it was like an electric shock went off under everyone. All of the girls jumped up to dance along with a couple of the guys who were there with their girlfriends. I did my self-pat-on-the-back move and figured I would see if the group was primed enough for a slow song and would let the song after Crocodile Rock play called High Flying Bird.

Just as Crocodile Rock was finishing, Sherry came over and grabbed my hand and dragged me over to Tina who was still sitting on the couch watching the action, and said, "Quit being a party pooper and dance with Derek." I was hoping that Tina who was 14 or 15, thought I was in grade 8 like Sherry and not some 12-year-old grade 7 kid. I kind of stood there looking for Tina's expression and she looked at me trying to figure out if I was ok with Sherry's attempted matchmaking and I gave her the reassuring head tilt, smile with eyebrow raise that signalled, 'Why Not'. In an 'I like you', not 'I can't believe I have to dance with you' sort of way.

I was pretty sure no one was aware that the next song was a slow song, especially Tina. I did not grab Tina's arm or hand yet, I just kind of walked beside her for the 6 feet to our makeshift dance floor. We turned to face each other when the song started, and she realized it was a slow song. As everyone else bolted from the dance floor, I reached down and took her hand and placed it on my shoulder. Her other hand found my waist and I then did the same. I looked at her and could tell she was a bit out of her comfort zone and smiled and said, "Thank you."

"For what?" she said with an inquisitive look."

"For staying and dancing with me rather than head to the couch because it's a slow song. It's usually tradition to have a couple of fast dances before we dare engage in a slow song," I replied.

She gave me this strange look that I was trying not to interpret as 'What are you my father speaking like that?'

We had automatically begun to sway back and forth to the song and the girl had a natural rhythm and I could also see everyone was watching us, all by ourselves on the dance floor. As we turned, I spotted Rob, he was flashing me a thumbs up and mouthing something, I was sure was disgusting and crude. We exchanged just the right number of smiles with each other and eye-to-eye contact. Tina had a great smile *(Perfect white teeth, but not as perfect and white as yours Dimples)* and these stunning hazel eyes. She was about 4 inches shorter than I was. We stayed as one until the song was completed and I realized I needed to put another song on, so I told Tina to come over to the stereo and help me, DJ. She smiled which I assumed indicated ok. I grabbed an eight-track and threw it in and switched the dial over to tape from Turntable. My selection was the Beach Boys, Endless Summer. If that wouldn't pack the dance floor again, I would not be the great DJ, I claim I am *(haha)*.

As soon as 'Surfin Safari' started, I knew I owned them. Before I could say anything to Tina, Sherry ran over and grabbed her hand, and pulled her to the dance floor to dance with her other girlfriends. As she was being kidnapped, she turned and smiled with an expression that said, 'I really want to stay with you, but I am not being given a choice'. I actually didn't mind, because it would give me a chance to go through the rest of the music and plot out my DJ program for the night. As I was flipping albums, I turned to take a look at Tina dancing. Her backside was to me, and I had the opportunity to do a more in-depth analysis. Wow, she had a great sense of rhythm, and I did not realize how small her waist was. When she turned sideways, I got my first analytical view of her top side. I knew if I ever see her again, I will have to channel my inner 'Christian Dior' and buy this young girl turning into a beautiful young lady, a 'DD' clothing makeover. I would guess she was around a 34 B plus-C with a Jenifer Aniston shape. Ok, 8.5 on the Rebecca scale *(Please be smiling)!*

As I was gawking, Luke appeared and gave me a male, side of the bicep punch along with one of his favorite responses, "Nice", complete with the eyebrow raises and head bob. Luke and I had developed our own language complete with a bunch of single-word expressions that replaced a few hundred-word detailed explanation. The facial expression and the head moves changed each single word expression depending on how it would be used and often what degree was chosen.

I gave him a push back and said, "She is still no RH."

"R who," he said with a confused look.

I just smiled and responded with, "Exactly."

I was sure my Freudian slip indicated I was still dealing with some deep-seated guilt factor. I asked Luke, "You see anything you like?"

"There are a couple, but I think the girl that just came in, Mary Lou likes me," Luke confessed.

I took a look around and spotted who Luke was talking about. Mary Lou has been secretly checking Luke out at school for a while. Mary Lou had an older sister the same age as my sister who was considered one of the hottest girls in High School. Mary Lou was no slouch either but was very shy. My guess is her sister is upstairs at Ted's get-together and Ted most likely used Sherry's party as an excuse to get her sister over. Now we had 3-grade Seveners here all pretending to be grade Eighters. So, I told Luke, "Why don't you go and ask if she would like a drink?"

Luke was not Mr. Aggressive when it came to the girls. He always sat back and let them come to him, which did not disappoint as Mary Lou spotted us chatting and made her way over.

"Hi, Luke. Hi Derek," Mary Lou said with a cheerful tone.

"Hey Mary Lou, I didn't know you and Sherry were friends," I commented.

"Well, my sister was invited by Sherry's brother, and Sherry called to see if I want to come to her party," was her answer.

"Glad for the grade seven reinforcement Mary Lou, we were feeling a bit outnumbered here," I joked.

Luke was just standing there smiling so I switched and became his wingman and asked if I could get the two of them a drink. Mary Lou said, "Yes please, Ginger ale if they have it."

"Luke?"

"Sure, a Mountain Dew if there any left," he added.

I left and headed to the pop area and proceeded to get the requested drinks when Ted came down and walked over to me. "Hey, Derek, one of my friend's upstairs is trying to put a fundraiser together and I was wondering if you could come up for a few minutes and talk to him about how you did your cancer thing."

"Sure, Ted but give me a minute to deliver these drinks," I replied.

I took the drinks over and told Luke, "I have to head upstairs for a couple of minutes. If for any reason I get delayed, after 4 or 5 Beach Boys songs, put this album on, side 'B'," I instructed. Luke nodded ok and I headed upstairs.

I was hoping to be here for song 8, 'In my Room', to have another dance with Tina, but I guess the Rascals may have to do. When I got up to the living room, the party had moved to the back of the living room where a very large den was located. I looked around to get a quick review of who was there and how many I recognized. I counted 4 guys I knew, and I identified 3 girls, 2 that were most likely the 2 hottest girls in High School, and the other who went to my church. One was Mary Lou's sister Maureen. She was already doing part-time modelling and worked in the summer as a lifeguard at the outdoor pool. She looked like a young Rachel Welch with a Farah Fawcett body.

She could have easily been on Baywatch had it been around. Back in my earlier days during round 1, I had a huge crush on her in grades 9 and 10 (Pre Rebecca 1.0). Unfortunately, she had no idea who I even was back then. I spotted Ted who was waving me over and when I arrived, he introduced me to his friend. "Derek, this is Kent, Kent this is Derek."

"Hi Kent," I got out first. "Ted says you're planning a fundraiser of some sort?"

"Hi Derek, yes I am, and I was very impressed with what you accomplished with your cancer charity work," he replied.

"Thanks, but it was mostly Mr. Simpkins and all the other volunteers that made it possible," I explained.

"I want to raise some money to start a program to help troubled teens who run away from home. I currently volunteer at a home for troubled youth in Hamilton. After High School, I plan to go into medical school and it will look good on my resume," he said.

"I guess my only advice Kent is to suggest you need to build yourself a network. Raising money is all about building a network of like-minded individuals who hopefully share your vision and passion. From there it's easy," I told him.

"How would you suggest I start?" he asked.

I had a grin as I was also processing this a bit differently. Here is this grade 7, thirteen-year-old, giving worldly advice to a 17-year-old grade 12 student. "Make a list of family and friends. Then speak to each and ask if they would be able to either refer a prospective candidate or maybe themselves would like to volunteer their time or services. Next, you need to have the network go out to anyone they can think of and make a pitch to raise money. It's all about having a pitch that is designed where the 'Pitchee' cannot say no to the 'pitcher'. Everyone listening was slowly nodding like they understood exactly what I was saying. Then Kent said, "Anyone you know that may be interested?"

I paused for a minute and looked around the room thinking when I spotted a beautiful baby grand in the corner. "Nice piano" I said out loud. "There is one person that may have an interest. He's a local lawyer who is wanting to raise his profile here in Hamilton and he is fairly well connected within the downtown business community. If you have a piece of paper and a pen, I will write down his contact information and you can certainly let him know I referred you.

"My dad was at the Charity gala and for the next week he kept talking about this young kid who was thirteen but spoke like he was 40. Now I get it," Kent said. Everyone gave a bit of a friendly laugh along with the male slap on the side of the upper arm.

"Since you are obviously 40 Derek in the body of a kid, would you like me to sneak you a beer," Ted said.

I smiled and said, "I greatly appreciate the offer Ted but at my age, I would prefer a nice single malt scotch, preferably a 30-year-old in a crystal snifter and maybe a fine Cohiba," with the added straight face.

These are the times I miss not having a cell phone with a camera. The guys just stood there with a somewhat stunned looked not knowing how to respond. “Sorry guys, but there is a very attractive young girl downstairs that I hope is waiting for me and I should get back,” I broke the silence with.

Ted said, “Thanks man. That was awesome advice.”

“Ya Derek, I will pop down in a bit when I find a paper and pen. Thanks again for the help,” Kent said.

I turned and headed for the stairs when Maureen grabbed my arm. “Hi Derek, I am not sure if you remember me from the skating rink last summer.” Oh my God Luke, ‘I think it moved Jerry’ *(Ya Ya, I used it again).*

Did I! They do this couples roller skating thing when you skate hand and hand, then every 30 seconds a whistle sounds, and you stop holding hands and the guys start to skate faster hoping to reach the next girl and grab their hand before the music starts. Kind of like musical chairs on roller skates. Well, last summer I got dragged up by Katie Wilson for the event and I ended up being the last man standing holding Maureen’s hand.

“Hi Maureen, absolutely, how could I forget such a handsome couple that night,” I said with a slight grin. She did not know that was Derek 1.0 and she is now talking to Derek 2.0.

“My sister Mary Lou is down there. Can you please keep an eye on her for me,” she requested?

“Certainly. It would be my pleasure,” I assured her. Funny thing, Derek 1.0 would have either fainted or worse had a Sarah experience in his pants at that moment. But Derek 2.0 was more interested in getting back to seeing Tina. I smiled at Maureen and disappeared down the stairs. When I got back to the basement, I spotted Luke up on the dance floor with Mary Lou dancing to ‘Little Deuce Coup’. Great, time to get my dance in with Tina. I scanned the room and spotted Tina over talking to Rob. Great, God only knows what Rob would be talking about with Tina. Rob lacked a personal filter most of the time.

I came up beside Tina and looked at Rob and said, “Would you mind Rob if this beautiful young lady and I grabbed a quick dance?”

I knew Rob would take a minute or two to figure out a response, so I grabbed Tina’s hand and we walked to the makeshift dance floor just as the song ended. Luke gave me a friendly bump as he left the dance floor with Mary Lou and I quickly grabbed his arm and said, “You promised me a dance” and pushed him and Mary Lou back on the dance floor. He can thank me later.

Tina was still holding my other hand as the next song started. I don't think she had any idea it would be another slow song. As the song started, I used the old Collins slow song move. I also don't think she had any idea I would sing along with the song to her;

There's a world where I can go
Tell my secrets to
In my room
In my room (in my room)........

I did my best to keep a slight grin to let her know I was not some nut job but just having a little fun. I got her to smile and eventually, she put the side of her head on my shoulder. I was having so much fun. No worries, no pressures, just being a thirteen-year-old kid, playing 14-year-old. The song finished and I whispered in her ear, "my DJ duties needed me for a minute" and took her hand and led her to the stereo. I took the album I asked Luke to play and loaded side A. The Album was Wings Band on the Run. I wanted a chance to talk with Tina without the loud music. I asked her if she knew where we could find a little less noise so we could chat. She now grabbed my hand and led me to where I certainly was not expecting, Sherry's bedroom.

She knocked and waited to see if anyone would be yelling, 'Occupied'. After the required 30 seconds of no reply, Tina opened the door, and we went in. The room was big and there were two chairs by the corner which also housed a basement window. I assumed we would go sit in the chairs, so I walked over and sat in the one without a pile of clothes piled on it. Tina had already taken a seat on the bed with her legs crossed facing me. She said, "You can sit up here if you like, it's ok."

Being the perfect gentleman, I elected to pull the chair over and go into a semi-reclining tilt on two legs with my now sock feet resting on the edge and said with a smile, "You trying to take advantage of me?"

She blushed and fired back, "No! I just thought it would be more comfortable than a wooden chair, besides, I know you are a perfect gentleman."

We stayed in the room for about 30 minutes and talked about all sorts of stuff. I found out she had turned 15 in February, and I told her my birthday was in January but did not tell her I just turned 13. I was as big or bigger than most of the grade 8 guys there, so was not too concerned. She was telling me about Mount Mary and some of the nuns that taught there as well as her catholic upbringing when a knock came from the door. I felt

Tina and I were comfortable enough with each other now that I could not resist being a 'little shit' and replied, "Just a minute, we need to find all our clothes first."

Tina let out a short laugh and followed up with, "It's open Sherry or whoever, you can come in."

The door opened and it was Sherry. She poked her head in first just to make sure and quickly figured out nothing was going on. "I was wondering what happened to you two," she said with a smile at Tina.

"Derek and I wanted to talk without all the loud music and this is the only place available down here," Tina replied.

"Well, the crowd needs our DJ since we are currently without music. Also, Derek, a guy named Kent came down looking for you," Sherry said as she held the door open suggesting our talk was over.

I put my shoes on and Tina got off the bed and put her shoes on. We followed Sherry out and it seemed there must have been a lot of gossip going on in our absence. Every eye was checking us out and snickering. And right on cue, Rob was attempting some childish pelvic thrust dance. I figured it was about time to give them a show. I walked over to the stereo and put on the Rascals album and put the needle to track 5 on side one. I loved this song, and I once wanted it as my wedding dance song. I quickly walked over to where Tina was standing with Sherry, who I am sure was peppering her with 100 questions and grabbed her hand and led her to the dance floor. Once there I said, "let's have a little fun and try to follow my lead if you can."

I was assuming Tina never heard of the song let alone heard it played before. I grabbed her hand and said, "we're about to pretend to waltz, please let me lead and just have some fun with it."

I started to move right, step one two slide, step one two slide, and was pleasantly surprised that she appeared to know how to slide-waltz. We started off going slowly but as my grin was growing, so was hers. Damn, she has taken dance lessons. Well, as the song continued so did our speed on the floor, we were now adding 360s as we traversed the floor. It must have looked like we had secretly practiced this for months just to put on this show for our gawkers. As we came to a very special part of the song, I would test her dancing prowess and added a stationary spin. That is where I stand and hold her hand high while she continues to rotate 360 degrees as I slowly rotate 360 degrees. I don't get surprised too often but tonight Tina did just that. We were having so much fun, I wanted to play it again. But I knew, we just peaked tonight.

Having just performed a flawless dance worthy of a golden buzzer on dancing with the stars, one would expect we would exchange a kiss after the dance. What Tina did not know; I was starting to experience a major attack of the guilts. Fortunately, my valves were solidly in place and the only move that I felt comfortable with while not offending Tina was to perform a royal-like curtsy bow. With my leg extending back I enter the curtsy position and taking her hand and give it a gentle kiss with a "Thank you me'lady" for added show.

Tina gave me a warm smile and said, "What is the name of that song?"

I looked at her with a serious look and responded, "How Can I be Sure."

While I would have expected all the guys to give me the gesture of putting their fingers down their throat, pretending to hurl, and the girls all rolling their eyes thinking 'who do they think they are'; We would be wrong! We got a legit applause. Well, 25 people worth. I quickly went back to the stereo and put on the only Led Zeppelin 8-track they had, hoping for a change in the music vibe. I felt we needed some head-bobbing stuff for a bit. As Black Dog started, I walked over to the pop area. I also need a few minutes to run upstairs to give Kent the info. I figured I had 15 minutes before the last song of the night for me would play. I needed a drink and grabbed a mountain dew. Luke wandered over and with a big smile said, "You Dog."

"No, Black Dog," with an added wink,

Hoping to change the conversation direction, I asked, "How's it going with Mary Lou? When I was upstairs earlier, Maureen asked me to keep an eye on her little sister," with an added grin.

"No Way, Maureen spoke to you?", Luke questioned me.

"Not only spoke to me but also refreshed my hand-holding event at the roller rink last year," I proudly boasted.

"So why didn't you stay upstairs and try to make a move on her?", my inexperienced young wingman asked.

"Simple, Tina was down here. Maureen is not in my league, or should I say, I am not in her league and you of all people know I hate rejection. Besides, I promised I would keep an eye on her sister. So, quit avoiding my question, how is it going with Mary Lou?"

"Great. We had a few dances, and she just went to the washroom after your big dance. Where did you learn how to do that?" Luke asked.

"Isn't it obvious, that I am secretly a young Derek Flint," I said with a chuckle.

Luke and I laughed, and I took a few gulps of pop and then told him I had to shoot upstairs. I saw Tina was over with about 4 other girls in some type of scrum while most of the guys were loving my recent selection and of course, old Rob was up dancing by himself. I will have to say one thing about Rob; he does not care what anyone thinks of him. I knew I had about 13 minutes to my last big dance, so I bolted upstairs. Kent was over standing at the piano with about 15 other people. I heard someone playing something on the piano and walked over and tapped on his shoulder. Kent turned and saw it was me and reached in his pocket and pulled out a piece of paper and a pencil. I wrote down the info and handed it back. I moved my position to see who was playing and it was Maureen and another girl trying to figure out the cords to the song 'Close to you' by the Carpenters.

Damn, 'just when I thought I was out, they pull me back in'. Well, that's what I should have been thinking! If it was not for Maureen, I would have simply left, but geez, it was Maureen. Yes, I was way too young for her I am sure, but there is nothing wrong with planting seeds for the future! *(I know, I am showboating some more.... I will address it while walking home Rebecca)*. I moved around the group and made my way in behind and tapped Maureen on the shoulder and said, "May I," and reached over and around her as she moved her hands to her lap, and I showed her the correct cords and fingering for the song intro.

Her friend immediately said, "That's it. Do you know the whole song?"

"I think I do, but I may be a bit rusty, and I don't know the words," I replied.

"Slide over Maureen and let the kid in," she instructed.

Did she just call me a kid? Let me show what this kid can do Miss Redhead who was around 17! I sat between them and started the song. I was kind of hoping Maureen was the singer, but I get the impression she was more there for moral support. As I started to play, old Red started to sing. I hate to say it, but she was not that bad. No American Idol level but at least she could stay in tune and had the correct vocal intonation. When the song was over the old gang up here were a bit more civilized, I think, and they all clapped, and a few gave a concert-style whistle. My kryptonite struck as Maureen said to me, "do you know any good songs?" Well, this one is fairly new, and I can actually handle the vocal range.

I was also hoping this would not get ugly later with some of the guys wanting to beat the crap out of me for ruining their shot at Maureen. But Red just insulted me and I had to defend all the kids out there! The song had no intro, just right into lyrics and twinkling the ivories. I announced to the group, "If anyone knows the words, please join in and try to make me sound great."

Long long time ago, I can still remember.....

There is a BT Barnum saying, 'Always leave them wanting more'. I stopped playing after the first verse and quickly jumped up and announced to everyone, "Sorry but I just realized I have a dance with a very special girl downstairs in 2 minutes."

As I was hurrying out of the room, I heard Tim say, "Hey, can't you finish the song and then go?"

I turned and replied, "We have a dance floor going downstairs."

I headed down the stairs and was dead on. 'The Battle of Evermore' was about half done. I could tell that not everyone was a Led Head, and this song probably needed a few beers to appreciate. But it did make sure the dance floor was empty. I went over to where Tina was standing with a bunch of girls and asked her, "would you be available for my last dance tonight?"

She gave me a sweet smile that said, 'Of course'. I extended my hand and she reciprocated and grabbed it. As we turned to head in the direction of the dance floor, I could see a bunch of people from upstairs coming down the stairs.

In the middle of those coming down was Maureen. I turned to Luke and yelled, "Meeting on the Dance Floor in 1 minute." Someone must have turned down the volume for one of the last Zepplin songs, so I had to detour past the stereo to crank it up. We reached the dance floor, and I could tell everyone was waiting to hear what song was coming on. Everyone knew before the first bar had finished that it was 'Stairway to Heaven'. I was officially down to my last 7 minutes and 55 seconds with Tina tonight. I had a great time tonight with Tina and she is a great girl. I would like to see more of her, but I had a bigger problem. When the music started, I was holding Tina like I once held Rebecca at the Collins. All I could do was imagine I was dancing with Rebecca. I was going through a major crisis in my head, but my heart said, finish your dance with Rebecca and then get the hell out of there.

I did just that. I would allow myself to feel guilty about what I was secretly doing to Tina, but my heart was clearly winning this battle. Suddenly, I accidentally bumped into someone and noticed that the dance floor was packed. Almost everyone that could fit downstairs was dancing. The only one standing against the far wall watching me dance was Maureen. Our eyes did make momentary contact and she smiled at me. I felt a bit sorry for her and as the song was about to end, I needed to figure out my swift departure route and story. I was so preoccupied re-living my Rebecca dance that I did not realize I was dancing close with Tina, just like I did with Rebecca. The song was down to the last 15 seconds, and I grabbed Tina's hand and led us off the dance floor. I whispered in her ear, "This was a really special night for me, and I am glad I met you. I know we just met but I would like to see you again sometime if you happen to feel the same way about me."

Tina looked at me and gave me a warm smile and then a sweet kiss on the cheek. I said, "I am sorry I have to go; I have to get up real early tomorrow."

She leaned in and said, "I will get your number from Sherry and give you a call tomorrow night."

"Great. I can't wait," I said with a big smile.

I know I should have said goodbye to Luke and a bunch of other people, but it would have to be only those I would pass leaving. My coat was upstairs in the front hall and as I passed Maureen, I said, "Mary Lou is in good hands with Luke." I passed by Sherry and gave her a quick peck on the cheek and said, "Thanks so much for the invite and for introducing me to Tina." I caught her off guard and she appeared very confused that I was leaving. I progressed up the stairs and reached the kitchen. Ted was in the Kitchen doing a little tidying up. I said to Ted, "Great party Ted and sorry I can't stay and help clean up."

"Hey, don't worry, got it covered, and thanks for helping Kent and great job on the piano," he replied.

I made it to the door and grabbed my coat and left as quickly as I could. My heart was finished for the night and my brain had taken over. The rain was done, and it would take me about 30 minutes to walk home. I would need that time to figure this out. Once I got a few deep breaths of the evening air, I was able to gain some mental composure.

UPDATE – Confessional PART II

(April 1st – April 30th, 1974)

****An important message to Rebecca:****

36 ***The Walk Home:*** *[I inserted this warning once I was able to get past what I wrote next. This section is a continuation of the prior section. If you're reading this, then I finished the guide. It's not necessary to read this section. It will not have any real bearing on what I am asking you to do. I know you're thinking, 'then why leave it in'? Because I needed to have it here, just in case at any time in the future, I need to remind myself of this issue. My suggestion is to skip it because it is going to expose you to a very dark and disturbing side of me. I had no one to vent too, get advice, or help me figure major stuff out. I will apologize for my language if you do read it. I always made a special effort to avoid swearing around you. It was never our thing. But I was angry and alone. I hope you will understand my circumstance and find a way to accept it for what it was at the time]*

As I began my walk home, all I could think about was what an absolute asshole I was. Wow, look at the 63-year-old man who is disguised as a thirteen-year-old kid, manipulating a bunch of other kids. I knew better but just had to go and play the bigshot. Hey, watch me dance, hey, listen to me sing and play the piano. But what I am most disgusted with, was my total lack of respect for Tina and her feelings. The thirteen-year-old me really liked her, but the 63-year-old perv was trying to live out some childhood fantasy. Yes, she looked a lot like Lindsey Wagner; Yes, she was a natural beauty, yes, she had a great personality, but she was still just a 15-year-old girl.

When I first came up with the whole do-over idea, it was solely motivated by the idea that I could come back and not make all the mistakes I made with Rebecca the first time. Mr. 'Beat the System' has once again come to life! Sure, justifying it on the basis of a greater good and hoping I would be able to right my perceived wrongs. She was my 'it-girl' and all I wanted to be, was her 'it-boy'. How can something that sounds so wonderful, and innocent, be so sick and deprived now. Because I am no longer that same kid. I will never be that kid ever again. I am, and always will be an old man hiding in the body of that kid. Yet, for a few moments tonight, I was just a kid. When I was first introduced to her, I had real thirteen-year-old butterflies. When we had our first dance, I was a thirteen-year-old kid, nervous and excited all at the same time. The 63-year-old man was gone. When we went to the bedroom to chat, I was a thirteen-year-old kid, not some perv envisioning this beautiful young girl wearing her school uniform in pigtails. And yes Rebecca, every single guy ever in existence has that disgusting thought buried deep, deep in their pervy brain. Call it DNA if you will. If they claim they never would think like that then they are the ones to watch out for!

It was almost like I had a split personality. One moment I am a thirteen-year-old kid and another moment I am a 63-year-old time-cheating paedophile. Really, what determines a person's age anyway. If I had sex with Tina, I would never be charged or held accountable as a thirteen-year-old kid. I haven't even had my first wet dream for god sake. But if a 63-year-old man had sex with Tina, he would be a paedophile and rapist and I would most likely put him on my list. Does that mean I am no better than fucking Peter Bernard? And what the fuck happened when I went from dancing with Tina to suddenly pretending, I was reliving my dance at the Collins with Rebecca. And when realizing I was doing it, refused to stop.

I am in big trouble right now. What the hell should I do? Go off myself and end the do-over? Yes, my parent's 2.0 would be devastated, but I wouldn't have to deal with this feeling I am some paedophile. Or do I embrace the whole paedophile thing and go and bang all the girls in my past that I use to think were hot! Because 'I'm Derek Devon, male prostitute'! Fuck Dan Aykroyd as well! Hell, why stop there; I could easily bang everyone; hot hockey moms, sisters, twins at the same time, up-and-coming movie stars. There would be no end, right? Hell, money will soon be no object. Buy my own jet, a few Lamborghinis, and work as an actor when I want. Pick all the great roles. And Music! I could have my own stolen music catalogue that would be the biggest and best ever.

I will tell you why! I would have to become a mother fucker, egotistical narcissist, loser, low life for the remainder of this life. I guess they haven't come up with the 'Party Store' concept yet or I would be heading over tomorrow to get myself a canister of balloon helium. I don't think I have ever felt this alone Rebecca. Utterly alone. No one to talk with about this. And we all remember what happened the last time *(a play on words intended)*, I had become emotionally compromised! Should have asked my new friends to turn me into a Vulcan!

I was about halfway home and just about at the end of Lover's Lane when I was starting to believe there may be a God. As I got onto Fiddler's, the sky opened up and God's tears of laughter came raining down on me. I was completely drenched by the time I got to the lights. As I reached the halfway mark up Fiddler's, I had to stop for a moment and think. I wonder if it is possible to segregate my mind into two zones. The kid Zone and the 'Wise old Man' Zone. It happened on its own at the party. I wonder what the triggers were that allowed the change in the thought process. I recall the sudden shift from 'The Kid', to 'Love Sick Kid' was my thought about you and 'Stairway to Heaven' did not help. But my dance with Tina and the bedroom chat. How was I able to enter the kid zone without any interference?

It was somewhat ironic that I was now standing in front of Sarah's house. I gave myself a brief respite with a solo giggle. If there was ever a time to congratulate me for being a bit of a TV'oholic, it was right now. I think I may have a solution!

> *'Why did it all turn out like this for me? I had so much promise. I was personable, I was bright. Oh, maybe not academically speaking, but ... I was perceptive. I always know when someone's uncomfortable at a party. It became very clear to me sitting out there today, that every decision I've ever made, in my entire life, has been wrong. My life is the opposite of everything I want it to be. Every instinct I have, in every aspect of life, be it something to wear, something to eat ... It's all been wrong.* ***Yes, I will do the opposite****. I used to sit here and do nothing, and regret it for the rest of the day, so now I will do the opposite, and I will do something!*
>
> *My name is George. I'm unemployed and I live with my parents.*

Yes! My main man George Constanza has the solution. The last time I was faced with an emotional crisis of similar proportion, my decision to handle it myself did not turn out that great. *(It was something I never talked with Rebecca 1.0 about and always regretted that)*. So, this time I will do the opposite! I will seek out a therapist to help me deal with all this shit! The only problem is; I would need my parents' consent. Hmm, what to do?

I continued my walk to my house and went inside. I had to use the hidden key from the garage which meant my mom was in bed already. It was around 11:30 pm and I had no idea if my sister was home or out. After I unlocked the front door I put the key back in our hiding spot, on top of the mailbox. I entered quietly and went to my room. I was drenched head to toe and stripped out of my clothes. I grabbed a towel and dried off, put on some fresh tighty-whities, my PJs, and a pair of socks. And to keep my self-promise of always brushing my teeth to make sure they would be as white as yours, I did just that.

I closed my door and climbed into bed. I sure wished at that moment I still had the video my friends made of us at the Hermitage. So, absent that, I just stared at the ceiling thinking over the idea of getting myself some psychological help. Finally, it came to me. A bit slow for my usual quick-thinking brain, but it was clear to me. I would have to do what most 13-year-old kids would do when faced with a similar dilemma. I would need to get an ex-parti court order authorizing me to hire a therapist/Psychologist without any parental consent. Simple! I can start work on writing my draft Court application tomorrow and hopefully, I can find a family court judge to hear my motion in chambers. If all goes as I hope, I could have my order in under two weeks.

This solution would truly be the opposite for me, but I would need to select the right person to provide the counseling. That step I will devote some time to over the next week. My other issue is what to do about Tina. She will be calling me tomorrow night and I don't want to be that guy who completely avoids her. It would be easy since we don't attend the same school and I don't think she would confide in Sherry, her potential deep disappointment in my not speaking with her again. However, I like Tina and she was the only person so far, I can point out that allowed me to forget the old man and be the kid. I think the right approach would be to continue to chat with her on the phone. Try to stretch out any face-to-face for a while. I should be able to be in therapy at the most, in 3 weeks. I have a hockey tournament next weekend so that is a good excuse. Tina goes to a different school so it might be good to get to know each other over the phone for a while. I remember we used to spend a lot of time chatting on the phone Rebecca, until one of our siblings or a parent would pick up and tell us to get off.

It was a very tough day. An emotional rollercoaster. I am feeling a lot better now that I have a plan and even more reassuring, I am doing the opposite. Sorry babe, no Hudson Bay fur-lined hooded coat for you this time *(Sorry, an inside joke to myself)*. So, first thing tomorrow, start drafting my court papers.

UPDATE – Student Mentoring Initiative

(May 1st, - May 31st, 1974)

37 It was amazing how fast time was passing. I had less than 2 months before the summer holidays started. Hockey was done and baseball was starting. I needed to determine if I want to play summer hockey in the next couple of weeks. Tina and I have been chatting on the phone a lot and it's been a welcome distraction. I completed my court paperwork and have filed what needed to be filed. I was hoping for a little faster turnaround on a date but the best I could get was Thursday, May 30th, 1974. I was able to find a Judge, Justice MacKenzie who has agreed to do the matter in Chambers but due to my age, the court is required to have at least two court clerks present. I am not completely sure that Justice MacKenzie is fully aware I will be appearing to represent myself. If he's not, I am sure it will make for an interesting update.

The other big news is my soap and dryer sheet manufacturer was so impressed with the oxi-clean 'cheat formula' that he has agreed to manufacture 25,000 sample packs, provided I allowed him to file a provisional patent for the formula. I agreed with the only change that I would receive a lifetime royalty on all production of 7.5% after he had recouped any upfront costs with my production needs. I received last week the first batch of 5,000 samples and have already been able to distribute them to my army of paperboys. Each of my guys rec'd 20 samples. They are going to give the sample pack to the best 19 prospects and give one to their mothers. If the customer was impressed with the sample, we would then ask them for a monthly order. Our monthly package would give them 20 loads. Eventually, we would increase it to a 3-month supply or 60 loads. That would lower the amount of handling we would need to do.

I had my mom try it and she was ecstatic at how well it cleaned and absolutely loved the dryer sheets. Mom would get her supply free *(Yuk yuk)*. I had already used my own route to test the system. Out of the 40 I gave sample packs to, 36 elected to continue with the monthly program. If I can get my guys to generate a 50% conversion rate, then I will double my initial sales forecast. I did run into a little resistance by a few carriers and they in turn had their parents call the Spec and complain. But since the success of the 'Kids 4 Cancer Cure', no one questioned my activity. I hired Blane part-time to help with distribution. I had signed up 30 people to handle product distribution on a part-time basis. I am currently renting a small warehouse in Westdale. I have a transport truck come in from Acme

Manufacturing *(Yes the real name)* and Bottling Co., the company handling the manufacturing.

They unload the stock into my warehouse where I break the load into smaller shipments. I have Luke and Stevo working part-time on this task. It is a fairly efficient system. I give a handful of Spec management a free supply to keep them happy and ignore any complaints. Most of my guys have been excited to add the extra income. My next big battle is with insurance coverage and taxation. I have hired Mr. Mattson to do the books and a friend of my dad, Mr. Cousins is looking into the insurance.

By the end of July, I forecast I will be making a net profit for yours truly of $7,500.00. Not bad for my first business venture.

[Tina called last night and asked if I would go and see a movie with her and a couple of friends. Her parents would also be attending since they wanted to see the movie. I have briefly spoken to Tina's mom when I called a couple of times, but I have not spoken to her dad. I am sure they are aware that Tina has been talking exclusively with some guy *(I think exclusively?)*. I just don't know if they have been given any additional info. The movie was The Great Gatsby. I would have preferred to go to see 'Thunderbolt and Lightfoot'. I agreed, and she asked if I wanted to drive to the theatre with her, a couple of friends and her parents. I said sure and told her I would ride my bike over to her place. I will let you know how it goes.]

UPDATE – Grade 7 Graduation and Camp

(June 1st, - July 15th, 1974)

38 ***The 'friend experience' with a girl!:*** First, I had my ex-parti in chambers hearing regarding my obtaining a court order allowing me to seek therapy without any parental consent. I had gone to Mr. Angelo and had him make me another suit. This one was a more traditional suit. As a result of the success of my first suit, and everyone asking where I got it, Mr. Angelo added a couple of dozen new clients. Some had some very deep pockets. So, it looked like this suit was a freebie too. It was a dark grey pinstripe with a full lapel and vest. I like vests. It was another work of art and Mr. Angelo made sure to include a couple of Egyptian cotton super fine white dress shirts as well as one all-black satin-styled shirt. And perfectly matched ties. The suit did make me look older. At Least 15 *(he he).*

When I showed up for the hearing the Judge was not aware that I would be representing myself. When I was taken into the Judge's Chambers, the Judge was sitting behind his desk in Robes and one male clerk and a female stenographer. When I entered, I stopped and made the traditional bow when entering the chambers. The Judge welcomed me and asked, "Where is your lawyer?"

"You're looking at him your honor," I replied.

"The male clerk let out a bit of a snicker and the Judge then asked, "Where is the person who prepared your filings."

"You're also looking at him your Honour," I replied again.

"So, you are telling me that you prepared everything filed to date?", challenged the Judge.

"Yes, your honor, I have prepared all the material in my brief myself. I also did all of the required case law research as well as the addendum containing my expert witness report. Just to add your Honour, I am what people refer to as a 'Gifted Child'. I read, write and think like I am 40 years old. It's a curse on some level and that is why I am here today seeking the order," I explained while taking a seat.

The judge looked at his clerk and at the stenographer then back at me. He began to read my filings again, which I was certain he had only glanced at before this hearing. I knew I had his attention as he flipped pages and would look up at me each page turn. After flipping through the entire Motion material, he asked me, "So can I conclude that your parents are not aware you are here today or that you are seeking this order without their consent?"

"That is correct your honor," I replied.

"And you are currently thirteen years of age," he asked.

"Yes sir. My birthday was January 9th," I responded.

"And you prepared every page submitted, did all your case law research, prepared the addendum, and filed all the material completely on your own. No help from anyone?", the judge asked.

"Your honor, if I may. It might be easier if you think of me like some 40-year-old seasoned lawyer in the body of a young kid. I have to deal with this situation every day. At school, at home, no matter where I go, I created a great deal of uncomfortableness for people sitting in front of me. I did not ask to be this way, it just happened. When I started the charity 'Kids 4 Cancer Cure', I also faced a great deal of resistance and plenty of trepidation in people I needed to work with. But over time, they adapted and overcame their biases. Eventually, they learned to look at me as a colleague and not some very smart gifted kid. I know I am an anomaly and I find myself often in a state of confusion and extreme anxiety. But I am also smart enough to know that it would be extremely beneficial for me to seek counseling at times. If I go to my parents with my concerns, it is unfair to them. Parents will often blame themselves or worse, think they can fix the issue themselves. I have great loving parents, but I want to deal with my issues without burdening them or making them feel they are not great parents. My supporting case law I believe is more than sufficient for your Honour to grant my request. I am happy to answer any questions you may have, but my written submissions should stand on their own, I plead," as I now sat back and waited for a response.

Justice MacKenzie just sat there and stared at me for the better part of 3 minutes. He then shifted his seat and started reviewing the motion material in extreme detail. After about 20 minutes, he got up and walked over to a bookcase, and removed a textbook. He returned to his seat and started reading a section of the textbook. I knew exactly what text he was reading and the section. My main argument was based on a very old and obscure section of the Mental Health Act of 1894. The section I referred him to, dealt with a case between the Catholic church and their authority over children in their care at their facilities. A judge had granted one of the older children to act as an adult without parental consent or knowledge when having to provide an affidavit pertaining to one of the school priests sexually assaulting children under his care.

Justice MacKenzie then asked the clerk to fetch him another book from the courthouse law library. The clerk got up and left. The judge continued reading the book he pulled and was comparing my argument with the text of the book. He then looked up at me and said, "The authority you are relying on was subsequently replaced by the 1934 Act. There was no provision given in the 1934 act to grandfather any of the 1894 act."

"You are correct, except for one exception. The supreme court in 1972 adopted the language from the 1894 decision in Ham versus The Catholic Diocese of New West Minister. That decision, which was upheld both on provincial appeal as well as the federal appeal did grant the exact relief I am seeking, provided the court is satisfied that the circumstance contained in the requested motion, met the same specific concerns and potential damage. I believe my argument addressed and provides your honor with that exact foundation," I countered.

The clerk returned and handed the book to Justice MacKenzie. He did not even bother to open it and confirm what I just told him. He sat there for another couple of minutes staring at me. I sat and returned the look. He then shifted his chair and addressed me formally. "Mr. Devon, this court having reviewed your submission is satisfied that the relief you are seeking is appropriate under the circumstances, however, as a parent myself, I would like to ask that you consider discussing this matter with them. You may be pleasantly surprised by their depth of understanding and capacity to understand your wishes. This court grants your motion, and this matter is now adjourned," the judge announced.

I stood up and said to Justice MacKenzie, "Thank you your honor and I will take your suggestion under advisement. I am heading into unchartered waters, and I will assure you that if my therapist advises me to do the same, I will certainly comply," I added.

"My clerk will type up your order. I see you provided a draft order. It should be ready for you in about 30 minutes. There is a very interesting case being argued right now in courtroom 3, if you are looking for a place to kill 30 minutes," the judge advised. I did the official bow and left his chambers. I took the judge's suggestion and went and sat in courtroom 3.

After 30 minutes, I returned to the Judges clerk's desk and picked up the order. Just as I was leaving the Judge, appeared out of gowns and said, "You should consider a career in law young man," with an added smile.

"I think I may prefer to make the laws your honor rather than enforcing them," I rebutted.

And that was it. I had my order and all that was left was to finalize who I wanted to try out as my therapist.

Well, it was almost the end of grade 7. It was a great year and from a 10,000-foot level, I think I hit, all of my major objectives so far. I was getting used to my new skin and although I did have that one hiccup, my opposite solution will hopefully help with my ongoing problem. I have been invited to a bunch of different graduation parties. Grade seven parties are all parent-driven and grade 8 parties are more like a real graduation party since they are graduating, complete with a graduation ceremony at school. Tina had her own party she was going to with kids from her school. I know she would like me to go but we have kind of settled into our arrangement of keeping those two worlds separate. At least for now. I did go to the movies with Tina, her friends, and her parents. Her mother liked me, but her dad was a different story. He was constantly probing me with questions. Not uncomfortable questions, just ones that he was hoping would give him any advance warning that 'This Kid' was bad news. Kind of what I am sure your folks will want to do Rebecca with your pre-me guys *(I am smiling)*.

Most telling for me was the selection of the seats for the movie. Tina's dad sat right beside me and Tina to my right. Her girlfriends are to her right and her mother is to the left of her dad. This was our first physical get-together since Sherry's party, and I did not have a comfort zone established with what I should expect. We talk all the time on the phone just like an old married couple. We discuss all sorts of stuff, but I never got a girlfriend-boyfriend vibe. When I first saw her at her house when she answered the door, she had a nervous smile, probably just like I did. I was the last to arrive, so it made it less uncomfortable when she introduced me to her parents. Her dad gave me a very firm handshake while her mom gave me a big smile and the natural reply, "Very nice to put a face to the voice Derek."

I knew better than to try some Eddie Haskell line and just said, "Same here Mrs. V." 'V' for Van Houten! I used that on an earlier phone call exchange when I called Tina. I met her friends, a couple I thought I knew from hockey but was more focused on not doing or saying something stupid, I mostly listened in on the other discussions. We chatted for about 20 minutes and then Mr. Van Houten said, "Let's roll in 5."

We all got in their suburban which was huge. Tina made sure to sit me behind her dad's seat, and she was beside me, with two more jammed to her right, and 3 more in the very back. As soon as the truck started to roll, I got a light elbow in the side from Tina. I looked at her and her eyes made a gesture that directed me to look down. She had her hand sitting on top of our legs which were tight together considering the seating arrangement. And it was open and in the up position. I knew immediately she wanted to hold hands secretly without her folks seeing. I got those wonderful butterfly's again and elected to do a variation on her request, and I grabbed her thumb and held it in my hand. She tried to remove it, but I would not let go and I knew she did not want to make a scene with her parents right in front. I sat quietly with a slight grin and eventually Tina gave in, and we both grinned as her mother was talking about Tina going to summer camp for the first time this summer.

Apparently, it was a summer camp that her mother had once gone to. Mrs. 'V', I would guess was in her early 40's while Tina's dad was closer to 50. So, as I held Tina's thumb with the periodic attempt on her side to free herself from my grip, I took in all the details and one activity that grabbed my attention was they did horseback riding. I love horses and use to own a couple as you know Becca. As we arrived at Jackson Square, Mr. Van Houten parked underground with the truck barely fitting under the ceiling and all the hanging pipework. Once we got parked, I let Tina's thumb go and she gave me a loving elbow to my side again, along with her new sweet sinister grin. We all climbed out and walked as a pack to the theatres. It was fairly new, and with it attached to the mall, was always full. I was not really looking forward to the movie as much as I was getting to spend some time with Tina.

I brought my own money of course and paid for my ticket. We never discussed the ticket paying arrangement so I assumed each person would pay for their own seat. I was wrong. Mr. Van Houten had planned to pay for everyone and when I was first in line and handed the ticket person a $10 bill, I am sure it caught him off guard. As the attendant handed me my change and ticket, Mr. Van Houten put his hand on my shoulder and said, "I was planning on treating everyone today. Especially with you kids allowing Mrs. Van Houten and me to join you."

I replied, "Sorry Sir, Tina didn't mention anything about that to me. But I do appreciate the thought."

We all got our tickets and Tina was now at the back of the pack with one of her girlfriends and I could tell they were trying to plot some seating order. Mrs. "V' asked all us kids if we wanted any popcorn. Everyone but me said yes. She looked at me and said, "Derek, do you not like popcorn?"

I replied, "I do like popcorn, but my folks are having a big dinner tonight and I better leave plenty of room, or I may offend my mother." Truth be told, I didn't want to sit there and stuff popcorn in my mouth on a first date! Not to mention having butter-covered fingers. We did the concession thing and went to the theatre and found a row that would accommodate the group. I would have suggested 2 rows with a more center of the theatre seating location, but Mrs. 'V' had the lead. As we started the musical seats routine, I got the distinct impression that Mr. Van Houten had already in his mind selected the seat right beside the young boy that apparently his little girl really liked.

When we all settled in our seats, Mr. Van Houten turned and asked me, "How is the 'Kids 4 a Cancer Cure', going these days."

I was caught a bit off guard by the question but was not shocked since he was a surgeon at the hospital that was the benefactor of my earlier plan. "Well, Mr. Simpkins has been handling most of the day-to-day things and we hired an accounting firm to look after the accounting stuff. We are meeting once a month and have already started planning next year's event," I explained.

"I must say that I am very impressed with such a young boy having the thought to do something for such a noble cause. I see what cancer does every day at work and you would be surprised how many lives are impacted," he added.

Mrs. 'V' at this moment felt the time was right to add her perspective to the discussion. "I have a very close friend who is fighting breast cancer and it's such a shame to see that disease hit such a young lady in her prime."

"Yes, that is terrible, and I hope that one day we will discover a cure," I threw into the discussion.

Suddenly I get an elbow in my side and Tina chimes in with, "If you guys are finished chatting with Derek, we have a kid discussion going on, on this side."

Her mom and dad exchanged glances and then turned and in a parental friendly tone said, "Sorry honey, we didn't mean to ruin your outing," adding a grin.

I turned to look at Tina, who was looking a bit jealous that I was chatting with her parents rather than her. So, I turned and said, "I am all yours" with a grin and my eyes telling her to look down. I had my hand on the armrest and my thump pointing up in the 'Fonze' position. She looked down and then gave me that sweet devious smile and then gave the thumb a gentle smack. I started to get caught up on the discussion from my right. The girls were all talking about the summer camp, and 2 of her friends were saying they were going to talk to their parents to see if they might be able to go. As I like to often say, a seed was planted. Geez, maybe I should go? This summer would be probably my last 'Kids Summer' with me being 14 next year. Summer hockey would be a must and I would be getting ready to go to high school. I had once gone to a summer camp for 4 days with my sister when I was 9. It was fun and it was the first time I was scared shitless, *(Pardon the language)* when one of the camp councilors told us the story of the old witch lady that lived in the woods nearby and would try to steal kids from the camp.

Plan Change! I think I may want to go to the camp this summer! What could go wrong with a bunch of emerging young adolescents just coming through puberty, raging hormones, and no parents around for a week? The movie's pre-show stuff started and as soon as the lights dimmed, I felt an elbow and looked over at the armrest. Tina had positioned her hand on the armrest with her thumb doing 'The Fonze'. We dared not look at each other, just stared at the screen. As I moved my hand into position to 'accost' Tina's thumb, I felt another light nudge on my left side. Oh-oh! Busted, I turned to look at Mr. 'V' *(I am more comfortable using that tag now)*, and he gestured with his eyes to look down at his armrest. Great, all I would need now to freak me out, is to see him holding his hand in 'The Fonz' position. Fortunately for me, he had a box of Glossette Peanuts and was offering me a handful. I smiled and joked, "Thanks but I am watching my waistline."

Don't ask me about the movie because I don't think either of us watched it *(Tina and me that is)*. First, I would hold Tina's thumb and then after a bit, she would grip mine. By the middle of the movie, we had started to introduce the modified 'Fonz' with the new 'T&D' move. We added the art of the squeeze. Almost like our own morse code. What made it so special for me and I hope as well for Tina, was the continuous butterfly feeling I was having. The only momentary 'Old man' moment was a split-second thought, which scared the hell out of me, 'What would I do if she started to slide her closed fist up and down on my thumb'? Thank you know who, that that never happened to ruin our innocent kids' bonding moment.

When the movie ended, Tina and I immediately stopped our joining and assumed or attempt to give a look that said, 'What a great movie, and Derek and I never did something completely inappropriate with our thumbs'. She walked out with her girlfriends, and I was upfront with her parents. When we got to the car, I opened Mrs. V's door for her. I knew it would piss Tina off. We all took our same seat selections and once again after a good elbow and a brief death stare from Tina, I was doing the 'T&D'

all the way home. When we got to the Van Houten's house everyone got out and I tried to jump ahead of anyone else and said my thanks and goodbyes. I just gave Tina a wave, got on my bike, and started my ride home.

I want to try to best describe how I was feeling, and the closest example I can compare was our third date when we met at Sandy B's house in Dundas for a party. You went with Sandra, and I went with Luke. Do you remember how we would stand listening to different people talking and you had your hand behind your back, and I was right behind you holding your hand with the old finger circle around your palm. No one knew we were dating yet, and no one knew of our secret hand touching all night. We did that all night and since there was no dancing, we must have stood and listened to a dozen conversations that night. Some I was behind you and some you were behind me. No conversation, just touching each other in a very intimate and secret way all night. Sorry Rebecca, I just realized it was another Becca 1.0 experience I was recalling.

I had to pass in front of Luke's house and for a split second thought I might stop in for a quick hello and tell him about the 'T&D'. But I decided I just wanted to enjoy the feelings I was having. I arrived home and walked in the door. Mom said as I hit the hallway, "That girl, Tina just called."

I said, "Thanks" and went to the phone and called Tina. Tina answered and before she could get a word in, I said, "Hi Tina, this is Derek, and I am here in the kitchen with my beautiful mom."

"I just wanted to call and say thank you for coming to the movie. My folks liked you as well. I had a really great time, and my thumb wants to thank you too," she said with a cute tone.

"Well, I hope that your thumb does not get too swollen," I quipped.

Tina was starting to get more comfortable exchanging little innuendo-style jokes as she replied, "I should be saying that to you."

That was all we needed, and she said, "Don't try thumbing without me."

I let out a chuckle and had to have the last word as usual, "Wait till you discover the big toe," and hung up. All in all, that was a great day. I was able to get the butterflies and the 'dirty old man' stayed, for the most part, hidden. I would try a do a little research about Tina's summer camp. I like the idea but want to get a few therapy sessions under my belt before I go too much further down this emotional road. I knew our relationship was moving towards a girlfriend/boyfriend declaration. It happened with us, and I felt like it was heading in that same direction.

UPDATE – What About Derek?

***(July 15th - August 15th, 1974*
*)***

39 ***Therapy 101!:*** The summer was flying by, and I had already had two therapy sessions. I selected a gentleman, Doctor White. He was a 60-something male clinical psychologist who had co-written a text on adolescent behavior. He also worked at a building near the Psych hospital, on a bus route I could access near my place. When I booked the appointment, his secretary thought I was trying to pull a prank on him and would not book an appointment. Finally, after the second try, I hopped on the bus and went to his office. I had the signed court order with me and walked into their reception area, which was a shared area with three other doctors.

I went to the woman at the front desk area, and she asked, "How may I help you."

"I have called here a couple of times trying to book an appointment with Doctor White, but the lady I have been speaking with would not make the booking," I explained.

"Are you the person who has some Court papers" she replied?

"Yes, I am. Here is a signed copy," I said as I handed it to her.

She sat there and read the Court order and then asked me to take a seat for a moment. I assumed she must have called Doctor White on the intercom line when she got up and went to an office door with Doctor White's nameplate on the front of it. I quickly scanned the waiting area and noticed a stack of magazines. I walked over and took a look to see if anything was interesting to read, and near the middle, I came across a Magazine titled 'Scientific American Mind.' It had a neat picture of a dissected brain on the cover. I grabbed it and sat in the chair beside the table. I had just started flipping through it when the lady from the front came out and asked if I would follow her. I got up, and she took me into Doctor White's office.

It was a classic-looking office of an academic—large, woody, with books everywhere. As I entered the office, the reception lady asked me to take a seat which was located in front of the Doc's desk. The Doc was on the phone, and I picked up almost immediately that he was talking to the court. It was the Judge himself. I took the chair, and the receptionist lady sat off to the side of the office in another chair. The Doc sat quietly for a couple of minutes, then laughed. He sat and listened, then laughed again. Finally, he thanked Justice MacKenzie and hung up the phone.

He shifted his position, got up, and turned to open the office drapes. The office became a lot brighter. He then took his seat and addressed me. "As you probably heard, I spoke to the Judge who issued this court order. This is a first for me, and I needed to verify that it was legitimate and to get some added direction from the Judge. My name is Doctor White, and this is our receptionist Miss Gale Westerbeeke. I am sorry that you had some difficulty trying to book an appointment, but we have never had a situation like this before. I have another appointment shortly but would like to chat with you for a few minutes, and Gale will fetch my appointment book."

"Thank you, Doc; if you don't mind me calling you Doc, or if you prefer, I am happy to call you Doctor White, but with this being our first meeting, I would be uncomfortable calling you Harold," I said with a smile.

"Doc or Doctor White is fine with me," he replied with a slight chuckle.

Miss Westerbeeke got up and left the room. She was in her mid 30's, hair pulled up, and was about 30 lbs overweight. She had what I would call a natural stern look. Not very inviting, and her actions were very robotic-like. The Doc grabbed a notebook of some sort and started writing. After a couple of minutes, he stopped and looked at me with a smile. He moved a couple of items in front of him and then said, "My hourly rate is $150 per hour or part. I will assume you will not be paying by way of a cheque from your parents, but I prefer to be paid before an appointment. As per the order, I am required to have at least one additional adult present during your appointment. This will increase the hourly rate by $50, making the total per hour $200. Is that acceptable to you?" he asked.

"That is fine, Doctor White, and I will be issuing you my own cheque. To lessen my bank fees, I will issue you an initial payment of $1,000.00 which will cover the first five sessions. I have no idea how many sessions I will need, but I am sure it will be at least five unless you have a red or blue pill for me to take," I replied.

He looked a bit puzzled and said, "I do not generally like to prescribe medications and have no idea what meds you are referring to that are red or blue."

"Sorry, Doc, I was trying to lighten things up. It was a reference to a movie scene where a person had to decide if they wanted to return to their present life or take the red pill and start a whole new life," I explained.

"Oh, interesting reaction," he replied and started writing again.

"I would like to schedule an appointment this week if you're available. When Gale returns, I think I have time at 4 pm this Thursday," he told me.

"I have a paper route doc, and it usually takes me until 4 to get the papers delivered. With the Bus schedule, the best I could do would be 5 pm or weekends," I replied.

"Ok, I keep later office hours on Tuesdays and Thursdays. I also teach a class at Mohawk in the evenings those days. To give you a bit more time, let's try to pencil in 5:30 to 6:30 next Thursday. I think we will need a couple of meetings together before we can look at a longer schedule. If I may ask, how are you going to address your absence with your parents" he asked.

"I will tell them I have a business meeting. I tend to have a fair number of business meetings and appointments. They are used to me having to go places after school. I am sure mom will ensure I get fed before I leave as all mothers would do," I answered.

Miss Westerbeeke entered the room and sat in the seat at the far end of the office. The Doc said, "Please pencil Mr. Devon into Thursday at 5:30 pm as well as the following two Tuesdays and Thursdays. Ok, Derek looks like we got this all straightened out, and I look forward to seeing you Thursday at 5:30 pm.

As I got up, I reached into my pants pocket and pulled out a cheque I had already prepared, signed, and handed to the Doc. As he took it from my hand, I could not resist the temptation and said, "Baby steps, doc, baby steps," with a grin.

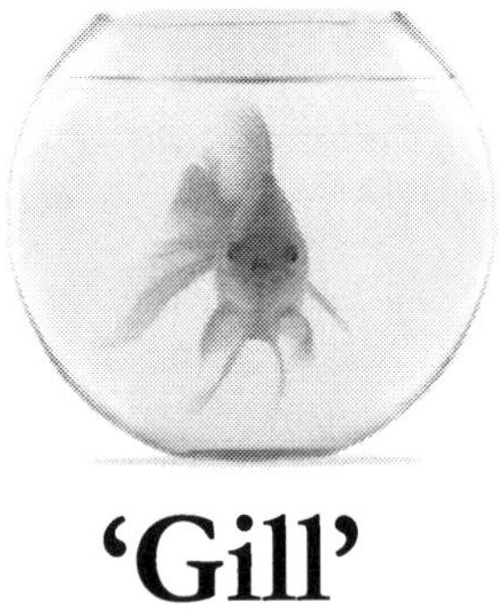

'Gill'

UPDATE – Summer Camp and Rebecca Spotting

(July 15th - August 15th, 1974)

40 ***Sarah 2.0!:*** I will fill you in after I get a few more sessions under my belt. The other exciting news was I had an entirely accidental Rebecca sighting. My first since I got back. Last Sunday, I was down at the Conservation area with Luke doing some hiking and general kids' stuff when I spotted a couple of people biking along Mineral Springs near the gatehouse. As soon as I spotted you, I knew it was you. Kind of a small red bike, but it was you. Not sure who was with you, but it was another girl. I turned and yelled at Luke, "Luke, Follow me now!,"

I thought if I ran full out along the gatehouse trail and then diverted towards the road along a deer trail, I knew was there, I could reach an incredible rock formation not far from the road you would ride by. I ran full out, and I was immediately fuelled by butterflies. Luke was going to be the issue since I did not want you to see me. To reach the rock formation, I had to get through an opening before you got to the top of the small hill. If you did that, you could see me in the woods. I wouldn't want to have our first meeting with you thinking I was some perv in the woods peeping tom. I knew I would get to where I needed to be, but Luke was too far behind me and would enter the area at the worst time. When I reached the rock, I wanted to hide behind, I stood up and watched the road to see when I would pick up the top of your head. I was hoping to wave Luke off at the last leg. We had already developed our own army ranger-type hands signs, and all I needed was for him to see mine. As soon as I spotted the top of your head coming over the crest, I spotted Luke and gave him the sign to immediately hide in place.

As you got to the crest, I had positioned myself behind a large rock with a bush providing additional camouflage between the road and me. I was at best 75 feet from the road. I stared at the road waiting for you to reach the angle that I could see you with a good front view. Back then, we did not wear bicycle helmets, just hair on our heads. You came into view, and the first thing I thought was, 'she is coming down a bit of a hill and would be moving pretty fast." As soon as I could see your whole face, my heart stopped. God, I wish I could have taken a picture of you. You had a sweatshirt and what looked like cut-off jean shorts that someone hemmed. You were standing up while you peddled, and the girl behind was sitting on her seat. You turned and said something to her, but I could not determine what you said. As you turned back, I had the best view of you yet.

I've never seen you this young. You were adorable and had that great smiling face. You have what I call a natural smiling face. Your natural disposition is a smile, while Miss Westerbeeke was a bit of a frowner. I know you had on a sweatshirt, but I was pretty sure you had not started any significant development. But please forgive me for this; I stared at your butt as you rode by. You were now past where I was, allowing me to sit behind the rock and have a clear 'rear view' *(I hope you smiled)*. You were still pumping the peddles, and I was in this pervy trance watching your butt shift side to side, No TEA, but you still had some filling out ahead of you. The whole Rebecca spotting lasted maybe a minute. But when you were finally out of sight, I just sat there and smiled. Eventually, I got up and returned to where Luke had taken shelter behind a huge rock. As I reached his location, which was about 150 yards from mine, he asked, "Who were those girls?"

I must have had this childish look on my face when I replied, "My future wife." I took a bit of razzing from Luke, but I had already etched my first picture of Rebecca in my mind! I don't think I ever asked you about that day and who the other person was. I am sure it was not your sister, but I did not etch her face in my mind.

UPDATE – Summer Camp Part I

(July 15th - August 15th, 1974)

41 ***A Changing Plan!:*** So, I want to tell you about my experience at the camp. Yes, the same camp Tina went to or was going to. I know you're much older now, and I am sure there wouldn't be a jealous bone in your body as far as Tina is concerned *(I am grinning)*. I had to do some arm twisting with my folks to get the approval to go, and after a lot of guilting and begging, including my offer to pay, they finally gave in. I tried hard to get my wingman to come, but their family vacation was that same week. I would be at the camp for a week. My folks had planned a trip to drive up and drop me off, then head over to South Hampton to stay overnight. Mom's family used to go there when she was young. Tina knew I would be there, and we both agreed not to tell our parents that we would be there at the same time. I told my parents I wanted to learn to horseback ride, and they had decent fishing in the lake. The drive up was 3 hours.

When we pulled in, I was concerned that we would be there when Tina showed up. To hopefully alleviate that issue, I told my parents I needed to arrive a half-hour before when the camp told me. I was not the first kid getting dropped off when we got there, and I counted three other cars. This was my first time away alone *(no sister)*, and mom being a mom, started with the rapid-fire 'Do you have…..' list. I was out, suitcase in hand and waving bye to my folks in less than 10 minutes. An older gentleman met me in his 40s, and he introduced himself as Pete Davies, the camp director. He handed me an information package and stuck a name sticker on my chest. He directed me to go over and see a girl *(a young lady)* who was in her early 20s to get my building assignment. They indeed appeared well organized, and I got my first whiff of the smell of horse manure. It must be an east wind.

I walked over to the young lady, who was very pretty. She looked sort of like Marsha Brady but had a healthier set of lungs *(Not that I was looking)*. She introduced herself to me, "Hi Derek, I am Maryanne, and I will be your counselor for the week. You are in cabin six along with seven other boys. Each cabin is gender-specific, and the only rule we have is boys do not go in the girl's cabins, and girls don't go in the boy's cabins. Take your stuff and go pick out a bed in the cabin and then come back to the welcome area and grab yourself a refreshment and meet the other campers," she instructed.

I did as she asked, was the first person to arrive at Cabin Six, and did a quick search. Each cabin had a room with two single beds with four rooms. There was a less than modern washroom in the middle of the cabin layout. I decided I wanted to be the farthest I could from the bathroom door. I chose room 2 and the bed on the right. I threw my suitcase under the bed and returned to the Welcome area. I was already in Tina's parent's search mode, and when I emerged from my cabin, I had already formulated an escape plan if needed. Tina and I had already planned to pretend we did not know each other and would keep our prior relationship as secret as we could. I am sure eventually the councilors will figure out that we like each other, but we were hoping it was from meeting at the camp and not a prior secret relationship that was about to go to the next level!

I walked to a picnic table and grabbed a pop from a cooler. I looked around and spotted a couple of guys sitting at another picnic table. The problem was they were too close to the drop-off area, and I needed a temporary shelter location if the Van Houten's arrived. I scanned the rest of the site and thought about taking a walk to check on the horses may be in order. I went to Pete and asked if he would mind if I walked over to look at the horses. Pete told me to go over to another building and speak to Stephanie. He thought she was going over to the barn to do something. I thanked Pete and walked over to the other office-like building. I knocked on the door when a young girl who was 20 at best came to the screen door and said, "Hi, are you lost?"

"No, I was speaking to Pete and asked if I could go take a look at the horses, and he directed me here to ask for Stephanie," I replied.

"Well, you are in luck, Derek, I am Steph, and if you hang here for a second, I need to wrap something up and will be out shortly," she said.

I smiled and nodded. I turned to see how the arrival was going and still did not see Tina's suburban. After a couple of minutes, Steph came out carrying a bucket of something. Now that she was out from behind the screen door, she was very cute; she looked just like Sally Field. If you want a better representation, look up the movie 'Stay Hungry' with Jeff Bridges. Oh, oh, I am going to be tested this week. I asked her if I could carry the bucket for her. She smiled and said, "Aren't you the perfect gentleman."

She passed me the bucket, turned, and said, "Follow me, Derek."

There is something about a girl in tight western-style jeans that fit perfectly. She did not realize she was forcing me into the absolute worst position for a girl. Me walking behind her! Immediately I did my instant analysis and studied her gait. The jeans were wranglers and had the western stitching on the pockets. She was about 5'5" and had a waist around 23 inches and a very balanced set of hips in the 36-inch range. She was a heelto-ball foot roller that produced a butt cheek pattern that allowed a twitch at the top of the step. No TEA, just a perfect fit. You know I could go even more pervy with my analysis, but instead will simply say, a Rebecca 8.8!

When we arrived at the stables, she opened the half-door and entered. As every horse person knows, I followed and closed the gate behind me. Steph turned and said, "Can you please close; Oh, you beat me to it."

She turned, and as we walked down past the stalls, she started to give me a brief overview. She said, "The stalls on the left have all the beginner horses, and the stalls on the right are for more advanced riders. Are you comfortable around horses, Derek?", she asked.

"Yes. Had me a few pony rides in my day," I said with a private chuckle.

"I will be giving the horse riding lesson, and I hope you will like the big boys now," she said while opening a stall door. "This is TJ. He is my favorite fella in here."

"Looks like a walker to me" I said.

"Steph turned and looked at me and said, "What do you mean a Walker?", as she grilled me with a stunned look.

"Well, I am guessing a Rocky Mountain rather than a Tennessee by his pattern, head shape, and the Rocky Mountain Horses are bred for gait, conformation, and disposition, but they are sold often because people love their color and long manes. The Rockies can come in any solid color but are best known for the chocolate colors. TJ has a beautiful long main and a great chocolate color. Almost like a Dairy Milk bar," I replied.

Steph looked at me, and a slow smile emerged, and she said, "Pony rides my ass."

"Sorry, Steph didn't mean to mislead you. We had horses, and I am very comfortable around them. I love to ride, and we owned a Tennessee Walker named Riley. He had such a smooth and easy gait," I confessed.

"Well, if I can get old TJ feeling better this week, you will be more than welcome to give him a go," Steph said.

"What seems to be the problem?" I asked.

"Not sure, but it may be a stomach issue. I'm giving him a mixture of some different grains and some antibiotics," she explained.

I went to the stall wall and grabbed a hoof pic hanging up high. I walked over to TJ and let him give me the horse stare down. We exchanged scents as I blew air out of my nose into his nose while I rubbed gently under his chin. I then stood tall in front of him, smiled, and said, "Hi TJ, hear you're not 100%." I then walked over to his right front side and gently leaned on him while lifting his leg to expose the bottom side of the hoof. I took the hoof pic and gave him a good cleaning along with a sniff of his frog.

I did that for each foot, then put the pic back on the wall, went back to TJ's head, and gave him an ear rub. While gently massaging his ears, I said to Steph, "His back right hoof may have a bit of an infection. Hard to tell without poking the poor guy, but if you have any alcohol-based ointment here, I will give his frog a good soaking and see if he flinches. If he does flinch, then I think you can assume an infection."

Steph left the stall, returned with a bottle, and handed it to me. I let TJ get a sniff of it and then went to his back right and raised his leg again to expose his well-cleaned hoof. I sprayed the ointment all over the frog, and as soon as it made contact, TJ's leg flinched. I was expecting that reaction and had a good grip on his leg. I reapplied more ointment, and this time he was used to it. I put his leg down and went back to his head and gave him another short ear job, and said to Steph, "Yup, a minor infection, and he should get this done three times a day, especially before he is put to bed for the night. No outdoor night-time pasture for him for a few days as well."

I smiled at Steph, who was giving TJ his bucket of stuff, and I walked out of the stall and did a quick walk to the end and back, looking at the horses. When I got back to TJ's stall, Stephanie came out shaking her head and said, "Well, Mr. Pony Rider, you just got yourself a camp job assignment for the week helping me."

I laughed a bit, smiled at her, and said, "Yes, Boss. I will be here at '0 six hundred' to give my new buddy TJ his next dressing" if that is ok with you, boss?", I added.

"Let me chat with Pete and see what we can arrange. I will let you know later. I will assume that from all your pony riding, you can sit a good seat," she said with a grin.

"I hope so. I have not been in a saddle for a bit but am looking forward to learning from a pro," I replied.

Steph and I left the barn and headed back towards where all the kids were gathered, and as we hit the split on the path, she grabbed my arm and said, "Thanks Derek and I do appreciate what you did for TJ, and I am looking forward to getting to spend a lot more time with you. It will be nice having another horse person in the mix. I have to head back to the office but will catch up with you later," as she released her grip and walked along the other path. I turned, headed to the other area, and tried to see if Tina was here yet.

When I got to the first table, I spotted Tina, her mother, and her father over talking to Pete. I quickly turned and sat at the table with my back to them. I was a long way away but was a little nervous that they may start doing some tour of the place. I did my best to keep an eye on them while not giving them any good view of me. After about 5 minutes, Doctor Van Houten and Mrs. Van Houten turned and walked back to the parking area. I turned a bit more to make sure I could watch them drive away. After a few more minutes, I watched their suburban drive away down the driveway.

As I got up from the table, I heard Pete yell for all the campers to join him at the fire pit area. I kept an eye on Tina and decided I would sneak up on her. After a bit of manoeuvring, I managed to walk right up behind her. As soon as Pete started to give his welcome speech, I took my thumb and gently ran it down Tina's back while whispering in her ear not to turn around. As soon as she figured out it was me, her back arched a bit, and she moved backward a bit, closing the gap between us. When my thumb reached the belt of her jeans, I continued it down to the top of her butt. Suddenly I felt her hand grab my thumb, and I knew we had a T&D going. She raised my hand from where it was to the swell of her back and was now almost leaning on me.

After the usual welcome stuff, Pete announced that there would be a three-legged race in 10 minutes and asked everyone to find a partner for the event. The age of the campers was 13 to 17. You could attend, apparently, even if you turned 18 after the camp week. I figured most campers would peg me at 15 or 16. The mix of boys to girls was about 60/40. Sixty being the girls. Hard to know yet the age spread. When Pete finished the three-legged announcement, I released Tina's thumb and gave her a polite tap on the shoulder. "Excuse me miss, but would you be interested in being tied up with me?"

Tina slowly turned around, and our eyes finally met for the first time here. We both, I think, were suppressing the urge to hug each other and maybe have our first kiss. When you consider how long it has been since we met at Sherry's party, I hope, us not having our first kiss yet wasn't too concerning for Tina. I know I wanted to get some therapy before deciding on the 'Kid verse Old-man' issue. She had such beautiful, friendly eyes. Tina replied, "Well, sir, there are a lot of very eligible kids here that may enjoy being tied up with me."

She was getting good at the kibitzing, but I was still a few notches above her. I replied, "I agree with your assessment, and perhaps we should find alternate people that may be more compatible with our inner butterfly?", with an added Mr. Spock attempted eyebrow raise.

Now, if there was ever a perfect 'timing moment' example, it was right now. I could never have orchestrated or manipulated this setup, even if my friends hurled me back a dozen times. Just as 'butterfly' came from my mouth, I felt an arm around my shoulder, and a beautiful older girl said, "Is this handsome young man taken for this event, or can I steal him away from you so we can teach the rest of the kids a lesson in how to be good losers?"

I knew it was Steph, and before I acknowledged her, I needed to watch Tina's reaction. Her facial expression went from giddy and oozing affection to shock and confusion. I was not prepared to send her on an emotional rollercoaster this soon in our secret getaway, so I took the lead and, hopefully, used it to my advantage. I turned and said, "Stephanie, I am truly sorry, but this very nice young lady whose name tag says 'Tina' asked me first, and I think it would be polite to ask her if she would prefer a different partner or take her chances with the Pony Rider", with an added grin.

Now I am not saying Stephanie was hurt or jealous by my reaction, but while I had assumed from the start of this exchange that Steph was playing around and having some fun with me, or maybe even being a bit of a wingman if she observed Tina's and my prior T&Ding. When I turned back to smile at Steph, she did look a bit confused by my response. I think women can uniquely sense other women's thoughts and emotions. When I returned my stare to Tina, her look changed from shock and confusion to a more serious but controlled look. When our eyes met, she responded while staring directly into my soul, "I am sorry, but he's; what does his name tag say? Oh yes, Derek is mine." Tina's expression had shifted from serious but very controlled to determined and devious and maybe a little 'in your face, older, beautiful, Rebecca 8.8 type'. Ok, a writers' over interpretation of the event, but as I said earlier, I have the advantage of being the person writing this guide *(Big grin).*

Steph shot back with, "Well, you guys better be prepared to lose cause I am the 'camp champ' at the 3-legged race."

I wanted to change the tone before any potential 'cat fight' over me *(Made you laugh in disgust)*, and said, "Tina, this is Stephanie, and she is the head honcho in charge of riding here. She gave me a brief tour of the barn earlier. Steph, this is Tina, who, to my surprise, just so happens, comes from my part of the world."

"Very nice to meet you, Tina, and we will have to chat later because I need to find me a 3-legged partner to whoop your butts," she said with a smirk as she turned and walked away.

"So, I am not even at camp for an hour, and you're already going off to the barn with an older and very cute girl," Tina said with a woman-scorned tone.

"Actually, I was trying to stay as far away from the parking lot as I could so your parents would not potentially see me. She just happened to be walking that way. Besides, why would I have any interest in anyone else here when I am standing in front of the cutest, hottest, and soon-to-be 3-legged champ that is dying to be tied up with me" I countered with.

Yes, it was corny and schlocky as it sounds, but it was the kid responding, not a measured old man. I have come to realize that my way of talking and even thinking is filtered through the mind of a 63-year-old, but the emotions and thoughts are that of a thirteen-year-old. When my brain searched for the right words, it had a much larger thesaurus to choose from. I will never be able to sound like a thirteen-year-old ever again. For me, to fake it, would come out sounding fake. Eventually, my age will reach a point when my vernacular word smithing is no longer a differentiator. But all that was important, did the underlying message make its way to the intended receiver.

I was smiling and feeling giddy at that moment, and I think it was reciprocated. Tina and I continued to look into each other's eyes with our adolescent glow. Suddenly she raised her hand and gave me her best 'Fonze.' I smiled and gently curled my hand around her thumb. It amazed me that something that would most certainly be defined as utter childishness and immature could give me the most excellent butterfly effect. The T&D was short, and we ventured over to the three-legged race area and got ourselves all tied up. Pete was with a few other camp councilors, and I immediately noticed Stephanie had secured herself the biggest kid from the lot as her partner. Tina and I did a little pre-race practicing with a couple of short walks and circles and then made our way to the starting line. Pete divided up the campers into three groups. The winner from each group would race for the coveted bragging rights and a camp t-shirt!

We were in group 2, and Steph was relegated to group 3. We lined up with the other stiffs, and when Pete pressed the horn for group two, Tina and I were off. We were like a well-oiled machine with perfect rhythm *(Almost like we were dance partners, could not resist)*. Our timing and step distance were perfect, not too long or too short. Like a good 'coxswain' *(I could not resist using that term)*, I was calling out the run count. One, Two, One, Two. On one, our outside legs went, and on two, our inside tied legs went. All we needed to do was slowly increase the count speed. When we crossed the finish line, there was no one even close. Pete, who had a megaphone, announced, "We have our second winner and looking like the team to beat."

As we turned back to look at the rest of the field struggling, Tina and I gave each other a look, and it was the first time I got to see her competitive side. She was an outstanding athlete with excellent coordination and balance. But I now got to see she also had a real competitive drive. We stayed tied and walked back to the starting line area, receiving a few pats on the back as we passed other campers. I was very comfortable with my arm over Tina's shoulder, and she loved having her arm around my lower back. I knew at that moment that this week would be very special.

I won't bore you with our eventual victory other than to mention that Steph was pissed at losing to us, and I think she was thinking, 'I wish that kid was 17'. I didn't need to say anything to Tina about my thoughts on the topic because she made sure we would walk over after the win to Steph, and her want-a-be jock partner, and deliver a friendly but very possessive, "Sorry, Stephanie, but you know the old saying, 'May the best WOMAN win.' I know Rebecca that you think I just added a little wordsmithing and that Tina never really said that, but I am telling you that she said exactly that. It both shocked me and made me think she was not as young as I had thought. Yes, age is age, but her attitude and demeanor were a very mature 15 year old or older. You can talk on the phone all you want, but you will never really know a person until you see, touch, and feel that person *(I hope that got an eye roll)*.

Tina's cabin was about as far away from mine as possible. The campers were divided up by Pete, and something Tina and I did not think about was happening. We were in separate groups. Activities would be divided into groups. I was in the Snowy Owls; Tina was in the Eagles, and the other guys were called the Red Tail Hawks. Not my choice, but it was not my camp. We would eat together at dinner, but lunches would vary, depending on your group and the activity. At first, I thought it sucked being in a different group, but I soon discovered it made the time we could get together much more exciting, and I know Tina was feeling the same way. Steph had taken me on as her 'during the week' 'cabin boy', getting me to do a bunch of horse chores. TJ healed quickly; on Wednesday, Steph let me use him for our riding lesson group.

I was middle of the pack by age in the Owls. When it came to riding, there was one other girl in our group that had been riding Hunter for a few years. Everyone else were first-timers. The Hunter girl was Debbie, and I spent most of the time helping Steph teach the group how to tack up the horses and strip and clean them up after the lesson. However, on Wednesday, Debbie and I got to head out of the teaching arena and ride around the camp together. She had Big Red, and I was on TJ. Big Red was a quarter. I am sure TJ liked me because he responded perfectly to my leg commands. We ventured on the trail down to the lake and back to a logging road. We eventually returned to the arena. When we entered the arena, Steph walked over and asked if Debbie and I would show the others some of the riding techniques and gait differences between the two horses. As we would ride, Steph would explain to our classmates the difference between the breeds and riding styles.

My Buddy TJ

TJ and I were exactly like Tina and me. We knew what the other person was thinking before the other person could say it. I loved riding, and for a brief moment in the ring, I felt sad that I never got to ride as much as I had hoped last time. I knew I would eventually want to own and ride my own horses again—this time, hopefully with you Dimples. For a few minutes that day, TJ and I were one. Even Steph, after, complimented me on my seat, and ease of handling TJ. I will give the most credit to TJ.

UPDATE – Summer Camp Part II

(July 15th - August 15th, 1974)

42

The kid becomes a Big Kid"!: After riding, we would have some free swim time at the lake before dinner. I spotted Tina the day before going to the lake for a swim when I was heading out canoeing with my group. The canoes were at least 100 yards from the swim docks, so getting a good look at Tina in a swimsuit was hard. Today, her group would be swimming at the same time as our group. I went to my cabin and put on my bathing suit. I bought a black suit with a runners split along the sides and a dive flag crest on the front right leg. I got them at a dive shop and was going to be doing scuba classes as soon as I was 15. I have always loved black. As I was heading along the path to the beach, Stephanie emerged from the office cabin wearing a bikini. Call it bad timing or good timing because Tina's group had just gotten back, and she was on her way to change when she looked over and spotted Stephanie walking over to me.

I said earlier that Stephanie was attractive. I think I used the Sally Field doppelganger reference. Wow! Could she fit a bikini perfectly! I know she knew she was one of the hottest councilors, if not the hottest here. It was never in any flaunting sort of way. It was more a self-confidence in herself and her abilities that emanated from her. As she reached me on the path, she said, "Great dive shorts."

"Thanks. I am planning on taking Scuba lessons in another year," I replied. Well, technically, a year and a half.

"Great job on TJ today. I had no idea you could ride that well. You must have been riding for a few years."

I smiled and said, "I have ridden a lot, Steph, but we don't have a horse right now. A money thing, I think," this was my excuse.

"That is a shame, you're a natural, and the horses all love you as well," she added.

We walked and chatted to the dock area and split directions at the dock. I went to grab a chair to sit in and wait for Tina, and Steph dropped her towel and walked to the diving board area. Man, she had a great backside! Not as great as yours, but it was up there *(Grin or grimace?)* She climbed the ladder and reached the top. She was very athletic-looking, and I would guess she was an 'A' cup, not a full 'B' cup. She used the springboard like a pro and entered the water without any real splash. If I had a card, I would be holding up a 10. It was about that moment that I turned my head to see if I could see Tina, and I wish I had sunglasses on because about 100 feet from me was Tina walking towards me wearing a tan color bikini with a towel around her shoulders. The last suit she had on was a one-piece. Unlike me, Tina had a light tan, and I have always joked I am half Italian and had a dark tan.

I knew she was keenly watching for a facial expression from me. I am sure if I were observing the other guys on the dock, they would all be gawking at her with their jaws on the ground. But fortunately for me, I could not take my eyes off her. She got to my chair, and I immediately got up and offered it to her. She smiled back and did not say a word but made sure to turn her back in my direction, bend over to remove my towel, and hand it to me, then turn around again and bend over slightly to put her towel over the back of the chair.

I guess I was like some deer in headlights, having been just subjected to my new kryptonite, when Tina said, "Are you going to stand there or go and grab another chair before they are all taken?"

See, this is where sunglasses help. She could read every thought I had, even the X-rated ones, and I am sure all through my eyes and facial expressions. I turned, probably looking somewhat catatonic, and went and grabbed a chair. During my walk back, I think I got a little composure, and when I returned, I put the chair right beside Tina, and then I proceeded to place my towel using my best 'Autin Powers' butt gestures from the future movie 'The Spy that Shagged Me’. As I eventually put my 'behind' in the seat, I looked over at Tina, who had her eyes closed, face taking the warmth of the sun and a grin on. I slid my leg over, took my big toe, and put it on her big toe, hoping no one would pick up on the move. Her grin increased as my toe touched hers, and I said, "Remember my Big Toe warning."

At that moment, we were two love-struck kids, discovering for the first time that feeling of losing some of our innocence to a new and exciting feeling emerging from once dormant regions of our bodies. As I slowly rubbed her toe, she said, "Let's swim to the rocks on the other side.” Without any need to confirm, we both got up, walked to the dock's edge, and did near-perfect shallow dives. We did not need any communications to guide us now. We knew the plan and would execute it flawlessly. As our competitive instincts kicked in, we went from an easy swim stoke to a full-on Olympic speed front crawl. The rocks across from the docks were a couple of hundred yards, and it was not unusual for campers who were good swimmers to venture over. We were both thinking the same thing, 'I hope no one else decides to swim across.

I, of course, allowed Tina the victory by holding back a bit *(Just kidding)*, and as we arrived at the rocks, Tina selected a spot that was more of an underwater seat, allowing us to sit our butts on the rock and the water was up to our chest. We both got seated, and without saying a word, we slowly slid towards each other, eventually having our thighs come together. I had the worst *(or best)* case of butterflies, and I am sure Tina was experiencing the same thing. We scanned the area, ensuring we were the only ones there. After the scan, we both looked at each other. We knew precisely the other's thoughts, and Tina decided to go first. She reached over, and instead of a T&D, she grabbed my hand and interlaced our fingers. As soon as she had my hand, I detected some movement! *(Oh, oh Jerry, I think it moved again).*

I was so excited and in a great way. Yes, that way, but also, I had the same feeling I once had so long ago, standing on Rebecca 1.0's front porch. I know I wanted it to be with you my first time, but it was happening now, and it felt right. No dirty old man thoughts, just two young kids about to discover something extraordinary that may become something more. I would have thought from my years of experience that this moment would be lost to a more mechanical, robotic-like feeling and, worse, the emergence of the pervy old man. But it appears that my new adolescence would cause a whole new set of pathways to form. Not re-tracing old ones, but brand new ones. Is this the secret, Becca? That my journey just taught me that this is not a re-do. This is about a new-do. Is this the secret to getting rid of the old man?

We held hands for a few minutes, and then we both did another scan for people. After we were satisfied it was all clear, Tina moved our hands to her special spot and pushed the back of my hand into her. I felt her legs open more, and I knew I had achieved full movement myself. She had a smile and grin on her face all at the same time. I know I was watching her. As the hand pushed a bit harder, I pulled it back a bit and said, "Are you sure? This is a big next step for us."

She smiled and pushed the back of my hand back into her and said, "I have wanted this since the movie. You make me feel so special, and you give me the greatest butterflies."

I looked at her and said, "I am a virgin, and this will be my first time."

She giggled and said, "I will be gentle, and it is my first time with you."

She released the hand hold and guided my hand under the top of her bikini bottoms. She was now sitting more erect and took her left hand, slid it under her bikini waistband, grabbed my left hand, and slowly moved it down to her special area. I could not believe we were doing this, like this.

I had a momentary flashback to the first time you and I had a similar situation happen in your pool, or I should say Becca 1.0 and me.

I had imagined a bunch of other scenarios, but never this one. After a minute of Tina helping guide my hand to the best spots, I felt her right-hand reach over and touch my special area through my suit. As she gave it a bit of a grip, I thought I would lose it right then. Luckily, she stopped for a minute and returned to her guiding help. After another minute, she looked at me, and this time I knew that look, and suddenly she found the waistband of my shorts with her right hand and slid it in. As her hand found my other thumb, she seemed to know what to do. I was looking at her, and I said, "I think I am about to make a mess on your hand."

Her face also started to scrunch up, and her left hand moved my fingers up and down quicker and quicker. Suddenly her eyes opened wide, and she said, "Kiss me now."

I immediately leaned over, and our lips met. As soon as our lips had fully sealed, she let out this incredible moan. Suddenly I was doing the same. We kissed for a few seconds as our bodies went into minor convulsions. When we finally stopped the kiss, we lost our sitting balance and slid into the water entirely. We both used our free hands to grab the edge of the rock seat to prevent us from going completely under. But what was remarkable, we continued to keep our other hand in the same last position.

What do you say to someone who has just introduced to you one of the greatest feelings we get to achieve in life? We both began to smile, and I was glad she said it first, "I always wanted this to be with someone special, and I got my wish. And now I will never let this thing go," as she gave me another squeeze and her cute little devilish grin.

I am sure some of me wanted to try and make some clever remark. Maybe some stupid movie reference or silly immature quip. But I let my inner kid take over completely. I moved closer and looked at her completely, free of any thought of the old man ever emerging again, and said, "I think things will be getting more complicated," with a grin.

Her hand released me, and she brought it up to my shoulder. I followed suit, and we both repositioned ourselves to sit on the rock seat again. I felt a chat coming my way and sat there with my head tilted towards her, allowing me to see her eyes. We were studying each other's faces looking for the next response when the splashing sound was getting louder. We both turned to look in the direction of the sound and spotted Stephanie swimming our way. We both had this immediate panic look like we had been caught and instinctively moved further apart. I was even more concerned because I didn't know if I got out of the water or if my bathing suits would now be stained with you know what. Without thinking, I let myself slide back into the water, leaving Tina on the rock seat, and did my best to use my one hand to try and wash, you know what, out of my suit.

As Steph arrived, she said, "I thought I spotted you love birds over here."

My quick-thinking side of my brain kicked in, and I replied, "You must be mistaken. There are only owls and Eagles here, Pegasus Girl."

"Steph smiled and commented, "You two look more like a couple over here than campers."

"Oh, Steph, we were just plotting how we could embarrass you at the next big sporting match. You're mistaking us as a couple rather than a team," I replied.

"Derek challenged me to a race over to here, Steph, and I needed to teach him a lesson," Tina chimed in with.

'Steph replied, "That-a-girl, another win for the women."

"Well, my two beautiful sporty spices *(They had no idea the joke I made)*, why don't we have a little race from here back to the dock" I challenged.

"What are the stakes Pony Boy?", Steph replied.

"If either Steph or I win, you're our slave boy for the rest of the day; If you win, we will be your slave girls," Tina suggested.

"Wait one second, Tina, he may be mature for his age, but I don't think he's man enough yet for the two of us," she said with her own devilish grin.

"Ok, let's do last place serves first place, and second gets to watch," was her counteroffer.

There were no shortages of innuendos flying, and a lesser man would have immediately gone in the direction of fantasizing about a threesome. But not me *(gigglely gigglely)*! "Everyone must have one hand on the rock to start," Steph said.

"Let's go one better; let's dive in off the rocks unless you're afraid to dive," I added.

"Rocks it is," Steph took the bait. I can hold my breath a long time and should be able to get a good lead off the start. We climbed up, and as I got out, I looked down at my bathing suit to ensure there was no prior evidence. I let myself get out last so I could watch my two losing beauties climb out in my full glory view. As soon as I got out, Tina said, "We go on Three."

As I started to position myself, Tina yelled, "Three" and proceeded to dive in, followed almost immediately by Steph. As soon as I could get a good foot position, I made my 'Phelpsian' dive. When I broke the surface, I was about half a length ahead of Tina. While Steph was older, she and Tina were about the same size. Tina may have had an inch on her. Steph exerted more energy, but my girl had the technical nailed down. I had my best crawl going, and it took me about three-quarters across to establish a full-body-length lead on Tina. Steph was close to Tina's waistline, but I knew this would be all me. I have been working out for hockey a lot, and there are a lot of muscles common in hockey to swimming. None of us swimmers could see that everyone on the dock spotted us and quickly figured out it was a race. As I got closer to the dock, I could hear a bunch of guys cheering me on and a bunch of girls cheering on Steph and Tina. This was going to be our camp's Bobby Riggs versus Billy Jean King's battle of the sexes. As I tried to look back to assess the competition quickly, I had Tina now by two body lengths, and Steph was at Tina's feet.

I landed the first hand to a large cheer of the testosterone groupies; when I turned to look at who was next, I was pleasantly surprised to see Tina was now in third place. I knew immediately that she had thrown the race between her and Steph. There was no way now she would have allowed Steph to be my slave girl. As Steph's hand touched, she looked and saw me now sitting on the dock. She was pissed and, even realizing she was not last, gave me a look that said, 'This ain't over, Ponyboy'. She continued to stare at me, and her pissed-off look turned to a grin when she swam over to me and placed herself between my legs. I thought if only she knew what had just happened down there a few minutes ago. Tina's hand hit the dock, and when she brought her head up, she spotted Steph between my legs. Usually, you would immediately conclude that Tina would be jealous, but what we just experienced together created a bond even greater than Steph could break.

To try and get under Steph's skin just a bit more, I yell and put my hands up and announce to the dockers, "Champion and Still Undefeated swim master, able to easily defeat two beautiful and somewhat athletic girls and win Tina as my slave girl for the rest of the day." Steph gave Tina a look, and those girls had their chick telepathy going, and suddenly Steph hauled me into the lake again and, between her and Tina, pulled my swim shorts off. Steph then swam to the dock, jumped out, and held her trophy up for everyone to see. As the laughter caught on, I looked over at Tina, and she gave me her best devilish grin to date. I was sure to have a bit of a blush, and there were a few cat calls from the gawker girls. I swam over to the dock, and Steph said, "Here you go, champ," she also had a devilish grin as she placed my swim shorts on the step of the lifeguard tower.

Not to let the moment go to the girls. I swam over to the dock ladder and could climb out while cupping my hand over Tina's new favorite toy. I walked upright and very stoic to my chair, grabbed the towel, and put it around me, never letting anyone see the water was cold! After the towel, I went and retrieved my shorts. Steph was toweling off and gave me a cute smile, and I could not shake the feeling she was not done with me.

I returned to my chair, slipped my shorts back on, and sat in the chair. I wanted to take a few minutes and process the last half hour. As I was sitting there, one of the other older camp girls walked by and said, "Nice butt, champ," with an added grin. It seems hockey workouts had started to give me a hockey player's butt! Tina approached the chair, grabbed her towel, and proceeded to dry off in front of me. She knew she owned me now and turned around, so her butt was about 2 feet from my face and slowly dried it with the towel.

Our swim time was almost over, and we would have to return to our cabins to change and get ready for dinner. Tonight, was an outdoor barbecue with a campfire, and I was sure there would be a scary story or two. After Tina was dried off, she sat down, looked at me with her innocent devilish grin, and said, "Slave girl ready master, just ask, and it shall be."

I gave a big smile, and we both wanted to sit back and relive what we had just done in our minds. I really wanted to hold her hand, but we both knew it would be better to keep our little secret a secret. After another 20 minutes of sun, the main house bell rang, indicating 30 minutes till dinner. Tina put her hand on my arm and said, "I think I will go and get ready."

I replied, "Ok, slave girl, I want you on your best behavior," with my devilish grin. Tina walked away, and I looked at her from behind and thought, wow, what a lucky guy I am to have someone so great. I had no idea she was as mature for her age as she was. And she had this whole other side to her that just made her that much more beautiful. I was already trying to figure out how we could get some more alone time later, so I grabbed my towel and walked back to the cabin. When I hit the main path, another camper girl named Bev came up and said, "A few of the guys and girls from my cabin are going to take a walk tonight, would you like to come with us?"

"I didn't know they allowed us to go off for walks at night," I replied.

"This is my third year here, and a camp counselor always offers to do a ghost-sighting walk into the woods on BBQ night. Usually, only a handful of kids want to go. The councilors have a stash of beer in the woods and usually have a fire pit as well," Bev explained.

"Sounds like a plan, Bev; thank you for letting me know," I said with a smile. We parted as we reached her cut-off, and I went to my cabin. All my cabinmates were there, and I had to field a few questions, including a couple of the guys asking if I had some secret affair going on with Steph. As much as I would have loved to stroke my ego and tell them some whopper about some tryst, I was a had-man now—only one thing on my mind. I changed, and tonight I put on my authentic cowboy jeans *(Levis)*, boot cut, and my new pair of cowboy boots I bought just for this week. I had a western shirt along with a great-looking bolo tie. I was tipped off that the BBQ night was when everyone dressed up. I hope Tina was also told, but she looked great in everything she wore, even though her pants were not always tightly fitting.

VOLUME I

Book Two

"The future is not set, there is no fate but what we make for ourselves."

- *John Conner*

UPDATE – Summer Camp Part III

(July 15th - August 15th, 1974)

43 ***'Urban Cowboy':*** Our whole cabin went to the BBQ area together, and most of the guys had dressed up. Two guys even had cowboy hats. I had thought about one, but the Clint look would have to wait until I was old enough for a scruffy beard and could smoke backwoods. As our cabin passed the office area, Steph suddenly popped out and looked like she was going to walk with us to the BBQ. She had on a different set of jeans and different boots. She had a low-cut top that showed a little cleavage but was tasteful. Her hair was done up a bit differently, and she even used a little makeup which was a first for me to see. As she reached us guys, she said, "You fine-looking folk, mind if this old cowgirl walks with you?"

There were a few guys who giggled and gave a yes reply, and a couple said no problem, but I could not resist taking it up a notch and replied, "Well, young Miss Stephanie, it would be the honor of the men from cabin 6 to escort you to the big hoedown," together with my devilish smile.

I expected a good comeback, but she did something I was not expecting and said, "My Pony Boy is looking like he's more 18, especially with the extra inch from your great-looking boots," and she put her arm around my arm. I knew immediately the other guys would be snickering and talking behind our back. I was more concerned about Tina seeing this, so as I usually do, I came up with a plan, "Men, this attractive young lady is expecting a proper escort. We need guys on either side and someone to take her other arm. The guys jumped into action; Timmy, the oldest and geekiest in our cabin, quickly grabbed her right arm. Two more flanked Todd, and I saw an even better opening, young Michael, who was my age but 8 inches shorter and was already showing some tough acne, looked left out, so I let go of Stephanie's arm and replaced me with Michael. He went a couple of shades of dark pink, and Steph smiled, but I could tell she was expecting just her and I to make the trip arm and arm. I came in on Michael's flank, and the formation was complete. The walkway was not wide enough for all of us to walk on the cement, so the outside guys had to walk on the grass. It was about a 5-minute walk to the BBQ area, and we looked like the last cabin to arrive.

I scanned the area trying to find Tina, and I spotted her just as she got a look at cowboy Derek. The fact that Steph was with us did not bother her the least. As we entered the picnic table area, Pete looked at us and yelled,

"Steph and her Stephettes have arrived." Not bad for a quick off-the-cuff. I laughed, as well as the rest of the guys. They had one large picnic table per house that sat four on each side. They made it extra special tonight and added long tablecloths hanging down and touching the top of your leg. My table was on a bit of an angle, and using my rapid-fire trig superpower, I calculated that the far left seat would afford me the best direct view of Tina at her table, which was about 20 feet away. She was seated, but I could tell she had dolled herself up but could not see what she was wearing.

Pete gave his dinner welcome speech along with a couple of short stories about past BBQs here. At the end of the speech, Pete added, "It has come to my attention that earlier today, there was a swim race that took place down at the lake. It seems Mr. Devon was able to beat our Stephanie and won himself the first dance with our 'Horse Gal' later. Congratulations to Derek, if he would not mind standing up so we can see the lucky gentleman." I immediately looked at Tina and tried to get guidance on what I should do. That was never the deal, and she knew it too. She just looked at me and shrugged from afar. The guys at the table started slapping the table, and I had no choice but to stand up and give a polite nod to Pete.

I sat down, and of course, all the jeering started. This was not what I wanted tonight. After Pete finished, each table was called to the buffet line to load their plate. I could see Tina get up, and she had this beautiful, pleated chocolate brown skirt that came down to her knees. Her top was a cowgirl-looking vest that allowed open arms and buttons to run up the front to a spot that allowed her to show she was not a little girl. To finish off the look, she had a pair of cowboy boots on to boot *(Pun intended)*. When it was our time, I made a point of walking past Tina's table to give her a closer smile. As I made my way past her table, she kept her eyes down. Oh, oh, I am in trouble for this Steph dance crap.

I ate at our table and was unusually quiet. I wanted to stand up and profess my love to Tina and tell Steph she would need to find another dance partner, but that would never be allowed. After dinner, we had to do the same, but this time it was dessert offerings. Tina was definitely ignoring me, and when I passed in front of her table again, the only thing I got was another girl smacking me on my butt. I went and grabbed a fruit bowl and sat back down. After dinner, there was going to be a trivia contest pitting cabin against cabin, and the councilors had their own team. I felt pretty confident we could win, but I wanted to ensure that I was not always saying the answer. Pete would ask a question; each cabin would discuss and then write down their answer on a piece of paper, and one person would have to stand and read their response aloud. After all the tables read their answers, Pete would say what the correct answer was. If you got it right, you sat down; if you got it wrong, one person from each losing table would have to go to the firepit and wait.

The trivia challenge went pretty quickly, and in about half an hour, we had all our guys, and the councilor table that included old Steph was still full. Over the course of the next 20 questions, we were down to 3, and the Councillor table was down to 3. Tina's cabin was down to 2, and Cabin 5 had 1. The questions were getting much harder, and the last one stumped everyone. "Next question," Pete announced. "Name the first human to make it to space?"

I grabbed the pad and wrote down Yuri Gagarin. I handed the paper to Timmy, and Timmy stood up. They went around the tables, and every other table answered Neil Armstrong, and the councilor table said Alan Sheppard. As Pete asked cabin 6, Timmy said Yuri Gagarin. I knew Tina was in her competitive mood, and she broke her demeanor and shot me a grin that said, you lose. I held my look as Pete said, "The correct answer is Yuri Gagarin. As soon as Yuri started coming from Pete's mouth, Tina's look changed to a more intense look. I did not flinch and hoped she was feeling the same thing I was. God, I want her/him here and now *(Like before! Not how it sounded)*. The count was now 3, 2, 1. Derek, Timmy, Grant, Paula and Stephanie, and Tina was solo.

"Next question; what is it called in ballet when a dancer is positioned on one leg with the other leg raised behind the body and extended in a straight line?". All I heard was a big moan from the entire room. I looked over at Tina, and she had a smile. Damn, she took ballet. Timmy slid the pad over to me and smiled. I took the pad and wrote down, Arabesque *(Ah rah besk)*, including the phenetics, to help Grant say it correctly. I whispered it into Grant's ear so he could hear how it sounded. The councilors had no answer. Pete turned to Tina, and Tina said, "Arabesque," and turned to give me her attitude look. This time I threw her a curve ball and gave her a big grin. Peter asked Grant, "Arabesque, the same as her answer." The place was dead silent, and as Tina and I looked at each other, she let herself slip for a second and smiled at me. "The correct answer is whatever the last two said. Some Arab thing," Pete responded with.

We held our look, and I knew she was thinking what I was thinking. The count was now 3, 1, 1. Derek, Timmy, and Grant; Stephanie was solo, and Tina was solo. "Next question; What is the capital city of Turkey?", Pete asked. Timmy grabbed the pad and said, I know this one, and he started to write it down; he handed me the paper, and I looked at the answer, 'Istanbul.' I smiled and said to Timmy, "Are you sure?"

"100%, I love geography and plan to major in it," he said super confidently.

"Grant, what do you think?", I asked.

"Sounds right, but I haven't had one right so far, so let's go with Timmy," he replied.

I stood up and looked at Tina, and she had another; 'I so got this, look going.' Then I looked at Stephanie, and she also gave me a somewhat devilish grin. Pete asked Steph, and she said, "The capital of Turkey is Ankara."

"Tina?". Pete asked.

"Ankara," with her, I want you look!

"Derek?", Pete asked.

"Istanbul," I said with a grin.

Tina shot back with an added nod. "The correct answer," Pete said, "Is Ankara"!

I gave Tina an eyebrow raise as a salute and then turned to look at Timmy. He was stunned, and I thought he might cry, so I gave him a high five and told him it was a great try. As I sat down, Timmy already knew his penitence and got up and left the table. Grant and I gave him a pat on the back as he began his walk of shame, mumbling; "I was sure it was Istanbul." I knew the correct answer was Ankara, but I wanted to be in a position if Tina lost, I would leave and let Grant and Timmy go down in flames to Steph. That way, I would have a win, win, win! I got to be with Tina, Tina got to be with me now, and Steph would have finally beat me at something. The count was now 2, 1, 1. Derek and Grant; Stephanie was solo, and Tina was solo. Next question; "What do they call the V-shaped part of a horse's hoof?", Pete asked with a snicker. I looked at Tina, and she was hesitating, so I needed to make the same move again. I turned to Grant and slid him the pad. He gave me a blank look. "Hey man, I have no idea but give it your best answer, and you can give it this time," I said.

Grant wrote down something, and I gave him a reassuring nod. Pete said, "Stephanie, and if you get this wrong, you will never live it down."

Steph smiled at Pete and then gave me the look, knowing I knew the answer, "The frog, of course."

Pete said, "And Tina?"

Tina held her head down and slowly brought it up with a new dramatic look for my benefit and said, "The frog, of course," displaying her piece of paper.

"Ok, Grant, you're up," Pete said.

"The V spot," Grant said with an unsure look on his face. Everyone listening in on the final questions broke into laughter. While everyone was laughing, I looked at Tina, and she had a puzzled look while her brain was processing what had just happened. She knew I knew the answer, so why would he throw the game like that. My girl was really smart and perceptive. She knew exactly my plan and suddenly shot me this 'I want you even more dirty look.' I had to look at Steph for her read, and it was a look of confusion as well. Why was he losing? The count was now 1, 1, 1. Derek was solo, and Grant just left the table; Stephanie was solo, and Tina was solo. Pete looked at us and said, "I think we have another showdown carrying over from this afternoon's swim championship. "Next and maybe the final question for our trivia battle of the night," Pete said, "Name the first Doctor to perform a human heart transplant?"

I was watching Tina closely and wanted to see her reaction. She sat there in deep thought and then wrote something down. I turned to look at Stephanie, and she was blank. I wrote down Christiaan Barnard; if Tina got it wrong, I would say Doctor Kevorkian. But Pete threw me his curveball and said, "Let's change up the order and ask Derek first." I looked over at Tina and didn't know what to do. There was a good chance she did not know the answer, and I was sure Steph had no clue. As I looked at her, a smile came to her face, and she gave me the Nod. "I am not 100% sure, Pete, but I will go with Dr. Christiaan Barnard."

"And Steph?" Pete asked.

"Sorry guys, no clue on this one," Steph confessed.

"And Tina?" Pete asked.

I knew we knew the game, and Tina was all in, "Christiaan Barnard" she replied.

We did not need to hear the final answer when Pete said, "Sorry Steph, it is Christiaan Barnard."

Steph looked over at me and smiled and then yelled at Tina, "you kick his ass, girl." The count was now 1, 1. Derek solo, and Tina was solo. "Next and hopefully the last question. What are the world's Highest Waterfalls" Pete asked?

"Ok, Tina, you're first this time," Pete said.

"Angel Falls, Venezuela," Tina replied with a grin.

"Derek, it's do or die, young man. You won the swim match; can you make it a double header?", Pete challenged me.

I scrunched up the paper and put it in my pocket and gave my best look of disappointment, and said, "Sorry, cabin six guys, I wrote down 'Tugela Falls in Kwazulu Natal, South Africa.'

"We have a new Champ, Tina Van Houten, and the girls from Cabin 1. Let's give them a big cheer, and if the girls can come up front to get their prizes and we need a picture," Pete instructed. "Derek, if you can come up, we have a runner-up prize, especially for you."

I was glad I would finally get to be close to Tina. As I got up and started to walk to the front, my cabinmates all came up and gave me a high 5. They knew I was the one that had every single correct answer, but they still liked the brief limelight, I suppose. As I passed Steph, she gave me a pat on the butt and said, "Seems you went down to a woman Pony Boy." The stage was, at best, a foot off the ground, and luckily it was small, which caused us all to be tightly standing together. I worked my way beside Tina at the front, and our arms touched. We already knew we could spontaneously explode at any moment. Pete came over and put a sash on me that read, 'I lost to the girls in Trivia.' I am sure they have one that says, 'I lost to the boys in Trivia' as well. Everyone laughed, and I was going to be a good sport as well. After all, my girl just won. Pete then handed each girl a small paper bag full of all sorts of neat stuff, including weird candy, skin oils, soaps, etc. Glad I didn't win that!

The final step was a photo shoot. I was well aware that I could not be in a photo that could find its way back to the Van Houten's. I went over to Pete and said in his ear that I needed to go to the boy's room. I left the stage and knew they would take the pictures, and I would be nowhere in them. I walked to the building with the bathrooms, guys on one side and girls on the other. I decided since I was here, why not empty my bladder. I finished up, washed my hands, and went to stand out at the side and allow enough time to pass for the photoshoot. I was just looking out into the woods when I heard footsteps and looked to see who was coming to take a leak. It was my girl. She had a devilish look in her eye, grabbed my hand, and led me into the boy's bathroom. She surveyed the layout and led me to the last stall on the right. She pushed me in and locked the door. She said, "Sit."

I looked first to make sure the seat was down and proceeded to put the lid down as well. I sat, and Tina immediately straddled me with her legs hanging down, facing the back of the stall. She grabbed my face, and instead of a huge kiss, she said, "You knew the correct answer and threw the game, didn't you?"

I smiled at her and, trying to use my most sincere and comforting voice, said, "No, I only knew the second-highest Water Falls in the world." She was on a mission of some sort and ordered me to stand up. I complied. She took her hand and put it in my right pocket, while my other brain started thinking, oh-boy, I realized what she was doing. She saw me put the piece of paper in my pocket after scrunching it up. Her fingers reached the paper, and I was not going to fight with her. She pulled it out and told me to sit on the toilet again. She went back into her straddle position and un-scrunched the paper. She looked at what I had written and started to tear up. I was frozen. All I could think was I hurt my girl. As tears came out of her eyes, she smiled at me and said in the cutest way possible, "Are you trying to make me love you?"

When writing this, Rebecca, you would think that my first reaction would be to have a flashback to the time in my living room when Rebecca 1.0 said, 'I think I'm falling in love with you? But that thought was nowhere to be found. This was a new thought. No cross-referencing, no comparisons, no creepy old man. And it was a kid's thought as well. Not a pure thirteen's idea but hormone-influenced mature thirteen-year-olds thoughts. I smiled at her and moved my head toward hers to complete the kiss. We kissed one of the most passionate kisses I had ever had. We stayed in the stall for around 15 minutes until we heard feet enter the bathroom. We then stopped and held our position in silence. Somebody just went into the first stall and decided to have a dump. Not a pretty dump, a loud disgusting dump, complete with all the added sound effects. I am sure my face was saying, 'This is so embarrassing, but Tina found it funny and struggled not to laugh. We both knew the intimate stall moment was complete, and as soon as we heard the bathroom door close, we made our move to exit as well.

As we came out and looked to ensure the dumper had gone, I turned to Tina and said, "I want to hold your hand so bad; I want to touch you like earlier so bad, but we can't, and it's killing me." She gave me a sweet smile and said, "I hear there will be a Ghost walk in the woods later. Let's go."

"I heard the same thing, and I am in," I replied.

"How do you want me to handle the dance with Stephanie later?", I asked somewhat sheepishly?

"You have a great dance with her. If she tries any funny business with you, then she will answer to me," Tina told me with her kickass woman tone. Maybe her nickname can be 'Mindy'!

I smiled and said, "Ok, but I am sure I will hate every minute of it."

Tina slapped my arm and said, "I better not see you enjoying it."

We decide to return to the fire pit area and act like ordinary campers. As we entered the area, one of Tina's cabinmates ran over and asked Tina to introduce her to me. Tina, fully knowing our connection was secure and could not be breached, said, "Morgan, this is Derek Devon. He lives not too far from where I live, but I go to a catholic school, and he goes to the non-Catholic school."

Morgan gave me a look that said, 'Do you need a girlfriend'? Then she said, "Hi Derek, I watched you ride, and you're an excellent rider."

"Do you ride yourself, Morgan?" I asked, being the perfect gentleman.

"Yes, I have two horses and have been riding my whole life. I want to go into veterinary horse work after school. Oh, do you have a girlfriend?", she asked.

"Yes, Morgan, I have a fantastic girl back home. I wanted her to come here as well, but her parents didn't think it was a good idea," I replied. "Do you have a boyfriend?"

"Not now, we broke up at the start of the summer, so I am a single gal. I was hoping there might be some hot guys here this year," she said with disappointment in her voice.

"Morgan, Derek, and I were going to go hang a bit at the fire pit if you want to join us," Tina said.

"Thanks, Tina, but I am going on the hunt," as she gave Tina a look.

Morgan walked away, and Tina said, "Some guy tonight is going to get laid. All she talked about at night was how horny she was with the other girls," Tina added.

"You know Tina, I am willing to help out any of your friends if you asked me," I said with a playful grin.

"There's only one person in your life now, Mr. Pony Boy," she said with that devilish grin/smile. We walked to the pit area and sat on a wooden 'home whittled' bench-like structure. It had to be 20 feet long. Everyone was either talking or just staring at the fire's flames. It was getting close to dusk, and I knew the dance was about to start soon. I understood from repeat campers that the dance is a line dancing lesson that anyone can try to do. Mostly the girls get up and do it. I loved the butterfly's I was having sitting right beside Tina and not being able to touch. I knew she had the same feelings. She got up and went and got a couple of pops for us and sat back down. She handed me a pop and said, "I think there may be a nail in the seat. Can you put your hand behind me and feel around?"

I was worried about her getting jabbed by a nail and getting blood poisoning. I slid over just a bit and reached around behind Tina with my right arm and hand. I moved my hand over the board lightly and could not feel anything. I said, "I don't feel a nail or anything that would poke you."

"It's more under where I am sitting. Let me move forward so you can check there," she instructed. She slid almost to the edge, and I put my hand down and slid it around where her butt was. Without any warning, Tina raised herself just a bit and then sat back on top of my hand with my arm now fully extended behind her back. As her bottom landed on my hand, I knew instantly, that she had no underwear on. She turned slightly and said in her quiet voice, "Do you feel anything now?"

I gave her a look that probably said, 'You're about to cause your guy to have a huge stain in his new jeans,' but chose instead to say, "I have never wanted you more than I do right now, but unless you and I are going to do the 'Morgan' right here, I need my hand back."

She had a devilish grin with those hazel eyes; she said, "Just a second." She moved her bottom, so my favorite place was right on top of my hand. She gave a kind of butt squeeze and then got up and walked over to some girls across the pit. I had to stay there and think hideous thoughts to get myself under control. I knew if I stood up right now, everyone would know what was happening to me. I took a few gulps of the pop and switched my thoughts to wanting to talk to Tina openly about what we were going through and explore some boundaries. That Rebecca was something that I never did with Rebecca 1.0. We had to learn by doing and only set one boundary. But we never really talked about how we felt being with each other intimately or how we could improve it. Assuming there were any areas of improvement *(Smile break)*.

With Tina, everything was different. Her personality was different, her smell was different, and her attitude was different. She was nothing like Rebecca 1.0. She was simply Tina. My new girl. I am not sure if any of this is helping or pissing you off, but I am going through a process, and that process is making significant changes in my thought process and making me question everything.

They announced the dance was about to start and called everyone over to the covered section opposite the fire pit area. It was a huge wooden structure measuring 75 feet long and 50 feet wide with a log roof system with an overhead of about 10 feet. I got up and made my way there and knew I would have that first dance with Stephanie. When I got to the dance floor area, I spotted Pete, who gestured for me to come over. I walked over to Pete, and he put his hand on my shoulder and said, "You're up, kid, and I need a song you would like to dance to with Stephanie."

"Pete, any good 2-step works for this old dog," I replied with a grin.

Pete chuckled, gave me that eye roll he always gave me, and said, "I got one you will like."

I spotted Stephanie walking over with a big smile, and she said, "You ready to give these guys a show, Pony Boy?"

I said, "Hope you can 2-step, Steph, because I told Pete to put his best 2-step on."

She gave me this look and said, "You sure you're only 15?"

Before I could reply, Pete hit the microphone and said, "Without further ado, I would like to open the dance tonight with our two runners-up from the trivia contest, Derek Devon and Stephanie Miller." As the song started, I grabbed Steph's hand and led her to the center of the dance floor, and said, "I may be younger than you, but please allow me to lead."

The two-step, also called the Texas two-step or the country two-step, is a fast-traveling dance. The movement of the dance is similar to walking, so it's relatively easy to learn. You start by getting into your dancing position, with one partner leading. The easy way to remember how to do the two-step steps is to learn "quick, quick, slow, slow." Take two quick steps, then two slow steps. As the music started, I took the lead and moved my right foot forward, and Steph was right there with her foot moving back. It only took a few seconds for us to size each other's dance ability, and by the end of the floor, we were very comfortable with the basics. I figured I would do the first lap with a simple stepping move. We would start changing positions in lap two, allowing me to turn and move backwards. By lap three, we would begin mixing it up and start doing twirls and fast studder steps for show. If you ever want to watch it in action, Becca, watch the movie Urban Cowboy one day.

I know the dance would have looked like we were two old pros whipping around the floor, but I was more concerned that I would somehow offend or hurt Tina. I knew if I was 3 or 4 years older, Steph and I could have been a couple, but the fake 15-year-old me was already hooked on Tina. As the song ended, I gave Stephanie a bow, and she gave me a curtsy. Pete jumped on the mic again and asked everyone to give us a hand. As my final showman move and to try and make the moment a bit lighter. I grabbed Stephanie's hand and took her to the middle of the dance floor and proceeded to do our best Broadway bows. After 3 or 4, we walked off the floor to the far left, and I said, "Thanks for a fun dance, Steph; I hope I didn't step on your toes too much."

She finally gave a look that I thought was coming. 'How dare you be 15 years old’. She leaned in, and before I could move, she kissed me on the lips and turned and walked over to the other co-worker's table. I went into a bit of panic mode and started my slow pan of the room, hoping no one saw that. I think every guy in the camp was glued to that moment. I looked out, smiled, and went to try and locate Tina. She had watched the whole dance from a spot on the far side, along with a bunch of other girls from her cabin. I returned to the pop area and waited to see if she would come over. I had just opened a can of Mountain Dew when my girl arrived. She also grabbed a can of Mountain Dew and stood in front of me. I was ready for some attitude and plenty of groveling. But my girl surprised me again and said, "I have never wanted you more than I do right now."

I was stunned, and she knew it. I had to touch her now. I walked over and stood to her left, and let my arm touch her arm. We both were becoming addicted to our little teasing episodes, and I think we both needed a release to clear our heads. It was dark enough now that we could probably sneak past the washrooms into the woods. I told Tina, "Woods on the far side of the bathroom in 5 minutes.” I tried to look nonchalant and walked away. I made it to the snack table and grabbed a handful of nuts just to make it look legit. I then walked over to the path that led to the bathrooms and stood there to see if I was being watched by anyone. After being sure I was not observed, I walked to the boy's side and went in quickly. I wanted to clean up any pre-mess that may have happened and check to see how bad it might be. Luckily my tighty-whities had some excellent absorbency.

I left the bathroom and looked around again. No one was near, and I made my move into the wooded area. It was not that dense for the first 20 feet, but after that, some big trees could give good cover. I stood behind a medium-sized tree and waited. About 2 minutes later, I hear a faint voice saying, "Derek, where are you?"

I popped out from behind a tree and said, "Tina, over here." With my quiet voice.

She spotted me, or my profile, as it was dark out here, and made her way over. When she was about 6 feet away, she said, "This is so exciting."

We finally grabbed each other and looked at each other for a while with huge smiles. She was the first to speak and said what I did not expect, "I am so hot for you right now; you have no idea."

"I pulled back again and said, "if you give me a sexy look, I will lose it right now, but I want to talk about our feelings first. I want to make sure we are doing the right thing and not something that may hurt our relationship."

This time she heard what I said and looked at me longingly, and said, "I have never been in love, so I am not sure what it is actually like to be in love. My longest-boyfriend was about a year, and we broke up about two weeks before Sherry's party. We had sex but never had intercourse. He wanted to, and I knew he was not the person. He was not my first boyfriend, either. I had a couple when I was younger, but they introduced me to kissing and getting felt up, not always in a good way. With you, it is so different. I never had that feeling like the one we had at the lake today before. When your body touches mine, I get these incredible butterfly's that I don't want to end. I trust you and know you would never hurt me."

"Today, Tina, was my first time having that happen to me. I have not even had my first wet dream. I have never touched myself, if you know what I mean. I wanted it to be with someone special, and I tried my best to hold off. But with you today, you took my wet dream," I said with a smile. "I just don't want to rush into sex too quickly and maybe lose all the other great feelings and emotions we have been experiencing."

We were having our most intimate and revealing conversation while standing behind a tree in the woods. She pulled us together and gave me a gentle kiss on the lips, then said, "Let's do this; Let our desires and emotions guide us moving forward. I know you will look out for me, and you know I will look out for you. I may be a bit more experienced than you with the whole sex stuff, but I won't ever push you into something you are uncomfortable doing. And I know you will tell me if I do without hurting my feelings."

I wanted to tell her that I was not a real virgin; it was my thirteen going on fourteen-year-old self that was. But I also was cherishing these first-time feelings my body was giving me. I knew we would need time to let me get a bit older before we would introduce the whole parent and going steady thing. My parents still look at me like I am a little kid at times. I know her parents like me, but they probably figure we maybe have once held hands. I was ok with the plan, and before we committed to going any further, I said, "Let's keep our relationship secret for a while. We can find time to be together when we get home, but I don't want to complicate our lives by adding our parents to the mix. My parents would freak out if they knew I was sexually active, and I am sure your dad would kill me if he knew what we did and what we would be doing in the future. Finally, no intercourse till I am older. Are you ok with that?"

"I am more than ok with that; it's what I wanted as well," she said as we knew it was about to get very hot and heavy.

She backed away and began to undo her vest shirt. I have not yet seen her upper region, and without any light, it would most likely be more of a touch thing. As her top opened up, I could see her shape and was taking in every feeling and emotion. She took my hand and brought it to her chest. If what we experienced at the lake was a 10, then this was a 20. It did not last long, but it was the most incredible feeling ever. I was smart enough to bring some paper towels from the bathroom, knowing we would need to do some clean-up. She was so gentle with me, but I did feel a bit deceitful that she thought she was the teacher, and I was the student. We had chosen to be together in a standing sort of way, similar to our last episode, just a tree instead of water, so no dirt stains on either of us. It was also great that we were still in an exploratory phase and hand exploration was good enough; neither of us wanted to rush what we were enjoying.

After we got ourselves put back together, we decided to head back to the bathroom building; Tina would go left and look like she came from the girl's side, and I would go right and look like I came from the boy's side. It sounded good, but as we emerged from the woods and just reached the bathroom cement, Bev popped out from behind the bathroom side with some guy and said, "Ah-ha, caught you red-handed. I knew you guys are into each other."

I knew that both Tina and I did not know, based on what she said, if she had actually watched us at the tree or simply jumped to that conclusion because we had emerged from the woods. As usual, 2-step Johnny replied,

"We thought we saw some people heading to the so-called Ghost walk and went after them, but the bush was too thick."

"Oh, sorry, we want to go to that party as well. Can we go with you guys" Bev asked.

"Sure, Bev, who is your friend," Tina said?

"This is Stu or Stewart, and he is with the Hawks. He is a second offender here," Bev laughed.

"Hi, Stu, or do you prefer Stewart," I asked?

"Hey guys, Stu is fine," Stu responded with.

We all headed back as a group which gave us great cover and started asking around about the Ghost walk. Eventually, a guy said, "the Ghost seekers are gathering over at the pit. Bring a flashlight if you want to go," the mystery camper explained.

I did not have a flashlight, and it looked like Bev and Stu were no better off. As we all thought about it, Tina said, "Bev, there is a flashlight in the cabin under the sink. Why don't you and Stu use that one and Derek and I will try to find one and see you at the pit," followed by Tina's elbow to my side and a grin. What was she up to now?

Bev and Stu liked the plan and took off for cabin 1. As soon as they were out of earshot, Tina said, "Let's go down to the dock and sit in the chairs and look at the stars."

"Probably because it's cloudy, and we can't see any stars," I told her.

"Then let's go to the Dock chairs and make out," she said with her hypnotic devilish smile/grin. I am thirteen, going on fourteen, but I don't know if my newfound systems would be able to replenish themselves as fast as my girl seems to recover. Maybe the only way to know for sure is by testing.

She started in the direction of the lake path, and I caught up and playfully lifted her skirt, exposing her perfect butt to the night air. She gave me a look, and I lowered it back, resulting in her reaching to my front side and giving me a gentle, playful grab.

I will end this section simply by letting you know that for the rest of our two days and two nights, we will explore every potential hiding spot at the camp, including a few car back seats. My system appears to recover as fast as Tina's. Also, we had slowly been expanding our exploration and were discovering a bunch of new and unbelievably satisfying new emotions and feelings. I was no longer just a kid!

I am sure Rebecca; you are wondering why I just shared these experiences with you. Especially some of the most intimate. It's because my original plans were changing for me, and I wanted you to understand why. My return was to be with you, not Tina. I never planned for Tina and never even knew who Tina was the first time. I do not want to offend you by sharing this, and I certainly do not want to piss you off. But what you are being asked to do, it is only fair that you know the entire story. At the time of writing this, I now was wondering if Tina may end up taking your 'It-girl' pedestal. Only time will figure that question out.

Task 6 – Hockey & Grade 8

(September 1st – December 30th, 1974)

44 ***'Being your best':*** I am sorry I spent so much time on my summer camp experiences. Still, they were so transformational that you needed to understand what was happening with my development altogether. I have started my next significant chapter, grade 8, and seeing you at school for the first time. Tina and I have become even closer, and while we are still keeping our parents in the dark about our relationship, we decided to share our situation with only a few very close friends. Luke knows *(as of mid-September),* and Tina, I thought, would have told Sherry but told me that Sherry could never keep a secret. Tina had another close friend at school who I had not yet met named Theresa Summerville. I will get into that first meeting shortly. The 'Student Mentoring Initiative' was hugely successful, and my manufacturer Mr. Petrovich had put me in contact with a young up-and-comer in Toronto who was interested in taking my program national. We have had two meetings, and I hope to finalize a deal early next year. If I do this, it will significantly increase my earnings, far beyond my original expectations.

The other big news is my ongoing training for hockey. I am starting to think that I may be able to get my game to a level that would allow me to go to a university on a full hockey scholarship. Luke has also started working out with me a lot, and we have developed some great training programs to elevate our puck control and handling significantly. Nothing like bringing a little baseball to the rink! I have also started work on my Fort 2.0. I decided I wanted to keep this private and have not exposed it to Luke yet. I may in the future, but for now, it was a solo endeavor. I selected a location deep in the conservation area that I knew would never be developed or see any groomed trail systems near it based on my prior knowledge of the area. Don't forget, I have watched the area transform for the next 45 years.

My goal was to dig an initial underground hole as phase 1. It would be roughly 10 feet long, 6 feet wide, and six and a half feet high. It would have a liner and dirt roof, and I would make sure it was near a deer trail so it would help mask any traffic during the wet months or winter months. It had to be close to some big trees but far enough away to avoid any significant root system. Once I had the initial structure complete, I would slowly expand it from underground. That way, I could work on it all year round without people stumbling on my new fortress of solitude. I will share more details later, I am sure, but for me, it was part of my hockey training program. I would ride my bike down to the conservation area, hide it in the bush and then hike to my secret location and dig a hole. If you ever tried to dig a fresh dirt hole, it is a workout. Not only did it help with the upper body, but it was great for finger strength and wrist strength. I was able to get half of it dug out so far and part of the time issue is the amount of time it is taking me to cover up the hole so no one would know about my excavation.

On my return ride home, I would pass Luke's house and often take time off my workout at his place. Luke's dad was a fitness freak and had a full gym in the garage. Often, Joe would join in on our workouts. I had a naturally larger frame than Luke, and building muscle for me was always easier. Luke's genetics were leaner, proving highly beneficial in his later years. Sometimes I would even have to make a quick pit stop at the field across from Luke's. Tina knew about my rides to the conservation area but not about the building stuff. When we were chatting at night, she would ask if I was going for my ride down to the conservation area the next day. If I confirmed I was, she would add to my schedule, "Let's meet in the field at 'X' time."

We had selected a location that was secluded enough that people who were maybe playing in the field or even riding their dirt bikes would not venture to our spot. We had dug a hole and buried a couple of blankets, complete with a plastic-wrapped plywood cover. I would detour off Lover's Lane, where the lower field trail met the asphalt, and ride the path to a great spot to ditch the bike and complete the journey by foot. It was always a special time because I got to see her, and it was also somewhat risky. Our get-togethers varied in length from a quicky 5 minutes to as long as 30 minutes. A lot depended on the weather! Our sexual relationship had matured to the point that even if Tina were having her time of the month, we would work with it.

I was well aware that my sexual development was occurring a good two years before it happened last time. I was also aware that Tina was almost two years older than me, and as far as adolescent sexual development goes, that time frame is significant. I am still trying to decide if it was better to have a fully matured sexual and mental perspective or if learning by doing was better, as had happened with Rebecca 1.0. I certainly felt Tina was a considerable benefactor of my immense knowledge *(I made you smile)*. However, from the physiological perspective, I was still a horny 13-year-old that struggled to control, you know what. Sometimes it only took a look, and sometimes a simple brushing of our arms to get me to attention. Do you know that 30% of females will have had intercourse when they are 15-17? Our sex life was great, but I knew that soon the intercourse issue would come front and center for us. I did not keep condoms on me specifically so we would not succumb to temptation and do it because we had protection.

On a couple of occasions, I would ride to the fort, dig for an hour, meet Tina for our 20-minute workout, usually with at least a couple rounds, and then head to Luke's for an hour workout. Then get home and do my papers. I still had two neighborhood guys helping with the route, so I was down to about 30 minutes. I kept the route going to maintain the illusion that I was a hard-working young future entrepreneur.

This hockey season, Luke and I started to play together on the Sherman Falls select travel team. It was the highest level available for us to play at our age. It was also great our folks could share the driving chores and even watch games together. Mom and dad still loved the hockey parent activity, and Luke and I, 'head and shoulders' above our teammates, gave them a special status with their fellow parents. Luke and I knew we would be jumped to first-year midget next year, an entire two-year older age group, due to our playing ability. This year we would most likely set new scoring records!

Now, what I am sure is of most interest to you was my first look at you entering grade 7. If you are wondering, why would I even care now that I am in a relationship with Tina? Especially knowing that I am at least a year or two ahead sexually of my peers. It's rather a simple answer, and I hope you will get it right away. You know about my whole 'It-Girl' analysis. Well, as great as things were going for me, and they were great, when I asked myself the test question, 'If I had to be stranded on a deserted island with one person for the rest of my life, who would I choose? The answer was still you. I probably, on many levels, loved Tina, and maybe over time, one day, I would be able to answer 'Her' to the question. But here, now, it was still you.

On the first day back, starting grade 8, we were the seniors now and the cool kids. A lot of my classmates continued to mature and grow both emotionally as well as physically over the summer. I know that other kids in grade 8 were sexually active, and if the old Timeline was not disturbed too much, one of the grade 8 girls would become pregnant by March, which would cause a whole new awareness campaign for us grade eighters. When I arrived with Luke *(we rode together)*, it was typical for all the returning grade 8's to gather in one spot, and the newly arriving grade 7's would hang on the outside of the scrum. When Luke and I approached our school buddies, some we had not seen all summer, they certainly noticed the results of our hard work getting ourselves to be the best we could be. What is great about guys, we adopted at a very young age the ability to assign nicknames to everyone. There were guys in my class that I still could not tell you their birth certificate names. Last year I was battling some who called me 'DD,' and my hockey buddies called me 'Cap.' I dreaded the day someone threw out 'The D Man,' and it stuck. Nicknames are tricky. Luke was easy; his name was Lucas. Our buddy Squiggy was easy, he looked like Squiggy from Laverne and Shirly, and I gave him that nickname. It will be funny to see his reaction when Laverne and Shirly starts in 1976.

Derek Devon was a tough one. I hated anyone calling me 'Dev,' too close to sounding like 'Devil'. There was nothing you could do with Derek or Devon. My middle names were 'William and Henry.' Truth be told, my birth certificate reads, 'William Derek Henry Devon.' Mom and dad hated the name Bill, thus, the use of Derek as my spoken name. William was my dad's dad's (Grandfather's) name, and his dad was William as well. Gramps once told me that his family's birth origins were from Devonshire, England. Back then, people would refer to a person as 'so and so' from Devonshire. I gather any other Devons in the world may have come from Devonshire. Anyway, during our first meet and greet, it was obvious that Cap had been the chosen name. Everyone except Cam 'T' called me Cap. Another interesting observation was everyone greeted Luke and me with a fist bump. It was funny to see some of the variation's guys adopted, but it was official, I started the fist bump generation for this Timeline *(Well truth be told, Stan Musial was the first)*.

As we went through the pre-entry rituals, I constantly scanned the area where the newly minted grade Seveners huddled, hoping to catch a glimpse of you. It has been a while since I spotted you on your bike, and I was curious about what entering grade seven may have altered. I spotted your brother and his other Dundas buddies, but I did not see you. The bell rang, and it was time to enter the shrine. I went to my assigned classroom, and as I walked through the halls, any teacher I saw, I would give them a fist bump and a 'Great to see you, and you're looking great for a year older,' along with my patented friend smirk. When I got to my homeroom, everyone knew and respected that I wanted the front left seat by the window. As I entered, a guy was in the seat, and Kyle, or as I called him 'Shultz,' was over, telling him he was in the wrong seat. The kid quickly grabbed his stuff and moved to another seat.

I made a point of detouring over to the new kid and thanked him for relinquishing the seat for me. My dad always tried to instil the old adage, 'you can catch more flies with honey than with vinegar'. My rule and the rule that I made my friends adhere to was simple. Treat everyone with respect and how you would want them to treat you. Never pick on someone weaker than you and break your word; you will be 'Excommunicado.' I never had to use any brute force yet, except that time back at the camp when Tina and I eventually made it down to the spot the Ghost Seekers had set up their bonfire and were enjoying a few beers. When Tina and I arrived after our dock chair workout, Bev and Stu spotted us and came over.

"Where did you guys end up? We have been looking for you guys," Bev asked.

"We could not find a flashlight and made a wrong turn on the path leading here," Tina explained.

Good girl! She was learning the art of putting on the 'Tap Shoes.' We all stood there checking out what was going on. A lot more older kids were there, and almost all the councilors had made it. Steph spotted me and came over, which did not bother me anymore, considering Tina was my 'Super Top Secret' girl! As Steph met us, she knew everyone and said, "Glad you guys could make it here. I hope you don't mind if I steal Mr. Pony Man for a few minutes, one of the camp councilors had told us that this guy was responsible for starting 'Kids 4 Cancer Cure'. Funny, he had never mentioned anything to me, and I was his boss," Steph said in a somewhat bitter tone.

Tina looked at Steph, who I think was sending out a test flair to see how Tina would react. I am sure with the amount of time Tina and I have appeared to be together, Steph had her suspicions. "Take away, Steph, Pony Boy, is not mine. I am into the older mature types like Clint Eastwood," she said with that devilish grin.

"Great, let's go, Pony Boy," Steph ordered. I thought her calling me Pony Boy was initially endearing, but it had run its course, and I was now finding it more irritating. As we headed over to a bunch of guys about 30 feet away, Steph put her arm around mine again like before. She guided me over to a guy sitting on an inverted barrel with a beer in his hand. There were two other guys standing who also had a beer in hand. As we got there, Steph said, "Dwayne, is this the kid?"

Dwayne smiled and said, "Yes. I was at the event with my dad Derek. It was quite the night. You must get a lot of attention after starting that Charity."

"Nice to meet you, Dwayne, and I think I recall seeing you there. Weren't you talking to that older good-looking blonde lady at the after-party?" I asked, fully knowing I had no idea who he was and had never seen him before.

"Ya, that was me," he replied, not knowing I knew he was lying through his teeth.

"As you know, Mr. Simpkins was the main man for everything. He did all the heavy lifting while I was given credit for the concept," I added.

"How much did you guys raise?" Steph asked.

"Just over 4 million, I believe," I answered.

"You raised over 4 million dollars for cancer, and you're only 16," Steph asked.

"As I said, I just had the initial idea, Mr. Simpkins and his family are the people responsible. That is why it is now named in their son's honor, Trevor," I said, trying to deflect the direction of these questions."

"Hey, kid," the guy to the left of Dwayne said. "You old enough to drink a beer with the men," he challenged?

Everyone was waiting to see my reaction, and I did not want to disappoint, "Thanks for the offer, but we already had a few scotches earlier at the 14 and younger secret fire, and I hate mixing a fine scotch with beer."

There was that familiar moment of silence as everyone was processing my comment, and then as usually happens, Dwayne let out a laugh and said, "I can't wait till you're a couple of years older, and I hope you will keep coming back to the camp so we can do just that."

"Well, I am going to get a drink from the cooler," Steph said. "You guys keep my young man company while I am gone."

I already had a bad vibe from the guy to Dwayne's left, and I knew he was already half in the bag. As Steph walked away, he staggered over to me and did what nobody should ever do to me, he began to poke his finger into my upper chest and said, "Listen here, Mr. Charity boy, Steph is with me tonight, so when she gets back, I want you to tell her you need to go back to your little friends. Got it."

My first thought was from an incredible radio bit called 'The Champ.' The Champ was a former heavy-weight Boxing Champ, and if anyone said something to the Champ that he would misinterpret, he would lose it. Here is an example Becca; 'The Champ goes to the racetrack with Mrs. Champ to watch the pony races. He is looking around the terraced table seating area when the waiter from the lower terrace says, "Hey, Champ can I help you. The Champ says, "Me and Mrs. Champ are looking for our table?" The waiter replies, "Champ, below me." The Champ says, "Pardon?" The waiter says, "Below me." Well, the Champ loses it and gives the waiter a flurry to his mid-section and then a huge uppercut." I guess you needed to be listening as I did. I busted a gut, anyway, back to Dwayne's drunk buddy.

Now, most 14-year-olds would likely have wet their pants or soiled themselves. But as you know, there are two things in life I can't stand; first is someone poking my chest with their finger and the Dutch! *(I had to add that, and I am laughing, Sorry, Austin, for the lift)*. I know I should have been the bigger man and just walked away, but since I was with a bunch of other guys and I knew my capabilities, I did what I knew was very juvenile.

"Well, my friend, I hate to tell you this, but Steph has much higher standards, and the best you will get tonight is anal probing yourself with your empty beer bottle," I replied. Everyone was stunned, and no one knew what to say except the finger-poking boy. I knew he was around 20ish and was considerably bigger than me, but I knew pressure points. I had ten years of extensive training.

Buddy Boy let out a snort, took his finger again and started poking the bear, and said, "Maybe I should make you try it first."

The other guys knew what direction their friend was moving, and I could tell they were getting ready to jump in and shut the dink up. But not to ruin my fun, I took my right hand and grabbed his upper forearm. I moved my hand exactly where it needed to be and pushed my thumb hard on the spot. Old Buddy Boy dropped his half-full beer and went down on one knee. The other guys all sat back and watched. I was much more a lover than a fighter this week, but I did not mind a bit of extra testosterone fun. Dwayne had a grin going as well as the other guys. I applied a little more pressure, and Buddy Boy let out a muffled, "Jesus Christ, that hurts."

I told him in front of his friends, "I am sure you had a few too many tonight, and it was the beer talking and not you. I am sure when you're not a drunk obnoxious finger-poking asshole; you're probably only a prick. You will not touch Steph, and most certainly, your buddies will make sure that you get home alone with zero contact with Steph because if they don't, I will make them cry. Just Kidding, Dwayne, I know you guys will do the right thing and watch out for Steph. So, Buddy Boy, I will release my grip from your arm, but I will change pressure point locations which will cause your whole arm to become paralyzed. I would not want you thinking it would be smart to take a swing at me because then I would have to rip your cock off and stuff it in your mouth."

I quickly shifted my pressure point location and watched Buddy Boys' face scrunch up in pain, and then his arm went completely numb. He dropped down on both knees, and his left arm grabbed his right paralyzed arm, giving me the look of 'What the fuck just happened'. I looked at Dwayne and said, "Remember our deal regarding Steph, and thanks for supporting the Charity. I hope I will see you again next year." I let the dink go and he completed his fall to the ground and was on his back holding his paralyzed arm in obvious pain. "Give it 5 minutes and it will return to normal."

I turned, walked away, and I saw Steph heading back over with a beer. She intercepted me and said, "How come you're leaving?"

I said, "One of the guys there seemed to think he was your guy and made a lot of rude and frankly disgusting comments about what he would do with you tonight. It was making me uncomfortable, and there was no way I could kick his ass, so I left."

"I wish I were either four years younger or you were four years older. You will be one hell of a catch," she said with a disappointed look.

I smiled, kissed her cheek, and whispered in her ear, "I will be in university in 5 years, and you will only be 25." I walked away, feeling exactly what I wanted to avoid. I am sure I won't be chatting about this with the Doc. I walked back to my gang, and Bev said, "You're the kid that started that Kids' cancer charity?"

"I was just the idea, guy Bev," I said with a smile and added, "Let's head back to the dance area and see if there are other after-parties. Tina was noticeably quiet, and for the first time, she and I walked up the path holding hands and grinning at each other. We could afford to let Bev and Stu see us. Heck, only two days left.

I made special arrangements last year to get into Mr. Hodgeson's class as my homeroom class. He and I had become good friends because of our after-school monthly hockey games between the teachers versus the students. Last year we never beat them but came close a couple of times. This year, a whole new ball game. I had put on another 10 pounds and grew almost 2 inches and was now 5 feet 8 ½ inches. My shoulders had broadened, and my strength was much improved. After our student-teacher hockey match, we would all go to Jocko's and enjoy a dinner together. I went to my seat and turned sideways to chat with Veronica. I had not seen her all summer, and I certainly noticed she had started to fill out. Many girls over the summer seemed to have filled out, and a lot, in a significant way. I asked what she did over the summer and if she was dating. We had last year sat near each other in a couple of classes. As I was telling Veronica some of my highlights, who walks in but Todd Hamlin. I had messed with the Timeline, I guess, with my homeroom request. Tonka Boy was never in my class before. He came in and looked around and saw a chair near the back in the middle. We did not make eye contact, and I watched him take his seat. He had also grown a lot and had a bigger mop of hair going. He was still not that tall but bigger than last year.

Mr. Hodgeson walked in and, as usual, went to his desk, sat down, put his binder on the desk in front, and then turned to scan the class. We all knew his format, and by the time he finished the scan, we were all sitting facing forward, ready to hear our classes plan for the day. He did his usual speech, and when we got to the 'BB-Bat' reward question, I knew he would try to throw me a curve ball of sorts after last year. This was a Derek versus Goliath-type match. He was a reasonably dull teacher, but he was good at teaching English.

"Your chance to win this coveted prize," as he held out his 'BB Bat', "will go to the first person who can answer, 'Would you please bring me the head of Mr. Devon?', would refer to what type of grammatical structure?"

I gave him a grin, and he maintained his poker face. I looked around the room, and after about 30 seconds, Nancy Henderson raised her hand and said, "Is it Imperative?"

"Not bad but not correct. Imperative would be a type of this."

No one else attempted to answer, and Mr. Hodgeson turned to me and said, "Did I beat you this year Mr. Devon?"

“Well, Mr. Hodgeson, as it appears my head is on the proverbial chopping block in your statement. I would have to defer to a more whimpier answer than Miss Henderson’s and guess you may be looking for a ‘whimperative,’ hybrid type answer,” I responded with.

He maintained his poker face, and everyone else was watching our stare down. After about 30 seconds, he tossed the BB Bat at me, and I proudly grabbed it, with an extra grin added.

After that, as he dismissed the class, I went over to Todd, said "hello" and gave him my BB Bat.

He smiled and said, “How did you ever know that answer?"

“My dad is a major bookworm and forced me to read a lot of English textbooks whenever I was bad. It turns out I was bad a lot, I guess,” I replied with a grin. “You ride to school still or busing it,” I asked?

“No, still ride with Frank and the guys, at least until the winter weather starts. My sister is starting grade 7 and is part of the gang now,” he said.

“Oh, so you have a sister,” I replied.

“I have two sisters and an older brother Mike who is starting High School,” he remarked.

“Well, I have to head to Chemistry now, so I will see you around. Welcome to Mr. Hodgeson’s class. He looks like a bore but is very good at teaching English,” I told him.

Ok, time to go for my first scouting walk. I left the class and had no idea where you may be. Classes were all spread out, and you could be anywhere. When I ran into Mary Lou, I had not made it 10 feet. “Hi Derek, how was the rest of your summer,” she asked.

"Hey Mary Lou, it was great. I went away to a horse riding camp and did a lot of bike riding, and went to the French River for two weeks with the family. And you guys?” I asked back.

“We go away in July for a couple of weeks to a cottage up in the Haliburton area. We have gone there for the last few years. After Sherry’s party, my sister asked all sorts of questions about you. I think you really impressed her with your piano and singing,” she replied.

OMG, Maureen knows who I am. I could not wait to find Luke and tell him. “Do you know where Luke is?” she asked.

“Funny you asked. I was hoping to bump into him on my way to Chem. He has math as homeroom class in the west wing,” I said.

"When you see him, please tell him I say hello and not be a stranger," she added.

I told Mary Lou, "I will," and continued my hunting. As I arrived at the end of the hall and had to turn towards the west corridor, I spotted Luke walking my way. We spotted each other, and Luke turned towards the wall, out of the way of everyone walking to class, and waited for me. "Any prospects in homeroom," I asked?

"A couple. Remember Sue Graves; you need to see how much she has filled out since last year. She looks completely different. And I mean in a good way," Luke replied.

"I ran into Mary Lou, who is on her own hunt, buddy. You better make a decision or else. She also told me that her sister was asking all sorts of questions about me after Sherry's party," as I gave him the OMG eyebrow raise and wide-eyed stare.

"No way! Maureen was asking about you? Get out; she's in grade 10 this year," Luke responded.

"I'm telling you, she wants me," I said with a grin. I still have not told Luke, but in a couple of weeks, I will be taking him as my wingman on a blind date with Tina's friend, who I have not yet met, Theresa.

"Well, I have to get to my next class. Let's compare notes at lunch, at the same table," Luke said as he left. I turned and was walking down the hall when I finally spotted You. Not from the front but from behind. Honest to God, I spotted your backside and knew immediately it was my Rebecca. I had memorized that view, which was permanently etched in my mind. You had dark blue pants on, a grey sweater, and were carrying a couple of texts and a pencil case. I did a quick speed walk to get myself within 10 feet and then hit the cruise button. I just stared and had this unbelievable butterfly hit me. Not the same butterfly's as I get with Tina. These were different butterflies. I never thought Butterflies would be specific to a person.

You turned to go up the stairs, and I knew I could not follow, but I wanted to see you climbing the stairs. It was hypnotic, and I was lucky that my buddy Mark was walking down the stairs and stepped into my Rebecca view to snap me from my trance. Hey Cap, who you checkin out?" Mark asked.

"Have you seen how many girls from last year have changed?" I asked.

"I know. Do you remember Clair and Linda from French last year? You will not recognize them now," Mark gushed.

"Hey, got to get to class, but Luke and I will be at our table for lunch today," I told Mark. We exchanged a fist bump, and I took off to make my class. I spotted you! And you probably don't even recall when you first noticed me. I got to chem and took my regular seat, and this year I was pleasantly surprised to have Kerry Unger as my chem partner. She is one of the smartest kids in school. She goes on to be a doctor in the USA and becomes a bigwig at some multinational pharma company if the Timeline stays true for her.

My new goal was to get a frontal view of you. I wanted to see how much you may have changed from my bike ride visual. I finished classes and grabbed my lunch and headed to the cafeteria. We had our table, and everyone in the school knew it was our table. If someone sat there, a grade 8 student would go over and give them the heads up. I was not first to the table, but as was customary, I gave each of the guys a fist bump. Luke was already seated, and I usually would sit across from him in the last two seats at the end of the table. The table would allow about 12 guys to sit—six on each side. I usually biked or ran home for lunch but being this was the first day, I had to be there for the checkin-out views. Luke had the best seat to view the rest of the cafeteria, so I had to turn and straddle the seat to allow myself a view, hoping to see Rebecca. There was no guarantee she would come in since a lot of kids at this time of year would go and eat outside somewhere.

I spotted Todd and Frank about mid Cafeteria but no you. I was listening to everyone's summer 'best of' stories, and now and then, I would laugh when someone said something funny. The tallest guy in our group, we called Korky, always had a humorous outlook on life. He was always good for a laugh or two with his observations. Suddenly my Spidey senses were tingling. I caught out of the corner of my eye your backside again. You were in line going to the cafeteria counter, and it looked like you were with three other girls. I could pick you out from 1,000 feet, I bet. I knew after you paid for whatever you were buying, you would loop out, and I would have a full-frontal view. I automatically went into stealth army ranger mode and got up without saying a word. I calculated the best vantage point and quickly went to the table and immediately squeezed into a small space at the table. I said to the people at the table while never taking my eyes off you, "Hey guys, sorry to crash your party, but I need to sit here for a minute or two. Hope you don't mind.; By the way, I am Derek Devon and if you're new here, Welcome."

"Hi Derek, I'm Peter, you know my brother Nick from hockey," Peter said.

While I kept my eyes on you, I said to Peter, "Hey Peter, Welcome to grade 7. Do you play hockey?"

I know Peter said something, and I felt terrible not listening, but you had made the purchase and were about to give me the big reveal. My eyes were glued, and then you made the turn. You walked straight toward our table, then turned to Todd's table. You stood and chatted until the girls you were with came over, and the group of you left. I was in a trance, processing everything I had just seen. I memorized every square inch and recorded it in memory. I must have looked like I had a stroke when the guy beside Peter said, "Who is that girl you're staring at?"

So much for secret agent Derek Flint, stealth army ranger moves, so I replied, "What girl?", with a grin.

I got up and returned to the table, and I guess unbeknownst to me, the entire table of my guys had stopped everything and were watching my every move. As I arrived at my seat location, I noticed everyone had a grin going and looking at me. It was Korky that broke the 'grin down'. "I see you like the young ones now", what happened to your dream of dating Maureen Cap?"

So, being me, I replied to the table, "How could you guys know that in 20 years that that young girl is not a doctor, lawyer, famous movie star, or even a great downhill skier. And maybe even my wife. Wouldn't you want to take a look at your future famous wife when she was in grade seven?"

I gave them a big smile and said, "I was looking at the girl in the far hallway that you can't see from here. She was super-hot and, I swear, had at least 36 c's. I have never seen her before. Do any of you guys know who she was?"

"What girl?", Korky asked.

"The babe in the hallway with the great rack," I said. Immediately half the guys got up and headed to check out the hallway. Incredible what a suggestion of a girl with 36 c's will do to guys.

Anyway, my diversion worked fine except for Luke. He knew me, and I could not get that past him. He gave me a kick under the table and a head nod signifying, 'What's up with her?' I simply said, "Later."

I could now have some peace to process what I saw. I wonder if you ever recall that moment, your first day in grade 7. I was right there watching you. You had gotten even cuter; you were starting to fill out and had become a very beautiful young girl. As much as I would have loved to go to you that instant, it would be a colossal failure. We both know it would have been a disaster. But there was a big part of me that I would have to fight constantly to overcome the urge. Anyway, my memory of you is etched in my mind forever *(Made you smile I hope).*

Task 1 – Complete and Updates!

(January 1st – May 30th, 1975)

45 ***The $500,000 kid!*** Great news: Mr. Petrovich and I have signed a contract finalizing the National roll-out of the 'Student Mentoring Initiative.' I will get three seats on the board, and Mr. Petrovich will get 2. Mr. Hank 'Henry' Derkson gets 4 for his group. That means Mr. P and I will control the board for a while. I retain an in perpetuity Royalty of 7.5% of net sales. Derkson and his people will pay a one-time bonus to Mr. P and myself of $500,000 spread out over 12 months.

My seats will be filled by Mr. Simpkins, Mr.Agro's nephew Albert and yours truly. I will receive the first $250,000, and Mr. P will get the remainder. I hired an estate lawyer to assist me with my will, setting up an educational trust fund and a unique academic scholarship program. Finally, I arranged a memorable trip to celebrate for Tina and myself. Tina has an aunt in Vancouver and had arranged a special 'girls' ski trip over March break to Whistler. I booked a room for just Tina and myself and one for Luke and Theresa, who were a hot and heavy couple now! Last October, Tina and I started going on secret dates downtown; Theresa would be Tina's wing girl, and Luke was my wingman. Tina and I wanted some private time, so we arranged a blind date for our wing people. Tina got her license in February and was now driving the family Suburban or their other smaller Mercedes.

We would meet them downtown at Jackson Square. They would go see the movie, and Tina and I would go and make out in the back of the car. If we had enough making out, we would walk the mall and do other stuff until the movie finished. Before Tina drove, we had a couple of movie make-outs sessions in the theatre. Thank God we had winter coats to put over our laps. Anyway, it was still exciting! Unfortunately for us, Luke and Theresa liked each other, and after, I think, the end of our February movie date, Tina told me Theresa wanted to use the back of the car to make out with Luke. So, it was flip a quarter to see who went and watched the movie and who got to make out. Luke and my trip to Whistler would be the first time we would be parent-free, with our own rooms to do whatever we wanted and with our girls. It was a great week, and to think, two guys our age, in whistler with a couple of gorgeous16-year-olds. Life was great!

All is great at home these days. Gramps is great; Gram's, Ian, and even my sister seems to enjoy high school life. My 'playtime' with the neighborhood guys had diminished. I was so busy with my new schedule that I was hardly around to play road hockey, football, or hang out like we used to.

I still see Mr. Agro every two weeks, and my trip now includes me sitting and having a bite with him and his boys at the shop. No new suits, but I need to see Mr. Angelo for a let-out and maybe a new suit for my growing collection. The 2nd annual 'Kids for a Cancer Cure' was held last week and was another huge success. It seemed to attract a bunch of new sponsors, and I think every politician in the region. It was great to sit at the head table beside Sean, and the most memorable surprise for me was seeing Mr. & Mrs. Van Houten seated at the table beside my folks and my girl looking like a million dollars. She kept it from me. I gave Mr. Mattson tickets so he and Mrs. Mattson could join the festivities, and I made sure Luke was there with his date, Theresa, who was also Smokin Hot.

The format was much more polished, including a dance during the schmooze with a band, and after spotting Tina, I decided to add a minor change to the format. My main man Phil the audio tech, was back on duty, so it did not take me long to get him to do his part. Knowing she would love it, I told Betty my suggestion and asked her to do her stuff. While the speeches were taking place, all the behind-the-scenes stuff was happening. Tina had this smug look on her face when I looked at her. Our parents knew we liked each other from the number of phone calls each week but never expected in 1,000 years what we were regularly doing behind their backs. We had never had dinner at our houses together, and with all our top-secret planning, we had done a commendable job of keeping our secret. But I thought it was time to change our relationship. We had already exhausted our sexual exploration without doing; you know what.

It was starting to feel a bit more 'routine' like. Don't get me wrong, it was still unbelievable, and I can say that our sex life was the best I ever had *(Sorry Girl).* Just around Christmas, when we were in the back of her Suburban in Jackson Square underground parking, I was sure that she accidentally used the 'L-word while we were kissing. I recalled a mumbled lip to lip, "Oh God, I love you." She might try to argue it was. "Oh God, I love this," but I am sticking to my version.

I had the prime rib, as did Luke. When dinner was being served, I took the opportunity to step down and check on my folks, and since the Van Houten's were right beside our table, I stepped over and welcomed them to the event and said, "Great to see you guys. Tina never mentioned you would be coming."

"You look like such a handsome young man in your suit. I love the style. Tina asked us to keep it a surprise Derek," Mrs. V said.

"Hi Tina, you look lovely tonight. I don't think I have ever seen you in a dress before; I hear there are a few young single guys here tonight," with a grin.

"Thank you for the compliment, Derek. And if you run into any nice-looking single young boys, please send them over my way," she countered.

Doc V jumped in and said, "Don't be silly; you two could be the proms, King and Queen," with a smile.

"Don't embarrass the kids, Hal," Mrs. V said.

"Well, I have to get back up to my seat; I will chat with you folks later. Tina, I will keep a look out for your special guy, " as I quickly left, ensuring I had the last word.

I returned to my seat, and the staff switched empty plates with dessert selections. I had the usual fruit bowl. The final speeches and presentation took place after the dessert plates had been removed. It was about 30 minutes, and rather than another plaque this year, I was only asked to stand and was recognized as the founder. I sat back down and realized that Tina had never seen me in my fabulous suit. And a few people commented how much older I was looking. It was great that Luke had already introduced Theresa to his folks, who were a couple now. I quickly looked over to Tina's table; she and her mom were gone. Crap, what a timing issue to have to go powder her nose. I quickly wrote a note on a piece of paper and asked Sean to pass it along to Mr. Simpkins, who had the podium. As the message got passed along like we were still in school, it arrived at the podium. As Mr. Simpkins explained the rest of the night's format, he read the note, hesitated for a second, and looked down at me.

He smiled, and I gave him a nod. After he wrapped up the intro stuff, he held up the note and said, "I have been requested to tell you a brief story about Trevor. I sat there with a grin, thinking Tina had figured out my plot and thought she could beat me at my game. Although I knew she had no idea. While Mr. Simpkins told a story about Trevor's first attempt at riding his bike, Tina and her mom returned to their seats. Mr. Simpkins' story went a bit long, but the crowd liked it. When he finished, everyone gave him a respectful applause for sharing his memory. I was sitting there knowing what was about to happen and had a monster grin on my face when Tina looked up at me and realized something was up. Her stare went from, 'What is happening now' to, 'I am going to kill you!'

"As you know, this amazing event and Charity was started by and supported by our youth. I think it is only fitting that we acknowledge their contribution by asking our young people here tonight to come up to the dance floor to have the first dance," Mr. S announced.

Tina's head dropped as she knew I was responsible for this, and she fully suspected I would use one of my old standbys just for the occasion. I got up and went over to her table and said to Mr. and Mrs. V, "Would you mind if I asked Tina for a dance" with a perfectly straight face?

"We think you guys make a perfect young couple tonight," Mrs. V responded.

"Miss Tina, would you please do me the honor tonight of having this dance with your phone buddy," I said with my best southern accent voice.

Tina had become very good at the whole kibitzing thing and figured I got her good but wanted her own dig as well and replied, "Well, sir, since you failed at finding me a nice young man tonight, I guess I will have to settle for you," she said while throwing me her 'In your face' look.

I had Betty go around the tables and force anyone 18 or younger to go to the dance floor. Once we got to the floor, Mr. Simpkins told everyone to get a partner for the dance. There were about 12 kids that partnered up to 6 couples, including Luke and Theresa. I led Tina by her arm, and she said as we got to the center, "You really going to do this?"

"I guess maybe you should have thought about there being consequences for keeping this night a secret from me. I am lucky I did not invite my other teenage lovers," I replied with my 'I want you so bad right now' look.

The lights dimmed, and suddenly a new set of lights lit up the dance floor and a giant disco ball. I turned to face Tina, and she looked up at me, and I said, as I put my hand on her shoulder, "I love you."

Yes, Rebecca, the Rascal's it was again. 'How Can I be Sure.' We owned the dance floor, and as all the other kids were dancing in the middle of the floor, Tina and I owned the outside. And my main man Phil did not disappoint as the spotlight hit us and followed us as we traversed the floor like an old married couple who had been dancing for years. What was special this time, Tina was much more confident than at Sherry's. As we continued our 360s, we kept our eyes locked on each other. I was sure we were giving Patrick Swayze and Jennifer Grey a run for the hottest dance number because Tina and I were having 'The Time of Our Lives'. She knew what I had just said and was waiting till the end of the song to give her reply. As the song ended, I did not know what we would do. Mrs. V was right; Tina and I were King and Queen of the Ball! I figured we would get some clapping from our parents, but I never expected a standing ovation. And to cap it off, my girl said to me, "I love you too."

I had Tina by the hand, and with my stage manager hat on, I walked her towards the other kids, and I told everyone that we were going to do a group bow as they do on Broadway. All the other kids gave approving smiles, and we lined up in a row, 14 strong, holding each other's hands, and then I said, "Bow." We all did the bow, and the crowd loved seeing a bunch of kids deliver a performance of a lifetime. We separated and started to congratulate each other, and my fist bump was in full form. Mr. Simpkins grabbed the mic and said, "Folks, aren't our youth amazing"!

I walked Tina back to her table as the band started to play their first number. I guess we inspired many people to want to dance because it did not take long to fill up the dance floor. When we got to her seat, Mr. and Mrs. Van Houten had ear-to-ear smiles, and Mrs. V said, "I don't know why you kids are not boyfriend and girlfriend? I know Tina had taken dance lessons, but where did you learn to dance like that, Derek?"

I smiled and said, "Too many Fred and Ginger movies, I guess."

I asked, "Would you mind if I took Tina over to meet my folks?"

They both looked at Tina and smiled. Tina was smiling and got up to come and meet my folks for the first time. My mom was still drying her eyes, and my dad had a parental glow-on like I have never seen before. Both my parents, that seldom hugged me could not wait to welcome Tina into our lives with big hugs. So, Rebecca, it was now official; your little bird who left the nest had found himself his first official girlfriend as Derek 2.0. We ended the secrecy pact and were entering a whole new relationship phase. I can't wait for next year's Gala to see how we can top this year.

Oh, before I forget, our hockey team won this year—both of them. Luke was the top scorer, and I won the best defenseman honors. Our dads were approached by a couple of scouts and one USA university recruiter.

Update – Grade 8 Graduation and Rebecca!

(June 1st – August 15th, 1975)

46 ***End of my favorite school year and an Unexpected Rebecca Encounter!*** It was the best year of my life. I had a great gal, the school was better than last time, and that was great. I was getting comfortable in my 'New Shoes.' I was enjoying 'you know what all the time' and had money. I had built a great network of kids I planned to nurture into my older years, and my home life was perfect. We had our graduation, and I won Athlete of the Year honors and the highest grade point average. Yes, I cheated, but it was why I came back to do this. I think we all but eliminated school bullying. After the graduation ceremony, I finally met your parents. I spotted Todd and went over to congratulate him on graduating. Tonka Boy saw me as I approached and put out a fist for the old bump. He said, "Derek, this is my mom and dad; mom and dad, this is Derek I told you about."

"Hello, Mr. and Mrs. Hamlin, it's a pleasure to meet you, and it was great having Todd in homeroom this year," I replied.

"We have met you briefly at the Charity dinner in January," Mr. Hamlin said.

I recall meeting them briefly, but I was sure no last names were exchanged. They were talking to another couple beside my mom's table where she was holding court! "I do recall seeing you there. I saw you were talking to another couple I didn't know," I said.

"Yes, that was friends of ours who brought us to the event. You should be commended on your accomplishments," your mom said.

"Well, it is Mr. Simpkins who is the main man. I am now just his sidekick," I responded with a smile.

I hope I did not give your mom any creep vibe, but I was checking her out in detail in an attempt to figure out the DNA distribution that built you. Your dad asked, "What are your plans for the summer Derek?"

"I have a junior hockey camp to attend for two weeks, and I am racing motocross this season. Other than that, I guess the usual stuff kids do over the summer," I replied.

Our chat continued for a few more minutes until Vice-Principal Ross came and grabbed me for a photo shoot with the 'Dignitaries' that attended that night. As I was being dragged away, I said, "Let's try to get together this summer, Todd, and it was very nice to meet you folks."

After the pictures, Luke came over with Theresa and asked if I was attending any parties tonight. I said, “Actually, no. Tina had a function at her school, and it was not open to outsiders.”

Phil Peters came over and put his fist out for a bump and said, “Hey Cap, there is going to be a bush party later behind our place on Powerline Road. Any chance you can make it? A bunch of the guys from hockey will be there, and I hear a few babes as well.”

Phil’s place was as remote as you can get in our town and backs onto conservation land. I have been there before for his older brother's parties a couple of times. I replied, “Let me see if I can get out of what my parents have planned and get out there.”

“Great, and don’t worry about you know what, Tim bought a few cases for us,” he added.

Typically, at these bush parties, we all stand around and ‘shoot the shit’ until someone does something stupid, and then we all laugh at them. I have found that hanging out like I did the first time was completely different, and the old saying ‘Been there, done that’ would apply. I was not into drinking a bunch of beers, acting stupid, and then throwing up. I usually would have one, maybe two tops, and Luke was the same. I would have instead spent the evening with my girl. As the schmooze wound down, I was able to pull my folks away, and we loaded in our car for the 5-minute drive home. As we drove home, Dad said, “Would you like to order some Lee’s Chinese food tonight?”

As tempting as that sounded, Derek 2.0 was trying to eat healthily, and I used the party as an excuse to say, “Thanks, but Phil is having a get-together at his place tonight, and I promised I would show up.” I knew mom was disappointed, and it most likely meant she would not be enjoying sweet and sour chicken balls with fried rice. When mom was at the nursing home, she always loved when I visited her along with some Lee’s as a treat.

We got home around 8 pm, and I figured Tina was already on her way or already there, so I did not try to call her. I was hoping that Tim would also be asking a bunch of his friends over since he was in Grade 10 and usually had a bunch of attractive ‘A-listers at his parties. With me entering High School next September, I figured no time like the present to start networking. I already knew a ton of High School kids. Since they started moving me up a level or two in hockey, I played with kids two or three years older than me who were already in grade 9 or 10. I changed out of my new Mr. Angelo creation and put on my jeans, jean shirt, and brown leather suede vest that looked like it had been through two wars.

I owned two motorcycles; a Yamaha 125 trail bike that I have had for three years which I completely rebuilt last summer, and my CanAm 250 motocross bike. While my folks were not a fan of me riding the bike in the survey, I often would take it over to the school, where I could connect to a series of trails that spanned a bunch of potato fields. From there, I could get to another trail that got me to Shaver's side road. There I had to cross the street, but I would pick up another trail less than 100 feet on the other side. I was going to take the 125 tonight since it was the quieter of the two and had turn signals and lights. While not happy, my folks would look the other way so they would not have to drive me there and pick me up later.

I arrived at Phil's around 9 pm, and the sun was almost down for the night. I parked the bike beside the garage and headed around the back. They had a pool that overlooked the woods, and there was a ravine at the bottom where the bonfire usually would be. If Tim were also hosting a few friends, then the pool would also be in play. When I emerged from the side of the garage, I spotted Tim first, and he said, "Hey, glad you could make it. Junior is down getting the fire ready. Can I get you a beer?" Tim asked along with the usual fist bump.

"Thanks, man. That would be great," as he handed me a Colt 45 *(beer)*.

"You havin anyone over tonight?" I asked.

"Well, the folks just headed to Grand Bend to the cottage for the weekend, so the answer is, absolutely," he replied with a grin.

I walked over to the pool deck rail, yelled at Phil, and waved. He gestured for me to come down, so I thanked Tim for the beer and made my way down to the fire. There were already about 15 people: 10 guys and five girls. The girls were all together, and the guys were broken into two groups of 5. I spotted Rob, figured he would be good for a few laughs to start the evening, and walked over to his group. It was ok hanging out, but I did find a lot of the discussion was just plain dull and primarily juvenile. But what would you expect from a bunch of 14-15-year-olds? I sipped the beer for about an hour and had heard every guy tell every other guy whom he thought was the hottest girl in school. After getting bored with the guys, I walked over to the girls and figured I would crash their party. As I arrived, I said, "Ladies, wonderful to see you all tonight, and congratulations on graduating today."

"Congratulations to you, Derek, on winning those awards," said Kim.

"Thanks, Kim; I think I only won them because I let the teachers beat us in Hockey," I quipped. Truth be told, I am sure it did play some role in my relationship with my teachers.

I knew my presence would cause the girls to change the discussion since they were probably talking about who the hottest guys were in school. They all knew I had a girlfriend, so I did not have to deal with any actual flirting by any of them. The girl's group had grown to 8, and my neighborhood buddy Kathy showed up and stood beside me. Kathy and the old Rebecca became friends when Kathy was in grade 10. It will be interesting to see if that remains constant. I asked everyone about their summer plans and if they would all attend the High School. Two of the girls were already attending grade 9.

I had been down by the fire for about an hour and a half, and I went over to Phil and told him I needed to take a leak and asked where he would prefer, I do my watering. He laughed and told me to head over to a big tree and go behind it. I said, "I am going to head up and see if I can steal another beer from Tim; you want one?"

"Sure, tell him to take it from my box," he added.

I walked up the hill to the pool deck area and scanned for Tim. I spotted him over talking to Kathleen Richards, an outstanding athlete and one of the best track and field kids in High School I have been told about. She had her own look and a very athlete-type body. Not much up top and lacked any shape due to her no hip chiseled legs. When I approached, Kathleen said, "Hey, it's our new minor niner, Tim."

"Well, officially, it will be a couple of months, Kathleen," I replied.

"How's the fire going down there," Tim asked.

"Great, I think we are up to around 25 down there," I said. "Phil asked me to grab a couple of beers from his case."

"They're over under the table with the tablecloth almost to the floor," as he pointed to the other side of the pool.

I thanked him and smiled at Kathleen. I made my way over to the table, lifted the tablecloth, and spotted a few cases of Colt 45 and two coolers with beers on ice. I grabbed two cold beers and stood up to survey who Tim had at his party. The pool was already in full use, and there were about eight people in the pool. I was just about to leave and head back down when I spotted Maureen climbing out of the pool using the ladder. OMG! She had on this red bikini that fit her perfectly. I had drooled many times at the pool in the summer when she was lifeguarding, but she always had on a one-piece *(Which she also looked great in)*. She was a full 35 B-plus-C and had the perfect dimensional body; 35, 24, 36. Her hair was wet and pulled back, and her skin was flawless. If I could stop staring and take a look at the rest of the guys around the pool, I would guarantee everyone was watching her get out, along with, I would bet, a couple of girls.

I took a calculated chance that if I left now and headed back to the side gate to return to the campfire, I may intercept Maureen if one of the towels on the railing was hers. With two beers in hand, I made my move. I had to make sure that it looked like I was completely unaware she was there. I started to head for the gate when I felt a hand grab my arm. I stopped and turned to see Maureen looking at me. "Hi Derek, I did not expect to see you at Tim's Party."

"Hey Maureen, long time no see. You must be cold," I responded.

"I am, can't you tell" with a grin. "Come with me to my towel and tell me what you have been up to. I don't think I've seen you since I waved at you from the car when you were out running a couple of months ago," she added.

I followed Maureen *(yes, walked behind her, Smile time)* over to her towel. She grabbed her towel and started to dry off. She said, "Is one of those for me," with a grin?

"Why, of course, Maureen, but hang on while I fetch one for Phil. He's down at the fire pit," I said.

I handed her a beer and made my way back to the table. While walking there, I scanned the area, and every guy, including Tim, was watching me. I am sure a few were trying their best to cut me in half with their laser beam eye looks. I did my best to make it look like it was no big deal. I grabbed another cold beer for Phil and walked back to Maureen, who was now looking over the rail at the fire pit.

"Hey, would you mind escorting me down to the fire pit so I can warm up" she asked while taking a sip.

"Well, it's mostly a bunch of young kids down there, and I can't promise you that they won't all be staring at you in your bikini," I said with a grin.

"Hang on a second," she replied as she reached for a pair of jeans that had been on a chair. While I was standing there, she started to put them on. I knew every guy's eyes at the pool were watching. So, I said, "Give me your towel Maureen." She stopped and gave me an odd look while she handed it to me, and I immediately opened it up to provide her with a bit of a privacy screen.

She smiled warmly and said, "Aren't you the perfect gentleman."

I just smiled and looked away, trying to look very nonchalant. She finished pulling on her perfectly fitting faded Levis and then pulled a top on and slipped on a pair of flats. When she was done, she grabbed my one hand and said, "Thanks, Derek, I will take the towel now." She folded it up and put it on the chair. She grabbed her beer, and I grabbed my two unopened beers, and then she grabbed my arm. "Lead away, my cute young man," she instructed. I knew I was in love with Tina, and it never crossed my mind that Maureen would ever have any of those types of thoughts about me. But when I was last in High School, she was like a goddess. Every minor niner worshiped her. And she knew it and loved it. She was not a tease; she just knew what gift God gave her and was not afraid to let people gawk. I used to be one of those gawkers. I would hate to think how many young boys back then, in grade nine, found themselves fantasizing about Maureen while they tested the functionality of their thing! Not that I would have ever done anything like that.

So, now, Derek 2.0, with the hottest girl in school on his arm, is walking down to a fire where everyone there will be in shock and awe. Derek 1.0 had not started the whole sexual exploration phase, but Derek 2.0 was already light years ahead of his fellow guys in that department. For a brief moment, I had a 'Hermie' flash from the movie 'summer of '42', and Maureen was my Dorothy. I wonder if Maureen knew what Tina and I did with each other, would she look at me differently? Maureen huddled in close as we arrived at the fire and put her hands out to get them warm. I walked over and handed Phil a beer and gave him a private wink that Maureen would not have seen.

When I returned to the fire, I could tell Maureen had a bit of a shiver going. So, I did what any awestruck 14-year-old would do with a stunning 16-year-old; I put my arm around her and said, "Would you like me to find you a blanket?"

"She smiled and said, "Thanks, but I think your arm is doing the job," She shifted her body and was now almost leaning on me. I won't lie, Becca; I was on cloud nine at that moment. I was the man! Every guy there was watching and wishing he could be me. But what gave me the most excellent satisfaction and confidence was Maureen knew that I would never attempt some creepy move to alter our current situation to suggest I wanted something more from her. And that self-confidence was powered by knowing I would never cheat on Tina or do anything to hurt her. I am sure she would not be thrilled with my chivalry right this moment, but I knew that was all it was.

This was the first time I had a conversation with Maureen. We chatted about Sherry's party and roller skating, and I asked about her modeling and future plans. She asked me a bunch of questions, and I was caught a bit off guard when she asked me about Tina. I told her that I first met Tina at the party, and we have been going steady since the last Gala. She said, "She is a very lucky girl. I wish I could find someone like you."

I was gobsmacked by her remark and said the only thing that I could think of, "You're the most attractive girl in High School, and I know I am not telling you something you are not aware of. Every guy here tonight is wishing he was me right now. That must be a very difficult and often an unwanted burden for you. But rest assured, you will find your 'It-guy' one day, and it will be worth the wait. I hope you don't have to kiss too many frogs getting there."

"What is an 'It-guy', she asked while still chuckling at my frog reference?

"Ask yourself this question; If I had to live out the rest of my life on a deserted island with one person, who would it be," I said. "That person would be your "It-guy."

She looked at me in a very loving and warm way and then kissed me on the cheek and said, "Thank you for that." We spent the next hour talking and laughing, and after that, I told Maureen I was heading home. She asked if I wanted a ride, and I told her I had my motorcycle here. She gave me a sweet goodbye kiss on the cheek. I thanked Phil and Tim and rode home. I got back around midnight and went inside. A note on my bed said, 'Tina called around 10:30. Call her tomorrow'.

I got up around eight and made myself some breakfast. I was trying the healthy juice shakes these days. Dad came up and asked if I would help him in the basement. He was trying to finish off the three-year bathroom project. I went down and surveyed what he was working on and did not have the heart to tell him to leave and let me finish it. He needed to re-route plumbing before installing a partition wall between the sink and the workbench. When we got into it, we discovered he needed a few fittings, so I said I would walk over to the hardware behind the church and get some.

As I entered the hardware, I quickly surveyed available signage and spotted the plumbing section. I walked over and started to scan the aisle of my fittings and needed to go to the next aisle. As I turned at the top of the aisle, I was standing about 6 feet from you! Yup, young Rebecca was filling shelves with stuff. She did not see me, but I was locked in place and just stared at you. I had been watching you at school all year, and a few times, I had to do a u-turn to avoid running head-on into you. My butterfly's kicked into full gear, and I had to do a new updated etching. I am not sure how long I was staring, but eventually, a man came over to me and said, "can I help you find something?"

I unfroze and said, "Yes, I need a 45, 90-degree street fitting, two joiners for 1 ¼ abs, and a bag of ½-inch copper pipe holders." As I was giving my list, I knew they would be almost opposite where you were kneeling, and as I was led in your direction, you shifted to let me by, and without any notice, you looked up at me. That was the first time we looked at each other, eye-to-eye. I can guarantee I would have stared at you for far too long, but it was our first time, and I could not help myself. You extended a gracious smile to me and then went back to stocking the shelves. The man said, "Here you go, son; they are right here."

I grabbed everything I needed and went up to the cash register. I paid, and as I was leaving, I decided to take the route out that would take me past you. I did not know that you had finished and left, and I guess you were in the back stock room. I went up and down every aisle until I figured things out. Then I left to return home. All the way home, all I could think about were your eyes. You have such beautiful warm, and tender eyes. So, there you go, we have officially had our first eye contact!

Update – The Breakup ☹

(December 27th, 1975)

47 ***My first big hurt; Ok, second!:*** The summer flew by. I did the hockey camp; we did a family vacation for the last two weeks of July. Tina and I spent a ton of time together and became like some old married couple, except we could not keep our hands off each other. My motocross racing wound up for me at the end of September. I started grade 9, and it was not as scary as some thought it would be. Many older kids liked me, and as a sports-oriented first-year student, I was big enough that I was never really hazed. I played on the football and basketball teams, and Luke and I decided to also play for our school hockey team. Luke and I played midget and were listed spares for the junior team. I added another wing to the fort, which looked incredible. I had carried in ten car batteries to power the place and installed a mini wind generator in a tall tree.

In December, the juniors were scheduled to play in a tournament in Quebec. They would be at the Tournament from December 20th to December 23rd. Teams from all over Canada and the USA play at this event. On December 15th, Coach called and asked if I would be able to come to the Tournament. They had a couple of guys out with injuries and wanted Luke and me to go. I was thrilled at the opportunity, as was Luke, so we committed to going. I was also aware that the High School has a special Christmas Dance on Friday the 19th, and Luke, Theresa, Tina, and I had planned on going. I called Tina immediately after the call and broke the bad news. She was not happy but understood how much the opportunity meant to Luke and me. I will assume Luke went through the same with Theresa. We would take a bus and leave on the morning of the 19th. Tina and I hung out till about 11 pm on the 18th. She had mentioned that she and Theresa may still go to the dance anyway and asked if I was OK with that. I told her sure. I was feeling guilty for stiffing her at the last minute anyway.

We left in the morning, and it was a rough tournament. We had guys 4 and 5 years older than Luke and I; in hockey, size does matter. The coach was pleased with our play, and Luke had the most goals on the team. He and I had our own system that was new to the game, and we enjoyed exploiting it. I would pick up the puck at the point. If the opposing player positions offered me a route, I would skate down into the corner, turn to head behind the net, and as I reached the first net post position, I would cause the puck to roll onto the blade of my stick, and I would then pitch the puck like a ball over the top the goal tender having it fall about 5 feet in front of the net.

Meanwhile, Luke would be out front cruising and waiting for my pitch. When he saw the puck coming, he would skate across the front of the crease and bunt the puck into the net, never above his shoulders, usually at chest level. We had practiced that move for two years in our backyards. We knew eventually that other's would copy our move. But for a brief while, it was all ours.

We lost the Tournament and ended up in the middle of the pack. The bus ride home was less than celebratory, and Luke and I shared a seat to chat. When we got home to the rink, my dad was there to pick Luke and me up, and we drove Luke home, and then I went home. I was looking forward to taking it easy and giving my girl a call. It was 3:30 pm, and I called Tina. She was not home, and her mom said she would give her the message to call me. Tina called me at around 6:30 pm and wanted to come by in the suburban and go parking somewhere. I could not turn down such an offer, and she rolled by at 7 pm. I jumped in the front passenger seat we exchanged a heavy tongue-filled kiss. We had a variety of spots depending on the weather, if it was dark or light out, and the temperature. Being a cold December evening, we decided the underground parking at Jackson square was best. We were very familiar with the underground lot and knew we could find an area that would be private.

When we reached our parking location, we were like animals in heat. We crawled over the seats, eventually making it to the very back. Tina had prepped for the occasion, and we had a couple of wool blankets back there. As soon as we got under the blanket, it was a race to see who could strip fastest. I won as usual. As soon as we were clothing free, we entered into a very passionate hug and kiss. After that, she pushed me onto my back and reached for something in a side pocket. She brought out a condom, tore it open, and proceeded to put it on me without looking at me. I was not sure where this was headed but assumed it was a 'Mess Control' issue. Once I was 'Contained', she straddled me and said something I was entirely unprepared for, "I want to make love with you tonight. I am ready, and I think you are too."

She reached down, assuming I was OK with her suggestion, and started the move. I could not help but feel something was off tonight. The whole thing felt like desperation, and I was not ready to take that next step yet, especially without having a really good talk about it. I knew we loved each other profoundly; believe me, I also wanted it, but not like this. I would have liked to go away for the weekend to the Piller and Post or something. Not in the back of the suburban in an underground parking area. I raised my legs, causing her to be unable to complete the move. When her eyes reached mine, she looked like she was about to cry. I stopped and just stared at her, and I was not sure why I said what I said; it just came out, "What happened?"

Her look went from looking like crying to now crying. She dismounted, straddling me, and was sitting beside me with her knees to her chest, arms around her legs, and sobbing. Instinct kicked in, and I went and put the blanket around her and said, "I am sorry, Tina, but I don't want our first time in the back of a car," thinking I was the cause of her distress. Her sobbing was now even harder, and she said what any boyfriend or girlfriend never wants to hear, "I made a huge mistake." I was still trying to process everything and understand; was she saying I was the mistake, or wanting to do it was a mistake, but what I did not think I would ever hear was her confessional. "I went to the school dance Friday with Theresa and never planned any of it, but my old boyfriend was there. He is the guy I dated for a year before you. I had not seen him since I broke up with him. I forgot he was going to Sherman Falls High, and suddenly he was standing in front of me. He was older now, and I guess I was feeling a bit alone, and we ended up sitting together."

I did not need to hear anything more. I had already played in my mind the full details of her night. I was stunned, to say the least, and just sat there, bare ass naked.

"He offered to drive Theresa and me home after the dance, and we agreed. He dropped Theresa off first and then asked to go and park somewhere so we could talk. I said OK, and he took me to some side road off Binkley."

I was taking it all in and had a pretty good idea of how it would end. I was coming to terms in my own way and was already working on my formulation when it came time for me to speak.

"He started to confess his love for me and his regret breaking up, and he was crying. I don't know what happened, but we ended up holding onto each other crying."

The male part of me was thinking, 'Great move, buddy,' but the other part of me was thinking, 'she is not my 'It-girl.'

"I never planned on any of it. It just got out of control, and I ended up making out with him."

I wish I could say that I was devastated and hurt beyond belief, but the truth was, I was actually feeling more relief. Our relationship was, in fact, heading towards her maybe being my 'It-girl.' I was prepared to let her be the one who took my virginity. Just not this way. Whatever initial pain I felt had given way to my valve system being fully engaged. I began to look around for my clothes and started to get dressed.

"Say something, Derek. I love you more than anyone else, and I want to fix this. I can't lose you," Tina said with a sobbing anger in her voice.

"I love you too, Tina, and I am sure you love me. I know you made a huge mistake, and it is something you will have to learn to live with. But I know now that you're not my 'It-girl.' She knew it was over when I said that to her. She continued to sob as she got dressed, and eventually, we ended up sitting in the front seat, and she asked if I would drive her home. I was more than capable of driving us home even though I was not licensed yet as long as we don't get pulled over. It was a long and lonely drive taking all the back roads to avoid the police. Not a single word by either of us. I pulled into her drive and told her, "I will walk home." I got out, and she remained in the suburban, and I could hear her go into an entirely uncontrolled bawl session. I did not go back to comfort her; I simply walked home.

When you have a long-term relationship, you also develop relationships with many other people as a result. When the relationship ends, it means you have to go through a breakup-like situation with each of these new friends/relationships. Over the next few days, I got a call from her dad, her mom, Theresa, and even Luke tried to get me to reconsider. It was funny; even my folks wanted me to reconsider. But it was not in my DNA. I still cared about Tina but not the way I used to. Her mom tried to set up an intervention-type get-together with them and my parents. I was done. It was over, and I had a job to do. Tina knew me and did not attempt to call me. She knew it was over the moment she did what she did. She knew if I were indeed her 'It-boy,' her indiscretion would never have happened.

Well Dimples, when I decided to tell you this, I always wondered how you would feel. Anger at her hurting me, joy she was no longer part of my life, disappointment in me, even jealousy. In my own way, I was glad we never talked about our old relationships, other than 'Pulled it out Boy*"! (Made you smile!)* [Update: Tina got back with her old boyfriend about 2 weeks later according to Luke]

Update – Road Worthy!

(January 1976)

48 ***I got my motorcycle license!:*** It was Friday, January 9th, and I drove my newly purchased 1975 Triumph Bonneville 500 up to the driver center on the mountain. Last time I had an old Honda 350. This time I treated myself to a new bike. It was a cold January, but no snow that day. I passed without any issues and was now a fully licensed motorcycle driver at the ripe old age of age 15! Back then, you could get a bike License at 15.

My plan is to get myself a Harley when I turn 18.

[Gala 3: It was another successful night, and I was attending as a single guy this year. It was great to have Sean make it to the night, and we spent a lot of time catching up with each other. Sean's private members' bill in 1975 gained recognition for the beaver as Canada's official animal symbol. I was certainly caught off-guard when he confided in me that he was considering leaving politics and was seriously thinking about becoming a priest. I told him that he was a needed voice in Canadian politics, but he felt the backroom BS and backstabbing along with the two-faced political class was something he did not want to become a part of. He thought if he stayed any longer, he would need to sacrifice his principles to remain competitive.

Mr. and Mrs. Van Houten attended, and we briefly exchanged pleasantries but no mention of Tina. I also bought a few tickets for select friends to come, including Mr. Angelo and his wife Mary, Mr. Agro and his daughter Patricia and her husband Antony, Mr. and Mrs. Mattson and Luke and Theresa. Funny side note; Since my Tina incident, Theresa and Tina appear to be no longer friends. I never said anything about it to Theresa, but I appreciate the sign of loyalty. Finally, my sister decided to attend with mom and dad, and she brought a girlfriend from school as her wing woman. All-in-all, it was a great night. For me, it had a little added specialness when Mr. Simpkins introduced me to a visiting family member from England who was over for a week to visit and check out U of T as a possible school. Sandy was the spitting image of Linda Hamilton from 'The Terminator', which won't be made for another ten years. She also had what can only be described as a 'Bubbly' and infectious personality.

There was an instant attraction, and Mrs. Simpkins picked up on it immediately and arranged for me to come for dinner in a couple of days. I always loved an English accent, but with Sandy, she also had a Kate

Beckinsale sounding voice. I knew I was in trouble for the remainder of the night and would be fixated on giving most of my attention to Sandy. Mom and dad had tried in the English sort of way to provide me with a pep talk about getting over a breakup, including the old 'Get back on the horse' speech. I was actually fine. I understood that Tina was a great part of my life, and I will always cherish what we experienced and learned together, but she was not my "It-girl. That means my 'It-girl' was still out there somewhere, which made it all okay.

Sandy was in grade 13 or their equivalent to our grade 13, and after graduation was thinking about taking a year to go to school here. What I appreciated most about Sandy was her perspective on life. Not a negative bone in her body. When the dance portion of the night started, we danced together for most of the night. Fast or slow. My mom, at one point, had to remind me that I needed to spend some time talking with my friends and guest, so I took her advice and dragged Sandy around for the Schmooze tour I went on. I did not realize that we were holding hands almost all of the time. Luke made mention of that fact, and I realized it was a mutual thing. I always loved holding hands, as you know, Rebecca, and this was no different. At one point in the evening, a reporter from the Spec took a picture of me and Sandy dancing which found its way into the Spec's weekend special insert all about the gala. The caption read 'Young love at the gala' *(I wish I cut that out and saved it, smile alert).* I knew it would find its way to Tina, giving me a brief smile.

At the end of the Gala, Sandy said, "I am glad you will be coming for dinner this week. Any chance you would have time to take me to a movie?"

"Well, if you don't mind taking the bus, I would love to go and see a movie with you," I replied.

Sandy was a gamer and loved the idea of taking the bus. She said that was her primary mode of transportation back home, well that and using the subway system they call the tube, and she enjoyed people-watching. We did not exchange a kiss goodbye that night but rather a simple handshake.

I went for dinner, and after, we grabbed a bus to head to Jackson Square to watch 'The Outlaw Josey Wales'. I always loved Clint movies, but this would always be one of my favorites. I would rank his top three westerns as The Outlaw Josey Wales, The Good, the Bad and the Ugly and then Unforgiven. I felt terrible because I was so into the film that I ignored Sandy. She could tell I was way into the movie and let me enjoy it up until about the scene when Clint leaves Granny's son's home to face the Comanches. We had been holding hands when I suddenly realized that Sandy had moved my hand from the arm rest to her lap. Yes, I had a momentary flashback to the lake with Tina. What was different was that she placed my hand on her thigh, then put her hand on mine, and began to gently stroke my leg. Never coming close to you know who, just a gentle back and forth. I found myself doing the same, giving us a new connection. I guess it was our version of the old 'Fonze.'

What gave me some hope *(Smile time)* was at no time did my youthful exuberance get the better of me and come to attention. It was an innocent connection, letting us know we had moved to the next level. After the movie, I wanted to talk about it, but Sandy, I could tell, was really not that excited about it, so I backed off, and we talked about her and what she wanted to do with her life. We took the bus home and went back into the Simpkins house. My dad was scheduled to come and pick me up, which I did appreciate. We chatted about the movie, and when my dad arrived and honked the horn, I got up, and that was when Sandy gave me a polite kiss on the cheek and thanked me for a beautiful evening.

I got in the car and drove home. Dad asked me about the night, and I told him how great the movie was. I spoke to Sandy each night on the phone until she departed, and we had agreed that if she decided to come here for school, we would see each other again, and if I ever made it to England, we would see each other again. Finally, we also agreed to write to each other once a month, and I was actually looking forward to having a pen pal.]

Task 7 – Flamboro Downs

(March 1976 – October 1978)

49 ***And They're Off!:*** When I was planning on how to leverage my time knowledge, Flamboro Downs was my first thought. This would be a do-over, so to speak, because I used to hang out with the drivers *(Derek 1.0)*, and I would get a tip every now and then. I also had a couple of regulars that were more than happy to place a small wager or two for me. Back then, $20 was a big bet. I still had the paper routes but had my two 'kids' doing all the deliveries now. I just handled collecting for visual purposes.

This time around, I would become friends with a couple of the drivers, especially old Mac. He was a full-blown alcoholic, always had a 40-pounder of Whisky hidden in the hay somewhere that only he knew where it was. But, as big a drunk that he was, he was the most honest drunk. I needed to find a guy like Mac because I was too young to place bets on the races, so Mac was my 'drunk bet mule'. One of the memorizations I made was several triactors *(Ok, a lot)*, that would happen at Flamboro shortly after it opened in 1975. I would have preferred a lotto win, but the current lotto at the time issued a pre-printed ticket with pre-generated numbers, rather than like lotto 649, that allowed you to pick your own. A trifecta is a parimutuel bet placed on a horse race, in which the bettor must predict which horses will finish first, second, and third, in the exact order. Known as a trifecta in the US and Australia, this is known as a tricast in the UK, a tierce in Hong Kong, a triactor in Canada, and a tiercé in France. My memory system was to memorize the date, by day, month, year *(last two digits)*, race number, and race results.

On May 24, 1977, 3rd race, the finish order was 4, 11, 7. It paid, if memory serves, just over $3,600. 24-5-77-3-4-11-7. The size of the pay-out was based on the odds of each horse in that race. I only memorized those race results with the highest pay-out. I memorized a total of 100 of those combos spanning 10 years or 10 per year.

I started working there part-time in March 1976, the year after it opened. I got my motorcycle license in January of that year and bought my new 500cc motorcycle. I had the option of using either the motorcycle to get to and from work, or my preferred choice, my bicycle. Just so happened, I would use the Mineral Springs route to get to the track. Gee, wonder why? *(Smile time)*.

After each win, Mac would collect my cash, and I would tip him 10% and a bottle of Whisky, which he would have to buy himself. Based on the pay-outs I remember that occurred initially, after the first 6 or 8 wins, he started to bet my same numbers on a second ticket since the pay-outs got lower. He was not allowed to bet on any race he drove in, but as it turned out, that just interfered in 4 of the 100 races I committed to memory. I arranged for an alternate mule, Luke Mattson's Dad Joe, for those races.

It turned out that Joe loved the ponies, and each time I got Luke to suggest a trip to the track, he jumped at the suggestion purely on a social basis. A guy's outing thing. He was more than happy to place bets for Luke and me. Whenever I 'won big', I would take Luke and his dad out for a nice steak dinner to celebrate and, of course, keep it secret from my folks! By the time of our first date, I had managed to sock away in my private bank accounts over $65,000 in winnings. Not bad for a 15-17-year-old time-cheater *(I giggled)*.

But when it came to wealth, it also meant I needed to be careful that I flew under the radar. A young kid, winning every time would draw unwanted attention. So, I made a pact with myself, never tell, or more importantly, show anyone! It was hard at times, but fortunately, wisdom and discipline come with age. And, as a soon to be 65 year old 15 year old, it was easier than I thought it would be. I even kept a paper route, always kept part-time jobs, and, as you know, started my own businesses while in High School.

You didn't see how I 'Worked' my money. Sports betting! Not the way you think, I had to use bookies because of my age, and the book-making world was just as sleazy as depicted in the movies. Again, because I could only commit so much to memory, I had to be selective and strategic. My focus was not on who won an event; I only cared about outcomes where a big underdog won. This offered me the best bang for my buck. I also had a rule that I would win three and lose 1. That way, I kept the bookie's attention at bay. My usual loss would be roughly 10% of my winnings. I also used more than one bookie, and I think the best idea I came up with was pretending to place the bet using a local 'mobster's' family name, and I was simply the 'bag guy.' I would call in the bet by phone using a voice-altering device I made from radio shack parts. It was a simple EQ like device that allowed me to clip the high frequency making my voice lower. Then, I would personally drop off the wager money for my made-up mobster want-a-be 'Micky Paletta', and after the win, I would pick up the winnings *(money)* for Micky Paletta' as his 'Bagman'.

If you're wondering about some of the mechanics, I once played hockey with Nicky Paletta. Nicky was just a so-so player *(Right Winger)* back in Bantam, and I think most parents believed he made the team only because the coach didn't want to end up in the bottom of Hamilton Bay wearing cement galoshes *(Yes, I am smiling)*. Big Gino Paletta lived more off a somewhat over-exaggerated reputation than being a hardened mobster. If you wanted a hardened mobster, you would go to the Papalia clan. Big Gino, as everyone liked to call him, except to his face, was a nice guy when you saw him not playing a mobster want-a-be. I was never friends with him during the first go-around, but I ensured we would be pals this time. We would do the old sleepovers, home and away, and fortunately, Nicky enjoyed hanging out with me, especially since I was the team captain and had two motorbikes to ride.

In order to access the illegal bookie market, I needed someone to get me in and give me sufficient 'cred' to ensure I was not taken advantage of. That is where old Big Gino came in. To get the party started, during one of my pre-planned sleepovers at Nicky's, and as a side note, Nicky's sister Angela was smoking hot and only a year and a half older than me. I made the first move with Gino, not Angela *(I am smiling)*. Hanging out at their home had fringe benefits *(I am grinning right now)*. At dinner, I worked in a story about how I overheard a couple of drivers talking about a supposed fixed race next Saturday. And right on cue, I joked, that I wished I could place a $10 bet on it. Well, as I expected, after dinner, which at the Paletta's took at least 2 hours, and the food was always incredible, Big Gino pulled me aside out in the garage where I was helping Nicky practice shooting the puck more effectively. As Nicky was going through the exercises I designed for him; I figured the 50 pucks would take him a good 15 minutes. That gave Mr. Paletta and me more than enough time to discuss my intel.

Next Saturday came and went, and I was at the track, having Mac place my wager. I knew big Gino would be using a bookie, so the pay-out would not be impacted. I figured I would run into Big Gino at the next hockey game on Tuesday night at 7 pm. When I got to the dressing room, I was the second guy. Coach Rick was always first, and his son Jeff, who played on the team, was always the first. I was usually always second. I enjoyed the pre-game time chatting with everyone. Another important lesson I learned the first go-around was the value of developing an extensive network of friends and acquaintances. You never know who may grow into a very successful business leader or politician.

My early arrival allowed me to spend a lot of time with my fellow teammates, and I made a point of maintaining those relationships beyond our hockey bond. When Nicky came in, he went to his usual spot in the dressing room. We each had our favorite spot; mine was on the bench between the showers and the bathroom. If you think it was stupid to be so close to the toilet, rest assured that no one ever took a dump; sorry, a 'number two' in the dressing room toilet. It is one of those unwritten rules I have never seen broken in my many years of playing the sport.

The bench was large enough for two people, and as Captain, I got to select who I wanted to share the bench with. My choice was always our goalie. I knew darn well the value of positive thinking, and the last 10 minutes before we left the dressing room to hit the ice, I was a masterful motivator and, I will add, a good Psychologist.

Nicky came over to me and said, "My dad wanted me to give you this. He said you and he discussed something about the best cheese to use for some dish the last sleepover."

Nicky handed me what appeared to be a block of cheese wrapped in butcher's paper, complete with a string keeping it closed. I knew what it was, and it was not cheese. I said thanks to Nicky and stuffed it into my hockey bag, in a little pouch inside the bag, usually used to hold tape, skate sharpening stone, and other odds and ends.

Glen, our goalie, looked at me and said, "You gonna eat that after it sat in your stinky bag all game."

"Absolutely not; I am hoping it will age further; being in my bag for the entire season should make it even tastier," I replied while tightening my skate.

Fast forward, we win the game, I get two goals, and Glen earned his 4th shutout. It seems my pep talks paid off. Glen 1.0 had epilepsy, and every now and then would have an attack, suddenly skate out of the net to the corner and stare at the lights. Since my pep talks this go-around, no attacks, and he went from just a so-so goalie to the top goalie in the league. I think his newfound confidence helped him overcome the attacks. As I exited the ice, I looked up at the stands and as always, waved to my mom and dad with a nod and smiling eyes. I also could not help but notice Mr. Paletta standing to the right of my dad, and when my eyes reached his, he gave me a big wink and a thumbs up. Mission accomplished.

When I got home and took my hockey equipment to the furnace room to spread out to dry, I grabbed the block of cheese and opened it up. Inside was a stack of cash and a note. The note said, 'Thanks for the tip, Derek. I placed your $10 bet and just happened to make a fairly large one myself. I have topped up your winnings and want you to know that I appreciate your discretion and information. If you get any more tips, please let me know'.

The note was not signed by Big Gino, as he had a habit of never signing anything with his name. Not even Christmas cards or birthday cards *(That last part was a joke)*. Sorry for the long and drawn-out explanation, but I thought it would serve you, knowing not only about having the results memorized but seeing how I could execute using them. Needless to say, Gino and I would have periodic, mutually beneficial exchanges over the years until his heart attack in 1998, assuming the timeline remained true. He was also my primary source for finding bookies for all my sports betting.

[Sean has quit politics and is becoming a priest. We chatted about his decision, and while I will undoubtedly be losing valuable access to the political elite in our country, it was the right move for him to make. It should make for some interesting discussion about my views on God.]

[Hockey Update: Luke has been asked to try out for another team, and I was not invited. My feelings were not hurt, but it did bother me that our dynamic duo could be coming to an end. I loved hockey, and my game had greatly improved, and I was starting to believe with continued hard work, I could have a shot at making the show. But I also had my tasks to complete, and I knew that I could not do both. The next few months would prove to be difficult for me as I had to transition from my dream of playing in the NHL to using my hockey skill to get a scholarship to a very strategic school, Harvard.]

Update – Rebecca Contact!

(June 1976 – July 1976)

50 ***She knew who I was!:*** Just a short update. I am sure you remember it anyway but enjoy the revisit. I was out with Luke, and we had my bikes out for a ride in the fields across from Luke's house. I let Luke use my 125 while I rode the 250. There were a few short trails and the makings of a motocross track, including two jumps. I was teaching Luke to jump; it was not uncommon for other kids to come here and ride their minibikes or even bicycles.

We had been riding for about an hour when I spotted Tonka Boy and his sister *(YOU)* riding their bicycles to where we were jumping. You came over from Lovers Lane's side. Todd did not recognize me immediately with my helmet on, and just as you got there, a guy on a minibike coming from the opposite side of the field showed up and went over to Tonka Boy and you. Seems a friend of your brothers who I did not know invited him to stop by and take his minibike for a spin. I found out later that you and Todd were riding home from your dad's hardware store near my house. Yes, I just had to show off, and I did a few big jumps. Luke was getting better and could get good air off the one jump, but I wanted you to see me do a double humper complete with a front-wheel side to side for show. Plus, I always looked good in my leathers.

Tonka Boy was out riding the minibike, and you were standing with the kid who owned the minibike; I know I wanted to keep myself invisible to you, but I could not resist the temptation and rode over to where you guys were standing. When I pulled up, I did not remove my helmet and asked whose minibike your brother was on, "Hey, is that Todd on the minibike?"

"Ya, it is. Nice jump! I love your 250; it's a beast," the young guy said.

"You know how to ride a motorbike with gears and clutch" I asked?

"Ya, my brother has a bike, a Yamaha 100" he replied.

"Well, why don't you take it for a spin to see how she feels" I offered.

"Are you serious?" he said with a huge smile.

"Sure, but no jumps, okay," I replied.

I did that so that I would be left standing with you alone. I took off my helmet; I was sure my head was soaked with sweat. I handed him the helmet, and he got on and was visibly excited. He drove off somewhat cautiously, which made me feel better. Once he was far enough away, I said. "Hi."

"You look like you have been riding a motorcycle for a while," you said.

"Yes, I raced motocross out at Copetown for the last four years," I replied while watching junior ride my baby.

"I think I saw you in my dad's hardware store last summer buying plumbing parts," you said.

"You must be Rebecca, Todd's sister," I countered.

"Yes, he has mentioned you a few times and about your Charity work. My parents were at the gala last year," you added.

Wow! I was in shock. You knew who I was and even remembered our brief first eye contact. I was sure I had a significant smile going, and I wanted our chat to continue, so I asked, "You looking forward to going to Sherman Falls High in September?"

"How do you know I am going to Sherman Falls High?", you asked.

"Well, I recall seeing you when you were in grade 7, and I was in grade 8, so I assumed you graduated this year," I replied.

"You knew who I was in grade 7?", you challenged me.

"Kind of; I saw you with Todd talking a few times and assumed you were family," I quickly qualified.

"Yes, I am looking forward to school in the fall. You will be in grade 10 next year like my brother?", you asked.

"Yes, officially no longer a minor niner, unlike you," I joked.

I would have loved for the chat to continue longer, but Tonka Boy pulled up and saw me talking to you and rode over. He took off the helmet and said "hello" to me and then asked you if you wanted to take the minibike for a ride. I was surprised when you said, "Sure."

"Just turn this to go faster or too slow down, and this is the brake. Take it easy, and you have to put the helmet on," Todd instructed you.

"You can really jump your bike Derek," Todd said as you put the helmet on.

"Four years of practice and a lot of almost broken bones, buddy," I replied.

You got the helmet on but did not have the chin strap done up. I am guilty of watching you raise your leg and straddle the bike. In my defense, I was in a bit of a dry spell *(Did you smile?)*! I had to seize the moment and walked over to you and did the honors of doing your chin strap up. You raised your head and looked into my eyes as I fumbled a bit but got it attached properly. I smiled at you, gave you a tap on the top of the helmet, and said, "Take it easy. It's your first time."

That was the first time I got to see your devilish side and you did a bit of a concealed laugh as you overturned the throttle and burned out, shooting dirt into the air. I looked at your brother, and we both rolled our eyes, figuring this would not end well. Soon you went out of sight on a trail, my young admirer riding my CanAm returned and handed the reins back to me. He was gushing at the bike's power and thanked me repeatedly. I turned the bike off, and Luke came skidding to a stop beside me. He turned the bike off, took his helmet off, and said, "Hey Todd, good to see you man."

Todd introduced us to his buddy, and I hate to say it, but I do not remember his name. While we were chatting, I was listening to the sound of the minibike, and then suddenly the sound stopped. Call it instinct or whatever you want; my girl was in trouble and needed me. Without saying anything to the other guys, I jumped on my bike without putting my helmet on, kicked it to start, and took off to see what happened to you. I was thinking the worst, but as I reached the crest of the hill, I saw you were okay and standing beside the minibike, trying to push it. I came up to you, stopped the bike engine, and said, "You, okay?"

I must have had a worried look on my face because you said, "I am fine, you don't need to worry, but I think it may be out of gas?"

I could have taken some gas from my bike and put it into your minibike, but I could not resist the urge to give you a ride back to the guys. I asked you to hold my bike as I pulled the kickstand on the minibike out with my foot and parked it where it was. I grabbed my 250 and said with a huge grin, I am sure, "I'm sorry, Rebecca, but this bike does not have a passenger seat; you will need to straddle me for the ride back." I gave you a few instructions, and after 15 seconds, I had you straddling me facing backward, just like Cameron Diaz and Tom Cruise in Knight and Day *(A movie example, in case you have never seen it)*. I kicked the engine over with your arms around my neck, and the bike fired up. I smiled at you, and can you remember what you said?" "Please, no jumps, Derek," and smiled at me. You never said anything about a wheely!

I confess now that I could have taken one trail that would have gotten us back to the guys fairly quickly, but I had you in my arms for the first time and decided to go for a bit of a trail ride. You knew what I was doing, and I got the official okay from you when you smiled and said, "This does not seem the fastest way back." I smiled, and you have no idea the butterfly's I was experiencing, but rest assured, I will be asking you one day what, if anything, you were feeling. Eventually, I got us back to where the guys were standing, and they were initially concerned you were hurt when they saw you draped around my neck, straddling me. As I stopped the bike, I grabbed you by the butt *(I have to pause while I recall that memory in vivid detail…… smiling big time)*, lifted you off the bike, and let you down onto the ground. My first thought was, 'I will never wash these hands again!' My second thought was, 'It moved Jerry'! *(Smile time for me, and don't forget my drought).*

I am unsure if you were feeling a bit uncomfortable arriving back in that position and just wanted to deflect from the moment we were having, but you said, "I think the minibike ran out of gas." I was so in awe that I did not say anything for a while, and eventually, Luke offered to pull some gas from his full tank and give it to the minibike. Luke gave the kid a ride to his bike, and you and Tonka Boy had to get home for some family function. I smiled, and when your brother said, "See you around, Derek," I smiled and nodded and looked again into your eyes when you got on your bike. Rebecca, it was the first time I felt we had a real connection. Yes, I was always trying to check you out whenever I could, but that was the moment in my mind that started it all this time.

Task 8 – Save Tonka Boy Part I!

(September 1976 – June 1977)

51 ***Anger and Euphoria!:*** I was initially glad to spot you at school, but that suddenly changed when I saw you hanging out with old minibike boy *(Yes, I still can't remember his name, and no, I don't want you ever to tell me either! Maybe it was Biff?).* The school year was sailing by, and between classes, hockey, school sports, my business interests, and work commitments, I had no social life anymore. Luke and I came to school at 7 am to work out every day. We tried to get an hour and a half in, shower then classes. Luke made the Guelph junior team, and I was going to stick with just the school team this season. Other than our workouts and a few trips to the conservation area, Luke and I hardly saw each other. He was still going hot and heavy with Theresa, which also took up Luke's time.

By the time Christmas was all most here, the winter dance was next week, and I had not even thought about going. What made things even more challenging for me was you were no longer seeing minibike boy; you were now seeing old 'He Pulled it Out' guy from Rebecca 1.0 days. The f'ing timeline wanted to bite me in my ass to remind me I was playing with fire! I was in the library doing some studying and also trying to avoid having to see you and 'Mr. Pulled it out Boy' walking hand and hand through the halls. That used to be me once! Whenever I got depressed enough, all I had to do to bring me back to civilization was to think, 'She is going to one day rip your heart out, 'Mr. Pulled it out Boy' without warning!'.

I was writing something out when I got a tap on the shoulder, and it was Maureen. I was now in grade 10, and Maureen, who was still goddess of the school, smiled at me and said, "Are you going to the dance?"

"Hey, cute stuff *(I know I use that with you, suck it up Mr. Pull it out dater)*, to be honest, my life is so busy that I have not had time to even think about it," I replied.

"Troy Adams asked me, and I think I will go with him as friends"; why don't you join us?", Maureen asked.

Great, I thought if only Maureen knew *(maybe she did already)*, but I gave Troy his nickname on the hockey team 'Stump.' And Rebecca, it was only from a casual observation in the hockey showers. There was no way I would be the third wheel with Maureen and Troy. If Troy got her to agree to go to the dance, I know he had one conquest on his mind, and I was not going to be there to watch it. It was bad enough I had to deal with 'Mr. Pulled it Out!'

"I appreciate the invite, Maureen, and let me see what my schedule looks like, but I would like you to maybe attend my charity gala in January with me, as friends, of course," I asked while studying her reaction.

I think we had progressed our prior periodic friendship into a new type of cat and mouse flirtation experience as she replied, "Wow, me with the man of the evening on my arm sounds enticing; let me get back to you on that," she replied with a new grin happening. I was feeling a bit down Thursday, and after I accidentally spotted you and 'Pulled it Out Boy' kissing in the hall, I decided I would go to the dance solo. I was single, popular, best shape I had ever been in, and was part loner anyways. Friday came, and after school, I was like some first dance chick trying to figure out what to wear. Most people got semi-dressed up, and lately, the old jeans with a sports coat was taking off. I was not a fan and decided at the last minute to debut my new Mr. Angelo creation I was saving for next month's gala.

I decided to walk to school rather than take the motorcycle and would not have my parents drive me. It was only 20 minutes anyway, and the fresh air gave me time to mentally condition myself to become Junior 'Derek Flint' for the night. As I walked in the main doors, Mr. Summers spotted me from my gym class and came over to say hello. He has been trying to recruit me for the gymnastics team, and I just don't have any time for another sport in my life. We chatted for a few minutes, and then I left to hang up my overcoat, which was 100% Italian-made and looked so cool.

I walked into the gym; the lights were in dance mode, and the stage had a DJ and some band equipment set up. One of our own homegrown bands was scheduled to play a 45-minute set later. I scanned the gym and decided to go to the refreshment window and get a pop. I took my pop and headed to the opposite side of the gym, where I spotted Kathy and her date Steve. Steve was a nice guy, and they seemed to be happy. I think they started going out in September. We exchanged greetings, and Kathy and Steve both commented how cool my suit looked. Suddenly, I spotted you know who entering the gym with 'Mr. Pulled it Out'. I hate to admit this, but I had severe jealous thoughts and was now pissed at coming. I never figured a minor niner would come to the dance. I never went to this dance when I was in grade nine. I guess 'Mr. Pulled it Out' being in grade 11, wanted to show off his new beautiful grade 9 conquest. You were considered by many guys as a potential catch!

I turned my back, so I did not have to watch and continued to chat with Kathy and Steve. I was now down by the stage area when I felt a tap on my shoulder. It was 'Stumper' and Maureen. When I turned to say hello, I noticed Maureen gave me a thorough up and down checkout. Stumper gave the old fist bump, and we started chatting about who else from the team was there. Maureen just stood there and smiled and then said to Troy, "Would you mind getting me a drink, please."

Troy smiled and said, "Sure, do you want one too, Cap."

I shook my head no, and off he went. As soon as he was out of earshot, Maureen said, "I am glad you decided to come, and I love that suit on you. You look like you could be in grade 12," with a cute devilish smile.

For any grade 10 kid, being told they look like they could pass for a grade 12 was the highest form of compliment. Not to allow our new flirtation cat and mouse to go by unused, I reply, "Gee, maybe I am old enough tonight to attract the attention of another gorgeous grade 12 girl. Let me take a look around," with my version of a devilish smile.

Her smile said, 'game on, junior.' We just smiled at each other, and I countered, "That is a stunning dress, Maureen." She smiled and gave me an eyebrow, indicating a thank you without having to say it. Stumper arrived with drinks, and I thought it was about time to leave for a bit and let Maureen check me out from behind! I walked over to a couple of hockey guys about 20 feet away and offered a few fist bumps. I was feeling much better now that Maureen was here, and I knew that she and I would be playing that game all night, but my inner jealous man was also trying to gain some space in my head. I scanned to see if I could spot Rebecca and "Mr. Pulled it Out', and they were not in the gym. My jealousy level spiked, and I suddenly needed to check out what I was hoping was not occurring. I left the gym and went upstairs to my locker. I grabbed my homemade door lock lifter and went to room 212, which was locked. I opened the locked door with my secret tool, went to the window, and began scanning the parking lot. I knew what car 'Mr. Pulled it Out' drove and kept searching. Suddenly I spotted the car, parked facing the window off to the right where I was.

I could confirm what I was afraid of, and I turned and walked out of the room. I put the door latch lifter back in my locker and returned to the gym. I needed to process this in my head, and I walked over to my hockey buddies and just stood there pretending I was listening to the discussion about how hot Miss Wayley looked. I assume I was there for 15 minutes or so. I remember how I felt the first time Rebecca 1.0 told me about the

'He Pulled it Out' incident and her willingness to take things to the next level. I have never asked you about that night, and I am sure you had no idea until now what I was aware of and that I watched you do it. It was part devastating, but it was also a good thing. Based on my first go-around, I knew you two did not last. I was hoping I did not interfere with the timeline enough to cause that to change.

I walked back over to where Kathy was now standing, and when I was too close to change my route, I realized that you were talking to Kathy but was blocked from my view by a big fat dink. When I arrived, I asked Kathy where Steve was. "He's out with a couple of buddies, I think, sneaking a drink or two in the parking lot," she replied. "Do you know Rebecca Derek?" she asked.

"Yes, Rebecca and I are a former motorcycle daredevil riding team," I said with a grin.

You laughed, and Kathy needed a little bit more info, so you explained our encounter in the summer. I asked you, "How is a minor niner able to sneak into the dance?" with a bit of a smirk.

"A grade 11 boy invited me if you need to know," you said defensively.

"And where is that lucky grade 11er" I asked?

Your demeanor changed, and you looked at Kathy and then looked at me; then Kathy jumped in and said, "He was a bit of a jerk to Rebecca tonight and left for some other party."

I looked at you, and you tried to put on a 'no big deal' face, but I knew your look, and you were hurt. It took every ounce of willpower to keep my composure and remain calm. I looked at you and said, "I am sorry to hear that, Rebecca. Do you need me to go and beat the living crap out of him for you?"

I hope you remember the look you gave me because it was the first time, I think you actually looked at me as 'potential' boyfriend material. I believe Kathy picked up on the vibe and said, "You two motorbike daredevils should go and have a dance before the night is over."

You gave me a welcoming smile that said, 'it's your move.' I was not ready for this and was still processing the whole 'Mr. Pulled it out Boy' and what he might have done to you, but my inner obsessed voice said, "I would love a dance but let's wait till the band is finished their set and we have the DJ back if that is ok with you?"

"That would be nice," you said.

I know it was wrong, and I always wanted to tell you about what I did next, but I never wanted ever to have you feel that it was not a special moment for us. I said to you girls, "I am going to get a drink. Can I bring you back something?"

Kathy said, "No, I am fine," and you said, "A water if they have any."

I left, and you must already know what I did; I went to the DJ guy and asked him to play 'Stairway to Heaven.' If you're pissed at me telling you after all these years, then too bad. I wanted to have 7 minutes and 55 seconds with 'my girl' again.

I returned with two glasses of water, and we continued to chit-chat, waiting for the DJ to strike. I knew the first song and said nothing. As soon as he started to speak into the mic, I grabbed your plastic glass of water and put them on the table beside us. I then extended my hand, and for the first time, we held hands. I led you through a bunch of people to the middle of the dance floor and turned to wait for the first song to start. What you did not know as well, I asked him to make a personal announcement. I told him I would get lucky tonight if he did this for me. That's how you bribe a DJ.

"Let's give a big hand for 'The Hawkers', and our first song is a special dedication to a special girl here tonight with the beautiful dimples," my DJ main man said. I have always wondered if you ever figured out that dedication was you.

As the guitar started playing, I looked at you, and you looked at me with your beautiful dimple smile and amazing smiling eyes. You figured out what the song was, and I could not resist and used the old Collins move again. We assumed the positions and started to dance. I was searching for those old feelings the last time we danced to this song when you suddenly changed our dance position back to a traditional position. I had enough therapy sessions under my belt that I was sure the 'old man' would not appear like he did at Sherry's party.

At first, I wondered what the hell was happening, but I soon realized you wanted to look at me. We spent the next 7 minutes dancing and staring at each other, eventually splitting apart for the fast part but assuming the slow dance position for the end of the song. When it ended, you said to me, "Thanks, Derek. Please don't take this the wrong way, but you're very different than the other boys." I did not know how to interpret what you said, but I was concerned when I didn't get any of the old butterfly's.

We returned to Kathy, and her boy toy Steve was back, and we stood there chatting, having to smell his beer breath. The DJ announced it was the dance's last two songs, and everyone went to the dance floor. They were two fast songs, and it was more of a group dance than a couple's thing. A few people were bouncing all over the floor, acting like idiots.

When the song finished, I walked with you back to the table and asked, "How are you getting home?"

"Kathy and Steve are going to drive me home," you said.

When Kathy was back with Steve, Kathy asked me, "How are you getting home, Derek?"

"I'm doing a nice evening walk," I replied.

"We're driving Rebecca home; why don't you come with us, and then we can drop you off on the way to my place?", she asked.

I looked at Rebecca *(You)* to see what your reaction would be, and I think it was an 'it's ok' *(Drive me home, I smiled).*

"I don't want to be a burden on you guys," I said, trying to look sincere while inside, I now had significant butterflies emerge again.

Let's skip to the next part, which I know you would prefer I skip. The drive was great, and we all chatted about our holiday plans. You were going skiing in Ellicottville; Kathy was heading to Ottawa to see her cousin, and I was home alone. I knew where you lived, and as we entered your driveway, another car was parked and running where your grandparents used to park their airstream trailer. I knew as soon as I saw it, it was 'Mr. Pulled it Out' guy. You then realized who it was, and I immediately said, "Let me deal with that asshole."

Oh, how I wanted to go and beat the shit out of him. Not just for this time but for the first time. I guess I was harboring that feeling for 50-plus years! You put your hand on my arm, smiled, and said, "No, let me go and speak to him first."

I said, "If he does anything or says anything that makes you uncomfortable, just look at the car and nod," I instructed.

You got out and went over to his driver-side window. You were chatting for a few minutes, then you came back over, and Steve rolled his window down, and then you said, "Thanks for the ride, but I think things are better now, and we need to talk about tonight." You looked at me in I think a bit of a sad way and said, "Thanks Derek for everything, and I will see you guys back at school in the new year."

Steve put up the window, and I watched you go and get into the passenger side. I was sure he would never do anything in your driveway, and I figured your dad or mom would eventually come out and tell you to get your butt inside. But as we backed out, I can tell you now that I was once again devasted but could not show it. Kathy and Steve dropped me off at my place, and I thanked them for a fun night. I went in and went straight to my room and just wanted the night to be over. As I lay there doing my usual analysis of every second of the night, I began to compare my Rebecca 1.0 experiences with my new Rebecca 2.0 encounters. My first time seeing you was your bike ride heading home on Mineral Springs. I had butterflies galore! Then, when I saw you for the first time in grade 7, more amazing butterflies. Then when I saw you at your dad's hardware store, again, more crazy butterfly's. And then our minibike encounter, the biggest butterflies yet. But, the first time I got to dance with you again to our first intimate slow dance like at the Collins the first time, no real butterfly's.

At first, I thought it was because I was still kind of pissed that you decided to talk to 'Pulled it Out Boy', instead of letting me beat the crap out of him. And why did I get similar butterflies with Tina or, for that matter, a few times with Maureen? I usually am much quicker at figuring the obvious out, and I know you have already figured it out. Every time I got butterflies was when our encounter was new, not an exact do-over attempt. All my butterflies came from having a first-time experience. Whether it was with Tina, Maureen, or now with you, damn, it was so obvious now. How could I be so blind for this long? Here I thought I came back for a do-over, or a re-do of my past, thinking and believing I could re-capture that magic. But, I realized that you couldn't re-create the first time feelings or experience. A first-time is precisely what it says. It's the first time. All my butterflies came from a new first time. That is why my friends viewed anything other than the leading edge as a waste of time.

Task 8 – Save Tonka Boy Part II!

(September 1976 – June 1977)

52 ***Anger and Euphoria!:*** Christmas came and went quickly. Nothing too exciting to report. No tournaments this year for me, and it gave me some time to spend with the folks. We played a lot of music, and I got down to the fort a few times to continue getting it finished.

School started, and it was a new semester with all new classes. This semester I had grade 12 chemistry. I had already taken grades 9,10, and 11 sciences over the last three semesters. When I showed up to the class, I knew I was getting a bunch of odd looks wondering why a grade 10er was in the class. I knew over half the people well, and to my surprise, Maureen was sitting at the back desk without anyone beside her. I walked back, and she knew what I was about to do. As I reached the desk, which in chemistry was a two-person desk where we often worked in teams.

"Excuse me, young lady, but would that seat be available for a young man who prefers older women?", with my usual grin.

"Only if you promise to do all my homework," she quipped.

I took my seat and we exchanged a few grins and smiles… I was looking forward to chemistry this semester. I knew every guy in that class had a whole new level of respect for me! It turned out, we also had a history class together at the other end of the school, so we would do an hour in chem every day, then walk all the way over to the other side, do an hour of History, and then lunch. I had asked Maureen before Christmas to consider going to the Charity Gala, but as it turned out, she was doing a photoshoot in New York that weekend which was a big deal. I joked I should go along and carry her bags so I could see and meet all the other supermodels.

I think our relationship became more buddies than potential future lovers. I always felt we could shift into full-on sexual deviants at any time, but it was just working how it was. Rebecca *(You)* had made up with 'Mr. Pulled it Out' and I always enjoyed the walk after chem because Maureen and I would have to pass your 2nd-period classroom, and I know you used to watch me every time we walked by. Ok, almost every time and I was secretly hoping it pissed you off on some level.

I got my license on January 9th and was now able to drive a car. I was pondering when I would buy a car but for now, using old Betsy was fine.

The year went fast, and I knew we were approaching the Gibson Pond day. I was concerned that the timeline was no longer exact to my original timing. I started watching for your bathing suit exposure through your top beginning the Monday before the Friday. I could not afford to miss any sign of any changes to the event. You must have thought I was some creep that week with me constantly bumping into you with Maureen. Even Maureen started to wonder what was going on. I was fortunate that the timeline was not altered, and on Friday, I spotted the suit.

Game time. To be safe, I left school right after chem and blew off History. I headed down to Gibson's Pond to stake out the area and do a pre-inspection of the rope, branches, and depth of water. I know you're asking yourself, why not just remove the rope or attach it better thereby avoiding the event. Simply; I did not know if I did that if there would then be another event that would be completely new. I knew exactly what would happen and could prevent it. But if I altered the event now, who knows, maybe they would decide to climb the tree and jump off the branch that eventually breaks, causing your brother to hit the rocks. I had to deal with what I knew.

You guys would be there in about an hour, so I took a break and lay in the only spot where the sun was shining. I had stashed my bike back by the road, and when I heard you coming, I would take another route from the pond over to my bike and pretend I had just arrived. About the time I expected your arrival, I heard you approach. I jumped into gear and exited the area at the far side where you would not see me. You guys arrived, and I knew it would be a while before I would be needed, so I waited for about 20 minutes before I rode my bike to the pond and parked it by your bikes.

The guys spotted me and, at first, thought, they may be in trouble for trespassing, but as soon as they recognized me, they all laughed and said hello. Everything went exactly as I expected. I swam over and got my first authentic look at you in your one-piece, and the butterflies were plentiful. You and I had our chat and you filled me in on the whole 'Mr. Pulled it Out' saga and you were not seeing him anymore. I was so preoccupied with staying alert for my big run around the pond that I did not get a chance to study your expression to see if you might be interested in me. You asked me if I was going steady with Maureen, and I told you we were only really good friends.

Show time! I got up, ran around the pond, grabbed the lose 4-foot end of the rope, and tried to wrap it around my waist. I heard your brother make a Tarzan-style yell, and I knew he was beginning the swing. Suddenly the branch gave way, and we all listened to the big crack. The line went limp but not entirely because I was holding it, and your brother dropped into the water right where I figured he would. Everyone was figuring out what happened, and at first, I am sure they thought I had done something, but when they traced the rope, they figured out what just happened. Todd was going through a little pain squeal, and I came around to get in position to watch you run around the pond to us. Wow, what a view! Butterflies, more wonderful butterflies.

I am sure you noticed my staring, and when you touched my back, I was hoping you felt something too. You were only 14, turning 15 in September, and I was already 16. We only had less than a month until school was done, and I would not get my daily view of my hopefully future 'my girl'. After we all sat in the water discussing the whole ordeal, we decided it was time to leave. When you got on your bike, I touched your hand and said, 'I will be keeping my eye on you," with a smile.

I rode home and needed to decompress from the whole event. I just completed my first life-changing task, saw my girl in her bathing suit for the first time, and found out she was no longer seeing 'Mr. Pulled it Out'. Today was a perfect day. That night I laid in bed reliving part of the pond event; the part when I first came upon you sunning in your one piece. I studied that image in my mind for a long time. I just could not figure out what or when would be our next encounter.

Gibson's Pond

Task 9 – Save Elvis!

(August 1977)

53 ***Long live the King!:*** The summer was busy, and this task was the first one that I had not finalized a plan for. I figured I would work on it over the past few years, and truth be told, I was so distracted with everything, including the time it took to write the guide entries, that old Elvis was still a work in progress. The information I had; he died of a heart attack induced by severely impacted constipation. He was most likely taking a dump and, while trying to force something out, ended up giving himself a heart attack. They found him at 2:30 pm and called for an ambulance. They got him to Baptist Memorial Hospital in Memphis at 3:30 pm, where they could not revive him. That means I need some form of intervention around noon to 2 pm. I planned to tell my parents I was invited to go with Luke to the cottage his folks had rented. Then I would drive down to Graceland and cause a fire outside the house around 1 to 2 pm, which would cause the staff to call the fire department, and then I would also put a call in to get an ambulance to go there with a reported cardiac arrest.

I did not want to be on the premises during the day to do this, as I am sure he had security. I needed to do a recon on the facility to know what I would be facing. I would have to enter the property around 4 am, just before sunrise. Elvis was a night hound and was known to be up all night. I also needed a few days to buy the necessary supplies and equipment for the job. He died on Tuesday, August 16th, which meant I needed to be down there no later than Friday. I was sure the place had a lot of fans mulling around on the weekends. I planned to take old Betsy as it would fit right in, but dad said it was acting up and maybe I should use my motorcycle. I went out the next day and worked on figuring out what was wrong with Betsy. She was as good as new, a fresh set of plugs and wires *(I smiled)*.

I left Friday morning, the 12th, at 8 am. I knew I would get there around midnight. I would sleep in the car overnight at a rest area, then do my recon on Saturday and buy my supplies. Sunday, I would do security monitoring and determine their schedule and procedures. I brought with me my high-powered binoculars, my all-black outfit, complete with a full hood, and a remote detonator that I would use to set off the explosion/fire. I had a box of surgical gloves I stole from my visit to see Dr. Crossgrove, and I had built last year my parabolic mic that was good from over 500 feet. I forged a letter from the University of Tennessee inviting me to get across the border for a football try-out. I figured that would be good enough at the border. I had a passport and forged a letter from my parents permitting me to travel to the University.

When I reached the border, they gave me a look. I handed them my paperwork, and they wished me well, and I was through in 15 minutes. The drive was long and boring, and I only had an old cassette player in the car, and I had only made one tape. It felt like I ended up listening to Bony M's Rasputin 100 times on the way there. I pulled into the Memphis area at 11:30 pm and parked in a trucker's rest area. I crawled in the back and was out cold almost immediately. With all the trucks firing up their rigs, I was awakened in the morning. I went to the restroom, washed up, grabbed my map, and headed to see the King! I drove through Memphis and came out on 51 and headed south. He was about 9 miles away from my current location. I planned to go to a street about two blocks away and walk over so I could get a good look at everything. I wish I had some small recording device, but nothing will hit the market for 20 years. I found a house that looked like the people were away. There was mail in the mailbox and two papers on the front porch. I pulled into the drive and waited for 30 minutes. No one came out, and none of the neighbors came over to question what I was doing there.

I left the car and headed over to Elvis Presley Boulevard. I walked down the street, mentally recording everything. Funny how different it is now. I was here when I was in my late 40s when I attended a convention in Memphis. Back then, the whole area was now a large entertainment complex, including a hotel, Museum, and the King's own tour plane. As I approached the front gate area from the other side of the street, a group of people were already standing there, conversing with what appeared to be a security guard. The gates were closed, and a security camera was mounted on top of the gate wall. Another camera was mounted on a pole just east of the main entrance, aimed towards the street. That camera could pick up everyone within 100 feet of the front gate. I spotted one more security guard on the other side of the entrance near a guard house.

I could hear music playing, but it was not that loud. I did not want to get within the camera view, so I stayed back. I then headed further down the Boulevard from the other side of the street. When I reached what appeared to be the end of his property, I was now entering a survey area. There was a large fence system surrounding the entire property. I spotted another camera at the corner mounted on the top of the wall pointing east along the wall. I assume it could pick up trespassers from that wall location.

I turned into the survey and walked along the street, looking into the backyards and tracking the fence. The fence had a black meshing that blocked anyone from being able to look into Graceland. When I reached a cul-de-sac, I noticed a massive tree near the wall with limbs that extended over the fence into the King's backyard. I also could see some outbuildings not far from the fence. So far, this looked like the best entry point. The only thing I was not sure of, did he have any type of motion detection along the fence. That was something I would test out tonight.

I continued my recon and surveillance for a couple more hours and had several spots that appeared poorly protected, and most of the so-called security looked like it was focused at the front gate. There were two other utility roads into the property. One had well-worn tracks, and the other looked like it had not seen a vehicle enter for a long time. I went back out to the Boulevard and returned on the route I took to get here. When I reached the main gate again, there were now twice as many people and what appeared to be a person selling merchandise. I slowed my pace and watched the interaction between the security personnel and the crowd. It looked friendly and I guessed they were handing stuff to the people. I continued to make my way back to the car and stood at the end of the street to see if there was any action around old Betsy. Once I felt the area was clear of anyone, I went to Betsey, backed out of the drive, and headed back towards town. There was a sign for a motel a couple of miles back toward town, and I pulled into a gas station to fill up. When I went in to pay, I spotted an Elvis souvenir section. I wandered over, and to my surprise, there was a map of Graceland, including actual photos of the entrances and several outbuildings. I grabbed two maps, some Elvis souvenirs and added them to my gas purchase.

I left the garage and headed back to where the motel sign was. I located the motel, a bit of a dive, and pulled in. I went to the office location and entered. An old woman was sitting at the desk knitting and said, "Hello, can I help you."

I told her I needed a room for three nights and asked how much that would be.

"$39 per night, and no party's allowed. Are you single, or will there be other people in the room," she asked?

"I am here for a try-out with the Memphis University football team," I replied.

"You want to be a Memphis wolverine," she asked.

I said, "I don't know any Memphis Wolverine; I am trying out for the Tigers. I am a kicker down from Canada."

"Just checking, son. We get all types come through here. We usually have at least one crazy Elvis fan staying here on the weekend," she replied with a grin.

I pulled out my cash and proceeded to pay her the total amount. "Do you want housekeeping daily or just keep the room as is?" she asked.

"Is it extra or included?" I asked.

"We charge $10 per cleaning, which includes fresh bedding," she replied.

"Well, let's go with keeping it as is. If I decide I need a change, I will let you know if that works for you," I said while finishing giving her the cash.

"Need you to fill out this card, and I need to see your driver's license," she requested.

I filled out the card and showed her my driver's license. She looked at it and said, "Got a cousin in Ontario. She is in a town called Sudbury. Do you know it?"

"The Big Nickle is about 5 hours north of me," I told her.

I finished the card info, and she handed me a key; and I thanked her and moved my car in front of my room. Three other vehicles were in front of the hotel and one beside the office. I opened the door and went in. Yup, a dive. I could spot a cigarette burn hole in the pillow from the door. I cased the exterior and did not see any camera system. I brought my bags in and closed the door. I needed to review my plan and see what additional info I could garner from the new maps. After working for an hour, I decided to grab a bite to eat. I went to the office and asked if there was a decent eating place nearby. The manager handed me a pamphlet with four eateries listed.

"Tommy's is probably the best if you want my opinion. They got some good southern food there if you like southern food," she added.

"I love southern food," I replied. I took the pamphlet and left with a parting, "Thank you."

It took me about 3 minutes in Betsy to reach 'Tommy's,' and I parked and went in. It was more like a diner than a restaurant, and I walked to a table that allowed me to watch the street. A young girl about 15 came over and asked if I wanted a menu. I looked at the menu, and when she returned with a glass of water and cutlery, I asked her for their fried catfish dinner. It took about 20 minutes to hit my table, but it was delicious. I also ordered a glass of chocolate milk, and it came with what appeared as Hershey's syrup squirted into white milk. I asked how their breakfast was, and she rifled off their entire menu from memory. I smiled, settled with a generous tip for the young girl, and said I would try breakfast tomorrow. I returned to the room and decided to grab a nap since I would be out early for my evening inspection.

I did my early morning canvas of the entry area and could confirm there were no motion systems. A dog in the third house down started barking when I climbed up the tree. I would need to be a bit quieter. I was back in my room by 5:30 am and was back in bed for a couple of hours of sleep. My alarm went off, and I returned to 'Tommy's' for their breakfast. The young girl was now replaced with what I guess may be her mother or even grandmother. She was a friendly waitress pushing 60, and I kept finding her grey hair all over the table and figured it would be in/on my food. I finished breakfast and returned to my room for another work-through on my plan. I also needed to assemble my incendiary device and test the remote.

As you know, Rebecca, I was successful with my plan and bought the King more time. The last thing I did Wednesday after the big event was drop off a package at the post office addressed to the Kings 'Ex'. It was a letter I wrote, pretending to be a young man in his 30s, and his mama, from the Bayou, used to have premonitions. She had seen Mr. Presley having a heart attack while trying to poop out 50 pounds of crap that had accumulated from all the pills he was taking and was unable to poop ever again. I included a Saint Christopher medallion saying my mama wanted Mr. Presley to have it as a reminder of how precious his life was and that I was sorry for blowing up some of his place. I would keep an eye on the King and wait to see if I ever see that medallion around his neck in the future.

As I was driving home, I figured the radio would be a non-stop chit-chat about what happened at Graceland, but it didn't matter since I only had a cassette working and one tape. I stopped for gas halfway home and bought the most recent national paper, and the front-page story was about an explosion at Graceland and the King being rushed to the hospital with significant heart issues. The FBI and ATF *(Bureau of Alcohol, Tobacco, Firearms, and Explosives)* were investigating, and there was a 24-hour vigil at the Hospital. The last doctor's report was they were going to operate shortly. The drive home was solemn, and while you would think I would be glowing at what I had just accomplished, I knew I needed to improve some of my approaches, having gone through an actual task like this. This was the first time I put myself at risk of being captured, and I was well aware of the ramifications. I needed new and more effective tools and much better recon procedures. I needed to get some old electronic schematics out and fire up the soldering iron. My fort was now complete, and it would now be my preferred place to build my equipment.

I was driving in silence for a while, wondering what you would be doing right this minute. I was leaning towards you working at one of your dad's two stores. Hopefully, on a dating dry spell like me *(Grin just happened)*. I passed a road sign that said, 'Let Jesus come into your heart and save your soul.' I started to laugh when my depraved mind started to think the sign should have read, 'Let the hand of Jesus reach in and pull all that old poo out and then save your soul.' Because without me, Elvis would be singing at the Pearly Gates right now. And as it so often happens with me, I started to search my 'Greatest Playlist Ever' for an appropriate Elvis song to sing. Found it;

Wise men say
Only fools rush in
But I can't help falling in love with you………

By the time I got home, I had mastered singing that song to you, Rebecca, flawlessly without needing any instrument but my voice *(yuk yuk)*. I even taught myself to sing it using the King's voice, complete with a quivering upper lip. I was received by all as if nothing much had happened, and I told everyone I had a great time at Luke's cottage. I would get Luke to back up my story next time he was over to add some more fluff to the big lie. My dad asked me if I had heard what happened to Elvis? My uncle Ian was a doppelganger for young Elvis, and his music was always a part of our family singing sessions. As a newspaper boy, I could read about the story every day, and then as most stories go, it faded. The King had a few surgeries. They removed his compacted poop, and I am sure it shrunk his gut since the last time I saw a picture of him, he looked rather rotund. He left the hospital after three weeks and returned to Graceland to continue his recovery.

The papers reported that the King was grateful that he did not die and was trying to change his old ways. The FBI and ATF were following up on a few leads but thought it was just a crazy fan trying to scare the King at this time. All the Elvis souvenirs I put in the blast zone area paid off. I felt a bit bad. My explosive calculation was a bit off, and I took out a large wall section. Fortunately, no one was hurt. Moving forward, I planned to maintain a date listing that I wanted to honor annually for my various tasks. I already went every April 14th to the Hermitage with a rose. Now I guess I will try to take a walk down to Gibson's Pond every June 3rd and every August 16th; it would become my Elvis music day!

Task 10 – Cancer Intervention!

(September 1977 – ongoing)

54 ***Try to make a dent!:*** Grade 11 has started, and I have been swamped of late dealing with the 'Student Mentoring Initiative' and started implementing my plan for introducing 2023 cancer treatments and detection into a 1977 science and academic research world. Many of the needed treatments will require extensive development time, and, to have any potential value to our moms, I will need to work on this task over the next few years actively. You will recall my 'Networking' value claim; here is an excellent example of utilizing it. One relationship I have been nurturing for the past three years was with Doctor Eugene Crossgrove from McMaster. I meet with him quarterly as part of my duties with the 'Kids 4 a Cancer Cure' charity work. This fall, I will start working with him in his lab under a new educational program I started with him, whereby High School students can work under a co-op program to earn 'experience credits' which will now be included in their High School transcript.

I worked with Eugene for the past two years, developing that program specifically to get me into his lab. This fall, I will be part of the first '8 selected students' from a variety of different High Schools. The Charity will provide each student with a transportation and meal allowance. They will need to provide 40 hours of co-op experience time to receive the new special credit. My selected schedule is Tuesday evenings and Sunday afternoons. Each shift will be 3 hours. We will be assigned a senior grad student to shadow, and they will be responsible for overseeing our selected work duties. The program is not simply to have free High School student labor washing test tubes; it is intended to provide real, practical experience. We hope our 40 hours will supply roughly 30 hours of hands-on contribution work on top of the grad students' expected work output. After my 40 hours, I expected Eugene would keep me on as a non-paid volunteer.

Over the next couple of months, I will slowly get a detailed overview of their process and how they develop among themselves the targeted testing and experimentation in choosing what direction they wish to research further. Once I have that information, I hope that I will be able to periodically feed into the system certain data that will shape their desired direction in my planned development of 2 essential drugs and three early detection methodologies. I am hoping I will fit in well with the team and will be able to gain a certain trust level allowing me the necessary freedom to do my thing.

The other major issue that will be a bit riskier and more difficult is my need to infiltrate the Doctor's office for both my mom and Mrs. Hamlin. I need access to personal medical information and regular check-up data to alter specific tests, including blood work, periodically. I will need to modify some blood work to generate results that will allow them access to special treatment programs that will soon be available from McMaster. It's both complex and will be personally very invasive. I hope, Rebecca, that you understand my need to do this and that my access to your mom's medical records will be protected and kept confidential, even from you, at all times.

[Rebecca Update: Rebecca is starting grade 10, and we now have our homerooms on the same floor this semester. I wish we were closer, but at least we run into each other almost daily. I did not run into Rebecca this summer after Gibson's Pond, and I was surprised we never bumped into one another at least once at a party or somewhere. My Elvis prep did take up a lot of time, and while I would love to force more contact, I am doing my best to let that process happen organically. I have decided to ignore any of my Rebecca 1.0 known contact dates and times and just roll the dice, I guess. You look a bit older *(In a great way)*, and I think you have completed filling out as much as you are. And before I forget, Happy Birthday, Beautiful]

[Big Gino has invited me to take a trip with him and the family to Vegas in December. When I was over the other week for a visit *(wink wink)*, Angela was checking me out, and I think she even tried a bit of flirting with me. Anyway, since you don't seem all that interested in me these days, maybe I will head to Vegas in December and see if what they say in Vegas is true *(Made you roll your eyes)*.]

[I have been corresponding monthly with Sandy; it has been a welcome distraction and allowed me to use words as a form of relationship building. Sandy will be coming for a visit next summer, and I told her I would be in Europe for six months starting September 1979. We plan to meet next summer, and she said she would make time for us when I get over there]

Update – Same Time Next Year Deal!

(July 8th, 1978)

55 ***'The Last Time I Felt Like This":*** Another year has passed, and I am starting to feel like I did about time before I leapt. From about 55 to 63, time for me was accelerating. My days seemed to be getting shorter and shorter, and there is not enough time to get what I want done. When I was this age for the first time, there was always plenty of time. Now I am finding the same thing here; even though I am now 17, I think the tips of my 'eukaryotic chromosomes', specialized DNA caps *(called telomeres),* are also linked to my mental system.

Today I was riding down to the fort to do some work when low and behold, little Miss Hamlin came out from Lovers Lane direction, where it meets Mineral Springs. I was coming from the library downtown, where I had dropped off a book. I will assume you recall this chance encounter vividly. As we noticed each other and after we were close enough to speak, I said, "Hey stranger, what brings you this way?"

"I was at my dad's store working. I work there each Saturday. What brings you this way" you asked with your always beautiful smile.

"I am heading down to the conservation area to get a run-in. I try to get there a couple of times a week. I used to do it with Luke, but he is away at his hockey camp and won't be back for a couple of weeks. How is everyone doing in your household" I asked?

"Everyone is good. My grandparents are visiting and have their airstream trailer parked in the drive. How about you?" you countered.

"Well, my grandfather just bought a cottage up in the Muskoka's, and I am scheduled to head up to hang with him in a few weeks," I replied.

It was a scorching Saturday in the high 80's and it was around 3 pm. We rode side by side, talking all the way down the hill, mostly coasting, catching up on how our year at school went, and as we were approaching the Gate House parking area, I asked you, "Hey, why don't you stop for a bit and take a brief walk to the Hermitage with me? I have not spent any time with you since Gibson's or the Christmas dance." This was my way of determining if you were involved or single. If you said no, then probably involved. If you said yes, maybe single.

You had your blue pants on that I always loved, that fit you perfectly. You had your dad's business-named t-shirt on and a pair of sneakers. I studied your facial expression after I posed the idea, and I think I detected a slight, 'Why not' look developing.

"Unless you have something else you need to do," I added.

After a brief thought processing period, you turned and said, “I really don’t have anything I need to rush home to do, and it would be nice to get out of the direct sun and cool down" with a slight grin. I knew you were still processing your decision and did not say anything else until we arrived at the spot where I usually would lock my bike. You did not have a lock, so I used my lock for both bikes. I had a backpack on and what you did not know, it had a bunch of electronic parts I was going to use on a couple of devices I needed for my current task. I was scheduled to do a B&E into your mom’s doctor's office in September. Around your birthday.

I asked you, “Do you know the history of this place, Rebecca?”

“Not really, other than this is the gatehouse for the main Hermitage ruins. People say they are haunted,” you replied with a smile.

“There's a story that tells of the Ives family coachman (The Ive’s owned the property before the Leith Family who actually built the current Mansion that is now the ruins), William Black, falling in love with Angelica, one of the Ives daughters, and they began an affair. When Black asked Mr. Ives for permission to marry her, he was denied. The next day, Black did not appear with the carriage and was later found hanging from the rafters of the stable. As suicides were not permitted to be buried in a churchyard, Black was buried at a crossroads where Sulphur Springs Road meets Lover's Lane - which is now named after the tragic event. Legend has it that on moonlit nights, the sound of Black crying for his lost love can be heard, and some have reported seeing him wandering the grounds of The Hermitage,” I explained.

“How do you know all that?” you asked.

Derek 1.0 worked here once as the gatekeeper to the museum the conservation authority would soon build. “I love history and did a paper for history class last year about this place. I love to come down here and hike all the time. Did you know there is a pond not far from here” I asked?

“No, I had no idea,” you replied.

“Well then, follow me,” I said. I wanted to grab your hand for the short walk, but you were still trying to process this whole chance encounter with the guy that might have saved your brother’s life. The Hermitage pond, which is about halfway along the gatehouse trail to the old ruins, was generally hidden by the heavy tree foliage. When I arrived at the spot to exit the path and enter the woods, I looked at you now ‘eye-to-eye’ and said, “Don’t worry about old Jacob the ghost; he only comes out at midnight,” with a grin.

A rock formation that ran east to west and sported huge rocks with significant gaps between them was always a neat feature of the property. It was this feature that Luke and I once exploited in the first go-around as the basis of our first fort. In order to get across a couple of these mini ravines *(about 6 – 8 feet deep)*, I had strategically placed two large tree branches shaped like a 'Y' in the two ravines we needed to get across. When we reached the first one, I gave you a quick explanation of why they were there and proceeded to demonstrate how to use them. I would hold the two ends of the giant wishbone, place one foot into the 'Y,' and with the other end firmly positioned into the bottom of the ravine, I would simply push off, and it would allow me to glide across the ravine from the one large rock to the next rock with an approximate arc to traverse of 8 feet.

I went first, then turned around and came back to where you were watching what I did with a little bit of a grin, but also a little nervousness since you knew I was going to ask you to try it. I knew you were a great skier from the first time, and you were always very athletic as I handed you the giant wishbone. You took it and were in your calculating mode, and as you were standing there, I came up behind you and began to hold you by your waist for added encouragement. I think that offended you, and you suddenly sprung yourself across the ravine, like you had been doing it longer than I. When you landed on the other side, you pushed the 'Y' branch back to me so I could follow. By the time I got across, you had already used the next branch and were looking at me across the last ravine holding the giant wishbone and said, "I guess I am in control now, smartie pants," with your cute devilish grin. I was so happy that you showed you wanted to move into a playful type of exchange with me now.

"The way I see it, we need each other; since if I choose to return to the prior rock, you will be stranded here and will be at my mercy," I explained with my own devilish grin. We both knew that we could simply climb down and walk through the ravines using smaller boulders as steppingstones at any time. My way was just cooler. You sent the branch back to me, and I arced over to you. I showed you my preferred route off the top of the bolder, and we headed towards the pond about 100 yards ahead. As we arrived at a little clearing area I used to either fish from or go in swimming; you took a long scan around the pond. It was your first time seeing it, and you lived so close to this place; I was sure you were asking yourself how you never knew it was here. The pond was regularly stocked by the owners that lived in the stone cottage just past the ruins. I rarely saw them at the pond, but I was respectful with the fishing and only took a few rainbows each season.

"Wow, this is a beautiful area. And the pond looks so inviting," you said.

I saw an opening and could not help myself. The butterflies were now back in full form, and I just decided to say it. "You game for a swim? It's hot and would feel great to take a dip," I asked with anticipation.

I watched your face, and you were calculating the offer, and between a grin, then a smile, then a curious look, you replied, "I would, but I don't have a bathing suit."

"Well, there is only one possible option, and that is to go in with our underwear," I proposed. "Unless you are too uncomfortable seeing me in my tighty-whities," I said.

You smiled at me and were obviously on the fence, and I figured I needed to do one last nudge. "Hey Rebecca, I can see you are scared and uncomfortable with my suggestion so let's pass on the dip altogether."

That was all that was needed, and you said, "You first."

I knew this would go one of two ways. I would strip, and you would take my clothes and put them up in the rocks, forcing me to walk through the woods in my wet undies, or you would follow. I benefited from wearing running shorts, a T-shirt, socks, and runners. You did not know that the runner shorts had a built-in package holder, and I had no undies on. Ya, I could have simply kept the shorts on since they were practically a bathing suit, but where was the fun in that. I took off my shirt, folded it neatly, and put it on a fallen tree trunk. I sat on the trunk, took off the shoes and socks, and was now down to the last piece of clothing. I stood up, and you were about 6 feet from me. I was grinning just like you were and said, "One small problem for me, I don't have any undies on."

I made the move, turned with my back to you, and removed my shorts with my bare ass staring you in your face but made sure not to bend over to pick them up or I may have scared you off! I was not prepared to turn and give you a full frontal view. I walked to the edge and made an excellent shallow dive into the pond. Hoping to show off a bit, I remained underwater almost to the other side of the pond. When I broke the surface and turned, you already had your pants off and were pulling your t-shirt off. I began to swim back to your side, and when I could touch the bottom, I stood with water up to my neck. This was the first time I saw you in just those cute white cotton bikini undies and your white bra with lace. I quickly etched the moment when I heard you say, "Turn around and don't look," with a bit of a do it or else stare.

I took the order verbatim and waited to hear you enter. It was not long, and I had already realized that I could no longer float on my back without giving away my inner feelings. I heard you dive in, and as I remained in my non-gawking position, I felt you swim right past me underwater. I looked down, and a lessor man than I would have lost all control at that moment. The great part of this pond was the fact it was spring fed and was absolutely crystal clear. It was like looking through glass. I stood there at attention in more than one way and took your underwater view in completely. Another etching. You had decided to take all your stuff off, and we were now officially having our first skinny dip together. The first of many, I was hoping at the time. You came up about 4 feet in front of where I was standing, and you were forced to tread water which you could do flawlessly.

It did not take long to realize that the water was so clear that even 4 feet allowed us both full view without any reduced visibility. It was the first time I saw your breasts in over 40 plus years. It was also your first time seeing me; fortunately for me, there would be no 'cold water excuses'. My butterflies were out of control, and all I could think of to do was to say, "Race you across and back."

I took off, and you turned and started swimming as well. I beat you to the far side, but you decided to use your cunningness and tried to drown me purely in a playful way. As you tried to force me under, all I could do was mentally count every time certain parts of your body came into contact with mine. I was sure you had made accidental contact with you know who, and when you finally got me turned around, I felt your feet make a giant push off my back as you started the final leg of our race. You made it back first and had taken your championship position sitting on the shore with the water just covering your chest. I arrived to your big smile, and you said, "Teach you to mess with me, Mr. Devon," along with a cocky smile.

"I think there may have been some illegal contact that took place. I will have to defer to the judges," I joked.

Do you remember what you said next? I know it's been a very long time Rebecca, but it was a defining moment for us. "Why have you never asked me on a date?"

I sat there and just looked at you trying to figure out the right thing to say. I knew it would be a significant moment and could shape our futures. I was studying you, and you were studying me. You made no effort to hide yourself checking out the entire package, and I was doing the same. I finally decided to tell you the truth. "I think it would be amazing to go out with you, and believe me, I wanted to ask you since the first time I saw you, four years ago, when you were riding your red bike on Mineral Springs with another girl who I did not recognize. You had on a sweatshirt and jean shorts that had been hemmed that fit you perfectly. I was down with Luke hiking when I spotted you back near the gatehouse corner. I ran all the way to the rock formation near the road and hid there so I could take a look at you riding by. From that moment on, I knew that something inside me was telling me, One Day, you will date this girl."

"I remember that day," you added while listening intently to my response.

"The problem back then was you were way too young and hadn't even grown those things," as I nodded towards your chest area with an added smile. "I remember your first day in Grade 7. I spotted you in the cafeteria buying something. The most challenging time for me was back at the school dance when you were dating you know who."

"Why did you not say something to me when we were dancing or standing and talking that night," you asked with a look of disappointment.

"Let me ask you something first. When was the first time you ever noticed me" I asked?

You paused for a bit and then said, "I think it was when you came into my dad's store and I was stocking shelves. We looked at each other, and I actually had this wonderful butterfly feeling. When you went to pay, I had gone back to the office where my mother was and told her to come and look at the boy at the cash register. That mirror behind the cash register was a one-way mirror. I watched you, and then my mom said, 'That boy is Derek Devon, he started the 'Kids 4 a Cancer Cure' Charity; your father and I met him at your brother's graduation at the end of this past June. I think he's looking for something?'"

"As you walked up and down the aisles, I knew you went back to look for me. I wanted to go back out and say something to you but you had left. After that, I started looking for you at school. I would never want you to know I was looking for you. You were so popular, and I was just some grade seven kid that wore a training bra. But I watched you all the time. Then you left for High School, and I did not see you again till the summer and the minibike encounter. That was the first time you put your hands on me. You have no idea the feelings I was having then. And when you grabbed my behind to lift me off the bike, I didn't want you to let go," you confessed with an anguished look on your face.

"Why didn't you say something or give me a clue that you knew who the hell I was," I asked with mild desperation in my tone?

"Because you were so out of my league. I was just this young girl who didn't know how to express those feelings at that time," you said.

"When you got to High School, you were a very popular girl and had a bunch of boyfriends. At the school dance, I looked for you at one point and could not find you. I wanted to know where you were, and I did something I am not sure you will be too thrilled to learn. I went up to room 212 and looked out the window to see if I could see you with your boyfriend, and to my disappointment, I did spot you guys in his car," I said with some hurt in my voice.

"You spied on us?" you immediately asked, sounding like I violated you.

"No, not exactly. When I spotted you in his car's front seat, I only needed a second to know what was happening, and I had to leave. I know I had no right to feel jealous or be mad at you. But that is what I was feeling. You had no idea how happy I was when later Kathy told me he had left you at the dance. I hope you understand my obvious anger when we arrived at your house, and I said I would deal with the asshole. Then when you returned and gave me that look, it hurt like hell," I confessed some more.

"That night, just so you know, was the first time a boy had pulled out his you know what right in front of me. I was young and inexperienced, and while I felt great pressure to do what most boys in High School would expect from a High School girl, I told him I was uncomfortable touching him in the parking lot. After a few minutes, I wanted to go back into the dance. He was angry and called me a tease, and I just got out of the car and went back into the school. He drove by me and said he was going to another party, and I could find my own ride home. I went back into the gym, straight to the bathroom, and cried briefly in a stall. I told Kathy what happened, and you know the rest. I wanted to tell you how I felt, but you were more interested in that girl Maureen, and she was three years ahead of me," you explained.

It's funny if you really think about it. I was secretly watching you, and I now find out you were doing the same. I just wanted to swim over and take you in my arms, and I was sure you were feeling the same, but I also knew it would be a mistake. My best chance with you would be at a later time. And that is when I decided to do a deep dive into my movie memories to come up with the proposal. It wouldn't be released until next November and was called 'Same Time Next Year'. Set In 1951, George *(Alan Alda)* and Doris *(Ellen Burstyn)* have an affair at a small California inn. Instead of writing it off as a one-night stand, the pair decide to meet at the inn every year for a romantic retreat, away from their respective spouses and families. In the following decades, both George and Doris face their own struggles and hardships. Together, they develop a level of love and intimacy that exceeds those found in their marriages.

My version would be a bit different because right now, I am single, and I never asked you about your status. Since you were sitting naked in a pond with me, I thought you were probably not dating. "We can agree we obviously like each other and there is some special attraction. I have to go to Russia next year for a four-month exchange student trip, and I plan to go to Harvard for University after High School. I am a very busy, and you could say, complicated person. My proposal is that we maintain this special friendship, and if we are so inclined, we can go on a date or two if we are both single. No long-term commitments or expectations, just two people who will let our futures dictate what this may or may not become. I think it is important that you can enjoy High School to the fullest possible, and if you decide to go to university, you should also experience that to the fullest," I explained watching your expression intently.

"And one final condition; We both agree that we will meet here once each year on this date regardless of our relationship status. That way, we can let fate guide us and determine if there is something more. If in the future, either of us determines that there could be no possible future, we will meet one last time and say our permanent goodbyes," I proposed looking for your reaction to my crazy idea.

I knew I had piqued your interest, and you were processing the entire proposal in detail. "So, if either of us is in a relationship, we still have to show," you asked?

"Yes. I am not suggesting our meeting here would be anything more than two friends talking about what happened in their lives over the past year, kinda like we are doing now," I replied with a grin.

"And we tell no one about our annual meeting here," you asked.

"Absolutely no one, ever," I added. "So, are you in or out on this cockamamy idea?"

You sat there just looking at me, and we had grins going. I knew it was a long shot, but right then, right now, it felt right. After a few minutes, you moved yourself over to my location and proceeded to now straddle me almost like when I put you onto my Canam 250 at the minibike encounter, but this time there were no clothes between us. I had been losing that feeling, but as soon as you straddled me, I was sure he was back to full mast. You arranged yourself so that our two private areas were basically munched together. No entry or anything, just pushed together super tight. I was pressed up to my belly which was a bit uncomfortable under the current conditions, and your legs wrapped around me, giving me a full-on leg squeeze. Your arms went around my neck, and you just sat in that position and looked into my eyes.

Suddenly, your head turned, and you said, "Shush, did you hear that?"

I gave a quick scan and did not see anything and figured you were hoping to get me to react to some fake unannounced intruder to our moment.

After a few minutes, you said what I will characterize was the most mature thing anyone had ever said at 15, soon to be 16. "If I agree, and I will not commit to it until you come here next year. If I am here, then you will have my answer. As crazy as it sounds, I do want to find out. I only fear that someone may one day get hurt, very hurt, and that scares me."

I looked at you and simply nodded my agreement to your terms. Then the most significant thing that happened to me since my return. We had our first kiss. It seemed to last forever, and I know it was special for both, but I think a bit more special for me. We remained with our spots glued together for another 15 minutes, just looking longingly at each other like a couple of first-time adolescents that may have found love but were not 100% sure. There was no 'look the other way' instruction when we got out. We both were comfortable with our nakedness, and considering we just spent the last 20-plus minutes with our most sacred regions stuck together, it would have seemed juvenile to make such a request when we reached our clothes. I took my t-shirt and began to dry you off. You allowed me to dry every inch and even forced me back to full attention when you parted your legs so I could dry your mushed region.

I handed you your bikini underwear and then your bra. You dressed without any apprehension with me watching. Once you were dressed, you came to me, took the wet t-shirt, and began to dry my excited little fella. I knew it was more symbolic than sexual, but there was a slight sexuality to it, and I could tell by your expression when I dried yours. We walked back to the bikes and, at first, did not try to hold hands, but when we emerged onto the main path, our hands seemed to find one another on their own.

When we got to the bikes, I took the lock off and placed it back on my bike. I still needed to head to the fort.

"Looks like you're staying," you said.

"Yes, I need to go for a long run to get some of this unspent energy used up," I replied with a smile.

"What now?", you asked.

"Well, if you are not doing anything in a few weeks, and you are not in any meaningful relationship, maybe you would like to come with me to my grandfather's new cottage in the Muskoka's," I offered.

"Define meaningful," you quipped with a devilish grin.

I gave you a puzzled look, I am sure, and then said, "If you decided to come, then I know you are not in one, and if you decide not to come, I know that you are; Because Rebecca Hamlin could never bring herself to ever cheat on her guy," was my response.

We did not share any kiss goodbye, just a big smile and we parted. At least for a couple of weeks *(wink wink)*.

The Secret Hermitage Pond

Task 11 – Iran Hostages Part I

(January 1979 – December 1979)

56 ***Pre-Putin!:*** You and I had begun to selectively spend time together from the first time at Gramps cottage and including a few secret dates over the school year. We actively explored our feelings for each other while letting our junior libidos go nuts. It was funny that our first time being with each other was almost the same time frame as the last first time. What we didn't do the first time was ask each other what was great and what missed the mark. We spent a lot of time discussing our sexuality and always wanted to make the next time better than the last. And yes, I was still respectful of our decision not to go all the way. It was odd seeing you at school and not being a traditional girlfriend and boyfriend. No hand holding or other clues at school. Our relationship was 100% confidential. It certainly added a new level of excitement, especially when we snuck off for a meet up during school hours. My favorite was the library stacks! I know Luke had noticed I was spending a lot more time around you or looking at you. I just told him we were good friends, but I was sure he could read between the lines. It was more an issue when a few girls asked me out and I had to use the excuse I was seeing someone else. I knew it could blow up on me if they ever got together talking about it and realized it was a dust off. But I think I pulled it off.

The next task would be the most dangerous for me as far as exposing myself to high-level intelligence people. I knew there would be no way to have a shot at preventing this any other way. For me to be overseas when I needed to be, I had arranged for a student exchange program in Russia. I did not want to deal with my parents, and get them to agree to let me, take off for Iran next October. So, I devised this plan to get me away for 4 months, and also, it would be of great importance for my Putin Task.

I applied to participate in a student exchange program that will get me into the outskirts of Moscow at a private school that also hosts children of some of Russia's great hockey players. I was qualified, not just with academic grades, but more importantly, I played at the Junior level of Hockey. The Russian hockey federation used these student exchanges to see what training techniques and skill sets we had developed here in the west. It also cost a pretty penny which I had no issues covering. The security clearance requirement had me going to Ottawa for a half-day interview at the Russian Embassy. After passing the security clearance, I will need to get Canadian government clearance to travel there for the school term. I was offered a full-year option but chose a half year so I would not be away from you for a whole year. I would leave on September 2nd, 1979, and would return if I don't get myself captured or killed on December 15th, 1979. I hope Rebecca, you can appreciate why I did not want to be in any committed relationship with you. Imagine if something did happen to me, how it would impact you and your family. I was prepared to take the risk, but I wanted to minimize any negative impact my action could have on you or your family.

Last March, I visited Sean, and I told him my plans *(going to Russia, that is)*, and we had a chance to discuss his plans. He seemed happy with his decision, and I was pleased for him as his friend. The main reason I needed to chat with Sean was my future need to get him to help me get an audience with our Canadian Ambassador in Iran, Mr. Ken Taylor, who would be stationed in Tehran. I would need Ambassador Taylor to get me into the USA Embassy so I could warn them of what was potentially coming.

Luke has been drafted by the Blues and leaves for St Louis at the end of July and then on to their farm team. He and Theresa, it seems, have called it quits after four years which came as a bit of a shock. I have not had a one-on-one moment with my bud since the news. I sent him a funny get-well card to cheer him up.

The only other news occurred on July 8th when I went down to the gatehouse to see what your answer would be. I arrived at 2 pm, and I did not see you anywhere. By 2:20 pm, I decided to go to the pond and have a moment alone thinking you made your decision. As I left the path and approached my wishbones, I saw they were both on the other side. Someone had used them to get across. I scanned the area and could not see you or anyone else for that matter. I took my alternate route through the boulders and emerged on the other side. I walked towards the pond when I spotted your arm now extending from behind a tree with what I think was a gift box of some sort. I went into full smile mode, and the butterflies were released. As I got to the tree, I grabbed the box and took it over to the same log that was there last year. I sat down and just stared at it.

"I want us to have this box, and each year we will have to bring some small item to put in as a reminder of that year. Open it," you said.

I had seen that box before. It was the same box Rebecca 1.0 had given me many years ago. I smiled and opened it and looked inside. There was some sort of cash register receipt. It listed six items and a total, and at the top was Printed your dad's hardware store name along with a date. It was a copy of the plumbing parts I bought when we first made eye-to-eye contact. I smiled and closed the box. I was speechless and was processing the significance of this. I then stood up and said, "come with me."

You gave me an odd look like you had done something wrong, and I was mad, but you followed me. I was moving with authority through the bush and did not take your hand. You kept up, and after about 15 minutes, we arrived at the spot I wanted to show you. We were both breathing heavily due to the pace, the hill we just climbed and were dripping wet with sweat. I turned and looked at you with sweat dripping down my forehead and said, "Come over here beside me."

You had a 'what are you up to' look on your face but came and stood beside me. I gave you a cocky smile and pulled out a little device from my pocket. I pushed the red button three times, and suddenly the ground in front of us began to rise. You jumped back at first, and my smile grew to its max. You were trying to figure out what was happening as the square 3-foot by 3-foot piece of the field exposed some form of elevator device. I got on the metal base and extended my hand to you. You looked shocked but accepted the offer and joined me on the base. "Keep your arms and hands in," I said.

I hit the blue button three times, and the platform we were standing on began to lower back from where it emerged. As we entered the underground chamber, lights kicked on, and you simply stared, trying to figure out what this was. I knew you had no words, so I took the lead. "This Rebecca is my fortress of solitude. I have spent the last four years building it by myself, part for the workout benefit but also as a place for me to hang out in private. It has a comfy bedroom with a queen bed, a small kitchen, a composting toilet, a recirculating filtered shower, and a few other neat features. I dug the entire thing by hand using a shovel and pickaxe. If you're wondering where some of my muscles came from, you're looking at it."

I knew I needed to let you take all of it in, and I expected your first question, combined with a look of astonishment, "How do you have lights and electricity down here?"

"I carried in 10 car batteries and have a small wind generator hidden at the top of a tree not far from here. I filter the shower water, which you are not allowed to pee in, please, and when I need water, I haul it from the creek in a backpack. I have a fridge, hotplate and freezer, so if you're thirsty or hungry, I would be happy to whip you something up," I explained like a proud poppa.

"This is unbelievable, Derek. I can't imagine how much time this took," you replied, still walking around looking down the other two wings in utter amazement.

"Other than me, you are the only other person who has ever been here or knows about this place," I said. I went to a drawer and took out another one of those devices that I used to open my fort. I opened the box and dropped it in. "This is our place now. But the only request, show no one. I was always worried if I ever died in some tragic accident, no one would ever get to enjoy my place. Now that is no longer an issue."

It was extraordinary that our very first activity was a nice long warm shower together. Rebecca 1.0 and I only enjoyed one shower together in their basement bathroom one afternoon when we were the only one's home at that time. And the rest of what we did that day was also pretty awesome.

We agreed to meet there one more time before I left for Russia, and I could tell you were not thrilled at my going, but we knew our arrangement. At our last time together before I left, you teared up a little. I spotted you wiping your eyes and pretended not to notice. I wanted to join but could not. I needed to close all my valves, and I am sorry I was already in my task mode. I told you to use it, and if there was ever a battery issue, what would be required to temporarily band-aide it.

Task 11 – Iran Hostages Part II

(January 1979 – December 1979)

57 ***My Connections!:*** I arrived in London at Heathrow and had to get a connector for Moscow. When I arrived in Moscow, I was met at the airport by two gentlemen that escorted me to the school facility. It took about 2 hours from the airport. When I got to the facility, we went in, and I was shown to my room. I would be sharing it with one other student. My pickup crew did not speak a speck of English, and I had to rely on my rusty 'conversational Russian' for any discussion. I was hoping this term would help me improve my Russian. I studied the language for the last two years privately along with some Arabic, and it was a tough language.

I unpacked my bags and made my way to the cafeteria for dinner. Not all the students had arrived, but there were around half there. I sat by myself for a bit, and eventually, a couple of people came to sit with me and try their English while I tried my Russian. It took a week, but finally, I was fitting in, and when it came time for our first skate, my fellow students had a whole new level of respect for me. My roommate was Vladimir Olegovich Potanin from Russia, and his family was considered part of the country's elite and notable families. My research showed three individuals I wanted to establish a relationship with for use in my future 'Putin' plans. It was just dumb luck that one on my list would be Vladimir. When Russia as I know it now falls apart in a few years, Vlad will become a very important businessman and friend with a man named 'Vladimir Putin.'

The other small item you need to know is my plan to have my parents meet me for a week's holiday in Austria the first week of November. Of course, I created another elaborate ruse and paid for the cost myself. The school was aware of my leaving for a week, and I made sure that a letter from my parents with the request and a detailed itinerary was delivered to the school superintendent when I arrived.

The school arranged transportation for me to the airport, and my flight was on Sunday, October 28th, with a connector through Rome. My parents would arrive on November 1st, and I had booked a room in a small resort town called Ischgl. I knew the area well from my previous ski trips here as Derek 1.0. It would not be ski season yet, but I knew it was safe, away from prying foreign intelligence eyes, and the people in Ischgl are super friendly.

It was a great hub location, and I could drive in under 2 hours to Innsbruck for some site seeing later with the folks.

My flight was uneventful, and I arrived at my hotel, The Adler, which dates back to the 1600s. It had a rich history and hosted famous faces from Albert Einstein and Ernest Hemingway to Alfons Walde until the 'Goldener Adler' finally became what it is today. I checked in and had one day to kill before my flight to Tehran. I walked the town and tried to spot some old haunts from my last time. I spotted a little eatery that was not here in 25 years, but the waitress I spotted through the front window had on the classic 'Dirndl,' consisting of a dress with a tight bodice, *(originally)* long sleeves, and a full, calf-length skirt. The dress is then adorned with a shawl *(sometimes a jacket)* and an apron. The name Dirndl Rebecca refers to its wearer in Bavarian *(and other German)* dialects 'dirndl' simply means 'young woman'. My young woman was a blonde beauty and looked a lot like Colonel Klink's secretary, Fraulein Helga, on 'Hogan's Heroes'. It was their slow season, so I assumed I would be their only guest, and that would give me time to simply chat with the locals, something I always loved to do when I travelled.

My young waitress's name was Sofia, a very common name in Austria, and she spoke 'not too bad' English. She wanted to become a stewardess in a few years and travel the world. The place was her parent's, and after about 30 minutes, I was able to get her to sit with me, at least until the next customer came in. Her folks were okay with my arrangement. I ordered my favorite Austrian dish, Tafelspitz, with a side of Austrian Spaetzle with cheese and caramelized onion. So much for my no or low-carb diet this week. We chatted for over an hour, and eventually, I asked Sofia what was there to do in the evening. She explained it was their off-season and there would not be much open, but the Adler had a great sitting room looking up at the ski hill. I think her parents had sized me up and figured I was a harmless Canadian; when I asked Sofia if she would go for a walk after her shift and show me the town, they thought it would be a great way to demonstrate their Austrian approachability and appreciation to foreign visitors.

I arranged for my return at 7 pm and met Sofia outside her place; she was still wearing her Dirndl. The temperature was around 8 Celsius, and Sofia was sporting a winter coat. I had stopped after lunch and bought myself a winter coat better suited to the weather. We walked around for an hour, and then I invited her back for a hot beverage at the 'Goldener Adler.' She was initially a bit hesitant but eventually agreed, and we went to my hotel. We sat in the restaurant lounge area facing the ski hill and sipped a hot chocolate-type drink with a shot of some local liqueur. After an hour and a half, Sofia said she needed to get home. I walked her back to her place and exchanged a firm handshake and big smiles. That was a great day. Good food, great company, and no desire to try and have sex with my new young Austrian beauty-friend *(Made you laugh).*

Task 11 – Iran Hostages Part III

(January 1979 – December 1979)

58 ***Mr. Intel!:*** The following day, I took a taxi to the Vienna airport, which was over 6 hours away. It was expensive, but money was never an issue. My flight was at 8 pm, and when we arrived, I decided to stow my bags at the airport and then head into the city for some walkabout time. It is truly a beautiful city and will bring you here hopefully one day Rebecca. I was back at the airport and boarded my plane to Rome for my connecting flight to Tehran. I arrived at Mehrabad International Airport, the only international airport serving Tehran, Iran's capital city. It will be interesting to see if they will construct a larger Imam Khomeini International Airport in the future. I had never been to Tehran, which made it my first time. I *(Derek 1.0)* was a seasoned traveller who navigated many third-world and middle eastern airports. There was no primary security screening yet, and I was able to get through immigration when I showed them my letter inviting me to attend a special lecture at the University.

I selected a young local cab driver that owned his car and hired him for the day. I knew I had a few stops to make and did not want to find any taxis or drivers who were unavailable when I needed them. Darius, my driver's name, spoke excellent English, and I would not need to fumble with my very poor Persian myself. I was much better at understanding than speaking. First stop was my hotel, and then I wanted a brief tour of the city. We drove around, and then I told Darius to take me back to the hotel. I thanked him with a huge tip and arranged for him to come back tomorrow, and I would hire him for the day. After I got to my room, something Darius said when we were doing the tour stood out.

Darius was telling me about Jalal Al-e-Ahmad's idea of Gharbzadegi—that Western culture was a plague or an intoxication to be eliminated; Ali Shariati's vision of Islam was the one true liberator of the Third World from oppressive colonialism, neo-colonialism, and capitalism; Since the Shah fled last January, the country was being transformed, but they were still struggling to dismantle the Western influence that ran the country. It wasn't that I felt at risk, but the attitude of Darius' showed it was only a matter of time. I laughed to myself when I thought about Darius's current views as I handed him a tip equal to 1 week's work driving a cab. That evening I placed a call to Sean and asked him to call his connections in government and let Ambassador Taylor know I would be coming to the Embassy tomorrow and needed to speak with him urgently.

Sean was not shocked he got my call from Tehran, and after I briefed him using my story of what I had overheard, he told me that he would do his best and that I should go straight to the Embassy tomorrow morning. If he were successful, I would find my name on a list, and if he was not, then plan 'B.' I got up early and reviewed the story I would tell in my head. Darius arrived on time, and I told him I needed to go to the Canadian Embassy and get some papers. When we got to the gates, I presented my passport to the officer, and he immediately gave me the 'OK' to enter. I turned to Darius and gave him a thumbs up with a hand to the head, symbolizing a phone to let him know I would call him when I needed to be picked up. We did not have cell phones then, and he would have to wait at his house for the call.

When I got to the front door, an older gentleman stood there and asked to see my passport. He took a look and then asked me to follow him. I was escorted into a conference room, and another young lady entered and asked if I would like a tea or coffee. I accepted the offer of a tea, sat at the end of the table, and waited for my meeting. The first person to enter was a man in his 40s in a full suit and tie. He introduced himself as the Special Envoy to the Ambassador. Three more people joined, and finally, I spotted the Ambassador coming in. He came over to me, introduced himself, and thanked me for contacting him. We had a brief chit-chat, and it was apparent Sean still had some cred back in Canada. What did bother me was when the ambassador opened a fairly thick file folder, and I could see my name was on the front. He must have reviewed it earlier, and I guessed it was likely assembled in the last 24 hours. He looked at me and said, "You should be proud of your cancer charity work Derek."

"I am Mr. Ambassador," I replied.

Over the next hour, I began to tell my tale of sitting at the airport in Rome when I overheard three men arguing about some upcoming plan to take American hostages when they returned to Tehran. A lot of fluff and detail was added that you don't need to hear, Rebecca. About 20 minutes into my story, a gentleman to my left said, "Excuse me, Mr. Ambassador, I need to ask Mr. Pettigrew a quick question. "Kayf yumkin lihadha alshaabi 'an yafham thalathat rijal yatahadathun bialearabia," he said in Farsi.

I knew what they were waiting for, and I would not disappoint. "Binafs altariqat alati 'aerif biha ma sa'altah liltawi alrajul almuhtaram almuqabil lak," I answered *("The same way I know what you just asked the gentleman across from you")*. The two men took a look at the Ambassador and gave him a nod. That was our dance, and I was now confirmed. After our meeting, I was escorted to a waiting room and told to hang tough for

30 minutes. After 30 minutes, I was escorted to an underground garage and put into a sedan. I sat for 10 minutes when the Ambassador climbed in with his assistant and one security official. The Ambassador said, "We have a meeting in 20 at the USA embassy and will be taking this car to avoid any attention."

We arrived at a small building outside the Embassy, drove into the double garage, and parked. We got out and were escorted into another room with a set of stairs. We had four armed servicemen escort us underground through a tunnel system to what I assumed was the US Embassy. We took an elevator up three floors and then into a large meeting room. As we entered, the room already had half of the 20 seats filled. I was asked to sit beside Ambassador Taylor, and at that moment, the Chargé d'Affaires for the USA, Bruce Laingen, entered. He was the top dog there, I gathered. After he sat, there was a brief exchange of pleasantries, and then the lights went off, and a projector displayed a picture of an Iranian man. The man next to Laingen, who identified himself as agent Thomas, asked me, "Do you recognize this man Mr. Devon?"

"No, sir, I don't," I replied. The picture changed a few times until a face I was familiar with popped up. "I know that face; he was one of the men I overheard talking in Rome." A few people I noticed were making notes. We reviewed about 30 pictures, and I identified three men for my audience. Agent Thomas addressed everyone and said, "The three men Mr. Devon has identified are all believed to be high up in a revolutionary movement at the University. That was all that was needed. My story sounded plausible, and Mr. Laingen said to me, "On behalf of the US government as well as the staff and members of the Embassy, I want to thank you for your decision to share this information with us."

I smiled and replied, "It was an honor and my duty as a Canadian to do what I did, sir. If I can just offer you one last piece of information; I would quietly evacuate the Embassy tomorrow through that wonderful tunnel system I came through. I would ensure I had as many cameras as possible and recording devices available, recording everything and faces that would take place in two days if what I heard was correct. I would not tip my hand to the Iranians you know of a possible attack. As I predict, if two to three thousand students arrive on your doorstep, this place is gone anyway. You cannot start shooting student protestors, and who wants to see the Iranians get a hold of a large group of US hostages. Park one helicopter on the roof for a skeleton force to be able to evacuate and wait to see if I am right or wrong."

I then got up, and the rest of the Canadian attaché I was part of got up, and was escorted back to our waiting car. I returned to the Canadian

Embassy, and Ambassador Taylor said he would love to have me over for dinner, but the Canadian Embassy needed to make emergency plans due to my intel. As we went to part, the Ambassador said to me, "Sean said you would surprise us. You did not disappoint. When you are back home in Canada and I am back in the near future, we will do dinner. If what you have told the US Chargé d'Affaires Bruce Laingen turns out to be true, you will have some friends south of the border."

We shook hands, and I asked to use the phone to call for my ride. Ambassador Taylor's assistant said she would arrange a ride, but I told her I preferred to use my driver. I called Darius, who was a bit shocked at how long my visit was and was at the gate in about 20 minutes. I had him drive me back to my hotel, asked him to wait, and then drive me to the airport. I told him that I had received information that my father had suffered a heart attack, which was why I was so long at the Embassy. They were trying to arrange for me to fly home. I boarded the plane and was off to Rome. I had a 6-hour wait for my connecting flight to Vienna and would be meeting my folks tomorrow morning. I was starting to come down from my adrenaline high and elected to just sit at the airport and wait and people watch.

The following day I got up, went to my parent's room, and knocked on the door. Dad answered and was sure happy to see me and did a very non-English greeting and gave me a big hug. Mom was next, and it was great to see them, although it had not been that long. They were completely unaware of my last few days and thought I had arrived directly from Russia. We had a great few days, and then it was time for me to get back to school, but they still had a couple more days to sightsee before returning to Canada. Everything I had predicted during my visit with my folks had unfolded exactly as I said. The limited newspaper reporting I got to see also suggested they took my suggestion. It was not without one unfortunate event: three diplomats had been grabbed at the airport. I was sure Bruce Laingen would one day buy me a beer if our paths crossed.

Task 11 – Iran Hostages Part IV

(January 1979 – December 1979)

59 ***The Intelligence Recruit Dance!:*** I arrived in Moscow and was looking forward to returning to the ice. I was sure Vlad, and the boys missed my great sense of humor. When I got off the plane and entered the terminal building, I was met by four men in suits. The one gentleman approached me and asked me to follow them—two in front, two behind. I was laughing to myself, thinking that the school had upped their game on the transportation back to school, but I knew they were not taking me to school. We arrived at a Russian-made van, and I was given a seat in the middle along with one of my new buddies on each side. As we were driving, I knew exactly where we were headed after a few minutes. It was about a 40-minute car ride from the airport to downtown, which meant the Kremlin. When we arrived, we passed through two security checkpoints before arriving outside a set of stairs leading into the side of the Kremlin. I had never been here before, and my only recollection was from movies, with the best one coming from Tommy's Mission Impossible sequel.

I was escorted now by only two men, and we maintained the front and back positions. At the end of a long hall, we took steps to the next floor up, and at the top of the stairs was a waiting guard in dress who opened the door for us. We walked in, and I was asked to please take a seat in Russian. I took the seat offered and said, "Spasibo za soprovozhdeniye, moy drug" *(Thank you for the escort, my friend).* After about 10 minutes, two new gentlemen came in and sat across from me. They, too, had a thick file folder. It seems they have spotters in Tehran watching the Embassy as well. I kind of expected this may happen. What makes these moments so easy is the fact that I can simply tell them what I did. Yes, I may sometimes add some fluff if it served me in any capacity, but it allowed me not to lie. I also assume they have an external camera monitoring my body temperature and facial gestures.

I spent the next two hours explaining everything that had happened to me, who I met with at the two embassies, and how I came to be at the Rome airport. After a few follow-up questions, I was given what I suspected was the last one. My interviewer asked me in English, "If you had heard that it was the Russian Embassy and not the American Embassy, what would you have done?"

"Simple" I replied. "I would have called my roommate Vlad and asked him to get me in touch with his dad, so I could tell him what I heard," I replied with a straight face. At this point, one of two things would most likely occur. One, they take me back to school or two, keep me in Moscow for a night, and the KGB will attempt to recruit me as a potential informant. Well, two it was. I was put up at the Cosmos Hotel, located in north-central Moscow, which was brand new. I was assigned a young man and lady as my hosts, and they took me out for dinner and then to a nightclub. I wish I could tell you that the young lady then took me back to my hotel and did naughty things to me to entice me to become an informant, but it was nothing like that. This was simple, their first meet and greet to size me up socially and get a feel for my potential political leanings. What was most interesting to me was; the girl was used to keeping me in a very social vibe while my comrade friend would ask me a question now and then. Notably, many had dealt with the US Embassy and the people I met. I think he only asked me one question about Taylor.

The next day I was back at school, and it was my last month here before heading home. Task 11 was a success, and I was looking forward to getting home and hopefully seeing you. The reason I never wrote was simply my concern of dragging your name into my files. I had developed four good friendships, with my roommate Vlad as the best. We had agreed, and his father was supportive of Vlad coming for a visit next summer. My other three buddies and I would maintain contact, but I was not sure if I would be able to use them in my future plans like I would Vlad. Mom and dad had gotten home safe and sound and, I assume went back to their regular routine. My flight from Moscow had me going back to Rome, a connector to Heathrow, and then on to Toronto. The first stop was uneventful, but when I arrived at Heathrow, as I was being processed through immigration, I was asked to follow an immigration officer to an interview room.

I sat there for about 15 minutes and knew what would take place. A gentleman entered accompanied by a lovely lady in her mid-30s. He had the typical English bad teeth going, but she was beautiful, and what made it worse, she wore librarian-looking glasses and had her hair pulled back in a ponytail exactly like Liz Hurley in Austin Powers. They reviewed my paperwork and passport, and then the young man said that they couldn't hold me, but the assistant director of national security had asked if I would volunteer to head over to the government building for lunch and that they would make all the necessary arrangements to reschedule my flight back to Toronto. I knew the drill now and was happy to agree. Miss Livingston escorted me to a waiting car, and we got in the back seat and were off to most likely MI6 headquarters. The ride there was full of useless chit-chat, and I mostly just enjoyed the smell of her perfume.

When we arrived, we went into an underground garage area, and then I was escorted into the building to the sixth floor to a small conference room. A white-haired gentleman sporting a bow tie came in with a file folder, most likely dealing with me. He extended his hand, and we sat opposite each other at the table. He asked me how my trip was so far, and then he wanted to know my family's background. He knew my dad was from England, and I assumed he already had an extensive brief in front of him. I told Mr. Sunderland that my gramps told me we came from the area at the north near Newcastle called Nags Head. I mentioned our family fish-mongering business around Whitley Bay pre-war and then sat back and listened to him give me a detailed account of my entire trip from the school to Rome, Austria, Tehran, all the way back to the Kremlin. It seems I am becoming popular these days.

"If I may ask, where did you get most of your intel? Canada, USA, or self-developed," I asked?

"Actually, I would say a bit of a mixed bag," Mr. Sunderland replied.

"And are we going to do a recruitment dance now?" I asked, which made my interviewer smile.

"Your file is accurate, Derek, and I guess I will simply ask you if you would volunteer to stay one day for a short interview process tomorrow.

I returned a polite smile and said in a sincere tone, "Yes, I would be honored to accept your interview offer, but I hope it's better than the Russian's," with an added grin. "I hope I am not asking for too special a treatment, but I would love to stay at the Savoy tonight, and my biggest request, I have a young lady friend that lives here, and she has no idea I am stopping over, and I was hoping you could have one of your people track her down and bring her for dinner at the Savoy tonight."

Mr. Sunderland smiled and said, "Do you have her name and address, and I will give it to Miss Livingston to assist" he replied.

I knew it was a yes across the board, and I replied, "One small problem, her address is back home in Canada, but I can provide her name and enough details, it should be a no-brainer for Miss Livingston to locate her, assuming she was in town."

I wrote down what I thought they could use, and Mr. Sunderland and I shook hands, and he thanked me for what I had done in Tehran. After my visit with Ambassador Taylor, he had called the UK Ambassador to give them a heads-up as well. Professional courtesy, I was sure. Miss

Livingston then took me to the Savoy, and I checked in. Yes, Rebecca, I was going to take advantage of what I was presented with this time. After all, I wanted you to appreciate all I could have had a long time ago *(I made you smile)*! As Miss Livingston was offering her hand for a shake goodbye, I said to her, "I hope this will not interfere with your afternoon, but why not stay here and keep an eye on me and we can go for a walk around town, and you can show me the sites, after all, it's not every day I get a fully comped offer like I have."

Miss Livingston smiled and grinned and said, "I am sure my bosses would want me to make sure you are safe here, but I will need to put someone on your other request."

I suggested Miss Livingston escort me to my suite, and I told her I wanted to freshen up. I had seen enough movies in my day that the first stop I needed to make was the hotel concierge desk. After a brief chat with my new best friend, Andrew, I went to the room. I asked Miss Livingston if she would like a drink or anything while she waited for me to freshen up, and she said, "A tea would be great." I picked up the phone and asked for room service. I ordered two teas and a small selection of finger sandwiches if they had them. Miss Livingston took a seat at the window and made a few calls while I went into the huge bathroom and turned on the shower. No, Rebecca, Miss Livingston did not decide to strip and come and shower with me! Although that would have been hot and certainly given the Brits a lead in the recruitment dance *(Eye roll detected)*.

My luggage arrived at the door; dressed only in my towel, I thanked the bellboy and handed him a 10-pound tip. I took the bag to the bed and grabbed some slightly used fresh clothes. I went back to the bathroom and finished getting dressed. When I got out, the tea and sandwiches had arrived, and we sat and chit-chatted some more. I was mostly asking questions about Miss Livingston and how she came to work for British Intelligence. The rest of the afternoon went as expected, and I was back in my room at 5 pm. I thanked Miss Livingston, and we arranged for a pickup tomorrow at 8 am for my interview. We shook hands and smiled at each other, and we parted. When I got to my room, I spotted the suit bag on a rack and a pair of shoes and socks.

A note on my room desk read, 'All has been arranged, Mr. Devon, and your dinner reservation is confirmed for 7:30 pm, Andrew'. I called the desk, requested a wake-up call for 6:30 pm, and crashed. The call came in. I got myself all done up for dinner. I arrived in the main lobby, and Andrew was still on when he spotted me and waved for me to come over.

"Your young lady friend arrived about 10 minutes ago, Mr. Devon, and I took her to your table and left her a bouquet with a card that said, 'For my favorite English pen pal' as you requested."

I smiled, thanked Andrew for his assistance, and walked to the dining room. Sandy knew it would be me, and I was sure this last-minute surprise was exciting for her. As we spotted each other simultaneously, she jumped up and met me halfway. She threw her arms around me and gave me a big hug. We parted and walked hand and hand to the table. I pulled her chair out, being the perfect gentleman, and she sat. We had a great dinner together, and she told me she had a flat near Piccadilly that she shared with a flatmate. After dinner, I invited her to my room to see the suite before we went out. I don't see the need to go into details, but we never left the room that night. She took something I was hoping to save for you. It was not planned, but I would be remiss if I didn't acknowledge I was feeling a little into myself, and this I thought was going to be the closest I would ever come to having a real-life 'Derek Flint' fantasy moment. It was not Sandy's first that way, and I must have known in my subconscious that I would not be the one who was your first. It always bothered me that Rebecca 1.0 had justified her decision to abstain from that one act, justifying it by claiming she wanted to save it for the person she would marry which turned out to be not true. The reality was simply, I was not the guy. I had to learn this fact the most uncomfortable way possible, through guys bragging about their conquests. It still makes me angry now! I don't know if we will talk one day about our firsts, but if we don't, I will now be wondering in the future just how special it would be with you that way. I always said our way was more special, but now I may have to rethink that!

The next day, I left before Sandy and told her to take her time and leave whenever she wanted. We were now saying our goodbyes with kisses, and she said she might be in Montreal in July for a business function. I went and had my interview, which I would characterize as having gone smashingly. They must have enjoyed my interview because I was no longer flying home on a commercial plane; I had a seat on a private jet of a Toronto Businessman named Carl Dowser. Carl was a commodities trader; apparently, his firm worked extensively with the newly formed BP. I never asked Carl how I came to be on his plane, he just knew I missed my last flight, and he was doing a favor for the company president. The story I was told was I was friends with the President's son from school.

I arrived in Toronto, and as I expected, I was met by a couple of gentlemen from the RCMP and CSIS at the plane's gate. They escorted me to a downtown office tower, and I had one last dance. This one was far easier, and most of the time, it was more a praising session than a recruitment attempt. When I finished, I was handed a handwritten note from Ambassador Taylor inviting me to Ottawa for a meeting and dinner in two weeks. Finally, I was driven home in a limo, and when I arrived in the driveway, my parents came out to meet me and wanted to know how I scored a limo ride. I needed a couple of days to decompress, and it was Christmas next week, and I was hoping I would get to see you. Maybe at the fort!

Update – Someone has a Boyfriend :(

(December 18th, 1979)

60 ***Lows and highs!*** I found out the school December dance was next Friday, the 21st. I called your house to let you know I was back and to see if you may be interested in taking me to the dance *(Smiled)*; with the returning Derek Flint, that is. Todd answered, and we chatted for a bit, and I told him all about my trip to Russia, the stuff I could say to him. I asked him how grade 13 was going for him and if he knew if you were going to the dance on the 21st. He told me that *(your/his)* family were going to Ellicottville for the week skiing, leaving Friday. I asked Todd if you were going, and he said yes, but also told me that you had a boyfriend now and that he was coming too *(A guy leaves for Russia for four months and look what happens)*. I was starting to think it might be karma for my little 'Derek Flint' moment with Sandy, although we both know as a scientist, I would never buy into the whole concept of Karma. Trying not to let him hear the hurt I was immediately feeling, I told him we should try to get a drink sometime but knew it would never be arranged *(Oh, I feel a song coming on)*.

Finding out that way and never considering that it would happen sucked! I was feeling like a bit of a hypocrite with my 'poor me' feelings when I had just been with Sandy. I knew our deal, but I was still feeling like crap, and since we have not had any snow yet, I decided to head to the fort for a check-up and some exercise. When I arrived, I went down in, and when the lights came on, I slowly got a huge smile. It seems my housemate decided to 'Rebeccaize' the place. A few pictures, plastic flowers, and my favorite, a miniature fireplace complete with fake flames and the sound of crackling. Seeing what she did made me even more 'pissed off' at the situation and in myself.

But it was not the end of the hurt. I found on the bed an envelope that was addressed to; 'The Boy that Can't be in my life.' I knew from the outside that the inside would be adding to the hurt. It was not long but was indeed painful.

Derek,

I once said, 'our rules' may one day hurt one of us, and I am sorry if that day has come. I want you to know that it hurts me as well, but we both agreed to the rules, and here is where it has brought us. I met a boy at school who is in my homeroom class. I was not looking for a

relationship; it just grew slowly. We like each other but not the way we do. I am in my second to last year of high school, and as you told me, I should enjoy it to the fullest. I know you have your reasons to travel, and I am also aware that you will be off to Harvard next September.

This is still our place, and I will honor our pact. I hope you can find someone that you can share yourself with.

Love
Rebecca :(

It hurt Rebecca, but not like my last time being dumped by you *(I had to add that)*. I knew it would eventually happen and to be honest, it kind of needed to happen. If we would one day have a shot at being a couple, it would happen later. We both subconsciously knew we need to stress test our relationship. I had too much to do to risk it now. It did however ease my guilt feeling about Sandy seeing you were in a relationship when I had my 'Derek Flint' experience moment. I was feeling down, and I am unsure if it was because my girl was giving herself freely to another guy or if I was just mad at myself for trying to justify what I was doing for the greater good. Regardless, I was feeling really lonely and wanted a distraction.

I did not want to stay at the fort now with all the visual' Rebeccaizes' and left for home. I decided to stop in at the Mattson's to say hello. As I got to the door, Luke opened it with a big smile, and we both did the best bud hug. I said, "What the hell are you doing here?"

"I had a few days off and came home for a short visit. We play over Christmas, and I won't be here for it, so we are doing one here early. When did you get back from Ruskie?"

"Yesterday. Long flight, and I still have some jetlag. I just went down for a hike to try and get the blood flowing," I told him.

I went in, and we chatted and got all caught up. I saw the whole family, including Lukes younger brother JJ and sister, who had blossomed into a beautiful young woman. They invited me to stay for dinner, but I wanted to eat with my folks. Luke and I agreed to grab a drink tomorrow before he had to head back. I walked home and inspected the neighborhood as I walked by each house to see what may have changed. When I got home, I was surprised by Lee's Chinese food for dinner. Ann was also glad to see me for a few days. After dinner, I decided to do something I never thought I would have the balls to do; I called Maureen Ferreiro. She must be back from her New York school, and I figured if I didn't get a meet and greet with her, at least I got to say hello and Merry Christmas.

I grabbed my address book, and when I dialled her number, I actually had some butterflies. The phone rang a few times, and I think her younger sister Patty, not Mary-Lou answered. When I asked for Maureen, her sister said, "Who can I say is calling?"

I hesitated, then said, "Her Chemistry Partner."

I could hear the phone being put down, and I waited. After a minute, a voice came on and said, "You burn the school down and need me to bail you out?"

As soon as I heard her voice, I smiled and said, "No, much worse, I have been abandoned this Christmas; I have no one. Even Santa is passing me by. One short trip for six months to Russia, and I return to a ghost town. I went through my entire address book, and it came to this, you are the last person left that can go toe-to-toe with me."

"Whose toes are up and who's toes are down?" she quipped.

"Both are in the same direction; the question is whose toes are at the back?", I chuckled.

Maureen shared the laugh with me. "I have to go to a modeling show this weekend in Montreal and won't be back till Monday. Besides, don't you have the Christmas dance on Friday?", she asked me.

"If I may be so bold, who are you going with?", I asked.

There was a polite pause, and then she said, "No one. I am taking the train there and back."

"Would you like a personal bodyguard for the weekend?" I asked with significant Butterfly's.

Another longer pause, then she gave me a typical Maureen response, "Well, I can't pay you with money, but if there were another form of payment, then I would say sure. Except you should know, I am sharing a room with three other gorgeous models."

"I think we can work out some arrangement. When are you planning on leaving?", I asked.

"My train leaves Friday at 10 am, and the show is Saturday at 1 pm, and a second one at 7 pm," she explained.

"Ok, let me pick you up at 9 am on Friday," I said.

"You're sure you want to be stuck on a train for 'like-ever' with me and then having to hang out with a bunch of other me's," Maureen shot back with.

"When I agreed to take the Chemistry partner oath, it said, through the good and the bad, you will never let your partner down," I said, chuckling.

Maureen laughed, and we agreed I would pick her up at 9 am. I told my folks I was off to Montreal for the weekend with a last-minute invite by some friends. I sat in bed that night and tried to figure out what I wanted to do with this trip. After about an hour, I went to bed grinning. The following day, I got up, grabbed a business card from my card holder, and made a call. "Hello, is this Carl" I asked?

"Yes, it is," Carl replied.

I told Carl it was me and then asked him if I could rent his jet for a run to Montreal on Friday. I explained what I was doing, and after he had a bit of a chuckle, he said OK. It was not cheap. $7,500 each way was his breakeven cost. I also booked a suite at the Queen Elizabeth Hotel for Friday through Sunday. Another $3,000! Your new 'boy toy' Rebecca was proving to cost me a lot of money *(Made you smile)* so I could ease my pain.

So, Friday arrived, and I went to Maureen's with good old Betsy. I knew she would take one look and die. I went to the door and knocked to be met by her mother. "Maureen, your car is here," her mom said. "She will be right out." I smiled and decided to play the role. Maureen came to the door with a suitcase and huge clothing bag, and as soon as she saw the old blue station wagon, she looked at me and said, "You got to be kidding me."

"Hello, I am your driver to the train station Miss that the modeling agency has sent. I would have brought the Ferrari, but they said you had a ton of luggage," I replied.

That reply was enough to shake the snob out of Maureen, and she didn't want to disappoint and replied, "I had asked for a full panel van," with a fake look of disgust. Her mother had no idea who I was and that we were actually sparring right in front of her. I grabbed her suitcase and tried to get a grip on the clothing bag, which I thought weighed more than the suitcase. Thank God I had a station wagon!

"I went around and opened the door for Maureen like some chauffeur and waved goodbye to her mother at the door. As we pulled out, she let out a little laugh and said, "I didn't know you would play this hard."

We both grinned at each other, and I said, "Thank you for letting me come. I have wanted to spend time with you since Tim's party," I confessed. "I just felt you thought I was too young for you."

She had on her faded blue jeans, low-cut style, a jean shirt, flats, a fat brown suede belt and a blue cool-looking choker. She used almost no makeup and had flawless skin. When I reached the highway, I decided there was no time like the present, and I reached over with my right hand, grabbed her hand, and said, "I love to hold hands if you didn't know."

She gave me a smile and altered our hands to an interlocking finger grip. I asked her about the how, who it was for, the format, and how much time she would have free. She needed to be at the convention center by 11 am for fittings; she would have off from 2:30 to 4. After the last show, she only needed 30 minutes, and that was it. So, we would have all Friday afternoon, evening, breakfast Saturday, rest between shows, and then all evening Saturday and Sunday to hang out. As I passed the turn-off for the Via station, she looked at me and said, "You know you just missed the turn-off?"

"I looked at her with a fake panic on my face and said, "Oh no! I think we are going to have to drive the whole way now," with a slowly growing grin.

She knew me better than most and smiled and sat back to see what I was up to. We continued chatting and holding hands until I reached Mississauga and headed north off the highway. It was only another 15 minutes when I pulled into the private corporate airport, where most of Toronto's wealthy plane owners kept their jets. Maureen did not look as shocked as I thought, but she did shoot me a grin and said, "Why, Mr. Devon, aren't we full of surprises."

I know the attendant had to do a double-take at the car, and I quickly fixed that concern with, "Sorry man, I was blocked in at the movie set and had to take one of the stunt cars." He nodded like he understood the situation and directed me where to park. He came over with a golf cart and proceeded to load our luggage, and a second car came for Maureen and me. It took a bit of work, but I managed to keep a straight face all the way to the private hanger where the plane was. As we arrived at the plane, the co-pilot who was standing on the plane steps smiled and said, "Good Morning, Mr. Devon, Montreal as usual, Sir?"

I knew Carl must have put them up to it, and I could not let it go unappreciated and said with a grin, "That is correct, my right seat, friend."

We climbed in, and a young lady met us and showed us to our arranged seats. We had the two on the right side, with me facing back towards Maureen. The plane had seating for eight, but it looked like it was just us. She came by and asked if we would like a drink, and Maureen surprised me by asking for Champagne. I asked for a coffee with cream and a banana. We did not say much at first to each other, but we kept always looking at each other with a smile. The captain came on and gave me a warm personal welcome and even threw in for show a mention of my recent flight back from the UK. Once we were airborne, Maureen said, "Is your family wealthy?"

"Not at all. You know where I live," I replied, sipping my coffee.

"Then how," she asked?

"Let's just say I have an extensive network of friends and business associates, and every now and then, I get a few perks thrown my way for all the work I do," I said.

I won't bother you further with the details, Rebecca, since you are probably reminiscing about your fabulous week in Ellicottville *(You know I am doing my darndest to piss you off).* We arrived in Montreal, and the Pilot Captain Mike told me he would meet us here Monday morning. We took the limo I arranged to the Hotel when Maureen said, "I have a room I was going to share with three other girls at another hotel."

"Oh, sorry, Maureen, this is where I am staying. I just wanted to drop off my stuff before I take you to your 'sorority room'," I replied with a grin.

We checked in, and I had the bellboy take our stuff up. When we got to my suite, we walked in, and even I was in awe. This was not a $1,000 per night suite; this was a $5,000 per night suite or more. I did not want to let on to Maureen, it was not the room I booked when Maureen spotted a bottle of Champagne on ice and a card. She walked over and opened the card. I watched her read it, and then she poured two glasses and brought one over to me. What she did not know was that I was not a fan of Champagne. As I took the glass, she said, "Who is Mr. Laingen. He said thanks for everything and hope you'll enjoy the weekend on him."

I gave a big smile and then made a toast. "To a wonderful and maybe even magical weekend with my Chemistry partner." The suite had two bedrooms, and the bellboy had put Maureen's bags in one room and mine in the other. She took her glass, walked around checking out the suite, and then went into my room. After a couple of minutes, she came out and then walked into what was supposed to be her room. I walked over to the window and took a look at the view. After about 5 minutes, Maureen came out wearing a fluffy white bathrobe with the hotel emblem on the lapel and said, "I think I will take a bath."

I must have had a grin going, and I was concluding she would make this her home base. If she wanted to hang with her girls all three nights or one night, that was fine with me. I was just glad to be away and welcomed the Rebecca distraction *(You pissed at me yet)*. I walked over to the phone and called room service. Since the room was comped, let's splurge a little. "Can I have a large fruit and cheese plate, a bottle of Taylor Fladgate 30-year-old, and a dozen long stem white roses?" Ordering Red Roses just seemed wrong *(Partial Smile?)*.

After I hung up, I heard Maureen call for me. I went to her room, poked my head in slowly, and said, "Yes, young lady, do you need your toenails clipped."

She giggled and said, "Not yet, I am trying to make them a bit more pliable first, but I would like a refill of Champagne." I went and grabbed the bottle, returned to her room, and walked through to the bathroom. It was huge, and a sizeable triangle-shaped jacuzzi bathtub was in the one corner. I went over with a smile on, and Maureen stood up and held out her glass for me to fill. I began a staring contest, and I knew she was waiting for me to stop and check her out, standing there naked with only a grin. I had already caught a brief glimpse and knew she was hairless *(I was sure I was having my own 'Trance' moment)*. I refused to let her win and kept looking into her eyes. When I reached her outstretched arm, I poured her a glass and kept my eyes on her the whole time with my grin. I turned and started to walk away, leaving the bathroom, and I knew I had won that round and she would be checking my backside out as well.

After about 15 minutes, there was a knock at the door. I went and greeted the services person and directed him to roll the cart in. I signed the chit and gave a generous tip with a hand note at the bottom that said, 'Thanks, Bruce!" I rolled the cart into Maureen's bathroom, and she was reclined and enjoying the bubbles. She opened her eyes and surveyed what I was doing. I pushed the cart beside the jacuzzi and opened the bottle of port. I knew my palette was not ready yet to fully appreciate the port, but my brain, I hoped, would compensate. I poured myself a glass, grabbed a piece of the Reggiano, and put it in my mouth. I savored the saltiness and then took a sip. Heaven! My brain had compensated enough, and I loved it. At that moment, Maureen stood up, bubble coated and all, and stepped out on the mat. She used her finger and gestured for me to come over to her. I took another piece of cheese and walked over. I put the cheese halfway in my mouth and presented it to Maureen to sample. She did not miss a beat and put her mouth on the cheese, and I finally had my first kiss with Sherman Falls High's hottest student ever *(Other than you, of course Becca, hehe).*

Our lips had touched until she managed to bite off her piece. She chewed it slowly, smiled, and said, "Yum, salty" with an added devilish grin. She then grabbed my hand with the port and guided it over so she could take a sip. After her drink, she began slowly and systematically removing my clothes. I had graduated from my 'Tighty-Whities' and had on Italian speedo-style underwear, which was all the rage in Europe these days. I was in a mental place that few people would ever be in. I had secretly worshipped this girl for years the first time, and she never knew I existed. Now we were true friends, and I was also about to discover lovers. There was no hiding my attraction for her as she stripped me down to her level. Once I was the same, she took my glass of port from my hand, moved it to my lower region, and stuck you know who in it. She reached over and grabbed another piece of cheese and handed me back the glass and proceeded to move down onto her knees.

I won't go into any more detail, Rebecca, but I would like you to know a few things. Besides, I am probably six feet under by now and this happened many years ago from your read now. It turns out that Maureen was not going to school in New York; she was living in a Manhattan condo overlooking central park. She still modeled but was, for the most part, a 'kept woman'. She said he would come to the city every so often, never more than twice a month. His wife and kids lived out on Long Island in a community called Oyster Bay. He was rich and liked beautiful younger girls. Maureen initially said she thought she was falling in love with him until he made the offer. After that, she was just a piece of meat. A very expensive piece, but she knew what she was. She was getting too old for modeling and knew it was only a matter of a few more years, and the jobs would end. She was smart, decided to try and sock away as much as possible, and wanted to eventually move to Hawaii. I planned to help her one day with a special set of numbers.

Maureen became a teacher of sorts to me. She showed me things and even made me practice a lot *(hehe)*. I always thought Tina and I had pushed the envelope in this area. She showed me what women want, like, and where to find those magic spots. I doubt there was a position or movement I had not been subjected to by the end of our weekend. This relationship worked because it was never about us being anything more than Chemistry Partners. I gave her, her needed distraction from feeling like some high-priced call girl, and she gave me my needed distraction from thinking about you.

I did not know how long this new arrangement would last, but it would continue as long as I needed to forget every now and then.

[When I got back, I went down to visit with Mr. Angelo and Mr. Agro. I also went to see Mr. Simpkins and popped in on Eugene to let him know I was looking for some volunteer hours for the spring]

A Perfect Pairing

Update – Graduation and Harvard

(January 1st, 1980 – September 1980)

61 ***Schools out for Summer!*** I was in the final stretch of my High School do-over, which was bitter-sweet. This month was my 6th Gala, and we had raised over $25 million since its inception. The 'Student Mentoring Initiative' was fully national, and my end of the sales was over $250K annually. My stock portfolio was unmatched in growth. It seems I was able to pick the higher fliers only. Maintaining a humble and simple life appearance was getting harder, and I decided it was the right time to have my parents win the lottery. The first chance would be the summer of 1982 when Lotto 649 is launched, which is not that far off. I know it would change their lives, but I would never forgive myself if I had been killed and they never got to sample the benefits of my superpower directly.

When school started back in January, everyone asked me about what it was like to attend school in Russia. I told them it was very much like here, but teachers would drink vodka in class. Then I would tell them that it was a joke. I was lucky that my classes, and your classes, could not be more out of sync. I remember the first time I bumped into you coming out of a class. You were heading to the girl's bathroom after you told me you had a bit of a 'girl's' accident. When your eyes directed me to look down, I knew what you were talking about. What a day to have that happen wearing white pants that I will admit fit you so incredibly.

I told you to wait by your locker, and I ran to my locker downstairs and grabbed my clean track pants and brought them to you. I told you to change into my track pants for your next period *(Pun intended with a grin)* and to give me your pants. You knew I was going to clean them, and we did not say that much to each other. I took your pants and headed to my Chemistry classroom at the other end of the school. Mr. Stubing was in the class doing some work at his desk when I came in. "Mr. Stubing, I was wondering if I could impose on your chemical storeroom for a few chemicals."

"What are you in need of Derek," he asked?

"Hydrogen peroxide and Tetrachloroethylene or a benzene derivative if that's all you have," I replied.

"Sounds like you want to do a little dry cleaning," he asked.

I smiled, showed him your pants, and told him a friend had cut herself and got some blood on her pants. I figured that was all he needed to know. He smiled and told me to follow him to the locked chemical room. He grabbed what I needed and told me I was welcome to use the fume hood at the back. I took the chemicals and cleaned your pants as if they had never had a stain.

I cleaned up and thanked Mr. Stubing. "No, thank you, Derek. It is rewarding to see a student that studied as hard as you have and has already grasped so much about the world of chemistry."

I smiled and laughed to myself when I thought about what he would have done if I had given him my list for C4. I took your pants to the janitor's closet and opened it. I took the vacuum cleaner and put the hose on the discharge side. I turned it on and began blow-drying the crotch of your pants. After a few minutes, they were perfectly dry. I went to your locker, opened it, and put the clean, nicely folded pants in. I closed the door and drew a happy face in pencil on the door. Later, I found my track pants in my locker. No note, just them folded up. I had a very brief moment where I thought about smelling them but immediately thought that would be so disrespectful. Not gross, disrespectful. I just wanted to smell your scent!

I was asked by a couple of girls if I would like to go to the dance and the prom, but I was just not in the mood to go without you on my arm. That weekend I drove down to New York to forget for a few days.

I finally decided it was time for me to get my own car. I had driven many different cars over my lives, but one that I always wanted but could never afford was a Lotus. Specifically, a Lotus Turbo Esprit. Unfortunately, it would not be in production for another year, so I took the next best choice, the revised Series 2 *(or S2)* Esprit. I had worked hard for a few years and had more than enough money to buy 10. I was worried that my folks would be slightly put off with the cost and the type, but that was not the case. They both thought I deserved to get whatever I wanted. That weekend I made a call to a friendly contact in the UK named Miss Livingston and asked her if she would track me down a new 1978 Esprit S2 edition in white. She said she would love to. It took a month to reach me and get all the paperwork completed finally. The steering wheel was on the opposite side, but that was not an issue for me. I loved that car, and it indeed turned eyes around town. Unfortunately, it did not arrive before July 8th.

This was going to be a very different day today. You had a guy in your life, and I heard you were very happy through my school sources. I was no longer a 'true virgin' and had completed the most substantial task to-date. Maureen and I needed fairly regular distractions, and I had 'files' in a bunch of countries. Soon, I was heading to Harvard. In December, I was going to save John Lennon. I rode to the gatehouse around 11 am and decided I needed a good long run to help numb my feelings. I ran a few laps of the headwaters trail and finally got to the fort around 1 pm. I knew you were already there. I had a couple of little tracker techniques that I never told you about. As I was lowering, I could smell food. It looks like you were cooking. As I landed, you turned and said, "I figured after your run you would be hungry."

No hi, no hello. I knew we were both in an awkward place, and I did not have any solution. All I could think of was, "It smells great but maybe turn the recirculator on high. I could smell it a long way away. I am going to grab a quick shower."

There was not going to be any rendezvous in the shower this time. I dressed, entered the sitting area, sat, and watched you finish cooking. I had not really seen you since the stain incident. I stared and watched. You brought over a couple of plates, and it was your fettuccine alfredo with chicken dish I loved. You sat and finally looked at me, smiled, and said, "Thanks for the stain removal."

I nodded and said, "No problem. I Just needed a few chemicals from Mr. Stubing."

"You cleaned them at the school?", you asked.

"Yes, I had Mr. Stubing give me the necessary chemicals to do a basic dry cleaning on them," I told you.

"A chemist now, how amazing," you replied with a slightly condescending tone.

We ate without much discussion, and after lunch, we decided to take a walk. We went down to the pond, and I brought my pocket fisherman. I spotted some rainbows mulling by a fallen tree and made a cast. It was only the second cast when a 3-pounder was on. I got it to shore and said, "You want fresh Trout for dinner?"

Your less-than-happy face finally showed a brief smile and said, "Sounds good."

We walked back to our place, and I got my fish cleaning gear and headed into the woods to clean our dinner. I was back in about 20 minutes, and you had already cleaned up the lunch dishes and had the table set for dinner. I brought out a new VHS machine. It wasn't until 1977 that JVC developed their own VCR system known as the Video Home System or VHS. I also had a small color TV stashed, which I brought out. I proposed we watch a movie and eat a bit later. You agreed, and I would bet you can recall my movie selection! I set up the TV and VCR, and we went to the bed to lay and watch the movie. My choice was *'Same Time Next Year'*. I knew you had most likely not watched it before and thought if there ever was a good time to introduce the movie to you, this was it.

We did not do any cuddling or holding hands. We exchanged looks at certain points in the movie that we knew were lesson-learning moments for us. When it was over, you turned and said to me, "Do you see them as being us?"

"No," I replied.

"Then what is your version?" you asked, staring at me.

I did not have an immediate answer, and usually, when boxed in, I will fire out a return question to buy time, but I felt that would be unfair. After a brief pause, I told you, "I truly believe that two people can love each other, but they are not a true 'it-couple'. They will love, laugh, cry and one day it will suddenly end. They may even have kids, which adds a whole other level of complexity. You can have one 'it-person' ,without the other person being their 'it-person'. In that case, there will never be true happiness for either; they may stay together for a while, mostly because the 'it-person' does not want to lose the person they thought was their 'it-person', even though it was not reciprocated. But at some point, it will end. I think the more pertinent question is 'how do you know when both people are 'it-people' together'? Or maybe even more relevant, when or how does a person transition from just a person in love to a true 'it-person?'"

I was looking at you, trying to figure out if you were understanding my ramblings or not. "Look at us as an example; I don't want, just to love you; I want you to know that I am your 'it-boy'. You should want to know that you are my 'it-girl'. I don't believe it can be forced and I don't want to lose the chance to transition from a non-'it-person' to an 'it-person'. I do think you need to start with a foundation of love, but eventually it will either die and wither or if you're lucky, transform into an 'it-relationship'. I don't know if you are in love with your current guy, only you will honestly know that, and to be frank, I don't want to know. But if you want to do the test I am talking about, all you have to do is ask yourself, 'If I had to be stranded on a deserted island for the rest of my life with one person, who would that be?'"

"Am I your 'It-girl' Derek?" you asked, your eyes getting watery.

"That is irrelevant, Rebecca. What you need to figure out first is do you have an 'it-person' in your life. Once you can answer that, then you will want to know if your 'it-person' feels the same", I explained. "When two people become each other's 'it-person', which is extremely rare, they will know, and it will not require a question to determine it."

I felt we had enough heavy talking and suggested we should start dinner. We went through our playing house, and I think our talk got us both thinking and reflecting. After dinner, we cleaned up and then got ready for bed. I didn't know if you would stay the night or wanted to leave. Our arrangement never required a sleepover. The fact you wanted to remain told me all I needed to know. We both had pyjamas now in our house. You had the adorable Micky mouse with the full booties, and I had my adult red flannel two-piecer. We laid in bed, each on our own side, and you finally asked me how Russia was. I told you a 'Cole's Note' version, including my visit with my folks in Ischgl. Eventually, we wanted to sleep. I turned off the light. I kept a night light on just in case someone needed to use the bathroom. After about 30 minutes, you reached over and grabbed my arm and draped it over you as you snuggled up against me. You fell asleep, but I continued to lay there, smell your hair, and enjoy the feelings I was experiencing.

I got up early and decided to go out for a short workout, grab a few freshwater backpacks and let you sleep. When I approached with the second load, I could already smell the coffee. When I got down inside, I saw you were having a shower and got myself a cup of coffee. I sat down and was sipping the coffee when you finally came from around the corner, and you were all dressed and ready to leave. You gave me a brief smile as you looked over at me and asked how I slept. I smiled and told you great, although that was not really true. I was hurting and kept it concealed.

You told me to take a shower and got yourself a tea going. I showered quickly and dressed for our departure. We put our house 'back to bed' and left. When we arrived at the gatehouse, I asked, "Would you like me to walk you home?"

"No thanks. But I would like to see you here one more time before you leave for school", you said.

"Ok, I would like that," I replied. I knew we would work out a date for that, and when it was time to leave, we did exchange a long hug. We were both thinking at that moment, 'Why not let ourselves try it and see what would happen'. I went to where I hid my bike and rode home. The ride did me good, and I think with the frustration I was experiencing, it made me clock a new personal best time from the gatehouse to home. I had told my folks I was going hiking and might camp overnight at the conservation area. They knew I loved it down there, and it was not uncommon for me to secretly camp down there.

We returned two days before I would be driving down to school. When I rode into the parking lot, I spotted your Gremlin. The old Gremlin has surfaced. Part of me wanted to go over and burn it to the ground, and the other part realized you would not be staying overnight. I rode over to the car, and it was about that moment you walked out from the trail and spotted me. You had on jeans and a t-shirt and your running shoes. No makeup, just natural beauty.

"What do you think of my car?", you asked.

"I won't lie. It's you," I smiled and replied.

"My dad bought it for us kids to drive a little while ago. I think he was tired of us always taking his suburban on him," you said.

"I gather you're not able to stay the night?" I asked.

"I am sorry, but no. My boyfriend's birthday is today, and we are seeing a movie later. Maybe you would like to join us?" you asked with that 'woman scorned' devilish look?

"I would consider it if he would not mind me holding one of your hands during the movie, and you know I need to be on your left," I replied with my own 'I can play this game as well, look'.

Knowing it was his birthday and you were taking time to be with me for a while, I wanted to show you my appreciation by respecting your decision and I made sure there would be no outwardly showing of affection. No hand-holding, no hugs, just two people who loved each other but were waiting for the sign.

We did not go to our house; we sat in the parking lot on a picnic table and did something we had never done before. We started to reminisce about our lives together, recalling each special moment and some of the painful ones, and I was sure to mention old 'Mr. Pulled it Out' a few times. It was about a two-hour visit, and when we said all we needed to say, I walked you to the Gremlin, opened the door, and you got in. I detected a weak moment when I thought you were about to hug me, but you quickly found your composure and did not want to offend my offering. I know there was no hug, but you placed your hand on mine, smiled sadly, and said, "I am going to miss you."

That was it. Off you drove, and I rode back home to finish packing for my trip to Cambridge, Massachusetts. You did not know that I was about to start my next Task prep. I would save John Lennon in a few months, meet a very important cancer research grad, and hopefully see Luke play in the NHL for his first time!

The Rebecca Mobile

" I Hate F'ing Gremlins."

\- ***D. Devon***

Task 12 – Mark David Chapman

(September 1st, 1980 – December 9th, 1980)

62 ***John 10:10:*** The drive was incredible in the Lotus, and it was my first long trip with the car. It still had the new car smell, and the border officer got out of his booth to take a detailed look at it. The car had no storage, so I had already shipped all my bulky items like my hockey equipment. I was looking forward to competitive Hockey again and was told there were a couple of Canadians on the team roster. There were a couple of stretches of road where I rolled the dice and opened her up. In one stretch, I hit 180 mph, but the white knuckles got the better of me when my brain said, 'What are you going to do when a deer runs out'? I made the trip in 6 hours and, fortunately, no tickets. I had been to the campus before and knew the general layout. I was scheduled for a hockey try-out tomorrow and wanted to get settled in. I elected to stay on campus the first year, and mom and dad were going to drive down at thanksgiving to visit *(US Thanksgiving)*. Dad was especially proud of me for attending Harvard. The only reason I was here was to meet a unique science grad student that would be developing a cancer treatment 20 years later. It was also helpful that New York was only 4 hours away.

I got settled in, met a bunch of hockey guys, and got an excellent tour by a few seniors on the team of the best places to party and meet girls around campus. You could say that many students here came from the cream of the crop: future senators, fortune 100 CEOs, top lawyers, actors, and even research scientists. If you wanted to build the most powerful and efficient nuclear bomb, you would not go and recruit community college people, no disrespect; it was just a fact. I was able to get a single dorm room by pulling a few favors. In exchange, I was scheduled for an on-campus recruitment meeting in November with the CIA.

My recruiters had been keeping tabs on me, including the Russians. Vlad and I have had a couple of home and away get-togethers, and I knew that made my other recruiters nervous. They did not know that in about 15 years, Vlad would be a huge deal in Russia and would be able to open up doors that I would never be able to do on my own. The only negative about my choice to attend here was that I would have to become a great student. My studies were not some time-cheat. I would have to learn almost everything. There was the odd advantage, especially when it came to my minor in computer science. But for the most part, I had to crack the books daily and burn the midnight oil often. Hockey was proving to be a pain in the butt with how much it interfered with my studies. My particular hockey talents were a welcome addition to the team, giving me a full ride and occasionally getting a scout or two approaching me.

December was near, and I needed to make the necessary arrangements to be freed up to go to New York for a few days. I was aware we had a game that Saturday the 6th, and I cut a deal with the coach to play that game, then I would leave right from the rink to New York. I had my Lotus in storage for the winter and had rented a car. We played and won, and I was off for my next task. When I arrived in New York, I arranged for a room at the Sheraton Hotel, 790 7th Avenue, and West 52nd Street, Manhattan, where my target was staying. I had tons of details from my research and could have simply offed him that night and returned to Harvard. What I was struggling with was your suggestion once that maybe rather than simply kill a person, I should try and intervene and point them in a new direction. That was my quandary. Do the Rebecca approach or the simple Derek choice? I decided I wanted to first observe the guy before making that decision. I was safe till the 9th, which would give me time to figure out what to do.

After I checked in, I went to grab a bite nearby. When I was doing some restaurant peering to see what the place looked like inside, I noticed a male person in the reflection of the window that was watching me. Damn, I am being followed. Seems, my friends, were not satisfied with our interview last month. I decided to pick a place with poor visibility to see inside from the street. That would force my watcher to come in. I took a seat that would allow me to watch through a glass reflection. That way, it would put my watcher more at ease. As I looked at the menu, a young lady came in and sat at a table by herself. Damn, I was tag-teamed. If I attempted to sneak out a back way, then they would know I knew. So, I decided to let them have their watch. I ordered my meal, ate it while reading a day-old newspaper, and then left.

I needed to understand the surveillance setup better, so I returned to my hotel to start my process. I called the front desk and asked for a wake-up call in an hour. I closed the drapes and laid in bed on my back with two pillows under my head. There were two vents in the room that were visible. I needed to see if they had a camera on me as well. I hit the light switch from the bed, and the room went dark; I immediately turned the switch on. I did not see any diode glowing from the first vent. I repeated the process for the second and was reasonably sure no cameras were watching me. But just to ensure, I went over and peered in with my flashlight. I then went to my suitcase and removed my homemade sniffer device. I turned it on and began to sweep the room. I found three mics carefully hidden and was satisfied that was all.

If there were no cameras, then they were externally watching. With the lights out, I went over to the window and made a small crack in the drapes. With daylight outside and me in the dark, they would not be able to see anything unless I opened the drapes another six inches. Any motion detection would not work. I scanned the building directly across and spotted my peeping tom. I could see two people, which made four that I was aware and I am guessing they also had a mobile unit. This would make my options of what I wanted to do with Mr. Chapman much more challenging. I was satisfied they did not know why I was in New York, but it was apparent someone did not trust me as much as I thought they would. If my American friends were all over me, I should also consider I may have a couple of other admirers this weekend.

My one advantage is they do not know I know they are watching. I know they have listening capabilities, and the only concern is any hallway cameras. I already assume they have the room next to me. I would need to check the hall thoroughly the next time I leave. If you are wondering, Rebecca, how I know about this stuff, a lot of my knowledge has come from watching Tv and Movies. Many people don't realize that well-made movies often hire consultants for certain aspects of the film to try and bring as much authenticity as possible. Thank Hollywood for some of my education and the dark web for the rest. After an hour, I received my wake-up call and decided to see the mobile unit at work. I went down to the front and exited the Hotel and waved down a cab. There was one waiting just up the street that came and grabbed me. I told the driver to take me to the Staten Island ferry terminal.

When the cab pulled up to the terminal entrance, I paid the driver and got out. I went to the ticket outlet and asked for the next ticket to St. Georges Terminal. The Ferry was leaving in 30 minutes, so I took a seat in the waiting area and started to see how long for my watchers to get in. It was about 3 minutes, and I spotted my fake watcher couple from the restaurant. They went to the ticket counter and purchased a couple of tickets, I assumed, for the next ferry ride. The weather was cold and wet today, and I was sure they were less than thrilled with my decision to take off for Staten Island. The Ferry arrived, and I boarded the boat and took a seat at the back so I could check out the Statue of Liberty when we passed her. Once we arrived on the other side, I went to a small restaurant in St. George terminal's east side and grabbed a seat. I order a salad and a tea.

My couple watchers arrived and came in and sat down. It looked like they were ordering something. I quickly ate my food, and as soon as the waitress came out with the watcher's meal, I got up, handed $20 to the waitress, and thanked her for a great salad.

My ticket was a return ticket, and I walked back to the terminal and jumped back on the Ferry for the return trip. I was sure my watchers were pissed they never got to eat. When I returned to the Manhattan terminal, I hailed a cab and had him take me to the Empire State Building. This time I kept an eye out for the trailing vehicle and spotted it reasonably quickly. When I got to the entrance to the Empire State Building, I paid my driver and went in. I went to the ticket counter and paid for a ticket to go up to the observation level. I hung out for about 30 minutes, saw my watchers arrive, then went back down and got a cab back to my hotel.

My little excursion took about 3 hours, and I had seen all I needed. There were no cameras in the hall; yes, they had a room beside me. As soon as I got to my room, I called for a 1-hour wake-up call and did my entire sweep process again. Tomorrow, I needed to be at the 72nd Subway station to observe his confrontation with James Taylor. I was not interested in intervening; I just wanted to watch how he conducted himself. It would give me a better idea of what I may encounter at the Dakota on the evening of the 9th.

On the morning of the 7th, I planned to order room service and make it look like I was staying in the room. With only the mic active, I felt I had a good shot at slipping out the back of the building for a while. At 8 am, I placed my room service order and got my backpack ready for my departure. At 8:20 am, my room service was delivered, and I handed a note requesting a Hamburger and fries at 11 am. I thanked the service person and gave him a $5 tip. I made some noise while checking out my food and then turned on the TV reasonably loud. I went to the door where I had left a shoe jammed into it to hold it open when the service boy left, and I slowly entered the hallway closing the door quietly. I went to the opposite end of the hallway and pushed for the elevator. The car arrived, and I selected the 2nd floor. I got out and went to the far stairs that led to the back pool area and went down. I walked through the corridor to a service door that led to the garbage bins. From there, I simply walked out to the street on the opposite side of where the mobile unit was.

I walked over to the entrance to the 72nd subway stairs and looked around. My research indicated that Chapman would confront Taylor while walking up the stairs to the street level. I did a couple of laps around the immediate block to get a sense of the layout and, if needed, where I should run and where not to run. No one ever wants to run up an ally that is a dead end. After a few laps, I went back to the stairs and went down to the first landing. If I wanted to get to the platform, I would need to buy a token. I walked over to the ticket window and bought two tokens. I went to use my first token and went down to the platform level. It was moderately busy with a busker on the opposite platform. I would guess about 45 people were standing down there. I started to mill about, and when I reached the middle of the platform, I spotted Chapman. He was a heavy guy with little to no chin. He wore glasses and had a blue-looking half trench coat and a scarf of some sort. He was passing by me about 30 feet from my current location, and I wanted to get a different view and, if possible, make sure I was below his position when he confronted Taylor. He moved over to a pillar, and I lost sight of him. I stayed where I was and waited to see if he would emerge from one side of the pillar.

I stayed where I was for over 10 minutes and was about to move back to my previous position when I saw his coat poke out a bit. He was leaning against the pillar, but I only saw his jacket side. As I moved further right to try and improve my angle, Chapman started to follow another man, and I heard him say, "Mr. Taylor, are you James Taylor? Excuse me are you James Taylor mister?"

Strange how stories change over time and what I saw was James Taylor turn and say to Chapman, "Ya, I am." Chapman did not pin Taylor to the wall, in fact he simply appeared to go up and want to talk with him. Maybe this was different than their encounter in Derek 1.0's Timeline. I was not close enough to hear much and I was more interested in watching Chapman's demeanour. He was certainly excited and was talking fast, he may have been high or coked-up by his movements, but he appeared harmless from my position. Just a mixed up guy who just wanted to talk to Taylor like he was a fan. After about 3 minutes, Taylor said something and turned and continued to walk up to the street. Chapman followed him to the top, and I was about half a staircase behind. When I emerged into the sun, I heard Chapman who was about five feet from me tell another guy leaning up against the stair railing, "That is James Taylor, did you see him talking to me."

I was glad to see his actions. My research had me thinking he was a nut job and was about to blow. My read was he was a somewhat of a confused guy who was a music lover that was able to spot James Taylor in a crowd. I walked past and continued to the street corner and waited to cross. I turned and looked back; Chapman was walking the other way back towards the Dakota archway. I crossed the street and went back up to a street vendor and bought a bag of roasted peanuts from him. I walked to a spot by a garbage can and started to eat my shelled nuts and throwing the shells into the garbage. After about 20 minutes I finished my nuts and knew I had to head back to the Hotel to make the next room service window. Chapman was just walking around looking lost and could easily pass as living on the street.

I returned using the same route but needed to wait until a staff person came out the door. It did not take long, and I flashed my room key and entered while the staff person took a bag over to the garbage bin. I had to kill about 15 minutes, so I took the elevator to the second floor and went into an empty meeting room that had the door ajar. I sat at the table and was thinking about what my plan was going to be on the 8th. When it was getting close to the time I requested my next meal, I went up to my floor and waited at the far end. The service staff used a different elevator closer to my room. I figured that once I spotted the cart, if I started to walk from my location, I would get to my door after they would have knocked and announced themselves.

They were a few minutes late, but I spotted the cart and started to walk. I heard a knock followed by "Room Service." My man had just knocked again when I tapped him on the shoulder and showed him my key. I opened up the door and pointed to him where I wanted the cart put. I walked over to my dresser and grabbed a $10 bill and went back and tipped him. I said, "Thanks for bringing up my lunch."

"Thank you, sir, for the generous tip," he replied.

He left, I closed the door, and the fake-out was complete. I turned off the TV and decided to grab a shower. I was still thinking what I wanted to do. I needed to keep my watcher detail on their toes and guessing what I was doing there. I wanted to phone Maureen to see if she wanted to come here and hang for the night, but I knew better and would never want her to be added to my friends 'Who are they list' for their analyst to profile. I felt it would be easy to shake my watchers if I really wanted, but this was my first task where I would be personally confronting a person, I already knew had a loaded 38 in his pocket. I figured that if I let my watchers watch, if things got ugly, I knew they would intervene, and it felt good knowing I could have backup if I wanted.

After an evening popping around town including a great Greek dinner of Gyro meat, walk-in Central Park and eventually back to my room, I had decided I would try your way this time, Becca. I would always be prepared for a worst case scenario, but I would try the non-killing approach. I got ready at 9:30 pm and planned to walk there. I put the stuff I wanted in my Backpack and left my room. It took me a bit longer than I expected to reach the Dakota and just like I researched, there was a small scrum outside the front entrance. I counted a photographer and I think two fans with albums they must be hoping to get signed and Chapman was talking to another guy about 20 feet away leaning up against the brick work.

I spotted my 'backup' doing a stroll, arm and arm, looking like a couple out for leisurely walk. I figured I may as well do it now. I would have liked to see Lennon, but to be honest, I was not a big fan. McCartney on the other hand, big fan. I put my Backpack down about 30 feet away. I walked over and said, "Hey, aren't you the guy that got Lennon to sign his album earlier?"

"Ya, that was me," he replied with a proud grin.

"Would you have a second to tell me how I could get one too," I asked?

"Sure," he answered.

"My backpack is over there, why don't you follow me over," I suggested. Chapman was excited that I noticed his earlier interaction with Lennon and took my bait. He told the other guy that he would be right back. When I got to my backpack, I put my hand out to shake his and said, "Hi Mark, I am John and I have something for you."

He seemed to hesitate and said, "How do you know my name," with a suspicious look as well?

I reached in my backpack, pulled out a bible and handed it to him. He took it and said, "What the hell is this for man."

"I want to propose a trade with you Mark," I said.

"Well, there is no way I would trade my signed album for a bible man," he replied.

"I don't want to trade for the bible," as I pulled out the Rosary and handed it to him as well.

"What the fuck is going on man? Are you a nut or something," he said with some agitation in his voice.

"No Mark, I am John and Gloria said a prayer for you the other day asking that you come home safe and sound," I said with a smile. "Open the bible where the bookmark is and go to the section marked John 10:10," I instructed him. I knew he was both confused and trying to figure out how I knew his wife's name. I smiled at him and said, "Go and take a look Mark, this is a message from your wife."

He opened the bible and followed my instruction and I said, "Read her message to you."

He looked at the passage and then at me then at the passage. "Mark, please read it out loud," for us.

"The thief comes only to steal and kill and destroy; I have come that they may have life, and have it to the full," he read aloud.

"Here is my offer to you Mark; I will trade you this bible and that Rosary for the loaded 38 you have in your pocket. You will take the bible and the Rosary and go home to Gloria. And when you get home, you will get help to deal with what you are feeling. Just know that you are not alone and that you are special and loved," I preached to him.

I knew he was struggling to process everything, and I said, "Read the verse again my friend and tell me, do you love Gloria and are you capable of being a great man?"

He looked at me with my smile and I knew I had broken through when his eyes started to well up. I put my hand on his shoulder and said, "You will be a great man one day Mark, don't throw it all away."

"How did you know about my gun? How do you know my wife's name? Who are you," he asked with a pre-cry look of utter confusion?

"Just a friend Mark. Someone who knows what you are going through and someone that can see greatness in you. You're not a loser and sinner, you just need to be nudged in the right direction and Gloria asked for help," I replied. At that moment I was going to make the last move and if it failed, I would give him to my watchers. I put out my hand and smiled at him. He was processing everything and was visibly shaken by what I said. I maintained my smile and kept my hand out.

He looked at the bible verse again and then took the hand holding the Rosary and passed them to his other hand. He reached into his left coat pocket and started to pull out the gun. I was ready to pounce the first sign that it was turning towards me. When it was fully out, he turned it on its side and looked at it and said, "It was supposed to make me famous," he said softly.

"Mark, you are already a famous man. You just have to figure out why." I replied.

He handed me the gun slowly and then moved his position to a full ass-on-the-sidewalk. He was reading the verse again out loud when I got up and put the gun in my Backpack. I put the Backpack on and said, "Gloria is expecting you soon."

"How can I contact you if I need some help?" he asked with a puzzled look.

I just smiled and said, "Ask Gloria." I walked away and when I compared Tehran to this moment, this rated so much higher. In Tehran, it was truly just giving information at the right time; here, it was me confronting a known nut-job killer dude in person. On the adrenaline scale, this was a 10. I was laughing to myself for the next 10 or 15 minutes while I was thinking, 'If there was an award for the greatest bullshitter, I just won it'. If Chapman knew what a con-job I just pulled off, he probably would kill me! I was feeling pretty cocky right then. The task was masterful, extraordinary and even Oscar worthy entered the laugh thought zone.

I was cognizant that my watchers had just seen everything and were now aware I had a gun in my Backpack. Not to disappoint, my route home had a slight detour over to the Central Park Lake, a few minutes' walk. When I got there, I picked a private spot and opened my backpack. I put my hands in and removed the bullets and tossed them one by one in the lake. I then had to wait to make sure no one was watching other than my watchers when I would toss the whole gun into the lake. I would have preferred to break it down further, but I did not have a screwdriver to remove its yolk screw.

After the toss, I put the Backpack back on and walked back to the hotel. I planned to leave in the morning early to get back, as I had 2 finals I needed to study for and our usual practice tomorrow afternoon. The drive the next day was uneventful, and it gave me time to run through the whole task and try to determine an area that I could improve on or maybe missed. I got to the car rental place about a block from campus and dropped the car off. When I got to my room, I was spotted by Pete, a fellow Canadian defenceman. He came over and asked how New York was. I had told everyone I had an interview for a co-op position with a pharma company. I jumped on my bed and told him to grab a couple beers from my mini-fridge. We chatted for a bit, then I told him I had to head to the library for a study group. Pete was in a business admin program that was not overly difficult. He asked me what my Christmas plans were, and I told him I was flying home for a bit and then had an invite to fly over to London for a few days. Task 12 was rewarding on many levels. I was able to prove Rebecca's no-whack option is a viable option, but the downside was I would now have to listen to John and Yoko's music every December 9th *(Wonder if you laughed).*

The first term ended, and I was looking forward to getting home for a rest period. I forgot how much energy studying required. I was not sure what Maureen's plans were. So far, Tonka Boy, Elvis, Cancer work, Iran and now Lennon. Next up, next term; Stop 'Dutch' from getting shot!

Update – Luke Makes the Show!

(December 18th, 1980 – January 5th, 1981)

63 ***Living the Dream!:*** As a young kid growing up in Canada, there is probably no greater dream than one day making it to the NHL. I know for Luke and me, that was once a dream. Luke 1.0 found his way to the NCAA on a hockey scholarship, but new and improved Luke 2.0 finally made the show. He called me last week and told me he was scheduled to play in Detroit against the Wings this Saturday night. The game would not be televised in our area since the Leaf's were home against Montreal, which is always a big rivalry. There was no way I would not be there, and as an added touch, I was treating his family and mine to take a limo bus to Detroit to catch the game. Unfortunately, we would not see Luke other than at the rink since they were flying out right after the game. But it was going to be a special night.

I was home on Thursday, and we would be heading to the game Saturday afternoon. The plan was to drive to Detroit, have dinner, then get to the rink pre-warm up to see Luke for a half hour. I was out for a walk Friday late afternoon when I noticed the Gremlin at Rebecca's dad's hardware store. I assumed one of the kids must be there and maybe working. I walked by the front on the sidewalk to see if I could spot anyone. No Luck. I turned around and decided I would go in and pretend I wanted something to see if I could spot the Gremlin user. I walked in and looked around and could only see one man behind the cash register, who I did not recognize. I did a little mulling, grabbed a can of white primer, and went to the side counter to pay. The gentleman rang me through and asked, "Can I put that in the shaker for you?"

"Sure, that would be appreciated," I replied.

Just then, I heard a voice say, "I will look after that, Bill."

It is funny how we remember certain things by sound. For me, it has always been the voice. I could tell who a person was simply by hearing their voice. That is why it had always bothered me back in Derek 1.0 days when I forgot the sound of your voice Rebecca. I don't know when it happened; just one day, I no longer could remember what your voice sounded like. I contemplated the day I sent a text to your other self, who did not feel comfortable accepting a phone call from me, to send you a follow-up text asking you to leave a voice message saying hello. You have no idea how much that would have meant to me. But my more mature and not to creep you out any further inner voice declined the urge.

As you emerged into sight, my butterflies spontaneously exploded again. It had been 4 months for us. Our eyes met, and you gave me your cute smile, dimples and all. You grabbed the can of paint from Bill and walked over to the area where the paint shaker machine was. I made sure to wait for a few seconds so I could walk just the proper distance behind you so I could take in my favorite view. I always knew you knew I had this obsession with the world's most incredible butt, and today, you seemed to know exactly what I was doing, and I think you gave me your best runway model walk. Rebecca 1.0 once sent me a postcard with a Tennis girl walking towards the net with her left hand scratching a bare buttocks with her caption, *'From your 1st favorite set of.... 😊'*. You loaded the paint can in and turned it on when you got to the shaker. I watched as you set the timer and suddenly grinned when you turned it to the longest setting possible on the machine.

"When did you get back?", you asked.

"Thursday," I replied.

"How long are you home?" you asked as you started checking me out to see if there were any changes.

"I fly back out of Buffalo on the 5th," I replied as I, too, reciprocated the checkout.

"How was Harvard?", you followed with.

"It was a lot harder than I thought it would be. I had to study and learn," I replied with a grin. "How's grade 13 going for you?".

"Ok; I broke up back in October with my boyfriend and have been focusing on my plans for next year," you said with a bit of disappointment in your voice while moving your look towards the shaking can.

"I am sorry, Rebecca. I am sure that sucks having to go through that in your final year," I replied, pretending to show some empathy while inside; I was doing cartwheels and cheering the news.

"I did not meet anyone last term," I quickly added.

"He did not like that I was planning on going to Europe next summer alone for a few months to travel before I start University," you explained.

"Europe? When did you decide to make that trip?" I asked, already knowing the answer from Rebecca's 1.0 experience.

"I always wanted to see Europe and figured with going to University, I doubt I would have the ability once that part of my life started," you replied.

"Do you have dates yet for the trip?", I inquired.

"Yes, I fly out on June 30th and get back on August 15th," you replied.

I had a few things running through my head. Like are you going to miss July $8^{th?}$?; was there still a school Christmas dance? "So, I guess you won't be here for July 8th?", I asked.

You gave me a bit of a sad smile and said, "I am sorry, the Euro-pass I bought would not change the dates for me so I could accommodate our arrangement."

"Are you going with anyone else?", I asked. Rebecca 1.0 went solo, and I was hoping it would be the same.

"No, just me," you answered. Although Rebecca 1.0 had a friend or cousin named Louise, if my memory is working that was with her for much of her travels.

"Do you know where you will be on July 8th?", I asked.

I saw you doing some memory searching, and you replied, "I will be in Scotland, I think Edinburgh, that week."

"Do you have a piece of paper and a pen or pencil?" I asked.

You went to a drawer beside the shaker, pulled out a notepad and pen, and handed them to me. I said, "Thanks," and began to write something on the pad. I then tore off the top piece and gave it to you.

You looked at it and said, "The Witchery by the Castle, Castlehill, Edinburgh. What is this for?"

"Well, unless you're prepared to break our sacred July 8th, pact; I will meet you there on July 8th. Go to the front desk after 10 am, and they will give you a key to your room. I will meet you in their courtside restaurant for high tea at 11 am, and please honor my gramps and don't drink your tea black," I instructed you while giving you my best serious face.

"You're going to fly to Scotland on July 8th, just to keep our arrangement intact?", you asked with a grin.

"I made a sacred oath, and I will not be the one to offend Aphrodite unless you don't want us to keep our record flawless?" I replied while maintaining my best fake serious look.

You knew me well enough that I would be there without wanting details. You folded the paper and put it into your right front pant pocket. I looked at the timer, knew the shaker was close to finishing, and said, "Are you going to your Christmas formal at school?"

"No, my ex is going with his new girlfriend. Take a guess who it is," you replied with a forced smile?

"Your sister," I replied with my grin.

"Yuk, No, he's dating your best friend's sister," you said while reaching for a stir stick.

"What a small world; I am going on Saturday night with Luke's entire family to see Luke play in his first NHL game. You should come," I said, knowing your response.

"Wow, that is great news. Please say hi to Luke for me," which told me your answer. "My sister and I will be down in Ellicottville for a girl's week skiing from New Year's Eve to January 7th. It's not that far from the Buffalo airport. Why don't you come for a ski on the 4th before you head back to school?" you proposed.

I smiled and said, "That's a date. Look at me, tag-teaming the Hamlin girls." You gave me a look along with a pretend slap on the arm. Suddenly the shaker stopped, and you turned, pulled the can out, and put it on the counter.

"Your paint is shaken, sir," you said.

"Actually, miss, I never really wanted it in the first place. I am sure you can donate it to a worthy cause for me," I confessed.

We all have sometimes made a particular facial expression, some knowingly and some unknowingly. I think this was one of those times for you. You looked at me and then began to write something on the paint can sticker pad. I watched and waited as you wrote. You then peeled the sticker off the pad and stuck it on my chest right where my heart was and smiled with a first-time look for me. I looked down and had to interpret it upside down, and I was sure it generated a smile. The sticker had your address in Ellicottville and a smiley face with Merry Xmas and five x's under it. Not X's and O's, five Xs.

It felt like such a special moment that I did not want to disturb it with a suggestion that we should meet at the fort sometime. I simply smiled, turned, and left. I hope you remember that day like I do, Rebecca. I never asked you if that was the day or not, but I always wondered. For me, it was a great day. My girl was single, she asked me to go skiing, and we had a date arranged for next July. I knew that could always change if you ever fell in love with someone else, but I was counting on some of the original timeline stuff to remain unchanged.

Saturday was also a great day, and we all had a blast riding down to Detroit to see Luke. I elected to sit beside Luke's sister on the way down so I could get some historical intel on your ex. I didn't know him from my days at school and never did any prying when you were with him *(Wink Wink)*. The parents seem to be having a good time. I knew Joe was a super proud dad going to see his son play his first NHL game. The moms were busy gabbing about mom stuff, and Joe Jr., was fixated on talking to his date. JJ *(as we call him)* was more into golf than hockey and had secured himself a scholarship to Texas to play in the NCAA next year. You and JJ are the same age by roughly a month. JJ was dating a girl Sandra from his same year. I once thought that if we never became anything, she would be one to watch. I don't see that working; Sandy is far too sweet for JJ. I always figured JJ would end up with some young hot gold digger who came from money. I am sure he will find it in Texas.

The whole trip could not have been better scripted. We got to see Luke pre-game, the dinner was a hoot, and Mr. Mattson picked up the bill. What was the icing on the cake was Luke netting his first goal in the second, which turned out to be the game-winner that night. The team equipment manager, after the game, brought the puck over to Joe and told him Luke wants you to keep it for him. Yet, with all the excitement and being with family and friends, I still missed you. We did not talk over Christmas, and the only contact we had was you beeping your car horn the week after when I was out shoveling snow at the end of the drive, and you must have been coming from work at your dad's store. The time between Christmas and the 4th went fast. I loaded up my rental car with my suitcase and ski equipment and was on the road by 7:30 am. With the border, I figured it would take me 90 minutes or so. I had not arranged anything, but I had planned on you bringing my ski stuff back home for me.

I got to town which I already knew well and went to your house. I pulled into the drive behind the Gremlin, went to the front door, and gave a knock. You answered already in your ski outfit. White turtleneck, red ski pants, and I was sure a white jacket would be added.

"How was the drive," you asked with a smile.

"Easy. The border went quick," I replied.

"We are just about to eat some breakfast, so come on in and give me your gym bag," you directed.

I went in, and the place looked exactly like the last time I was here so many years ago. Felt like I was just here a few weeks ago. I said hi to your sister Brenda, and we chatted for a while. You finished getting breakfast together. We did our usual continuous 'pretend not to look' glancing, and it was extra special when you put your hand on my leg and squeezed it under the table while eating. I helped clean up the dishes with your sister, and then you showed me to my room. I changed and was ready to head over to the hill. You were always such a smooth skier to my more aggressive style. I was more a mogul guy, and you loved to carve up the slopes. The day skiing was great, and it was good to see you chatty on the chair lifts. I could tell you were excited about your trip in the summer and did most of the listening, which is rare.

I trust you recall me cooking dinner for us *(and your sister who was becoming a very attractive girl)*. I knew we would not be abandoning your sister tonight, and we all went out on the town for a couple of hours. When we got back, I could tell the ski hill wiped us all out, and bedtime was around 11 pm. I needed to be on the road by 9 am to make the car rental return and my plane. We had shared a bed many times before this but tonight was, for me, the best. I can remember you slowly opening the door and pretending to sneak in. You knew I was awake but still acted like I was still asleep. I went along with your role-playing, and when you slipped under the covers, I was complete! There was no sex that night. No groping, no rubbing on each other. We just assumed a sleeping position with me behind you; my one arm draped over you and your two hands holding my arm. I wanted to utter the 'L-word' in your ear, but there was no need. I truly felt it was understood without verbal confirmation.

I was smelling your hair when I heard what sounded like clapping. Do you remember me whispering in your ear, "Did you just hear someone clapping?"

I remember your response, "No, and go to sleep."

Funny how when I think back to that moment when I am writing this section, it did not dawn on me that the sound was very similar to the sound my friends made once when I told a joke. I was sound asleep when you decided it was time to sneak out to your own bed before your sister got up. As you pulled the covers back to climb out, I grabbed you, which I am sure you never expected, and pulled you back onto the bed face down.

I threw most of my body on top of you to hold you in place as I proceeded to pull your pyjama bottoms down just far enough to expose your perfect butt. I then quickly positioned myself in such a way to keep you pinned as best I could and placed my mouth on your left butt cheek. As soon as you knew what I was up to, your attempt to break my hold stopped. I probably gave you the longest hickey I had ever given you, and I wished I had asked you how long my brand remained on you.

When the sucking stopped, you returned to your prior getting out of the bed and turned and gave me a look that I read as, "How dare you brand me but thank you, and I love you." Well, that is how I will record it *(That got a smile, I am sure)*. I laid in bed for a bit, waiting to hear other doors opening and closing, and then I got up, made the bed, packed up, and did a bathroom stop to clean up. When I got to the kitchen, you were still in your pyjamas, and your sister was sitting having a bowl of cereal. I said good morning to all and sat for a few minutes. I spent most of the brief sit talking to your sister, and then I announced I needed to hit the road. During our walk to the door, you pushed me, saying, "Just go already," with me pretending to resist. I did not know what to expect at the door, a hug, a kiss, a handshake, or just a smile. When I turned to thank you, you came up and gave me a gentle kiss on the lips, grabbed my right hand, guided it to your butt, and pressed it to the cheek I just branded. You looked into my eyes, smiled and said, "It was a good visit."

I drove to the car rental place on cloud nine. I was so happy that you were single again, but I knew there were no guarantees that something unexpected could happen. I tried to justify that possibility as slowly testing and hopefully removing any obstacles that would interfere with our being one. If there was any one thing that gave me hope was the look in your eyes during our last exchange. Strange, now that I think about that moment at the door, I also heard clapping for a brief moment. I returned to school by 4 pm and was sound asleep in my bed for a needed power nap. I got up, grabbed a shower, and headed to the rink for our first post-Christmas skate.

A Great Day!

Task 13 – Dutch!

(January 6th – June 15th, 1981)

64 ***Taking one for the Team:*** Starting the second term was much easier than the first. Routines were in place, friendships were established, and classes this term were much lighter. Hockey was a needed distraction, and we had a competitive team. Our 'D' was solid, but our goaltending was shaky. I still had to figure out a schedule for my trip to Washington. My research provided me with many details, and my only real access to get myself into a position to intercede was to follow Hinckley to his location. There had been excellent eyewitness accounts, and I felt comfortable with precisely the steps I needed to take. I checked the hockey schedule, and we did not have a game on Monday but one on Wednesday. I knew I would be extensively interviewed after the event and had no idea if I would make it back for Wednesday's game.

School went as expected, and I still had the Lotus in storage until I knew the weather would not throw an unexpected snowstorm at us. I would rent a car. After thinking over the drive time of 7 plus hours each way, I decided to fly. I booked a ticket to arrive in the morning and leave in the evening, although I knew the return trip would need to be rescheduled. I had already concluded it would be a simple move for me to grab Hinckley's arm as he was going for his gun, and since he would already be moving into a kneeling position, it should be easy to topple him over and pin him while yelling gun. To aid my story, I joined a pro-union local liberal political action group and even volunteered for a couple of events to make it look legit. The American Federation of Labor and Congress of Industrial Organizations (AFL–CIO) was the group at which the President would be speaking. I ordered a ticket well in advance, and if anyone reviewed my activities before the event, they would assume that I was attending like many others. Although I am sure, a real analyst would have issues with a Canadian kid, going to Harvard playing hockey, joining a liberal political group, then deciding to attend some event in Washington would set off all sorts of alarm bells. Especially when you add in my Russian connections.

I don't need to bore you with the preliminary stuff, so I will get to the actual interceding. I attended the event and caught part of the President's speech but left and went outside at 2:10 pm, took out a pack of cigarettes, and made it look like I went out for a smoke. I walked around the hotel to the area to the west where I knew Hinckley would be. As soon as I rounded the walkway, I spotted him immediately. He looked exactly as was described in the eyewitness accounts. He was part of a larger group, and because I came from the direction of the hotel, the secret service person stationed by the wall ignored me. As I walked by, I smiled and nodded while still looking like I was enjoying a smoke. The time was now about 2:15 pm, and I wanted to get closer to Hinckley. He was about 5 feet 11 inches and of average build. I was sure he would be pumped up with adrenaline, which could give him some added strength. To be honest, my biggest concern was being shot by an overzealous secret service agent after I yelled gun.

After Chapman, I was thinking I could do anything! I was able to get myself right beside him on his left side. He would draw right, and I wanted to push his arm away as it would be the weakest position for him holding a gun. I removed the camera from my jacket pocket and put the strap around my neck. More fluff. It was now 2:25, and I heard the commotion as the President was leaving the side from the 'President's Walk' on Florida Avenue. I turned my attention from watching the area I expected to spot 'Old Dutch' walking from and was glued on Hinckley. I watched as Hinckley put his hand in his pocket, knowing he would pull the gun while dropping to the ground on one knee. My timing would be perfect, and I was just about to lunge when I felt a hand on my shoulder and a man said, "Mr. Devon?"

I turned and saw my old watcher from New York and gave him a push backward and turned back to Hinckley. That brief delay by the watcher allowed Hinckley to get the gun completely out of his pocket, and I had no choice but to launch myself on top of him. As I leapt, I yelled, "Gun," as loud as I could. As I was knocking Hinckley over, I felt a sudden burning in my gut area. I finally got a hold of his hand holding the Röhm RG 14 .22 LR blue steel revolver. The barrel stuck into my gut and my weight coming down on his wrist caused him to release the gun. By the time I was entirely on top of him, I felt another person landing on my back. It was my watcher. He yelled at me, "Where is the weapon?"

My own adrenalin had kicked in, and I turned my head to the side and said to him, "It's wedged between the shooter and me. I have his arms pinned. Reach under me and grab it."

As the watcher followed my instructions, I could feel him grab the weapon, and he pulled it out. By this time, two other secret service members had piled on, and one reporter was knocked over during the scrum on top as well. I felt a hand grab one of my arms and another hand grab the other. I was now being dragged off of Hinckley, and I felt two more hands grabbing my legs. I was now face down and taken to a clear spot on the sidewalk. I was dropped to the ground with my face taking most of the initial weight. The two hands on my arms moved to my wrists, and they were pulling my hands behind my back. I felt the handcuffs being locked into place, and then I was flipped onto my back. I could now take a look at the people who had grabbed me. I was trying to see if I could spot my watcher so I could get his attention as I could feel warm blood flowing from my head over my face and eyes making it harder to see. I assumed my head was cut open with the face first drop to the ground.

The one secret service agent closest to me brought his wrist to his mouth and said, "We have a possible gunshot wound and need medical assistance and an ambulance immediately."

I heard a voice say, "I know this man, and he is not the shooter. The other person was." As a side note, Rebecca, my hand never touched the gun, and fingerprint examination would show only Hinckley's prints were on the gun. My watcher crouched beside me and asked, "Do you know the other man?"

I was starting to really feel the pain in my gut area and said, "I think I am shot," with an added grimace and grin. "The guy's name is John Hinckley, he told me earlier; I thought something looked off, which is why I was so close to him." It was about then that everything went fuzzy, and I must have passed out for a bit. The next memory was waking in the ambulance and seeing my watcher sitting beside the medical attendant, who was busy putting something against my gut area. They had an oxygen mask on me, and I reached up and pulled it down. "Get me the secret service detail supervisor and have him meet us at the hospital." I returned the mask to my face and laid back. I was conscious for the rest of the ride, which was not long. This was my first gunshot wound, and it felt just like it's so often portrayed in the movies. It burned, and it stung and hurt like hell.

When we arrived, my stretcher was pulled out, and I was wheeled directly into emerge, and I could hear a bunch of people giving orders to others. I must have passed out again. The next memory was when I awoke in a hospital room, and I could see a nurse, a doctor, and two men in suits talking.

I did not recognize the men, but the older gentleman spotted me moving and walked over. "I am special agent Carruthers, and I am the senior detail agent assigned to this case. Special agent Mitchell over there is with the CIA, and we would like to ask you a few questions as soon as you feel up to it. I smiled and wanted a few minutes to survey everything in the room. I was on a few IV drips, and my chest was covered with electrodes and wires. The monitor information did not look that bad, although my systolic blood pressure was low. I said to Special Agent Carruthers, “Can I have a word with the doctor first, please?”

The agent gestured to the doctor, and he came to the bedside. “What’s the damage, doc,” I asked?

“You took a frontal entry gunshot to the lower thoracic area. The bullet luckily hit your vertabrochondral number eight before exiting the rear left side. A fragment clipped your kidney, but we expect it will survive. You are a fortunate young man. An inch either way, and it could have been much worse,” he explained, as doctors always do.

“Do you think I will be able to play hockey this Wednesday, Doc?” I said with a grin.

“You will be out in a week; that’s about the best we can do,” he added.

“Special Agent Carruthers, do you think I could have a private one-on-one with you for a couple of minutes?” I asked.

Special Agent Carruthers emptied the room and came to the front of the bed. “Ok, Mr. Devon, I am all ears,” he said, holding a thick file folder with my name on the front.

“First, thank you for getting me here and patching me up. I hope I won’t have to pay for the stay. Second, and most importantly, I want absolutely no press coverage about this. I am sure your investigation has already determined the man who told me his name is John Hinckley was most likely going to try and shoot the President and likely a nut-job, judging by his actions. I noticed him putting his hand into his right coat pocket, and it looked from my angle he might have been grabbing a gun in there. I am sorry that I waited to see if my hunch was correct and probably should have alerted you guys a few minutes before the incident. I am just glad that I was the only one injured. I want to propose the following to you; deputize me now as a member of your detail. Call me a junior member of your detail in training—that way, you are permitted by law to protect my identity, including from Congress and any congressional hearings. By deputizing me, you will be able to take credit for the intervention, making you guys look good. Finally, please get in touch with my school dean and give him a good story about why I have to remain in DC until I can return to school,” I requested.

Agent Carruthers stared at me, and I could tell he was mulling over the whole request in his head.

"I have had the opportunity to get a full briefing from Bruce Laingen and special agent Samuel. He was the agent who was assigned to 'observe' your activities. You seem to have a knack for ending up Mr. Devon in the strangest places. Apparently, you have some analysts frankly stumped. Regarding your suggestion, I will run it past legal to make sure we can accommodate your request. You certainly seem to have an excellent knowledge of how things work around here," he said.

"Must be all the recruitment meetings rubbing off on me," I replied with a grin. "And please, no calls to my family. That is the last thing they need to hear."

I guess we could say Task 13 was a success, all-in-all. I spent the next week in the hospital, but I had different people coming to interview me every day, and I must have answered hundreds of questions. Most answers I shot from the hip, and a few I could give facts. My political affiliation, pre-booking the ticket, and the camera around my neck helped give my story credibility. The only one that never bought any of it was Samuel. I made one mistake in that task. I turned and looked at Samuel before Hinckley had drawn his gun, and when I yelled 'Gun,' he had already seen in my expression what I was about to say before Hinckley had even drawn the weapon. He never forgot that, and it made him my number one concern moving forward. He was a nice guy, but I could tell he knew something was not as it appeared with me. On day 7, I was told I could be discharged, but no hockey until I got all the stitches out. I was assigned to a specific agency-cleared doctor back at school. My face was still bruised up from being dropped on it and made me look like I had been through 15 rounds with Mike Tyson, who would not have his first match for another four years.

A nurse rolled me out to the front to an awaiting Secret Service car. After all, I was now a special deputy of the Secret Service. I was being flown back to Boston on a 'company' plane. I felt great, and other than a bit of tenderness around the stitches, I felt I could play hockey. As we drove off, the driver said to me, looking in the rear-view mirror, "Sorry special deputy agent Devon, but we need to make a short detour," with a sarcastic tone and grin.

Not to be out sarcasm'd, I replied, "It's about time I got fitted for my suit and gun." I was looking out the window, and as a few landmarks passed me by, I figured out where I was being taken. As we drove down Pennsylvania Avenue, I thought about what I wanted to say. I chuckled to myself when I thought about the irony that here, I am saving one President, and in another 15 years, I would be killing a future President. My car pulled up to the gates, and we got the official nod to enter. I was taken to the rear Secret Service entrance, not the White House's official front. I smiled at the driver, who knew I had figured out what the detour would be. When I walked in the entrance, I was met by special agent Carruthers and my old acquaintance Bruce Laingen. I extended my hand first to Bruce, and we had a hearty shake and then the same with Special Agent Carruthers.

Bruce said, “Please follow me, Derek.” I was led to a small meeting room area and not the oval office. A meeting like this needed to be off-camera, and I did not need to see the oval office. We sat down, and a young lady came in and said, “It will be a couple of minutes. Can I get anyone a coffee?”

I replied, “Tea if you have it, please, and my friend Special agent Carruthers will have a coffee with just one cream, and my other friend Mr. Laingen will have a tea-like me with milk on the side.” As the young lady turned and left, I gave my friends a look, and the two of them just looked at each other and shook their heads with a minor chuckle. The drinks arrived, and we were chatting about the current state of affairs in Russia. They knew I had attended school there and had a friendship with a few fellow hockey students. I told them that Brezhnev was not going to last and that my bet would be on Yuri Andropov to replace him, but I also said that the person to watch was Mikhail Gorbachev, an up-and-comer. It was about that moment when the wall opened up, and in walked the President, old Dutch himself. He was a much bigger man than I thought, but he had that instant charisma when he entered a room. We all got to our feet, and Bruce was first to say, “It is a pleasure to see you again, Mr. President, and I would like you to meet the young man that was shot after your speech.” The President was all smiles and was in a somewhat politician-like mode when he extended his hand for me to shake.

“It is an honor, Mr. President, to meet you, sir,” I said, trying to stand at attention.

We shook hands, and the President said, “Bruce, good to see you, and thanks for taking the time to make the trip here as well. I have had the opportunity to read your file on this young man, and I thought it was fitting that you be here as well. Now, Mr. Devon, first, I want to ask how are you feeling?” he asked.

"Well, I am sure it looks like I just went a few rounds with Old Tex Cobb, but I assure you the look is worse than the bite," while sporting a grin.

"Thank you for what you did. I know that a very disturbed young man wanted to take a few pot shots at me over some crazy idea it would win him some actress's heart. I am sorry you ended up taking the shot meant for me. What I really wanted to ask you was, why no press or publicity? I am sure you know the type of attention taking a bullet for a president would mean. Imagine the fame and probably the wealth that would have come your way. Probably even some movie about you would be made."

I smiled as humbly as my smile could go, and I said, "I guess, Mr. President, that I prefer to keep my life as simple as possible. Yes, fame has its appeal, and I might even be able to get a date with Lindsey Wagner *(Ok Rebecca, I made that part up, but I made you roll your eyes)*, but I would have to give up my privacy. I have a lot of goals that I want to achieve in my life, and the fame you refer to would directly impact those dreams and goals. I am happy where I am in my life, with a great family, and good friends, and no one knows who the hell I am," I replied.

"Well, Derek, if you don't mind me calling you by your first name, most people would take the fame; very few would want the privacy. I know you are now a special Deputy on my personal detail," complete with a grin and a look at Special Agent Carruthers, "is there anything I can do for you" the President asked?

"Well, Mr. President, there is one thing I would like to ask you for. I know you will not always be President, and your job can change from republican to democrat or vice versa. I was hoping I could get some letter or document that could get me immediate access to the head or top person heading up intelligence, should in the future, I stumble on some intel that I would not want to have exposed to the lower levels first, and have to work its way up," I requested.

The President looked at Bruce and then at Special Agent Carruthers and then at me. He was thinking and had a semi-smile going. "Please leave that with me, Derek. I am sure we can figure something out for you. It would not shock me that in the future, as you do come to us with important information; you always seem to pop up in places that have proven invaluable to our country's security. On that note, gentlemen, I have a meeting I need to get back to, and I will have to say goodbye to Mr. Devon," as the President held out his hand for a goodbye shake. We all rose as the President got up and stood until he left the room through the wall. At that juncture, Bruce asked, "How was Montreal?"

We left together, and Bruce walked us to the door where my car was waiting. Special Agent Carruthers was going to drive to the airport with me as he had to fly to another location. We continued to chat about Russia all the way to the airport, and I was sure that information would end up in some report. When I reached my plane, we shook hands, and special Agent Carruthers smiled at me and said, "Don't forget Special Deputy Devon that you're on my detail. I expect nothing but exemplary service from you." We both smiled, and I knew it was purely a title for privacy purposes, and there would be no future pension. I enjoyed the flight back to Boston and I found an envelope on my seat and opened it. It was an overview of the story that was concocted for my absence.

You are far too bright, Rebecca, not to be asking yourself, 'Why did I not just do a simple intel dump, and no one needed to be shot or worse, killed? This was never about saving the President, this was only about getting me that letter I requested. You see, I will need that unfettered access in 1993, 1995 and 2001.

"Dutch"

Update – Finished First Year and Scotland!

(April 10th – August 30th, 1981)

65 ***The big moment!:*** When I arrived back at school, everyone wanted to know what happened to me, and I followed the planned storyline and told everyone about the car accident. Once I got cleared to play, all the guys wanted to see the scars that were still reasonably fresh. Our season was almost over, and I was able to play the last two games. I was a bit rusty the first, but I was in full gear by the second. The only issue I had to deal with was a call I got from Maureen. She asked me to come to New York the weekend I was scheduled to drive home. She was upset about something but did not want to discuss it over the phone. I called my folks and told them I had to delay my arrival home for a few days as I had a work placement interview in New York. I told Maureen I would drive there right after I packed up everything at school and stuck it in storage. Next year I was going to get my own place off-campus. I loved the dorm, but I did not have a task until Air India, and that was going to be an intel info play anyway. I would not get my hands dirty until January 1986.

I had the Lotus out of storage since my return to Boston and was headed to New York. Maureen was adamant that I get there no later than Thursday the 30th. I arrived at her apartment at 1 pm and had security call her room. I was cleared to head up and took the elevator to the 23rd floor. I walked down the hall to Maureen's door and gave a light knock. Maureen opened the door and immediately hugged me and did not want to let go. I could hear her crying softly, and I began to rub her back to try to comfort her, knowing absolutely nothing. She eventually let me go, wiped her eyes, and told me to come in. I followed her in and went to the kitchen to get a glass of water. Maureen's eyes were red from crying, and I said, "What happened to my Chemistry Partner?"

She gave a forced smile and said, "I'm pregnant."

Yes, Rebecca, that was exactly my first thought, and I can tell you it was a very uncomfortable feeling hearing those words with no warning. I was trying to figure out the right way to phrase my question when Maureen said, "I am about a month along, they say, and my 'keeper' (my term for the dickhead) told me to get an abortion immediately.

"Are you sure it is his?" I asked as gently as I could.

"Yes, I had only been off the pill for two weeks when he made an unscheduled afternoon get-together. I thought I made sure he did not get any of his stuff in me, but obviously, I was not careful enough. I had to go off the pill for an unrelated medical test on my thyroid for a few weeks," she explained.

I put my glass down, walked over to her, and held her for a while. Then I said, "What do you want to do?"

"I definitely don't want it, especially if it was his, and I have already booked an appointment at a clinic later this afternoon to have an abortion. I asked him to come, and he said it was all my fault and that I needed to look after it on my own," she said with tears starting to flow again.

"First, you are not alone, and second, if you want to go through with it, and it's ok if you want to change your mind as well, I will support you either way. But when you are well enough, I am driving you home for a rest and let you think about what you want to do moving forward with your life," I told her in a parental sort of way.

She smiled and just needed to be held for a while. I eventually made her a cup of tea, and she asked me how school went. After our tea, she took a shower and got ready to head to the clinic. "Thanks, Derek, for being a real friend. Funny how I don't have any close friends here. I have a few model friends, but none that would qualify as my Chemistry Partner," she said with a forced grin.

It was a tough afternoon for both of us. As a Catholic, it was even more of a difficult decision for her, and the fact her keeper was a real dink to her, I would certainly be suggesting she alter her future plans on our drive home. We returned to her place by 6 pm, and I ordered some Indian food for dinner. I could tell the whole process was unpleasant, and she needed to rest for a day or two. We watched tv and talked about the old days at school for a while, and by 10 pm, we headed to bed. The last thing I expected was Maureen wanting to have sex. I suspected it was more her feeling she owed me for what I did, which bothered me, but I knew she was under a lot of stress, so I decided to tell her I just wanted to cuddle tonight. The truth, Rebecca, was I did not want to have sex with Maureen anymore. At least, while I thought our situation had changed.

The following day, I got up and went for a shower. While I was in there, Maureen came in and joined me. I think she still thought I needed some attention, but I was happy just to wash each other and call it a win.

She spotted the scars and asked what had happened. I told her the story. I took Maureen out for brunch, and we talked about when she thought she would feel well enough to travel home. She thought she was able to go now, but I suggested one more day of rest. After brunch, we went for a walk, and she seemed fine from a physical perspective. I cooked a great salmon dinner, and we retired to the couch to watch a movie *(I chose 9 to 5 to keep things light)*. When bedtime came, I brought my workout shorts as my pj's and a t-shirt. I was reading a magazine article when Maureen emerged from the bathroom with nothing on and climbed into bed. I was concerned that she would try to escalate things again and did the only thing I could do, tell her I wanted just to cuddle again.

We left at 10 am the next day, and I figured I could get us home in about 9 hours. Maureen had not seen the Lotus and loved it. She asked what happened to Betsy? She told me the Lotus was so me. She was feeling better, I thought and was just happy to get home to family for a while, and she didn't want to hold hands either *(That's the story I am going with again)*. I often wonder how I could have ended up good friends with Maureen. As a guy, we always thought she could have whoever she wanted and were too afraid even to say hi. Even now, when she walks into any restaurant or shop, every guy takes a look at her, often at the expense of a woman's slap. The drive was uneventful, and I got us home by 9 pm and dropped Maureen off at home. She kissed me, and I told her if she needed a shoulder to cry on that I was only 5 minutes away.

I had a month before I would be taking off to Scotland, and I wanted to call you to say hi and let you know I was back. The family was happy to see me, but I was tired and told them I would tell them all about the school year tomorrow. I was out in no time and didn't get up until 8 am, which, for me, was unheard of. Dad was in the kitchen when I wandered out, and I sat and chatted about hockey with him. Mom then came in and did what all mothers do, make me breakfast. Bacon and eggs! Ann was not up yet, and I asked how things were going with Ann, and I got a bit of a mixed response. Ann was going to college, taking some 'arts program' of some sort. I don't think she ever figured out what she wanted to do with her life. We had breakfast, and I helped clean up. Before I left, I took my shirt off and showed them my scars. I wanted to get out in front of the issue since they would see me one day without my shirt. Mom was mad that no one called them, and I told her that I was fine and did not want to worry anyone and was out of the hospital the same day.

Dad had mentioned the old Caprice was having engine issues, and I told him I would take a look at it. I was looking forward to getting my hands under the hood for a while. I changed into my work stuff and headed to the garage. I parked my Lotus across the street at the church and pulled the car out. I had been under the hood and did not hear a Gremlin pull up behind. I was pulling all the sparks out to replace them when you came up behind me. I guess my shirt was riding up high enough that you could see my scars. At least the ones on my lower back. "Oh my god, what happened to you" you suddenly said rather loudly.

My head popped up and hit the hood with a good whack sound. You started to laugh while saying you were sorry for startling me. And I was rubbing the top of my head to try and reduce the pain. I turned and saw you, and that was all I needed. I grabbed you, gave you a huge hug, and said, "God, I have missed you."

You let me have the hug, and then you asked me again, "how did you get those scars?" I stuck to the plan and told you about the car accident I was in. With mom, I played it down as being no big deal, but I wanted a little sympathy with you so that I may have hammed it up a bit. Anyway, it's irrelevant since you know exactly how I got them.

I stopped working on the car, and you said you were on your way to work and spotted the Lotus. You only had 5 minutes, so I asked if you wanted to meet later at the fort. I hope you remember your answer. We agreed to meet at the fort the following weekend, Saturday night. That would give you time to figure out which girlfriend's house you would be staying over at. We exchanged a polite goodbye kiss, and I gave you a gentle pat on the butt, and you turned and gave me that 'don't touch the merchandise, mister' look with a grin.

I was so looking forward to seeing you Saturday that I splurged on a rack of lamb, a bottle of sparkling rosé wine, a couple of European cheeses, and a fresh French stick. Salad was always a given, and I even bought a bottle of port for myself. I went early to open the place up and get it aired out for your arrival. Once again, I was pleasantly surprised to see you had been using the place and had added a few homey touches, including new bedding. I had to do a few runs to replenish our fresh water supply and needed to climb up the tree to do some regular maintenance on the wind generator. I was up the tree when I saw you arrive on the deer trail. You still followed the route I showed you exactly. As you got close to the tree, I called down to you and said, "Hey, did my girl call Avon."

You looked up and gave me the 'really' look, so I finished up and climbed down. When I arrived in the fort, you had already inventoried my special supplies and smiled at me. It felt different. Almost like we were a happily married couple. We had not been intimate for a long time. In fact, since July 8th, 1979. We cuddled in Ellicottville and that one night at the fort last July 8th, but it had been a long time for us. I had a ton of butterflies going, and I think you did too. I made the dinner with you as my sous chef, and it was spectacular. I love a rack of lamb. We cleaned up, and I asked, "You want to go for a walk?" You gave me a look that I knew immediately said, 'There is only one place we are headed to after this'. I wanted to delay the big moment for a bit, hoping it would be even better, so I asked you how school was going. I knew you had a few weeks left and was curious if you *(maybe)* had any dates since Ellicottville.

The delay did not work a bit, and I wanted one last thing before we climbed into bed. I wanted a dance. I went to the bookshelf, flipped through a few tapes, and found the one I wanted. You know it was not Stairway to Heaven, and I would never insult you with Meat Loaf, knowing you now knew its origin when you read this guide. No, it was a song I also loved and would become even more popular in a few years, 'Unchained Melody' by the Righteous Brothers. I popped it in and rewound the tape to the first song. I made the tape, so I knew exactly where to find it. I pressed play and then turned with an outstretched arm. No Collins move, no re-do, or some attempt at some historical re-enactment. Just a first time. We held each other while constantly looking at each other's face.

Woah, my love, my darling
I've hungered for your touch
A long, lonely time………………

The only downside was its length. I wanted our dance to continue, but when it ended, I went and pressed the stop button. I was ready now.

I don't need to write about what we did next since you were there *(Big smile, girl)*. But I want to mention one thing that may be an issue, perhaps to both of us. I know it was always important for us to kiss at that magical moment, and I know that you now know that it started with Tina, but it was much different than with Tina. If I had to compare the two, with Tina, it was a five; with you, it was a Ten. What I never had with Tina was the ultimate emotional and spiritual connection we now had. Love was at best a 5, but 'it-love' would always be a 10.

I don't know if you ever felt what I felt just after we had reached that moment, but I felt we were giving a show to people. When we both collapsed into each other's arms, I could swear I heard a clapping sound. Keep in mind that I am writing this account near the end of August. For the past few months, I have been thinking about this in more and more detail. I'm sure I can recall you saying, lying on the bed, "That was noisy." I thought you were referring to you yelling, "I'm ready" *(Made you smile).*

In fact, if you search your memory, I had the same feeling each time we were intimate before you left for Europe. Slight variations but always the feeling we were being watched. And for me, it peaked in Scotland. I know Scotland was the most significant moment for us, and I would never want to detract or cause it to be anything less than our ultimate expression of our love for each other. Try to see if you can recall that moment. We had talked about our get-together at the Witchery being like a honeymoon. I will never forget that night. But if you think hard, I was sure as you guided me in for the first time, I could hear and feel like there was heavy breathing somewhere in the room. We were so into the moment that I never gave any external distraction a second thought. But when I returned and stripped the emotional cloud away, I had those feelings and concerns.

It had been almost ten years since my transference, and I guess I was now pushing 74. The first time I experienced the clapping sensation was when my friends and I devised a plan to allow me to assign laughter to them. That was the same type of feeling I was now starting to experience again. Almost exclusively when I was with you. I returned to my memory of the Hermitage Pond when we first went skinny dipping. You were straddling me, and 'our things' were munched together. We were having our first real kiss when you stopped and started looking around and said, "Did you hear that?"

I should have said, "Yes," but I was so consumed by that moment that I could only process one thought, "I am going to marry this girl." I heard that clapping sound now that I have returned and revisited that moment. But what would my friends be doing coming back to this divergent timeline? It was meaningless to them, and I could feel how pointless it was to them. The last time it was very noticeable for both of us, was my last night with you in Scotland. We had been exhaustively experimenting with our new form of showing our love for each other when we first used the 'L-word' at the peak moment. Then we collapsed on the bed, maintaining our connection for the next 5 minutes. You looked at me and said, "I think there is a concert going on nearby." Remember now? I heard the applause as well. I have since gone back and researched that night, and nothing was happening at the hotel or anywhere in earshot.

Moving forward, we will need to be intimate even more to test this new theory *(Made you smile).* The problem is, I could never tell you any of this. It is a concern because I can't figure out why it might be true.

Task 14 – Air India, Brinks-Mat, Harrods, and the 'Relationship'!

(September 1981 – June 23rd, 1985)

66 ***Living together apart!:*** We had a wonderful reunion at the Fort when you returned from Europe in August. You were about to head to university, and I was on my way back to my second year. I wanted you to change your school and come to Harvard. I told you I could pull in a few favors, but you will recall how you wanted to finish what you had already planned to do on your own. So, a long-distance relationship would have to be. I was sure that we would keep talking about your future plans over the next year or two. We made sure to try and split the home and away visits. It was the hardest scheduling I have had to do! The only other major issue was our decision to keep our relationship a secret from our parents, especially during the summer months. As far as they knew, we were just very good friends. It was also time for me to give my parents a winning Lotto 649 ticket. I will use my mom's birthday as the vehicle to deliver the ticket. I still remember my dad's call telling me about their unexpected windfall and offering to cover any of my educational expenses. They knew I was already doing well with my finances and didn't need their help.

When I decided to be an 'intercedealist' I always knew I would have to pick and choose events. It was a complicated decision-making process. I wanted to act with the Clifford Olsen serial killings, but it would have been extremely difficult from a logistics and potential exposure perspective. I only had 22 days to select, learn and then memorize. I decided to divide the tasks into two categories; One hands-on and the second was a pure information supply process. I know you are asking, 'why not do more information supply events since it was simply supplying intel before the event'. Two reasons: It would potentially expose me to the intel community negatively. When I say negative, I would have been watched at a level that would have removed my ability to do any of my personal 'hands-on' tasks. Second, intel info would have to pass through a vetting process, and that would also have made me a target by other intel factions since the analyst would have concluded I must be an inside man to have that intel.

Can you recall our return trip back to the Witchery in November 1983? That was not just a random, last-minute idea for us to go back and have our own re-enactment; it was also for me to drop off some intel to a friend, Miss Livingston. I was already on their radar and did not see any downside in ensuring I would remain on it. We went for a massage on Saturday and flew home on the red-eye Sunday. We decided to pass on the couple massage and get our own since we already were giving each other massages during our bedroom time. My massage was a 30-minute briefing with Miss Livingston. I recall you commenting after my massage when you got a look at Miss Livingston, "There better have not been any happy-ending or else," with your grin. Yes. Miss Livingston was a very attractive lady, but my heart was already under lock and key. During our briefing, I told her that I had obtained some information from my private sources, which I made her think was the Russian's. I told her there was a planned robbery on 26 November 1983 at the Heathrow International Trading Estate near Heathrow Airport in West London. The only lead name I had was a security guard Anthony Black. The second intel I provided was a potential IRA bombing that would occur on Saturday, 17 December 1983, in front of Harrods or Sunday, December 18th.

British Intelligence summoned me through a Canadian Intelligence contact. They asked that I fly over on January 8th, 1984. I was still on school break and was able to make the trip. Once again, Carl and I would fly over together. I was now suspecting that Carl was a British Intel plant here in Canada using his commodities brokerage as a front. I was met at the airplane hangar by Miss Livingston and driven to a remote country estate just outside Nottingham. When we reached the town of Nottingham, I asked Miss Livingston, "Would you mind if we stopped for a drink first? I am feeling a wee bit parched, and I know of a small pub not far from here." I guided Miss Livingston to the 'Ye Olde Trip to Jerusalem,' a public brew house in Nottingham which claims to have been established in 1189, although there is no documentation to verify this date. The building rests against Castle Rock, upon which Nottingham Castle is built, and is attached to several caves, carved out of the soft sandstone. These were reputedly used initially as a brewhouse for the castle, dating from the medieval period. What I loved about the place was the ceiling height. Most of the carved-out cave sections had a 5' 5" ceiling which in the 1200s was sufficient height for most of the patrons.

We stopped and went in, and I led the way to a private table at the back of one of the carve-outs. We sat down, and Miss Livingston asked me, "how do you know about this place?"

"I once came here with my wife," I said with a grin.

"But you're not married; you just have a serious girl, Rebecca," she replied with a puzzled look.

"Keeping tabs on me, I see," I said with a smile.

"And you should also be aware that we were fully briefed on your unfortunate injury in Washington," she added.

I was ok with the two governments sharing intel, and I was sure they were both trying to figure out how I came by my own intel. I had hung out in the summer for a week with Vlad and his family, who came to Canada for a holiday at my request. This was one card I had that would keep the intel analyst constantly guessing. I quickly spotted all three watchers when I took Vlad and his family to Niagara Falls. They all stuck out like a sore thumb. Canadian, US and British. I did not spot any Russians, so I concluded Vlad's dad was the government's eyes and ears for the trip. I looked at Miss Livingston and said, "I like to keep a few secrets from you guys."

I ordered the house stout and Miss Livingston had a glass of the house lightest ale. I was hungry, so we split a Yorkshire meat pie. Two spoons. We chatted about a lot of stuff that was not intel-related or shop talk. I found out Miss Livingston was engaged and had received a promotion due to the last intel dump I gave her. I felt my history with Miss Livingston was one that was comfortable for both, and that was why she was picking me up and not a lower-level person, which would have usually been the case. I felt some chemistry between us, especially over the last couple of years. I was much more mature and carried myself with extreme confidence. She started asking me about you, Rebecca, and I could tell there was slight jealousy. She was trying to figure out why you and not Maureen. I enjoyed keeping her guessing and asked, "Why the meeting out here?"

She looked at me and said, "You know that is confidential, and if I said anything, it would not look good on me."

"Then let's make a mini-pact. Give me enough info, but not everything, and I will extrapolate and figure out the filler. In exchange, I will agree if things don't work out for Rebecca and me, and you and your bloke split, we will go out on a date," with a bit of a playful grin.

I made her smile, and she said, "A surprise birthday party."

Ok then. Mission accomplished with my stop. I knew what I was walking into. A birthday party was an excuse for a full-on attempt to recruit me to come and work with British intelligence. Yes, there would be a bunch of pomp and circumstance one would expect at a birthday, but the underlying game was getting me. We finished up, and off we headed. The last leg of the drive was about 30 minutes, and we pulled up to a rather large farmhouse that was also an Inn. There were about a dozen other cars parked around the place. The beautiful, thatched barn roof looked like it was just re-done in the past month. The grounds were impeccable, and there was a cute stone wall encircling the main house, about three and a half feet tall and looking like it dated back 500 years.

When Miss Livingston and I entered the front door, a young man asked to take my suitcase. I handed it off, knowing they would be rifling it before it reached my room. I was led into a quaint sitting room to the left of the main hallway, and I spotted my old friend, Mr. Sunderland sitting in a leather wingback chair and sporting his bow tie as usual. "If it's not our Canadian guardian angel," as he rose to offer his hand.

We shook hands, and I took a seat beside him. It was just the two of us and one waiter type. He wheeled a cart over with tea and assorted sweets. He asked if I would like a tea, and I nodded. Mr. Sunderland asked me, "How was your drive here. Miss Livingston take good care of you?"

"Always. I had her stop for a pint at 'Ye Olde Trip to Jerusalem'," I replied.

Mr. Sunderland did not reach his position for being a mediocre intel man. As soon as I told him about the stop, he knew that I most likely already knew why I was here. Not that it would ever result in any fallout for Miss Livingston, he just knew me very well and probably saw a bit of him in me. He smiled and said, "A stout, I presume?"

"Always," I replied with my own grin.

"Well, the fun and games will be starting at 6 pm, and I look forward to a more formal get-together with you," as he got up and extended a hand. I retired to my room and laid in bed for an hour, mostly thinking. It was already around 3 pm, and I knew it would be a late-night, so I tried to close my eyes for a bit, but it was mainly lying there. I took a shower and got dressed for the gathering. I had brought one of Mr. Angelo's latest masterpieces and wanted to show off his work. Most of the guys had their own tailors, and it would be interesting to hear the comments I would get. I arrived in the main hall, and as I entered the room, I received a welcome British cheer, "Hip-hip-hooray, Hip-hip-hooray, Hip-hip-hooray." The room was full of about 30 people. I guess the wives got to attend as well, or fiancés in the case of Miss Livingston. I stood at the entrance and received the cheer with a wide smile. I knew I was the man of the hour, and any recruiting would be subtle and well disguised with the wives there.

I was taken to my seat, and I was sharing a table with Mr. Sunderland, Mr. Sunderland's wife, Miss Livingston, and her Clark Kent-looking fiancé, Mr. Pool who I had just met, and his wife, and finally, to my shock, Sandy and her husband, Calvin. When I first met Sandy's eyes, I could tell she was concerned about how I would react. We had stopped writing the month after you and I had the great fort moment, and I explained my new situation. I knew she was dating but did not expect to see her here and married, for that matter. It seems Sandy was recruited after my last visit with her. I won't bother you with any details. They tried hard, and I humbly declined all offers but one.

Mr. Sunderland on Sunday had a breakfast arranged for just the two of us. At breakfast, after saying how he admired my resistance to the many attempts, he told me, "On behalf of the British government, we would like to thank you in a 'very special' way, and you can thank Miss Livingston for the idea. We know your grandfather's departure when the war ended in 1948, and his family moved to Canada. Simcoe, I believe. We also know that he could not take most of his money from the country when he left, and he only received a minimal stipend as a pension. While we certainly cannot do anything directly for you as you requested, we would like to honor your grandfather with an honorary 'Special Apology' for the withholding of his money and give him what he would have earned had he remained here along with a special medal of 'Exceptionalism' for his work as a heavy machine mechanic during the war. We will fly you and your family here in July for a special ceremony and rooms at the Savoy, of course," with a grateful smile.

"Mr. Sunderland, I have never asked you for anything, and anything I may have done for your country was done unconditionally. I have always considered my roots as being English, and your offer would mean the world to my grandfather and my dad. You probably already know that my father was the breadwinner for the family when they first got to Canada, mainly because my grandfather had a severely broken arm and knew nothing about farming. I don't know if you could arrange one more thing; if you can't, I will certainly understand. I would love my grandfather; my mom, dad, and uncle could have high tea with the Queen at Windsor Castle? Again, if it can't be done, I thank you for what you have already proposed," I asked with a sincere look.

Mr. Sunderland returned a smile and said, "No promises, my boy, but I will make a few calls to see if that is in the cards. Have a safe flight home, and once again, I thank you for your service to our country." We stood and exchanged a handshake, and he departed; I sat back down when Miss Livingston entered the room and took Mr. Sunderland's chair. As she went to sit, I stood and grabbed her arm, drew her towards me, and gave her a sweet kiss on the cheek. She smiled and knew I was told it was her idea. We chatted, and I did not tell her about my added request. She was very excited about my accepting her idea, and this moment was about her.

So now you know the background about our trip to England that July. As much as I loved watching my grandfather and parents receive the British government's offer, there was no way it would happen unless I had you there with me. I know it increased the rumors with my family about just how close we were, but it was such a special occasion, I wanted my future wife at my side. The only thing that sucked was separate bedrooms. I want you to know that I wanted you to attend the high tea with the queen, but it was best that you did not know about that. My grandfather, uncle, and parents were sworn to secrecy about the tea with the queen, and I elected to pass so I could be with you for the morning. But you don't know that at 6 am, I heard a knock at the door, and a young man holding riding attire said, "Here are your riding clothes, sir; please change, and I will take you to the stable."

Bloody Sunderland: I knew what he arranged, and I was on cloud nine. I got changed and left with the young man who drove me to the stables. It was a short drive but afforded me a different view of Windsor Castle. When I got to the barn, I was led into the main building, where another young lady introduced herself and proceeded to introduce me to Sir Lancelot. Not the knight, the horse. A beautiful thoroughbred stood at just over 16 hands and had highly developed front chest muscles. She led Sir Lancelot and me to the rear of the barn and offered me a leg up; I was in full English attire, complete with red jacket and helmet, vintage Jodhpurs Breeches Pant, and a leather crop. While I preferred western, I was also very comfortable with the English mount. As Derek 1.0, I had participated in a few fox hunts in my youth. My horse handler told me to ride to a gate and wait for my fellow rider.

As I waited, I spotted another rider approaching, and she was riding traditional side-saddle. I knew who it was long before the arrival and just sat there and smiled. As my riding partner arrived in front of me, the queen said, "Good Morning Mr. Devon. I understand you will be accompanying me for my morning ride."

"Please forgive me, your Majesty, I am not sure the proper protocol and whether I should dismount and offer a bow?" I asked.

"You did just fine with your Majesty, and I would not want to force you to have to mount Sir Lancelot on your own. He can be a nasty boy at times. Well, let us see how well you ride," as she turned her horse and began to ride out toward the pasture. So, now you know something I never told you before. I spent the start of that morning having a ride with the Queen. We rode for about 45 minutes, and for someone approaching 60, she could sit an excellent seat. Side Saddle was always an awkward look for me, but the queen rode wonderfully. We did not talk much, and the few times we rode side by side, she acted more like a historian and travel agent telling me the history. It was something I will remember for the rest of my life, and I am glad I could finally share it with you. I hope you are not pissed at me for ducking out for a ride rather than sneaking into your room at 6 am.

On the flight home, I had never seen my grandfather have such a 'glow.' That was the most incredible day of his life, other than his marriage to his wife, who passed away long before I was even born. While I tried to test the waters to see if you were interested in joining the 'Mile High Club,' I am pretty sure by your look that you knew what my various head gestures meant and that it would give away our relationship status. It was a small plane, after all. I had a year to kill before my next intel dump, and I was heading into my final year. As you know, I have been working as a research assistant 'undergrad' for the past year and will continue in that job for the remainder of my term. I was working on introducing some needed technical expertise on an experimental delivery system for the target antibody formula Dr. Crossgrove was developing. Since entering Harvard, I have continued to keep my relationship active with Dr. Crossgrove.

The technology I was developing was a nano-emulsification process that would allow Dr. Crossgrove's formula to be administered orally. I knew I needed to devise a 'ghost' method to administer the experimental doses to our moms. We also decided to end our secret relationship and let our families know. The other thing I need to tell you is my decision to put pressure on you to change career paths. Business Administration was not your calling. I know you thought it was having been exposed to your family's entrepreneurial life—especially your dad's business sense. You were a natural for the pharma industry. You had great people skills, and no one had more empathy than you. While being a hands-on healer was not for you, managing the healing process opportunity would be. That recruitment meeting you thought was the result of your favorite professor at school was me. I arranged for that meeting and interview, and I also manipulated your prof indirectly to select you for that interview. I hope you are not mad or disappointed with me, but I wanted you to be in a position to help others and be closer to me. I could assist, and you would have the ability to sell it.

So, I decided that at our July 8th annual rendezvous at the Fort, I would propose to my 'It-girl'. I don't need to rehash the whole event, but I wanted you to know that this was the single greatest day ever in my two lives. I wanted it to be simple, no huge show or staged pre-dance stuff that I like to do—just a simple expression of my love for you and, hopefully, your acceptance. The night before I got down on my knee, I had a memory dump of my life with Rebecca 1.0 and the differences this time. I would never know what could have been, having never met at the Collins that night. I wondered if we would, at some later time, have some chance encounter that would have led us to an eventual date. I knew I did not want to be in your high school learning phase. I wanted to know you after that. And this time, as much as I hurt at times not being your boyfriend through high school, watching you be with other guys, I knew that if it were meant to be, it would occur on its own schedule. Not mine or yours.

But the main reason I am bringing this up with you now was my concern that my old friends may be spying on us. Or even a bit scarier, the post-transference friends finding out they were now in a divergent timeline and no longer on the leading edge as they would have thought. How would they react to such a discovery? Not to take away from that moment when you replied, "There is no one else, and there will never be anyone other than you, my 'It-boy'. We had officially become a true 'it-relationship'. That kiss we shared right after we proclaimed our love for each other, I heard voices this time. It was like a bunch of people trying to whisper secretly but were not doing a very good job hiding it: no clapping sound, tiny voices. I wanted to ask you if you heard anything, but you know I could not say anything. I kept looking for any sign or response from you that may suggest you heard or felt something. When we finally consummated our love in what was one of the best or the best 'Kiss me now' moments, I could not shake that feeling we were some sex show for prying minds.

I know you wanted to finish university before we would have a wedding, and I agreed that we would do a bit of a show for our folks by pretending to go on a few dates and keep our planned marriage to ourselves. After the first time you came for dinner at my folk's house, I never told you that my mom later that night said to me, "It's about time." A mother's instinct, I guess.

The year went fast, and it was great that our home and away visits could now include family activity time. I finally got to ski with my girl in Ellicottville, not in secret.

It was coming up to May, and I had some work I needed to do in prep for my intel drop to my contact at The Canadian Security Intelligence Service (CSIS). My research showed that there had been several individuals who approached both the RCMP as well as CSIS, and both complaints were ignored as being unsubstantiated. I was concerned that my intel might receive the same reaction, so I decided that I would deploy a backup plan as well. My backup plan would include a self-contained box that houses a fully automatic homemade .22 long rifle and a remote activation mechanism. My range for the remote activation was just over a kilometer, allowing me to position myself far enough away that I would have ample time to depart the area. If I could not get the RCMP or CSIS to intervene and search the plane as planned, I would have the option to use plan 'B' to shoot out the plane's tires while it taxied to the end of the runway. Montréal–Mirabel International Airport has a unique configuration where its two runways form a 'V' shape. The problem for me was knowing which runway would be utilized the day of the flight. I did not want to rely solely on forecasted wind reports, so I built two boxes. One for each end of each runway. That way, I would be able to cover both options.

I built my boxes at the Fort and did my best to conceal them from you. I had always wondered if you had spotted them at some point when you were at the Fort. I needed to leave on June 20th, 1985, and drive to Montréal-Mirabel International Airport to do some recon and deploy my backup boxes. I had also sent via a courier an information package addressed to Mr. Gordon Edwards, who was a CSIS agent I had selected as the receiver of my intel. If they took my intel seriously, I would see the flight would be canceled at the Montréal-Mirabel International Airport. If it were airborne, I would assume it was most likely ignored like the other intel they had.

The plane arrived in Montréal-Mirabel International Airport at 01:00 UTC (9:00 p.m., 22 June). There, it became Flight 182. Flight 182 was scheduled to depart for London Heathrow Airport at 1:00 am as a 'Red eye' flight, en route to Palam International Airport, Delhi, and Sahar International Airport, Bombay. Three hundred and twenty-nine people were on board, including 307 passengers and 22 crew. Captain Hanse Singh Narendra served as the captain, with Captain Satwinder Singh

Bhinder as the first officer and Dara Dumasia as the flight engineer. Many of the passengers were going to visit family and friends. I left the airport at 8 pm and repositioned myself at my watching location, allowing me to see what runway would be used. I knew the plane was not scheduled to depart for a few hours, and I needed to periodically move my location to avoid anyone becoming concerned with my stationary presence. My box had a remote trigger device with a 3-second delay signal. I had calculated that I could take a maximum of three separate rounds at the plane. Each round would use approximately 20-round bursts.

I had my binoculars out, and every 15 minutes, I would look at the plane at the gate to see what activities were taking place. Just after 11 pm, I noticed the ground crew starting to perform their routines, and that told me that CSIS was not taking my intel seriously. I had increased my watching after 12:30 to almost steadily watching with the binos. Based on my weather analysis, I figured they would likely use the east runway. I moved my position slightly to get a better view of the end of the east runway. The plane was loaded and was being pushed from the gate. I knew I had less than 10 minutes. I armed my remote and waited for the plane to reach the needed location for my first burst. The plane suddenly stopped before entering the main taxiway. I continued to watch, and suddenly the plane changed direction and headed in the opposite direction. Thank God CSIS finally intervened. I was relieved and planned to retrieve my boxes once I observed the aircraft was being searched.

It would turn out that my short-term relief was just that, short-term. The plane was not returning to the gate; it was now heading to the west runway. Great, now I had to relocate my visual angle. I decided to leave the car and head on foot to the best angle for me to see the turn at the west runway. The plane and I were having a bit of a foot race, and I was getting concerned I may lose that race. I lost sight of the aircraft for a brief moment, and when I finally reached my location, I saw the plane start its turn. I took the remote and armed it. Three, Two, one, press and hold for 3 seconds, then release. While the boxes did a fair job of muffling the sound, I still could hear the rapid-fire. The plane was still rolling, and I pulled the remote trigger again for three seconds; the plane suddenly stopped. I waited a minute to ensure it was not moving, took my binos, and looked at the landing gear area: Bingo, direct hit. Every tire was flat. I turned and ran back to my car. Time to leave before all the action started. I knew CSIS would be notified of the attack on the plane, and with them already sitting on my intel and other intel, I assumed they would have the plane do an emergency evacuation right where it sat.

My boxes would stay, and I knew they would be dissected to figure out why someone would do such a thing. I also assumed that once they found the bombs in the luggage, they would be arresting the list of people I had identified for them in the info I sent in my intel brief. When I built my devices, I selected gun parts from all over, including most from the USA. I assembled my gun with just parts, never having bought a complete weapon. Any identifying marks were removed, and there were no fingerprints anywhere. I was proficient at my work and was proud that I had accomplished Task 14. Now back home to my girl!

[On October 14th, 1985, I was riding down to the Fort when I noticed two cyclists behind me that didn't look like they rode much. My Spidey sense went off. If I were being followed, I would change my route today and see how good a shape they were in. I quickly picked up speed heading down the Mineral Springs hill and was at my top speed. As I rounded the last bend at the top of the last hill, it allowed me a clear view of the turn at the Gatehouse, I quickly began to add brakes. Two vans were parked at the corner facing each direction, and four men were standing at the front with their arms raised, indicating I should stop. As I slowed and was about 30 feet from them, I recognized one of the men as Mr. Gordon Edwards. When they lowered their arms, and I coasted up to them with a smile, I knew I was not about to be gunned down. I stopped, dismounted my bike, and said, "Hello, Mr. Edwards, what do I owe the pleasure for this meet and greet?"

"Well, Mr. Devon, we would like to ask if you would please come with us for a meeting," he asked with a bit of a serious face.

"Right now, or can I finish my ride and meet you somewhere for lunch?" I asked.

"Unfortunately, right now and we will put your bike in one of the vans," he explained.

"I am a bit sweaty already, so I will have to apologize if I stink a bit,", I said with a grin to my escorts.

I handed the bike off to one of the other gentlemen and was directed into the van's middle seat facing the direction I was riding. As I got seated, another of my escorts handed me a towel, and I said, "Thanks."

The encounter and departure from the corner in front of the Gatehouse lasted maybe 3 minutes. I was now on Governors Road heading towards Dundas and asked, "Where is the meeting, Mr. Edwards?"

"We have a location downtown Hamilton that we are heading to," he replied.

I would typically try to do a little chit-chatting to lessen the tension, but this time felt different, so I just stayed silent like my escorts. We arrived at Jackson Square, which I knew intimately from my Tina days, and as we drove through the underground parking lot, the van came up to a steel door that I had always thought was access to some utility room, and it opened. We drove in, and it was another parking area with several different federal vehicles with various markings. We all got out, and I was escorted to an elevator and went up to the 9th floor. As I exited with my new buds, there was a large meeting room directly in front that we entered. I was told to please take a seat in a particular chair, and another young lady approached and asked if I would like a coffee or tea.

“Coffee today, please, and the usual,” I replied with a smile.

I sat, and in short order, my coffee arrived when a large contingent of people entered the room. I counted 6 East Indian-looking individuals and one female who was Indian. Mr. Edwards’ group consisted of 5 gentlemen who were new to me and, to my surprise, my old friend Mr. Samuel from the CIA. When our eyes met, he smiled, and I got up, walked over, extended my hand, and said, “Great to see you again. I trust my detail is doing excellently,” with a smile.

“Good to see you, Derek; you’re looking like you are keeping yourself in shape, but I would have thought you would have changed into something more appropriate,” he replied with a grin.

Another man’s voice said, “Please, everyone, take a seat and let’s get this started.”

“My name is Mr. Fielding, and I am a special attaché to Director Thomas Finn. In addition to Mr. Samuel, who is sitting in at Mr. Devon's request; thank you, Mr. Devon, for volunteering to sit in at this meeting. I would also like to welcome the Indian Intelligence members that requested this meeting.

After Fielding spoke, each person introduced themselves except for me. Samuel identified himself as being strictly here as an observer just in case it was determined that there would be a need to request something from the USA during the meeting. After the first few minutes, I knew this was related to the Air India incident. I was most interested when they started to discuss the ‘incident’ at Montréal-Mirabel International Airport. The papers had reported it as a plane having a major tire malfunction resulting in the flight being rescheduled. There was never any mention of any bomb being found on the plane. The agent heading up the Mirabel part started to describe the actual events that night/early morning.

"At approximately 1:30 am, as the plane was taxing to the west runway, a hidden device approximately 200 yards away in a treed area was remotely activated. In the box was a sophisticated, fully automatic, modified 22-long rifle that was used to shoot out the plane's tires. The trajectory of the weapon strongly suggests that it was never intended to do anything but shoot the tires of the aircraft. We have thoroughly analyzed it, and there is a detailed report in your accompanying brief. As you are also aware, after an extensive inspection of the plane, two suitcases contained homemade bombs with a timing device that would have most likely resulted in the plane being downed mid-flight. Before the flight, our department had received information from two known individuals and an anonymous brief sent by courier specifically to Mr. Edwards. We have been conducting a thorough investigation, and as a result of our current intel is why we are meeting today. I want to ask Mr. Ahuja from the Indian delegation to now update us on their information.

Not to bore you with too much detail, Rebecca, I will jump to the information included in the file they gave me. The first two pages told me all I needed to see to understand why I was there. First was a security camera photo of me in a side profile picture at the airport time-stamped at 7 pm. The second was a security photo of me at a gas station about 1 hour from the airport, time-stamped at 3 am. Finally, there was a picture of me exiting a gun repair shop in Boston carrying a bag and a copy of a cash receipt for purchasing six boxes of .22 long rifle cartridges from 1983. Attached to the front of the two pages was a handwritten note that read;

Dear Mr. Devon,

I recently spoke with two close friends of yours, Mr. Sunderland and Mr. Taylor. It was a very insightful discussion, and I would like to extend my thanks to you personally for your assistance, and I hope we can build on this relationship in a meaningful way.

Regards,

Ted

What was apparent, Rebecca, was that the intel community wanted me to be aware they knew who I was and what they seemed to know I had accomplished. This was their way of telling me things would be different between us now. That would mean constantly watching for surveillance, and all my travel would be heavily monitored. They still had no idea how I obtained my intel, just that I was willing to help, even when they ignored it. The way they brought me into this meeting told me they were willing to work with me to a point, but it was their job to continue trying to find out how I did what I did. I was ok with that arrangement for now. When Mr. Edwards finished his presentation, he introduced me as an outside contracted analyst working with Canadian, British and USA intelligence agencies. He then said, "Mr. Devon will discuss his analysis of the couriered intelligence material and what additional information he may have uncovered."

“Thank you, Gord, and welcome to our visitors. The only additional information I have recently identified is the following: The Babbar Khalsa separatist group is the primary group behind the activities here in Canada and, I suspect, in India. Mr. Ahuja, you will want to locate Ajaib Singh Bagri, who will be accompanied by Talwinder Singh Parmar. They are planning an attack on your government as we sit here; As the courier package suggested, Inderjit Singh Reyat should be closely surveilled, and he uses a location not far from his place in Duncan, BC, to conduct bomb tests. That is all I have at this time,” I replied.

The meeting ran about 2 hours with one break; by the second hour, I felt like I was part of the team. When we got up for a break after the first hour, Agent Edwards came over to have a brief chat with me. “I want you to know that the couriered information that I received was appreciated, and I am sure you have concluded with my presence here that I was not the one that decided not to act. My prior boss, I believe, is now working at an Embassy in central Asia.”

“Well, Gord, I hope you don’t mind me calling you Gord now; I assumed exactly that. But I would be grateful if you could privately convey a message to Mr. Finn. Please tell him that he should not proceed with mass wiretapping. There are less than friendly people in the BC office, and I will assume he has stepped on a few toes in the past month or two. He also needs to go back and tidy up his wiretap requests, especially those related to Singh,” I requested.

“I will do that as soon as we get out,” he assured.

“Are you in town tonight?” I asked.

“Yes, we fly out tomorrow afternoon,” he replied.

“Great, let’s have dinner tonight at my favorite steakhouse, Shakespeare’s. On me,” I said.

“Ok, sounds great,” he replied. As we stood there chatting, Agent Samuel came over to say hello.

“Hello Derek, thank you for requesting my attendance, and it’s great to see you’re doing well, although I am not sure if your clothing choice is appropriate,” he said with a grin.

“Hi Chris, this is Gord with CSIS, and I guess you can call him your Canadian equivalent. We are going out tonight for a steak dinner; Any chance you can join us, purely social since you are in my territory now,” I invited.

“I happen to be laying over tonight and appreciate the invite, provided I can charge it to Uncle Sam,” he insisted.

“Well, I am not going to argue with the CIA, are you Gord?” I asked.

“I would not want to insult our neighbor,” Gord added.

"Regarding the invite today, that was courtesy of Mr. Sunderland, not me, although it's great to see you."

So, we all met for dinner, and it was different to finally have a chance to get to know these guys that had been in my life for the past few years. I even had a chance to have a few laughs discussing my trip out to Staton Island with Chris. I did not know how long those relationships may last when I wrote this, but for now, I would consider them friends.

Task 15 – Bernard!

(July, 1985 – December 1986)

67 ***Getting my hands dirty!:*** I could not believe that we would finally be breaking the news to our families about our engagement. And I am sure you have figured out who sent your mom the birthday card with the lotto 649 ticket. I knew your folks were doing just fine in the financial department, but I figured, if your dad thought he needed to pay for your wedding, then why not help out, especially with the size of the reception. Besides, they would be family soon. Where and when was all on you as long as we got to do the honeymoon on the Amalfi Coast on a Sailboat that I would charter. Trying to narrow down the invite list would be the greatest challenge.

It was finally time for me to get my hands dirty, really dirty as far as the tasks are concerned. I remember years ago being stoked to do this one, but as I have matured and am now about to become a husband, my inner niceness was at war with my inner 'Paul Kersey'. I had long ago come to accept my decision to simply eliminate Bernard from the face of the earth. My struggle was how did I want to do it. A few years ago, I was still all gung-hoe on the plumber's torch, but I seem to be a bit soft these days and was thinking maybe something simple like a good old fashion OD.

These days I was working almost fulltime with Doc Crossgrove and his team as a senior grad student while working on my Masters. I was now monitoring our mom's blood samples myself using the marker test I developed at Harvard. My best shot for success would be my ability to start the treatments as soon as the first markers are detected. What we have learned in the 2020s, was cancer that our moms had to deal with, use to lay hidden for many years as a hidden memory cell. These memory cells contained the information needed to create the cancer cells and would continuously multiply slowly over time. In our current timeline, everyone was focused on trying to detect specific cancer cells and then attack those cells using chemo or radiation. My 2024 knowledge was going to allow me to locate those memory cells first and then use a targeted mRNA strand that would seek out those cells as hosts to a nasty bloater cell. Those bloater cells which I like to call them, are sitting ducks to our own immune systems. So, the theory is, that once I detect the presence of the memory cells, then add my mRNA concoction and then let the body do its own thing.

Task 14 I had decided would take place at the beginning of October just as the leaves would be falling. I already recon'd Bernard's house and

I had also surveilled him a couple of times already. Strange that whenever I saw him, all I could do was remember the videos that had been shown at his trial and fight the urge to go back to the plumber's method. He used to like to go out on Saturday night to nightclubs and he drove an old Chev 4-door. My plan was simple. I would place a needle device under his car seat and when he sat down, the needle would inject him with a 500 mg dose of propofol. By the time he figured out he just sat on a needle, he would become unconscious.

Once he was out, I would drive the used van I bought a year ago beside his car and transfer him from his front seat into the van using a highspeed electric winch. All I needed to do was place a strap around his midsection and hit the remote. I did not care about injuries he may sustain with such a violet transfer, just speed was important. The entire transfer took less than 3 seconds. Once he was in the van, I would load his car up with a few gas cans and place a time-delayed device that would go off in the early morning. I would then transport him to an awaiting plastic 45-gallon drum I had buried in a remote wooded area a few years ago allowing for sufficient natural growth to return and hide the barrel burying activity. The barrel had a couple of bags of lime in the bottom, and I would be adding water to the top. At the bottom of the barrel was a cellulose bung that would be dissolved by the lime after 60 days allowing the liquified contents to seep into the ground. The lime would completely dissolve Bernard including his bones, teeth, etc. I had loaded some carpet cleaning equipment and supplies into the van and had a few rolled-up old carpets in the back as well. I would roll up Bernard in one of the carpets and add it to the pile at the bottom just in case I was ever pulled over. Any inspection of the rear of the van would simply look like I was in the carpet cleaning business.

I had already arranged to drop the van off at a wrecker the next day and negotiated to have it cubed up for a film I told them I was shooting. I was paying them for the filming plus they got the scrap value of the van. Well, Rebecca, I can now report that you are going to be marrying a murderer. It was harder than I thought. Not the actual killing but having to convince myself that what I had become was for the greater good and was not something I actually enjoyed. When my conscious started to bother me, all I had to do was remember the tapes of the murders he committed or would have committed, and I returned to my good place. I guess only time will tell if this would be a future deal breaker for us!

Update – Wedding, Task 16, and my 'Friends' Part I!

(January 1987 – May 1988)

68 ***Win, Win, and lose!:*** We finally had time to focus on ourselves, and I was so looking forward to the wedding. I was now 26, and you would be 25 come September. But the most meaningful thing to me was our July 8th night at the Fort. It used to be pretty simple; just ride my bike to the Gatehouse and go to the Fort. Over the last few years, I have been surveilled by my CSIS buddies on several occasions. I was starting to think I was part of a standard new recruitment training class at one point. If you could stay with me, you passed, and if you couldn't, you took the course over. I was now using several different routes to get to the Fort, and I also had to teach you a few options, if you recall. No more bikes at the Gatehouse meant it took us up to an hour to reach the Fort once we lost our followers. Most of the time, it was more like a game, but I wanted things simple and quick today. Today for me, was Martin Side Road, and then ditch the bike at the old Iron Ore bog west of Eneral Griffin's place. Then hoof it from there. Sorry boys, you failed today!

I recall your route was the old Train Station, the east headwater trail, and then up to the top of the hill and wait to see if you had company. I only recall one time a year ago spotting a helicopter buzzing about, but I did not think I was currently at that level of demand. I was there first, and I still get butterflies when you arrive on the lift. I hope that we will both continue to have the same feelings we still enjoy now for many years to come. After our big hug and kiss, it was our usual shower time together. I had no idea what you wanted to talk about that night. Thinking back, I missed a few signs, I guess. After our Rack of Lamb dinner, we retired to our bed to sit and chat about the wedding in detail. August was coming soon, and while I knew you had everything looked after, we still needed to pare down the wedding invite list by 12. We both agreed that 250 was the max, and we had people coming in from all over. I had my British friends, Harvard friends, and US Intel friends. You had your Pharma friends, and University friends, and we both had our high school friends. We had family coming from all over, and our own families now had their families; well, your brother did. I hated the coin toss, and you hated rock, paper scissors. So, drawing names from a hat it would be.

It was a tough battle, but I think we were both thinking the other person won the day. After that, you asked me the big question; "Have you thought about when we should start a family?"

“Well, I was thinking we should get the marriage out of the way first unless you’re ovulating right this minute,” I replied with a chuckle.

“No, Seriously, Derek, we both have careers, and family planning is important. We have always told each other we want to start a family, and we are not getting any younger old man,” you teased.

“Money is not an issue for us, so I am ready anytime you are ready to get huge and lose that amazing figure. But I will most likely continue to be your ‘hickey monster’ no matter how ginormous you become,” I said with a smile. It was right then I heard that damn voice in my head again. They had not been around for a while, but this time I was prepared to try to confront whoever they were. “I think I need to pop up for a minute and pass some gas,” I warned as I got out of bed.

“Oh gross. Hurry up, and I want to finish this talk with you, and don’t go running off or no Hickey Monster for you ever again!” you warned me with a grin. I put my runners on just in case I ever needed to take off for any reason, kind of standard protocol for us. I hit the button, and up I went. I always returned the lift immediately, no matter what I was doing. I had installed an excellent fire suppression system years ago, and a fire was never a genuine concern for us. When I got to the top and stepped onto the field, I immediately turned on my privacy mode and thought, ‘Ok, I know you’re spying on us, and I have known for a while. Please drop the charade and identify yourself’. I waited and had no response mentally to my request. ‘Last chance, friend, you know who I am, and you know why I am here, don’t be afraid; I won’t bite your ass, assuming you have one’, I thought. Suddenly a tiny single person clap could be heard.

‘Hello Derek, it’s Tank from the lake,’ I heard in my head.

‘Hi Tank, it’s good to hear from you my old friend, but I am a little confused; I thought you were not allowed to make a trip back and cause a new timeline to occur?' I asked.

‘There have been a few unexpected developments that have happened that have forced me to make this covert trip back to see you,” Tank replied.

Here I am, supposed to be farting up a storm, and you were waiting below for our chat about kids to continue.

‘Where is your pod, Tank?’, I asked.

‘In your pond,’ he responded.

‘How much time do you have left in the pod?’, I asked.

‘I just arrived about six hours ago and tracked you down when you were on your bike. I have plenty of pod time left, but I can only stay for another day then I am scheduled to return’, Tank told me.

‘Clarify, please; I thought you could not return to the leading edge once you have gone back in time?” I asked with a bit of a confused attitude.

‘That is not entirely accurate, and it's part of why I needed to come back and speak with you. There are a few developments that we need to chat about as soon as possible,” Tank cautioned.

‘Ok, buddy, we will have the whole morning to chat but right this minute, Rebecca is waiting to talk to me about starting a family, and I do not want to keep her waiting,” I responded.

‘Derek, we have only been exchanging thoughts for less than .0036 nano-seconds. Rebecca’s heart has only beaten once since you stepped off the platform.

‘Sorry, Tank, it’s been a while, and I forgot how efficient our discussion time is, so let’s do this; Let’s chat for 3 minutes my time, and then I need to return to Rebecca. Does that work for you, Buddy?” I proposed.

“Ok, Derek, but I only need a maximum of 30 seconds but would love to chat about other stuff if you like,” Tank replied.

‘Ok, Tank, the floor is yours,” I quickly said.

‘Back when we first joined our consciousnesses at the lake, you had been asking about why so many of us had been asking you questions about Rebecca. I know that you were told it was to give context to memories, but what you were not told was that the emotional component of your memories had opened up a long closed-off part of our consciousness. We told you that we had adopted a kind of open mind policy. Since we had collectively shut off that part of our mind, we did not experience emotions like you understood emotions to be experienced. It turns out that some of our people started to experience completely new feelings and thoughts and eventually could fully experience your actual emotions and feelings simply by replaying your thoughts, especially your Rebecca thoughts. Would you let me perform a brief experiment so you can better understand what I am attempting to explain to you? It will not hurt but maybe messy.’

‘Ok, Tank, now you have my curiosity, I replied.

Suddenly I was experiencing this again like it was really happening;

‘Tina selected a spot that was more of an underwater seat, allowing us to sit our butts on the rock, and the water was up to our chest. We both got seated, and without saying a word, we slowly slid towards each other, eventually having our thighs come together. I had the worst *(or best)* case of butterflies, and I am sure Tina was experiencing the same thing. We scanned the area, ensuring we were the only ones there. After the scan, we both looked at each other. We knew precisely the other's thoughts, and Tina decided to go first. She reached over, and instead of a T&D, she grabbed my hand and interlaced our fingers. As soon as she had my hand, I detected some movement! *(Oh, oh Jerry, I think it moved again).*

I was so excited and in a great way. Yes, that way, but also, I had the same feeling I once had so long ago, standing on Rebecca 1.0's front porch. I know I wanted it to be with you my first time, but it was happening now, and it felt right. No dirty old man thoughts, just two young kids about to discover something extraordinary that may become something more. I would have thought from my years of experience that this moment would be lost to a more mechanical, robotic-like feeling, and worse, the emergence of the pervy old man. But it appears that my new adolescence would cause a whole new set of pathways to form. Not re-tracing old ones, but brand new ones. Is this the secret, Becca? That my journey just taught me that this is not a re-do. This is about a new-do. Is this the secret to getting rid of the old man?

We held hands for a few minutes, and then we both did another scan for people. After we were satisfied it was all clear, Tina moved our hands to her special spot and pushed the back of my hand into her. I felt her legs open more, and I knew I had achieved full movement myself. She had a smile and grin on her face all at the same time. I know I was watching her. As the hand pushed a bit harder, I pulled it back a bit and said, "Are you sure? This is a big next step for us."

She smiled and pushed the back of my hand back into her and said, "I have wanted this since the movie. You make me feel so special, and you give me the greatest butterfly's."

I looked at her and said, "I am a virgin, and this will be my first time."

"She giggled and said, "I will be gentle, and it is my first time with you."

She released the hand hold and guided my hand under the top of her bikini bottoms. She was now sitting more erect and took her left hand, slid it under her bikini waistband, grabbed my left hand, and slowly moved it down to her special area. I could not believe we were doing this, like this.

I had a momentary flashback to the first time you and I had a similar situation happen in your pool, or I should say Becca 1.0 and me.

I had imaged a bunch of other scenarios, but never this one. After a minute of Tina helping guide my hand to the best spots, I felt her right-hand reach over and touch my special area through my suit. As she gave it a bit of a grip, I thought I would lose it right then. Luckily, she stopped for a minute and returned to her guiding help. After another minute, she looked at me, and this time I knew that look, and suddenly she found the waistband of my shorts with her right hand and slid it in. As her hand found my other thumb, she seemed to know what to do. I was looking at her, and I said, "I think I am about to make a mess on your hand."

Her face also started to scrunch up, and her left hand moved my fingers up and down quicker and quicker. Suddenly her eyes opened wide, and she said, "Kiss me now!"

I immediately leaned over, and our lips met. As soon as our lips had fully sealed, she let out this incredible moan. Suddenly I was doing the same. We kissed for a few seconds as our bodies went into minor convulsions. When we finally stopped the kiss, we lost our sitting balance and slid into the water entirely. We both used our free hands to grab the edge of the rock seat to prevent us from going completely under. But what was remarkable, we continued to keep our other hand in the same last position.

As quickly as the memory played in my head, it was over. I knew immediately I had just filled my clean underwear. 'Tank, you SOB, you could have warned me I would make a huge mess in my pyjamas,' I said angrily. I quickly pulled the pyjama bottoms off and removed my underwear and did my best to clean myself up. Thankfully there was little mess on the pyjama bottoms themselves, but the undies were done. I put the bottoms back on and said, 'Never do that again without giving me a detailed description of what you meant by a mess,' I instructed.

'Sorry, Derek, I did not understand how you would react fully, but I hope you can better understand the power that thought contains for a person. Imagine if I had placed the Tina thought, followed by the Maureen thought, followed by the Sandy thought right after each other," Tank explained.

'Well, Tank, I can tell you my European undies would not have been able to handle the load, *(Pun Intended)*,' I added with a concerned snicker.

'Since your interface, we had a number of people breach our privacy rules, and they retrieved your original Rebecca thoughts as well as your fabricated Rebecca thoughts. We do not have a physical reaction like you just experienced as if it was happening right now, we have a mental equivalent, but it is about ten times greater than your experience. They started to form small private groups where they would share those moments together. It got to be so bad that the higher-ups began to issue a general ban on the entire activity. They began to assign groups to monitor and look for that activity. Eventually, a few of our people decided they could hide from the leading edge by secretly transporting back, forcing a new transference timeline, get their fill of you and Rebecca, and then returning without letting anyone know what they did.

'So let me try to recap the current state of affairs, Tank. Your people have been secretly warping space and coming back to this timeline, getting their rocks off secretly watching me and my girl be intimate then after they have their mind load blown, they warp back to the leading edge and act like nothing had changed," I laid out somewhat sarcastically.

'I wish it were that simple, Derek, but it's much worse. Each time they warped back; a new timeline was created. That is the problem. Not the 'mind load blowing' you called it. Partitioning time has a theoretical limit, and the more timelines diverge from the leading edge, the more unstable the leading edge becomes. That is how our people discovered the activity. Our scientists developed a method recently to measure the degree to which the timeline has been fractured. The last count was just over 2 billion. Our scientists estimate the theoretical maximum is around 4 trillion, Tank explained, sounding anxious.

'That's a lot of mind loads, my friend. We're lucky you guys don't have a physical response, or my world could have been jizzed into extinction,' I replied, now laughing.

'It's no laughing matter, Derek, you don't understand the severity of the situation now and what our scientists are proposing to fix it,' Tank said, emitting a sense of fear.

'Sorry, Tank, I don't mean to make light of the situation, but I have no idea how to react. I am guessing their fix will somehow wipe out Rebecca and me, or you would not be here. I also know you guys are so far advanced compared to me that I have absolutely no ability to offer any solutions to fix this, so I do what I always do when forced into a no-win situation, I make jokes', I confessed.

'I am so sorry for being the one to break the news to you, however, I myself and the others you saved felt an obligation to come and tell you. We have a couple of ideas, which is also why I came back. I want to discuss them with you and get your thoughts', Tank said.

"Any ability to give the time frame in terms of my time measurement from the current two billion to the projected four trillion' I asked?

"That is less relevant to you; you need to know the time frame for the fix from this moment. I would estimate not more than 10 years," Tank replied.

'Ok, my friend, let me get back to my girl, and we will continue this tomorrow. And Tank, you are a real friend, even though I still don't know how ugly you are," I said with a forced grin.

'No uglier than you, my friend,' Tank rebutted.

I hit the button, and the lift came up. I got on and hit the button to lower.

"That was sure fast," you said when I hit bottom.

"You have no idea the amount of gas I was just subjected to," I replied, trying not to show any signs of stress.

"Can we finish our discussion now?" you asked.

"Only if I can hold you while we talk," I said, climbing over to you.

I wanted you to know what I was having to deal with since I was sure you thought I was not taking our kids-talk seriously enough. I can assure you after my chat with Tank, I was now trying to figure out if we should even have kids but could never tell you.

I kept my privacy setting active and I know that Tank would never violate that trust. Our lovemaking was great, but my brain was now in full-speed mode of trying to figure out a solution. I know you accused me of being distracted more than once that night. I was hoping you would simply assume I was stressed a bit about the whole family planning stuff.

In the morning we did a needed cleaning of our place and I made sure we were out of there by 10 am. We split at the bottom of the rock formation hill, and I headed to my bike. As I got to my bike, I checked for a small stick that I had placed on the tire to see if anyone touched the bike. The stick was gone, and I knew my watchers had most likely stuck a tracker on the bike. After a brief inspection, I found the device inside the frame under the seat. I carefully removed it and placed it on the tree near the bike. I walked the bike through the woods west and emerged a fair way down Mineral Springs Road. I would take a different route out through Copetown today and hopefully, a couple more trainees would have to take the course over again. When I mounted my bike, Tank connected with me again.

"Good morning, Derek, is this a good time to continue our chat?" he asked.

"Hey Tank, I guess it's as good a time as we got," I replied.

"Before you start, I have a few questions I would like you to clear up for me," I requested.

"Sure Derek, shoot," Tank replied.

"Yesterday when you implanted my Tina memory, I was there and was experiencing that moment like it was live, I mean physically there as you found out, not just a visual watching party like the old Hermitage video of Rebecca standing there naked. Is the infection you are referring to the same? Do your people get the 'doing' rather than the 'watching' experience?", I asked.

"Interesting way to frame the issue Derek, but I think I need to better explain what our people are actually doing so you better understand the underlying issue. We do not care about the sex, physicality or the visual. What we are only interested in is the emotions your mind constructs. When you are making love, there are 3 major processes occurring; there is a visual or sensory component, looking, touching; then there is the physical response, your body experiences changes such as enlargement, secretion, hair standing on its end as you like to call it, and then there is the emotional; The butterflies! We don't share the underlying physiological constructs as you, so any of the other non-mental aspects are irrelevant to us. Did you ever wonder where those wonderful butterfly's come from?" Tank asked.

"I never really thought about that Tank, it was always just there, it was part and parcel of the process," I responded.

"So let me ask you this question, if you could only experience one of the components I described, what would it be; Arousal, Orgasm or Butterflies?" Tank posed.

"Interesting proposition Tank," I replied with a thinking look on my face.

"Orgasm, while very intense and powerful, it is limited in duration and let's not forget the mess. Arousal is ok, but when compared to butterflies there is no contest. Butterflies have the longest duration, and the other unique aspect of butterfly's is your ability to generate them simply by thought. When I used to look at a picture of Rebecca 1.0 sitting at the front of my fishing boat, years after it was taken, it could still produce butterflies for me. I bet if you showed me that picture today, it would generate Butterflies. So, my answer my friend is butterfly's," I explained in detail.

"We want the butterflies as well," Tank admitted. "Butterflies are actually generated when the mind begins to search out a variety of engrams and creates a new linkage. It is this process we share that is unique to each individual. I can have all the same memories of Rebecca you have, but my mind will figure out its own new pathway linking those engrams that will be different from yours. It's this individuality aspect that we want. And this is why it is so dangerous to the people responsible for maintaining our harmonized system of existence. Once our mind begins to enjoy this 'individuality' emotion, it wants more. Eventually, our minds will start to seek out new methods to generate these 'Butterflies' and we would eventually swap collective harmonization for individual consciousness. This would destroy our system of existence which took hundreds of thousands of years to evolve," Tank said with trepidation in his thought.

"Tank, this is really heavy my friend and I will need time to do my own processing and I think I need you to jump to the really big question; What do the keepers of your way want to do as far as a fix?" I asked, really not wanting to hear it yet.

"To keep it somewhat simple or as you like to say, Coles Notes, here it is. First, they identified you as the cause of the first infection. Second, they have a complete record and trace of the entire infection routing. Basically, they have traced every infection from you to each of our people that have been infected. Third, they have examined methods that would only involve our people to eradicate the infection, and as fast as they come up with one, those infected figured out a workaround. The result was the concept of a full reset. Simply put, they need to conduct a complete purge at the same time eliminating the ability of our infected to pass the infection around in order to keep it active," Tank paused to see if I was keeping up.

"Well Tank, it makes sense and is probably something even I would come to the same conclusion to do after running my 'what if's'. I guess my last question for the day is this; When we detect a cancer, we usually want to remove all of it, and just to make sure, we also cut out all the surrounding tissue just to make sure we got it all. If I was you, I would also want to remove the source of the infection, especially after all the work that would have to go into a full reset," I let my friend know I figured it out. "That is really why you are here isn't it my old friend?" I asked.

"You never disappoint Derek, my new friend. But we may have an idea or two that we want to run past you," Tank offered.

"Tank, I have a wedding coming up and I would like you to round up the old gang and be my guest that day, it will be a great day and I can think of no other friends I want there than you guys. After the wedding we will chat and that way it will also give me some time to process everything. But I want you to make me one promise and I am asking you to give me your word on this one. No matter what eventually happens, under no circumstance can anything ever happen to Rebecca. And that goes for Rebecca 1.0 and my future wife. Because if you can't give me your word, then I will take matters into my own hands and that is something your people do not want to see," I said with my best Outlaw Josey Wales attitude.

"We anticipated your request and we have already agreed that we would 'go to the mattresses' for you my friend, and me being here is proof that we put our money where our mouth is, if you knew where our mouths are," Tank said in Derek speak.

"Thank you, Tank, I needed that. See you at the wedding and it is formal so come well dressed. Wear a tie, assuming you have a neck," I finished our chat with a grin.

Well Rebecca, hate to put this cloud over what was the most amazing day for us. No need to go into details since you were there my love, but I will point out now, your first contact with my friends. It was at our wedding. Do you remember when we had our first dance, it was a custom arrangement joining my three favorite songs; The Last Time, Unchained Melody and How Can I Be Sure. What you did not know, the vocals you heard were not the bands, it was my friends singing to you. They over-rode the band's vocals and replaced them with their telepathic voices. It was their little wedding gift to us.

[Finally, the other important news. At the wedding, I dosed our moms for the first time. I had put their treatment into their first Jello shooter. Theirs had no alcohol, at least the first one. I detected the marker in late July and decided the time was right to start. I will be administering three more treatments over the next three months. Let's hope all the work will pay off babe!]

[July 1988, I will get into a bit more detail later when I get a chance to see my beloved Leaf's finally win the Stanley Cup but suffices to say, I was successful on orchestrating the trade of Gretzky from Edmonton to the Leaf's rather than see him end up in Los Angeles.]

Update – Wedding, Task 16, and my 'Friends' Part II!

(July 1988 – June 1989)

69 ***Making Adjustments:*** I know you are wondering Rebecca what transpired from my chat with Morpheus, Tank, Trinity, and Cypher after the wedding and also when did I speak to them. We had 2 sessions that day. One before the wedding ceremony; when I was sitting alone in my dressing room trying to take it all in. A two lifetime dream was about to happen. I know this was nothing like would have ever happened with Rebecca 1.0, and we both know that Becca 1.0 and Derek 1.0 could never be anyways. I will always cherish the time we had, and for producing my first and only 'It-girl'. Without that ever taking place, this would never be. The second discussion was in the airport bathroom; when I said I needed to use the boy's room. Both discussions were extensive even though they occurred in mere minutes, and I will admit that I like some of their ideas, but as usual, I needed time to mentally process them. Morpheus explained that space warping was now being closely monitored and that their frequency of monitoring trips here had been greatly reduced, at least until the future reset takes place. There was no way for us to pre-schedule a meeting time in the future. They used to monitor semi-annual but now their monitoring was every couple of years, and even that could change in the future.

We spent a lot of time discussing or I guess more accurately, they spent a lot of time trying to explain the reset process. "Tank, you need to dumb down your technical explanation a bit more for me my friend; remember you're talking to an amoeba," I half-jokingly said.

"Derek, you are far from an amoeba my multi-cell friend, we would classify you closer to a cockroach," he replied with a round of clapping.

Some people may be insulted, but I took it as a compliment. The evolutionary advancement from a single cell amoeba to a cockroach is huge. "I accept your comparison with pride, my friend, remember, cockroaches will survive everything. Nuclear, famine, flood, and even a reset," I returned with a chuckle.

"Let me try a recap so you can see if I am understanding my pending doom," I said.

"The great 'Reset' is planned once your people have built sufficient storage systems and mind-mapping tech to house all of your people's brain mappings. The idea in very simple terms; is to pick a specific date in the past, map each individual's brain as at that date and store it until all individuals have been recorded and stored. Then your entire population will transfer the stored mappings back into the entire population at the exact same time, thereby eliminating any one individual from hiding one of the infection memories, while another person is being re-imprinted. Prior to the mass re-imprinting, someone will go back in time, take a copy of my brain, then modify my memory causing me to never go to the Collins on that night I first met Rebecca 1.0. Finally, they will modify the individual that was responsible for the botched landing the night you first contacted me for help, preventing that event from ever occurring', I restated to my friends.

"Yes, that is close," Trinity said.

"Ok, then using our old Q&A format, I have a few questions I would like you to answer to help fill in some missing information for me," I replied.

"We are all ears, assuming we have any," Cypher replied with a clap.

Q: 'Why not simply go back and prevent my birth?'

A: 'They are trying to minimize the interference in order to limit the negative impact to our 'Prime Directive' as you like to call it'.

Q: 'So they are prepared to breach the Prime Directive, pull a Captain Kirk?'

A: 'Yes, but as little as possible is the goal'.

Q: 'Will the modification to my brain which causes me not to go to the Collins not create some potential future ramifications when you consider what my life experiences actually generated/created'?

A: 'Our scientists we believe already did such a test and went back and altered your brain in a new divergence and monitored its impact. They must be satisfied that the consequences of your brain dump was less damaging than the Rebecca and Derek infection'.

Q: 'Is the re-implanting tech a one-to-one tech or does it do multiple implants through a single device?'

A: 'Multiple. Currently 5,000 per device. I know your next question Derek so here is some additional information. The reason for so many to be hooked up to the same device is the belief that a majority who want to fix the problem will be able to keep an eye on anyone wanting to try to beat the system. It is a lot harder to slip one by 4,999 people watching you'.

Q: 'I understand the re-set process but how do you retract or remove all of the divergent timelines that have been created?'

A: 'They will all be terminated at the same moment the reset is done'.

Q: 'What do you mean by terminated?'

A: 'They are looped back to their original divergence spot. Remember the explanation of warping space using the pencil lines during our first encounter. Try to envision that each line is looped back to the spot at which it started. This looping will cause the timeline to collapse back into the precise moment it was first generated. Now imagine that you start this loop process at the last known divergence. It will create a cascading loop effect that will eventually collapse every divergence back to the very first divergence that was created to return you to your very first transference'.

Q: 'I have to believe if my particle physics is not too rusty, the process of collapsing these divergences would have some mass energy impact on the originating timeline or something to that effect?'

A: 'We may have to move you up the evolutionary scale from a cockroach to a mouse', Tank joked with a round of clapping.

Q: 'So here is a little mouse question for you; What would prevent you from taking a mapping now and storing it somewhere and then at a later time, simply re-imprint that memory thereby restoring you to a much more current memory-sucking moment?'

A: 'Great question but you are missing two pieces of information. To answer your previous question, there is a substantial energy discharge when they collapse a timeline. How they handle that, is to direct that energy into a micro-size black hole no larger than the size of a tip of a sewing needle. They then direct each of the micro-size black holes towards an existing black hole which will absorb all the micro-size black hole energy. There are a few black holes large enough to handle the total energy output created. For your second question, they will be splicing the leading edge, as well, back at the point in time when the memory mapping was done. Everything that occurred after the splice point will also be collapsed into a micro black hole. I expect, that would be the day you first met us. Once that occurs, time will have been reset back to that moment and we would have a new leading-edge beginning from that moment. Everything that had occurred since that moment is gone and sent to the black hole as well,' Morpheus took lead on and explained.

Q: Why not loop the Leading-edge like the divergences?

A: A Leading-edge cannot be altered or directed, just spliced. If a Leading-edge could be looped back, then everything would no longer exist. This is why we only care about the Leading-edge. It's responsible for everything.

Q: 'What happens to any new additions to your population that occurred after the splice point?'

A: 'They will cease to be, but new one's will emerge again in the normal order of our civilizations development' Trinity replied.

Q: 'What if we parked our mappings before that point in time?"

A: 'Another insightful thought but as soon as we go back, we create a new divergence, which they are monitoring closely and would also end up being looped, or spliced out' Tank said.

Q: 'Can you provide a realistic description of what will occur to me and Rebecca at the moment that the timeline is looped back?'

Suddenly a very strange silence. Silence usually meant that the answer was going to be a very uncomfortable explanation.

Q: 'Guys, you all know me well by now so I will let you know my valves are all closed, and I prefer you give it to me straight'.

A: 'At the moment the loop meets the initial divergence point is when the micro black hole is created. It immediately begins to absorb all the energy which from your perspective would manifest in your entire planet collapsing into itself eventually ending in a singular micro black hole. The collapse will occur exponentially but from your time frame perspective, it would occur over a 4-hour period. Your air is the first thing to go and all life that relies on the air will essentially suffocate within the first 20 minutes. Anyone using artificial means to breathe would have the supporting technology ripped away and would follow fairly quickly to those already who are no longer living. I am sure you are thinking, Derek, how can a civilization as advanced as us, do something so barbaric? Well, we do our best to minimize the physical stress associated with suffocation by deploying a series of satellite-type devices that emit a specific wavelength that will essentially knock out every living thing on your planet. That way, you would not experience any potential pain', Tank further elaborated.

Q: 'Well that is mighty nice of you guys! I guess that is better than having my asshole pulled out through my mouth as I get sucked into the micro black hole', I replied sarcastically. 'I will assume that the entire process must be simultaneous if you're collapsing so many divergent timelines," I added.

A: 'As we have told you before, Time is a relative construct and from our perspective, the entire reset occurs instantaneously and with the micro black holes being directed to the main Black hole, there is no direct impact on time as a result of the massive energy build up. From your perspective, you will simply blink, and everything will continue as it would', Cypher responded.

Q: 'Except one important thing, I will no longer ever meet Rebecca according to you," I replied with definite attitude.

A: 'No but maybe you end up with Tina or Maureen or someone else', Trinity suggested.

Q: 'You guys know I would trade 1,000 Tina's and a 1,000 Maureen's for one Rebecca. And let's not forget the huge loss that Rebecca will never know she is experiencing. Imagine how disappointed she will never know she would be without her 'It-boy', I said starting to try and deflect from the actual pain I was experiencing with joking.

A: 'That is why our idea is the best approach, Derek'.

Q: 'But your approach also has the greatest risk to you guys as well. And it does not solve the issue of the Leading Edge time disruption consequences'.

'Guys, I have a honeymoon awaiting me and as much as I would love to continue this wonderful discussion, I also need time to think and process. Let's regroup as soon as you can return. I am sure that you will be able to get back long before my ass passes by my brain! But when you get back, please have a solution for how we can fix the multi-divergence problem', I added.

Well Rebecca, that was my wonderful experience just before we boarded our flight to Italy. I know initially I must have appeared distracted to you or lost in thought. I was glad you were able to fall asleep during the flight. I never could sleep on a plane so that gave me a few hours to process what I had learned. I was a big sci-fi fan all my life and especially loved a good time travel or paradox-type story. I especially loved a series called the Time Travellers Wife. I can tell you Becca that at one point I thought maybe a solution was to simply take off and find another planet to live with you on. Finally achieve the ultimate 'it-people' dream of living out the rest of our lives on our very own planet, all to ourselves. I knew there were a few candidates from my 'mind meld' with my friends when I first met them. Surely my friends could make that happen. But I knew that would mean having to tell you the entire story and then leaving all our family and friends to be 'Black Holed' to oblivion. Yes, another version would continue but our version would be gone. And I knew we would never agree to abandon our family and friends. We would rather die trying to fix it.

I grabbed a piece of paper from my computer bag and began to chart out a ten-year time chart. I wanted to visualize what the next ten years would look like based on Tank's warning. The Tasks I still have to complete during this time frame would be the ones that occur from 1989 – 2000 give or take a year. Funny how my original memorization has been so well maintained in my head after all these years.

1. *Blackberry Investment 1991. 25% Ownership.*
2. *1992 – Spyglass Investment, acquire 25% Ownership.*
3. *Place Bet on Blue Jays to win world series.*
4. *World trade center bombing, Friday, February 26, 1993*
5. *1993 – Bre 'X' investment – Sell when stock hits $200.*
6. *OJ Simpson hidden camera – June 12th 1994.*
7. *April 19, 1995- Timothy McVeigh and Terry Nichols*
8. *Dunblane massacre - 13 March 1996*
9. *Aug 15th 1997 – Death of the World's Most Dangerous Narcissist*
10. *Princess Diana Aug 1997*
11. *April 20, 1999, Columbine High School*

The 1990's Task list above could be subdivided into 3 categories; Investment, Intel dump and hands-on. 1,2, 3, and 5 are Investment decisions. 4 was the only intel dump and 6, 7, 8, 9, 10, and 11 would be more hands on with 9 being another murder like Bernard. The only reason

I could do 9, was the fact that Derek 1.0 had personally attended the 1997 PGA Championship at Winged Foot where I personally observed the Narcissist at the event. I knew when and where he would be for his demise. If the Princess Task interferes with the Narcissist, I can always move him to a later date. He does not become President until 2016.

I was well aware that my friends would not be back again for a couple years. It gave me some comfort that I had friends looking out for me, but I also knew at the root of all this was my decision to have a do-over. I spend a lot of time thinking about that issue and wanted to assess my own potential culpability. After my analysis, I was satisfied that it was not my fault or responsibility to have foreseen my new friend's reaction to me and my Rebecca thoughts. I even asked them if my request would cause any issues and they assured me it would not. I sat in thought looking at you Rebecca, sleeping, and knew there would be only one outcome, fixing this mess and preserving our two timelines. I had no attachment or mental connection to any of the other divergent timelines. That was on my new friends and their kind. All I knew was I had a couple of years to figure out a plan.

We landed in Rome and I hope I was not to distracted. But once we got out on the open seas, I was in a much calmer state of mind. My biggest concern was the fact that you got seasick on the first day! I could not have my wife be a non-seafaring gal! Let's hope it was just a small adjustment thing.

Tasks – 17, 18, 19!

(July 1989 – October 1992)

70 ***Investment Guru and the Jays!:*** Our honeymoon was spectacular, and I was able to compartmentalize the whole world-ending crap after a day at sea. I was mentally working on running never-ending 'What ifs' and wanted to have a bunch of options ready when my Friend's returned. I would not have any warning when they would get back, and there was always the risk that they would be discovered by their own people and never returned. I did not see any benefit in altering my plans moving forward and even supported having kids, as you know, Rebecca. I was glad that we decided to start a family right away. Having had five girls, I knew you were a natural from Rebecca 1.0 days.

It was shortly after Roxanne's first birthday that I made my investment in Blackberry. My broker was getting greedy and mirroring far too many of my investment buy and sells, and I needed to part ways with him. I would have to start switching my investment broker yearly to ensure my stock buy decision would not become too obvious and lead to speculation that I was getting insider tips. I met with Mike in January, and we agreed on a silent minority partnership arrangement with an initial $1.5 million investment, with me having the first right of refusal on all future investment opportunities. Essentially, I became their private banker. I was constantly asked to sit on boards over the past two years, and I have always refused. Mike wanted me on the board, but I was satisfied with his management for now. I may want to take a seat in 5 years, assuming we were still around.

In hindsight, I never told you enough, was my appreciation for your input and willingness to act as a sounding board for my suggestions. I know you gave up your career to raise the family, not unlike your former self from my prior timeline, but we were both adamant that children should have the chance to be raised the way we had chosen. With the second on the way, we had to head over to Russia for Vlad's wedding. I knew that my watchers would be aware of the invite and my decision to travel to Russia, but it would also be the first time you would get a brief taste of my arrival process in Russia. I knew what they would do, and I was very comfortable that you could easily handle the situation. I was pleasantly surprised to hear my Russian interviewers compliment you on your demeanor during the interviewing process. What made it special for me was the fact I did not prepare you or coach you. I just knew you well enough, and there was no need to worry. My interviews on arrival were more routine these days, and I even had a regular interviewer who did not mind chatting off the record about international hockey events, especially Russia versus Canada or the USA.

What I never told you was the evening before the wedding, when the men all got together at a private gentleman's club for a bit of a Russian-style Bachelor party, was who I met. You had gone off with all the ladies, and Polina was babysitting for us. When I arrived with Vlad, there were approximately 50 guys there, with a split of 35 younger men like Vlad and me and roughly 15 older gentlemen that were friends of the parents. I knew Vlad could drink like a fish and hold his own with the best, but tonight I felt he would be driving the porcelain bus. As soon as we entered the room together, a waiter handed us a shot glass of vodka and a group cheer, followed by downing the shot, the first of many.

Vlad introduced me to the group, and I fortunately already knew about eight former students and fellow hockey players from school. I also assumed that the KGB was watching me, but at first, I did not know who it was until I spotted this somewhat smaller man sitting alone in the corner. After we had our first eye contact, I knew exactly who was watching me; Task 33 himself. He must now be with the First Chief Directorate, where he monitored foreigners and consular officials in Leningrad. He sat there with a glass of something in his hand, and I could tell he was trying to look inconspicuous but was not pulling it off. I knew Vlad's dad was connected with the Kremlin, but never did I think I would be meeting my future target so soon.

I spent the first hour trying my best to chat with my old school teammates, and we argued about the Canada Cup series of 1987. Andrei played for Russia, as did Sergei and Igor. I tried to meet up with them in Hamilton during the event, but the Russian team was off-limits and locked down after each game in their hotel. I told them the story of the Great Simcoe match, which they all got a kick out of. The most animated argument was who was the better player, Gretzky or Lemieux. I held the line on the 'Greatest One' while noting Mario was a strong second. Andrei, who played defense, thought Lemieux was the tougher player to knock off the puck. Eventually, as the vodka shots increased, we all wanted to find a rink and have a game ourselves for old-time's sake. It was about this time I ventured over to say hello to my watcher and see his reaction. He gave me a polite grin and a head nod as I approached. I took the seat on the other side of a small table and said, "Privet, ya Derek Devon is Kanady, otkuda ty znayesh' Vlada? *(Hello, I am Derek Devon from Canada; how do you know Vlad?),* I announced while taking a seat.

"Zdravstvuyte, menya zovut Vladimir, ya soratnik ottsa Vlada i drug sem'i. Otkuda ty znayesh' Vlada?" *(Hello, my name is Vladimir and I am an associate of Vlad's father and a friend of the family. How do you know Vlad?),* Vladimir asked while knowing exactly my history with Vlad.

"YA byl student PO obmenu neskol'ko let nazad, i Vlad byl moim sosedom PO komnate. My stali khoroshimi druz'yami i podderzhivali svyaz' na protyazhenii mnogikh let" *(I was an exchange student a few years back and Vlad was my roommate. We became good friends and have stayed in touch over the years),* I replied.

"Chto ty delayesh' v Kanade?" *(What do you do back in Canada?)* my KGB friend asked.

"YA rabotayu v oblasti meditsinskikh issledovaniy, a takzhe upravlyayu sobstvennym investitsionnym portfelem. A vy? *(I work in medical research as well as manage my own investment portfolio. And you?),* I answered.

"YA rabotayu v pravitel'stve v otdele vneshnikh svyazey. YA prismatrivayu za vysokopostavlennymi gostyami" *(I work for the Government in the Foreign relations department. I look after visiting dignitaries),* my new friend said.

"Khotya ya ne sanovnik, no yesli vy igrayete v shakhmaty, to cherez vsyu komnatu ustanovlena doska, khotite li vy sygrat'?" *(While I am no dignitary, if you play chess, there is a board set up across the room, if you would like a game?).*

He gave me a nod Rebecca and a slight grin. We got up and walked to the table where the chess board was set up. It was a beautiful board with hand-carved pieces. My new friend grabbed a white and black pawn and held out his closed hands. I selected his right hand, and he showed me a black pawn. We took our seats according to the pawn selection, and I put out my hand for a pre-game shake. He smiled and gave me a single firm shake. I played a lot of chess over the years and studied the game back in my Derek 1.0 days. I was no grandmaster but was also no slouch. I was looking forward to studying my future target's mental prowess.

He made a standard Queen pawn opening, and I decided to play the Petrov Defense, also known as a Russian Game, to see my opponent's expression. It is a chess opening characterized by the moves: e4 e5. Nf3 Nf6. My target grinned, and I knew he knew my initial plan. The game progressed as expected for the next eight moves. Vladimir had decided to employ the Cochrane attack, which showed me he had studied chess. Unfortunately, I had the 'Devon counter-attack' move on move 20 that killed his offensive and put him in a defensive position. By this point, we had attracted quite a crowd, including Vlad and his dad. Vlad's dad was an excellent player; we had a few great marathon matches. Tonight, however, would be handled slightly differently. My KGB friend was trying to search for a draw move, and I wanted to throw a bit of a wrench into his plans. On move 26, I took his rook and was now six moves away from checkmate and a win. Everyone was watching intently as I very slowly removed the rook and placed it with the other taken pieces. I stared at Vladimir and was hoping to get an eye-to-eye stare, but he grimaced and sat back in his seat. Vlad senior looked at me and gave me a smile. He knew I had the win.

But I did not want to humiliate my Russian watcher in front of his fellow countryman, who most likely all knew what he was and did. No, I would do one better. I would throw the game. Let him win, but he, I, and Vlad senior would all know I lost on purpose. I moved my queen to bishop 6, held my finger on it for a few extra seconds for show, and then let it off. I sat back in my chair, grabbed my glass of Starka on the rocks, and took a sip. He looked at my move, then looked at me. He looked again and then back at me. I played my role and did not make any facial expressions. I simply took another sip of my Starka. Vlad senior's expression, who was standing behind Vladimir, went from a smile to a look of concern, and he attempted to give me a head gesture suggesting I should not throw the game. Unfortunately, Vlad did not know my end game, or he would have understood and agreed my move was brilliant.

Suffices to say, Rebecca, that I had to surrender the game in 4 more moves, and those four moves were the greatest moves I ever played. My opponent was not a happy camper but could not show it then. Once I toppled my king, the room burst into cheers for Vladimir for beating the westerner, complete with a vodka round of shooters. It was supposed to be all in fun, but I could sense this was much more than a friendly game. At some point during our visit, I knew I would get a lecture from Vlad senior about my brashness. But I was ok with that. It showed he cared about me, which was essential to me in the long game.

Once the game was over, across the room, doors opened, and a dozen or so ladies walked in. It appeared the night was just getting going. When Vladimir and I rose from our chairs, I extended a hand for a congratulatory shake. This time I did get my eye-to-eye, and he knew I just made a fool out of him in front of Vlad senior and maybe one or two other chess aficionados in the room. But as he was trained, he played his role, and the shake was robotic, and the smile was forced. I said at the end of the shake, "Mne ponravilas′ Nasha igra. Odnazhdy Nam pridet·sya provesti match-revansh" *(I enjoyed our game. We will have to have a rematch one day).*

"YA nedootsenil vas, mister Devon, v sleduyushchiy Raz ya khochu nastoyashchuyu igru" *(I underestimated you Mr. Devon, next time I want a real game),* with a forced grin.

It was a fun wedding, and I was glad we could leave Roxanne with Vlad's sister Polina, acting as our babysitter. I love to dance with you, and even if number two forced us to forgo the 'old grind', it made us stare into each other's eyes and remember all our prior dances together. It was also great that you got along with Vlad's family, and I appreciated that my friendship with Vlad was now 'our' friendship with Vlad and Oksana.

I was expecting another encounter with my KGB friend, but it never happened. I was usually pretty good at my guesses, but this was a mystery and caused me a minor concern. The departure was clean and uneventful, and I was sure you appreciated the first-class reclining seats for the trip home. I was amazed at what a great traveler Roxanne was. I could not wait for her little brother to arrive in 4 months.

It was October now, and I had pre-booked every Jay's home game for the series against the Braves (Game 3, 4, and 6). I had our seats behind home plate for 3,4, and 6. I bought 12 seats, and it was great to have the entire family there for the last game. I knew our dads were not huge baseball fans; our mothers had never attended a game before, but my mom was a huge fan at home and watched every game on TV. I had placed an enormous bet in Vegas at the start of the season, and one with old Gino and a few different bookies. I think Gino thought I was some gift sent by God to him for being such a great wop and never whacking anyone.

Anyways, it was a great game, and I was sorry you were just too big now to fit in the seats.

I missed my old friend Sean and I always had to beat myself up every now and then for not being able to do anything to prolong his life. I never prepared to deal with Leukemia, just the cancer our moms would battle. I know when we began the discussion of names for number two. You wanted to go with Derek, which I said absolutely not. You also liked William, Douglas and then the 'trending names', Owen, Tyler and the least favorite of mine, David! But I want you to know that I was so appreciative and loved you even more when you agreed to call our first son, Sean *(I think I just welled up).*

[Update on our mom's health: I have gotten your mothers latest blood work from the lab *(or I should say stole it)*, and my intervention is showing promise. Unfortunately, my mothers blood work was not as successful, and I would need to tweak her treatment. The counts and markers were down, but I was hoping for a better result]

Tasks – 20 and my Friends Return!

(November 1992 – March 1994)

71 ***A Faster Clock and Problems!:*** I can't believe we're in our early 30's and I have been back now for over 20 years. I was shocked at how big Sean was now and I was sure he may have avoided my slow twitch muscle with the amount of movement he had. Roxanne was proving to be a great older sister and I was the happiest person on earth these days except for the lingering total annihilation feeling I got every now and then. I know you are wondering why I purchased that property north of Perry Sound, but that is the property my old friend Al once owned back in my Derek 1.0 days. That is where this all began. I felt guilty that my old buddy would no longer get this property, but I am sure he will find another private lake somewhere. I needed it for you, Rebecca!

My next task was to prevent the bombing of the World Trade Center in New York. While the original explosion did not topple the buildings as the terrorists thought it would, it did do substantial damage. On Friday February 26, a truck bomb detonated below the North Tower of the complex, the 1,336 lb *(606 kg)* urea nitrate–hydrogen gas enhanced device was intended to send the North Tower *(Tower 1)* crashing into the South Tower *(Tower 2)*, bringing both towers down and killing tens of thousands of people. It failed to do so, but killed six people, including a pregnant woman, and injured over one thousand. The attack was planned by a group of terrorists including Ramzi Yousef, Mahmud Abouhalima, Mohammad Salameh, Nidal A. Ayyad, Abdul Rahman Yasin, and Ahmed Ajaj. Ramzi Yousef was the organizer behind the bombings, and Eyad Ismoil drove the truck carrying the bomb.

Yousef, aided by Mohammed A. Salameh and Mahmud Abouhalima, began assembling the 1,500 lb (680 kg) urea nitrate-fuel oil device in his Pamrapo Avenue home in Jersey City. I knew his address and I planned to go to his home to do a brief recon on Monday the 22nd. I wanted to see how far along they were progressing and wanted to make sure I gave my friend, Special Agent Samuel, enough lead time to meet me there so I could hand it off to him and his team. That trip Rebecca, I had told you that I had meetings pertaining to my investments in Spyglass and that I would be in New York for the week. I figured I would have to go through the usual debrief and interview crap for at least 2 days before they would let me leave. I was sure CSIS would call me in for a meeting the week I got back.

I flew into Newark this trip out of Buffalo and had a room at the Hudson Plaza Motel which was 5 minutes from Ramzi Yousef's home.

Being so close I could blend in as a local jogger and kill two birds with one stone as they say. I checked in at 4 pm on the 22nd and decided I would take a run after dinner around 7 pm. That would provide me with enough daylight when I ran by. If they spotted me jogging now, it would allow me to better blend in if they spotted me again on another day jogging'. I planned to call Chris Wednesday afternoon and request his presence for Thursday. I would simply tell him I got a last minute dump of some reliable intel on a possible bombing and popped into town to verify.

When I ran by on Monday night, I did not see any van. The place actually looked deserted when an Arab looking woman in her 50's came out of the house. I think that was Abdul Rahman Yasin's mother whom he shared the home with. I decided to go for a longer run and would loop back in an hour for a final look. As I passed by again at 8:15 pm, still no Van, lights or movement. I returned to the motel and grabbed a shower and called you Rebecca! The next day, I rented a car and decided to do a drive by and see if anything had changed. Still no van or movement. I returned the car after the day and had booked a van rental for Wednesday. I picked up the van and returned to my motel. I had a one-way mirror like window covering for the rear windows of the van. I also hung up some partitioning material to hide any prying eyes from seeing into the rear of the van. I was planning on doing a long duration stakeout down the street and would watch them from the rear window using my binoculars.

I parked the van at 6 pm and assumed my position in the rear. I had winter clothing including ski pants, toque and gloves and bought two lawn chairs and had drinks and snacks along with a pee bucket if I needed it. I rigged up a 12 volt fan to a heavy duty battery I bought so I could limit any condensation from my breath. I sat and watched for a couple hours when I finally saw the van pull up. I knew when it arrived that it was already full of the urea nitrate–hydrogen and the other bomb parts due to the compressed suspension view. This was a concern since it was my understanding that they did not pick up the material until tomorrow morning. I wonder if my information was faulty. I watched 3 men exit the van and it was odd that they all exited the right passenger door. They all walked into the townhouse and lights went on. I planned to wait until later to do a personal inspection on the truck. As I was watching the house another car drove up with 3 men. One man went in and the other two sat in the car. This was going to be a problem if I wanted to inspect the contents of the van. As I was sitting there, I got a very uncomfortable feeling when I started to think through the timeline and began to imagine that I had now disrupted the original timeline or perhaps the timeline was being impacted by all the divergences. I decided to stay put and continue my surveillance. I knew they would not try to enter the underground this late in the day. My concern was what to do if they were going to blow it up tomorrow. I needed to get in touch with Chris Samuel immediately. I grabbed my cell phone and looked up our special phone number. I press the call button.

"Morning Side Maintenance Service. How may I direct your call and may I have your service number please," the voice on the other end said.

"This is serviceman 34988KT, I need an immediate clean-up on site," I responded.

"One moment and I will try to connect you to your service manager," the voice replied.

I sat on the phone and waited. "Sorry, but we will have to try another line, please hold," came the voice.

I was guessing Chris would be in DC and my late call would mean he needed to get a company plane to bring him tonight.

"Hello Derek, this line is not 100 percent secure so I will need to call you back in 5," Chris informed me.

I hung up and waited for the call. As I was waiting, a man emerged from the house and went to the car parked behind the Van. The men in the car handed a briefcase to the other man and he returned to the house. One of the men in the car then got out and went into the Van through the passenger side door. Suddenly the cell phone buzzed, and I grabbed it.

"Hey Chris, sorry for the last minute call but I am sitting in New Jersey, and I need you to get your ass down here immediately. I got a last minute intel dump from my overseas source and came down immediately to check out whether it was accurate or not. I have a group of middle east boys, Jordanian I believe, who I think have a rather large bomb in the back of a Van I am currently staring at. I don't want to spook them, and the site is active. My intel said they plan to use the Van to deliver a bomb Friday to the World Trade Center, but by the looks, I am concerned they may try to do it tomorrow. When can you be here?" I asked.

"I should be able to get there in 3 hours. Will that work or should I call in the local cavalry?" he asked.

"If they have the Van packed with Nitrate and other goodies then we are talking about a full block blast radius which would level 30-40 homes, not to mention you will find my parts somewhere in the Catskills. I don't know what the detonator situation is yet. I would suggest you get here and have a team ready and stage them incognito at Value King Department

Store between Old Bergen Road and Ocean Avenue. I am currently parked 100 yards down the street on Pamrapo Avenue in a Budget Rental Van. I have my S&W 44M with about 24 rounds, and a set of big balls," I informed him with my added humour to diffuse the seriousness of the situation.

"What will you do if they decide to move," Chris asked?

"There is no way they are going to get into the underground garage tonight. Unless they have a closer staging area, then in that case I will follow them to get a location for you. If I suspect they are making any move to place the Van for an evening delivery, then I will have to do my best Dirty Harry I guess," I said trying to offer him some assurances I had this under control.

"I am on my way. Expect a call from our local bomb unit commander. I don't have a name, but he will identify himself as Willard Whyte," Chris said with his attempt at a 'Devonesk' play.

I continued my watch and there was no more activity for about two hours. At around one am, the man that had entered the Van emerged from the passenger side carrying a box and placed it in the trunk of the car. My cell phone buzzed, and I answered.

"Is this Ernst Stavro Blofeld?" I asked.

"Ah, no. This is Willard Whyte and the line is secure Mr. Devon. We have been briefed by Agent Samuel and we are in position as requested. We would like to send a man to your location to replace you. Is that possible?"

"I would rather you stay ready in your location. If they accidently detonate, then your guys will be ok there. I know the situation better than you guys so it's best if I stay here till Chris gets here. If they decide to move, we need a better location for a takedown if that becomes necessary that will cause the least amount of potential collateral damage. Assume it's a 1,200 plus pound nitrate grade bomb and they used compressed gas cylinders to create fuel-air and thermobaric explosive characteristics that release more energy than conventional high explosives just like the 1983 Beirut barracks bombing," I explained.

"Our guys are ok with the risk, and it may be helpful to have another set of eyes and if you have to move, someone to man the comms," Willard Whyte suggested.

"Ok but send him through the rear of 116 and ask him to bring a scoped LG *(Long Gun)* with an armour piercing high capacity mag. I will leave the front passenger side unlocked and watch out, the people in 112 are still up and the front window is open," I advised.

Still no movement and in about 5 minutes I heard the front passenger door open. I pointed my 44 at the door and waited to see who entered. My man was dressed in civilian winter clothes and had a large briefcase. He entered and turned and gave me a nod. I smiled and nodded back and said, "Thanks for volunteering. I gather you're the single guy in the group?" I quipped.

"Yes, good read. My name is Thomas, but everyone calls me TJ," he replied with a whispered voice.

"Hi TJ, Derek, and the van down the street is the suspected mobile bomb. By the looks of the shock compression, it must have a fairly heavy load," I advised.

"Yes, I agree with your assessment. I have the Scoped LG here. I need to assemble it," he advised.

"Any word on Agent Samuel?" I asked.

"Yes. Should be here in about 30 minutes," he replied.

I did my watching and TJ put the long rifle together. After a couple minutes I asked him, "How long have you been with ATF Special Bomb unit?"

"Five years this June," he answered.

"Something I did not check was the weather. Any idea what the next 8 hours looks like?" I asked.

"Should stay like this. Around 40-45 tops and no snow until Saturday," he explained.

I grabbed my snack bag and pulled out a Slim Jim and offered one to TJ. He declined and pulled out a radio set with a special muzzle microphone similar to what a court reporter would use so we can communicate without anyone hearing us. TJ put the muzzle to his mouth and provided 'WW' with an update. I ate my Slim Jim and continued my watch. After about 30 minutes TJ got a call and Samuel was making his way to us using the same route as TJ. We heard the side passenger door open, and we both trained our handguns at the door and waited to see Samuel's face. He sat in the front seat and gave a nod. I smiled and gave a nod and added wink. I was actually feeling a lot better now that I had TJ and Chris with me. I was not really a field man but loved to pretend I was. These guys really had no idea my principal training was from watching a lot of movies and TV. In fairness to myself, I also taught myself a lot of stuff and even came in second in the South Florida Rifle Shooting Tourney in 1980 when Derek 1.0 went to Miami U. Because I could slow my heart down, I was an exceptional shooter. But I don't think they want to hear about my qualifications at this moment!

We all settled in for the rest of the early morning and I asked Chris what the plan was. "The team is in position, and they will not let them enter the Holland Tunnel. They are planning on evacuating the area around the Hilton on Washington Blvd and will create an accident scene just before Thomas Gangemi Drive causing a choke point. When they slow down for the accident, we have snipers on either side of Washington that will takeout the driver and passenger. We just need to make sure there is no one in the rear. I sure wish we could determine the detonation mechanism," Chris explained.

"My best guess based on the fact one of their people was in the back of the van for about two hours is they are low tech and were fabricating a delay fuse line. It would have to be shielded and they would need about 8 feet to give themselves enough time to get to a safe distance. That would mean a 10 minute fuse. With the van being parked underground they could not rely on a remote electronic device and a timer device can always fail, but a lit fuse is almost always reliable, and they look like low tech guys," I replied.

"Let's hope that is the case," TJ chimed.

At 7:30 am four men emerged from the house. They went to the car and the two men in the car got out and they all began a hug fest with some cheek kisses. It looked like I was right that the timeline is fucked up now. What we did not want to see happened. Three men got in the van through the passenger side. The other men got in the car and began to leave slowly. The van appeared to follow. TJ was on the comms and was providing detailed information to the team. I put our van in drive and began to follow from a distance. It never dawned on me to ask Chris if he minded if I drove or, did he want to drive. Anyway, the van was heading down Pamrapo Avenue. When it reached Old Bergen, it turned left heading towards Merritt. Suddenly when they reached Merritt, they turned left, not right. I looked at Chris and said, "440."

TJ was talking with his team and conveyed my comment. We had a second unit about 100 yards behind us as well that was at the previous staging location.

"TJ, what is the alternate plan if they get on 440?" I asked.

"There is no way we can get the team moved in time to stop them from getting to 139 from 9. They are moving everyone to Washington and 12," TJ relayed.

"TJ, ask them to get a few cars onto I-78 before it becomes 12. If the van blows on top of I-78, the blast will have minimum impact since we are so high in the air at the turn. Ask for a confirmation that that is a good alternative location and see if they can slow the traffic down in the middle and left lane asap. We are about 20 minutes from that location if they get on 440," I requested.

"They agree Derek that if the Van was detonated on the top of I-78, it would cause the least collateral damage and they can have cars up there in 12 minutes," TJ replied.

"Ok Chris and TJ, here is my idea. We are going to get in front of the van and as the traffic slows, I need Chris to knock out the front windshield and when I tell you, I need you to shoot a hole in the radiator. Near the top. TJ, I need you to position yourself in the rear with the LG and Chris, you will need to position yourself to open the rear door giving TJ a clear view through their front windshield of the van. TJ, your job is to take out the guy in the back. Chris and I will focus on the driver and passenger. When our van overheats, I will bring it to a stop and get out. I will make a show and then will head to the van to ask for help. When I get to the driver's door, Chris, open the back for TJ. I will need to switch guns Chris. My 44 is too big to carry in my rear waist belt. Any objections?" I asked.

"Let me pass it by command Derek," TJ said. The van was headed toward the ramp to get on the interstate as I suspected.

"Seems we got a green light boy's" TJ replied with a grin.

"Derek, why don't I go to the van, and you open the back for TJ," Chris proposed.

"What, and let you have all the glory. Besides, you have kids and I do not trust you with the LG or I would have TJ go to the van since he is single and more expendable," I replied with a chuckle.

"You're a new dad also Derek," Chris challenged.

"Ya, but I am most likely going to have my brains pulled out through my asshole in a few years, so I think I win on the most eligible chump contest!," I replied with a smile.

"What the hell are you talking about Derek?" TJ asked.

"Don't worry TJ, just an old joke my friend. I hope you got a good grade in marksmanship, or we will be having words after," I joked.

Everyone started to do what they needed to do, and TJ decided the lawn chair would give him the best position and get him above Chris. Chris and I switched guns and we were now on 9 heading toward the 139 hook up. We all completed what we needed to do, and we all seemed to go into a little self-reflection mode for a while. I was thinking about you Rebecca and the kids, and I did not want this to me my final exit plan.

"Chris, if you don't have ear plugs, stuff something in your ears buddy," I said.

"What I can't hear you, I got ear plugs in," Chris replied with a smile.

Funny how I seem to elicit humor from my companions. I figured we were about 5 minutes from the overpass turn where I was hoping the traffic jam would start.

"Ok guys, I am moving in front so both of you get in the back till I get past," I instructed.

I took the outside lane, and they were in the right lane. As I passed, I did not look at them. Once I was a couple of lengths in front, I put my turn signal on and moved to the middle lane. I continued to hold my position about three car lengths in front and was hoping I could pick up visually the brake lights ahead where the traffic slowed.

"TJ, if you had to guess, how many of your boys do you think are somewhere in the mix of cars around us?" I asked.

It was both strange and reassuring to hear TJ start to laugh at my question. "You sure you're not one of us Derek," he replied.

"I wish my friend, but I am already taken by the Secret Service," I chuckled back.

"I would guess 4, maybe 6 are around," he finally answered.

"Then we don't need to worry about their lead vehicle which is now behind them?" I asked.

"I would suggest you keep one eye open, but I would bet my guys will have your back," he assured me.

I spotted the brake lights ahead and gave the 2 minute warning. Chris was in the passenger seat with a tire wrench he found in the back and was ready to take out the front window. I put my signal on again and moved into the right lane in front of the target van. I did not want to get too much of a gap between us and the van, so I took my foot off the gas and let the van slow on its own. This narrowed the gap and by time they figured out what was happening, the other lanes where down to a crawl and the van was about 4 feet off my rear bumper.

"Ok Chris, lets pull the windshield into the van," I instructed.

Chris took the pointy end and jammed it into the window at the top. It went through the glass and a large section shattered but remained intact. Chris then took his hand wrapped in a cloth and put it through the small opening and began to pull the shattered glass in toward us. It rained down on the dash, but the section directly in front of me stayed intact. Chris moved the pulling to the right and had a 2 foot by 2 foot opening now in the windshield in front of him. Our pace was down to a slow jog, and we were about 100 yards from the main bend in I-78. I could see the traffic was stopped about 200 yards ahead.

"Ok Chris, lets put a nice hole in the rad and don't hit the poor people in the Lexus in front or they will sue our asses," I joked.

Chris took the Glock 19 from the map holder where I had placed it and aimed it from the top of the van roof on an angle down. He pulled the trigger and as soon as my ears cleared the steam was away. I popped the van into neutral and began to press the gas to increase the engine rpm to force more steam out. We continued to slowly coast along, and the steam was increasing and was now sufficient that the van behind would have noticed it and figured I had an overheating problem.

"Ok guys, I am going to stop. TJ, let me get back to the side and watch for my left arm. When I drop it then you can take the shot but not before unless they shoot me in which case open fire and kill every one of those sons of bitches," with my best impression of Clint from Unforgiven.

I finally brought our van to a full stop. I saw in the side mirror that the van behind was about three feet off our back bumper and stopped as well. I opened the door and got out. I went to the front and stood far enough from the side of our van that Ramzi Yousef who was driving, not Eyad Ismoil who was in the passenger seat, could see me clearly. I began my pretend to be pissed off rant complete with arms in the air and then slamming the driver side door followed by a good kick to the back tire. I put my hands on my hips and looked at the ground for 30 seconds. I then raised my head and began to walk to the van behind us. As I approached the driver side, I began to gesture like I was in need of water for my van. I had my eyes scanning to see if either of them appeared to be reaching for a weapon of some sorts. When I looked at their face's, they both seemed normal and Ramzi rolled down his window and said, "Sorry, we don't have any coolant or water," in poor english."

I walked over to the side window and smiled while I reached behind and grabbed hold of the Glock 19. As I reached the window, I was about 2 feet from Ramzi and said in my best Arabic, "Ramzi wa'iiad la tataharaka wa'iilaa sa'utliq rasasatan fi rasaka. eabd alrahman yasin hu mukhbiruna wanahn nuraqibuk tawal al'usbuei. muezam al'ashya' almawjudat fi alkhalf laysat madatan eardiatan haqiqiatan. lil'asaf 'ana bihajat li'iikhraj sadiqik fi alkhalaf" *(Ramzi and Eyad, don't move or I will put a bullet through your head. Abdul Rahman Yasin is our informant and we have been watching you all week. Most of the stuff in the back is not real explosive material. Unfortunately, I need to take out your friend in the back)*, I told them.

As soon as I knew they were both processing my instructions and hoping my Arabic was not too shabby, I dropped my other arm. The rear van door opened, and I heard the LG fire. Both Ramzi and Eyad jumped as the windshield was pierced and without saying another word threw their arms in the air and froze. I opened the driver side door and said, "Ramzi wa'iiad hal lakuma salahi?" *(Ramzi and Eyad, are you carrying a gun)*, I yelled.

"la, la tutliquu alnaar, nahn lasna musalahin" *(No, don't shoot, we are not armed),* he replied.

Chris had jumped out of the back and was moving to the passenger side with my 44 magnum drawn. "Chris, they claim they're unarmed. I have both covered, make sure their other friends behind are not getting ready to let loose on us," I instructed.

Chris carefully moved to the rear and was out of site and suddenly I heard two silenced shots fired. I held my position and yelled, "Chris, update quick."

Suddenly Chris reappeared through the passenger side window and appeared fine. "TJ's buddies," he yelled over.

Within 2 minutes we were joined by 6 tactical officers and two bomb techs from the trailing vehicle and some of TJ's boys. The two tactical guys on my side grabbed Ramzi Yousef and pulled him to the ground. Chris had pulled Eyad Ismoil out and already had cuffs on him. The bomb techs entered through the driver side and wanted to survey the rear situation. The first bomb tech stepped out and started talking into his radio. The second bomb tech remained inside, and I assumed was making sure the fuse was removed and there were no secondary detonators. I felt safe since I already knew the make-up of the bomb from my research, assuming that had not changed. Chris handed off Eyad Ismoil to one of the tactical guys and came over to my location. Just as he got to me TJ came over as well.

"When the interviews are all done, let's go for a nice cold beer to celebrate," I proposed.

"Only if you're paying Derek," Chris said with a smile.

"Are we staying in New York or are you dragging me back to Langley?" I asked.

"Are you kidding me, Langley my friend," Chris laughed while telling me.

"Well, then I will insist that we drag TJ along or I am not going," I threatened.

"I am sure Langley will want to get their hands on all three of us," Chris replied.

"I am sorry Chris. I think you're about to lose your field work status and be relegated to supervisor after this," I warned him with a sad smile.

"Derek, I am ready for a simpler life-style, I think. I know the wife will be happier with that arrangement," he confessed.

"TJ, nice shot with the LG *(Long Gun),"* I commended him.

"That was the most amazing thing I have ever done. What a great plan and the execution was spot on. Your training in Canada must be first rate," he gushed.

It was at this moment that I had a memory flash back to a movie scene from a James Cann film called 'Thief'. I loved that movie. Cann's character Frank Hohimer had just finished cutting through an impenetrable safe's door using a custom made high temp torch. As his crew enter to empty out the contents of the safe, Frank steps away and lights up a cigarette and surveys his work. That was my moment. No thank-you's, no congratulations, no 'I just officially earned my Boy Scout Merrit Badge for Secret Agent'. You, Rebecca, are the only person that I hope is sharing that moment with me now. Even though I am not there to enjoy it with you, I will choose to smile this second believing you are smiling with me and saying, "If you ever risk your life again like that, no more Hickey Monster for you."

Well Becca, I won't bore you any further. We did two days of interviews and de-briefs and then a night of celebration, agent style. One day I may tell you what 'Agent Style' means *(made you smile)*. The only two requests I made was to have any press release mention that it was a joint USA, British and Canadian intelligence operation. I knew Sunderland would get a kick out of that. It would certainly add to my IOU stack at home. The second request was to let Ramzi Yousef have immediate access to visitors. I told my interviewers what I said to them and knew that they would eat their own and that cell would end. Yousef would provide additional useful intel and that Task was officially done. I would add watching Thief every February 25th to the list. They flew me home on a company jet and I was so looking forward to relaxing and decompressing after that Task. The adrenaline was still pumping, and I knew I needed a week to rest.

I picked up my car at the Buffalo airport and had just sat in the driver seat when I heard a familiar voice in my head. 'Tank, please, no more singing 'A Cappella' unless you start channelling Mandy Patinkin', my friend.

'Good to see you're in a good mood Derek', Tank replied.

'Well, it was a very productive and satisfying week and I am looking forward to getting home to my family', I responded with.

'That is why I am here Derek, there's been a major wrench thrown into our plans and we needed you to know as soon as we learned about it', Tank informed me with a serious tone.

'How bad Tank?" I asked.

'Please don't get mad or fly off the handle. Just let me finish what I need to tell you, then you can go nuts on me', my friend said with a tone that was new to me.

'Now you have me more worried than before Tank. I have never experienced you in this agitated state before', I told him.

'I am here by myself. I can only have the warp opened for a minute or two which will give you more than enough time to ask me everything I think I know you are going to ask and then I will have to depart. We are going to start setting up what we will call mini briefs. We have found a way to open a very small space warp fissure sufficient for our communications to pass threw but not us physically. I am back on my home planet in what you might refer to as my basement. Using this tech, we fly under our prying eye overseer's tech, but it can only be communications for now. Here is the serious news my friend. Rebecca is now here. On my planet and in the hands of a group that was formed a short while ago…', Tank was explaining when I interrupted.

'Wait Tank, did you just say, Rebecca is not at home right this instance? That she is off world there with you? Then who is looking after my kids?', I interjected with.

'Remember back when you joked about the Rebeccabot? Well, the Rebecca at your home is not the original Rebecca, she is a 'Beccabot'! But before you go ballistic, the kids are safe and the 'Beccabot' will function almost exactly like the original. She has all of Rebecca's memories implanted at the time of the insertion and as far as the kids will see and experience, it is their mom. And one last point before I have to deal with you, I can't tell you why they took your Rebecca or what they are doing with or to her. I can only say that based on my lifetime experience here, they would most likely never do harm to her, probably just examine and study. Ok now you can lose it on me', Tank said waiting for a major blow up.

I just sat there and did not say a word. I did not know what to say. My brain was trying to process all this information, but it was also trying to find the Rebecca valve and make sure it was turned off. But I could not find it. My first instinct was to start the car and get home to my children before the imposter mom blows a fuse and potentially harms them. I was actually frozen. I never experienced this feeling of utter helplessness before. The only other time I felt something like this was when my mom and dad passed away. I went through what I called the orphan effect. The orphan effect occurs when you lose your last safety net. For me, it never mattered how bad things may get, I always knew in the back of my mind I could go home. Back to mom and dad. They would always welcome me home and would never judge or complain. They would simply be loving and supportive parents. Rebecca was my safety net. She kept me from being an orphan even thou I still had parents in this timeline. I gave her my heart and soul and if I ever lost her, it would kill me. Especially this way.

'Tank, I have never been in this position before my friend. I am at a complete loss what to say or do. I do however want to thank you for taking the risk to come to me and tell me. I know it is putting you at risk as well. I will have to take your word that my kids are safe with 'Beccabot', but I am going to start the car and start the drive. I need to see for myself, and I need to hold my kids. While I am driving, please tell me what you would recommend I do about Rebecca and has the timeline for the reset changed?', I replied now going into a listening mode as my instincts would cause the car to drive me home.

'Derek, this is new territory for both of us. I wish I had a better answer for you but at this moment, all I can do is tell you that you have friends here. We are all working to figure this stuff out and please accept, that if I could switch places with Rebecca to get her home to you, I would do that in a nanosecond. Second, the reset as far as we are aware is still moving forward. I know you asked us last visit to get you some answers or information of the divergence reversal. I don't have any update yet but our best minds in our growing group are working on it. Finally, when you get home, you will need to act completely normal with Beccabot. Her memories after the switch will be extracted and added to your Rebecca on re-insurgence. If you act differently, they would see that in Beccabot and may take additional actions so please, try to just act normally. I know it will be weird, but we just don't know if her absence is minutes, hours or days', Tank ended his reply.

'Thanks, Tank, for your frankness. I will do my best, but I need you to push hard to find out where they have Rebecca on your world. I also want to ask one last favour before we end this chat. I want you to get me the tech that allows for the mapping and implanting process and the space warping. I want you to also upload the required knowledge to operate it into my pea-brain. In addition to the operational knowledge, I want you to pump into my brain with everything you have on the design of the tech and how it actually works down to the smallest detail. I want to know what your greatest minds know. Can you promise me that my friend," I asked?

Tank knew I was hurting and did the unexpected. He knew my greatest playlist of all time, and he knew my love for a good 'song of the moment' and started to sing to me with his best Mandy Patinkin impersonation;

Somewhere over the rainbow
Way up high
There's a land that I heard of
Once in a lullaby……………
Why then, oh, why can't I?

I knew Tank would pull my B.T. Barnum and be gone at the end and I also knew he would do his best to deliver my request. I made it home in an hour and a half and wanted to stop and pick up some Lee's Chinese food for dinner. Rebecca and I had bought the old Smith farm at a price they could not say no to. I wanted my kids to grow up in Sherman Falls like I did and experience somewhat of a small town lifestyle. We had renovated the main house to tide us over until our new house was completed. The property came with 200 acres, and we decided to build our place at the back of the property close to the tree line. Behind the place was about 30 acres of woods that backed onto conservation property. I was also building a large pond and an indoor full size skating rink. We had 2 pools. One outside and one inside connected with a wandering little fake stream. In the winter we can section off the outdoor pool and keep the indoor pool going year round.

As I pulled in the driveway, I spotted Roxanne playing outside which meant 'Beccabot' would be nearby. I really did not know how I would first react to 'Beccabot'. I knew the Alien dinks that took her would leave a first rate replica and I would not doubt, if Tank didn't tip me off, I may not have known. As I pulled up by the house Roxanne came running over and gave me a big hug and said, "Daddy, come look at the snow angels I made." I walked over to her spot and took a look and gave her a big smile and then plopped myself down beside hers and made one myself.

"Daddy, your too big to make snow angels, that's for little people only," with her pouty type grin.

"Sweet Stuff, where is mommy?" I asked brushing the snow off.

"She is in the kitchen making a pie for us with Sean," she told me.

"Well, let's sneak in and surprise them together, ok," I proposed.

"I don't think they will be surprised Daddy, they are watching us from the window," as she pointed at them.

I looked in the direction of the window and saw Beccabot for the first time. She certainly looked identical. We walked into the side foyer, and I took off my coat and boots and helped Roxanne out of her winter gear. We walked in hand and hand and Sean gave me a smile and a funny grunt type welcome.

"Hey honey, welcome home and I hope you have not eaten yet, we have a wonderful turkey pot pie in the oven that Sean and I made along with a blueberry pie using the berries we picked last summer," Beccabot announced.

I walked over to Sean in the highchair and gave him a kiss and then proceeded to give him his favorite vibrating lip attack. After a minute of that, Beccabot approached me and made the first move to give me a welcome home hug and kiss. Our lips connected and I tried not to be too analytical and more like I thought I would be but did not pull it off too well.

"Are you ok babe, you seem distant or pre-occupied," Beccabot picked up.

"Sorry, Becca, just a long week and a lot of stuff in my head which I am still processing. I am sure now that I am home, I will get back to my old loveable self," I replied with a forced smile. She smelled the same and her voice was spot on, and the figure was exact. I just did not know how I would handle her wanting to do you know what tonight once the kids were asleep. I guess I will have to cross that bridge when we get to it. I went upstairs and changed into my track pants so I could do a quick pre-dinner workout. I needed to process for a while and working out always was my favorite thinking place after the lawn tractor.

I finished the mini-workout and went to the living room when Becca called me. We all sat down and had our usual dinner. Well, more eat and clean than eat and chat these days. I still loved the whole daddy thing and knew it would never grow old. My Rebecca and I have already been discussing having one more child but Rebecca was also talking about maybe adopting. She knew I was adopted and thought it would be a wonderful thing to do, both for us as well as the kids. Whenever the topic came up, I would devolve into joking she wanted to adopt so she wouldn't lose her perfect body. She had rebounded from the first two without any changes. Not even stretch marks. Her breasts got bigger with Sean but shrunk a bit after Roxanne. The doctor said it was not uncommon for the first child to reduce breast size and the second to increase. Something to do with mammary memory gland stuff.

We got the kids off to bed and I told Rebecca that I was going to grab a quick shower before bed. As I was enjoying a hot shower standing letting the large rain head pour down on me, I felt a hand reach around and grab you know who. I was no longer alone, and I let out a brief laugh. I figured she thought I was just being playful, but my first thought was I hope she doesn't short circuit in here while she was handling me *(made you smile)*.

I can report that they did make a very life-like replacement *(and that is all I am going to say about that)*.

Tasks – 21 and my Rebecca Returns!

(April 1994 - January 1995)

71 ***A Juicing, and a familiar taste Returns:*** Life was far from normal. Every day I had to pretend with Beccabot. Not unlike the Terminator, seems dogs can detect a T1 as well as a Beccabot. Max, our German Sheppard was skittish around Beccabot. Max loved my Rebecca and would always be close to her around the house. And when she was carrying the kids, even I got the stink eye from Max when I wanted to rub her belly. Now, Max would shadow me and if Beccabot approached, Max would sit up. The kids appeared oblivious which was good and Beccabot seemed to pull off the impersonation to a tee. I was struggling with Task 20. The issue for me was to intervene and prevent a double murder or record the murder and make sure the murderer who was acquitted in my prior Timeline is sentenced to life. I know Rebecca, that you would see this as a no brainer, but I was concerned how to intervene that did not require me whacking the asshole.

I would be less concerned with the whacking option, but this dink was high profile. Whacking him would raise the stakes for me and subject me to all the resources of law enforcement and not unlike in many respects to Task 31, he to was a narcissist as it turns out. The only major difference between 31 and 20, was 20 was a beloved hero to many. He was a Heisman winner, NFL hall of famer and had everyone fooled what he truly was capable of. I still had a few months to figure out my plan. I also had to arrange a trip to England in late August to save a Princess. This to has its issues politically and there was no intel like connection available. This had to be all me with no outside assistance since she would be on foreign soil. Kind of like the Air India solution. I also had to factor in the altered timeline possibility that I experienced during the last Task.

It was not a simple time issue. Other things changed as well. Ramzi Yousef was driving not Eyad Ismoil. Why did that change? What possible action had I taken to change that aspect? Their routing was different. But today I had a different plan. I knew eventually that those who took Rebecca would have to return her to this timeline and it was not a simple mind transference type process. This was a physical movement exercise. They would have to bring my Rebecca here and pick up their Beccabot. And somewhere in that process they needed to suck out Beccabot's memories for the period Rebecca was taken and added them back into my Rebecca thinking no one would ever know what they did. I was counting on those responsible not being aware of my inside knowledge and they would not be looking for any potential interference in the process. This I was hoping would be my ace in the hole.

I spent the next two days buying the most sophisticated camera systems available today to the consumer. I am sure if I called up my CSIS or even my CIA buddies, they would furnish me with whatever I needed but one small problem, I would have to explain why I needed it. I wanted more than one type of camera as well. I wanted one with night vision ability, inferred as well as high speed film that would allow me to view things through a frame by frame analysis with the highest definition possible. My little shopping spree set me back $36,000 but I did get the best of the best. No radio Shack stuff for me Sheldon Cooper! My guess was they would do everything after Beccabot was in bed a sleep. I had no idea how they plan to deal with me, but I was sure they would have no problem keeping me unconscious during their whole swaparoo.

I had placed the camera's all around the bedroom and told Beccabot I was replacing some old light fixtures. I even installed a one way mirror over the dresser. In addition to the locally captured imagery, I also had two camera's, one high def and one inferred transmitting their information to a secure server I set up a few years ago. This way, if they ever found the local cameras, they would have to memory pump me to try to find the servers and I would have my privacy sign up. But I was no ordinary tech nerd, I was 'Derek Flint' now! To hide my server location, I had retained the services of a young future tech wiz I would eventually hire named Ryan Bowker to hide the location of the server even from me. In order to achieve this, he programmed a random generator server IP selector so even he would not know what server was being accessed. In addition, the data files were encrypted, and the data files were parsed for added security. I would be using this approach later when I started Facebook! Well, it was the best I could do on short notice and the waiting game began.

Next weekend we had a small family gathering for my mom and dad's 35th wedding anniversary. It was a small group of about 75. Thankfully Rebecca elected to have it catered rather than have me be the master chef. Although we all know I could easily handle *75 (Made you smile)*. No one could tell 'Beccabot' was a stand in. The following week I had to fly to Chicago to meet with the board and management with respect to Microsoft's interest in licensing Spyglass's Mosaic browser platform which would go on to be Microsoft's 'Internet Explorer' browser platform. In my prior timeline, Microsoft cut a deal to license the technology along with a royalty for all sales of the browser tech. Microsoft screwed Spyglass by bundling it free with Windows, thereby avoiding the royalty arrangement. As a major shareholder, I wanted to take lead on the negotiations and make sure our contract this time had buried in it, a royalty fee regardless of if its sold or provided free. I wanted to better position the company for their eventual sale in March 2000, to OpenTV who bought out Spyglass in my last Timeline in a stock swap worth $2.5 billion. With the added legal 'clausing' I would do, I figured we would move that number up to $5 Billion. In the deal, 'OpenTV' will receive both Device Mosaic, an embedded web browser, and Prism, a content delivery and transformation system and maybe even a Derek Devon on their board for a while.

After my return from Chicago, Beccabot surprised me with a ski trip she arranged out to Whisler for 4 days with her and me and her family. Time was ticking down for my trip to California in June, and I still had not finalized Task 20's solution. I decided to throw a bit of a travel variation and told Beccabot that I had to pop down to California on business the last day of our holidays. At least I would get to hang with her family for 3 days and it was a straight shot from Vancouver to LA. I figured I needed to do a recon on the house to better assess my options. Not to mention, I think the Leaf's were in LA for a game that I could not miss and say hi to Luke.

The Whistler trip was fun, and it was great to see Tonka, Mike and Brenda who brought her new fiancé with her. I knew Bill, who was now a cop from Highschool football, and while he seemed like a decent enough guy, he was not Brenda level material by any means. I recall Brenda 1.0's marriage to Bill and I did not want to see her go through that 'BS' again. She was such a sweet kid and deserved so much better than him. At some point I would have to intervene and make sure she got to her real 'It-boy'. The trip to LA was fast and informative and I think I may have figured out my angle to deal with the situation. I met with a local security company and made arrangements to have them contact Ms. Brown and tell her she won a free home security audit and $2500 in equipment and services. If they are successful with obtaining an audit date from her in the next 3 weeks, I would return to assist them with the review and install. To secure their assistance and discretion, I also had to buy $50,000 in equipment over the next year. I knew this would not sneak past the FBI or CIA and fully expected a request for an interview at some point after.

When I got back from California on Monday night, I found a note on my front seat of my car. It was instructions and a map to my storage facility in Hamilton. I got the impression this might have been Tank's handy work. Although I did not understand how he could write a physical note and get in my car. I guess I will address that with him next time we speak. The next morning, I headed down to the storage unit to see what surprises it may contain. I was hoping he dropped off my requested shopping list of gear for my first hands on inspection of alien tech. My storage unit was well known to me since Derek 1.0 in one of his earlier careers once foreclosed on the business here and knew it intimately. I also knew one unit backed onto an abandoned utility room that measured 12 feet by 6 feet by 9 feet high. It was completely blocked in on all sides and at the time I took possession of the property around 1998, no one knew about this room. I discovered it when I noticed a mechanical drawing did not match up to my measurement for installing a new security system.

I specifically requested the unit which backed onto the wall that was shared with the empty old utility room and over a period of time, I managed to open up a few blocks to allow me access to the secret space. This was where I hid anything that was sensitive, or I did not want accidental eyes ever seeing. I assumed this was where Tank would have put whatever he delivered. When I got to my unit, I opened the door, entered, and shut the roll door behind me. The owners really did not care what people did in their units along as they did not try to turn it into some overnight accommodations or other unseemly uses if you know what I mean. It was in Hamilton's Northeast part of town, so it was not considered first class storage.

I opened my secret door and entered the rear section and turned on the lights. I surveyed the room and was a little shocked with not what I saw but what I did not see. I walked over to my work bench and saw another note. This one was in an envelope and addressed to 'James Tiberius Kirk'. This was definitely Tanks' handy work. I sat on my workbench chair and opened it. I pulled out a full one page computer generated letter in Times New Roman 10 point font.

Captain,

Things here are not progressing well and I wish to inform you that we cannot meet your previous requested provisioning list. Our special group has recently experienced something that has not happened here for over 50,000 years. Our 'Societal Managers' have allowed a small group of our people to 'De-couple' from the rest of our society. This goes against everything we hold dear and sacrosanct. The one good piece of news is their actions have increased our numbers. The downside is, we are being watched and do not know anymore who, what or when it is happening. We have been doing our best to figure out a countermove but it's in development. In order to send you this letter, I had to warp through 6 alternate planetary locations just hoping I dropped any 'tail' that I may have had. I guess you could call me 'Alien Derek Flint' my friend. We believe we can make two more openings to you before we will no longer be able to contact you.

Now for the big ask as you would like to say Derek; We want to bring you here to our planet. We can keep you safe here and it will allow us to work directly with you on your plan. Our issue is the new surveillance and the secret watchers. Opening fissures to you is hard to conceal and getting harder. We need you to write down a date, time and place for the exchange. Yes, you heard me correctly. Exchange! We will be using one from your play book that our overseers usurped from you. We will be replacing you with a Derekbot! And don't worry my friend, we will add an extra inch and some girth this time (I inserted this Rebecca - I hope you laughed with me on this one. I think Tank just became my first off-world best friend)*!*

Finally, full disclosure. We may never be able to return you. And best guess, the reset is now set for December 31st, 1999, your time. They figure they can use the whole millennium technology fear factor to mask their intrusions. You also have the option to say no and just wait it out. Be with your Rebecca and family right up to the reset. But we both know that is not how you're wired so I will not even need to mention that option to you.

See you soon my friend. We will finally get to meet face to face!

Your main Alien
Tank Flint and company!

PS: *On my planet, I am considered handsome!*

To be honest and accurate Rebecca, I was partially laughing and partially hurting. Not crying hurting, this was different. I was having to process the fact that I would have to leave the kids. All my lives, I never had to deal with an emotion like this. Yes, you and I had many emotional lessons, some good and some bad. But I never had to deal with that feeling only your children could elicit. Part of me wanted to stay and have those precious few years with my family but Tank was right. I was never wired that way and it was not who I was or wanted to be. I was only wired one way and that was to fight to the very last breath, and when that was gone, try to remain a ghost and haunt the hell out of them for the rest of their lives and more! There was also a part of me that hoped I could find and save you from the alien kidnappers, but I still had no idea if Tank knew your location.

I sat and thought of the best date, and it didn't take long. I grabbed a piece of paper and a fresh envelope. I wrote down September 11th, 10 am, here. I knew it would give them the most options without worrying about having to deal with any external issues. Before I folded my reply, I grabbed the pen again and wrote at the bottom of the page one last request. Sorry Rebecca but that request I cannot share with you at this time. It will have to be shared at a later time. I folded my reply and stuffed it into the envelope and left it on the work bench.

The drive home was very sombre, and I was already trying to put a list together of activities I wanted to do with you and the kids before my departure. I was glad I selected that date. First, it meant I could finish a couple more Tasks. Second it would allow me enough time to do a few special things with you, the kids and our families and friends. My 'last' few months would be less a Debbie Downer and more a celebration of life with friends and family for me. I knew deep down if I was given the choice of ending the reset but never being able to return, there was only one answer, and we both know what it would be. Right this moment I was more concerned when my Rebecca would be back. I can't imagine they needed to keep her so long, unless she was enjoying the alien probing *(Made you smile and that is all I am going to say about that!)*.

When I was about halfway home, I decided to make a brief detour. My CSIS watchers had all but disappeared and I felt I was all alone these past few months. So, the gatehouse awaited. I pulled in and the weather was not that bad, about 10 Celsius with some cloud. I walked first to the Hermitage to take a look at her. It had been a while since I was there, and I knew the conservation authority was planning some restoration work on the old structure. When I was walking up the drive, I did notice barriers had been placed around the main building with a caution sign, warning of falling rocks. Note to self, if I get back, major donation to the conservation authority to do a major reno with a complete main building restore, money would not be an issue.

I took one of my own routes over to the orchard area and scanned for any prying eyes or unwelcome company. The place was deserted so I took to the headwater trail and looped up to my exit point to get to the fort. I took it slow and did a thorough examination of everything along the route to see what if any changes had occurred. So far, all looked good. The only major issue for me was always the hidden wind generator. I spent a lot of time designing it and making it as hidden as was possible. My fear was if anyone found it, especially the conservation boys, they could trace the electrical feed all the way back to the fort. Fortunately, that was not an issue yet.

I hit the button 3 times and the lift came up. I got on and hit the button again to descend. The lights came on and at first glance all was as it should be. I did a quick walk about and my level one inspection looked good. I took a closer look at the batteries and that is when I saw a problem. Two had finally died and two were on their last legs as well. Time for some fresh ones and I was looking forward to the switch out. I missed spending time down here and I know Rebecca and I since the kids have not been sticking to our July 8th date, like we had been sticking to the deal up to a few years ago. I think we will have to get a babysitter and have a night or two down here before my departure even if it's Beccabot.

I did a few little things and was out in about an hour and headed home. I took a route out on 52 and was home in about 20 minutes. Everyone was outside playing, and I saw an unfamiliar car. As I approached, I soon realized it was my brother in-law Bill who was a police officer. I pulled the car up to the garage and got out. Beccabot came over and was crying and gave me a long hug and did not say anything. Bill walked over and I knew there was about to be some bad news.

"Sorry Derek but your sister was in a car accident this morning and was killed," he informed me. "I heard the information on the radio and was coming off shift and wanted to be the one to let you know. Your mom and dad have gone to the hospital, and I think are expecting you. I will be happy to drive you guys there."

"Thanks Bill, but we will take my car. I don't know what the situation will be once we get there but if you and Brenda could watch the kids, that would be a big help," I replied.

"Already on it and Brenda is on her way here," Bill replied.

This was certainly not on my list, and I know my mom and dad are going to be devastated and it made it all the more difficult that the person hugging me was not my Rebecca. Beccabot and I got the kids all sorted out and did not say anything to them. They were too young still. Brenda arrived and she and Bill made themselves at home and we left for the hospital.

Beccabot held my hand all the way there and we did not say too much. She knew I was processing everything so when I saw my parents, I would be the strength for the family during this difficult time. I had all valves tightly shut and I knew seeing my mother cry would be the hardest for me. As we entered the hospital, the church minister Robin spotted us and came over to extend his condolences and to direct us to the hospital chapel where my parents were congregating with other friends.

Word got around fast. When I entered the chapel, Ann's closest friends were all there already and sobbing with each other while my mom was slumped over a pew with my father comforting her. As I approached, I sat beside mom and put my arm around her and just held onto her. She was sobbing and dad was doing his best to keep it together. There was nothing to say, just be there and let it finish its cycle. After a few minutes, Beccabot came and sat beside me and rubbed my back to comfort me I guess and we just all sat there until mom had cried herself empty. The first words from her when she turned towards me was, "She was going to the farm to ride. She was driving her new car and it was hit head on by a truck. The police said the driver appeared impaired."

I gave my mom a solo hug now and just said, "I will deal with that mom." I don't think my mother had any idea what I meant by that, but I think Beccabot who overheard me knew what I probably meant, and I was sure she would be giving me a lecture later. I knew the old timeline was now fully deviating from the first-time and while I should have been more concerned, with having the knowledge of the pending reset, I wrote it off as something I would address later, if there was a later. The next few days were hard as you would expect, and this was the first family tragedy for both of us. I know Rebecca 1.0 had to deal with the death of her brother in her arms and I could never truly know how devastating that could be. She and I never really talked about that. While I was sitting at the funeral service at the church with Beccabot and the kids, my phone buzzed and when I looked at the phone number, I knew I would most likely be hopping on a plane in the morning for LA.

The next day, I was flying to LA and would be back in four or five days. I knew what I wanted done and I was sure my security experts would appreciate me taking lead on this one. Other than get the area well covered with camera's, I also needed to find the best location that I would need to be positioned as well. I found the perfect spot and removed a bunch of foliage so I would have a clear view of the front door area. The system we installed would allow me to have a remote monitor and system control on me as well. I knew where he would enter the property, or at least based on my old intel, and I wanted to record his every step. I knew how he thinks since we shared this same trait. It's not easy to kill a person, especially your former wife. It takes a very unique mind to be able to condition yourself with the mental discipline to carry it out. It's virtually the same ability most great athletes have. That's what makes them great and different than the average person.

The last piece of equipment I needed to install, would be a tracking device that I would place on old 'If it does not fit, you must acquit' cars. I wanted to track his movement that night and I knew he would park his car in a laneway behind her house. It took less than 10 minutes for him to drive over from his house on Rockingham. The laneway behind the house was not well lit which is why he selected that location. If my plan was to whack him, that would be where I would have done it. I had only seen photos of Nicole and when she came out to the front yard to speak with Doug about the install, I could see just how beautiful she was. Funny how all Narcissists seem to want to cheat on their spouses and think they are doing the other women a favor. I am sure 'Julie Ellen Kitaen' owes me a thank you as well.

I was anxious to get home. I was even looking forward to seeing Beccabot and the kids. I only had two weeks before I had to return to LA for the big night. This weekend I wanted to take the kids to see their first drive-in movie. Roxanne was old enough to appreciate it, but Sean, I'm sure would be out cold by 8:00 o'clock. I expected to get some pushback on the idea from Beccabot, arguing the kids were too young. But I knew I would win the argument in the end with a simple condition that we would leave as soon as the kids fell asleep unless we wanted to stay and have our own fun.

On my return trip, I would be flying into Vegas and then driving to LA in one of my cars that I owned there, a van actually. I kept vehicles all over the country along with various items I knew I would need in the future. When I was in Vegas with Big Gino, I had rented a storage garage large enough to store a Van and a few other items if needed. It was charged monthly to my special credit card that was in the name of one of my false identities I kept. Also in the storage locker was a number of firearms. It was a hell of a collection. The one I would be using in LA was a little bit unique. It was a German built short rifle equipped with a silencer. What made it unique was the ammunition it would handle. I wanted a special round that on impact would shatter and do the most, soft tissue damage.

When I was done, Mr. Heisman would be using a walker or crutches the rest of his life. I was certain he would get some jail time, but attempted murder with good lawyers would most likely only get him five to Ten and out in two or three. Especially when they would keep bringing up the mystery neighborhood vigilante shooter.

You would think that simply hitting the master alarm button causing the place to light up like it was high noon along with the sirens blaring would stop him in his tracks. But I knew better. He would finish what he planned to do and then deal with the other possible issues. Once a person like him convinces himself to act, they don't have an off button. I know that personally. I wanted to be in town 3 days prior just to provide some buffer to the original timeline since we all remember the New Jersy changes. The major problem I would have, was the type of neighborhood they were in. This was upscale and no cars parked on the road overnight. So, I decided to attend the house during the day and stash my gun and ammo. I drove over with my white van and parked in the drive. I knocked on the door and was soon met by Nicole. I had on a ball cap, sunglasses and a shirt with the security company's name on it.

"Excuse me Ms. Brown, I need to check on a camera that appears to be malfunctioning. I will only be 30 minutes tops," I informed her.

"Oh, I was not aware of any problems but thanks for looking after it," she replied. What she did not know as well was my turning off the entire system before I entered the property. I knew I would leave CIA level clues, but I was not prepared to give the local police any help identifying me. I did what I needed to do and left after turning the system back on. I returned to my apartment that I was renting since my first trip and relaxed for a few hours. I had the trackers activated on the cars and was watching his vehicle movements. I expected to see a few daytime drive-byes by him. He would want to see if anything odd was going on and its kind of a ritual for the self brain-washing process he would be wanting to do on himself.

My original intel had him doing it on Sunday, June 12 and the bodies were discovered around midnight. It was a coincidence that on the night of the murder, Nicole had eaten dinner with her mother at the restaurant where Ron Goldman worked as a waiter, and her mother had forgotten her glasses. She called and asked him to drop them off on his way home, which brought him to Brown's that night. I was just as curious if any timeline interference by me potentially would change Ron's timing. My post Task story that I would leak was a written letter to the local newspaper explaining I had noticed this man driving around the neighborhood looking like he was casing the Brown's home and decided to keep a watch out thinking he was a burglar or worst, rapist. The cameras would tell the real story and my only concern was timing. The Nicole 1.0 autopsy determined that she had been stabbed seven times in the neck and scalp and had sustained a 14 cm-long gash across her throat, which had severed both her left and right carotid arteries and breached her right and left jugular veins. This would have been done after she was down on the ground, I was sure. The wound on her neck penetrated 1.9 cm into her cervical vertebrae, nearly decapitating her. She also had defensive wounds on her hands that must have occurred first.

This clearly shows a person who had entered the 'No return Phase', of the act. Once he started, he had a plan, and he would not stop until he completed his plan in his head. This was no impromptu or decisions on the fly. This was a detail step-by-step thought through process that he would have rehearsed in his mind, over and over. He would have been on autopilot. My computer went off with the program alarm and I went to look at his movement. I had no intel what Nicole did Saturday night or Friday night for that matter. Friday night, he drove past the front of the house at 9 pm and then turned down Dorthey Street to access the rear laneway. He did that again at 10 pm and 11 pm. According to the security camera's, Nicole was in Friday night with the kids and a girlfriend. I could see them in the living room watching TV. I always had access to the alarm speakers to issue a verbal warning or other information if need be.

Sunday was my big day. Well, I think it was about to be my big day. I waited until 9 pm and then parked my van off Gretna Green Way at a local church parking lot. I was in my jogging outfit and started to pretend I was a local jogger *(Yes Rebecca I know I use this approach a lot).* I ran along Gretna Green Way and then turned left up Dorthey. I then turned left again to run down the laneway behind the house. No sign of anyone yet so I turned and enter the rear of Nicole's property. I have one fence to climb and just before I started the climb, I took my portable controller out of my shorts and turned off the security system. I climbed over the fence and made my way along the rear fence to get to my position around the side where I had all my stuff hidden and reactivated the security system. I reached into the bushes and pulled out my gear. I opened my mini-laptop and turned it on in night mode. I took my cell phone and connected it to the laptop. I booted up my tracking software and settled in. I was lucky as Nicole just arrived home and proceeded to go directly into the house. There was a babysitter in there and in about 5 minutes, the young girl exited and walked left up Bundy.

I sat there for another hour when I saw the tracker marker begin to move on the screen. I watched the car do the exact same routing again. It did not stop in the laneway, it kept going. I figured he was in his psych-up mode and would do another drive around. I looked at my watch and it was now almost 11 pm. Nicole was in the kitchen now and I returned my look to the tracker screen. This time the car had stopped in the laneway, and I figured this was go time. I quickly put on my special outfit and got myself positioned to take the required shot. Timing would be everything. I turned the laptops camera view to the 6-camera view so I could watch him entering where I did and then could track him to the front door. I figured he would knock on the door and tell Nicole he wanted to chat with her about the kids or something. Once she came onto the porch, he would strike.

I was spot on, and I noticed he was wearing the 'famous gloves' and kept his hands behind his back clutching the knife. This was it. I drew my weapon up and was in my prone position waiting to pull the trigger. He knocked and I could hear Nicole ask why he was there through my earpiece that was feeding me the sound from the porch mic. Right again, he wanted to talk about the kids and told her he had to leave tonight for a trip to Chicago. He had his hands behind his back again and Nicole came out onto the porch and closed the front door, probably to keep the kids from maybe hearing any of the discussion. His angle was a little off, giving me a clear shot at his nut sack. I retrained the sight to his left knee. As he brought the knife out from behind his back, he entered his killer zone.

"You fucking dead bitch," the asshole told her as he pulled the knife from behind his back. Bingo, got him on tape now.

I heard Nicole say with alarm in her voice, "What the fuck are you doing?"

That was all I needed to hear. I pulled the trigger, and it was a direct hit to his left knee shattering it and causing him to rotate towards me. I pulled the trigger for the second shot which hit him square in his junk! That was for Nicole 1.0 and Ron 1.0 asshole; Ron 2.0 was now running up the drive having watched what was happening from the street. He yelled, "Nicole, get in the house and call the police."

Nicole yelled back at Ron, "Fuck, the asshole cut me. I'm hurt Ron, I am bleeding."

The Asshole was rolling on the ground screaming in pain. I think trying to decide if he should grab his missing knee or his missing junk. I was leaning towards the castration being more painful. Under my mask, I had a huge grin. Each task seemed to have its own Frank Hohimer from 'Thief' moment for me. This was it on this one. I left everything exactly where it needed to be and exited the bushes. The rifle was untraceable and anything I wanted to remove went in a small knapsack I was now carrying in my right hand. As I walked down the drive, I stopped once Ron spotted me. I had the remote in my pocket and hit the panic button. The place lit up, sirens started, and I was on full display for Ron but far enough away the cameras we installed would not pick me up. I turned and gave my vaudevillian bow. I then continue to walk to Bundy and turned right. After I got about 2 houses away, I removed my costume and quickly put it in the knapsack and tossed it on my back and entered my joggers act again. It only took me 3 minutes to reach the church and get in my van. I started it and exited left on Gretna Green Way and took it all the way to San Vicente Blvd and made my way to the 405. As I neared the 405, I could hear a siren or two and would be interested to see the news tomorrow. I was back at my apartment and was inside before midnight and proceeded to do a complete wipe down of the van and I burned my clothing in a mini-incinerator I threw together. I left at 2 am and headed back to Vegas to park the van and head to the airport. I had an 8 am flight out back to buffalo that I did not want to miss.

I had been listening to the radio and it certainly did not take long for the news media to report what had happened. First reports came out that the 'Asshole' was rushed to the hospital with gunshot wounds and was in critical condition. That did not seem likely unless Nicole decided to give him her own beating or maybe even stuck him with the knife. I would hope Ron would intervene and look after her until the police and ambulance(s) arrives. Nicole suffered a severe laceration to her left hand and was being kept overnight at the hospital. I was sure there would be plenty of news the next week or more once the surveillance tapes had been reviewed and I turned the radio to a music station. And as I always do after a Task, I replayed the whole thing over in my mind, dissecting everything to see if there were some possible improvements.

I landed in Buffalo and grabbed my car and headed home. I was curious how long it would take Chris to call me or maybe have me detained at the border, but it was a little too soon and this was more a Hollywood story and not a national security thing. I breezed through the border and was home for dinner. After dinner, I went to sit in the living room and flip through the mail. Beccabot came in and turned on the TV to ABC news. She said, "Have you been following any of this. You must have been there when this happened. The last news item had them trying to identify who the neighborhood vigilante was that wore a Guy Fawkes mask, dressed in black with a cape."

"No. this is the first I have heard about it," with a bit of a grin.

"You must know who her husband is. I think he even did one of those goofy airplane movies," Beccabot added.

"Who would have ever guessed he was capable of doing something like that," I replied.

"Like what," Beccabot turned and stared at me.

"Well, I assume he was there for a purpose at 11 pm. I think they were separated and there were some stories a few years ago that he used to beat her I think I read," I deflected.

"The hospital reported that he took a gunshot to his genitals and left knee. He also had a number of blows to the head and is in critical condition," Beccabot explained.

Guess what annual ritual I will do every June 12th, Rebecca? Yes, we are going to watch V for Vendetta, at least once it gets made!

The next day I got up and sat at the kitchen table with Beccabot running through a schedule for the next 2 months. I would have to leave on August 25th for London for a week. After our chat, I went to the barn and jumped on the riding lawnmower to do a grass cutting. I know we use a lawn service, but every now and then I just enjoy doing it myself. It was my thinking time. I was generally pleased with the outcome of Task 20, but Task 21 was going to be awkward. I had the benefit of seeing what life would be like after the death of the princess and I was concerned what changes may occur if she had not been killed. Her two boys turned out to be wonderful young men and William was on course to be a great king one day not to mention marrying a super hot girl, and my type to boot. Any interference by me could drastically change that future, and maybe not in a good way. Having thought it through cutting the grass, I decided there was really one course of action I felt comfortable with. I would have to bring Mr. Sunderland somewhat into my confidence but I had a good angle, and it would take any decision out of my direct hands. It may alter my relationship with Mr. Sunderland, but I would just have to roll the dice.

That evening, I took the kids for a short walk after dinner to wear them out before bed. It was usually a 7 pm bedtime and they were generally good sleepers. Sean would have the odd nightmare but usually would roll over and cry himself back to sleep in 5 minutes. As I arrived at the house, I spotted Beccabot in the kitchen window and it looked like she was in a baking mood. As the kids and I entered the kitchen, she came over and gave the kids a big hug and that is when I first noticed Max was now at her side. She looked at me and gave me a smile that was different than her smile earlier today. I was in a full analysis mode as I watched her every move. I went to Max, who's tail was wagging, and he seemed to be smiling, at least how Max smiles. I told the kids it was bedtime and took them to get ready. I was still processing what I had just observed but was thinking that maybe my Rebecca was back. They must have completed the switch when I was out for a walk with the kids.

I got the kids in bed and returned to the kitchen. I went over to give the person baking a test hug. I came up behind her and gently began to suckle on her right ear lobe. My Rebecca loved that. She said it was one of her erogenous zones. As I began to gently suckle, she tilted her head and said, "When was the last time I told you how much I love you?"

"Last year I think," as I came up from the suckle and whispered that in her ear.

"I am sure it was not that long but just to be sure, tonight is going to be Derek's night," she said with a grin.

I put my face into the back of her hair and took a deep smell. Her scent was different than Beccabot. In fact, it was the smell I remembered and so loved. I looked down to my left and finally knew that my Rebecca was back. Max was there looking at us hugging and was wagging his tail. The first wag in almost six months. God, I could not believe it was six months.

"Derek, is everything all right between us?" she asked.

"I hope so. Why do you ask?" I replied.

"I don't recall you and I being intimate like we use to the past few months. It has me worried," she confessed to me.

"Well Becca, I think tonight we will have to make a new deal that we will do our thing at least once a week no mater what," I suggested.

"Well, I am game if you're game my favorite Hickey Monster," she replied with her beautiful but devilish smile.

Once I knew Rebecca was gone, and I was having to pretend with Beccabot, my preferred intimate moves were put on hold. I hope you understand now Rebecca why. I played the role I had to play but that was it. There was no anything else. Nothing!

We had a very long and somewhat passionate kiss and even that felt different. Different in a good way. Seems my alien abductors could make a pretty good copy, but they could not match my girl exactly. It was good to know they were not perfect. Tonight, I planned to inspect every square centimetre of her, inside and out, to see if I can spot any other mistakes my new number one enemy may have left or done to her *(made you laugh, but I was pissed about that, and you know I would get my pound of flesh or what ever they were made out of at some future point)*. I can now safely report that the replacement was exceptionally well done from a visual aspect, but as far as smell and taste goes, I can tell the difference big time.

The next morning, I was anxious to get some time by myself to take a look at the camera footage. I always thought they would do it at night when we slept. I never thought it would be during the daytime. I went through every one of the tapes for the time it would have happened and would you guess, not a thing. There was no obvious tampering, just my $36,000 worth of video stuff pointing in the wrong spot. And don't worry Becca, I will remove the equipment and you don't have to worry that I would try to make some 'Special Tape' for us to watch in the future *(Made you nervous?).*

Task – 22,23,24

(August 1995 – September 11th, 1997)

72 ***Princess, Stout and Bond;*** Over the next two months, life was perfect. Family was great, work was great, and our moms were responding fabulously to my special treatment regime. When I first evaluated what I could accomplish when I made my "Wish List" on T-Minus 18 Days preparing for the transference, I had divided the list into two major categories: Information Dump and Hands on. There was going to be two major events that lent themselves to a pure information dump. First was the Oklahoma Bombing carried out by Tim McVeigh and Terry Nichols on April 19th, 1995, which killed at least 168 people, injured more than 680 others and the other was the Dunblane massacre on 13th of March 1996 that killed 16 young students and one teacher and injured 15 others.

My Friend Chris Samuel was now a senior supervisor and I know he appreciated my little information package, and I knew my identity would be preserved. Miss Livingston was also now a sectional head and also appreciated my tip, although her behavioral science team could not figure out how such a tip was possible. Nonetheless, a great success!

My flight to England was not by private plane this time. I wanted to enter the country a bit more under the radar. I knew they would pick up my arrival at immigration, but felt sure that they would not detain me, and may not even bother to meet up with me later. Immigration went smoothly and I rented an Aston Martin Virage for the week *(Don't ask the price!)*. I had booked a room at the Savoy and check-in went without any issues as well. I went to my room to freshen up and left to make my next stop. I drove out of town towards Walthamstow. I knew where Mr. Sunderland lived, and I wanted a very private and off the record so to speak chat with my Friend. Mr. Sunderland had a lovely old Tudor home on about 2 acres with a large metal gate at the entrance. I pulled up and rang his intercom.

"Hello, may I help you," a voice came from the box.

"Good afternoon, would you please inform Mr. Sunderland that a Derek Devon is here to see him," I replied.

"Just one moment please," was squawked.

I sat in the car for about 3 minutes when the gates opened and a voice came over the speaker, "A bit lost are we Mr. Devon."

"I was told you can get a wonderful pint of the local stout here at an affordable price," I returned.

"I will get a couple ready for your arrival," Sunderland told me.

I drove up the drive which was lined with a wonderful flower bed and a small stone partitioning wall about 2 feet high. As I arrived at the front circular drive area in front of the main entrance, Mr. Sunderland was standing there in casual dress but still sporting a bow tie. I pulled up and got out and approached my old friend. "Welcome to my place Derek, it must be important for you to arrive without the usual fanfare," as he extended his hand.

"Yes, it is rather sensitive, and I will trust that we can have a frank and off-the-record chat without anyone else being privy to it," I replied.

Let's sit in the back and have that Stout you have been so anxiously wanting to try," my friend responded.

We walked around the house rather than through it. There was a lovely stone patio with a quaint wrought iron table and chair arrangement. There were 2 glasses and a couple of bottles already on the table. We took our seats and we both poured out our dark and creamy liquid and we watched the cascading bubbles suggesting it was a nitrogen infused beverage similar to a Guiness or Kilkenny.

"Arthur, I have been given some very sensitive intel that I felt deserved this private meeting. You know me and I know you so there is no need for any dance my friend. On August 30th, a certain princess is scheduled to be assassinated and not by who you may think, and it will take place on French soil. That is why I am fairly sure you have absolutely zero intel on this. You know that my standard MO would have me either disclose what I know in advance, or I would handle the matter discreetly myself. However, this event has other potential consequences and I felt that it was proper to let one person make the call as to what I should do," I explained.

"Take a drink Derek and tell me what you think of our local specialty," Arthur replied.

I took a few gulps and savored the liquid in my mouth and finished my swallow. "Very rich and I love the hint of blackberry and truffle," I replied.

"First, thank you for your discretion regarding this matter, and second, I want to do a little snooping myself before I give you my decision on what I want to do," Arthur informed me.

Our discussion went from business to soccer. I knew Arthur was a big Arsenal fan and I could not resist the opportunity to bring up their last match against Chelsea that they lost. They were both middle of the pack this season, but Chelsea sat just above them in the standings. Our friendship was more professional, and I knew there would be no late dinner invite. I finished my stout and we parted. We agreed to meet again on Thursday at the pub in town. I drove back to the Savoy and was enjoying the Aston Martin. I kept the Lotus in storage and every time I try to get you to let me start driving it again, you give me the old family man speech.

I returned to the pub on Thursday and Arthur was already there with a half-filled glass of some ale. He was standing at a small table in the corner that was customary in British pubs and sporting his usual tweed bowtie. As I arrived at the table, we exchanged our customary handshake, and a bottle of stout was brought to our table by a lovely young waitress. "I trust you have been keeping yourself occupied, Derek," Arthur said.

"Yes, Arthur, the usual stuff," I replied jokingly. We both knew I was now under watch, and it was not on Arthur's request, but was now standard protocol for me, especially because of my Russian affiliations.

"So here are my two cents on the matter Derek. I could find no information on the topic anywhere. So, I am forced to take your word on this, and I don't offer that to many people, but you have always put our country's interest first. If what you say is true and I know you won't divulge your sources, but assuming it was related to her current companion, and let's also assume that his people are not happy with the situation; if it was to go down that way, we would potentially be put in a very difficult position both politically as well as economically. Your decision to meet with me first is to be commended and very much appreciated. I think I know your next question so go and ask it," Arthur requested.

"I want 'mum' to make the call. I know she had to dance around the whole divorce mess, and this is a kingdom issue not a Derek doing the right thing issue. I will either go home and let you handle it, handle it on a much more private level myself or simply fly home and let the chips fall as they may," I replied.

"If I bring her into this discussion, even if its only her and me, she will have to know you will also be privy and that may be an issue," Arthur countered with.

"Yes, she will have to trust me and only she can make that call. I came to you Arthur because I trust you, and for that matter her, because I have a deep respect for her role in your country's future and that such a decision will be something we will all have to live with the rest of our lives, but I am sure she will do what is best for the country first and foremost," I said somewhat assuredly.

"Well stated and I will make the visit first thing tomorrow. I will get you my answer by noon tomorrow and you will know it when you see it my friend. And thank you once again for your services to our country," my old teacher said.

We finished our drinks, and I gave him the latest update on marriage and the kids. I also told him a few concerns I had with certain changes in the old Soviet Union and a few intelligence suggestions. I drove back to the Savoy and retired to my room. Like the USA, I had arranged some private storage in the area as well as obtaining some special firearms over the years. If this was going to end up being a 'Devon only' operation, then I would use the semi with armour piercing rounds, and it was my plan to shoot out the engine, about two blocks from the Pont de l'Alma tunnel where the accident had previously occurred. By taking out the engine, the car should remain in the control of Henri Paul, even in his impaired condition. It simply would lose all power. I could position myself safely near their location and by the time they came to a stop, I would be in my car heading south.

I went for a walk around town to kill the time. I had a good idea how Arthur would send the message. I had not eaten any breakfast and decided to grab a bite in the Savoy. I was sitting at my table when the waiter came over and said, "The young woman over there wanted to buy you a Tea."

I turned my gaze over to the table across the room and I know a big smile was produced. Miss Livingston was here. Not sure if this was business or another reason. I got up and walked over to her table. "Hello Abby, what a pleasant surprise, business or pleasure?" I asked.

"Hello Derek and marriage seems to be treating you swimmingly," she replied with a cheerful look.

"Yes, I could not be happier, and I love the whole fatherhood stuff. How about you?" I asked.

"Well, work limits me a bit on the children front, but I am hoping that I will be getting a promotion next year that will get me out of the field and then start a family," she told me. "To answer your first question, I am here working. You have picked up a couple fans since you arrived, and I am simply watching your back supposedly. But we both know you have no need of any back watching," was her reply with a smile.

"Yes, I was aware of my admirers and until I am told you are no longer my guardian angel, you can always count on me expecting you'll be watching my backside," I said with a big smile.

"Are they good," she asked.

"Not really, I am thinking they are fairly green, but I will give them some fun maybe later," I informed her.

We sat and chatted for a few more minutes and then I told her I needed to retire to my room for a phone call. When I got to the room, I decided to call you Rebecca, not sure if you recall *(that particular call),* but it was the call that you proposed that we spend a weekend down at the fort like the old days when I got back. I had briefly mentioned it before I left, but I was so happy to hear you ask. Since it was getting close to your birthday and my departure off-world was in 13 days, I suggested that we celebrate your birthday at the fort. You told me you would see if you could arrange for someone to watch the kids for us.

When I hung up the phone, I heard a knock at the door. One of the front desk staff appeared and handed me a package. I gave him a ten-pound tip and retired to the desk chair and proceeded to open it. As I pulled the wrapping paper back a book title appeared Bentley's Miscellany. It appeared to be an original 1840's edition. Well, Arthur pulled a fast one. He actually was able to fool me which is pretty hard to do. I was sure I knew what his answer, or should I say 'mum's' would be, and it actually made me feel pretty good. I was always worried if I was told to leave that it may bother me over time. I would certainly understand that course of action, but it would still bother me. I was always working on saving people, not having political expedience sideline that requirement and sacrificing such a beautiful soul and wonderful mother. If you're wondering the significance of the book Rebecca, it was the first time my old alter ego Guy Fawkes appeared in print. My money was on Sunderland sending me an actual Guy Fawkes porcelain replica mask. But to send me such a rare book was his way of saying, "Thank you, and I one upped you my young protégé." If anyone could spot my handy work in LA, it would have been Sunderland.

I checked out of the Savoy and needed to get to Paris to do my job. I needed to get there by the 30th late afternoon at the latest. I was a bit concerned the French intelligence may have me flagged because of my Russian conncctions and that would potentially screw everything up. As a precaution, I called Miss Livingston and asked her if she could provide me with a clean ID and passport in 4 hours. She laughed at first then said she would put a rush on it for me once she knew I was serious. I had stashed my equipment in the car, and I met Miss Livingston outside MI6 where she handed me my documents. She had no idea what I was doing and knew better then to ask. She simply smiled and said, "Good Luck on what ever you are up to Mr. Devon."

I made my way to Dover to catch the Ferry and figured I would need four hours from Calais to Paris barring any accidents. I had more than enough time, and the trip was smooth with no issues. I did not take a room around Paris and was planning on driving South to a region called Lévis. There was a beautiful old Chateau down there that would accept me for an overnight stay without many questions asked since I stayed there a couple times before. I had about 8 hours to kill so I did what any tourist would do in Paris, I went to the Louvre to raise my cultural level a bit. I knew that would only take up a few hours and planned on a light meal at Café de Flore, right across the street from Les Deux Magots in the popular 75006 Paris cafe zip code.

I wanted to stay away from anywhere there may be cameras and I still had four hours to kill so I decided to drive around the town. I never really drove around Paris before on my own and figured it would give me something to do. I was not a fan of Paris and always preferred the region south. I always felt the Persian French were a bit snobbish to us Englishman.

It was my research that Dodi Fayed would be staying at one of his apartments on Rue Arsène Houssaye. This section of Paris was set up like a giant wagon wheel with the center of the wheel being the Arc de Triomphe *(A famous arch you would have seen in many films).* There were a bunch of roads that extended outwards. Driving in Paris was always a bit of a challenge and I wanted to retrace the fatal route, so I made my way up to Rue Arsène Houssaye. They would have to travel along the Av. de Friedland and around the Rue de Tilsitt *(Giant circle around the Arc de Triomphe).* They would travel roughly 280 degrees and then exit onto Av. D'lena. I continued my route looking for the best location available for my positioning. I travelled along Av. Marceau heading towards the final turn before entering the Tunnel under the Pont de l'Alma overpass, the site of the crash that resulted in the death of the Princess.

I was scanning each side as I drove and wanted to find a position that would also afford me an exit route. With all the one-way streets the last thing I would want is a position that after the shots, would then have me drive right past their disabled car. Finally, I spotted my position. Just off Av. Marceau running away, Av. Du President Wilson. The second shop on the right had a construction area secured by fences and a covered scaffold tunnel for pedestrians. I figured I could position myself on the top of the scaffold and after my shots, drop down, get in my car, and be heading in the opposite direction. This area was not a high night-time traffic area, and I was hoping would be public-free at the time.

I would do another drive by at 11:30 pm and would need to find an alternate location as well. I thought the worst option would be to park on the opposite side of Av. Marceau and as they drove by going in the opposite direction take the shots. I was sure that Av. Marceau would have some traffic and if there were public walkers at the time, it would most likely be along Av. Marceau. In hindsight, I should have also brought my 9×21mm Gyurza *(Russian for "blunt-nosed viper")* round designed to defeat body armor that was developed by 'TsNIITochMash' and my SR-1 Vektor semi-automatic pistol. That would have been my choice if I had to park on Av. Marceau. My next route to check would be my exit route. I did a lap so I could travel again down Av. Marceau and then made a right onto Av. Du President Wilson. My goal was to get myself as quickly as possible to A6 or A. du Soleil. That was, for the most part, a straight shot south to Lévis. It took a few laps before I found my preferred exit route.

I felt like some physical exercise, so I eventually parked my car on Rue le Tasse and walked over to Fontaine du Jardin du Trocadéro. I proceeded to do a few laps of the fountain and it also afforded me an excellent view of the Eiffel Tower. It was dark now and I was getting closer to my positioning time. I grabbed a drink and a pastry from a street vendor and returned to my car. I loved the car, but I was starting to rethink my choice with the amount of people that wanted to take a picture beside it. Maybe a Plain Jane car would have been a better choice. I sat in the car and ate my pastry and drank my juice. It was now 10:30 pm and I figured I have enough time to drive the exact route one more time. I also needed some time to install my disposable wireless camera along Av. Marceau that would allow me to see the approach of their Mercedes. As I passed by Rue Arsène Houssaye I slowed and spotted the Mercedes along with two men standing outside having a cigarette and chatting. I took a good look at the car using the sideview mirror hoping to better train my eyes to the front view of the car.

When I made it down to Av. Du President Wilson, I spotted a street parking opening that was perfect. I did a parallel park and scanned the construction area directly behind me. I could use the end of the scaffolding closest to me to climb on top and then climb down off. I took my sports duffle bag that had my equipment and went over to the scaffold. I scanned for any possible late-night walkers or smokers and did not see anyone. I climbed up the scaffold and proceeded to set up the rifle using the sports bag to lay on. Once I was satisfied everything was ready, I climbed down and went back to the car. I grabbed the disposable video camera and made my way out to Av. Marceau to find the best location to mount it. I had a limit of 300 yards but wanted the angle to give me the best side visual to make sure it was the right car I would unload on. I found a small balcony that I could reach from an entrance wall that was about 5 feet tall. I climbed up and quickly mounted the camera to the metal sub-structure.

I returned to the car to wait a few more minutes. This Task I was hoping had zero impact by any of my prior tasks or I may blow it. Suddenly I thought about the potential consequences for me. If I did not make the shot, and my timing was off and the accident still happened, Sunderland may think I was the cause of the accident. That was a scenario I would not want to see happen. The time was approaching midnight and I exited the car and made my way onto the scaffold. It was not a great lit side street but there was enough light for anyone out walking to spot me climbing. I did a very thorough scan of the area and felt I was safe to climb up. As I assumed my position, I felt comfortable that my prone position would make it hard to spot me from the street given the height of the scaffold tunnel. I turned on my mini laptop and activated the camera. The battery life on the camera was only 30 minutes due to the high-resolution output and the auto focus feature it had. When they trace the camera, I was hoping they would conclude it was most likely some pervert or secret security system for the area.

So far, knock on wood Rebecca, all my tasks had been collateral free as far as running into innocent wandering people or unexpected last-minute issues that could either stop me from completing the task or subject me to unwanted exposure. Unlike Peter Bernard, where I had time on my side, and removed the problem long before it would become a problem, this was more like the last task where timing was the difference between life and death. The car would be traveling roughly 60-70 km per hour and my available time to deliver the required shot to disable the motor would be approximately 2-3 seconds with the full side-to-side range of motion from my position. I estimated I could deliver 2-4 shots. I had mentally completed the math required to time the shots. Mercedes is built like a tank and I was sure the main passenger compartment was reinforced with added protection but the front side body panels where no match for my armour piercing rounds. The added noise suppressor would have a slight impact on the exit muzzle velocity, but I was confident at 150 yards, it would not cause any issues.

I prepared the rifle with the 6-round clip, and I had the screen brightness turned down to try and keep my location and activity private. Last thing I wanted to encounter, was some glow emanating from my position. At 12:15, I noticed movement on the laptop screen. I spotted a car, and it was not the Mercedes. It was traveling at roughly 60 km per hour. I counted off the time in my head that it took for it to move from the location I first spotted on the laptop to my delivery spot. I counted 4 seconds. I turned my head back to the entry view and watched for the Mercedes. Finally, I spotted it coming. Thankfully no other cars in front and I was right, it was moving pretty fast.

I assumed the firing position and placed my finger on the trigger. I took a deep breath and was ready for the delivery. As soon as I picked up the front bumper with my eye, I pulled the trigger while maintaining my tracking about one foot ahead of the front bumper. I did not use ear plugs because I wanted full hearing ability. The silencer helped but it was still a fairly loud release of propulsion gases. I would not know what round would be the one that killed the engine, it could be all 4 if my tracking was accurate. At 150 yards from the vehicle, I would not hear anything from my location. After the final trigger pull, I looked up over the gun sights in the direction of the Mercedes location to see what damage I had done.

There was a prominent steam discharge coming out of what I assumed was the entry hole. The car was still moving but I could tell the engine was no longer driving it. At that moment, I got up, packed up the gear and climbed down. I placed the sports bag in the back seat, threw the blanket over it and got in the driver side. I started the car and pulled out onto the street and began the separation process. My exit route was pre-planned, and I figured by the time Henri got out and inspected the front end and discovered the entry holes, I would be one kilometer away and only 4 kilometers from my entry onto the expressway leading me to A6. I was hoping that once they realized the holes were from a bullet, they would call in reinforcements and take a defensive position on Av. Marceau. I was also aware that the paparazzi was behind the Mercedes and that would also add to the hole confusion and distraction I wanted to create. It would also mean that the incident would be front page material tomorrow.

After Lévis, depending on the newspaper and television reports, I would decide when I would make my way back to England. My return trip would keep me away from France and I would ferry from Amsterdam over to Newcastle. I wanted to stop into Whitley Bay and see where my grandfather and father came from and before leaving Amsterdam I would have to load up on salted licorice. The next morning, I turned on the television and the events last night were the headlines, 'Princesse et tentative d'assassinat de Fayed' *(Princess and Fayed Assassination Attempt)*. I could not have written a better headline myself. The French tabloids went even further, and it was very telling that they all referred to an unnamed Interpol source claiming it was a Saudi backed group. I figured that was the work of Sunderland to get the focus off the Royals from the get-go. I really loved this part of France and decided to stay one more night. That day, I rented a bike and rode around the area and made a few stops checking out the local cafes and pubs. The reality of my pending departure had begun to really set in.

The ride from Lévis up to Amsterdam was wonderful and I was falling in love with the car. I stayed overnight in Amsterdam and did a walk-a-bout. The next day, I loaded onto the ferry, and we began the lengthy trip across the north channel to Newcastle. I had been to Newcastle once and it was just another English city. The last time Derek 1.0 was in Whitley Bay, the biggest challenge was finding a traditional Fish'n chip shop. My wife and I at the time ended up travelling down to North Sheilds to find a traditional Fish'n chip shop. That trip was by train and taxi. This time I had wheels, really nice wheels.

The ferry ride is rather long, but I love being on the sea. I spent a lot of time up on the observation deck until the squall hit. There was an onboard immigration officer that would do pre-arrival immigration clearing processing. I was still using the fake ID and was a bit curious what would pop up when it was scanned. I handed the 40-something-year-old immigration officer my English passport. He scanned the passport and immediately sat up straight in his chair and said, "Sorry sir, I was not aware we had any royal security officers travelling with us."

"We don't usually give any notice Mr. Oxley," I replied.

He handed me back my passport and stood up and said, "Welcome aboard sir and if you require anything, please let me know."

I smiled and put the passport into my coat pocket and returned to the observation deck. I doubt Sunderland would have picked up my decision to ferry across to Newcastle. Perhaps when we arrive and the immigration officer uploads the data he collected, but for now I was still under the radar. He knew my car and licence plate so with the drive from Whitley Bay back to London, it would most likely provide Sunderland with my whereabouts. I thought that due to the nature of the trip, it would be best, to let me be, and avoid any contact. One of those plausible deniability things. I knew my effort would not go unnoticed by Sunderland or 'Mum'.

As I sat at Gatwick waiting for my plane to board, I was reading a local newspaper which had a full section pullout detailing the events in Paris and the actions being considered by the Royal Family. I knew that most was pure speculation, but it was promising when I read about the princess returning to Buckingham Palace for a family meeting. I was hoping it may lead to some more stable arrangement for all concerned, especially William and Harry. As I sat reading, I noticed a tweed pair of pants on the man that just sat in the chair beside mine. I must have let out a slight chuckle when the man in the seat beside me said, "Something funny Derek?"

"No Arthur, just thinking about an old movie I watched many years ago," I replied.

"Just wanted to wish you a safe trip my boy and I have a letter here from an old friend; she asked that you only read it after her death. And last but not least, this is for you as well."

Sunderland handed me a small decorative box with very old looking embroidery on it along with the Royal Seal. I opened the lid and looked at the contents. As I stared at it, Arthur reached over and opened it all the way exposing a handwritten note on the inside of the box lid.

'I hope in the future, we will get another opportunity to ride together. I greatly appreciate your discretion and skill'. No signature, nothing special, just a note written by hand. I smiled and felt Arthur's hand grip my arm with a gentle squeeze and he got up and smiled and handed me a small paper bag and said, "This is from me, and I made the necessary arrangements for you to enjoy them on your flight."

I stood up clutching the box and extended my hand first to shake his and then take the paper bag. I knew what it was. I gave a nod and stared at him walking away. I wondered if this would be my last time seeing my old 'Sherlockean' sleuth buddy. I sat back down and opened the box up and stared at the medal. It was the George Cross Rebecca. You will find both the letter and the medal in my personals' box the lawyers would have given you. I only ask that you continue to honour the 'Mum's' request and don't open the letter until her death.

I sat in first class and asked for a chilled beer glass. I knew Arthur would make sure they had one for this occasion and the stewardess returned with an ice-cold glass. I took one of the bottles out and popped the cap off. I gently poured the stout into the glass and watched the cascading bubbles. As I was watching, a voice from behind me just to my right said, "Excuse me, where did you get that?"

I always prided my hearing on being able to identify a person by their voice. Well, if there was ever a voice that I did not need any talent to identify, was the man sitting behind me to my right.

I smiled and turned and said, "Well, just so happens that I have one more with your name on it."

I gestured to the stewardess to come over. I asked her, "Would you by chance have another chilled glass back there for me?"

She smiled and said, "Your friend gave us four glasses."

"Would you please grab me one more," I requested.

She returned with the glass, and I had already retrieved the other bottle Arthur gave me from the bag. I opened the bottle and got up and walked over to the gentleman sitting behind me to my right. I placed the bottle on his table along with the chilled glass.

"You must know people in high places to get those on the plane," my new drinking companion commented.

"I would tell you who gave them to me, but I would have to kill you after that," I replied with a smile.

I turned and grabbed my glass and by the time I had turned back to my new acquaintance, he had poured the stout and he raised his glass for a friendly cheer, "Here, here," he said.

I raised mine avoiding any crass clinking and said, "To Arthur."

Eventually we went from chatting about the stout and where it was made to golfing. Finally, I asked why he was flying to Toronto, and he told me it had to do with some new movie release called 'Just Cause'. We chatted until the beer was done and I told my new friend I needed to do a little work at my seat, and wished him a successful trip to Toronto, and encouraged him if he had time, to play the Hamilton Golf & Country Club. I returned to my seat and took out a note pad and started to make a list of everything I needed to do over the next 7 days. I guess six, if I don't count today. I spent about an hour and a half writing out a fairly lengthy list. Dinner was served, and after dinner, my drinking friend came over to my seat and handed me a glass and said, "Best I could do on short notice."

I took the glass, had a sip, smiled and said, "Glenmorangie Signet I would guess."

"I see you have just as good taste in your scotch as your beer Derek," he replied.

"I also prefer my Martini shaken not stirred," I replied with even a bigger smile.

I got up and we stood and chatted a bit more about the Bahamas where he lived in the Lyford Bay exclusive community of Nassau. He extended an open invitation to stop in and have a pint should I find myself in Nassau. He wrote down his Nassau phone number on the napkin and handed it to me. I told him that my next trip near his place would most likely be in my sailboat. He told me that he would love to have a few scotches sailing around the islands. We had a couple more scotches when the captain informed us that we would be landing shortly. My new drinking buddy and I shook hands and exchanged our appreciation to one and other. I took my seat and started to go into my departure planning mode.

The Departure!

(September 4th, 1997 – September 11th, 1997)

73 ***Is this the End of Derek 2.0?:*** I was both glad and sad to be driving up the driveway. I missed you and the kids but also had to carry the knowledge of my pending departure and could not look to you for comfort or support. If it was only going to be a short trip and I knew I would be back, I would not have the feelings I was having. I pulled into the garage, and as soon as the car stopped, you and the kids appeared at the door to the garage from the house. I didn't appreciate how much traveling my new life required. I was away a few times every month. Between Board meetings, investment meetings, Cancer research symposiums, and catching Luke playing out of town. You and the kids would give me those wonderful butterflies whenever I returned.

"Hey guys, daddy's back and might have something for you in my luggage," I announced.

For a brief moment, the kids did not care about any gifts. They just wanted to give me hugs and kisses. But that only lasted a few seconds before the questioning started.

"Wha-u get me, daddy," Sean asked.

"Well, you will have to let me get inside, and we can take a look after dinner," I qualified, with the kids giving me a bit of a disappointing look.

"Hi honey, missed you. Was the trip successful?" you asked.

"Well, I found an interesting stout and hung out with James Bond," I replied.

I retrieved my luggage, and we all went in, and I took it to our room. The kids, as usual, would jump on the bed and watch me unpack, hoping to get a pre-look at their gifts. Roxanne was becoming more like me, and Sean would take after you, Becca. Roxanne had this new analytical approach to things. Even at her young age, I could see how she would look at something, pause to think first, then proceed. I was very much the same. In my Derek 1.0 early days, my father explained how hydro workers were in an insulated bucket when they worked on the overhead powerlines. In order not to be electrocuted, as long as you were not grounded, you could handle 1,000-plus volt lines. When my mother's old canister vacuum cleaner on wheels stopped working, I thought I would surprise my dad by fixing it.

I know I was only 10, but I knew about electricity now. I proceeded to take the vacuum apart, eventually exposing the motor. I thought I would check to see if the motor would turn if it had power. Knowing the teachings of my father, I grabbed my pillow off the bed and stood on it to insulate me from the ground. I plugged the vacuum into the wall outlet, took the screwdriver, and started to turn the motor winding with one hand. With my other hand, I decided to check if any of the wires to the motor were loose. Suddenly a large spark and I found myself across the room, lying on my back, having felt like a baseball bat just hit me across my entire body. Between the sound of me hitting the floor and the sound of the crack from the spark I caused, dad came running down the hall and took a look in the room.

"What happened, Derek," my dad asked?

I was still feeling the effects of the electrocution and being more concerned about my dad being pissed at me for taking the vacuum apart; I replied, "I was trying to fix the vacuum for mom."

"Are you ok?" dad asked with some concern.

I slowly got up and could now officially claim I had been electrocuted. Yes, only 120 volts, but at 10, it felt more like 240 volts. I was prouder of the fact I never cried. It seems maybe embarrassment was an anti-cry mechanism.

"What is the pillow doing on the floor," my dad asked? Dad was brilliant and had already put the pieces together from our chat about the hydro worker.

"I used it to insulate me when working on the vacuum so I would not get electrocuted," I answered.

Dad laughed out loud just before he said, "No more electrical repairs without me, and I want you to read a book about electricity and how it works before your next attempt," he politely suggested.

Sean was getting much better at speaking complete sentences now being 4, and Roxanne was helping him when he was struggling with how to phrase a sentence. Lately, I would like to bring a thinking-type gift for Roxanne while Sean still gets some toy-like item.

"Can I see now, daddy?" Sean asked with big eyes staring me down.

"Ok, buddy, but only this one time," I replied while handing him a toy train in a box.

"Roxanne, this is for you. It's five magic tricks," I handed her a box, "it will teach you how to perform the tricks and how and why they work as a magic trick."

With the kids armed with their gifts, I returned to the kitchen to give my best girl a big hug and a long-awaited kiss. I wonder how well you recall that return and if you ever detected something was bothering me. I would have been extra lovey-dovey. And I know you would have told me more than once to stop all my inappropriate grabbing around the kids. I was on my countdown and did not know how to act. But more importantly, it was the first time I considered bringing you into my confidence. We had an hour to kill, so I did what I so often did when I needed to think: cut the grass. It didn't need it since my lawncare guy Scotty cut it two days ago, but it was where I could think. I was trying to figure out what I could do here before I left that may make the day you would have to read this easier for you.

I was on the fourth or fifth lap, and it came to me. What would I do if I was told by myself that I was not the original but a copy? A Derekbot! Not a clone, a copy. Once the switch took place, we would both be building our own memories, and most likely, our friends would not be in a position to combine our memories since they would share the same synaptic area in our brains. Editing would most likely be impossible. Once I was gone, I would never be able to be updated with any of Derekbot's memories. I realized this was almost like the movie 'The 6th Day' starring Arnold. I think I have a not perfect solution for this issue.

First, would I want to know, and second, how could I leverage that situation to my advantage? I used the next few laps to run through my usual 'what if's', and the answer was the same each time. YES! I would want to know. Finally, something I could now sink my 'mind' into. How would I want to find out? Letter, someone else tells me, or maybe a good old fashion video message. It worked for Houser *(a reference to Total Recall, and yes, that is the movie with the second greatest butt girl!)*; why not Devon? I decided to record a message at the storage unit just before my switch. I was not worried about my friends conducting the mind suck and download. I always figured they would do a little housekeeping removing all information and discussions I had with Tank just in case the Alien watchers ever got a hold of Derekbot. I knew they would view it as protecting the cause, but they did not realize my interests were the same, and this was where two Derek Devons were much more potent than one! I knew that if I were told I was Derekbot, I would be willing to off myself to protect the cause, especially if our family would be put in danger.

My brain was working overtime, Rebecca, and while I wanted to spend as much time as possible with you and the kids, I needed to do a few side things before my trip. I put the lawnmower away and came in for dinner.

"Daddy, I learned my first trick, and I want to show you," Roxanne announced.

"Ok, sweety, let's see the 'Great Roxy,'" I replied with a smile.

Roxanne showed me a four-pack of crayons with a little window at the top, exposing the top of the crayons.

"You see, I have a box with four crayons: one red, one black, one green, and one yellow. Daddy, I want you to put your hand in front of the crayon box so you cannot see the crayons with your eyes," she instructed.

I placed my hand in front of the crayon box she was holding in her hand. She said, "Abracadabra," well, something sounding reasonably close for a 6-year-old.

"Pull your hand away, Daddy," she said.

I pulled my hand away, exposing the box, "Where are the crayons?" I asked with a puzzled look for the show.

"Put your hand back up, Daddy, and I will make them reappear," Roxy instructed.

I put my hand back up, and Roxanne rotated the box in her hand lengthways, showing me the back, and she said, "Abracadabra." She rotated it again. It was so cute hearing her try to pronounce Abracadabra.

"Ok, Daddy, take your hand away," she said.

I pulled my hand away and said, "Oh my goodness, where did those crayons come from" as she gave me a proud smile.

"Let me show you how the trick works, Daddy," she said.

"Roxanne, a magician, never gives away the secret to their tricks," I informed her.

She continued to smile and look so proud of her accomplishment, and that was when you called us for dinner, Becca. Roast Beef and Yorkshire pudding! Wow was I hungry all of a sudden! We had a great family dinner, and Sean wanted to see if his new train would travel through his mashed potatoes. I did the clean-up, and you got the kids ready for a bedtime book reading. I was so going to miss this when I was gone. I was now more comfortable with the idea of Derekbot, especially knowing my friends would build him, unlike Beccabot, which strangers constructed for me. I wanted to spend the weekend at the fort but choosing you over the kid's bedtime reading session was getting harder.

After the kids were in bed and a sleep, I wanted us to go through our photo albums and school yearbooks. I was feeling somewhat nostalgic, not knowing my future, and needing a refresher. I also had you bring your old family album for me to flip through. I was always fascinated by your early-year pictures. I wanted to compare your photos with Roxanne and Sean and try to pick up genetic similarities. Do you recall when I showed you the 'Pulled it out Boy's' grade 12 photo? Or you showing me Maureen's grade 11 photo? Anyway, I am sure you remember that night perfectly well, so I will return to the important stuff.

Yes, I was looking forward to staying at the fort for your birthday and birthday night. But I had a few things I had to attend to the next day. I called up Doc Crossgrove in the morning and gave him a small shopping list for some equipment I wanted to get ASAP. He said he could help me out and would arrange for the equipment, but I would need to pay a same-day courier to bring it in from Toronto. I also needed a few hours to prepare a few electrical schematics for Derekbot and a lengthy shopping list of parts. That night I just wanted to hold you and stare at you. I think your eventual friskiness was a counter to my creepy staring thing.

The following two days had me all over the place buying things. I made sure to do stuff with you and the kids, and I was glad you let me take the lead with the bedtime readings. Part of me always wanted to know or was curious how you would react knowing you were about to be living with Derekbot, and if you would be pissed off at my decision or would be understanding. I was leaning towards understanding, especially with the great re-set hanging over us. It's funny how the male mind works, and even though I knew it was an exact copy *(almost identical)*, I still felt jealous. With my luck, you would want me to keep Derekbot on my return so you could enjoy a non-cheating ménage à trois *(made you smile, I hope)* and always have one of us at your constant beck and call! *(My turn to laugh)*.

I know you are wondering what I had been trying to do before my departure, so I figure that since you're reading this now, I will not have to face your potential wrath if you are pissed at my decision. So here it is; I had been playing around with the idea of building some headgear that could block my friends from simply accessing my brain/memories through an external radio wave-type process. This would then force them to have to do an in-person option. Back when my friends did the large memory dump at Al's lake, they included a lot of information and detail about how the system worked. I think they thought at the time it would ease my mind with what they had just done to me. Armed with this information, I had been working on this idea for a few years. One of the schematics was my design for a blocking system. I needed two systems. One built into a baseball cap and one that I could put near the head of the bed.

Now to the item that you may not appreciate as much. I was planning to suggest at the fort on your birthday that we try for child number three. If you agreed, I would only have a few shots *(pun intended)* at impregnating you before I was gone and maybe even permanently. The one thing Derekbot could not do is impregnate you. In fact, based on my experience with Beccabot, they added some sort of cherry flavor to you/her. I did not realize it until you returned, and I figured it out firsthand. I will always wonder what flavoring they may have decided on for Derekbot. Hopefully, not Pralines and Cream *(I made you smile)*. My call to Doc Crossgrove was to obtain the necessary equipment for me to store my seminal fluid safely *(sounds less creepy)*, just in case our attempts before I left were not fruitful. For the record, I was thinking only about us at the Hermitage Pond and our first skinny dip and not Maureen and the Port incident when I had to stock up! *(Made you laugh, or maybe cry at this juncture ☹).*

The second device I was working on, which was more of a last-minute idea, was a delivery system that Derekbot could use other than a turkey baster *(I am going for an eye roll and head shake)*. Our sex life was perfect, and other than that one thing we loved to do every now and then *(and that is all I am going to say about that)*, we never brought outside equipment into the mix. Well, not that I was aware unless you had your secret stash somewhere. So, I purchased one of those 'lonely lady' toys that I would be adding a fluid delivery system so you would have no idea that Derekbot would be attempting to impregnate you with me. I, of course, would need to bring him into my confidence about the whole thing, but it was important to me that I could leave you with one more child that was 100% ours. My only concern was the possibility that you would become too attached to it *(I needed to lighten the topic)*.

I don't need to tell you about our entire fort outing other than to say, it was the most memorable time for me ever there, and we had a lot of great experiences over the years. Before this, the first-time skinny dipping was number one for me. It was supposed to be your birthday event, and you turned it into a 'Derek Day'. The hardest part was our return home to the kids. I always loved when Brenda stayed with the kids when we needed alone time, and I think she would one day make a great mother. I was down to the last 24 hours and required 3 hours at the storage unit to do my last-minute stuff, so we were down to 21 hours. I read the kids an extra long story that night and laid in bed with them till they fell asleep. Next was my last night with you. I held you, and I am sure like it was the last time I would ever see you. I could tell you wanted to ask me if I was alright but chose to let me smother you with affection.

The following day was probably the hardest thing I have ever had to do. I had every valve shut tight and mentally lashed them down with stainless steel chain. My only defense from bawling like a little kid was my choice to go into angry Derek mode. That would give me the added strength that would keep the valves shut. I gave everyone an extra big hug and kiss goodbye, especially for a simple trip to the storage unit to supposedly fetch some stuff I said I needed. Once I was done with the hugs and kisses, I was out of there. The further and faster I could get away, the better for me. Driving to the storage unit, I made a few calls just to hear voices for perhaps the last time. I called my folks, my grampa, and uncle just to say hello; Sunderland to wish him an early birthday wish with the excuse I would be traveling on his birthday, and finally, Luke.

I got to the storage place and made my way to my unit. I entered, as usual, knowing I would not be the one exiting. I put a box on the bench for Derekbot and set up the video recorder on the desk. I would do the recording and leave it in the box marked with a large heart shape drawing, and in the middle would be the initial LM loves DA, and under the DA would be IDDT! I know if Luke ever saw it, he would also be busting a gut laughing. I knew that would get his attention immediately. I did not fully understand how the whole transfer process would work, but I was sure that once there, I could get Tank to make a few family-type home movies for me to watch externally when I was feeling lonely and missing my family. I looked at the clock on the wall and knew I needed to do my recording. I pressed the record button.

Hey Derek,

Before you get all worked up, make sure you watch this entire recording. This was not made and left by our friends; I made this for you without them knowing. Think of this as our 'Houser' moment! So here is the first piece of information you will need to digest. You are a Derekbot.

Yes, Derekbot. Suck it up, sunshine. I'm the original. I have a special blood test kit in the box, and the Microscope is ready over on the side counter, so why not get this issue off the table now! Do the test before proceeding. I took some of Beccabot's blood without her knowing and developed the test to isolate the nanobot tech. That is what you are looking for with the Microscope. I expect you to continue our work on the other samples while I am gone.

Ok, I am sure you are wondering why and are trying to search your memory for the answer. Unfortunately, it was necessary to scrub your memory just in case our friend's new 'Watchers' decide to get a hold of you for some intel. That is why I will be somewhat cryptic with some of the information I will be telling you; I hope only you and I would figure out the actual messaging. Just like I did with the Donna Anderson message.

I am sure you can figure out where I am going, and since you are here, it was a shuttle craft move, not a transporter beaming deal. The first thing you need to do is build the brain blocker devices. I have the necessary parts and the schematic in the box. I also have a schematic for a brain wave probing detector. None of this was ever tested, and for that, I am sorry, but I believe it will work. You may have to do some tweaking.

I don't want you to have to always wear a baseball hat or other cap, but you will need to have it in reach all the time. I can't tell you what I am doing yet to protect our friends. I am counting on you and me to work as a team; my friends do not know about this.

Rebecca and the kids know nothing, and you are to continue the Task work as planned. I left you a bunch of new high-tech video equipment, and I expect you to video a ton of stuff with the kids and family for me. You're my only eyes and ears now. You are on Task 25, just in case, any memory modifications deleted the last task information and if you need to, you can refresh yourself by reading the guide. There is always a chance that I will not be able to return, which means you will have the responsibility to become me, or, I guess, continue being you. I don't know your life expectancy as Derekbot, but I think it may be much longer than Rebecca's, so you will need to factor that into the future.

You can't go to the hospital, and you should do some testing on your cells, regenerating and repairing. Maybe try some new programming project for the moms and maybe Rebecca.

Tank has been my main man, so if you ever get contacted, it would be from either Tank or me, no one else. We will be on radio silence, and I have no idea if it might be permanent. My efforts are not unlike Harry S. Stampers in one of our favorite movies. I would hope for the AJ or Rockhound outcome, but if I believe it is the only way, you will need to build a school in our name for me.

If you want to know more about the issue, watch our old favorite 'Trek,' 'The Alternate Factor.' Think of me as good Lazarus and our friends' watchers as mentally ill Lazarus. If you have time (Wink wink), also watch 7 of 9 in 'Year of Hell'. For you and our world, it is that serious. If our friends' Watchers' get their way, our initial dream of a 'new-do over,' or worse, a Rebecca 'new-do' will be eliminated along with you and Rebecca. Their perception that it is an infection is simply short-sighted, but I have another option/plan. The problem is, I can't disclose to you, what it is, other than to say, I am counting on you being me. I mean, 100% me!

The single most important thing for both of us now is protecting our families. Rest assured; I am going to be doing everything in my power there to make it happen. I may have graduated to a cockroach in my friends' eyes, but I am a cockroach with huge balls and special tech like in the episode 'The City on the Edge of Forever'! They don't seem to understand such primitive tech. At some future time, I will need you to watch the video of the guy making the Statue of Liberty in New York City disappear in front of a live television audience in 1983. You will understand why later if you have not figured it out yet.

Finally, I want you to use our fortress of solitude every month on the day that is most memorable to us. Maybe we can have an ET moment if possible. I probably don't have to tell you this, but I will anyway. If you ever feel you might be putting our most precious things at risk, should you have unexpected interlopers, you know the helium is not the way. You will need to resort to the Deer Hunter method.

If you find yourself enjoying the new millennium, then please know our efforts were not for not! Rebecca and I are trying to have our third child. I have left you a special device and instructions on where the magic elixir is stored and how to load it into your/her new play toy. If that does not work, you can always use 'AI' by using the stored elixir.

I know at some point, you will also be wondering what will happen in the future if I return. Let's agree to deal with that at the time, and we can, for now, view that as a good problem to have. I am now almost 98 years lived. I can't say old anymore. There is nothing I would change. If things don't work out for me, my last request is this. If Rebecca is successful in having a third child, if it's a boy, I would like it to be named Derek David Devon. I want it to be named Nancy Joan Devon if it's a girl. Do us proud, Bot-boy!

Cheers,

The Original Derek 2.0

Well, Rebecca, if you're reading this guide and it ended here, then something must have happened to Derekbot. I know it would not change the emotional roller coaster you must be on and having to absorb all this craziness. If I am still alive out there somewhere, please know that I will always try to get back to you and the kids. That will always be my final act.

As my final entry into this guide, I put the CD in the box, sealed it up, and made the heart message. This was perhaps the end of my time here on earth, and I may never see you or my family again. I love the kids more than anything, and I know you will always tell them that, but Rebecca, the only love of my lives; nothing will ever change the fact that you are, and always will be, my 'It-girl.'

End of Volume One

A Letter Guide for Rebecca

Volume II

Coming 2023

If you enjoyed Volume I, I invite you to visit my website to register to receive a special pre-release discount copy.

www.ALetterGuideforRebecca.com

The Special Thanks Page!

Since this is my first ***'Thank you'*** page in a book, I am going to approach it from a time perspective *(Keeping with the theme of the book)*; noting my *'thank you's'* in the order that I engaged certain individuals throughout the process. When I finally decided to get off my ass (Hockey Player ass ☺) and commit to the exercise of writing this book, I decided that I would approach my fellow geriatric, recently retired teacher and hockey buddy Lou. Lou was a sci-fi lover like me, former teacher and reads a lot of books. I thought Lou would be a great first sounding board that could evaluate my writing style as well as the story. What made Lou the highest on my list of potential reviewers was the simple fact he only knew me from hockey for the past 5 years, but more important, never knew me in my earlier years, especially my 'Rebecca 1.0' years. So, to Lou, a big **Thanks** for reading my book, offering your opinions and making many suggestions and generally for being a great supporter of my endeavour. If or when they turn my book into a movie, I will make sure you have front row seats to the premier! My newest challenge is convincing Shawn Levy and Kevin Feige to make it!

To my friends whom I have known for most of my life and who also were keenly aware of my fixation on Rebecca, Thank you for your support and input without too many mental beatings…. Scrott, Kiana, Patrick, Jeff and to the original Luke Mattson, I truly was glad you could be a part of the process *(But not part of the royalties you cheap bastards! Except for Kiana of course)*.

I cannot leave out my buddy Chuck! He was not only a fun sounding board but also made our 3 pm coffee get togethers a little more animated with his somewhat personal opinion of Derek Devon who he constantly wanted to suggest I was secretly thinking was really me! And yes Chuck, I am secretly Derek Devon…. ☺.

When creating/writing the book, I do not have an individual to thank but they were also a major contributor to its *(Hopeful Success);* You Tube, Wikipedia, Microsoft, Descript and countless other software programs all needed for the process.

And last but not least, to the Original Rebecca *(aka N?)*; You were my unknown Muse and even to this day, still my ***'It-girl'***!

Citations

As this is a fiction ***'scifi'*** book and not a formal white paper on the 'Phycological Deficiencies' of Derek Devon *(Yuk Yuk),* I have elected to include this Citation page more out of an appreciation for their literary contribution to this book. I think it is important to acknowledge others who have also contributed to my book and hopeful success.

Photos

Most of the Photos used in the book are Licensed through istock photos, personally taken by me or reproduced from an open source license.

Music

As you can tell, I love music, both listening as well as playing. I tried my best to stay within the *'Fair Use'* criteria and even reached out to a few publishers to ask if they would send me a letter acknowledging it was "OK" to use their song lyrics in my book. I never got a reply and was forced to only use small excerpts. While including a small portion of lyrics does not make or break the book, I felt from a 'literary' perspective it was cool and different! So, here are the musical influences I have in my book (and can be found on my ***"Greatest Play list of All Time,"*** Spotify Play List);

1. Two out of Three Ain't Bad – Meatloaf – Bat out of Hell 1977
2. Stairway to Heaven – Led Zeppelin - The Song Remains the Same 1971
3. In My Room – Beach Boys – Surfer Girl 1963
4. Let's Get it on - Marvin Gaye 1973
5. Go all the Way – Raspberries – Raspberries 1972
6. Faust – Paul Williams – Phantom of the Paradise 1974
7. He Ain't Heavy he's my Brother – The Hollies - Hollies Sing Hollies 1969
8. How can I be sure – The Rascals - Groovin' 1967
9. Unchained Melody – The Righteous Brothers 1965.
10. Wise men Say – Elvis Presley - Blue Hawaii 1961.
11. What a wonderful World – Louie Armstrong 1967.
12. American Pie – Don Mclean – Don McLean 1971
13. The Last Time – Johnny Mathis and Jane Olivor - The Best Days of My Life 1979.
14. Come Sail Away – Styx - The Grand Illusion 1977
15. Lover Man - Billie Holiday 1945
16. All By Myself – Eric Carmen 1975

TV Quotes

As a first time Author I was initially unaware of the legal ramifications of using song lyrics in my story. My first draft of the book included all the lyrics to songs that characters sang in the story line. After researching the issue, I was forced to remove the majority of the lyrics and had to settle for a couple lines followed by the old …… (dot ,dot, dot). I really wanted to use the entire first verse of Faust from Phantom of the Paradise written by Paul Williams, but my numerous attempts writing them (the publisher) simply went unanswered. So, a couple lines and ….. would have to suffice.

As more of a homage to my favorite TV shows and not as a legal requirement, I wanted to include a couple major acknowledgements.

First and foremost; Star Trek. All the Star Trek iterations. If you are able to identify all of the Star Trek pop culture references, then you're a true Trekkie.

Second and almost equal is Seinfeld. My use of the George "Opposite Speech" is priceless. And not to be overshadowed, let's not forget the "It moved Jerry" and "He pulled it out."

Here is a partial list of other movies I mentioned in the book in no particular order;

1. Same Time Next Year.
2. Notting Hill
3. Thief
4. Outlaw Josey Wales
5. Unforgiven
6. John Wick
7. Kick Ass
8. Our Man Flint
9. The Time Travellers Wife
10. The Matrix
11. The Green Mile
12. The Terminator
13. Guardians of the Galaxy
14. Contact
15. Field of Dreams

16. Boogie Nights
17. Suicide Squad
18. Minority Report
19. What about Bob
20. Stay Hungry
21. Knight and Day
22. Mission Impossible (Tommy's version)
23. Urban Cowboy
24. Spy who Shagged Me
25. Waynes World
26. The 6th Day
27. Total Recall
28. ET
29. Armageddon
30. Phantom of the Paradise

About the Author

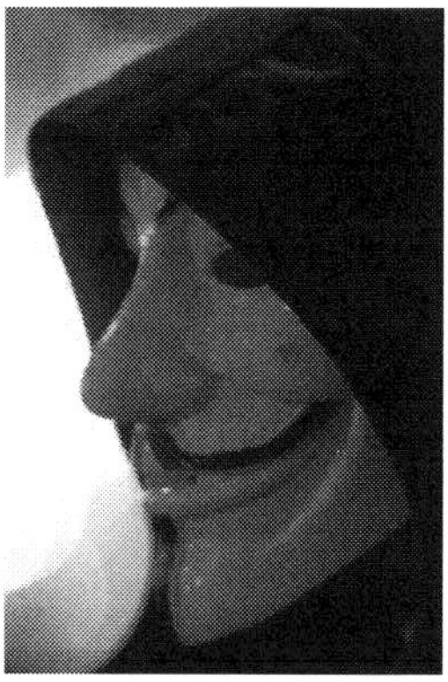

I find it somewhat humorous that I would ever have to contemplate referring to myself as "An Author." Since this is my first attempt, let's just refer to me as a "Potential Author in Training." Ultimately, you the reader will determine that title (Pun Intended) simply by the success or failure of the book (by way of sales). Books I purchase usually reserve the back cover for the self-promotion of the author. Since I am not yet one, I will use the back cover in a different and hopefully more entertaining way. As far as posting a photo of me, I think I will continue to use my alter ego's picture for now. After all, when an author in their ***'work of fiction'*** book includes whacking a few current living world figures….. let's just say it's a little bit of a self-preservation issue as well. Who needs a dose of Novichok at my age!

What I can tell you; I grew up in the fictional town I called Sherman Falls. Some people will easily figure out the actual name of my hometown, but I had to alter the name for legal reasons *(That could be a whole book on its own).* While it is a work of fiction, I did use many of my actual life experiences throughout the book as a framework for the fictional story and fictional characters. I am sure there will be a few readers who may claim they recall being at the Collins with me, went to school with me, played hockey with me or they are the real Tina or Maureen 😊. It was very important to provide anonymity to anyone that I chose to include in my story by way of a fictional character and I hope you're not offended by the name(s) I assigned.

Finally, the story is in fact a love story. My love story, and it is not yet finished….. While my journey continues to find a new 'It-Girl', my current 'It-Girl' remains firmly etched in my memories…. Now, never to be forgotten!

12757982 😊

www.ALetterGuideforRebecca.com

Or is it now ….. 13225476082? 😉

Manufactured by Amazon.ca
Bolton, ON

34401861R00278